I0674328

THE YOUNG OAKS

Book Two

UNUSUAL GIFTS

Christopher Laing

Copyright © 2012 By Christopher Laing
Signal Flag Publishing and Promotions, LLC
Madison, Wisconsin
Cover art courtesy of tonyschwartzphoto.com

www.theyoungoaks.com

1

For my wife and kids.

Willy knew Mae was dead when he saw the teacup on its side on the rug in the living room. One of a set, an heirloom from her mother, it was milky white with a pattern of gold, brown, and orange, a precious thing. Leaving the teacup on the rug was simply something that Mae would never do. The fact that she lay curled on her right side, knees up, ankles crossed, thin left arm behind her, was less shocking to him than the teacup on the floor.

"Oh, no," he said. "No, no, no, no."

He fell next to her, called to her. He took her soft face in his hands and shook her gently, saying her name. He felt her neck, felt her wrist, felt the bones of her narrow chest.

William McGregor came to himself after some time, leaning against the couch, his wife's head in his lap. Easing out from under her, he stood. Bending down, he clutched her to him, lifted her, and took her to the bedroom. Setting her on his side of the bed, he turned down the covers on the other half. He took off her slippers and her housecoat, leaving her in her pink flannel pajamas with little red flowers. Then he picked her up again, moved her to her side of the bed, and pulled the covers up to her chin.

Before getting in bed himself, he closed the door to the bedroom and opened the windows. It was still snowing outside; the pulses of wind at times shook the open windows.

Willy got into bed and pulled up the covers. He leaned over to kiss his wife on the forehead.

"I love you," he said.

Willy barely blinked, lying on his side through the hours, gazing at his wife's serene face. She was beautiful. Perhaps her chest would rise and fall once more. Perhaps she would open her eyes. Perhaps he would die in his sleep. He willed himself to die, but his own heart was obstinate, and kept beating, pointlessly. He thought he should assist himself, like Doc Ambrose, but he couldn't move. Wind gusted, and he could hear the shifting of the sheers and occasional rattling of the curtains. Later, the phone rang out in the kitchen, persistently, and eventually stopped.

Willy withdrew into sleep at last. He dreamed of Mae and the boys, smiling in the sunlight gold on the water of the river, where they had tied the boat up under heavy green foliage to have a picnic. Dan was there, too, although he was somehow larger, older, almost the size of Gordon and Chief, who had grown into solid teenagers. The boat was not his boat, and that bothered him for a moment, but when he saw them all laughing and smiling together, eating ham sandwiches, it almost broke his heart. He began to sob, and they all became concerned, gathering around him. He pulled them all to him in his arms, heaving with his tears in the cockpit of the strange boat. They soothed him, made him laugh through his tears. "See, Grampa?" Dan said, looking at him with very blue eyes, "it's all okay."

Willy woke up in the grey light just before dawn and moaned when he realized he was not dead. Mae lay beside him, her sweet face waxy in the half light of the chilly bedroom. He kissed her cold forehead and forced himself back to sleep. If he slept long enough, eventually he wouldn't wake up.

He ignored the commotion at the front door, of people coming in and calling his name, Mae's name. Emilio and Bob, they should leave him alone. Soon they were knocking on the bedroom door, louder and harder, and when they opened it, there was a moment of silence before Emilio said, "Call the doctor. Call an ambulance."

Willy pulled the covers over his head and curled into a ball. Emilio and Bob wouldn't leave him alone, shaking him and then pulling back the sheets and blankets.

"Get the fuck out of here and leave us alone," Willy said, struggling to get back under the covers. He was strangely weak, though, and they soon had him sitting at the side of the bed. He looked over his shoulder and saw Mae in bed. Groaning, he tried to get back under the covers.

"Willy!" Emilio said, "You have to get yourself together. Willy! People need you, you have to snap out of it!"

Willy saw fear on their faces, and wondered what it was they were afraid of. When he realized that he had soiled his pajamas, they were able to convince him to get into the shower.

"Jesus," Willy said, "just like a little kid. Don't tell anybody, okay?"

He shuffled off towards the bathroom, but when he looked back and saw Mae lying still in bed, his knees buckled. Bob put his arm around him and took him to the shower.

He yelled over his shoulder, "Emilio! You protect my wife, Emilio! Just... protect my wife! Bob! Do it! Protect her!"

Bob shushed him and got him into the shower. He tried to help, but Willy said sharply, "I can do it myself! Leave me alone!"

4

Willy came to himself somewhat. He watched his own hands, guided by the habit of twenty thousand repetitions, go through the ritual of showering. He did it as he always had, so ingrained was the procedure, and it was this simple action that brought him back from the very closest proximity of the edge.

When he combed his hair in the steamy mirror, he saw that his face was slablike and unreadable. In the cold hours in the bedroom, his body had betrayed him by living. Faced with that prospect, he made a checklist of what he had to do and simply worked through it.

Emilio and Bob sat in the living room, waiting to let the doctor in. Willy stood in the arch to the room for a moment, ashamed that they had seen him in such a state. "When that young doctor comes," Willy said, "maybe one of you fellas could call Sam Feeney."

As he dressed in the bedroom, he talked to his wife. "Everything's all right now, honey," he said. "I'll take care of everything. I'll look after the boy. You don't have to worry any more. You just wait for me."

When the new doctor came, Willy couldn't remember his name. As the young man- neat, dignified, professional- filled out the paperwork, Willy sat at the edge of the bed with his hand on Mae's calf. He was aware only peripherally of what was going on in the room, but soon had to focus his attention when Sam Feeney came in with his assistant.

Emilio and the doctor tried to get Willy to leave the room when it was time to transfer Mae from the bed to Sam Feeney's collapsible gurney. Willy got them to leave instead, asking them to wait in the living room.

Willy had covered up the soiled sheets, and now moved Mae gently into the bed's quilt, her favorite. He folded it around her, leaving her face exposed. With the gurney next to the bed, Willy took the corners of the quilt by her head, Feeney the edge by her middle, and the assistant the corners by her feet. At Willy's word, they slid her softly onto the gurney.As the assistant secured the belts of the gurney, Willy gazed at Mae's face.After a long time, Sam Feeney said quietly, "Willy?"

"Yeah," Willy said. "Okay."

He leaned over and smoothed back the faded hair from his wife's forehead, then kissed her. "Good-bye, my love," he whispered. "I'll be along." He pulled the top of the quilt up and covered her face.

Bob was sobbing in the living room as they rolled the gurney through it. Emilio stood by Willy, his chin quivering, tears running down his face. Willy touched them both on the shoulder, following Feeney and the assistant out onto the porch, holding the storm door for them as they took the cart down the steps to the driveway, Willy squinting against the brilliance of the white day, the sky deep blue overhead.

They slid the gurney- collapsing its undercarriage- into Feeney's van. Willy shook their hands and stood in the cold, watching them drive away. When the van was gone, he went inside and made coffee for his friends.

More people came over that day, as they always would in such times. Willy functioned as an automaton, looking after the needs of others, their food and drink, instead of letting his thoughts roll back into his head. When a young woman who waited tables at the bar sat down and started to play the piano, Emilio must have seen the look on Willy's face and went over and asked her quietly to stop.

Though the gathering lasted several hours, Willy would later remember little of it. Towards the end, various friends gave offers of assistance. Emilio and Solveig (who was hollow-eyed and dazed with grief), offered to have Willy stay with them. He told everyone he would be fine. Finally he was alone.

He stood in the door of the bedroom. Solveig and one of her daughters had put on clean sheets and a new quilt, which didn't seem to look right in the room. He closed the door, got a blanket from the hall closet, and went out to the couch.

An hour later, he found himself sitting there, looking at his distorted reflection in the black screen of the television, listening to the ticking of the kitchen clock. The most frequent image that came unbidden to his mind was one of Mae down in the basement of Sam Feeney's, there alone in the dark. He almost got up several times to go down to Feeney's and break in, so he could sit with Mae until morning came; then she wouldn't be alone. The imagined repercussions of this kept him on the couch. He wanted her here, though, wanted to hold her.

The images wouldn't go away, and even though he was exhausted, he couldn't sleep. He finally gave up and went into the kitchen and got a bottle of whiskey, drinking and listening to the radio, jotting things in a notebook, until he was bleary enough to pass out on the couch, dreamless, his consciousness temporarily at bay.

When he found himself blank, when he didn't know how to proceed, he imagined what his wife would tell him to do. "Have some breakfast," she would say. "Shovel the walk. Go to work. Come home. Don't drink too much."

He followed the words she spoke in his mind, and slowly, guided by habit, forced his way through the heavy days.

When Willy first discovered blood in his stools, he laughed. He had noticed sharp flickers of pain like lightning in his guts for some time, but he was old; his joints hurt, his back hurt, his head hurt, it hurt to get up off the couch in the morning. He had categorized the new pain with all the others, and ignored it.

He finally went to see the young doctor, who insisted that he go to the Veteran's Administration hospital in Black Marsh for tests. By coincidence, Stumpy and Nubby Schommer (Dwight and Don, as they preferred), scions of that prolific clan, had been recently in the same hospital, both having come home badly wounded from Viet Nam. They had forbidden anyone but family from visiting them, and Willy knew them both well enough to be sure they would be rueful and ashamed in his presence, after all the dire warnings he had drummed into their heads. Willy had written them on several occasions, though, and had managed to keep out of his letters any vestige of the sentiment he had wanted to scrawl on the page: I TOLD YOU SO. He knew that his own father had shown such restraint, the sharp-tongued old Scotsman. He also remembered Gordon accusing him of *wanting* to say it, all those years ago.

The lively Schommer brothers (were they still that way?) had been rehabilitated and released, whereabouts unknown, although there were rumors that they were both bikers. Willy faced his time in the VA by himself, surrounded by the freshly wounded from the current conflict.

"The only thing we learn from history," Willy had said to one young veteran in a wheelchair, "is that we don't learn from history."

"Got that shit straight," the legless young man had said, laughing.

Willy was diagnosed with a metastatic carcinoma of the colon. The doctor was careful to break the news to him in a tactful manner. He was quiet and respectful, and did not condescend to Willy.

"Oh," Willy said, once he had listened through the young man's rather lengthy explanation. The doctor did a subtle doubletake at his indifference.

"It's operable," the doctor said, "and you probably have many years ahead of you."

"Hey, that's great," Willy muttered.

Mae's absence caused an ache on the most basic level; his cells themselves seemed to be in pain. Suffering this condition, it seemed only a comparatively minor inconvenience to have his abdomen sliced open and the cancerous section of bowel cut out. Lying in bed after the operation, pinched sutures closing the incision in his belly (soon to be another scar), he was somewhat disappointed that he had awakened from anesthesia.

Willy was in accord with the Schommer brothers in his opinion regarding visitors. Against his wishes, Emilio and Solveig came to the hospital frequently, as did Bob Two Bears and most of the bar's employees. Julia, his next door neighbor (the aunt of Charlie and Jim) had been abroad since shortly after the visit of her nephews, and came to see him before he was released. Willy was almost angry when she walked in; the pity of his visitors made him uncomfortable. Julia's reaction upon hearing the sum of his suffering was one close to bafflement; she seemed to look at him almost as if he were a freak for even being alive.

Willy soon grew restless in the hospital, though, as he healed and was slowly put back on solid food. There was only so much reading he could do, so much television he could watch, so many conversations he could have with young, wounded men. The thought of the avoidability of their pain overloaded his mind until he was numb.

About himself, Willy didn't care one whit. If he stayed alive, he'd help the boy. The thought grew in strength as he got better. Emilio, apparently, saw it as a way to motivate him to stay among the living, to focus his will.

"You have to stay alive, you selfish bastard," Emilio said at one point. "You guys are all you've got."

Willy pretended to be watching a baseball game on the wall-mounted black-and-white television, but the words percolated in.

He hectored the doctors to have him released, and promised to stick to the regimen they had laid out for his recovery. After Emilio drove him home, he went back up to Maiden Bluff to gaze down at the river, its eternal flow and the vastness of the sky making him feel small and inconsequential, diminishing the importance of his sorrow.

His illness had stripped him of more than forty pounds; his pants were loose and his shirts hung on him. He tried to summon his will to work out, to maintain the habit of strength, but he had lost something that he knew would never return. Certain that things lay ahead which would call for the best of him.

"Find Dan," Mae told him one night before he fell asleep on the couch. "I'm worried about him."

Dan's welfare was the only thing he had left to worry about in his life.

Finding the boy wasn't easy. He had no idea where they were, and no records showed a phone in Ingrid's name, which would have been changed when she remarried at any rate. He had no idea what Mike's last name was, or where they might have met, things which would have told him where to look. If they wanted not to be found, it seemed that it would be easy for them to do. Back before life on the river, he'd have done it himself. Willy had no justification to call the police; Dan was legally Ingrid's son. He felt certain that the boy would eventually call him, though, and would continue to search for him while he waited. It became apparent to him that Bob Two Bears had told the workers (Willy called them "Our People") at the bar to treat him with kindness, not that they needed to be told. Willy tolerated it at first, but soon found that he missed the vulgarity and the rowdy humor always there among his people. He told them- a bit too grumpily, he realized later- to knock it off.

In the spring, Willy and Emilio went through the ritual of putting his boat in the water by Emilio's dock. They fired up the engine, cast off the lines, and Willy eased forward the throttle and took them out on the river.

The oaks along the shore were just budding pale green against their dark bark, the sky deep blue. Canada geese headed south in vees overhead, mallards bobbed in the more placid backwaters. Fishermen were out here and there among the islands. The wind was fresh, and, after a few pleasant moments of sensation, of an empty mind, Willy remembered that Mae was dead and the feeling of happiness collapsed. He looked over and saw Emilio smiling, eyes closed in the breeze, the wind in his dense grey hair. At least he's happy, Willy thought.

This made him think about how quickly people adapted to the deaths of those who were not in their immediate emotional vicinity, how (and he had thought of this before) it was as though the person had been plucked from the water of the river, their absence leaving only a few ripples as the roiling current instantly filled their space. He was sure he appeared to be the same person to those who knew him, who watched him as he moved forward through his days, but they only saw the outside of him. The inside had been gutted out, leaving only a chill wind to whistle among his ribs.

The boat's engine threw a rod and cracked the block the second time Willy went to take it out. His companion of more than forty years, the agent which had brought him up the river in the first place, borne him to his life, to his rebirth, was now gone. In the face of everything else, Willy was surprised at how little it mattered. The boat was too old to fix, and Willy watched blankly as it was towed away for scrap.

"Some collector might want to buy it and fix it up," Emilio had suggested.

"They can have it," Willy said. He knew he would never go back down the river and out into the world again. Not alive, at least.

It was reassuring to think that he was already in his seventies and could only reasonably expect to live so long. He watched the living around him, going about their business in the bright world, and he thought, *They can have that, too.*

All he had left to do was to see about the boy. He had to stay alive for that. It was the price of duty.

"I'll be along, Mae," he often said aloud, although he managed not to say it in front of others.

There are only two choices, he often thought: you either die young and become someone else's grief, or you live to bear the grief of the passing of others. He found, though, that after a point it didn't matter. After Mae's death, the deaths of others washed over him like fresh rain over saturated ground.

While he was struggling to adjust to his new life, a few deaths came in their predictably unpredictable fashion, and he greeted the news of each one as dispassionately as if a beer delivery had been delayed. He had no more room for it.

Wayne Romer, a young man who had been through the revolving door of employment at the bar, working there during his college years, had died suddenly. After getting through college, he had become an insurance salesman, had a wife and three children. He had been driving in the country northeast of Mt. Pleasant on a stormy day when a tornado sighting was reported over the radio. He drove on, persevering, until, among the roiling green and black clouds behind the thrashing trees at the side of the road, he had seen the formation of a funnel cloud. Leaves were torn from trees, branches flew, and the grey funnel approached. That was enough for Wayne, who, being an insurance man, knew the right thing to do in such situations. It was, after all, the kind of thing he habitually warned his clients about, and was even more consistent in the badgering of his wife and children.

"What do you do in a thunderstorm?" he would ask.

"What do you do in a flood situation, when you come upon a submerged roadway?"

"What do you do in a tornado? What if you're in a car?"

9

His clients responded in a variety of ways, from jokes to wrong answers. If he pestered them with questions until they responded correctly, they were rarely annoyed; they knew he was motivated by genuine concern. His family did get annoyed, however, especially his children, all of them almost grown, and having been grilled with disaster preparedness questions for the entirety of their lives.

They would have known what Wayne should do as the tornado approached, and he didn't hesitate a moment to do it. As the roar got louder and a branch thudded against the door of his car, he pulled over to the side of the road and got out, running around the car and into the tall grass next to a drainage ditch. He threw himself down in the ditch and covered his head with his hands, knowing that low ground was the safest place to be in such a situation, and that you should never stay in your car.

The roar grew even louder, and Wayne was thinking of what a great story this would make, what a fine illustration of his lessons in safety, when the nethermost cone of the tornado crossed the road, lofted his car as if it weighed no more than an empty refrigerator shipping box, and dropped it upside-down in the ditch on top of him.

Willy greeted this news with a grumble.

Bob said, "Wayne? Wayne Romer? Used to work here about fifteen years ago? Well, what the hell."

Willy attended the funeral in the old Coeur de la Riviere on the hill, going only because Mae would have told him to do so. He felt for the family, knowing it would be hard for them (in spite of the fact that Wayne had been well insured), but he had reached the hard bottom of sorrow, and walked down the hill after the ceremony dry-eyed and empty of emotion.

The next death happened in the bar itself. Frank van Wie had been a customer of the bar since before Willy had bought it from Ole at the end of his booze-running days. Frank wasn't a regular in the bar, the way he had been in the 1930s and before, but routinely came in for the Saturday night prime rib, most of which he took home in a doggie bag. One Saturday coincided with his ninetieth birthday, and Frank's amiably cranky wife had arranged for a large party in his honor. This kept all the staff jumping; the van Wie entourage numbered more than sixty, including grandchildren and great grandchildren. Willy was in the kitchen with Bob preparing a birthday cake large enough to support all the candles, which Frank's wife had insisted upon as a kind of joke.

"Trying to blow them all out might finally finish the old bastard off," she had said to Willy with a nudge of her bony elbow.

Willy and Bob had finished the painstaking placement of candles on the three-foot-wide cake and were signing a salacious birthday card with some of the employees when a furor broke out in the dining section of the bar. When someone called for help, Willy shot out the swinging doors and was stopped short by a wall of backs as impenetrable as a rugby scrum.

"He's choking!" someone cried, and they were right. Frank van Wie had taken his final bite of prime rib just as a grandson had told the punchline of a joke. He'd inhaled to laugh, lodging the dense piece of meat in his windpipe. The over-attentive crowd confused matters by shouting a variety of contradictory directions, and by the time Willy could get through the mass of people to help, old Frank was already dead.

10

"You're the center of attention now, aren't ya?" his newly-minted widow said to Frank's corpse as it was rolled out later through the crowd of stunned onlookers, some sobbing, some simply puzzled, grandchildren rolling balls back and forth on the pool table.

Willy envied the old woman's callousness as he walked down the hill, yet again, from the cemetery.

Willy had a dream that night that he was in his foxhole, a child in the war. It was during a barrage, and he was terrified, clutching at clods of dirt, pressing his face into the soil, as the explosions lit up the clouds from beneath, the silences between blasts torn by the screams of men. When the barrage was over, men were walking around in the aftermath, silhouetted against what had become a brilliant sunset. Several came over to look at him down in the foxhole, which he realized was actually his grave. They talked about him in a way that he couldn't quite make out, but no one had the decency to shovel dirt in the hole to cover him up. This made him angry, but he couldn't say or do anything about it because he was dead, not to mention the fact that he wanted to be in the river, where Chief went, where they all should go.

When he awoke from that dream, an hour before dawn, he knew he wouldn't be able to sleep any longer and walked down the empty streets to the park where he and Mae had been married by the river. After some time lost in thought, he went back to the bar and made some coffee, then some bacon and eggs. He was drinking coffee and watching the morning news, getting the paper when it thumped against the front door, and was in the midst of reading when it occurred to him how he could find Dan. It was so obvious that he was angry with himself for not thinking of it earlier. He waited until it was time for offices to start opening in the town where Gordon had died.

With surprisingly few phone calls, he was able to find out that Ingrid was not living in town, and that it was unknown where she had moved. He was able to find out from a sympathetic secretary- who apparently had known and disliked Ingrid- that a trust fund had been set up for the care of the boy, with Ingrid as administrator of the trust. Willy asked for the address to which the checks were sent, but the secretary, upon checking her records, informed him that it was deposited into an account with a bank which had branches across the state, north, south, east, and west; Ingrid could take the money out of any of them. Willy thanked her for her complicity, summoning some of his rusty charm, and hung up the phone to fume.

The sole chance he stood of getting the boy back was to prove in court that Ingrid was an unfit mother, but that point was moot unless he was first able to find where they lived. After another week of persistent phone calls, he had reached enough dead ends in his search that he was to the point of hiring a private investigator, and had begun to make prefatory calls.

These preparations were made unnecessary by a call from a young woman named Miss Robinson, a social worker from Greysport. Apparently there were enough problems in the household that the situation merited "the possibility of other placement" for Dan.

The phone call made Willy dizzy. He sat down heavily at the kitchen table, trying to get his mind to work, to think of intelligent questions to ask. He got a notepad from a drawer and jotted down questions while Miss Robinson talked, then wrote down her answers.

"So, if necessary," the kindly young woman asked him, "we could place Dan with you? For awhile, at least."

"Of course!" Willy said. "Permanently! I'd want to have him here permanently."

"And your wife would agree?"

"My wife died this last winter," he said, spitting out the phrase before he could dwell on it. He didn't say what he believed, that it was the final loss, the loss of Dan, which had killed Mae.

"I'm sorry for your troubles," Miss Robinson said, in a way that sounded genuine even over the phone. "Dan seems to think, though, that he might not be wanted there."

"That's...that's not *true*," Willy managed, aghast at the notion. He explained what he had been through in his attempts to bring Dan home.

Miss Robinson promised to keep an eye on the situation and stay in touch. Willy got the phone number for the apartment in Portview before he let her hang up. He immediately dialed the number.

Ingrid answered. When he said his name, she hung up. This didn't make him angry; he felt victorious.

Now that he knew where she was, he knew how to apply pressure, if only he could get her to talk on the phone. She hung up on him persistently for one frustrating week; once Mike had answered, said, "We don't want any," and slammed down the phone, but that was the only time he answered. Willy got around Ingrid's resistance by shouting an offer at her as soon as she picked up and he recognized her voice.

"Money!" Willy said as quickly as he could. "Ingrid! I've got money for you! Lots of it!"

That got her attention.

When he finally got her to talk, Willy sensed that she was at the end of her rope as far as Dan was concerned. He proceeded cautiously.

"I know it's been hard," Willy said in as soft a voice as he could manage. When she began to cry, Willy was surprised, and even a little moved.

Willy was tentative. "It *has* been hard, hasn't it?"

"*Ohhhh*, you don't *know!*" she bawled, her shell of composure breaking. Willy realized the she was drunk. "It's been *so* hard. I miss my dad and I...I miss Gordon. He was so smart and funny. And talented. I never saw anything like it until Dan, who's even better, the little shit. But I didn't know how good Gordon was. Mike made me see that."

"Mike?"

"Yeah. You know," she burbled, blowing her nose wetly, loud enough that Willy had to hold the receiver away from his ear. "Mike," Ingrid said. "Mike's an idiot. I married a guy named Krapczak. What was I thinking?"

"And how's my grandson?"

She sniffled. "He's good," she said in a suddenly chipper tone. "Kids are adaptable. He's fine. He went to the beach a lot this summer. He has a girlfriend named Betty."

She paused, then turned on a dime again and resumed sobbing.

"That's a lie! I don't know if he's good! I hardly ever see him! Him and Mike go at it hammer and tongs," she snuffled loudly and belched.

Willy rolled his eyes, but said in a soothing voice, "But is Dan okay?"

"It *has* been hard. *You* understand, I can tell. It's been really hard. Nobody cares about me, do they? What about *me*? What about *Ingrid*, huh? Somebody should take care of *me*, dammit! Dan'll be fine, he's gonna be big like alla you guys. Mike better watch it. What about *me*, though? What about *Ingrid*?"

It took awhile for Willy to get her settled down.

"Ingrid," he said. "Listen. Is Dan okay? I got a call from a social worker. A Miss Robinson."

That started her off again immediately, Willy realized with a wince. She started to sob once more, and Willy heard her slurp a drink. "Oh, goddammit, I don't know what I'm *doing*! How do *I* know what to do with a kid like Dan? That Robinson lady was right, I'm a terrible mother!"

"Did she say that?"

"She didn't have to. I *am* a terrible mother."

"It can't be that bad," Willy said, the meaningless, soothing words out of his mouth before he could stop them.

"It is," she said. "You don't know. They get into fights. Dan got a bloody nose, not that he didn't have it coming."

"He what?" Willy asked, keeping his voice quiet to counter the immediate rush of the desire for violence that shot to his head.

"You heard me," she said.

"Is he okay?"

"Who?"

"Dan," Willy said, amazing himself by not screaming.

"*I* don't know," Ingrid said. "He comes and goes as he pleases. Sometimes he's gone for weeks at a time. Sometimes it's a good idea, gives Mike time to forget to be angry. But *I* can't control the kid. If he really loved me, he'd stay home more."

"Listen, Ingrid, this is important…"

"Shit," she said, "Mike's home! 'Bye!"

And she hung up the phone.

Willy sat thinking for a few moments, weighing his options. He waited for another couple of minutes and called back.

The phone was picked up, and Willy heard an argument in progress. It sounded as if Mike had lifted the receiver, with Ingrid was across the room. Mike's voice said, "We don't want any." There was a loud clack, and the line went dead.

When Willy called back, the phone was busy. It remained busy until late that night, when he gave up.

He waited until the next morning to try again, lying on the couch and struggling to maintain his patience. At dawn, he went down to the bar and let himself in, there to wait until a time of day when he thought he might get results. He was about to fix breakfast when Emilio pulled up in front of the bar in his new El Camino, a vehicle Willy thought was ridiculous but which Emilio loved. "It has a Spanish name," Emilio had said. "Soon this country will be *un pais bilingual*."

13

Emilio came in the door and said, "I thought you were here. Time for breakfast?"

"Back in the kitchen," Willy said. Once there, he filled Emilio in on events.

Emilio hung on his words, interjecting with, "No!" and "Then what?" and "You're kidding!"

"I'm not kidding," Willy said after the final such interjection.

"What are you going to do?"

"I'm gonna go kick that Mike's ass and get that kid back."

"Jeesoos!" Emilio said, his accent still intact in spite of the decades. "You jus had surgery half a year ago! You're over seventy years old!"

"Seventy?" Willy made a fricative sound with his lips. "I could take most twenty-year-olds. Shit, I could take three twenty-year-olds and a ten-year-old. Pow. Out."

"You have to do this in a more intelligent way," Emilio said.

"I've thought of that," Willy said. "I'm going to use a two-pronged approach. A: implied threats. Two: bribery. Here's how it will work." He went on to explain as he fried bacon and poured Emilio a cup of coffee.

It wasn't a very complicated plan. As Willy cracked eggs on the griddle, Emilio frowned and nodded in approval. He wanted to go to Greysport with Willy, but in the end was sidelined when Solveig hit a deer with the El Camino while driving up the river road on the way to Black Marsh. She'd been watching a passing freight train down the embankment to her left when the deer, a ten point buck, trotted into the road ten feet in front of Solvieg and stared at her serenely for an instant before she hit it, screaming. The body of the deer (much more dense and destructive than many city people would believe) smashed the front end of the El Camino, bounced up and shattered the windshield, at which point Solveig completely lost control, allowing the vehicle to do a one-eighty down a slippery embankment, where it came to rest against the gravel of the railbed, three feet away from the passing freight train.

Solveig emerged without a scratch. The deer and the El Camino did not survive.

Passersby ran down the embankment to help Solveig from the wreck. When she looked at what had happened to Emilio's cherished vehicle, she didn't appear to give any thought to what had almost happened to her. Instead, she shook her head and clucked her tongue.

"Ding dong dammit," she said.

Willy's braggadocio diminished on the drive to Greysport. It seemed a long time before he got on the Interstate, which was boring until the traffic condensed on the freeway into Greysport. Then it got tense; Willy was completely unused to city traffic.

As cars streamed by him on either side, people honking and cursing, Willy bellowed back. When not doing this, he swore foully and blisteringly at a steady rate. If he drove too fast, he might cause an accident, and therefore be unable to save the boy. If he drove too slowly, he could have the same result. It angered him that the people zipping by him didn't understand the need to observe the speed limit, especially with the energy crisis. He flamed curses out his window, knowing, absolutely, how he looked.

Navigating the freeways was even worse, but Willy managed not to get lost and ended up down by the port. It was late afternoon when he arrived. He called the number he had for Ingrid from a phone booth and got no answer. He waited in the truck by the payphone and tried again. This time the phone busy, and remained so for two hours.

He gave up and checked into a place by the port with a blinking sign and a handpainted, misspelled placard beneath it: "Semen Welcome!" The fact that it made Willy laugh was enough.

Once the traffic was done with, the truck parked (everything of value removed and the doors unlocked), he enjoyed the liveliness of the port. The boy was nearby, but there seemingly was nothing he could do tonight. There were hookers on the street, other languages being spoken. Sitting in the second-floor window of his tacky room with its suspicious sheets, he watched out the window, smiling and drinking from a bottle of cheap whiskey.

When he thought that Mae would have liked it, he put the cap on the bottle, drank some water, and tried to sleep.

Ingrid answered on his first try in the morning. She seemed unusually focused.

"Mike's asleep. Dan's not here right now," she hissed into the phone. "Give me your number, and I'll call you when he shows up."

Willy waited, not daring to leave the phone. While he shat with the bathroom door open, he contemplated staking out the apartment at 718 Pier. To get Dan into the truck without Ingrid signing the papers in his possession would be, legally, kidnapping.

Indulging himself in the luxury of delivered Chinese food, he tipped the kid who brought it an amount that made the young man do a delighted double take. Willy felt pleasure and guilt using chopsticks to eat, while a sloppy fight went on across the street from his window. When one man clicked open a small knife and stabbed the other half-heartedly in the arm, and the two eventually walked away together, arms around each other, Willy just shook his head.

The next day, Willy was expecting the phone to ring, and was staring at it when it did.

Ingrid said, "Bring, you know, everything." She told him directions that he already knew. He left a mess but a ten dollar tip and hurried down the stairs to the truck.

In front of 718 Pier, a truck pulled out from the curb, and he backed into the space. Taking a deep breath, he took the papers and the cash and walked up the flights of stairs to the apartment. He heard the sound of someone running a blender, and found the door ajar. He tapped lightly on the door, and it swung open. Dan was standing at the sink, his back to the door, making orange juice. Willy's heart swelled. In spite of everything, the boy looked healthy and strong.

Walking into the room, he stopped in front of the kitchen table. Ingrid sat on the couch, her look unreadable. The blender stopped and the boy turned around. Seeing Willy, his mouth dropped open.

Willy knew that Ingrid was talking but barely heard her. The boy had black eyes but nothing appeared broken, and Willy was dizzy with relief. He told Dan to get his things, then forced himself to go through the details with Ingrid. All he wanted to do was put his arms around the boy.

Sounds of hurried packing came from Dan's bedroom as he got Ingrid to sign the papers terminating her parental rights. He gave her the cash they had agreed on, a sum that made her eyes glow a little, but which was almost useless to him.

Willy knew that he was too old and weak to face Mike if he came home. He tried to get Dan to move things along, and when the boy started arguing with his mother, Willy glanced at his watch and urged him to drop it.

The sound of heavy boots came up from the landing, and Willy knew from the look on both of their faces that it was Mike. Too late, he thought. He set himself, ready to try to be reasonable, but thinking that it probably wouldn't go that way.

The look on Mike's face told him he was right. When Mike bellowed, "*Why are you in my house?*" Willy put his stance solidly on the floor, but wasn't prepared for how weak he had become when Mike grabbed him by the shirt and hauled him back against the counter. His usual techniques momentarily deserted him, but in a flash of inspiration, he grabbed the pitcher of orange juice Dan had just made and slammed it into the large man's head. The glass was thick, and Willy was surprised and gratified when it broke.

And although he felt a little bad about it later, he was further surprised and gratified when Dan raced across the room and kicked Mike in the face. *Get him!* Willy thought, tensing his body when Dan kicked him twice more. He intervened and pulled the boy off when it was obvious he would have kept on applying his boot to the man's face until it resembled an order of corned beef hash with plenty of ketchup.

And his hands had been shaking with adrenaline as they had driven away. Adrenaline and jubilation.

It was before the shakes wore off that Dan asked the question he'd been dreading. At home, of course, it was different. People had moved on, as even the most compassionate will eventually do. He was left to his own devices, to walk around like a human being, although he had been eviscerated, left open, the cold wind blowing around his great new empty spaces.

Deflecting the question once bought him some time, although he knew it was pointless. He knew he would have to broach the subject eventually, but almost a year of thought had given him no way to convey the news to this kid who had so little left.

Fortunately, the boy was quiet, his bruised eyes pointed out the window. His glum silence was unnerving.

Willy took an offramp from the Interstate and onto the state highway that headed for the river. He drove for miles, wanting to talk to the boy about *anything*, but with the truth stuck there like a bone in his throat. He feared that Dan would think he was ridiculous if he made frivolous conversation.

There was a Dog'n'Suds drive-in that he liked at the side of the highway, and he pulled in, knowing that no sane teenage boy would turn down the food.

"Couple of chili dogs sound good?" he said.

"Yeah!"

The enthusiasm of his response reassured Willy. The car hop came over to the truck and took their order; Willy could see by the look on Dan's face that her cheerfulness made him suspicious. When she came back with the tray which hooked on the window of the truck, Willy handed over the food to the boy.

Dan seemed disappointed when there was no hot sauce for the chili dogs, but it didn't slow him down when Willy handed over the dogs, fries, and frosted mug of rootbeer. The boy didn't eat completely like an animal, in that he used his hands, but Willy was shocked at his ferocity. Having always been strict on manners, Willy nonetheless held his tongue.

"Want more?" he asked when the boy was licking his fingers.

"Yes, please." At least all civility was not gone.

Willy watched him eat, and finally saw his gusto wane. He paid and tipped the car hop, who took the tray off the window, and Willy backed out and drove off.

Feeling something like peace for the first time in recent memory, he drove the truck up into the hills, along streams, through valleys, the full October colors of the woodlands taking them in. They drove through Mt. Pleasant, down the winding road through the forested bluffs. When they emerged from the trees at the stop sign for the river road, there was the river before them, reflecting the blue of the sky, the colors of the leaves almost garish on the islands and the far shore.

It seemed to Willy as if the faint scowl left the boy's face, the expression replaced by a milder one.

He had intended to take Dan home immediately, but, on an impulse, drove to the base of Maiden Bluff and parked the truck.

"Come on," he said.

"What about my stuff?" Dan asked.

"We're not in Greysport anymore."

They went up the trail to the top of the bluff and looked out over the river. The view was splendid, as always. Willy sensed the boy's distance, but overcame his own shyness and put his arm around Dan's shoulder.

"It's okay," he said. "You're home now."

When he took Dan back to the bungalow, the boy went into his old room and set down his things, not bothering to unpack. He came back out into the kitchen, where Willy waited for him at the table. Dan looked around and opened his mouth to speak, but Willy spoke first.

"Your grandmother died," he said.

Dan's eyes widened a little, he pulled out a chair and sat down. He looked desolate. His chin quivered, then he seemed to will his face to be still.

"What happened?" he said at last.

Willy told him in simple terms, omitting any mention of his own response to Mae's death. He told his grandson that it had been painless, and the she had looked peaceful, wrapped, as she was, in her favorite quilt. He spoke slowly, leaving silence between each sentence to give Dan time to really hear.

Willy knew the boy well enough, even after the changes he had gone through, that he wasn't deceived by his appearance of emotionlessness. Dan's eyes were slightly widened, and he stared at nothing, breathing in small pants.

They sat at the table for some time.

"What do we do now?" Dan asked finally.

Willy took a deep breath and exhaled through his nose. "We have your grandmother's ashes. We have your father's ashes, too. I thought it would be good to scatter them together. Into the river, the way we did with your Uncle Chief, your Uncle Dan, I mean."

Dan sat at the table, his hands clasped. After a long time of sitting in silence, he cleared his throat and asked, "Do...do you miss her?"

Willy thought about it for some time before saying, "I hope you never know what it feels like."

Dan nodded, staring at his hands. They sat at the table for some time, saying nothing. Finally, Dan said that he was going to take a nap, and got up and went to his old room.

When Willy went to check on him later, thinking to bring him a sandwich and a glass of milk from the kitchen, the boy was asleep on the bed with his back to the open door.

They scattered the ashes from Maiden Bluff on a windy day at the end of October. There had been the memorials for both Gordon and Mae at the time of their deaths, and Willy thought (and Dan seemed to agree) that it would be better for them to perform their little ceremony in private. The bluff was a place of freedom, of beauty and majesty, Willy had explained. He told Dan about the history of it, that it had been his grandmother's idea, that they were water people and it was fitting. If Dan disagreed, he didn't say anything about it.

They ascended the trail through the woods to the top of the bluff, Willy carrying the cherrywood box containing Mae's ashes, Dan holding the box of his father's. It occurred to Willy that he would never have to do this again; if anything happened to Dan, Emilio would be scattering both of their ashes from this very place.

Dan was silent on his way up the bluff, and waited calmly, his eyes downcast, when Willy had to stop occasionally to rest. Once out on the clearing at the top of the bluff, they stood and looked out and down, the boxes in their hands.

Willy tried to remember what he had said when they had done the same thing for Chief's ashes twenty years ago, then the words stood in his mind in surprising clarity. He looked to make sure Dan was paying attention, wanting him to hear and remember the words.

"These are the ashes of those we love," he said to the sky and the water. "Wife and mother, father and grandmother and son. Wherever they are now, they are far

18

away from sorrow, far away from pain. They can never be hurt again, and are immortal in our hearts."

He opened the box in his hands and set it at his feet. Dan followed suit. Willy showed him how to tear open the packet, but stopped him from pouring the ashes. Willy cleared his throat and said,

Waves will run under endless sun
Long after deed of man is done

Take our loved ones, set them free
Softly, softly to the sea

The wind was at their backs out of the west, and Willy held the container of Mae's ashes aloft and shook them into the wind. So Dan did with the ashes of Gordon, his father. In a mist like smoke, the ashes swirled and mingled on the wind, drifting out and dissipating over the river far out and far below.

At a word from Willy, the two gathered kindling and firewood from beneath the trees, making a large bonfire. When the fire was high, they took the cherrywood boxes, which could have no other purpose, and put them in the flames. Sitting in silence, they watched as the fire transformed the old wood, watched the smoke drift out over the river, away from where they sat under the trees.

It appeared that Dan had little trouble readjusting to life in the little town. Although he seemed to lose some of his tension and wariness in fairly short order, he was never enthusiastic, and rarely smiled. When Bobby Dolan came nosing around one day, Dan saw him out the window and sighed bleakly. He may have had some exciting times in Greysport, but he rarely spoke of them, and even then only under direct questioning from Willy.

Willy soon saw that Dan had an ingrained habit of going out and wandering alone, especially in the worst of weather. This made Willy oddly proud.

"Going out for a bit," Dan said one night during a December blizzard, dressing as if he were going on a mission in his down coat and black wool watchcap.

"Pretty rough out there," Willy said, smiling over his book from where he sat on the couch.

"Yeah," Dan said, adjusting his gloves.

"Guess that's the point, huh?"

"Guess so," Dan said. "See ya."

"No dying of hypothermia!" Willy called as the front door slammed, but wasn't sure if the boy had heard him. When Dan did such things, Willy wondered what he might really be up to out there, but if he knew the kid was healthy for the most part, he was usually too tired to care.

When Dan returned to the river with Willy, it was as though he were walking into a story he had read about another person, a story he had fully imagined yet was not actually real. He would later understand that the shock of learning of Mae's death was so deep and permanent, that, at the time, it was too huge a concept to actually embrace and comprehend. He reacted as if this fact were something he simply crossed off a list: "Gramma's dead, check. Grampa's lost it and is sleeping on the couch, check."

The scattering of the ashes was also too large a thing for him to encompass. He went through the motions of it for his grandfather, happy to do as he was told and to simply follow; in that way, he didn't have to think about what he was doing. He had been surprised at the heaviness of his father's ashes, and he had occupied his mind with trying to appear strong and stoic. He had no idea what else he should do.

He felt dazed for a long time afterwards, and made lists for himself to follow, lists of things he imagined that a normal person would do.

Dan did well in school, seeming to look upon homework as a distraction. Asking Willy's permission, he took over Chief's old room as an art studio, further requesting that Willy keep the door closed and not peek. He was working on a surprise, he said. Often when Willy got home from the bar late at night on weekends, the light was on under the door.

Before Christmas, the two took the truck to some woods not far from Mt. Pleasant and cut down a pine tree from a large slope at the base of the bluff. As much as it had snowed already, the powder was still fairly deep under the pines, and Willy had to stop to catch his breath from time to time. They found a tree that suited them both, and Willy had no qualms about having the boy do the work.

"You're the trainee," Willy said, handing Dan the axe. "Have at it."

Dan smiled a little and hefted the axe, taking a chop at the base of the tree.

"What kind of trainee?" he asked.

"Trainee human being," Willy said. "It's like an apprenticeship program. Apprentices do all the work."

"Maybe you're just lazy."

"Maybe, maybe," Willy said. "Keep chopping."

After Dan had dragged the tree out of the woods and put it in the bed of the truck, Willy rewarded him by giving him a driving lesson, wanting to teach him some tricks for driving on the snowy backroads. The boy took to it immediately, and Willy wondered what kind of experiences he'd had with cars in Greysport.

They set up the tree in the living room, after Willy had Dan help him make some venison stew in the warm kitchen. Willy put some Beethoven on the record player, then broke out some hard cider, pouring them both pint glasses.

"You're on break," he said as he handed Dan a glass. "It's not a school night."

He'd thought that Dan might do something typically teenagerly like being sullen about the prospect of decorating the tree, but he went at the project with enthusiasm. Willy brought out the box of ornaments, many of them more than forty years old, and Dan took them out and inspected them with appreciation and interest. Seeing this, Willy was able to push out of his mind (for the most part) images of the Christmases that had gone before, right here in this room. He forced himself not to think that Mae had been here with him only a year before, and yet, with Dan gone, even that day had had its sadness. He concentrated on forging a memory for Dan to hold in the future, to show him the possibility of happiness.

They ate venison stew with cider in the kitchen. Afterwards, Willy broke out some old single malt whisky and gave Dan a taste, teaching him how to sip it, to swirl it on his tongue and let it oxidize to get the flavor. Dan smiled his small smile.

"Don't rush it," Willy said. "You're not pounding down a shot of something cheap. Go slowly. Appreciate it. You want to get a glow, not get shitfaced. Good scotch is a drink for philosophers, not drunks."

They both got slightly more than a glow, however, and Willy found himself pouring more cider and whisky and telling Dan stories about Gordon, Chief, and Mae. He disciplined himself not to get lachrymose, to keep the stories funny or interesting. When he thought he might be getting boring, he shut up until the boy asked him, "Then what happened?"

On Christmas morning, Willy gave Dan a pair of cross-country skis and a deluxe set of oil paints and an easel. Dan gave him a framed, eight by ten pencil drawing of Willy, Mae, Gordon, Chief, and Dan himself, at his present age. This was so reminiscent of the dream Willy had had, that, along with the brilliant and wistful execution, Willy's first response was to feel chills. In the picture, they all stood in the sun, faint smiles on their faces, the wind moving their hair. Behind them was the river, and any visible trees were bare. The sky had dark billows of cloud with rays of bright light shining through. It was obvious that the weather was cold, but they were all together.

Willy swallowed hard, disciplining himself not to weep in front of the boy like an old man. When he glanced up and saw the look on Dan's face, the look of guarded hope and anticipation, he pulled himself together.

"It's very good," he said, and covered his emotions by going down into the basement to get a nail and a hammer. He stomped back up the stairs and immediately put the picture in a prominent place on the wall of the living room.

Dan had also gotten something from the Gates family in Greysport. It came in a box large enough to hold a couple of record albums, some books and a large black sweater. At Willy's request, Dan held up the record albums, explaining that they were by someone called MC5 and the Blue Oyster Cult. The names struck Willy as ridiculous, but he nodded pleasantly. The books were from H.P. Lovecraft, which seemed to please Dan. The sweater was a heavy cable-knit, and Dan pulled it out of the box slowly and smelled it. A small, pink envelope with a black border fell out of the folds of the sweater, and Dan snatched it up and set it aside. If there was anything else in the box, Willy didn't see it, but didn't pry.

As soon as they had had breakfast, Dan excused himself, taking his new skis and going down to the river.

When he first took some of the acid that the Gates brothers had sent him at Christmas, the island town of MacDougal had a feel of intensely detailed surreality. It became too much, and, although he maintained an appearance of calm, it was all he could do to refrain from actually fleeing to the comforting darkness of the woods up on top of Maiden Bluff, or to the ruins of the hotel, or to a quiet stand of trees by the river. Instead, he forced himself to walk calmly and methodically to his chosen destination. Once there, safe from the cold next to a fire, he sat wide-eyed, his mind running in dozens of golden clockwork meshing circles about his predicament.

He distracted himself with schoolwork and went on binges of creativity in his little studio. During the winter, he got out on his skis, according to one of his lists. It was good to do solitary things; he knew that, at school and in the town, he was talked about, probably seen as strange, although he was obviously regarded with a certain amount of caution and left alone, even by those inevitable kids who comfortably filled the niche of bully. Taking on one loudmouthed kid who had made comments about his family and his grandfather had rectified that in short order. After the more dangerous environment of Portview, Bluffside High School seemed tiny, quiet, and ridiculous.

Dan regularly worked out in the basement with the old equipment, lifting weights and pounding on the heavy bag with a singlemindedness that often crossed the line into ferocity. When Willy gave pointers, the boy paid close attention. Willy imagined that he saw the face of his step-father on the bag as he hammered away, and wondered who else Dan might envision there.

"You want to be a boxer when you get older?" Willy asked him once while holding the bag for him. He hoped the levity in his voice didn't sound too forced.

"No," Dan said. He was sweating, his hair held out of his face with a bandanna used as a headband.

"That's good," Willy said. "You've got such talent as an artist. People need what you've got. Pugs are a dime a dozen."

If this sank in to any depth, Willy couldn't tell. He held the bag as Dan snapped his fists into it, rocking Willy on his feet.

Not only did Willy miss Mae miserably, there were times almost daily when he needed her advice. He had been in prison, after all, when Gordon and Chief had been

Dan's age, and he often felt too old and in need of rest, too lacking in know-how, to be doing the job of raising him. It was fortunate that the boy was so independent.

He often imagined discussions with Mae, and even talked aloud to her if he was alone on the river, up on the bluffs, or in the woods. If he spoke to her clearly, then tried to answer as she would, it often resolved questions in his mind which otherwise would have turned around and around, like a rat on a wheel.

It was an era in the country when the subculture of drugs was more visible than Willy could remember it being in his lifetime. He knew that some of his employees were part of this, although he forbade them from indulging on the job. Bob Two Bears told him in a tone of secrecy that Stumpy and Nubby Schommer, as recovered as they ever would be from their grievous wounds, were not only members of the Guardians of Nocturne motorcycle club, but were somewhere in the state making a living growing marijuana. Willy wondered why the young men never came to see him, and suspected that it might be their embarrassment for not following his relentless advice. This seemed a reasonable assumption; he'd thought the same of his own father.

When Willy scheduled some hours for Dan at the bar for a little extra money and the experience of the work, he wondered if Dan might get drawn in to the subculture, but thought that it was so much a part of the local environment that it would be impossible to avoid anyway, and Willy wanted him to learn the business. The only thing he could do was talk to the boy openly about drugs.

"People have smoked reefer forever," he said, simply barging into the subject as they sat fishing one day in early spring. He knew he couldn't maintain the boy's trust by lying to him; Dan already seemed suspicious of nearly everyone. "Did you know that it used to be legal? Yep. Way I understand it, it was a powerful newspaper man- way too powerful- who had lumber interests he wanted to protect by removing the competition. Competition was hemp, which was once used for all kinds of things, like making rope, clothing, even newspaper. So, this guy, already wealthy and powerful beyond all reason, was greedy enough that he wanted to wipe out the hemp industry. How was he going to do that? By whipping up a public panic about marijuana. It worked, too. Why do you think it's illegal?

"Never did much for me, smoking reefer, but it shouldn't be illegal. That's not to say that, if you ever smoke it, you should just go ahead and smoke your brains out. Moderation, moderation. And don't get busted; you'll be another victim of the hysteria."

He went on to tell Dan about those he had known who were lifelong smokers of reefer, including Steve Hansen, whom he hadn't thought of in years. "I guess it didn't matter in his case if he smoked every day. He was a man of modest talent. You're different. Don't waste your unusual gifts."

Willy was often sure that Dan *had* been smoking dope, however. He came home from one of his nighttime walks, sitting down at the kitchen table where Willy was reading a book. Dan began talking with unusual animation about the full moon and the river, and listened with interest as Willy explained the formation of both of them. At one point, Dan seemed fascinated with his own hands, flexing them and watching them work as he listened to Willy's talk about geology. His focus then changed to Willy's hands, and he squinted at them analytically. The boy's eyes were glassy,

23

Willy thought, and he was unusually talkative, but he didn't slur his speech or show any other symptoms of intoxication. He often went through periods of seeming disinterested in anything, so Willy found that he couldn't object to the boy's apparent state of mind.

"Hey," Dan said finally, "I know this is a weird question, but would you mind if I draw your hands?"

Willy was pleased to encourage the boy's talents. "Sure," he said.

Dan went to Chief's old room to get his supplies. As he drew, he asked Willy questions. "What's that scar from? There, on that knuckle."

"It's from a tooth, if I remember correctly."

"How about that one? Or that one?"

"I actually don't remember," Willy said after thinking about it. It puzzled him. "I used to have a story for every scar on my body. Now I only remember the stories of half of the ones that aren't faded or lost in wrinkles."

"Your hands are stories in themselves," Dan said. It was about as close as the moody kid could come to a compliment. Willy accepted it. He eventually put the framed results of Dan's efforts on the wall behind the cash register at the bar.

He was an odd boy, that Dan, but odd in a way that made Willy amused and proud. If Dan hadn't been his grandson, Willy would have wanted him to be.

One of the first things that came out of his little studio was a painting done with his new oils. "Still Life with Severed Head" was its title, depicting, against a dark brown background, a white ceramic pitcher on a matching platter, surrounded by several ripe peaches. Beside the pitcher and behind the peaches sat a severed head, the eyes half-closed, the skin yellow, a tiny pink dot of muscle visible from under a folded lip of sliced skin at the neck. It was beautifully executed, as it were, resembling the work of one of the Dutch masters; a nod, as it were again, to the Champmartin at the Greysport Institute of Art.

Willy couldn't help but laugh, which made Dan smile a bit. Willy had gotten the joke.

"Bit morbid, isn't it?"

"Yep," Dan said, and actually grinned.

Dan improved upon the joke by entering the painting in a contest put on annually by the Riverland Women's Art Auxiliary at the Ambrose Library, where the sometimes talented artists of local high schools were nominated by their instructors to exhibit their work. The art teacher at Bluffside, the lackluster Mr. Dubronski (who had fled a failed art career in Greysport), timidly suggested to Dan that he submit something. Dan had nodded mildly at the suggestion, and promptly tendered "Still Life with Severed Head", ignoring Dubronski's softly stammered objections.

Dan related this story to Willy as they walked through the exhibit at the library named after Willy's old friend. Some of the works showed promise, but most were insipid garbage. A particular standout was an acrylic painting done by Bobby Dolan called "Necromancer"; done in the Sword and Sorcery style of the day, it was a low-angle view of a cowled wizard on a bluff in front of a lurid orange sunset, hurling green flame with his hands. Willy grimaced when he saw it.

"Yeah," Dan said.

"Still Life with Severed Head" was far and away the most technically proficient piece there. Charlie and Jim's Aunt Julia, stopping off to check in at her *pied a terre* between Europe and India, saw it and pronounced that it was better work than that of many adults she knew who made their livings as artists.

"You've got a bright future," she told Dan affectionately. Willy nudged the boy and nodded.

The painting received no prize. This didn't bother Dan in the least. "I'm surprised they even put it up," he said.

If Dan had many friends, Willy didn't see them much. Occasionally, some long-haired kids in jeans and fatigue jackets came by when he was home. Typically, Dan brought them in and introduced them to Willy, they mumbled something polite, went to Dan's room for a few minutes of muted conversation and laughter, then left again. Sometimes kids came around to the back door of the bar while Dan was working, and Dan would go out to talk to them in the alley. It reminded Willy of the Schommer boys; maybe kids of this generation were simply like that. It made him a little sad that, as close as he and the boy often were, much of Dan's life was opaque to him.

He sometimes hung around with Bobby Dolan, out of pity and loyalty. The poor young oaf followed him doggedly and had even taken up painting, whether in emulation of Dan or as a quest to fulfill some interior vision, Dan didn't know. Perhaps he just liked it. The boy was not completely devoid of talent (with considerable coaching, Dan thought, he might be able to airbrush sword-bearing barbarians on the sides of custom vans), but it was Dolan's inept attempts at art that made Dan grudgingly admit that he himself might have some talent, even though he was a *maldito*, and worthy of nothing good.

It was pity for Bobby Dolan that prompted Dan to take him on an adventure. On a Saturday in spring, shortly before he got his driver's license, Dan had a craving for the kind of food unavailable in MacDougal, where the chicken cordon bleu as a special on Willy's menu was perhaps the nearest thing to exotic that one could find in or around the town. What he craved most wasn't exotic at all, nothing more than a simple Italian beef sandwich from Graziano's deli, but that was hundreds of miles away, and there was nothing remotely similar anywhere near. The next most satisfying thing he could think of was the Chinese restaurant in Black Marsh, Fung's Golden Dragon. Over the course of the week preceding that Saturday, Dan's fixation on making the trip to Black Marsh grew.

At first, Willy had said he would take Dan up the river to the restaurant, but had had to beg off in order to lend his assistance on a project of Emilio's. Dan was not to be deterred, however, and decided to hitchhike. He was on his way out of town, walking onto the bridge to the river road when he heard the wheedling voice of Bobby Dolan, who had been fishing at the base of the bridge. Dan sighed and looked around to see if anyone was watching, feeling ashamed of himself for doing so.

"Whatcha doing?" Bobby said, putting down his pole and lumbering up the gravel slope.

"Going to Black Marsh," Dan said, wondering if he cared more about the opinions of people in the town than he allowed himself to believe.

"Hey, I'll go!" Bobby said.

"You should stay here."

"No, I'll go. I'm just fishing. I can do that any time."

"Well, I'm hitchhiking," Dan said, trying to make it sound as if such an activity was undesirable.

"Oooh! High adventure! Brigands of the road!"

"Yeah, I guess," Dan said. He didn't dare mention to the chubby kid that the purpose of the mission was food. "I should get going."

"Wait!" Bobby said, "Let me hide my pole and my tackle and I'll come along."

It was then that Dan's pity and loyalty exerted themselves. He sighed and said, "Okay."

"I'll be your Sancho Panza!" Bobby called up the slope. Dan had no idea what he was talking about.

The concrete of the bridge was bright in the sunlight, and had no history to them. It was simply a bridge. They walked across it, ignorant of the impressions of years that had reverberated down through the concrete and rebar and now echoed up again, unsensed, unfelt, unsuspected.

Over the bridge, they walked through a long stand of trees by the slough, and up across the river road. Facing south, they waited for cars. Bobby stood with his thumb out, whether there was a car in sight or not. Dan winced and waited until he heard the sound of tires on asphalt from around the bend before facing south and putting out his thumb.

The first driver to pick them up was an old man with a seamed, unshaven face and a rattling old green Ford pickup truck with rust working through a forgotten, patchy job of Bond-O. He roared down the road, downshifted upon seeing the boys, and shuddered to a complete stop at an angle, both of his rear tires on the road, the front ones on the gravel shoulder.

"Where ya goin'!" the old man shouted unnecessarily as the truck finally came to a complete stop in a lagging nimbus of dust and a clatter of gravel.

"Black Marsh," Dan said.

"Hop in back!" the old man yelled. "I'm turnin' off to go to the blacksmith in Mt. Pleasant! I'll let ya off there!"

"Okay!" Dan shouted back, making Bobby giggle.

They had barely sat down in the bed of the pickup when the old man gunned the engine and patched out from the shoulder in a dual blast of gravel. Dan laughed and Bobby's eyes shot wide open. The old man hurtled down the road, obviously not being too discriminating about using the shoulder and the centerline in his progress, weaving back and forth as he went around curves at the bases of bluffs at a speed far in excess of the limit. When they hit a bump while going off onto the shoulder and partly into the weeds, Dan, Bobby, and the assorted junk in the bed of the truck all jumped simultaneously into the air. Dan howled in delight, although Bobby looked less than pleased.

At the turn-off for the county highway to Mt. Pleasant, the old man slid entirely off the road to a stop. Dan and Bobby hopped out of the bed of the truck, coughing in the dust.

"Here ya go!" the old man yelled from the dimly visible window of the truck.

"You were really hauling ass!" Dan said appreciatively. Bobby, still wide-eyed, didn't appear to agree with Dan's enthusiasm.

"What!" the old man yelled.

"You were really whipping!"

"What!"

"Fast! You were going really fast!"

"Nah, I wasn't," the old man said in a normal tone. "I was takin' it easy cause you kids were in back."

With that, he stomped on the gas and floored it onto the county highway and up into the bluffs, the legs of their pants tapped with a parting flurry of grit.

They stood at the side of the road for some time after that. Bobby wanted to walk backwards, thumb out whether there was traffic or not; Dan told him it was pointless.

"Anyone who would pick us up a quarter of a mile down the road would pick us up here," Dan said. "This way is more efficient and less pathetic."

Cars voomed by, most of the drivers pointedly staring straight ahead. A group of older boys passed them, jeering, driving a station wagon in the opposite direction. They did a u-turn and came back, slowing down and getting close enough to the boys that they couldn't avoid noticing that the windows of the car on their side were now studded with naked asses, and only five feet from their faces. Dan ignored this; Bobby pointed and laughed.

Dan was beginning to wonder if they would be recognized by someone from MacDougal. He didn't worry about how Willy would react (the old man knew that boys had to have, within reason, their adventures), but it occurred to him that perhaps the town didn't need another rumor regarding the McGregor clan. He felt stifled and anxious, and each car the passed them increased his anger.

"Maybe we'd get picked up if you didn't look so pissed off," Bobby offered as they stood at the side of the road waiting for cars.

"Maybe we'd get picked up if you didn't look like such a dork," Dan shot back, immediately regretting it when Bobby dropped his eyes. There was something about the kid that brought out his meanness.

They got a short ride from a chubby woman in her thirties who lectured them on the dangers of hitchhiking, that people got killed all the time.

"Didn't you hear about that man in Greysport who was picking boys up and torturing them to death in his basement? Boys just like you! He tied them up, shackled them! Beat them! Did things, oh! I don't want to say! They were helpless, and naked!"

Dan got the clear impression that their welfare wasn't her concern at all, rather it was her own horniness. Plump and clean and nicely scented, Dan caught a look in her eye that he was sure had more in it about her visualizing him naked in the quiet safety of her own home, instead of in a dank basement with a naked lightbulb in Greysport. If Bobby hadn't been along, he might have given it a shot.

She dropped them off, apparently as soon as she knew nothing was going to happen. There was nowhere for her to go, with the river on the left side and a bluff on the right. She didn't explain this, instead telling them with mock severity to be careful before giving a fluttery wave and a wink to Dan. "Maybe I'll see you again sometime," she said.

Dan gave a friendly wave back, along with a waggle of his eyebrows. He told Bobby about his suspicions.

"No!" Bobby said, giving Dan a disgusted look. "You've got one heck of an imagination."

The next person to pick them up (quite some time later) wouldn't have cared that Bobby was a dork or that Dan looked pissed off. Driving a fifteen-year-old International Harvester Traveler, he slowed down at the side of the road forty feet before he got to the boys. The driver sat there, idling his engine with a rumbling muffler, his face a dim silhouette behind the reflected images of leaves, bluff, and sky on the windshield. Although Bobby held up his thumb, wiggling it optimistically, Dan dropped his hand and watched the truck.

The truck pulled slowly forward until it was abreast of the boys, and the driver leaned over to roll down the window. "You boys need a ride?" he said. He was thin with greasy hair, wearing a sleeveless t-shirt with a dixie flag on the chest. His voice and pallor smacked of cancer.

"Sure!" Bobby said, getting in the back seat. "We're going to Black Marsh."

"I can take you there." He looked out at Dan, who regarded the man from the shoulder of the road. River rat, Dan thought, although that wasn't necessarily a bad thing. Dan could tell by looking at him that he had eaten raccoon and collected a bounty on rattlesnake tails. Beggars can't be choosers, he thought, and got in.

The man smelled of booze and sweat, and there was a hint of both decayed meat and cleanser in the vehicle.

"Like your shirt," Dan said.

"Thanks," the man said automatically, then looked at Dan with narrowed eyes, as if to detect sarcasm. Dan saw it coming and looked blandly out the window.

"What're you boys goin' to Black Marsh for?"

"Nothing," Dan said. "Fun of it."

The man gave another squinty look at Dan and grunted. He drove on for some time in silence.

"You don't look like you're from around here," the man said as they passed a gas station on the outskirts of Black Marsh.

"Actually, we're from…" Bobby began.

"Not you, tubby," the man said. "I'm talking to tough guy here."

Bobby was a nuisance, granted, but the fact that such a dirtball would pick on the unfortunate boy immediately made Dan feel hot and light.

"I'm from Greysport," he said, sensing it would needle the man's rural sensibilities.

"Greysport, huh?" The man whistled. "*City* boy. Must think you're pretty impressive."

"Not really," Dan said, "although it might seem impressive to *you*."

"It ain't," the man said with a vehemence that suggested Dan had succeeded in pissing him off. "Lots of fags and spics and niggers in Greysport, ain't there."

He's *that* kind of river rat, Dan thought. He also thought of Mike. And of Jorge, Adriana, Darnell. Of Hugh Gates.

"Yeah, I guess there are," Dan said.

"You sound like you like all of them, fags and niggers and spics and such. You like fags and niggers and spics?"

"Depends on the fag or nigger or spic," Dan said.

"Omigod, we got us a liberal," the man said, and turned to spit out the window. "You a *liberal*, boy?"

"I don't know," Dan said. "All I know is that if you showed up in Greysport in a t-shirt like that, you'd get your head sent home to your mama in a hatbox with your dick in your mouth."

Bobby gasped and the man stomped the gas pedal in an instant of shock. "You threatening me?" the man said.

"No." Dan could see that Bobby wanted him to remain silent; he looked like he was holding his breath, and was frantically, minutely, shaking his head.

"I'm not threatening you," Dan said. "You're not important enough to threaten."

"I got a gun *right here*," the man said, indicated the space between his seat and the door. "I could blow both your heads off and drop you in a swamp and nobody'd be the wiser."

"You have a gun on your left side?" Dan said.

"I'm left-handed, goddammit!"

"Okay," Dan said, smiling and looking out the window.

"I got a gun, so mind your manners!"

"I've got a knife right here," Dan said, slapping his right hip. He regretted not actually bringing his knife, and tried not to smirk at the thought. "I could stab you in the neck before you got a round off."

They were nearing the south side of Black Marsh. The man glanced at the road ahead of him, then at Dan, back and forth.

"Let's see the gun," Dan said. "Really. I'm interested."

The man glared at Dan.

"No?" Dan said. "Okay, we'll get off right here."

The man pulled over and stopped, the muffler rumbling. Bobby scrambled out and slammed the door.

"Thanks for the ride," Dan said with a smile, and got out of the truck.

"I'll be looking for you," the man said.

"*I'll* be looking for *you*," Dan said, and drew his thumb across his neck.

The man chirped his tires and pulled away, cutting off the driver behind him, who laid on his horn.

"Jeez!" Bobby said. "I almost crapped myself! Are you nuts?"

"That guy didn't have any gun."

"How do *you* know?"

"I just do."

"You're nuts, man," Bobby said, shaking his head. It took him a while to forget to be angry.

It was still a bit of a walk to the restaurant, along railroad tracks and past a used car dealership and an abandoned grocery store, weeds growing tall from the cracks in the asphalt. When they finally got to the restaurant, they were famished. Bobby was a stranger to the menu, but with a few suggestions from Dan, he ordered a great deal of food. Dan had his food spicier, but in smaller portions. In an attempt to broaden

Bobby's horizons, he tried to introduce the boy to the chili sauce he was using. Although the flavor wasn't all that similar to the sauces at the little tienda owned by Jorge and Adriana's parents, he thought that it hit the same region of the palate, and wanted Bobby to understand a bit of what he had learned while he was gone.

He knew it was a slim hope, but was nonetheless disappointed when Bobby ate a bite of food with the sauce (Dan had to admit that it was a pretty good dollop) and, after a moment's pause, went completely berserk. More amused than embarrassed, Dan chuckled watching Bobby's involuntary convulsions.

First his eyebrows came together, then his eyelids fluttered. He looked side to side, opened his mouth and fanned it, witlessly, with his soft, white hand. Sweat broke out on his face, which turned an unpleasant pinkish shade that Dan immediately categorized as puce. Dan realized that, although he had hoped for some kind of understanding, of union, this was much better. When Bobby ran outside, came up to the window, rapped on it, and pointed to his open mouth, Dan's sense of concern was obliterated by his mirth. He and the Chinese waiters shared a look of delight.

The amusement was not to end there. When it came time to return home, Bobby, apparently recovered from the chili overdose, revealed that he was too afraid of the man in the International Harvester to hitchhike on the return leg.

"I don't want him to find us on the road," he said.

"That guy won't do anything," Dan said. "He was full of shit."

"I'm not hitchhiking," Bobby said, adamant about something for once.

"What are you going to do, have one of your parents come and pick us up?"

"No! And tell them that I hitched up here? No way! I'd get grounded."

Dan contemplated ditching the boy, but thought the better of it. Like it or not, he was responsible for him.

"Did you give any thought about how we'd get back?" Dan asked.

"I don't know. I'm just not doing it with that psycho on the road. It's like that lady said. We could end up getting tortured to death."

Dan looked over at Bobby and said, "I know what to do."

There was a railroad switching yard south of town, and it occurred to Dan that they could simply hop a freight, something he had always wanted to do anyway. Bobby seemed willing to follow Dan's lead, as usual, and was cheered by the prospect of another adventure.

Dan envisioned a long wait in the switching yard, but realized that he hadn't understood the level of activity there. It was only twenty minutes before they were able to find a train with empty boxcars beginning to move south. The train crept along so slowly, in fact, that they were able to climb into an open boxcar with ease, even for Bobby, who was less than nimble. Dan was momentarily afraid that Bobby would slip while boarding and be maimed or killed by the grinding steel wheels, as happened from time to time in the area. He stood in the boxcar, holding out his hand and ready to pull the boy in by his shirt or hair if necessary. Soon the boy was aboard, though, puffing triumphantly.

The train gained speed so slowly that Dan was afraid they would be discovered by railroad men before they left the yard. He took Bobby by the elbow and got him to stand back in the shadows until they were safely on the rails south of town. They were soon making progress, and Black Marsh diminished behind them.

The boxcar was empty except for a flooring of straw and a few scraps of cardboard. An empty liquor bottle provided evidence that either someone had ridden the car before them or railmen had been drinking on the job. Dan took the bottle and threw it out the door, smashing it gratifyingly on the stones of the railbed.

Travelling by boxcar proved so pleasant that Dan was soon imagining riding the train all the way down the river to the sea, or up and up into the trackless arboreal forests of the north. He stood in the doorway enjoying the wind, the water of the river spread out before him, trees rushing by, all of it made somehow peaceful by the rhythmic steel percussion of wheel on rail.

"I have to poop," Bobby said suddenly.

Dan stared at him for several seconds.

"What?" he said.

"I have to poop," Bobby said.

"Poop? *Poop*? You have to *poop*? Fuck!"

"But I do!"

"So hold it," Dan said. "Goddammit! We're halfway home."

"I can't. Maybe that food did something to me. I really have to go!"

"Oh, *man!*" Dan said. He looked around the boxcar. "Just do…just…fuck! *I* don't know!"

Bobby solved the problem by taking a two-foot-square bit of cardboard and going off into one of the corners of the boxcar. He dropped his pants to his ankles and leaned back into the corner of the railroad car. There he shat onto the cardboard, runnily, noisily, as Dan glimpsed and howled, glimpsed and howled, laughing and gagging.

When Bobby was done, he pulled up his pants and said, "What do I do with it?"

"I don't know!" Dan cried. "Leave it!"

"But some hobo might come in here," Bobby said.

"So what?"

Bobby did the noble thing and took the cardboard slab of his own shit to the door of the boxcar. He erred only in standing in the door facing south, with the cardboard in his hands and the wind in his face. The cardboard in his face.

Dan thought he might actually die laughing. He couldn't catch his breath, and was soon choking for air. When he got control of himself, one look at Bobby's dolorous, splattered face set him off again.

Bobby took off his shirt and wiped his face, balling up the garment, and, after a moment's hesitation, tossing it out the door. Even the t-shirt he was left with was flecked. Dan felt a spark of pity at Bobby's humiliation, but pushed it down and covered it up easily with fresh mirth. The boys sat at opposite sides of the boxcar.

It suddenly occurred to Dan that the train might not stop as it headed south down the river, might just go hurtling past the road to the island. He knew that trains often stopped nearby, but had no idea whether this was one of them. The idea of being trapped on the train with the malodorous boy, of having to call his grandfather to pick them up somewhere downriver, of sitting with the smelly kid in the car on the way back, were all ones that he found to be less than attractive.

The train did, in fact, shoot by the road to the island, but fortunately slowed down with a shrill grinding and came to a stop a few miles south. Feeling reprieved, Dan got off and started walking north along the gravel of the railbed. He heard the occasional scuff and stumble in the gravel behind him, and knew that Bobby was following. After a while, he heard some sniffling, and realized that the boy was crying. He sighed and turned around.

"What am I gonna tell my mom about my shirt?" Bobby said.

Callous self-preservation wrestled for a moment with his better nature, and Dan said, "We'll think of something. Come on, we can get down to the river right up there and wash you up a bit. Just don't touch me." The boy's gratitude and relief made Dan feel ashamed, and he thought, *maldito*. Then he had to stifle laughter again, struggling though a cycle of pity, mirth, and shame as Bobby splashed himself in the muddy water of the river.

It was twilight when they got into MacDougal. They were lucky enough to go up back alleys to Dan's house unnoticed.

"My grandfather's at the bar, I think," Dan said as they went up the back steps and into the kitchen.

Dan stood back as Bobby washed up almost frantically at the sink, scrubbing and scrubbing with soap and water.

"What is it with you and shit, anyway?" Dan said, then found that he had to ignore Bobby's doleful look. He gave Bobby a clean t-shirt when he was done. It was obvious that Bobby wanted to say something as he stood by the back door.

"I forgot my fishing stuff by the bridge," he said finally.

"It'll be there tomorrow," Dan said.

Bobby went down the steps.

"Thanks," he said, only turning halfway towards Dan.

"Don't mention it," Dan said. "To anybody."

Bobby nodded, avoiding Dan's eyes, and left down the driveway, into the dark. Bobby didn't seem to want to spend much time with Dan after that.

Dan was self-possessed, though, and not spoiled in the way of many kids his age. Willy would see, especially among the summer tourists, ugly family arguments he would never have tolerated. A perfectly wonderful vacation, a day spent at hippie art fairs or farmers' markets along the river, would easily be ruined by pointless arguments between children with, as Willy saw it, an undeserved sense of entitlement and parents with little ability to communicate. Willy and Bob would witness such spats and give each other gravely deadpan looks of amusement.

This kind of thing wasn't a problem with Dan. He seemed old before his time, comfortable to sit around with Willy, Bob, and Emilio, willing to learn from them, but acting neither subservient nor cocky. Willy had a hard time imagining him throwing the kind of temper tantrum he had often seen demonstrated by the children of tourists. He often wondered what he would have done if such a case had arisen.

Willy had gone around and around with Stumpy and Nubby Schommer and other young employees about blasting the volume on the juke box, and was not going to do it again with Dan. If he found the boy rattling the glassware at the bar while sweeping up on a Saturday morning, he would tell him twice to turn it down before raising and sharpening his voice. As mature as the boy was for his years, he was still a teenager; sometimes it took a while for a message to sink in. When Willy came home one afternoon and found Dan vibrating the windows with a new stereo he had bought (the sound of the bass was audible down the block), he simply took the boy out and bought him headphones rather than starting an argument.

"You're not going to yell at me?" Dan asked as they walked out the front door.

"Nope. We shouldn't do that," Willy said, "we shouldn't fight." Suddenly remembering what Emilio had said, he added, "We're all we've got."

On Dan's sixteenth birthday, Willy took him up to the Department of Transportation office in Black Marsh to get his driver's license. Although the boy could drive the truck as if he'd been driving for years, they opted to take Mae's sedan, which was an automatic.

"Just to make things a little easier," Willy said, and Dan didn't argue.

Dan passed the test without difficulty, and Willy let him drive home along the river road. It was May, the trees leafing out, flowers in bloom at the sides of the road, boats moving up and down the river. Dan turned on the radio, but was unable to find a station he liked, complaining about the radio available in the area. There was a small college station in Black Marsh which played what Dan considered to be good music, but it had a weak signal which faded quickly as they drove south. Willy, whose most modern taste in music leaned towards the big bands, was relieved. He held his tongue, though, remembering his own father's contempt for his love of jazz.

"Put on the public radio station," he said. They had in common a taste for classical music; Willy had heard Dan listening to Beethoven's Seventh through the door of his studio on headphones, prompting a suggestion that Dan protect his hearing. He knew that the suggestion was immediately ignored.

Dan leaned toward the radio, and Willy said, "No, wait, I'll do it. You should concentrate on your driving. You're new at this."

"I'm fine," Dan said, but Willy tuned the radio anyway.

As they drove, Smetana's *Moldau* came on, and, to Willy, it sounded good even over the sedan's tinny speakers. The river glinted brilliantly in the sun, the trees with their fresh leaves moved in the wind. The swelling of the music blended with the nobility of the day.

"This is beautiful," Dan said.

"Concentrate on your driving," Willy said. His heart pulsed with the music, a tune Mae had first taught him on the piano.

As they approached the bridge to MacDougal Island, a truck coming from the other direction went over the centerline, straying a foot into their lane. Dan blasted the horn and went off into the gravel for a moment before getting back on the road. Willy's eyes widened and his heart clenched; he knew they had just passed a version of their own deaths.

"Jesus!" Dan cried out the window. "Be sure to take your half out of the middle!"

When Willy had first used the same expression in front of Mae, she'd laughed.

For his birthday, Willy was already going to give Dan his old service rifle, the Springfield M1903 Caliber .30, complete with bayonet.

Dan's stoic shell cracked; he was awed at the present.

"You can use that deer hunting this fall," Willy said, adding as a joke, "Not the bayonet, though."

He had also slipped out to the new record store owned by a long-haired couple who catered to the ever-growing population of hippies, but also had a sizable collection of classical music. The husband, a tie-dye wearing, bearded man with a beer belly nourished by frequent evenings at Willy's bar (and who went by the improbable name Skyhawk), demonstrated his knowledge of classical music.

"I studied in Greysport," he had once said in a dismissive tone.

"I'm looking for a copy of Smetana's *Moldau*," Willy told him.

Skyhawk, who smelled of reefer, stared off into space for a moment and snapped his fingers. He walked among the large racks of albums, went to a single row and riffled through it for a few seconds, pulling out an album.

"Just the ticket," he said. "Smetana's *Moldau*, conducted by Karel Encerl, another Czech. Second in a cycle of six entitled *Ma Vlast*, or *My Country*, by the composer. *Moldau* is German; it's *Vtlava* in Czech."

"Okay. I'll take it," Willy said. "What's a guy with your knowledge doing in a place like this?"

"Same thing as you," Skyhawk said. "Stickin' it to the Man."

After a small birthday dinner at the bar, Willy got up in the middle of the night to take a leak. The light was on under Dan's studio door, and when Willy leaned close, he could hear that Dan was listening to the *Moldau* on his headphones.

If it weren't for the boy, Willy would have followed the example of Doc and Harriet Ambrose. The days without his wife, his dearest friend, were hypnotic in their pain. The black cancer of loneliness he had suffered in prison was little in comparison, a mere warm up. If he didn't keep moving, he found himself staring off into space in a trance of misery. He slept on the couch and took his clean clothes from where he folded them in the laundry room, barely able to go into the bedroom at all. When he showed up at the bar for the first time of the day, he had a habitual struggle not to pour himself a large whiskey and simply keep on drinking. He would waver in front of the large racks of bottles, sometimes seeming to himself to be frozen in time, locked in that position, before leaning away and into the motion of making a cup of coffee. If he drank, it was at night, where he knew the activity would be curtailed by sleep. He listened to Mae's voice: Don't drink too much. Eat right. Get enough sleep. Take care of the boy.

"I'll be along," Willy would mutter.

Dan rarely talked about Mae or her absence. If he broke his general taciturnity, his comments were terse and controlled, but once or twice he started a sentence with, "When Gramma used to..." and cut himself short, giving a quick glance to his grandfather's eyes as if he had committed a transgression, strayed into an area which was forbidden. He never said anything about Willy sleeping on the couch.

Willy came home once on a Saturday afternoon, having forgotten some paperwork he had brought home from the bar, and found Dan, obviously just out of bed, sitting at Mae's unused piano. His long hair was in spiky disarray, and the bleak look on his face made him look years older. Unaware that Willy had come in through the back door and was standing in the kitchen, he sat at the keys, plunking haltingly. Willy recognized the notes of the first movement of Beethoven's Sixth, the Pastoral, one of Mae's favorites. Willy's chest thumped more with love than it did even with sadness.

Willy watched him sitting, his brow drawn tight, fumbling at the keys until he got the first eight or nine notes right. When Dan noticed that Willy was standing there, he didn't exactly jump, but his eyes widened, the look on his face as if he had been caught doing something shameful.

"I'm sorry!" he said, closing the lid over the keys as if to hide evidence.

"No, no," Willy said. "I didn't mean to startle you. Go ahead!"

"I was just messing around," Dan said. "I have to take a shower anyway."

Dan got up and walked toward the bathroom and Willy, trying to stand aside, stood in his way instead. They did this for a few seconds, moving back and forth, and when Dan finally got past him, actually looking embarrassed, Willy slapped him on the back so hard that he was sure that the comradeliness of it seemed forced.

"I'll never be too old for stupid," Willy muttered to himself when he retrieved the paperwork he was looking for and went back out the kitchen door.

When summer came, and Dan's grades were more than good enough to have earned him some freedom, Willy let him run wild. He allowed him work at the bar as much as he wanted, and the boy was usually willing to fill in for any of the other employees who wanted to go on vacation. He didn't want to overburden the boy with work, though; after what he imagined to be a bad summer the year before, Willy was glad to give him his freedom. He was needed most at the bar around the weekend and was a diligent worker, but there were times during the week when Dan might take a pack and a canoe and be gone for days.

To walk the streets of the town, especially when high, was densely unreal. When Bobby Dolan ran into him- bigger, acne-spattered, but still his goofy self- Dan had a moment when he was on the verge of freaking out. What was real? Was it Greysport, Portview, Jorge and Adriana and Darnell? Was it the beach, Graziano's deli, the warehouse ruins? The burglarized time that he had spent with Gigi in the Gates mansion, how could that have been real, he wondered, looking around him at the small town, where such things would be incomprehensible.

As his boredom increased, so did his creativity. He received vacuum-sealed shipments of marijuana and acid from the Gates brothers, weighing out the weed into convenient bags and parceling the blotter acid into individual hits, selling each out of the back door of the bar (in the tradition of the Schommer brothers) or after school by appointment, and then only to people he trusted. The excitement of doing something illicit gave his days a little more spice, and put more money in his pocket than he got from doing his work at the bar, although that job provided him a cover for this extra income.

When Dan was straight, Willy's deterioration made him anxious and then angry, a connection he, himself, did not perceive, much less understand. It was subverbal and unconscious, unseen waves which lifted and dropped his conscious mind. In that conscious mind was the knowledge that the old man disgusted and embarrassed him.

When he was high, though (having smoked some of his own product), or amicably drunk on beer, he often loved the old man, seeing, in flashes, the sadness and longing that had settled into his face, gravity and grief having seemed to draw on the strong lines he remembered from childhood, those lines now filigreed with puckers and scrimshaw. Willy's hard brown hands, especially under the light at the kitchen table, were still often fascinating, with their corded, wizened knuckling and forgotten stories untold.

The old man tried to give him advice on women, but Dan knew his own experience was unique. The old man could know nothing about women, married, as he was, all those years. Dan saw it as pointless to talk to him on the subject. In the usual environments where he spent time with the Willy- river, bar, woods, or home- the subject was either too awkward to speak of, or he didn't want to ruin the moment with a conversation that was too deep.

And so Willy didn't know about Dan's brief relationship with Karen, a petite blonde girl from a farm west of the river. Her dad, she said, raised hogs, but her mother had felt repressed and had left the farm to come to MacDougal, where she could work for a tourist-oriented art gallery, collecting unemployment in the winter. Karen was pretty and smart, liking Dan enough to make him feel awkward. Having the same streak of appreciation for art that her mother had, she liked Dan's work so much that it made him want to stop any involvement with art whatsoever. They had made out furiously after a party in a grove of trees by the river. Dan had shown up as the provider of smoke, sure that he would otherwise not have been invited. He had stood aloof, safe in that pose, refilling his plastic cup of beer from the keg set up by the enterprising hosts of the party, students at his school. Several people seemed surprised and pleased that he was there, but he was cool to them, engaging only cursorily in conversation until, one by one, they went away. Karen had finally approached him, nearly grabbing him, after half an hour of his morose inattention, and dragged him away into the underbrush.

After that day, whenever Dan was with Karen he felt paralyzed. She was sweet and sunny, happy and smart. She shouldn't want him, and he couldn't defile her. When he kissed her, he thought of Gigi, with her pale skin and black clothing, her cigarette breath and sexual wisdom. Kissing Karen came to feel like he was dragging his ass across fresh, sunlit sheets in a Sunday bedroom, leaving skidmarks, the only besmirchment in an otherwise cheerful room. He almost made a painting about it, but hesitated, wondering where the subject would go, what would be its point. She didn't so much dump him as fade away, saying that she had to spend time with her father on the farm that summer, never answering his letters packed with drawings.

There was Ellie, her brown hair threaded with auburn highlights, a pointed chin and merry brown eyes. Her father was a psychologist in Black Marsh, making the commute along the river road every day. She wanted to be a botanist, and was attracted to Dan, she said, because he was so different from anyone she knew.

At another beer party, they had slapped together as if covered with suction cups when the alcohol had overcome Dan's reticence and reluctance. Having no place to go, Dan had come up with the plan to sneak into the rear door of the bar and go up to the spare bedroom overlooking the alley. They slipped in cautiously, going up the back stairs and into the room, which was lit only by a dim light from the alley. Once there, they had sucked wetly on each others' mouths with a fervor that only teenagers can muster, Dan yanking off his flannel shirt and the black t-shirt underneath, Ellie taking off her sweater and working at the buttons of her blouse.

When she was down to her white bra and panties, Dan in his jockey shorts with a protuberant hardon, she laid down on the trapunto quilt of the old bed.

"Come on," she said.

It was sweet, it was perfect. There she was, hands spread, smiling, hair lashed across the white pillow.

Dan hesitated. *Maldito.*

Dan heard the tread of the boots coming up the stairs and knew it was Bob. It was the break he needed.

"Shhhh!" he held his fingers to his lips, then palms down to motion her to stillness. They watched each other, wide-eyed. Bob's footsteps receded down the hall to a small storage room at the end of it. Dan listened at the door, holding his breath. The boots came back down the hall and seemed to slow for just a moment outside the bedroom. The door had no lock, and Dan watched the doorknob, waiting for it to turn. After a moment, the footsteps continued down the stairs.

When Dan was sure Bob was gone, he said, "Okay, this isn't cool. We should get out of here."

"But…" Ellie said.

"No, really, we should go."

Ellie seemed disappointed, not to mention mystified, but got dressed. They went out the way they had come in, and Dan walked her home.

She seemed to lose interest in Dan not long after that, and it pierced him to see her with another boy some weeks later.

He told himself that it was good to be solitary; nobody in the little town could understand what he was about anyway. He was cool.

As the town became more and more stifling to him, Dan found the most solace in being alone in the woods or on the river. If he happened to be relishing a particularly melancholy mood, he went up to the old abandoned hotel (which seemed closer to actual collapse every time he went), or up into the old mossy cemetery under the huge old oaks. Feeling cleansed by these refreshingly mournful spots, he would then strike out for places with as few signs of human influence as possible.

As with the old warehouses or the beach in Greysport, he brought food and books in his backpack, along with other things to keep him diverted and occupied. It was at times when he was off alone, paradoxically, that he didn't think about his loneliness. He didn't know he was lonely, he didn't know he was desolate. He thought that people he saw who appeared happy were frauds and cowards for faking it.

To sit unseen on the top of a bluff, looking down with binoculars on the activities of those on the river, provided endless hours of entertainment. He made up stories about the lives of the people he watched. He witnessed arguments and affection, drudgery and boredom, little bits of drama, fishermen drinking beer and picking their noses and eating it. A couple once anchored their boat almost as close as they could get to him on the river below, then looked around a bit anxiously before taking off their clothes and lying down in the cockpit of the boat to go at it in the sunshine. Dan watched, laughing, holding the binoculars in one hand and eating a peanut butter and jelly sandwich with the other. People tended to look around but not up, he noticed, perhaps some adjunct of evolution on the savanna. He felt like a ghost, watching them all unobserved.

He sat like this one afternoon, watching the goings-on. When it began to get dark, he built a fire and made some soup, dropping acid with a gulp of water from his canteen. Storm clouds began to build in the west, and he put up his tent in the clearing under some of the sheltering trees. In time, he got off on the acid, and soon after, the storm poured slowly across the dark sky. Dan lay in his tent watching the thunderstorm rumble overhead and across the river in a slow-motion roll. Later in the night, the same storm would be raining down on Greysport.

He tripped. The rain came down and the sky was dark, but when the lightning laced white across the sky, or crawled swiftly out and down from the clouds and along their underbellies like neon spiders on a black ceiling, it revealed the structures of cumulus clouds otherwise invisible in the night. Flash, cloud, flash, cloud. Dan marveled at this. It was an image of the texture of reality unknown, towering structures revealed in brief glimpses to humankind. It was too much to leave untouched. He took off his clothes and left them in the tent, unzipping the screen and emerging naked into the rain, holding up his arms which appeared white and blue when the lightning slipped skeletal fingers through the clouds. He watched the storm until it ended, then slipped back, shuddering, into the warmth of his sleeping bag, falling asleep just before dawn.

When he got home the next afternoon, he started painting what he had seen, wondering about how Rene Magritte might have done it. Soon he was absorbed in the process and the afternoon disappeared. It took him a while to notice that Willy had entered the house and was standing behind him, watching. Willy leaned against the doorjamb with his arms crossed, his smile contracting in deep wrinkles around his watery eyes. Dan smiled back and continued applying paint to the canvas, distracted, and, for the time being, content.

Willy thought that Dan should exhibit the finished painting somewhere, like Julia's gallery.

"I can't," Dan said.

"Why not?"

"It's…personal."

"The painting?"

"Yeah."

Willy watched him for a few moments. "Don't do that."

"Do what?"

"Hide yourself."

"Why not?"

"You've got something," Willy said in his unreadable manner. "Give it."

Willy was stern, naturally, and still had something of his old authority.

"All right," Dan said.

Willy appeared to forget about the painting, at some point, and didn't pressure Dan to put it in Julia's gallery, or, worse, to enter it into another local contest for kids his age. Dan continued to paint, and the canvasses stacked up. If he'd cared more, he would've taken them out and burned them.

Willy worried when the boy was gone, unsurprisingly, and knew that every day they spent apart was one of a finite number. On the other hand, if he forced Dan too much, he might pull away entirely. He thought it best to let him go until he was hungry enough to return, in spite of how he himself missed the boy.

Emilio seemed to understand his plight. Although two of his daughters were still nearby, they and their children frequent visitors, the virtual estrangement that had happened years ago between Emilio and Katita was still in effect. Willy tried to reassure him that it was due to the habits of living that Katita had acquired, the routine of the life she had established, rather than any lingering animosity.

"We're almost through another war since then," Emilio said to Willy. "It's been so long since I've seen her, I sometimes think I wouldn't recognize her on the street."

Willy had nothing to say to that. He just nodded slowly.

Dan went fishing with them that summer, and hunting in the fall. Emilio had never had sons, of course, and his own grandchildren tended to roll their eyes when he tried to share his extensive knowledge as an amateur naturalist. Dan, on the other hand, was an observant student. Willy would watch as his old friend gave the boy an impromptu lesson, perhaps bending over a dragonfly with a magnifying glass, or inspecting the gills of a freshly caught fish. Dan was not talkative, but interested, often fascinated. Willy knew this was good for both of them.

Deer season came and they took to the bluffs upriver. Dan was groggy getting up before dawn, being on teenager time rather than old man time, as Willy put it. A cup of Willy's strong coffee did the trick, though, and they were soon dressed and ready to go out into the fresh snow just as the sky was turning a faint slate grey in the east behind the naked black trees. Dan carried the Springfield Willy had bequeathed him for his birthday. As they approached the tree stand Dan was to occupy, Willy gave him a reminder of what to do: to remain as motionless as possible, to look around by moving his eyes, not his body.

"Try to see with your peripheral vision," Willy said.

"I *know*, Grampa," Dan said, and climbed up into the stand.

"I give you one bullet because you get one shot," he said. "You can't be banging away like some fascist."

"I *know*."

It wasn't until the afternoon that Dan got his first deer. Willy heard the single gunshot from the direction of Dan's tree stand and came through the snowy brush to find Dan standing over a doe. He was reassured, in a way, to find that the boy was not jubilant; he'd hate to discover that his grandson was an asshole. The look on his face, rather, was one of puzzlement, of near-comprehension, as if he were seeing something in the form of the doe that he almost recognized.

"Well, good job," Willy said quietly, and when Dan looked up, the focus came back to his eyes. "Good shot. She felt no pain. Let's dress her."

Dan wasn't squeamish about the process of cleaning the doe, and nodded patiently when Willy couldn't resist an opportunity to lecture.

"Meat comes from somewhere," Willy said as he gutted the animal. "Somewhere that's not very pretty. If people eat meat and think that hunting is barbaric, they're not taking responsibility for their own carnivorousness. You got me?"

"Yes," Dan said, standing still and seeming a little sad.

A marinated tenderloin from the doe was served for Thanksgiving dinner at Emilio and Solveig's. Dan went out for a walk along the river as dinner was being prepared and those so inclined drank hard cider around the fire. When dinner was served, Willy made an effort to give credit to Dan for providing something for the table. Dan, whose appetite seemed immense, acknowledged the praise from around the table with a perfunctory nod as he ate methodically.

Bob Two Bears, who had overcome his old dislike of Thanksgiving (at least among these friends), seemed to think that it was expected of him to say something pithy and recondite about Dan's first kill as a hunter, although no one had asked him.

"So here's what I have to say, with my deep and spiritual native wisdom." He held up a glass of cider, and the table went silent.

Bob raised his eyes to the ceiling and intoned, "Please pass the mashed potatoes!"

Everyone laughed, even Dan.

The following summer, Julia's nephews Charlie and Jim came out to visit. Julia had been talking about selling her house and her arts and crafts shop and moving to Europe, and had told Willy that the nephews had wanted to get out to the river while they had the chance.

Both of the boys had grown since Willy had last seen them. They pulled up in front of Julia's house in a rumbling roadster with a paint job so dark green that it was almost black. The two had a changed demeanor, especially Charlie, the elder. Julia had said that Charlie had been in some trouble back in Greysport, but had not elaborated on it. Whatever had happened seemed to have made the boy harder, and, in his black t-shirt, frayed jeans and wild blonde hair, he didn't look like the local kids, except for Dan, perhaps. Both of them were muscling up, and taller, the older one a few inches over Dan's height, the younger one parallel to it. Willy noticed that, when Charlie shook his hand (respectfully, as always), a skull-and-crossbones earring glinted from beneath his hair. Kids, Willy thought. Trouble, he thought.

Upon seeing the Gates brothers, Dan was happier than Willy had seen him since before Gordon's death, when he had been a child and a different person. Dan almost ran out of the house, stopping short and opening the screen door of the porch slowly, walking across the adjoining lawns of the houses. The boys met in the middle of the lawn and shoved each other playfully, even competitively. They soon announced that they were going camping.

"Have fun," Willy told them, realizing much later that, if his instincts had been functioning properly, or if he'd paid attention to them, he might have had a feeling of misgiving. When the boys returned days later, barging into the bar for hamburgers, they were dirty and tired. Charlie and Jim seemed to want to hang around and listen to stories from Willy and Bob, but it was obvious that Dan was uncomfortable and wanted to get them to leave. They did, and stayed out late, so late that Willy was asleep on the couch when Dan got home. He feigned sleep as Dan tiptoed into his bedroom, and said nothing about it the next day.

Willy gave the trio the task of painting the front of the bar, offering a fair wage. He hadn't consulted Dan on the idea beforehand, and it was obvious that the boy was put out. Dan shook his head when Willy gave him the money to go to the hardware store for the necessary supplies. When he told Dan to bring him a receipt, the boy sighed gravely. It was only after they had left that Willy thought about his history in the hardware store. Surely the boys would not make the connection.

The Gates boys seemed to be fascinated with the bar and with Willy, who was positive that there were times when he came up from the basement or in from the back door that Bob was telling them a grandiose story of Willy's past. Charlie and Jim Gates would be listening, Dan playing darts or a game of pool. When Willy came in, there was a slight pause before their demeanors changed and Bob started a sentence with "So! Anyway!"

It seemed that Dan was happier but more tired when the Gates boys were around. He woke up late in the day, normal for a teenager, but always showed up for work on time. He was gone as much as he possibly could be, though, and Julia said that her nephews were missing just as much.

The three boys left for another trip on the river, the three of them in a canoe, but not before Willy gave them a cautionary talk. He knew that Dan was competent to take care of himself in most situations, but there was something about the wild-looking city boys which told Willy that they were capable of doing something imprudent. It didn't matter that they were polite and seemed actually interested when Willy spoke to them, taking into account a bit of glib con-artistry on Charlie's part. He recognized the simmering energy and recklessness just beneath their trained good manners, and the mistaken youthful belief that they could pull one over on someone as weary and wily as Willy. He clearly saw their capacity for mischief, but let them go, trusting Dan to be responsible and level-headed.

That was life with a teenager: optimism tempered by occasions of betrayed trust. When Willy got a call from the Sheriff's Department in Black Marsh in the early morning to inform him that Dan was in custody, he exhaled slowly through his nose and said, "I'll be there as soon as I can."

He'd gotten letters from Charlie and Jim, saying they'd been thinking of coming out for the summer. The idea became more distinct, eventually taking the form of actual planning. Charlie had gotten his license a year before, and had gone around his father's half-hearted objections to use money from a trust fund to buy his dream car, a Barracuda.

Dan had a dim hope that they would bring Gigi, but knew it was not going to happen. He made due, instead, by waiting until Willy wasn't home and taking pornography and Gigi's pink and black envelope into the bathroom, along with the slightly used panties she had sent him in a plastic bag, hidden inside the sweater she had sent as a present.

"I miss my naughty boy," said black ink letters on the pink paper.

The day Charlie and Jim showed up, Dan was in his room reading a book while Willy puttered in the kitchen. The phone rang, and Willy called, "It's for you!"

A phone call for Dan was a rarity. If it wasn't a call from the bar asking him to fill in, he got no calls at all. None from school, none from friends. None, ever, from his mother. Anyone who bought his weed talked to him in person, and then only people who he knew and trusted as customers.

The voice on the other end was Charlie's. "Be in front of your house in five minutes," Charlie said, and hung up.

Dan wasn't about to do what Charlie ordered, and sat in the shadows of the living room, waiting on the piano bench. Willy brought him a cup of coffee. In five minutes on the dot, a dark and lustrous Barracuda rumbled up in front of the house, pointing in the wrong direction, its driver's side tires just up on the grass. Charlie had staged it so that when he got out, it was he who Dan saw first. Dan nearly snorted coffee from his nose.

In spite of himself, Dan shot to the front door. Charlie leaned against the car inside the open door, looking like a rock star as he patted the roof smugly, squinting a little against the sunlight. Dan grinned then hid it, and forced himself to walk across the front porch and down the steps, slowly, as if not impressed. Jim got out on the passenger side.

"Hey, man," Jim said. He looked like the bass player.

Dan lifted his chin and said, "Jim."

He regarded Charlie and the car for a few moments and said, "Where'd you get this piece of shit?"

Charlie smiled and said, "You rippin' on my ride?"

They crossed the gap between them and shoved each other, back and forth, harder each time, laughing. Jim came across the lawn and Dan got him in a headlock, grinding his knuckles into the boy's scalp while Jim punched him in the kidney.

After repeating the cover story for Willy that the Gates boys had fed their aunt, they grabbing some gear and took off immediately in the car. Jim graciously yielded the shotgun position to Dan, who found a spare pair of sunglasses in the glove compartment and put them on. Charlie turned up the volume on the tape deck, which was playing a tune by Blue Oyster Cult.

They rolled down the main street, locals turning to look at them from the sidewalk. Dan pretended not to see them, but watched peripherally, putting a blasé expression on his face. When he saw Karen and Ellie (together!) with shopping bags in their hands, he deigned to notice when they stopped in their tracks, their mouths slightly open, and waved slowly. He lifted his chin expressionlessly at the girls as the Barracuda rumbled by. Only a block later the experience was repeated, when they passed a group of boys from the high school who imagined themselves to be tough guys. Dan, Charlie, and Jim all stared at them as they passed. One of them began to wave but stopped in the midst of the gesture. The others slowly lowered their eyes or looked away.

They crossed the bridge and took a left onto the river road.

"You gonna show me what this P.O.S. can do?" Dan said.

Charlie snorted and punched it.

Dan had never known the river road could be so exhilarating. The engine vibrated the vehicle as Charlie downshifted into curves, then up again as they came into a straightaway. Charlie stomped on the accelerator, and Dad was jolted back in his seat, his eyes wide.

Charlie saw this, smiled and said, "Pussy."

They pulled off the road at a corner gas station next to a county highway that led up into the hills. The driver of a black dumptruck they had passed for no reason a few minutes before roared by, sounding his air horn and holding a beefy red arm out the window to flip them off. The boys all laughed.

"Better get some fuel," Charlie said. He gassed the car and went into the station to pay. When he came out, he had a case of beer.

"Dude didn't even card me," he said, handing the beer back to Jim. "No one ever does. Got this beautiful fake ID for nothing."

Jim doled out beers and they raced up into the hills. They pulled over at a scenic overlook and jumped out of the car, ignoring a family next to a camper.

"We don't want to get all groggy from beer, now do we?" Charlie said, "That'd be irresponsible. So we should probably do some acid."

"Let's just do a hit apiece," Jim suggested, "so we don't lose our shit."

Charlie pulled a knapsack from the things packed in the trunk, among which Dan noticed two baseball bats and a length of chain.

"What, no guns?" he said.

"We were counting on you for that," Jim said.

Charlie laughed and handed out hits of blotter.

"This is shaping up to be a good summer," Dan said.

"You missed us, didn't you?" Jim said, grinning.

"You assholes? Fuck no," smiling and punching him on the arm.

They put the blotter on their tongues, which they stuck out to show each other the little white squares. Then they washed the hits down with beer.

"Here goes," Charlie said with a carnivorous grin. They got back in the Barracuda and hurtled off.

The city boys were not used to life in by the river, and Dan found himself explaining things as simple as silos. When they drove past a pig farm, the Gates boys howled at the stench.

"You like bacon? Ham? Pork chops?" Dan asked.

The boys agreed that they did.

"That's where it comes from, man," Dan said, spreading his hands.

They were halfway through the case of beer before they began to get off on the acid. The looming future of a shortage of beer threw them into a panic, although they did not slow their consumption.

"We've got to find a store," Charlie said.

"My anxiety is increasing in inverse proportion to our beer supply," Jim said.

They all cracked up at that.

They knew that they were tripping when they realized that they had entered what Charlie called The First Chapter of the Trip.

"You ever notice how tripping is like that? Episodic?"

"You mean like when you spend and eternity in one room, and as soon as you go into another, a new episode begins?" Dan said, laughing.

"Yes!" Charlie said, punching the steering wheel and sounding the horn. "Precisely!"

Jim said, "And this is the chapter entitled, 'The Lads' Quest for Beer'."

"Goddammit!" Charlie said, "They've always told me that you were a genius, and I did not, until this moment, believe it!"

"*One* of us has to carry the burden of intelligence," Jim said.

Charlie began to swerve back and forth on the curving road, going from shoulder to shoulder and back again. Dan and Jim yelled at him to be careful.

"Who's a genius!" Charlie cried, steering with his left hand on the wheel and a beer in his right, turning sideways to look at them both, the hilly road rushing by.

"Fuck!" Dan shouted. "*You* are! *You* are!"

"Was there ever any *doubt*?" Jim yelled. "Genius! Focus on the task of finding us a liquor store!"

That snapped Charlie right to.

"Oh yeah," he said. He finished his beer, tossed the bottle out the window to shatter on the road. It was minutes before he asked for another.

Down to their last three beers, they found a liquor store at the intersection of two county highways, along with a bar and a post office. It was only Dan's explanation of the lettered system of such highways that made them realize how much they were tripping.

"County X and County Z, man," Jim said. "We're at the edge of the known universe."

This struck them as funny, as small things will to tripping people, and they leaned on each other, laughing. It took considerable effort for Charlie to get it together enough to go into the store. When he came out, he brought two cases of beer on one trip, two styrofoam coolers and ice on the next.

"Make room in the trunk," he said.

They were far enough away from Dan's home turf that he wasn't sure where he was. This did nothing to slow Charlie down, however. He roared over the countryside, getting lift going over hilltops so that the beer sloshed in their bottles and Dan had tiny periods of weightlessness, his guts floating upwards in his abdomen, only to plop down again when they lit upon the asphalt.

They found the river again by heading towards the setting sun, and ended up in a small park on top of a bluff. They took a break from the drive, bringing several beers and a couple of joints over to a park bench. Dan's body tingled, both from the acid and the scary thrill of sizzling through the hills with Charlie at the wheel. The sunset was on the verge of becoming stupendous.

"This is relaxing around here," Charlie said. "I haven't seen a cop all day."

"I think they're pretty thinly distributed," Dan said. "My grampa says they stick to the highway along the river to make money off of speeders."

Charlie had mentioned in a terse letter that he had gotten into some trouble, but hadn't expanded on it. This was their first chance to talk.

"So, what happened with you, anyway," Dan said, passing the joint to Jim, whose look told him that this wasn't an entirely safe subject.

"Got busted for burglary," Charlie said.

Dan shot his eyes wide. "Shit!"

"Couldn't let you have all the good stories," Charlie said. He told Dan about how he had gotten the inspiration to burglarize cars from Dan himself, and thought that he needed to expand his own horizons. Apart from nearly constant acts of random vandalism, this gave him a new stream of income, independent of what Dan thought was his enviably lavish allowance. The sales from the thefts supported the purchase of pound bags of weed and hundred-lots of acid, which kept Charlie and Jim supplied with their favorite diversions for free, the profit from the sales covering their own large scale use.

They sold Dan his cut at no profit, and Dan didn't ask about his preferential treatment, although he wondered about it. As Charlie told the tales of his exploits, Jim only made occasional interjections or embellishments.

"Weren't you there for most of this?" Dan asked Jim.

"I was there for a lot of it," Jim said, a bit defensively.

"Gotta look out for my little brother," Charlie said.

Jim snorted. "Somebody ought to look out for *you*."

Charlie went on to explain that he'd advanced to burglary with some older boys from school, boys who came from a neighborhood closer to the port and who were much less privileged, and therefore, apparently, more desirable company in Charlie's eyes, Dan surmised. They'd done several B and E's (as Charlie called them) together, but he had been alone when he'd gotten busted.

"Whose house was it?" Dan asked.

"Ha! You know him! Scotty, remember that kid? Snotty Scotty? You almost beat the shit out of him at our house?"

"Him? What an asshole."

Charlie laughed. "That's why I did his house," he said.

"How did you get busted?"

"Got caught red-handed. I thought they were gone for a week, but they opened the garage door with their opener and drove in, just as I was about to lift some tools. I ran into the house and out the back door, but they saw me. The cops matched up my footprints in the snow."

"Wow," Dan said.

"No shit." Charlie gave a philosophical shrug.

To save face in the neighborhood and as an ethics professor, Henry Gates had let Charlie sit for two weeks in Greysport County Jail, where he had just turned old enough to be detained. It appeared to have been a transformative experience.

"So what happened in jail?"

Charlie abruptly shut the conversation down.

"Nothing much. It was boring. Let's get out of here."

"What, did you make some nice friends?" Dan said, smiling.

"Shut up."

"Ooooooh, like some nice boyfriends? Big horny ones?"

He couldn't help but needle Charlie, but was taken aback when Charlie shoved him, hard.

"Shut the fuck *up*!" Charlie grunted.

"Don't fucking *shove* me, man!" Dan said, shoving him back, harder. Charlie shifted his right shoulder toward Dan and snapped out a kick to his chest which landed him on his back. Dan looked up at Charlie, struggling to draw a breath.

"Think I forgot about that time you decked me?" Charlie said. "*I* don't forget." He walked forward, panting with anger.

Jim got between them. "Wo, wo, *wo!*" he said. "Be cool!"

Dan got up and found himself going at Charlie, but Jim put his hand on his chest, now holding both of them apart. "Fucking be *cool!* Jesus! You want to fight, let's go fight some rednecks! Fuck!"

Jim stayed between them until they settled down, then handed out beers all around.

"You guys can't be doing shit like that," Jim said, in a position to lecture for once. "We're bros, right? Droogs! Can't be fighting amongst ourselves! Come on!"

Dan and Charlie both hung their heads and drank their beers.

"Just don't make fun of me about being in the slams," Charlie said. "Makes a good story, but it pretty much sucked."

"Okay," Dan said. "Next time, you won't be surprising me with any moves like that. Where'd you learn that shit?"

"Later," Charlie said. "Let's get out of here."

They finished their beers and smashed the bottles on a boulder before getting back into the car. Dan would have loved to watch the remains of the sunset (maximally augmented, as it was, by the acid), but the drama was over and the beer-fueled trip with his friends was too exciting to pass up. He laughed in glee when Charlie stomped the accelerator and patched out of the gravel parking lot.

It got dark. Dan wasn't completely sure where he was until they got down on the river road, when he realized that they were forty miles south of MacDougal Island. They cruised north along the road, looking for any kind of excitement, some local kids with a muscle car, anything.

Rumbling slowly through one small town, they were eyeballed by a cop perpendicular to the road with his radar out the window. The cop watched the boys as they rolled past. Charlie kept his left hand on the steering wheel, a beer in his right and down next to the seat. He looked blandly over at the cop, then back to the road. Dan tried to appear casual in talking over the seat to Jim, whose face had assumed a look of appealing innocence. They drove past.

"Keep an eye on him," Charlie said, flicking his eyes to the rearview mirror.

"He's not moving," Dan said. "Not moving. Not moving. Shit! He's pulling out. Here he comes."

"Okay, stay cool," Charlie said, glancing again in the rearview.

The cop followed at a distance, then accelerated until he was ten feet behind them. Charlie didn't pretend not to see him, nor did he act furtively. They were almost out of town, back into the safety of the dark, when the cop flicked on his take-down lights.

"Fuckfuckfuckfuckfuck," Jim said.

"Be cool," Charlie said. "I'll pull over, and when he approaches the car on foot, I'll take off. He can't catch us."

"Shit," Dan breathed.

Charlie slowed and pulled over onto the shoulder, watching the cop on in the rearview. The cop pulled up behind them…and rolled past, turning on his siren and speeding down the road into the night, then taking a right and heading up into the bluffs, the cycling red lights making flickering shadows in the trees. Then he was gone.

"Well!" Jim said in a cheerful tone. "Holy fucking shit! Would you mind driving someplace where I can change my pants and wash my ass?"

The boys looked at each other and roared with laughter. They celebrated their escape by opening more beers and lighting a joint.

"Let's make a mental note to stay out of that town," Charlie said. "I think that guy was just fucking with us, and all he needs is probable cause to pull us over."

"He might just pull us over and make up the probable cause later," Dan said. "I told you about cops on the river road, man."

Even Charlie agreed that they might have pushed their luck for the night. They drove back closer to home to a place Dan knew in a grove of trees next to the river. The night was muggy, but they built a fire to keep away the insects, and sat drinking, smoking dope, and mildly tripping. They went home in the blue light before dawn, Dan creeping in through the kitchen to his room, looking into the living room to see Willy rolled over on the couch with his back to the room.

The brothers appeared fascinated with the idea of hanging out in a real bar, as none were available in the posh neighborhood where they lived, and they wouldn't have been allowed in one in any case. The fact that, as a family member of the owner, Dan was allowed to get behind the bar and serve customers seemed to impress Charlie and Jim even more.

"You are the luckiest motherfucker," Charlie said. "Pour us some beers."

"Can't," Dan said. "My grampa'd lose his liquor license."

"Who's going to say anything?" Jim said.

"Can't do it."

"Dick," Charlie said.

Dan leaned over the bar and stage-whispered, widening his eyes imploringly, *"We'll go get more later. Fake ID."*

The Gates boys met Bob Two Bears and many of the regulars, and couldn't seem to get enough stories to satisfy them. Dan was annoyed that they were so taken by this boring environment, and played pool while Charlie and Jim hunched over hamburgers and ginger ales ("You'll get beer when you're old enough," Bob had said with mock severity). It aggravated him further that the brothers asked so many questions about his grandfather, his father, and his uncle, when he had made it clear that there was nothing much to tell. They had a gleaming machine parked up the street and hundreds of miles of roads to explore, and here they sat, leaning on the bar and interrogating Bob and the patrons, all of whom succumbed to the questioning far too readily for Dan's taste. Vexed and embarrassed, he broke the pool balls hard, making a few of them jump. He would gladly have changed places with Charlie and Jim, spending the summer by the lake, at a mansion with a swimming pool, with Gigi (a mainstay of his masturbatory fantasies) nearby.

Willy's stories were never mentioned in his presence; he didn't like them talked about any more than Dan did. Once or twice Willy came up the stairs from the basement or in from the back door when Bob was telling an inflated tale, suddenly forced to change the subject and make the change seem natural.

Willy was old, Dan knew, but nothing much was lost on him in the world of adults. He eyed the room suspiciously at any awkward silence, seeming to know that something was up, but not sure what, exactly, it was.

Dan had a good idea of Willy's motives when the old man gave the three of them the task of painting the front of the bar. It was pure Willy to give the boys something constructive to do, and Dan could also guess that Willy thought the brothers were a little shiftless and unaccustomed to work. Even though they both had plenty of money, they cheerfully accepted the assignment, apparently relishing the chance to have a closer relationship to the notorious Willy McGregor.

Willy gave Dan some cash and a list of supplies, and sent them to the hardware store.

"Bring me a receipt, and change," he said.

As they walked the worn wooden aisles of the store, with its pleasant smell of fertilizer, chemicals, and varnish, Charlie said to Dan, "Is this where he did it?"

"Where who did what?"

"Where Willy killed that guy. Beat him to death with a hammer."

"I notice you don't call him Willy to his face."

"No shit. He's a badass."

"He's old," Dan said.

"He'll always get 'Mr. McGregor' out of us," Jim said. "And is this where he did it or not?"

Dan sighed. "Okay, I'll show you. We never talked about it between us. He probably didn't say much to my grandmother, either, and they were like *this*." He held up crossed fingers.

Dan showed them where he thought it happened. The boys bent over to look at the floorboards.

"Maybe that's an old bloodstain there, in the crack between the boards," Jim said.

"Oh, yeah!" Charlie said.

"Jesus!" Dan said. "It was, like, fifty years ago! Let's just get the shit and do the job!"

"That's a bloodstain," Jim said. "Right there in that crack. That could be some dried brains, right there."

"No it's not! Come on!"

They didn't say anything to the kid behind the counter, a senior from Dan's school, who eyed them a bit nervously as he bagged up the painting supplies.

Out on the street, Charlie wouldn't let it alone. "You guys have great stories. Your family's just cool, is all I'm saying."

"Our dad's a pussy," Jim added, at the same time that Dan said, "*What* family?"

It was when they were painting (something Dan had to show them how to do) that they were not in party mode and talked at length to fill the time. Gigi, apparently, had found romance in Provence, the location of which had to be explained to Dan. This item of information made Dan's heart sink, although he didn't want to let on. Hugh was working at a gay bar for the fun of it and to augment his trust fund money while he studied voice. He had also been seriously studying martial arts.

"Really? Hugh?" Dan said.

"What, a homo can't be tough?" Charlie said, his tone a bit defensive. "All kinds of warriors were homos throughout history."

"The samurai?" Jim said. "Major gayboys."

"How 'bout the Spartans," Charlie said.

"Okay, okay," Dan said, dipping his roller in the pan of paint. "Hugh just seems too...kind-hearted for that sort of thing."

What had motivated Hugh, the brothers revealed, was a series of gay-bashings. Young hoodlums had recently revived the practice of trolling the areas of gay bars down by the port, looking for victims to beat up and roll for their money. Hugh had been working at the oldest and most famous gay bar in the city, one founded by a former sheriff and his lover, a piano player (as the story went), although Charlie and Jim had known nothing of this aspect of the bar's history. Hugh would one day tell Dan the history of the place, that the sheriff and the piano player had fled the oppression of the rural area where they had lived, and had come to the city to find that oppression had simply taken a different form. The sheriff, a man who knew the law and might have been dealing with some past shame, had stood up to repeated raids by local vice squads, by beat cops, and by public health department lackeys, resulting in an eventual pitched battle with the police in front of the barricaded bar. Gays had begun to push back.

If this tale had ever been told to Willy, he might have shaken his head and laughed, finally hearing the end of the story of his old friend, Marvin Purdue, the Sheriff. The connection was never made, though, by any of the parties involved.

For Hugh's part, he had carried on the tradition of the bar, which was seen by the regulars as the town hall of its community. When patrons had begun getting rolled, a group of men had formed to get militant and fight back, getting training in martial arts, studying forms of organized resistance, legal and otherwise. Hugh was foremost among them, and came up with their ironic name, the Raging Queens. The group became instrumental in putting fear in the hearts of would-be gay-bashers. Hugh was often seen in community newspapers, and was even mentioned in a newspaper article in the Greysport Tribune, along with a photo showing him looking lean, muscular, and stern.

"So he's been teaching us some stuff," Jim said. "That's where Charlie learned that kick he used on you. Hugh wouldn't have liked that, by the way. He says we should only use such training to 'do the right thing', whatever that means."

"That's what my grampa says," Dan said.

"And that's where they're both *wrong*," Charlie said.

Willy inspected the job they had done when they were finished. Dan had made a point of correcting Charlie and Jim's haphazard work as they had gone along, the result being that Willy was happy with the finished product and paid them immediately. Charlie and Jim gave each other pleased grins when they took the money. Willy and Dan exchanged their own look: perhaps this was the first time they'd earned money for actual work. Dan thought he also detected a spot of pity, of compassion, in the old man's eyes.

That compassion might have dissipated quickly if Willy had known what the boys had gotten up to next.

As they walked back up the street to the bungalow, Charlie said, "So! Guns!"

"Oh, here we go," Dan said.

"We never get to shoot guns," Jim said. "You do all the time!"

"It's no big deal," Dan said.

"So then we should do it!" Charlie said. "Right?"

"Man," Dan said, shaking his head but laughing a little.

"We've got a list of things we want to do while we're on vacation here," Jim said. "A list?"

"Yeah, want to see it?"

"Just tell me what's on it."

"Well, tripping and driving at high rates of speed while drinking lots of beer," Charlie said.

"Check," Dan said. "Did it."

"Sure, but that doesn't mean we can't do it some more," Charlie said.

"Good point." It *was* a good point. He'd often been so bored in MacDougal that he tripped or climbed rocks or worked out to exhaustion just to alleviate it. Now that the Gates boys were here, he found himself acting like the old men he hung around with, just as his friend Darnell had once said. Why was he being such a contrarian, when most of him wanted to do everything the brothers suggested, and more?

He shook it off and said, "What else is on your list?"

"We'd like to get in a drag race or a car chase sometime," Jim said, "but so far none of the local yokels have seemed capable or willing."

"This is America," Charlie explained. "You've got to have a car chase."

"There are gearheads all over out here," Dan said. "What else is there to do? We just haven't found the right ones."

"What happened to those hoods from up at the hotel that one time?" Jim said. "The ones we got with the M-80s?"

They all laughed, agreeing that it had been great. "Those guys are all gone," Dan said, "I haven't seen them in ages."

"We also have to shoot guns," Jim said. "Hence the current topic of conversation."

"Gotta get some bang," Charlie said. "And for that matter, we have to blow some shit up."

"Molotovs?" Dan smiled, surrendering to the mood.

"How about dynamite? Can you get any dynamite?"

"Why would I be able to get any dynamite?"

"You live out here!" Charlie cried. "You've got connections! You get to do cool shit that we can't do in Greysport!"

Dan didn't mention that he had blown up tree stumps with his grandfather and Mr. Benitez, and that he knew where Mr. Benitez stored his dynamite. The idea of the Gates brothers with dynamite in their possession was hair-raising enough that it made their firing guns seem manageable by comparison, and put temporary brakes on his spell of recklessness. And he wouldn't steal from Mr. Benitez, ever. So he compromised.

"Okay, we can shoot some guns. You have to be cool about it, though."

The brothers cheered and slapped each other five.

The shooting of guns had to involve targets, and Charlie came up with a solid idea about that. Their laissez-faire Aunt Julia had been so busy with tourist trade at her little gallery that the garden in her back yard had gotten neglected. Charlie and Jim wouldn't know the first thing to do if she asked them to tend to it (and she wouldn't have), so she had told the boys to take anything from it that they wished. Much of the home-grown produce was too small to use, but there were a number of melons in danger of rotting, and, best of all, at least four dozen watermelons.

"I don't know what I was thinking," Julia said to the boys. "This is all more than I can do anything with, I'm so busy. Take all you want. Really."

The boys all looked at each other, an idea hatching.

"Target practice," Charlie said.

Dan squinted in thought and improved on the idea. "*Moving* target practice," he said. "Let's fill up the trunk of your car."

While Charlie parked the car in the alley behind the bungalows, Dan went in the back door and down to the basement while the other boys loaded the trunk with neglected produce. He picked out his rifle and two of Willy's twelve-gauge shotguns in their cases, pushing down a slippery moment of guilt. After packing a canvas satchel with plenty of ammunition for both, he went up the stairs and out of the house, through the back yard and over the fence to where the boys sat in the rumbling car.

51

"Moving targets?" Charlie said, once the guns were on the floor by the backseat.

"Yep," Dan said. "I'll show you where to go."

"*Guns*, man!" Jim said, glee on his face. "We've got *guns*!"

They stopped for beer along the way. Dan then took them to a bank of land facing upstream at a curve in the river where the current was strong. Trees grew by the banks, and there was evidence that the place had been used for partying, with packed earth between the trees and around the banks of the river, beer cans and cigarette butts everywhere.

"Back the car up to the bank," Dan said.

The brothers got the hang of the shotguns with a little instruction, although they were melodramatic about their use, especially Charlie, who stood with his legs braced wide as he racked a round into the chamber. He gazed coolly out over the river and said, "Time for some melon *payback*."

Jim laughed hard at this, and Dan's safety training and respect for firearms dissolved as he began laughing as well.

"Jim," Dan said, racking a round into his rifle, "toss a watermelon in the river."

Jim took a melon from the trunk of the car and did so, the melon splashing in the water and quickly moving away in the current. Dan sighted down the barrel of the rifle, took in a breath, let out half of it, and fired. The watermelon exploded gratifyingly in a column of pink and green chunks, the spray of water and melon bits going high into the air.

The boys cheered.

"Death to the melon aggressors!" Charlie roared.

It was almost the best time that Dan could remember having. Charlie and Jim were only fair shots, even with the shotguns, but anything they missed, Dan picked off as it went downstream. Charlie had to try firing two shotguns at once, missing both melons, but Dan exploded them before they could escape. As always happens, it all went by too fast, and they were soon looking into a trunk bereft of produce.

It was at that point, as the boys all stood around with their respective gunbutts on their hips, the barrels pointed in the air, that a rusty brown van with four surly-faced rednecks inside and some Lynyrd Skynrd on the radio drove past, perhaps coming to the bank to party. When they saw the boys with guns at the ready and beers in their hands, they slowly drove by, giving small, polite nods on the way. The boys glared at them.

"That's right, crackers," Charlie muttered, "Keep on driving."

When the rednecks were gone, Jim said, "That was great. We should always have guns."

Amazingly enough, Dan managed to get the three of them and the guns back to town before anyone got shot, or Willy found out.

Late the next night, though, on their patrol of the nighttime roads, they found a target of opportunity: a golf course with a Bobcat and a backhoe parked in the lot near the entrance. As energized as the boys were with beer and acid, they saw no alternative but to hotwire the vehicles and tear around the course, ripping up greens and fairways. As they left, satiated with destruction to an almost post-coital extent, Charlie drank a beer while driving, and Jim lit up a joint.

"Anarchic landscaping," Charlie said, exhaling smoke reflectively. "That's what we'll call it."

Their efforts made it into the newspaper the next afternoon. With great satisfaction, the boys huddled in a booth of the Eyrie and read the article. Jim had to be restrained from hooting. As the three were exchanging smug looks, Willy brought them hamburgers and soft drinks.

"Everything okay with you fellas?" he said.

"Couldn't be better, sir," Charlie said.

With the days of the Gates boys' visit winding down, they had to go all the way to Black Marsh to find a car chase. They'd had a few close calls, including passing, at sundown, a double line of bikers from the local chapter of the Guardians of Nocturne. The bearded, long-haired men in faded denim and black leather, large patches with skulls on the backs of their vests, thundered by on their Harleys, not giving the boys a second glance.

"Okay," Charlie said, "We probably don't want to mess with those guys."

Dan had thought one of them looked familiar. Long and lanky with a handlebar moustache and a prosthetic left arm, Dan was almost certain he was one of the Schommer brothers. He was gone down the road in a roar and a flash, though, faster than Dan could snap his head around and say, "Hey, I know that dude!"

He didn't have time to think about the absent Schommer brothers as they shot over a hill, got some lift, and came down laughing just in time to see a slow-moving farm vehicle directly in front of them, wide enough to be over the centerline.

"Fuck!" Charlie cried, cranking the wheel to the left and going off onto the far shoulder, cursing again as their arc around the tractor revealed an oncoming pickup truck. He yanked the wheel back to the right, just missing the front of the tractor, but still forcing the pickup truck to do some unscheduled offroading in the tall grass of the ditch at the side of the road.

"Holy shit!" Dan shouted.

"Jesusfuckingchrist!" Jim yelled.

"Did you see the look on that guy's face!" Charlie shouted.

"Maybe we should go back and see if he's okay," Jim said.

"Fuck that!" Charlie said. "He probably can't identify us now."

"Hit it, hit it!" Dan cried, his body flooding warm with adrenaline. "Go, go, go!"

With that, Charlie pounded the accelerator and took off. They all laughed at the hilariousness of it, and opened fresh beers. Dan might have felt a flicker of remorse, but didn't want to show it. He thought Jim might have had a hint of the same feeling, but Jim was now laughing so hard that any misgivings he might have had had apparently disappeared.

Some trace of caution persuaded them to stay off the river road, and they came down into Black Marsh from the bluff. Try as they might, they were unable to find any takers for a race. Jim spotted a couple of muscle cars parked outside a bowling alley, but they decided it would look ridiculous to walk into the lanes and find the drivers of the vehicles, then challenge them to a race.

"That'd be lame," Charlie said.

Parking the 'Cuda, they waited for the drivers of the vehicles to come out, but didn't have the patience for it. Soon they were back on the road, prowling slowly, looking out the windows of the car for anything that smacked of possibility.

They ended up pulling into a Dog'n'Suds for some chili dogs. Covering the current case of beer with jackets, they did little to conceal the ones they had open. The carhop brought their chili dogs and onion rings out on the window tray, flirting a bit with Charlie as she did so. Charlie thanked her coolly, and she left looking a little defeated.

"I guess I'd like some strange pussy," he said, "but the local chicks don't really do it for me. Kind of hickish."

"No offense," he added for Dan's benefit. Dan shrugged.

Charlie and Jim had concluded that Black Marsh was boring, and Dan didn't try to alter their perception. "I told you so," he said. "When I'm done with high school, I'm out outta here. Moving to Greysport. Done."

"Nice place to visit," Jim said, his tone diplomatic. Dan gave him a sour look.

As they backed out of their stall to leave the parking lot of the Dog'n'Suds, a white pickup truck roared by on the street. Two young men were in the cab, four in the bed, all with crewcuts, most wearing jeans and white t-shirts. The boys in the back yelled and swore at a family in a station wagon poised to pull out onto the street, two of them threw beer bottles at the wagon, although they were sloppily aimed and smashed on the asphalt.

"Now those look like our kind of guys," Charlie said.

"Ohhh boy," Jim said.

"Be cool," Dan said. "Let's hang back in traffic and see where they go."

The 'Cuda was undeniably conspicuous in such a town, so it was wise to proceed with caution, Charlie doing it because it smacked of deviousness. The pickup had a cracked taillight lens, which made it easier to follow at a distance. The rednecks in the truck kept up their yelling and tossing of beer bottles, the driver laying on his horn from time to time, once or twice swerving into oncoming traffic.

"They might be hicks," Charlie said, "but you gotta like their style."

"It's shocking that such rowdiness should go undetected by the constabulary," Jim noted, and they laughed. "You'd think that an arrest would be imminent."

"The cops are probably staked out for speeders on the river road," Dan said. "I keep telling you."

They almost lost the rednecks when they squeaked through a yellow light, leaving the boys to be caught by the red, but found them again, a quarter mile ahead, when they got on the bridge which went west across the river and a few islands to the next state. The bridge had no lights, but the cracked taillight lens was still visible in the dark among the few other vehicles making the crossing. Halfway across the bridge, in the midst of slough and marsh and thick stands of dark trees, the pickup took a right at a break in the siding of the bridge and out onto the slough, the white sidepanels and a cloud of dust visible momentarily in the lights of a passing car.

"Oh, I think they just pulled off onto Frenchman's Slough," Dan said. "There are roads and trails back there for hunting and shit. Boat landings."

"Decent!" Charlie said. At the break in the siding, he pulled off. There was a gravel parking lot for vehicles with boat trailers, empty at this time of night. The pickup was nowhere in sight. A two-rutted track carved by countless sets of tires went north into the woods. Dust was still settling in the headlights of the 'Cuda.

"That's the only way they could've gone," Dan said.

"Shall we?" Charlie said, waggling his eyebrows.

"Oh, shit," Jim said.

Dan was sweating in the muggy night, his heart squeezing in his chest like a rhythmic fist. They thumped down the rutted tracks, long grass and tree trunks the only things visible in the headlights. Charlie kept one set of tires on the hump between the ruts and one just off to the side to keep from bottoming out.

"Maybe we should get the bats and shit out of the trunk," Jim said. "Just in case."

"Ahhh!" Charlie scoffed, although Dan thought it might be a good idea.

Finally, they saw light through the foliage up ahead, the boughs of the trees lit from underneath, the dense leaves of the underbrush black in silhouette. The sound of country rock and loud voices came through the trees and brush.

"Man," Jim said, "we just passed a turn-around back there. "Let's back out and get out of here."

"Don't be a pussy," Charlie said, and drove forward. "You know what Dad says: 'The coward dies a thousand deaths, the brave man dies but one'."

"Yeah, but he's a coward."

"Then we should live that down."

They came into a large area of packed earth with a bonfire at its center. Four pickups and two vans were parked around the edges of the clearing, leaving space in the center. At least fifteen young men with short hair or baseball caps stood around drinking beer (a brand favored by rednecks, unsurprisingly) and smoking cigarettes, a few with girls in attendance. The white pickup was the most recent arrival, of course, and its driver, a leanly muscular redneck with a blond crewcut and a white t-shirt, was just closing the door of the truck and accepting a beer when the boys pulled the 'Cuda into the clearing. Crewcut narrowed his eyes at the appearance of the strange car. Others around the fire stood up or slid off the hoods of their vehicles, walking closer.

"Who the fuck are you guys?" Crewcut said. The others who moved closer had expressions ranging from puzzlement to hostility.

"We're not from around here..." Charlie started.

"No shit!" a redneck said.

"- and thought you guys might be fun to party with."

"We don't party with hippies!" another redneck called out.

"Why not?" Charlie said, smiling. "Hippies have the best dope. Besides, we're not hippies, we're rock stars."

The puzzlement among the rednecks immediately boiled off, leaving hostility. Rednecks approached the 'Cuda, muttering to each other. Even some of the girls looked angry.

"This might not have been the best idea," Dan said softly.

"No kidding," Jim said.

Crewcut came over to the car and leaned on the roof, looking into the window.

"You guys can party with us," Crewcut said, his tone amiable.

"Really?" Charlie said in a perky voice.

"Sure," Crewcut said. "We just have to give you all haircuts."

"Huh," Charlie said, furrowing his brow as if in thought. "You got any scissors?"

"*Charlie...*" Jim whispered. Charlie held up his hand.

"No, we don't have any scissors," Crewcut said. "We have knives."

"Okay," Dan said, "time to leave."

Charlie looked at Dan, and in the rearview at Jim.

Dan kept his voice quiet. "We've got to get out of here."

The rednecks' voices had become consistently louder, with calls of "Give 'em haircuts!" and "Fuckin' faggots!" and "Let's kick their asses!"

Crewcut leaned a little closer into the window, looking at all their eyes, one by one.

"You could all use haircuts," he said amiably. "You kinda look like faggots. Big city faggots."

The notion of getting dragged out of the car for a haircut by a crowd of young Mikes struck Dan as unappealing; the fear made his heart hammer and made him angry. The look on Charlie's face was difficult to read.

"We'll just be leaving, if you don't mind," Charlie said at length. Dan could see the bunching of his jaw muscles.

"Sure?" Crewcut said.

"Yeah," Charlie said, smiling. "We'll just catch up another time."

"Okay, then," Crewcut said. "You'll have to back your faggot asses on out of here."

"Right. Later." Charlie put the 'Cuda in reverse. He backed out.

"Motherfuckers," he said.

He pulled back to the turn-around that Jim had pointed out and did a Y-turn. He sat with the car idling, facing down the road. He sighed.

"Hand me one of those old paper cups from the floor in back," he said to Jim.

"What for?" Jim said.

"Just give one to me, for fuck sake."

Jim rifled through the detritus on the floor, finding a cup.

"Here," he said. "What's it *for*?"

"I have to take a piss," Charlie said. He slid forward on the seat and pulled out his penis, pointing it downward to piss into the cup. From all the beer he had consumed, he nearly filled the sixteen ounce volume.

Dan was wondering why he didn't simply hold it and take a leak in the parking lot when Charlie put the cup in the receptacle of the car's console and put the car in reverse.

"What the fuck are you doing?" Jim cried. "Let's go!"

Charlie backed into the clearing and to his right, the bumper of the 'Cuda just missing that of a parked van. There were barks of surprise and offense.

"Sorry, dudes!" Charlie called out, holding up his hands and smiling.

"Drag 'em out!" a redneck called.

"Yeah!" said another. "And fuckin' cut their hair!"

There was a chorus of agreement, but Crewcut shut it down with a word. He walked over to the driver's side of the 'Cuda and said softly, "What the fuck do you want?"

"Just wanted to buy you a drink," Charlie said. "To express the appropriate apology."

Crewcut leaned toward the car, too cool to look perplexed.

"You got some booze for us?" he said.

"No," Charlie said, "a drink." And tossed the piss at him. It missed his face but splashed onto his neck and chest.

Crewcut flinched back, his eyes going wide. The hot liquid, almost clear from Charlie's consumption of beer, soaked down Crewcut's white t-shirt.

"It's...*piss*!" he shrieked.

"Cheers!" Charlie said, flicking the paper cup to bounce off Crewcut's sodden chest, then popping the car into first and gunning the engine. The tires spun, and with squirts of dust, they were off down the rutted track.

Dan and Jim were nearly hyperventilating with laughter. When they turned to look out of the rear window, they saw rednecks scrambling for their vehicles. Some threw beer bottles, some bent down for rocks. In his haste, Charlie slid the tires into the deep ruts of the trail and bottomed out the car, getting stuck. A rain of rocks and beer bottles fell around the car, with two hits to the pristine body- a bottle shattering- and a rock hitting the rear window, spiderwebbing it.

"Goddammit!" Charlie shouted, punching the gas and getting the 'Cuda out of the ruts. They thumped down track and into the empty parking lot.

"Broke my fucking window!" Charlie shouted. "Those assholes!"

"Just go!" Dan said, watching out the shattered rear window. "Go, go, go!"

"They're coming!" Jim yelled. Bobbing headlights approached them through the underbrush.

Charlie pulled out to the gap in the siding and went to turn left, back to Black Marsh, but Dan said. "Don't go that way! There's lights and traffic and cops! Take a right! Take a right!"

Charlie patched out onto the highway just as the first of the pickup trucks bounced out into the lot.

As a stroke of luck, there was no traffic on the bridge. Charlie stomped the accelerator and took off down the asphalt, the engine cycling up to a howl, its fullest beauty. The line of vehicles was turning out onto the bridge from Frenchman's Slough, but they were a quarter mile behind and fading.

Charlie slowed down and pulled over.

"What are you doing?" Dan and Jim said at once, their smiles fading.

"That was too easy," he said.

Jim started laughing again, hard.

"Maybe we *should* get the baseball bats," Dan suggested.

"Too late now," Charlie said, as the headlights of the rednecks bore down on them. When they were close enough for their lights to brighten the interior of the 'Cuda, he stuck his fist and its protruding middle finger high out of the window and shot off again.

Over another two islands and through a marsh, up over a soaring cantilever bridge with a barge passing underneath, they were pursued by the gang of rednecks. Charlie let them get close, then easily pulled away. On the far side of the bridge, the road came to a T at the base of a bluff, a three-way stop. Charlie came to a halt.

"*Now* what?" Dan asked.

"Stop sign," Charlie said, pointing.

The rednecks came up behind, unable to pull around into the oncoming lane as a truck came through the stop sign and roared past. The rednecks stopped their vehicles and got out, though, and were running at the 'Cuda when Charlie punched the gas again, taking a left down the road and leaving them gesticulating in frustration before piling back in to continue pursuit.

"Morons," Charlie said, chuckling.

Dan had just begun to wonder when Charlie would end it when a state police squadcar came over a hill from the other direction. Charlie allowed the line of rednecks to get fairly close, and when he saw the cop, he laughed, said, "Perfect!" and accelerated hard.

They increased the gap between them and the rednecks, and the cop, predictably, pulled over onto the shoulder and did a U-turn in pursuit. Charlie floored it, and the 'Cuda became a bullet. The last they saw of the rednecks was the cop picking a more convenient target and pulling over the first of their line. Then they were over a hill and into the night, down along the river road in another state.

"Motherfuckers messed up my ride," Charlie said late the next morning, as they stood in the alley behind the bungalows, assessing the damage. The rear window was shattered, and there were dents and scratches in the gleaming body from rocks and bottles, more than the boys had anticipated.

Dan looked the car over, but the damage wasn't what he was really thinking about. It was Mike. "Can't let 'em get away with this," he said.

"Better think about it," Jim said. "After everything we got up to yesterday, the cops could easily be looking for us. Let's just cover the car up with a tarp and lie low until we go back to Greysport. Charlie, you're on probation. Why push it?"

Admittedly, it is not the first impulse of many teenage boys to refrain from pushing it, but Dan wanted time to think through the possible ramifications of their actions, and even Charlie seemed willing to delay immediate retribution. Perhaps the fact that he was on probation *was* something of a deterrent, although it seemed unlikely that he would ever admit such a thing. In the end, they decided to go camping for the night, being careful enough, first, to give Jim some credit and cover the 'Cuda with a tarp. After being busted for matching footprints, it appeared that Charlie was ready to believe that helping the odds wasn't something practiced solely by pussies.

They geared up their packs, gave cursory notice to Willy and to Julie, and headed up through the woods and onto the bluffs. The largest weight in their packs was their supply of beer, as food and other supplies were almost an afterthought.

"We're going to be tripping too hard to need much food," Charlie pointed out.

Indeed, seeing as it was one of the last nights the Gates boys had before their return to Greysport, they decided to "do it up", as Jim put it. They'd made a simple camp at one of Dan's favorite places on the bluffs, and dropped acid as the sun went down. To ensure a revelatory experience, they did twice as much as they would have done simply to keep them sharp as they cruised the roads.

The light faded from the landscape. Trees grew dark across the river, and the shadow of the Earth slid slowly up the pink and orange and golden clouds, turning them silver and grey against the deepening blue of the refracted sky. Dan watched this, enraptured.

The boys built a fire. Crickets chirped, and soon the fire was the only light, the flames magical, shifting, their nature made more fascinating and mysterious as the acid seeped up into their brains. Clouds moved in and intercepted the rising moon, and soon they seemed to be held in a rough sphere of breathing firelight, everything in their field of vision seeming to be composed of enlarged pixels, shifting in texture. If the pixels became too large, Dan thought, you could fall between them, through the darkness and into another reality. He mentioned this thought to Charlie, who nodded, lying with his fingers laced behind his head, looking up at the firelit, shifting leaves and the clouds moving in to obscure the stars beyond.

Jim was gamely attempting to read a comic book, in spite of the growing distraction of the trip. Charlie remarked on this and Jim said, "In life, Science provides the lines, while art provides the color. Each would be less interesting without the other."

This provoked a discussion on perception and reality, all three of the boys talking animatedly for an untrackable time. The conversation petered out for a while and they drank beer, staring at the fire as Dan used a stick to poke the logs and coals around into different shapes, imagining worlds in there. He felt himself in a near trance, lost in the world of visions in the flame, of burning buildings and holocaust, the final crumbling structures of all human work, the external world dissipated and unreal. Dan muttered these thoughts to Charlie and Charlie nodded, his eyes wide and glowing in the firelight.

Later, Jim snapped them out of their fascinated trance by saying (apropos only of the commotion in his own head), "In life, every time we acknowledge a mistake, we evolve."

Charlie thought about this.

"I can't evolve," he said, standing up by the fire and spreading his arms. "I'm already perfect. This is perfection. You're looking at it."

"Then the species, and the planet, are truly doomed," Jim intoned. This struck them all as funny, and they erupted into laughter.

After the gales of mirth had ceased, Charlie sat wiping his eyes and said, suddenly somber, "Truly doomed. We *are* truly doomed."

"What?" Jim said.

"Well, give it a little thought. We're wobbling on the precipice of a nuclear Ragnarok with the Soviets, balanced in a constant, teetering tension, and any false move that tips that tenuous balance will end *all of this*." He spread his hands again and tilted his face up to the sky.

"You become so poetic when you're tripping," Jim said, smiling at Dan, but Dan was listening.

Charlie said, "Most people are inured to thoughts of this nature. They live their lives and walk around and around somnambulistically in their little daily duties, enslaved by the habit of thinking that *that* is the world, *that* is reality. While actually they are only a *tiny* part of it, and it could all fall apart, all be swept away like taking a broom to a mandala of colored sand, all of it gone. And the eddies of it, the shockwaves of their final, shrieking terror, wouldn't even reach as far as the Moon.

The disappearance of all of this, *all of this*- hear me?- would bear as much consequence in the Universe as wiping out a bacteria colony in a toilet with cup of bleach."

Dan and Jim looked at each other. Dan smiled.

"Cheerful," Jim said.

"Real," Charlie insisted. "And that's only one form of our demise, this witless and ravenous species. If we don't wipe out ourselves and everything else, all the innocent life groping through its pointless evolution, if we don't sweep away the omnicolored mandala with nukes, we will do it another way. Consistent poisoning of the environment in cumulative ways that will lead to mass extinction- mark my words- dwindling and finite resources and an ever-spiraling population, what will that lead to? The structure of civilization is tenuous, tenuous. People will be fighting over the corpses of dogs."

"Makes you wonder why you want to go to college," Jim said.

"Yeah," Charlie said. "Yeah, it does."

"So why do you?" Dan said.

Charlie thought about it, his face underlit by the light of the fire. "Pussy," he said finally. "Pussy, and the remote possibility that I might meet someone there who can tell me what all this means, if anything, and why I should even bother to be as good as I am."

They were silent for awhile, watching the fire. Dan handed out more beers, and Charlie surprised the others by breaking out a bottle of tequila, which they enthusiastically passed around.

"Look at the stars," Jim said after a long time.

"It's gotten overcast," Dan pointed out.

"So that's why they're moving."

"And multicolored," Charlie said, and they all laughed.

With Charlie and Jim's time on the river nearly over, they came to the conclusion that they could not allow the actions of the rednecks in Black Marsh to slide. After some discussion, they agreed that they had to go on a mission to blow up Crewcut's truck.

"A cup of piss just isn't enough," Charlie said.

"No fucking hick is going to threaten to cut my hair," Dan said to Jim, who seemed the least convinced of the prospective course of action.

Charlie had an idea of how to blow up the truck. "I heard it somewhere," he said. "It'll be great."

At the dimestore, he bought a box of ping pong balls, but wouldn't tell the other boys what they were for. They went back to the bungalow, and down into the basement. Charlie took two of the ping pong balls and carefully cut off the top quarter of one and the top third of another with an Exacto knife. At Charlie's request, Dan brought him some Drano from under the kitchen sink. Charlie carefully poured Drano crystals into the three-quarters ping pong ball through a funnel made of a scrap of paper.

"I don't get it," Jim said. Charlie waggled his eyebrows.

He lit a candle found among the junk on the workbench, and when the candle had accumulated some molten wax, he put the one-third section of ping pong ball carefully on top of the three-quarters section containing the Drano. Holding the sections together carefully between thumb and forefinger, he dripped wax on the sections, forming a seal.

Dan watched throughout this process, finally laughing and saying, "It goes in the fill tube of the truck."

"Yeah," Charlie said, grinning.

"Oh," Jim said. "The gasoline eats away the wax. The sections fall apart."

"Boom," Charlie said.

"Okay," Jim said, "that's pretty cool."

Charlie made two more of the capsules. "Just to be safe," he said.

To make it a more interesting mission, and to avoid driving the roads with the 'Cuda, they opted to borrow a fast boat docked on the river. Dan knew a friend of Willy's who left keys in his speedboat in the chart compartment, having been out on the boat once or twice with the man and Willy.

"He'll never know we took it," Dan said. He wasn't so sure about that, but felt that he had to up the ante on Charlie's idea of the improvised explosives.

They reasoned that, it being a Saturday night, the rednecks would congregate in the clearing at Frenchman's Slough, which was obviously the place they liked to party. They would take the boat upriver, secure it at the boatlaunch, and slip like commandos through the woods to the clearing. Once there, Charlie would get to Crewcut's pickup and drop the ping pong ball into the gas tank.

"We need a distraction," Jim said.

"Why?" Charlie said, giving his brother a derisive look. "This'll work fine."

As always, Jim was patient and diplomatic. "There are just some angles which, in your fervor for revenge, you might not have considered. First, if there's a distraction, you can just walk up to the truck and drop the thing in the tank. There's much less chance we'll be spotted. Second, you don't want the thing to blow up when people are around, do you?"

"Says who?"

"You don't. Anyone gets hurt, like burn ward hurt, and the heat'll get turned way up by the cops."

"He's got a point," Dan said.

Charlie thought about it. "Okay," he said finally. "But I would have zero compunction about killing that cracker."

Dan thought about what Willy had said regarding the calculation of proportionate responses, but dismissed it.

Jim said, "The guy's just an asshole. All we want to do is teach him a lesson. Everyone knows you're a badass. Okay?"

"Okay, okay," Charlie said, but Dan could see that the gears were still turning in his head.

Their cover story to Willy and Julia and been that they were going camping in the canoe for the night. Willy had even taken them down to the boat launch with the canoe in the back of his truck, and had seen them paddle off upstream, hugging the bank to stay out of the strong current.

"Perfect alibi," Jim said.

"We won't need it," Charlie told him.

The boys made camp at a familiar spot and waited until after midnight to "commandeer" (as Charlie put it) the speedboat. They did a little white cross to stay awake, but were otherwise moderate, wanting to maintain focus until the mission was over.

"Then we can party," Charlie said. For that, he'd brought beer and tequila.

In black t-shirts, jeans and sneakers, slathered in mosquito repellant, they got into the canoe and pushed off. Using the current to their advantage, they were down to the boat slips in MacDougal in no time.

They tied up the canoe and slipped aboard the boat. Dan had an instant's thought that it might be best if the keys were not in the chart compartment, but there they were, right on top. He looked around to double-check that there were no witnesses in the park or by the boathouse, then put the keys in the ignition and started the engine. The boat turned over, and Charlie and Jim cast off the lines.

Dan eased the boat out onto the dark river, getting away from the shore before turning on the running lights. When they were out in the current, he opened it up and they roared north, bouncing across the water.

He had a short feeling of remorse, just a second, when he thought about what he was doing, but the amphetamine was slipping through him, making him feel light and strong, and with the wind washing over him and the speed of the boat beneath, he opened up the throttle and turned to grin at the other boys. They all howled; the feeling was freedom itself.

They passed small towns on either side of the river, the reflected lights from them breaking up on a thousand small waves. There was little other river traffic, and Dan wished he could just keep the boat pointed north, keep going until he was somewhere he'd never been before, someplace brand new.

Soon they saw the lights of Black Marsh to the north, and then they were underneath the bridge and heading for Frenchman's Slough. Dan had been here a few times before, but never at night, and never at the helm. He went slowly, worried about running up on a shoal, past marshes and dark stands of trees, the lush leaves looking black and silver and blue in the moonlight.

They prowled around for more than an hour looking for the right waterway to the boatlaunch at Frenchman's slough. Charlie began to curse, and Jim to fidget, although both of them tried to be helpful.

"I thought you said you knew this area," Charlie said.

"I didn't say I knew it *well*," Dan said. "And it's night out. Give me a break."

"Look," Jim said, "let's just blow it off. Let's get the boat back. No harm done."

"Jim." Charlie said. "I want. To blow up. The redneck's. Truck."

"Well, maybe it's just not going to happen this time. We'll get 'em next year."

Dan realized he was ready to give up. "Yeah," he said. "We'll get 'em next year."

"*Et tu, Brute*?" Charlie said.

"Come on, man. You already doused him with piss. They'll be calling him Pissy until he moves away or dies."

Charlie thought about that for a moment and chuckled. "Well. You've got a point." He laughed again. "Pissy."

"So, let's book," Jim said.

Charlie sighed. "Okay."

Dan was relieved, and the same emotion was evident on Jim's face.

"But in that case," Charlie said, "we have to get drunk while we still have this cool boat."

Dan and Jim agreed that this was a reasonable compromise, and Charlie went into the pack for the tequila and beer. There was a momentary discussion about taking the boat to Black Marsh, but Dan pointed out that it was one place on the river where Sheriff's Department patrols were likely to be more dense, so they headed south, away from the small city and into the darkness.

They motored along at a moderate pace, not wanting to bring back the boat too soon. The occasional barge loomed by in the darkness, but at that small hour of the morning there were few other boats out on the river. They drank tequila and beer, the buzz from both soon overwhelming the speed, which, they all agreed, was a nasty, gritty kind of reaction anyway, nothing like the power and beauty of acid.

If they had been tripping, the brothers might have been content to simply enjoy the ride, the sound of the motor and the waves, the feel of the wind. As it was, though, both of them began to agitate for control of the boat, even if momentary.

"Come on," Jim said. "How often do we get a chance to do something like this?"

Dan was a little surprised at Jim taking the role of instigator. He gave him a look, and set his eyes back out on the dark water, keeping his hands on the wheel.

"He's right," Charlie said. "We've got tomorrow night, and then we head back to our boring lives in White Folks Pointe."

"It's my grampa's friend's boat," Dan said. "Come on."

"Didn't you get to do some cool shit with us in Greysport?"

"Yeah, but that's not the point."

"Sure it's the point," Charlie persisted. "Furthermore, just let us take the helm for a bit, and we'll do more cool shit next time you're in G.P. Like, you can bone Gigi or something. She likes you anyway."

Dan almost did a doubletake at this; he had never mentioned anything that had happened with him and Gigi, and wondered how much Charlie knew, or even if he knew anything. He gave Charlie a glance in the dark; there might have been something hard about his eyes, something challenging, but it was too dark to tell.

"Okay," he said. "Shit. But be careful."

Charlie took the helm first, over Jim's objections, simply shouldering him out of the way.

"I'm the oldest," he said.

"Hugh's the oldest," Jim said,

"Actually, Six is the oldest."

"He's dead," Jim said. "Besides, what does primogeniture have to do with it?"

"I can kick your ass. How about that?"

Jim looked at him for a moment. "Well, if you have to be a dick about it, go ahead."

Charlie did. With his usual penchant for speed, he pushed the throttle forward, looking over to watch Dan's reaction. He grinned and wrinkled his nose, his look saying, Is this too far, is *this* too far? Dan stood by ready to pull him away. For a second, something his grandfather said flashed in his mind: "Any idiot who thinks he can drive a car thinks he can drive a boat, and most idiots can't drive a car."

63

Soon they were skipping over the waves, though, the pitch of the engine changing as the boat bounced up and down across the water. Dan laughed and drank from the bottle of tequila, handing the bottle to Jim.

"This is excellent!" Charlie shouted.

After a few minutes, Jim gave Charlie a knuckle slap on the arm and a hands-up gesture, Come on! Charlie slowed the boat down to idle, their own wave catching up and slapping into the stern.

"Fair's fair," he said, relinquishing the wheel to his brother. "Where's the tequila?"

Jim shoved the bottle into Charlie's chest and pushed him out of the way. Charlie laughed and drank.

"Okay," Dan said, "you know how to do it, right? Here's the throttle...."

"Of course I know how to do it!" Jim laughed. He eased the throttle forward a little more cautiously than his brother, but soon they were rocketing across the water. Jim howled with delight.

"Ahahahahahahaha!" Jim screamed. "I'm free, motherfuckers! I'm free!"

A barge laden with coal churned its way up the river in the opposite direction, the running lights on the powerful tug getting closer as they sped south. Jim hooted and drank from his beer.

"You're watching that barge, right?" Dan shouted.

"Of course I am!" Jim yelled back. Charlie simply yelled.

Over the years, Dan would often think what might have gone differently, as one frequently will. If the river had been as high as it had in the spring, nothing would have happened at all. If he had insisted that Jim slow down with the boat, crisis would have been averted. The final conclusion he would make was that, if he'd ever heard a thing his grandfather had told him, if he hadn't just sat there pretending to listen as Willy navigated the river, he might have handled the whole incident with a bit more knowledge, if not actual wisdom. As it was, he was drinking tequila and laughing when Jim passed the barge, albeit with a cautious enough berth, and the boat hit the first big wave of the tug's wake at full throttle, sending them all airborne.

They landed in a jumble in the stern, Dan stunned from hitting his head on the coaming. The engine was roaring, and they were bouncing across the subsequent waves of the barge's wake, the three of them howling with laughter until they realized that no one was at the helm.

"FUCK!" they all shouted simultaneously, and scrabbled on hands and knees to get to the helm and regain control of the boat, which hit a wave and was airborne, hit a wave and was airborne, each impact and liberation from the water changing the pitch of the boat's engine and bouncing the boys up from the deck. In spite of this, the boys were about to converge on their goal, each reaching for the steering wheel, when the boat hit the sandbar. The impact sent all three crashing forward. Dan's face crunched into the housing of the steering wheel, sending off a red light surrounded by black in his head. The next thing he knew, he was in an unanticipated position, Charlie and Jim groaning on either side of him. The boat was not moving and the engine had stopped. As they sat for a few moments in stunned silence, it began to rain.

"What the fuck happened?" Jim said.

Dan got to his feet with some effort, his ears ringing, and found out.

In the growing pre-dawn light, Dan could see that the boat had hit the sandbar at nearly top speed, leaving a long gouge in the sand before becoming completely airborne for a few yards. If they'd been aloft longer, or the water had been higher, they might actually have made it over the sandbar and back into the water. As it was, the boat had come to a stop with its bow in the water and it stern still up on the sand, where the propeller had bit in and stalled.

"Oh, shit," Dan said. It started to rain harder, and he laughed.

Charlie came back to the stern and looked over. "Wo," he said.

Jim joined them and began to laugh. Soon they were all laughing. When Dan turned to face them, Jim said, "Wow, you're really bleeding. Gonna need some stitches."

Dan raised his hand to his right eyebrow and pulled it back slick with blood and rain.

"You've got a pretty good gash, there. Right through the eyebrow," Charlie said. "Make a good scar."

"Shit," Dan said, flicking the blood and water off his fingers.

"What are we going to do?" Jim asked.

The only plan Dan could come up with was to wait and see if the rain would float them off. Any other of the ideas they had were too impractical.

"I'll just wait here," he said. "If we're lucky, the boat'll float off, and I might get it back before anyone notices."

"Yeah," Charlie said. "Guess that's our only choice." Jim nodded.

"Well, *you* guys don't have to stay," Dan said.

"Why not?" Jim said.

"Too risky. Suppose a cop or a DNR warden comes along. You're on probation," he pointed at Charlie, "and Jim, you're not, and want to keep it that way."

"Fuck that," Charlie said. "We're not leaving you hanging."

"Right," Jim said. "No way."

They argued back and forth as the rain got heavier and their surroundings faded from black to grey. Dan finally prevailed, depending on the logic of the two brothers.

"First of all, there's little chance I'll get caught. Second, there's no need for you to take a chance at all. It serves no purpose for you to stay here. This was my idea, it's my responsibility. Just get going."

Charlie and Jim finally agreed, but were downcast about it. Dan sent them on their way.

"Take the sandbar to those woods, there," he said, "and go over to the tracks. Head through the woods, you literally can't miss them. From there, you go down to the bridge and into town. Take the canoe back to the campsite and I'll meet you there."

The boys got ready to go. Charlie found a plastic bag in a drawer and picked up the empty beer cans; the tequila bottle appeared to have gone over the side when they first lost control of the boat.

"Might as well not leave any evidence," Charlie said, grinning guiltily.

The Gates brothers jumped over the side of the boat and onto the sand. It began to rain even harder, and thunder cracked and boomed overhead.

"See you in a little while," Jim said.

"If it doesn't look like this is going to float off," Charlie said, "just ditch it. They can't pin this on you."

Dan watched as the brothers trotted across the sandbar. They stopped near the bank of the river and the sheltering trees, turning around to wave to him. He waved back, and they were gone, into the woods, a curtain of rain dividing them. He wouldn't see them again for nearly two years.

For a while, it looked like the boat might actually be lifted enough off the sand to be freed. Dan hopped over the side of the boat to check the progress of the water's rise. I might be in luck, he thought. Thunder rumbled and the rain roared down on the dark morning. As he stood up and looked over the gunwale of the boat, he saw a Black Marsh County Sheriff's patrol boat idling in the water off the point of the sandbar. A deputy in a reflective yellow slicker and a rain hat was in the stern of the boat.

"Looks like you're in a little trouble," the deputy said. Dan sighed hard and nodded.

Willy was not in a hurry to get up to Black Marsh and have Dan released. He sat at the kitchen table drinking coffee and reading the paper. After a good breakfast, he took a leisurely shower and got dressed. Let the kid sit, he thought.

He took his time driving up to the familiar courthouse building. It was late morning when he got there. The storm had passed, and it was a warm and breezy summer day. The building was ominous to him, though, heavy with memory. He got out of the pickup truck with a sigh and trudged up the steps. Inside, a receptionist pointed him in the right direction.

He introduced himself to the young deputy in his office.

"Willy McGregor?" the young man said. "From down in MacDougal?"

"Yep," Willy said.

"Heard a lot about you." The young man smiled and nodded.

Willy let this pass without comment.

"What are you holding my grandson for?" he asked.

"He stole a boat," the deputy said.

"Shit."

"Yeah. You might know the victim. Sam Feeney? Undertaker? Or funeral director, as they prefer to be called these days, I guess."

"Goddammit."

"You do know him," The deputy said.

"Old friend of mine."

"Jeez, that's awkward."

"You're telling me."

"I have to say, this doesn't seem like the kind of thing a kid would do alone. We talked to your grandson for a long time about it, but he said next to nothing. Name, rank, and serial number. Know who he might have done this with?"

"No idea," Willy said.

"We'll get your grandson and release him to your custody."

"Fine. Say, do you have a phone I could use?"

"Sure, right here."

66

As soon as the deputy had left the room, Willy took a deep breath and called Sam Feeney, explaining the situation as far as he knew it.

"You McGregors have always had a lot of energy," Sam said, laughing a little.

There was damage to the boat, which Willy offered to assess and to repair.

"There's no reason it should come out of your insurance," Willy said.

"Well, you shouldn't have to pay for it," Sam said.

"I won't. Weren't you looking for a part time person? Might help the boy to see what you do for a living to make the money to buy the boat. He can pay me back from what he earns."

"What about his hours at the bar?"

"He can do that too." Willy said.

"Poor kid's had kind of a bad time of it, hasn't he?" Sam Feeney was nothing if not compassionate.

"Yeah," Willy said, "but that doesn't mean he couldn't use a good kick in the butt."

Sam Feeney had the charges against Dan dropped. Willy had a cup of coffee and chatted with the young deputy while Dan was processed from the holding tank where he had sat, the deputy told him, with two passed-out drunks and a man who had beaten his wife.

"Sat in there for almost two days until he gave us enough information to call you," the deputy said.

When Dan was brought into the room, he was muddy and sullen, butterfly sutures over a cut through his right eyebrow. Willy saw this but made no comment, then shook hands with the detective and turned to leave.

"Come on," he said. Dan moped after him.

Once in the truck, Willy explained how he had worked things out with Sam Feeney.

"So, congratulations," he said, "you're an indentured servant. If Sam wasn't such a good fella, you'd be in deep shit right now. Hear me?"

"Yeah, I hear you."

As they drove home along the river, Willy wasn't sure who to blame more, the boy or himself. He'd talked to the boy, again and again. Doesn't matter what you say, he thought, if no one's listening.

In spite of himself, he got angry, at least as much as he could muster. "What were you thinking?" he said. A sharp voice was the most he could manage.

Dan didn't answer.

"Seriously, what were you thinking? Don't you know Sam Feeney's an old friend of mine? I'm asking you a question. Don't you know that?"

"Yeah."

"Well, shit. What did the Gates boys have to do with this?"

Dan shrugged. "I think they went home."

"They did, huh? That mean you're going to take the rap for it?"

"Guess so."

"Okay, if that's the way you want it."

When they got home and Dan went inside to shower, Willy saw Julia next door on her front porch. He decided not to tell her immediately what happened, but asked, as blandly as possible, about the welfare of her nephews.

"Oh, they went back to Greysport," she said. "Early this morning, which is unusual. They're both such sleepyheads."

"Yeah. Kids," Willy said. He didn't laugh until he got into the house.

He didn't let Dan rest, although it was apparent that the boy had had little sleep. He walked with him down to Feeney's, into the carpeted hall with the ticking clock, into Sam's office. There, he made Dan apologize. The boy barely met Feeney's eyes, and Willy couldn't tell if his mood were sullen, angry, or morosely contrite. Maybe all three.

When they had worked out a schedule for Dan for the rest of the summer, Willy took him to the bar and set him up with a list of the most odious tasks he could devise, beginning with scrubbing the urinals and cleaning the grease traps. He worked the boy until five o'clock, then set him loose. When he got home from the bar later in the evening, the door to Dan's room was closed, the light out.

The Gates boys had gone back to the city, and Dan's fun was over for the summer, and for some time after that, as far as Willy was concerned.

Autumn came, and Willy kept Dan on a strict schedule. He was back in school, with only a year and eight months until graduation. Willy kept on him about getting into college in Greysport.

"You've got a lot of potential, son," he said, imagining this refrain being spoken ten million times a day across the country. "You have to try to live up to it."

"Well, I sure as hell can't wait to get out of here," Dan said, stinging Willy. "Why did you stay here so long, anyway?"

Willy usually dismissed such comments. "Guess I just liked it here," he'd say, or "What could be better than living here?" or "Just smart, I guess."

On one of the increasingly rare occasions when Dan was friendly and talkative, Willy responded to the question from a deeper place.

"There were a lot of times when I wanted to leave," he said. "I wanted to take your dad and your uncle and gramma and go down the river in my old boat."

"Where would you have gone?" Dan asked.

"I thought for a while that we'd reverse the course I took, and end up back at the St. Pierre et Miquelon Islands." He got an atlas to show Dan where that was.

"Why didn't you go? Seriously."

Willy shrugged. "Your gramma's family. The boys. Your dad and uncle, that is. Our friends. Our life. And there was the small matter of my being indisposed to travel for several years." Willy thought that Dan might have been darkly amused by the last comment.

"But think about it," Willy said. "If we'd done that, sure, your uncle and dad would've grown up speaking French, living on the ocean; that'd be an interesting difference. I grew up around lighthouses, and I would've liked to be around them again. But then you wouldn't have been born; your dad would never have met your mother. There might be some other kid named Dan McGregor, with different color eyes and hair, different interests, a different life."

Dan's eyes widened slightly, and Willy could tell that he had successfully spilled a mass of hot thought into the boy's mind.

"So there are advantages and disadvantages to anywhere you're going to live. And where you choose to live writes the story of your life. But the choice is the important thing. Remember: you might not get the life you want, you might just get the life you accept. I think that's the way most people live. You have to go after the life you want. You can do that, Dan."

Dan opened his mouth to speak twice before finally saying, "So, you won't be, like, sad or anything if I move to Greysport to go to school? That won't bum you out?"

"Nah," Willy lied. "I wouldn't *accept* your staying here if you didn't want to. This is going to be *your* time. You have to make *your* life. See?"

Dan thought about it. "Yeah," he said.

Any time Willy wondered about a kid Dan's age working at a funeral parlor, he wondered if he were doing the right thing, just for a second. When the inevitable thought followed- that Willy had been in a war at the same age- he adjusted his thinking. He could not remember what his mind had been like, what kind of safe and illusory notions had occupied it, before the crisp white morgue sheet had been yanked back, exposing to his young eyes the underlying and inevitable ugliness of the world.

People die, he thought, in more ways than could be predicted or imagined , even by the most febrile mind. By disease or bloody accident, by crushing, slashing, rending and smashing, by bullet holes and botulism, there were billions of forms of death in the world, more than the human mind could encompass. Although he didn't want the boy, who was already a bit morbid, to be stripped of all hope (as he had once been himself, before Mae), nor did he want him to be the kind of reality-sanitizing somnambulist who teemed the streets of every city and speckled the countryside, the kind who could not even bring themselves to look in objective curiosity at a dead deer at the side of the road. Charlie would have been with him on this, but would have missed Willy's following point: those people who shied away from death failed to understand the transient preciousness, the absolute limitation, of their own lives.

Perhaps, for Dan, seeing the kind of reality that existed in the basement of Sam Feeney's could permeate his mind a way that Willy's countless lectures never could. And Willy was realistic about how much time he might have left to lecture the boy, pointlessly or otherwise.

Dan kept his grades up. At least that wasn't a struggle, as Willy often saw with friends who were parents of kids the same age. He kept the boy busy with work after school and at Feeney's, and on weekends took him to Emilio's to work on restoring Feeney's boat. Dan made a few predictable, teenagerly attempts to slip out of his obligations, but Willy remained steadfast, knowing that, in the long run, years after he was dead, the boy would benefit from the knowledge that some obligations were unavoidable, and that was that.

It was during the afternoons on fall weekends, working on the boat, that Willy felt closest to the boy. Dan sometimes seemed to struggle with focus at first, led astray by his tendency to daydream (often with vertical lines between his brows), but with a reminder or two, he was soon working diligently. They might go for hours without talking, the smell of sawdust and varnish in the air, listening to the public radio station as leaves drifted to the ground outside the open door to the shed. While Dan rarely smiled, Willy could sense his contentment when he was engaged in a task, and knew that it was this mood, almost a trance, that took the boy when he was working on art late into the night.

Willy occasionally offered to let him off early to go to a football game or some other activity, but Dan never seemed interested in such things. He talked to him about dating and girls, but got the sense that Dan considered the local girls perhaps a bit bucolic, although this attitude might have been feigned. Perhaps it was something deeper, that there was something Dan didn't like in himself, although Willy couldn't imagine what that might be. He was intelligent, talented, and handsome (under all that hair), and to Willy it made no sense that that he wouldn't see these qualities in himself. Willy tried to be positive and encouraging in a way that he hoped would float the boy away from any adolescent self-doubt.

When, one evening at the dinner table, he launched in to a discussion about sex and the necessary precautions a young gentleman should take, he was met with a disgusted sigh, a rolling of eyes, and an unbelieving glare.

"So you know all about this," Willy said.

"Jesus, Grampa," Dan said.

"Okay, okay," Willy said. "Just wanted to make sure. And you're aware of what to do with the clitoris and everything, right?"

"Holy shit!" Dan cried, and actually laughed.

"What kind of grandfather would I be if I didn't make sure you knew about such things?" Willy said. "Your dad would do it if he were alive, but all you've got is me. And no grandson of mine is going to be the kind of pig who takes care of himself and not the lady. Ladies first! That's not just about opening doors, you know."

"I can't believe I'm having this conversation," Dan said, getting up from the table and taking dishes to the sink.

Willy followed him with more dishes, saying "So, it *is* a conversation! In that case, tell me about what kind of sex you *have* had."

"You're incredible. What an old lech. Let me tell you, I've had wilder sex than you can imagine."

"Well, that's just insulting. I can imagine a lot. I can *remember* a lot. You think kids your age invented wild sex? Shit, there was this one girl, after the war. Gunta...."

Dan washed dishes hurriedly. "Grampa, I don't want to visualize you...*doing* it, all right? Next thing, I'll be thinking about you and Gramma, and...oh, *man!*" He held up his hands and shook his head sharply.

Willy was laughing. "Let me tell you," he said, "your gramma was one hot tomato!"

"AH!" Dan cried, throwing down the dishtowel and covering his ears with his hands. "Enough!" He walked through the doorway to the kitchen and into his room.

Willy followed. "You ever have a threesome? You should try it before you get married. You've got plenty of time. Get married at thirty. You could have plenty of threesomes."

Dan slammed the door behind him.

"And don't feel guilty about beating off!" Willy called through the door, trying not to laugh. "Do it as much as possible, it gives you greater control!"

"Not listening!" Dan called through the door. Willy heard him turn on his stereo, heard muted music from the headphones. He laughed out loud and went back to the kitchen.

Dan remembered Willy saying something to him about how each consecutive year in a person's life represented a smaller proportion of it, that to a two-year-old, it was fifty percent of the child's life, but that to a fifty-year-old, it was two percent. There was a sensation, Willy had said, of increasing speed as one went through life, and that a year to someone Dan's age might seem like a month or two to Willy.

Dan had been high at the time, and the idea struck him as funny.

"So we're accelerating through life," Dan said, "like a bug into a windshield."

Willy laughed. "That's one way to look at it. But don't despair," he said, clapping his hand on Dan's neck. "We're amazingly lucky to be here at all. Each day is a glowing gift."

"Yeah." Dan said. "Right."

Dan would not often have agreed. Life in the little town was abrasively boring, and, at sixteen and a half, to be eighteen and done with school and free could not come fast enough. At his present age, a year (he had calculated it while high) was about 6.06% of his life. At Willy's it was about 1.37%. This struck him as unfair.

He partied occasionally with other kids who bought his pot, but found them boring and lacking in spark, culturally unalive and with terrible taste in music. There was no one in town who matched Charlie and Jim for excitement and intelligence, and when he told local kids about some of their adventures together, he was sometimes simply disbelieved. He came to the conclusion that their comparatively sheltered lives occluded the possibilities of the world to them. It was clear that almost all of them were going to spend their years within twenty miles of where they were right now, some of them thinking themselves fortunate to get jobs at the coal power plant up the river, or on the railroad or the river. Dan could not imagine such resignation. On the other hand, he admitted, many of them seemed happy at this prospect, and also appeared to have a sense of inclusion that Dan, a *maldito*, found somewhat enviable.

Would he trade what he knew of the world for their simplicity and peace? He thought of something Charlie had once said, "Better Socrates dissatisfied than a pig satisfied." He would rather be, he thought, Socrates dissatisfied. Time moved so slowly until he could be free, though. It sometimes seemed unbearable. He didn't belong here, maybe not anywhere. He wanted to scream and beat things, smash windshields and throw molotov cocktails. He would look around the quiet town, though, and see that it was beautiful and peaceful, see that it was the place his grandmother had loved, where her music had echoed down the street at night, and he would walk back to the bungalow, his only known home, to where his grandfather would sleep on the couch and make him breakfast in the morning. Walking home was as secure and cozy, he thought, as reassuring as a straightjacket.

On occasion, though, he had amused and alarmed some of the local boys by proving his wildness. He realized later that it was an attempt to lend veracity to some of the stories of things he had done in Greysport, and with the now-legendary Gates Brothers. He and some of the local boys had been drinking beer and smoking dope by the railroad tracks along the river, the beer in the back of a pickup truck in much the same way as it had been with the rednecks at Frenchman's Slough. The difference was that these local boys were all stoners, with the requisite long hair, flannel shirts, army surplus jackets and hiking boots. They were an uninspired bunch, but Dan often felt fairly uninspired himself.

They partied by the tracks, driving there in the pickup truck and another rusted beater. A pile of refuse sat nearby, the heap consisting of a large stack of underbrush, several empty five-gallon paint cans, two tricycles, and a cable spool about six feet in diameter, built of sturdy lumber. As they partied, they threw their empties onto the heap, something that struck Dan as a bit untidy.

The local boys knew his family's reputation, although few of them ever mentioned it to his face. They also knew that he had been taken in for boat theft, something that had buzzed through the community, causing outrage in its more conservative sections.

The fact that these boys still doubted some of the tales he told of Greysport annoyed him. They drank beer and passed joints, and Dan had lapsed into silence after trying to tell them about the warehouses, and about breaking into cars with Darnell, about the beach and the tienda. The locals had slid into their usual dialogue, telling the same old stories and the same old jokes, at best coming up with creative and filthy ways to insult each other. When Dan heard a train whistle from the south, distant but growing nearer, the welcome light of inspiration clicked on in his mind. Without a word, he set down his beer and walked over to the pile of refuse. From it, he pulled the cable spool upright, and, with a little effort, rolled it across the packed earth, up the gravel of the rail bed, over the closest rail and onto the tracks. The train whistle sounded nearer as he stood back from the spool, and was soon very close indeed.

"What the hell are you doing?" one of the kids yelled over the sound of the approaching train.

"Just watch," Dan yelled back, and moved away from the tracks.

The huge diesel engine bore down the rails, sounding its whistle more urgently. The local boys looked at each other in a mixture of consternation and delight; whatever their fear, they were still teenage boys. Dan picked up his beer and sipped it as he watched.

He knew that not only would the train not stop, it *could* not stop, at least not in time to save the well-placed spool. The whistle sounded continuously as the train hurtled near. The boys were frozen in anticipation, their mouths agape.

With the screeching of the whistle and the engine's roar, the heavy steel front of the train hit the spool, exploding it into splinters and chunks, bits flying high into the air and off into the grass. The train dopplered past, thundering, the steel wheels pounding the rails like triphammers.

Some of the boys cheered, some looked frightened. When the last piece of the shattered spool had landed, it was still several minutes before the final car of the long freight train passed.

"Jesus Christ!" one of the boys said.

"Holy shit, McGregor!" said another.

"Are you fucking nuts?" said a third.

The sound of the train receded, leaving silence. The boys looked at Dan.

"When I tell you I did something," Dan said, "I did it. Why would I lie to *you* assholes?"

There was a pause.

"Let's get out of here," one of the scared kids said. The boys made for the pickup truck and the beater.

"You douchebags go ahead," Dan said. "And give me some of those beers. I'm walking home."

It occurred to him to look up the Schommer brothers, Stumpy and Nubby, who had taken over their uncle's blacksmithing business in Mt. Pleasant, at least as far as rumor had it. He had a curiosity about them, a drive to find them, as if he were seeking two more brothers to fill his void.

The Schommer brothers were both members of the local chapter of the Guardians of Nocturne (he *had* seen Stumpy that day in the 'Cuda with Charlie and Jim), but Mt Pleasant was a ways away, and it was easier to tell himself that he would look them up in a week or two, appeasing this procrastination by getting stoned in the basement or garage and watching TV on the couch, even though the local stations were only a third as numerous as those in Greysport. Maybe Willy was right, he thought from time to time. Wherever you lived was a trade-off. Greysport was exciting, but then there had been his mother and Mike. Here on the river, it was beautiful, and he lived with his grandfather, who was almost as interesting as he was annoying. The people were boring, the television limited, the closest movie theater in Black Marsh. A trade-off. You had to make your own life, though, which he would do as soon as he left here forever.

The one thing which was not boring, which, in fact, made his hair stand up on his head, was working at Sam Feeney's. He had dragged his heels about reporting there for work, but Willy, in an unusually stern tone, had told him to "march himself down there" (Willy had lost patience when he used those words) and report for duty.

The fact that Sam Feeney greeted him kindly made him feel a bit ashamed. They sat in the quiet office where Willy and Mae had sat, and where Willy, finally, had sat by himself. Dan didn't know this, and it wasn't even close to what he was thinking about. He had been hoping that Feeney would act like a dick, but his kindness took Dan aback.

"I'm not going to have you do anything too heavy duty," Feeney said. "Just some cleaning and so forth, vacuuming the carpets, polishing and dusting. A funeral home has to be pretty neat, as you can imagine."

Dan had not imagined it, actually, but when he did, he realized that a filthy or disorderly funeral home might not inspire the confidence it should. Feeney gave Dan a list of tasks and set him to it, saying that he would be in the back rooms or the basement, at work. Dan imagined, again, what this might entail, but Feeney didn't elaborate. He padded away down the hall and through a door, leaving Dan alone with the ticking grandfather clock, some cleaning supplies, and the sense that Feeney was a deeply lonely man. Get over it, he thought to himself. Everyone's lonely.

At the end of two hours, Feeney found him at work vacuuming one of the reception rooms. Feeney smelled of chemicals and soap, and took Dan into his office, where he wrote down the hours that Dan had worked, showing him what he had written in order to be fair. Dan left and went down to the river, glad to be outside. On the bank, he knelt and scooped up a handful of muddy sand, scrubbing his hands with it, then washing them in the smoothly roiling and perpetual flow.

Trust developed between the two as Dan continued to work off his hours. When Feeney seemed comfortable enough, the aging, dapper man showed Dan the rooms where the preparation of bodies for burial was done, the cooler where the bodies were kept, the store room for coffins. Feeney had an assistant, Fred Turner, who was friendly enough, but usually seemed quiet and distracted, even during the periods when there were no "customers" as the dead were sometimes called behind closed doors. Turner was handsome enough to be a movie star, always dressed and coifed as perfectly as a mannequin in a Greysport department store window. It seemed to Dan that the man was perplexed and annoyed to be doing such work.

The first time Dan handled a body, Sam Feeney was out, and Fred had just pulled into the loading dock after returning from Black Marsh Hospital. Turner came in to the front hallway where Dan was polishing brasswork, and said, "Hey, kid. Gimme a hand, will ya? Got a customer. Big one."

Dan felt a flush of heat go to his face, and was aware of being a bit dizzy as he walked back to the loading dock. Fred had opened the doors of the nondescript work van used for hospital runs, and was hauling the gurney out of the back. The corpse was encased in a body bag of maroon fabric lined with rubber, the exterior napped almost like carpeting. The bulk of the body itself was enormous.

"This is a collapsible gurney, right?" Fred said. "I thought this fucker was *gonna* collapse it, seriously. Fuckin' whopper. Four-thirty-five or something. They weighed him on the loading dock scale, no shit."

In an attempt to seem worldly and cavalier about the cadaver, Dan said, "Where'd you get a big enough body bag?"

"No kidding, huh?" Fred laughed. "Packed in there like a fucking sausage."

They both took a side of the gurney to slide it out all the way, the legs snapping into place with a clack.

The gurney itself was up to the task, although the wide-eyed look on Fred's face told Dan that the man was dubious. What went wrong was that, when the whole contraption, corpse and all, thudded out of the van, the body itself was a bit off-center. Perhaps the straps of the gurney weren't tight enough, not to mention the fact that there was a slight slope to the concrete of the loading dock. Whatever the case, no sooner had they cleared the gurney from the van than the apparatus toppled over on its side with a crash and a heavy thud, the legs of the gurney sticking out sideways, the bulk of the customer also on its side and straining against the straps.

"Oh, *fuck!*" Fred cried, doubling over in laughter. He glanced around for witnesses, but the driveway and the loading dock were concealed by hedges on one side and the building itself on the other, so they were safe.

Dan was laughing so hard he couldn't breathe, and had to stagger over to the loading dock to sit down. They tried to stop, but whenever they looked at the body and the gurney and each other, they erupted all over again.

"Okay," Fred said finally, "We've got to get this fucker inside before Feeney gets back."

This involved unbuckling the corpse and collapsing the legs of the gurney, which was made more difficult because the corpse lay on the open straps. Finally, with some effort, they rolled the corpse over on its face, which was surprisingly difficult, the body being completely loose in death.

"It's like trying to move a four hundred pound raw turkey," Dan grunted.

"It'd be easier if rigor mortis had set in," Fred said, straining against the bulk.

"How long does that take?"

Fred looked at his watch, realized the ridiculousness of this habitual action, and started laughing again. "We don't have time," he managed.

With a great deal of tugging and straining, they got the body back on the gurney, strapping it in securely. It was more difficult to get the gurney back up on its legs, taking several tries. Finally they jerked the contraption upright and the legs clicked into place.

"I used to work out for football and shit, but Jesus," Fred said, lighting a cigarette. "Good thing you're a strong son of a bitch. Okay, let's get Fatso inside."

The rolled the gurney through the long tiled hallways to the preparation room. Once there, Fred unzipped the body bag all the way. The corpse inside was huge indeed, bloated, with a y-shaped autopsy incision on the chest and abdomen. The incision had been sutured closed only loosely, and Dan could look into the corpse's chest, seeing the fat cells there, resembling congealed tapioca stained with a red wash, a palm's width thick. The neck of the body was thick with fat, the mouth and eyes slightly open. The blood had settled in the back, thighs, and buttocks, leaving the coloration of bruising, whereas the rest of the flesh had the sallowness of uncooked chicken. The hands had been tied together to keep them close to the bulk of the body, something Fred told him was unusual.

"If someone is of normal size," he said, "their arms just stay by their sides like they're supposed to."

Dan felt the blood rush to his head again, along with a dizzy sense of surreality. It occurred to him that his history with hallucinogens made the whole situation more tolerable. When you trip, he thought, the bizarre becomes normal. With that thought, the rush and the sense of surreality faded.

"Ever seen a D.B. before, kid?" Fred said.

"D.B.?"

"Dead body."

"Oh. Yeah, sure," he said, although he couldn't remember when.

"Let's slide him over," Fred said, indicating the stainless steel table with a nod. "Just roll up and grab the sheet underneath him, like this, and yank. On three. One, two...."

"Three!" Dan said, and they slid the bulk over in a tumble of hollow thumps on the stainless steel.

"Most people shy away from death," Fred said. "Wash your hands over here."

As they soaped up at the large sink, Fred flipped a cigarette into his mouth, took a gold lighter to it, and continued. "People don't want to think about it. They'd rather just run around screaming with their hands over their ears, squinching their eyes shut. Then when the bad shit happens, and they're completely unprepared. And the bad shit will eventually happen."

"Sounds like something my grampa would say."

"Mr. McGregor? Now, there's one tough old fella knows what he's talking about."

"What's going on in here?" It was Sam Feeney, standing in the doorway.

"Got a customer," Fred said. "That one from BMH."

"I see that," Feeney said. "I was rather hoping Dan wouldn't be so exposed."

"Well..." Fred began.

"No, it's all right," Feeney said. "I can see Dan's no shrinking violet."

"Guess not," Fred said, punching Dan on the shoulder.

When they noted Dan's hours for the day, Sam Feeney put down three times as many. "This kind of thing wasn't supposed to be your job," he said, "although I suppose if I had a son your age, he would've been doing it. You deserve credit for it, though."

"Thanks," Dan said.

The first customer he saw that was the DB of someone he knew was that of Mickey Potts, a man he had known for years from Willy's bar. A handyman by trade, Mickey was a short, Mediterranean-looking guy with dense white hair, black eyebrows, large blackrimmed eyeglasses, and bandy legs. He was a frequent customer in the bar, but was usually lost in the general hubbub of the evening. Dan got to know him better in the spring after his return from Greysport. Willy had given Mickey the task of fixing a garbage disposal at the bar, and Dan suspected it was to pay off part of a bar tab, as Willy was perfectly capable of doing the job himself. When Mickey came in on a Saturday morning, Dan was mopping up the bar and listening to the jukebox. Mickey introduced himself. Dan immediately smelled vodka on his breath, and was amused by this.

Mickey told Dan how easy it was to fix the apparatus, showing him where to find the reset button. "It's like a little clit down here, see?" Mickey said, down on one knee and looking up at Dan, leering as he reached in under the sink to touch the device. "It's on the bottom of the disposal, and ya just gotta...*finger* it, see?"

"Sure," Dan said, unable to keep from smiling.

The disposal was fixed, and Mickey stood up and flicked the switch to prove it. The disposal ground away and the backed up water sucked down in a noisy vortex.

"So what do you do?" Mickey asked Dan.

"Finger it," Dan said.

"Finger what?"

"The clit," Dan said.

"*There* you go," Mickey said, giving Dan an evil, boozy wink.

Mickey had also worked on Julia's house when Charlie and Jim were in town, installing new gutters and doing other such work. During a particularly muggy day, the boys had sat on the couch Julia's living room, watching the Three Stooges on one of the Black Marsh stations after doing a series of bongs in her garage. Mickey, wearing only cut-off, rolled up jeans, socks, workboots and a tool belt, brown from the humid sun, rattled around outside with an aluminum ladder, and didn't seem to be having that good a time of it. The Three Stooges, as always, were funny enough, but when the boys saw Mickey struggling with an obstinate gutter through the sheer curtains over the window, it began to get funnier than what they saw on the television, mostly due to the scorching profanity loosed by Mickey, who thought he was unobserved.

"Ohhhh, you cocksucking motherfucking sonofablueballed *bitch*!" he snarled at the gutter, standing on the ladder with only his bandy legs in view. "Fucking motherfucking fuck fuck *fuck*!" There were sounds of clanging and rending, who knew what. Charlie had been about to laugh out loud, but Dan and Jim had cautioned him to silence.

When the hapless Mickey had climbed down the ladder, the gutter finally came loose on one end, swinging down and cracking him in the head with the sound of a gong. That really set him off.

"Fucking dyke Mary and that faggot Joseph and the cornholed baby Jesus! Fuck!"

The boys had clutched at each other and rolled around, trying to stifle their laughter. At Jim's suggestion, they put on straight faces and went outside to talk to Mickey. When they came out the side door, Mickey was at his truck, rifling through a toolbox, his dense white hair matted with blood around the part.

"Oh, hi, boys!" Mickey said pleasantly.

Only Charlie was cool enough to speak, stoned as they were.

"Wow," he said, pointing at Mickey's head. "What happened?"

Mickey touched the top of his head and pulled his fingers away bloody. "Oh, that? Heck, that's nothing. It happens."

Jim did a smart about-face and headed down the driveway to hide his laughter. Charlie, on the other hand, looked at Mickey appraisingly and said, "You ever smoke dope?"

Dan didn't have time to interrupt before Mickey said, "Sure. Got some?"

They had spent the next hour in Julia's garage, doing bongs and drinking cheap paisano wine from a giant jug which Mickey produced from the back of his truck. Mickey's lewd and leering line of jabber kept the boys laughing. It was apparent that Charlie and Jim had no access to someone like Mickey in White Birch Pointe.

Mickey finally left in time to avoid Julia coming home, leaving the gutter hanging from the house but promising to come back the next day.

"We'll say you got hurt on the job and had to get stitches or something," Dan offered.

"Great," Mickey said. "You boys are all right." He wove off in his pickup, apparently dreading going home to his fundamentalist wife.

"I like that old dude," Charlie had said.

Dan liked the old dude, too, but had his misgivings about Mickey's capacity for survival. The penultimate story Dan had heard about him involved his attempt to fix a van belonging to the owner of the record shop, the pudgy hippie who went by the name of Starhawk. Dan had been behind the bar (the only sober person in the place, aside from Bob Two Bears) when Mickey had offered to fix Starhawk's ailing van. The van had been sitting down by the docks for so long that it was covered with dust, with *Wash Me* fingered onto the windows, then covered with enough dust again to almost obscure this. The Sheriff's Department, no more than an occasional presence in MacDougal, had put enough tickets on the van to finally get Starhawk's attention.

Dan wasn't sure how it came about, but it must have originated with the mindset of the Energy Crisis, although the reasoning beyond that would remain murky to those not in attendance. With the knowledge of things mechanical at his disposal, it was surprising (and amusing) that Mickey would think it was a good idea to get gas out of the tank of the disabled vehicle with a drill, which he had done by running a dropcord from the boathouse to the van, sliding a large, flat receptacle underneath the van for the gas. Starhawk later claimed that he had not known what Mickey was going to do, but the locals were skeptical. Perhaps it was a morning saturated with vodka that blurred Mickey's reason, but that's what he did, took a drill to the gas tank of the van, possibly in some misguided effort to save the fuel. Predictably, the friction from the drillbit not only punched a hole into the tank, but ignited the freshly sprung gas leak as well.

It was summer at the time, and the gravel lot by the docks had been packed by the parked cars of boaters, some of them unusually posh vehicles from Greysport and out of state. When Mickey did his bit with the drill, the gas ignited but didn't explode, which it would have done if the gascap of the van had been off. Instead it had caused a flaming leak as thick as a stream of piss.

"Cocksucking motherfucker!" Mickey had cried, rolling out from under the van, running to the driver's seat, and cranking frantically at the ignition.

Starhawk had been at a nearby picnic table and jumped to his feet. "Hey, man, what the fuck!"

Heroically, Mickey started the van. "I'm sorry! I'm *sorry*!" he called out, before driving the vehicle away from the parked cars and the boathouse. As he drove, he left a trail of ignited gas behind him.

Perhaps he was trying to get the van to the street, but he never made it that far. With a small *fooomp!* the gas tank ignited, and Mickey finally heeded the shouts of witnesses and abandoned the van, which went up in a burst of flame so intense that the tires caught fire and exploded, the windshield melted, and an apple tree ten feet away was left half scorched. By the time Dan had heard the commotion and run down the street, the van was a smoking, gutted mass of metal, generating a giant black plume of roiling, oily smoke. The volunteer fire department showed up some time later.

The locals muttered, laughed, and shook their heads, all of them knowing Mickey. Out-of-towners resolved to vacation elsewhere.

None of the locals were surprised by how the handyman's story finally came to a close.

Mickey Potts was up fishing at one of the state's several Long Lakes one weekend, staying at a cabin owned by his wife's family. It was known that he didn't like the family, and that they returned the favor. Later it was discovered that he had tried to convince his wife and daughter to go fishing, it being a beautiful day. They had pointed out that it was too windy and choppy, and that fishing in the jonboat would be unsafe. He had laughed at them and left. Mickey was last seen out in a boat by himself, as reported by witnesses, two of whom said that he had smiled cheerfully and raised a beer as they cruised in to shelter on their larger, safer boat. The next thing anyone knew, Mickey's boat was empty, running in slow circles on the turbulent water.

There was almost no chance that Mickey wasn't drunk. Perhaps what happened was that he wobbled a bit when leaning over the side, that a wave lifted the boat and he lost his balance and went into the drink. The boat, with no one at the tiller, might have come around and bonked him on the head (another convergence of aluminum and his densely-furred cranium) sending him underwater just as he gasped in surprise and pain. Then he might have choked and panicked for a bit, taking in some water while trying to get his breath, then a lot of water, before suddenly coming to the realization that, hey, this isn't so bad, and relaxing to it and floating slowly down into the dim green depths as the boat described lazy circles overhead.

Divers were called to look for him, but their search was eventually postponed when thunderstorms rolled into the area. Dan would imagine Mickey's body, quiescent in the mild

currents, looking up through the dark water as the flickering thunderclouds rolled overhead.

The divers came back the next day, searched the frigid depths of the lake and found Mickey's DB, which ended up at Feeney's as a customer.

When Dan saw him, Mickey had been through rigor mortis and back again, the enzymes having worked through that part of the process. It was still Mickey, though, or at least the shell of him. The eyes looked like agate, and the tongue, visible in the open mouth, was almost black.

"You knew this guy, right, Dan?" Fred Turner asked him.

"Yeah," Dan said.

Turner said, not without compassion, "Any words?"

"*Sic transit gloria mundi*, man," Dan said, with a bit of a smile. It was a Charlie phrase.

"Fuckin' A," Turner said.

Dan wanted to touch the poor, hapless man's face, but that simply wasn't done.

A moment later, the corpse seemed to tug at recognition in Dan's memory, but something in his mind clicked and looked in the opposite direction. Instead, he found himself thinking about things Charlie had said, though, and wondered what the point of it all had been for Mickey, stretched out on the cold stainless steel with his agate eyes. He wondered what the point was for anyone.

While the days loitered by for Dan, the leaves and then the snow falling in slow motion, for Willy they seemed to scream by almost audibly. The trees became bare, then he was shoveling snow, then the holidays were gone, and then it was spring again. In one more spring, the boy would be eighteen, and off and on his way.

Willy shifted through emotions about this. He loved Dan, perhaps even more than he had Gordon and Chief, if such a thing were possible. It broke his heart to think of the boy's life so far, and he could only assuage himself with the hope that he and Mae (yes, and Gordon) had equipped him with enough strengths that, when he got older, he would be able to find some kind of happiness in life.

He knew his lectures and advice were generally disregarded, but he kept them up anyway, hoping that something would filter in, to eventual effect. It had been so with his own father, who he ultimately realized had been right about almost everything. Even lighthouses; Willy missed lighthouses.

That was the problem with humans, though; being told was not enough. In spite of any warnings, they would have to try the painful, again and again. And look at the results.

Often, he felt that old sense of purpose which only raising a child could bring out. It was that which kept him going. Doing something as simple as cooking Dan a good breakfast in the morning before the kid stalked off through the crackling pink and orange winter dawn to school, that was something. He offered to talk to the boy about anything (having learned from the negative example of his aloof father), although he was usually dismissed. He wanted to know what was going on in the boy's unusual mind. What had he seen in his life which might present questions? Dan, as always, was as reticent as Willy was willing.

When Dan had worked off his debt at Sam Feeney's, he turned down the offer of a job there. Willy was a little relieved; he thought that Feeney, having no children, might have wanted Dan to take over the business for him, whereas Willy wanted Dan to get off to Greysport and to college.

Dan's last day at Feeney's was in the spring not long before the boy's seventeenth birthday. Willy picked him up in front of the place and told him to come along.

"Where are we going?" Dan asked.

"What, are you busy?" Willy asked back.

"Nope."

"Okay then."

He drove up the hill to the old Coeur de la Riviere cemetery above the town, the hill he had walked up and down so much that he thought that, there in the springtime grass, he should be able to find his own personal rut. He parked on the asphalt lane between the gravestones.

"So, working at Feeney's," Willy said. "Think that brought on any epiphanies?"

Dan shrugged.

"When I was your age," Willy said, "I was seeing dead guys all the time. Made me look at things a lot differently, I'll tell you."

"Did it make a man out of you?" Dan said, gently mocking.

"No. Your grandmother did that. And your dad and your uncle."

They sat in silence for a few moments, looking out the windshield.

"What are we doing here?" Dan asked.

"You'll see," Willy said. "Come on."

Willy wondered if Dan gave any thought to the age of some of the stones, then remembered that he had done charcoal rubbings of them on newsprint when he was younger. If anyone would understand, the boy would, with his artist's eye. They walked among the rows, silent for a while.

He stopped at one stone, laid his hand on top of it. "Here lies Mollie Sletto," Willy said, the stone cool under his palm. "She was…our friend. She might have lived a long time. You would've liked her."

Moving on, they walked by other stones, and Willy said the names of those he knew, told something of their stories. Finally they stood in front of a large stone with two names on it.

"The dates of death are the same," Dan said.

"Very observant," Willy said. "Doc and Harriet Ambrose. He was like a father to me, as they say. He straightened me out when I needed it. When his wife died, he just didn't see any more point, and there was none, really. His golden span was over."

"Golden span?"

"That's why we're here, what I wanted to talk to you about. Not everyone has a golden span, a stretch of years that are their most beautiful, a time of someone's life that justifies any pain or sadness or burden in the rest of it. There will always be some sadness, but if you realize the preciousness of the golden span, that sadness is more tolerable.

"The worst thing one can do is to get so distracted by the sadness of one's life, or even the wearisome minutia of it, which is what most people do, I think, they're so sealed off. That not enough attention is being paid to the good years- or good months, or good minutes- while they last. I think that if one isn't careful, if one isn't observant, those months and minutes and years might be gone without even being recognized. I think most people wander around in a distracted daze, worrying themselves sick about the most unimportant shit. Then their days are over, sometimes suddenly, and they might not have had the sense to recognize the beauty of it.

"These people, buried here around us, are mostly forgotten," Willy said. "It's what happens. I'll be forgotten. You'll be forgotten, at least eventually. Think about it. Most guys your age don't know their grandparents as well as you know me. Your kids probably won't know me at all. Their kids will barely know *of* me.

"And if we don't have the sense to appreciate our brief time here, in this place, *wherever* we are, why, then, we've lost it all, any meaning we might have had.

"So, make a place for yourself, Dan, somewhere you find beautiful, a place that gives you a sense of peace. If it isn't beautiful, make it beautiful. Find a woman you really love, and I mean really love. A partner, a best friend, not someone you show off like a sports car or an expensive watch. And don't let any woman use *you* in the same way. Have a family if it seems right. Make connections, be a good friend. Corny as it sounds, love and friendship are what keep the emptiness at bay.

"Employ your good talents, goddammit, not your bad ones. Live in a way where you can look yourself in the mirror. Do something just, do something right, do something beautiful, bring some light to the world. And pay close attention to those good years. Enjoy them. They are not eternal. They are your Golden Span. It's a gift to know when you are living them."

Willy stared at the boy until he got a reaction.

"*Okay*," Dan said, widening his eyes and spreading his hands. Willy ignored this slight whiff of tired sarcasm.

"Come on," he said.

"Now where are we going?" Dan asked.

"We're going to pick up a shitload of saplings at the nursery and plant them. That'll put you right."

Dan snorted and shook his head.

"Come on," Willy said, lightly punching the boy's arm. "You like that kind of thing. Admit it. It's a holy act to plant a tree, a gift to the future."

"If you say so."

When they were almost at the truck, Willy said, "And Dan?"

"Yeah?"

"Don't ever leave me in a fucking place like this," Willy said, nodding his head at the cemetery. "The river, okay, boy? The river."

Mae would have told him to be patient with the boy; he could almost hear her doing so when he was awake, and did in his sleep. Sometimes he awoke on the couch at night having heard her voice, her breath still warm on his ear from where her shadow had bent over to whisper. With his eyes adjusted to the darkness, the only illumination that of a streetlight through the living room sheers, he would jerk, put his hands out to steady himself. What was that slender patch of darkness in the corner?

Rippling with goosebumps, he would say, "Mae?"

When he turned on the light, there would be only the bookshelves and the old reading chair, the lamp next to it. And yet he sniffed the air to catch some scent of her, and prayed to taste her on his tongue.

Then he would read until it got light out, and, when Dan got up for school, would fix the boy breakfast.

"Ham and eggs jambalaya?" he might say, referring to one of the boy's favorite concoctions, sautéed ham, onions and tomatoes, sometimes cheese, mixed with eggs. Not jambalaya at all, but that was their name for it.

"Sure," Dan would say noncommittally from his bedroom or the bathroom.

They ate silently together, listening to the public radio station. Dan would leave for school, pack over his shoulder, his long hair wet even if it froze on the way.

The traces of blood in Willy's stools again came as no great surprise, and the occasional flickers of shanking pain did little more than make him falter in midstep while walking to or from the bar. He said nothing about it to anyone, nor did he intend to. He went to an attorney, though, to revise his will, which had remained unchanged since before Mae's death. Even that he did only at her half-heard insistence. He also left a package for Emilio with the attorney, after having gone over it together page by page. The young man suggested doing a few things differently, but had surrendered to Willy's mildly contemptuous obstinacy and a large payment in cash.

"This is more than my fee," the young man pointed out.

"The rest is a tip," Willy said.

"Oh," the attorney replied. "Then, uh, thank you."

Dan came home from school on a fall day at the beginning of his senior year in high school looking a little more dour than usual. Answers to any questions were monosyllabic, as usual, and any attempts he made to engage the boy in conversation were fruitless. Willy was on the verge of telling him to go out to the garage and smoke some reefer to improve his mood, but didn't want to cross that line or encourage such behavior.

Instead, he improvised. Feeling a bit of a roiling in his guts, the threat of an imminent blast, he reverted to a routine which had amused the boy when he was small. Dan had just set down his pack in the living room and gone into the kitchen when Willy approached him.

"Pull my finger," he said, holding out the customary digit.

"Jesus," Dan said, but smiled a bit nonetheless.

"Come on. Pull it!"

Dan smirked, acting like he was about to touch something explosive.

The tired joke had better results than Willy could have hoped for. Dan pulled the finger. Willy lifted a knee a bit, squinted, and liquidly shat his pants.

"Goddammit!" he shouted. He stalked off to get clean underwear, jerked some off the pile, and walked into the bathroom with a clenched, sticky gait, slamming the bathroom door behind him. The fact that the boy was actually, literally, rolling on the floor with laughter was the only thing that made it acceptable when Willy found blood in the mess in his underwear. Willy even laughed as he cleaned himself up.

Things got less pleasant between the two of them, though, and Dan was often argumentative for no concrete reason, other than the obvious one, that he wanted his freedom from the little town, wanted to burst into his own life.

In his touchiness, Dan often overreacted to some minor correction of Willy's. One Sunday morning in the fall, they had a spat about gassing the truck. Although Dan was, in principle, supposed to pay for his own gas, Willy often topped the tank off for him before a weekend night, one of the small, unseen kindnesses he did for the boy. In this instance he had forgotten to do so, being busy at the bar. Dan got home that Sunday morning, saying that he had run out of gas somewhere off the river road and had taken that long to get a gas can, put more in the tank, and return home. Willy had awakened before dawn, realized that Dan wasn't back from his night out, and was sitting on the couch when Dan pulled into the driveway and came into the kitchen with a surly look on his face. They went back and forth about what had happened.

"Well, you could have at least called," Willy said finally. "Don't you think I worry about you?"

"No, I don't think you worry much about anything."

"Well, that's just…unreasonable. That's all I do, is worry. I worried about your dad, I worried about your uncle, I worried about your grandmother. My whole life has been worrying about people."

"Lot of good it did," Dan said, taking a banana from a bunch on the counter and going to his room.

"What's that supposed to mean?" Willy shouted after him.

"Think about it!" Dan shouted back, slamming the door. Willy then heard the muted sound of music playing through the boy's headphones.

Willy did think about it. He knew he had made mistakes all along the trail of his life, but now, with the circumstances as they were, he could not see a thing that he could do differently. His only task was to launch the boy into his own life, and hope that he had helped him to be happy and complete. Dan's words stung him, though; he kept this to himself.

On a late afternoon in November, Willy got Dan to work out on the heavybag, holding the bag for him, being his coach. The boy was now as big and solid as Gordon and Chief had been at the end of high school, and when Dan hit the bag, he hit it hard.

"That's good," Willy said. "Use your left. That's it. Good. Get some snap."

Dan hit the bag harder and harder, grunting with the effort until he was actually shouting inarticulately. A final right at chest height sent Willy back against the workbench. Willy caught himself and leaned against the bench, watching Dan, who stood pale and muscular, his sweaty skin gleaming in the light of the basement windows.

"Why didn't you come get me!" the boy shouted.

"What?" Willy said. "When? The time you ran out of gas?"

"No! Fuck! When I was in Greysport! In fucking Portview!" He slammed the bag with his right and sent it swinging wildly.

"I didn't know where you were," Willy said, the cold wind again in his empty places.

"How the fuck could you not know!" Dan shouted.

Willy told the story as far as he could remember it and said, "I didn't know where you were until I talked with that Miss Robinson from Social Services."

Dan watched him, chest heaving but slowing down. "You talked to Miss Robinson?"

"Yeah. They were going to try to place you with me anyway. I got the feeling that a kid your age wasn't at the top of their list of priorities."

Dan reached out and grasped the chain supporting the heavy bag, leaning on it.

"They deal with people who hit their *babies*," Willy said, "people who hold toddlers' hands over stove burners. I think they thought you were holding your own."

Dan's eyes went up and to the side, as if doing a fact check. He gave Willy a cool glance. Without another word, he went up the stairs and into the bathroom. Willy leaned against the workbench, hearing the crank of the faucet and the sound of the shower. Taking a bottle of whiskey from where it sat on a shelf between a circular saw and a drill, he sat on his old stool and took a drink from the bottle. He waited, listening to the sounds of Dan getting dressed in his room. Then the boy walked solidly through the living room and out the front door, across the porch, down the steps. Willy sat for several minutes in the quiet of the basement. When the silence began to roar and hum, he reached under the workbench and chose one of two trunks, sliding out his old trunk of dusty writing, his oldest poetry mingled with his most recent, the yellow pages and the white, sheaves of the things he had left undone.

Willy sat there for hours, reading in the naked light of the workbench bulb until the bottle of whiskey was done. Finally, he slowly creaked stiffly to his feet to shamble up the stairs, ignoring the knowledge that he should drink a large amount of water before going to bed.

In spite of his hangover, he got up to fix the boy breakfast in the morning. Dan was formal in his thanks, and left. Willy sat at the old kitchen table for some time, then walked slowly down the hall. He opened the door to the master bedroom, where everything was still in place. Leaning against the doorjamb, he stood looking in, then turned away and closed the door behind him. He took a shower- the endless ritual of reliable motion- and found himself walking exhausted down the street to the bar.

There were times when Willy nearly panicked about his life. On any given day, Dan might come home from school, or in for his work at the bar, and be so expressionlessly sullen and silent that Willy could only imagine what was going on in his head. There were times he felt sure that it was hatred the boy was feeling, certainly hatred for his situation, and probably hatred for Willy. This was another sick feeling to lance through his guts. Rather than doing anything to spook Dan, or to further anger him, he kept up his own habitual face of protective stone.

How did he lose his traction? He'd known the right thing to do and striven to do it, and yet it came out wrong. Two boys had slipped away from him, and now a third seemed to be on his way. How did he lose them? How much time did he have to correct it?

It was obvious to others that Willy was out of sorts, even depressed, and it took an organized effort by Emilio and Bob to get him to talk about it even a little. They had apparently waited until they had gotten Willy in the bar on a weekday morning, the early spring sunlight illuminating the details of the old oak floorboards in a way that the regular customers would never see. As they sat and drank coffee over plates smeared with the remains of eggs and dotted with toast crumbs, Emilio and Bob established what was wrong through a series of questions and Willy's terse answers.

"He's a kid," Bob said finally, spreading his hands. "Pretty *big* kid, but still a kid."

"He'll understand," Emilio said, patting Willy's forearm before standing up to gather the dishes. "He'll know who he came from, he'll know who he is."

"People misunderstand all the time," Willy said. "People fuck *up* all the time. You think that there's a rule that any particular life is going to end up *well*? Things go badly all the time! People come to bad fucking ends! Both of you are old enough to realize that! Fuck! You both are living in a dream world!"

Emilio came back from the kitchen and they sat in silence for some time, sipping coffee.

Finally, Willy said, "I guess I just figured that I'd someday reach an age when wisdom was effortless and everything went smoothly."

"Now who's living in a dream world?" Bob said.

Only Solveig made him feel truly better. Willy stood on their front porch one morning a few days later, waiting for Emilio to get organized so they could go fishing. As Emilio wandered through the house, muttering to himself in Spanish, Solveig brought Willy out a cup of coffee and an apple. They stood looking out at the pastel dawn together, watching the still water by the dock reflecting the orange light of the morning sun, the rose threads of mist rising from the water.

"It'll be okay," Solveig said.

Willy looked down at her, her white hair, sharp blue eyes set in smiling wrinkles. For a moment, it seemed as if he'd never seen her before.

"You think so?" he said.

"Yeah," she said, winking both eyes simultaneously. "Yep, I do. Know so."

She seemed so sure about it that it made Willy smile a little.

"Chief was different, that boy," Solveig said. "He took after Mae, had that sunnier disposition. But you, and Gordon, and Dan? You're all just the same, one after another. You just think too much."

Willy drank half the cup of coffee in a slow drag, then sighed through his nose. "Is that right?"

"Heck, yes. Can't just relax and be the good men you are. And you're all good men."

He looked at his old friend, her face and words so simple and genuine.

"Are we?" he said.

She made a fricative sound with her lips. "Of course you are," she said, putting her arm around his waist and leaning her head against his shoulder. "Don't you know that?"

The reassurances of friends did little to abate Willy's sentiments. Dan seemed angry most of the time he was home, and appeared to set up his work hours for times when Willy wasn't there. Willy's proclamation had long since been that Dan would work when he wanted to, as long as the work got done, this logical policy leaving Willy no room for complaint.

Dan's eighteenth birthday was supposed to be a surprise. With Spring again on the river, the water gigantically high, they had the party at Emilio and Solvieg's in spite of the flood, their house and outbuildings with their carefully wrought wood carvings high there above the heavy breadth of water.

A dinner was prepared of fish and game, early things from the garden. Solveig displayed drawings and other small pieces of Dan's art work around the living room and dining room, the accumulation of years. Dan smiled politely and seemed gracious on the surface, but was clearly preoccupied, perhaps even worried.

He put on a brave face, though, and made it through the dinner, saying something pleasant about each of the presents he had opened. He was the youngest person at the table by decades, and Willy struggled to keep from feeling sad for him, although he had asked Dan if he'd wanted any friends to attend. When Dan requested the keys to the pickup truck, Willy felt better. It was the first Saturday in May, and it was good that the boy appeared to have plans, even if Willy didn't know what they were.

Dan came home in the small hours very drunk. He braked the truck hard in the driveway, waking Willy up on the couch. When Dan came in the kitchen door and turned on the bright overhead light, Willy pretended to be asleep. Dan was usually considerate if he came in late, taking off his boots on the back steps and tiptoeing through the house to his room, so the fact that he turned on the light told Willy that something was amiss. When he began to slam cupboard drawers and bang around in the refrigerator, Willy couldn't ignore it and got up.

Willy could see Dan's condition by the look on his face. He wove a little as he stood with one hand on the counter, a glass of orange juice in his hand. Willy tried to keep his tone light.

"What's going on?" he said.

Dan dragged his head in Willy's direction as if it had weights strapped to it. He looked blearily at Willy, apparently having difficulty focusing.

"Havin' some fuckin'…" he looked at the glass, studied it, "…orange juice." He looked back at Willy, a little belligerently.

"You'd better drink that down, have plenty more and some water, and get yourself to bed. You won't feel as bad in the morning. You want me to get you some aspirin?"

"Don't get me anything!" Dan shouted, slamming the glass on the counter and slopping most of its contents. "I don't want anything! Just leave me the fuck alone!"

86

Willy held out his hands. "Okay, easy. Why don't you sit down at the table and we can talk. What's the problem?"

"Don't tell me what to do! I do what I want!"

Willy wanted to put his arms around him, but he was somewhat menacing, feral, standing under the kitchen light with his fists bunched, his long hair disarrayed, his chest heaving.

"Okay, okay. Just tell me what's the problem."

"The problem? The fucking problem? What the fuck do you think the problem is?"

"I don't know, son. That's why I'm asking."

"*I am not your fucking son!*" Dan shouted loudly enough that Willy thought the neighbors might hear it. "I'm *nobody's* fucking son!"

"Okay, now, settle down. Drink some juice."

"What the fuck are we doing here! What are we doing here!"

"What...on Earth?" Willy said, trying to be funny.

"No, goddammit! In this fucking shithole town!"

"It's where we live," Willy said, quietly enough that he hoped it would calm the boy down.

"Well, why are *you* here? Weren't you going to *be* somebody? What was it, something about poetry? You were going to be a poet? What the fuck! Look at you!"

"All right," Willy said, beginning to lose his patience, "let's not say anything we regret."

"Fuck that! I regret all kinds of shit! I regret being born into this fucking *family*," Dan said, making wobbly air quotes. "What's a little more?"

"That's enough, Dan."

"*Fuck* you. I mean, who *are* you? You're just some old motherfucker who lived out here in this shithole! *You're* a *poet*? The *fuck* you're a poet! Waste your fucking life out here, and you try to tell me what to do. *What have you ever lived through?*"

Willy watched the boy for a moment, sorry for the regret he would feel. Dan stood waiting, glowering, unfocused. Willy said slowly, "If you think I've fucked up, learn from it. Do better. When you've got something good, something precious, have the sense to recognize it, to preserve it instead of destroying it."

Dan talked over Willy's words. "Yeah yeah yeah. Blah blah blah. Whatever! And I *am* going to do better! *Anybody* could do better!"

"Goddammit, go to bed!"

"Don't *tell* me what to do! *Nobody tells me what to do!*"

Willy drew himself up and Dan squared off. Willy came closer, to put his arms around the boy and hold him in a bearhug until he was peaceful. Dan pulled back his fist. He was large and solid, the boy, and Willy no longer had the strength. Willy sighed, turned around, left the kitchen and went back to the couch. Dan stood in the kitchen for a few moments, then turned and went toward the door. Willy knew Dan had left the keys to the truck on the counter, and he did not retrieve them. Dan clomped down the back stairs and slammed the door, and Willy heard him shuffle down the driveway. He got up from the couch and went to the window. Dan walked down the street toward the river, visible for a moment in a cone of streetlight, then gone in the darkness.

Neither of them said anything about what happened in the kitchen. Willy thought the boy would feel better in the long run if he apologized, even though Willy himself agreed with some of what Dan had said. For his part, Dan, after coming in just before dawn and sleeping until the afternoon, avoided Willy's eyes for some time after that, his face hard and unreadable. At the bar, Willy rarely had to give Dan instructions, and when he did, it was something simple: "Bring up a case of the Greysport," or "Take out the garbage," anything Dan didn't know was necessary or that he might've missed. Dan would usually simply nod in reply.

One Saturday, Willy sent Dan to clean off the booth of some regulars who had finished their burgers and fries and were drinking pitchers of beer. Willy thought this was odd; Dan had cleared the tables around them. One of the regulars was a cute, although somewhat sleazy, blonde named Debbie, who was sitting with her large husband, a cop, whose name Willy could not remember. They'd had vocal arguments in the bar in the past, but seemed to be on good terms at the moment, smoking and drinking, talking to the other couple in the booth. Willy told Dan that he had forgotten to get the plastic food baskets on their table, and Dan, with seeming reluctance, went over to get them. Willy thought it might have been his imagination, but Dan seemed to give Debbie a brief look, perhaps a heated one, which Debbie either ignored or didn't see. When Debbie and the cop left, Willy didn't give it another thought.

In the last weeks of Dan's high school, Willy asked him occasionally if he wanted to go fishing, or to drive up to Black Marsh for Chinese food at Fung's, anything he could devise, but Dan declined quietly. When Dan received a letter of acceptance from Greysport University for the fine arts program, Willy only found out by seeing the letter open on the coffee table by the couch. Willy wanted to celebrate with Dan, but the boy remained scarce, leaving early in the morning and either coming home late at night or going straight to his room. When they ate together, it was usually in silence.

The ever-changing Ad Hoc Band arranged a visit by a travelling group of Irish musicians for a gig at the bar. As always, Willy was glad to have itinerant musicians, paying them generously, feeding them and buying drinks, finding them a place to stay. The Irish boys were a gregarious bunch, but when they sat down to play in a circle of chairs in a space cleared on the floor, they snapped into their roles as musicians with fluidity and ease. As if to dispel any notions that they might be tasteful and restrained, they started off their set with a song called *One-Ball Riley,* moving quickly on to *Seamus Shagged a Sheep*, which was, the leader of the band, Ignatius Muldoon, explained in his tart brogue, "an agricultural tune". With banjo and mandolin, tin whistle and bodhran and accordion, they went at it. The owner of the record store, the pudgy hippie Starhawk, danced a jig with such glee that he slipped in spilled beer and thudded to the floor, but got up immediately and hoisted his unspilled beer in triumph.

"Kiss me, I'm Irish!" he cried.

"Blow me, I'm Scottish!" someone in the crowd yelled back, and even the members of the band laughed, although they never stopped playing.

When the crowd seemed to be reaching critical mass, Ignatius Muldoon gave Willy a look and a nod, and changed the tempo down. They started with the lone plucking of a banjo, then the flickering notes of the mandolin, and Muldoon began to sing. Willy immediately recognized *The Streets of Laredo*, transformed by Muldoon's tenor, the thumps of the bodhran keeping the time of a dirge.

Willy looked around the bar at the people he had long known and seen age, at the young faces that had come to replace those of the dead, the young faces often those of strangers while he could almost see, through the shifting crowd, the likenesses of those he had known long ago, in a booth or on a barstool, lifting a glass or giving a smile. He had the sense that if he turned around at just the right speed (a sensation Dan would recognize), Mae would be beside him, smiling and wistful at the thought of the song. And there would be Doc and Harriet Ambrose, there Mollie, Barnacle Brad and even Steve Hansen. He turned to see Chief bring a case of Greysport up from the basement, realizing after a few dizzy moments that it was Dan. The boy gave him a dead look and went back to work. Suddenly choked, Willy excused himself and went around Bob's back, through the crowd and down the basement stairs.

Back among the shelves, he sat on two stacked cases of beer in the same place he had caught Stumpy and Nubby Schommer smoking reefer years before; he saw their faces, smiling and young, but they, too, were gone. After sitting there for some time, Willy realized he was weeping. He hunched forward with his elbows on his knees, his vision blurring as he watched tears drop to the concrete floor.

"Grampa," Dan said, standing at the end of the row of shelves. When Willy looked up, Dan saw his face, recoiling slightly.

They regarded each other for a moment.

Dan said, "I just wanted to ask if we could give Steve Connelly credit."

Willy snuffled and wiped his eyes with the heels of his hands, trying to appear nonchalant. He cleared his throat elaborately.

"Yeah, yeah," he said. "Steve's all right."

Dan stood there for a moment before saying, "I never thought I'd have to tell you to buck up. Jesus."

"Give me a break," Willy said, "I'm old."

Dan didn't want to attend his own graduation from high school, but allowed Willy to talk him into it, for the sake of Emilio, Solveig, and Bob Two Bears, among others. He insisted on not having a party, but Willy surprised him with one when Dan came in to work late in the afternoon the first Saturday in June after school let out. Willy thought that the boy actually was a little angry at the surprise. He was completely taken aback, and, for just a moment, seemed that he was even startled enough to be scared. After some minutes, though, he succumbed to the attention with terse words and pursed lips. It was clear that he didn't like being the center of attention.

Without fanfare, Dan left for Greysport as soon as he could. Willy had hoped he would stay the summer, but the boy was anxious to get started. He arranged a ride with Starhawk, who, long since equipped with a new van, was taking a trip to Greysport for a music store owners convention. Dan packed in such a hurry that it was as if he were fleeing. Willy watched his swift and harried action from outside his bedroom door.

"You call me when you get settled," Willy said.

"Yeah. Sure."

"Don't get into too much trouble living with Charlie."

"Yeah."

"Are you sure you don't need any money?"

This stopped him in his packing. He looked at Willy slowly, distance in his eyes. "No," he said. "I'll be fine."

Dan carried boxes out to Starhawk's van, refusing Willy's help. When everything was loaded, Starhawk started the engine and sat waiting.

Dan spread his hands and said, "Okay."

"You take care of yourself," Willy said. He went to hug Dan, and Dan stiffened, then raised his hands to give Willy exactly three pats on the back, as if he had counted them. Just as Gordon might once have done.

When the van backed out of the driveway, Willy could see through the sunlight and leaves reflected on the windshield that Dan was already laughing and talking to Starhawk. He didn't give Willy a last look as Starhawk put the van in drive and rolled off down the street.

Willy stood for some minutes in the driveway before walking slowly into the empty house.

When Dan came back to Greysport, Charlie had gotten an apartment on the top floor of a four story building of grey brick, the name Buckingham carved in the granite arch over the entryway. It became known among Charlie's (and subsequently Dan's) circle of friends as the Kicking Pig, and was the center for heavy partying, especially on weekends, in the two hours between the closing of their favorite clubs and the opening of the bars by the port at dawn, should they be so motivated. They often were. If the weather were particularly pleasant, Charlie and Dan and a crowd of others often bought carry-outs and otherwise scrounged the necessary ingredients for continued partying, then moved the whole thing to the beach, or beneath the large concrete arches of the soaring bridge which spanned the entrance to the port if the weather were inclement. In the latter case, Dan could often see in the light of the rising sun the area of abandoned warehouses across the water where he had often taken refuge in his time living in Portview. Among the crowd of partiers in leather and denim, torn t-shirts, ripped fishnet stockings, short skirts and combat boots, hair violently dyed or spiked into mohawks, Dan would sometimes find himself oblivious to the music pounding out of the speakers in the open trunk of Charlie's car, often walking slowly away from the crowd until it was a small knot behind him under the orange cone of a quartz-halogen streetlight.

The thought of Ingrid and Mike made him feel hot and light, made his pulse beat a little faster. He occasionally cruised the streets of Portview with Charlie in the summer when he first arrived, looking for Mike as a target of opportunity. Dan knew some of the bars where he might be found, but never felt committed enough to take it to the next level. There was plenty of time for that.

The apartment at the Kicking Pig was in the back corner of the building over an alley, with a wide, L-shaped wooden fire escape running along the side and back of it, giving them access to stairs to the roof. Their parties often spilled onto this fire escape and up to the roof, with a wonderful view of the lights of the city spread out around them, the moving lights of traffic on the freeway, buses roaring by below, sirens and sometimes gunshots in the distance. Dan never tired of it, and would often sit up on the roof alone at night until the quiet before dawn, when the partying had died down and the susurrant sounds of the city seemed relatively quiet.

When their parties were raucous, as they usually were, there wasn't much of anyone in the neighborhood who would've complained, populated as it was by young people like them, or the poor and the desperate, not to mention hookers, winos, vagrants, sailors, a shifting assortment that came to the surface at night when the surrounding businesses were closed and the downtown of Greysport was left abandoned for them. It was then that the dives and clubs and music venues revived yet again as if populated by the reanimated dead, creating scattered pools of light among the darkened skyscrapers reaching up to penetrate the fog, there among the empty and echoing alleys.

It was Charlie's beautifully written letters describing this place and its people that drove Dan to distraction with restlessness and a feeling of slow-motion entrapment in his last year in high school on the river. The records Charlie sent him- The Clash, the Sex Pistols, Richard Hell and the Voidoids, on and on- all filled him with the desperate feeling that there were exciting things happening in the world that would never be dreamt of on MacDougal Island, and that every passing day was one when he missed something thrilling, unique, irretrievable.

Along with this sense of attraction was another one, not constrained or described by the clarity of words: that of his grandfather's decay. He wouldn't allow himself to verbalize or analyze it, he only felt an unseen pressure behind him, pushing him, pushing him to flee. Any feelings of responsibility or guilt or love were washed over by this wavelike desire for flight, lifting him up and over these obstacles and depositing him on this fresh and unsullied shore, teeming, as it was, with its endless convenient distractions.

Starhawk had dropped Dan off at the Kicking Pig, and Charlie had come downstairs to meet him. Dan was as silently astonished by Charlie's newly changed appearance as he had been the last time, when Charlie had looked like a rock star getting out of his Barracuda on the front lawn of the bungalow. Now he was taller and more lankily muscular, his hair nearly white-blonde and spiky, wearing an earring which resembled a tiny man dangling from a noose. He was in a sleeveless black t-shirt and tattered, faded jeans, black boots with a chain around one ankle.

Dan and Charlie both grinned. They punched each other's shoulders, and embraced. They were insulting each other at length when Starhawk coughed, apparently to remind them of his presence.

Dan would later regret how cursorily he had thanked the kind man, as distracted as he was in his new place, his long awaited freedom.

"I'll keep an eye on your grampa," Starhawk had said in parting.

"Okay. Thanks," Dan said, barely aware of the portly hippie's departure.

As they carried the boxes and bags of his few possessions up the four flights of stairs in the open vestibule of the building, Dan knew he was going to have to change his appearance immediately, or he would stick out, looking like a hick from a pot farm.

Charlie understood this without saying a word. He took Dan first to get his long hair cut, at the same place where he had his own bleached and spiked. Dan was not as ostentatious as Charlie, of course, and settled on getting his hair shorn to an inch in length, with the concession to Charlie that he get it dyed black. The stylist, Candy, was a friend of Charlie's and member of his group. She had a voluminous hairdo the color (and seeming texture) of pink cotton candy, which went along with her short leather skirt and asymmetrically torn zebra-stripe shirt, which did little to conceal her hypnotic breasts.

When she was done, she smacked her black lacquered lips and said, "Mmmm, yeah. You're a cutie." Dan forced his gaze away from where it naturally wanted to go and looked her in the eye to thank her. His appearance in the mirror was completely changed; his grandfather might not have recognized him, looking, as he did, like someone from the cover of the kinds of record albums Charlie had sent him. Appearing like a different person provided him with a surprisingly hard push to *feel* like one. Charlie insisted on paying, and on the way out Dan wondered if the stylist lacquered her nipples the same color as her lips. When they were out of earshot, he mentioned this to Charlie.

"I'm sure it would be easy enough to find out," he said, grinning and punching Dan on the arm.

Their next stop was at an army surplus store where they got Dan a few pairs of black fatigue pants, some sleeveless t-shirts, a black hooded sweatshirt, and a black nylon flight jacket. All were Dan's choice; again, he had a feeling of transformation, as if he were leaving a body poisoned and useless, entering one that was cool and fresh. Charlie again insisted on paying, and when Dan protested, Charlie said, "Look, I've got more money than you, maybe I always will. Also, you took the bite for that thing with the boat. I'm not forgetting that."

Dan felt a little guilty, but allowed himself to be persuaded.

"The upside was that I got to work in a mortuary," he laughed.

"Yeah," Charlie said. "I bet the sex was great."

The apartment at the Kicking Pig was dilapidated, sprawling, and airy. Built in the late 1800s, it had twelve-foot ceilings, worn hardwood floors, giant rectangular windows bare of shades or curtains. The place had been painted so many times that any edges on light fixtures or moldings which had once been sharp were now softened by the accumulated layers of paint. There was a living room with a non-functional fireplace, a couch, a television on an orange crate, and little else other than a giant, old-fashioned steam radiator and many empty beer cans. The big dining room was spare, empty but for a scratched, second-hand wooden table with mismatched chairs, more beer and liquor bottles scattered on every horizontal surface. The bathroom had a clawfoot tub the size of a sarcophagus, although the rest of it was less than resplendent, with walls painted chocolate-milk brown, and floor covered with peeling, foot square pieces of adhesive-backed carpeting in red and black. The kitchen had a pantry with a little window which looked across a short hall to another of the large windows to the outside. There was an old stove and a large, ancient sink, stacked with dirty dishes.

"Nice," Dan said, and meant it.

There were books everywhere, naturally, it being Charlie's place. Roommates had moved in and out, but at all times, one of the three small bedrooms was reserved for stacks of Charlie's books, some on mismatched shelves, many in neat piles along the wall, the locations of each one filed away in Charlie's head in a system comprehensible only to him. The center of the room was dedicated to weights and a heavy bag. Dan found the set-up of the room amusing, pure Charlie.

Charlie had been at Greysport University for awhile, to his father's delight, but had dropped out when he realized that he had no particular goal in mind. He freely admitted that he would start a semester in a blaze of academic rigor, getting perfect grades and garnering the attention of his professors. He soon lost interest, though, his attention span depleted and attendance lapsed, and would have ended up with average grades or below, even failing, if he hadn't dropped the classes at the last minute. Jim, who was still in high school (and on the honor roll), would later explain his theory that Charlie was in search of a working-class, tough-guy credibility, the type which didn't come with his upbringing. Charlie got a job in a foundry south of the city in the steel town of Cary for awhile, long enough to generate some stories, but was apparently not too disappointed when he was laid off.

Dealing dope was an easy match for him, and provided him with the acceptable role of outlaw. There was an edge to such a lifestyle which no classroom could provide, and Dan was already somewhat familiar with the constant caution, suspicion, and even paranoia that such activities entailed. The easy money made Charlie loose with his cash. "There are always more people who want to buy dope," he said.

Although Dan knew he had to find a job quickly, Charlie persuaded him to take a week or two off to "get acclimated", as he said.

"I've got to watch my money," Dan said.

Charlie snorted. "Don't worry," he said. "I've got you covered."

Dan grimaced and shook his head. "Can't get into that kind of habit," he said.

"I respect that," Charlie said. "Just for awhile, though, until you get on your feet. Pay me back when you're a famous artist. Or don't, I don't give a shit. I can always hit up the old man for some cash, if things get really tight. Or if I just want to blow some money I didn't make myself. Did your grampa give you any money?"

"He paid me for working."

"Nothing else?"

"He offered. I just…"

"Didn't want to owe him?"

"Yeah."

"I don't figure I owe my dad. I figure he owes me." He paused for a moment, unusual for Charlie, and said, "Your grandfather is a great man."

Dan ignored this, and diverted the topic by means of going along with Charlie's general theme. "Any good bars around here?"

Charlie laughed. "In Greysport? Hell, no. Probably less than a million." he said. "Let's go."

They went downtown and had lunch at Charlie's favorite taqueria, Perrito's. Dan hadn't had such food since he'd left Portview, and, although it wasn't exactly the same as the food at the tienda of the Lopez family, it hit a spot he found to be ravenously empty. Eating a burrito, he thought for a moment about Lopez family, of their kindness, but immediately shut that down.

"Let's do a shot of tequila," Dan said, and Charlie let him buy that one.

They went to a German bar, one too expensive for Dan, but which had a legendary array of imports. The décor was medieval, with a giant wrought-iron chandelier, wall sconces, armor here and there, crossbows and swords mounted high up on the walls. It would become a place where they would go to celebrate. At Charlie's insistence, they drank whatever they wanted, sitting by large windows overlooking the city. When they started to get a little buzzed, Charlie broke out some blotter and gave Dan a hit, taking one himself and washing it down with a Hefe-Weiss. "Here we go," Charlie said.

When they had gotten off and the sky shifted through the last vestiges of a brilliant sunset fading to sepia over the factories west of downtown, they cruised in the Barracuda, tripping with a case of beer and a bottle of tequila, west and south around the port (driving right in front of Willy's old Semen Welcome hotel; how could they have known). They continued south to the industrial area along the lake, down toward Cary, a region large and despoiled. Although Dan had seen it in the distance from his redoubt on the beach, it was the first time he had actually been there.

That first night was only a taste, driving into the blighted miles of Greysport's industry. How sincerely they would come to love those dystopic industrial wastelands, the brown, grey, and black fields sprouting mutant weeds to fill the dead space between the flame-spouting refineries and rusted, science-fiction chemical plants where large nameless machines rumbled endlessly behind cyclone fences, bugeyed headlights of gigantic vehicles marking their progress in the necrotic twilight. The ugliness of the place, the desolation of it, made them happy.

They came upon lone bars, reassuring eyeblinks of jarringly colorful neon behind dirty windows in grey walls, places hunkered in the bottomlands, and there they drank, talking to the joyless patrons, probing their lives.

Over the next few years, Dan found strange and quiet solace in these surroundings; they seemed to be proof and vindication of his deepest futilitarian musings. With a visual shift to the future, this land was something dimly imagined by his hero Hieronymus Bosch, grim visions of a punitive hell, and here it was, real.

Charlie, on the other hand, became positively cheerful; such blight and squalor hinted at a future of unguessed destruction and chaos. Anything could happen, and probably would! He saw himself, he said, as a conscienceless cyborg in a movie, and this landscape was the intricate set. "Things can only get worse," Charlie cried at one point, before buying the bar a round.

"I admire your optimism," Dan laughed.

They rumbled back, that first morning, in the lake-fresh dawn as the acid and the booze wore off, parking the car at the cathedral square park near the Kicking Pig, wandering through the alley and trudging up the wooden stairs of the old fire escape to the apartment. Out of obligation and ritual, they opened a beer and smoked a joint on the roof in the light of the rising sun before tumbling down to sleep.

Dan woke up on the floor of his new room around one in the afternoon. He was in the sleeping bag he had gotten from Willy, burnt orange with a gold lining, a zone of portable comfort to him. The window was open to the breeze off the lake and the noise of a city, right there, alive, down the fire escape, all his.

Charlie's favorite club was Vnuk's, an old brick warehouse painted black and purple on the outside. Punk bands played there most of the nights of the week, usually local groups, and with multiple line-ups. They went to Vnuk's on the second night after Dan's return, to see performances by the Buggery Thugs and the Spewin' Humans.

They had to "frontload" as Charlie called it, going to other bars starting in the late afternoon or early evening; no one ever showed up early at Vnuk's, and although Charlie didn't say it, it was obvious to Dan that he had in image to uphold. They did more acid for the stimulant effect (both of them too hardened to the drug's force to be overwhelmed), and had pitcher after pitcher of cold Greysport Lager in a succession of dive bars near the port. The freedom of it made Dan want to laugh out loud; this was what he had been waiting for, and it was even better than he had fantasized in all those days of torturous boredom on MacDougal Island. Here no one knew who he was, and he felt unburdened.

When it was sufficiently late, they rumbled back up to the lower east side of town, past the Kicking Pig and up a dozen blocks to where Vnuk's sat on a hill over the Ashipinakwa River on its way to the harbor. The club was surrounded by warehouses and alleys, a weedgrown lot and a decaying bridge over the river just across the street. Charlie parked on a side street, and they walked down an alley, emerging a few doors down from the entrance of Vnuk's. There was already a crowd of people in spikes and mohawks and multicolored hair in front of the building, drinking beer and smoking joints. A bouncer stood at the door (purposelessly, Dan thought, considering the chaos right before his eyes), and Charlie shook hands with him, laughing, their speech inaudible under the pulsing wave of noise that blistered from the club.

It took too long, in Dan's estimation, to get to the bar. Not only was Vnuk's packed with sweating people, most of them seemed to want to talk to Charlie, and Charlie introduced Dan to almost all of them. There were so many that it was impossible for Dan to even come close to remembering their names (even when he heard them), so he lifted his chin in greeting and waited while Charlie and whoever he was talking to shouted across each other's ears.

The walls of Vnuk's were painted black, but were covered with posters new and old, fresh and torn, with the names and pictures of bands. The Buggery Thugs were on the at the moment, wearing black leather in spite of the heat, pounding out a sinister bass and rapid, crunching guitar. The tall, shaven-headed lead singer, black greasepaint around his eyes, screamed incomprehensible lyrics into the microphone. Dan laughed. This was what he had been missing.

They finally made it to the bar, and, once there, kept their precious space staked out. This began a flurry of drinking; the bartender was a friend and customer of Charlie's, and when Charlie lit up a joint and shared it (with no attempt at concealment), the bartender began setting them up with shots. Dan looked around to see if anyone seemed to care; no one did, if they noticed at all. Again, he laughed aloud at his sense of freedom. He laughed harder when he noticed that Charlie was leaning casually on the bar with his pants around his ankles, having an earnest conversation with a young woman with black lipstick and jet black hair.

With the acid and weed and continuous infusion of booze into his system, things began to seem…unusual. He went to the restroom at one point, Charlie saving their place, and shouldered his way through the crowd. He stood for a moment watching as people slammed into each other in the area in front of the stage, and stood out of the way, laughing, as a kid with spiked orange hair leaned over to snatch an empty pitcher from a table in front of him and fill it neatly with vomit, before placing it just as carefully back on the table.

"Pop goes the weasel," the kid shouted amiably, and staggered off into the chaos in front of the stage.

In the black hallway that went to the restrooms, Dan stood blinking for a moment at the sight of a young woman on her knees at the end of the hallway, giving a blowjob to a young man in a leather jacket, who stood with his head tipped back, slackjawed, staring at the ceiling. The sight was so out of context that it took Dan a few moments, in his buzzed state, to recognize what the couple was doing.

In spite of the acid in his system, the night became increasingly blurry. At one point he found himself at the base of the crumbling bridge across the street from Vnuk's sloppily kissing Candy, the stylist with the pink hairdo, holding her up against the wall by a stand of tall weeds. For a moment, his *maldito* reflex nearly kicked in, but he realized that she was as intoxicated as he was, and enjoying what they were doing. He found out that her nipples were not, in fact, tipped with black lipstick, but that her line of carefully-sculpted pubic hair was dyed to match the hair on her head. He spread her pale legs and held her against the wall, eating her enthusiastically until she came, then bending her over with her hands braced against the wall, pounding into her from behind until he came himself.

Afterwards, they found themselves to be too sober, and wandered back out of the weeds, across the street to Vnuk's, where little seemed to have changed, although the people sprawled on the pavement in front of the place might have been different.

The night turned into an early morning of partying on the beach until the sun rose, with Dan and Candy stuck to each other. Charlie, his arm around the young woman with the jet black hair, smiled at Dan and mouthed *Are they black?* Dan snorted and shook his head.

They straggled away as the sun rose over the lake, past a garbage truck idling in the beach parking lot, over to Charlie's car. When Dan got up in the early afternoon to pad down the hall to the toilet, he found Candy sitting there with the door open, reading a comic book and smoking a cigarette.

"Hi, sweetie," she said, before casually wiping herself and flushing the toilet. Rendered libidinous by their hangovers, they went at each other three more times, in increasingly imaginative ways, before going out for gyros.

It was in this haphazard manner that Dan found his first girlfriend in his early days of freedom in Greysport. They had little in common, and almost nothing to talk about. Dan persuaded her to go the Institute of Art one grey and rainy Saturday afternoon, the perfect kind of day to spend at the museum. Dan was eager to be inside the comforting halls, and almost ran up the broad old steps. Once inside, though, Candy quickly seemed so bored and distracted that Dan tried to ignore her at first, but soon began to feel contempt for her. Oddly enough, he found this sexually exciting. When he tried to interest her in one of his favorite paintings, she glanced at it, but her attention was torn away when a dwarf walked down the hallway crossing the end of the gallery. She snorted quietly and nudged Dan.

"Look," she whispered. "Dwarf."

This infuriated Dan, and he took her by the wrist and led her down a marble side passage to an isolated restroom, looking both ways before shoving her inside. When he saw that the stalls were indeed empty, he took her into one of them, bent her over the toilet seat, and fucked her punitively. He held his hand over her mouth to squelch her yelps when she came.

"That was hot," Candy said when they were done, and Dan shook his head and smiled in spite of himself.

They went back out to look at the art hung on the long, cool walls. If Candy's attention seemed to wander, Dan swatted her sharply on the ass, which seemed to make the activity better for both of them.

This became the thing he found refreshing about his relationship with Candy: he not only didn't love her, he often found her annoying. It was liberating; he felt that he didn't have anything to lose, didn't have to make a good impression, and didn't care in the least if she figured things out and discovered his fundamental nature as a *maldito*.

Willy never knew it, but it was Dan's having his heart wounded yet again which had sharpened his desire to flee the river. The damage hadn't come from a girl in his high school; he'd convinced himself that they were too puerile and he too much of an outsider for there to be any connection. When he had seen Ellie or Karen with other boys, he often found himself in an instant of wistful reverie before covering it up with a sneer. He was, as has been noted, cool.

It was a customer of the bar who would do the latest damage. Debbie Paulson was twenty-seven, brown hair and eyes, married to a man more than ten years older who worked third shift as a deputy with the sheriff's department. This meant that he had to leave mid-evening to get to work in Black Marsh in time for his shift, then reversed the commute after ten hours on the road. Dan had seen them together in the bar before. Debbie was leggy and attractive, and Dan had overheard customers and Bob Two Bears briefly wonder why the vivacious young woman was attached to such a surly lug. The fact that he was a sheriff's deputy (an unpopular job among the clientele of the bar), made the question more pointed. She seemed a bit old to Dan, but there was something about her raucous laugh, the way she held a cigarette while tossing down half a mug of beer, the way she treated her sullen husband with light disdain, that he liked.

Debbie wasn't the type to be pushed into staying at home, no matter what her husband said, and often came to the bar with friends when he was on the job. She worked afternoons as a checkout clerk at MacDougal's grocery store, and the group she hung out with were mostly fellow employees, using pool or dart leagues as an excuse to get out of the house and do something in their lives. The Ad Hoc Band was something that Debbie seldom missed.

A few of the coworkers were customers of Dan's, who understood their desire to smoke a little dope in order to make their jobs more amusing. When one of these regulars referred Debbie to him, Dan allowed it.

The first time he had sold her any weed, it was only a half ounce, and he did her the courtesy of going out into the alley behind the bar to smoke a quick joint together. It was winter, and they went out without coats, hunching and huddling over the joint against the cold. When Debbie had pressed her estimable breasts against his upper arm, Dan had thought it was an accident.

"Cold out here," she'd said.

"We should go back in," Dan replied.

She bought an ounce the next time, on a Saturday night when her husband was gone and the Ad Hoc Band was playing. She signaled to Dan her interest, catching his eye and discreetly miming smoking a joint by holding a thumb and forefinger to her lips. Dan nodded and told Bob that he was going on break, meeting Debbie by the back entrance.

"It's still pretty cold out there," she said. "Is there any place else we could go?"

"Sure," he said, and took her upstairs to the old spare bedroom

Dan would later think of what happened as the redemption of his misfired night with Ellie. It wasn't that *he* redeemed it, however, because Debbie had promptly taken control.

Dan sold her an ounce in the darkened room, doing the transaction by the dim streetlight coming in from the window overlooking the alley. He turned to lead her out, but she interrupted him.

"You're pretty solid," she said, putting her hand on his arm. "I'd never guess you're still in high school."

"No?"

"Nope. You look years older. Must be your build. I guess you McGregors are all like that."

"Guess so," he said, wondering what Charlie would do in such a situation.

"You ever look at me at all?"

"Sure," Dan said. He thought for a moment that she could read his mind; he'd already spent considerable time beating off over her mental image at home.

"You're so stoic," she said. "I like that."

He might have hesitated, he might have stammered, but Debbie removed all ambiguity from the situation by simply reaching out and cupping his crotch. At that point, Dan knew what to do, Gigi's lessons popping immediately into his mind. Pushing her back against the wall, he bumped her head slightly, and when her lips parted, he was kissing her, hotly, sloppily, in a way he thought would have been too unrestrained for girls his own age. Her beer and cigarette taste was exciting, no innocence there, a dark flavor with a hint of cancer. They slid off each other's clothes and he touched her everywhere, sucking her nipples, feeling her wet labia, clasping her almost roughly between the cheeks of her ass. She moaned and dropped to her knees and took his cock into her mouth.

He almost laughed. It felt like liberation, it felt like revenge. He watched her suck him for awhile, then pulled her hair back, threw her on the old bed, knelt down and sucked between her legs.

She gasped and thrashed. "Fuck me!" she said sharply, and he did. He did it, hard, until they both came.

Afterwards, they got dressed, attempting to look composed, and returned to the bar separately.

"Have a good break?" Bob asked over the din of the music.

"Yeah," Dan said as blandly as possible, trying not to laugh in exultation.

Thus began his affair with Debbie Paulson. They took full advantage of her loutish husband's hours, fucking until they were sore, doing everything in their imagination. It was far better than having a high school girlfriend, Dan thought, laughing silently when he sat in class. He didn't imagine that high school girls gave rimjobs. He snorted at this notion, getting a puzzled look from his biology teacher.

They went at it every chance they got. Debbie claimed that her husband, for all his manly demeanor, was something of a "limpwick" (her words), and had never, on his best day, had anything like the stamina or skill that Dan exhibited.

"I stand there at the store, checking people out, ringing up their groceries, and I'm on autopilot," she said. "What I'm really thinking about is how sore my pussy is, and what you're going to do to it next. I find myself wanting to say this to my customers."

Dan discussed it with no one, either, except in his letters to Charlie, who delighted in it.

"Fucking a cop's wife," Charlie wrote. "That's the greatest thing ever. It's the absolute subjugation and denigration of icons of power. Fuck!"

They did it everywhere, at Debbie's house, Dan slipping through the alleys after dark. They did it at the bungalow, when Willy was at work. They did it out by the river, and up by the slowly decaying old hotel. It seemed unlikely that the deputy would return home during his shift, as he was stationed in another part of the county, but the fact that the possibility existed at all seemed to heighten Debbie's desire.

For a few months, looking forward to his next encounter with Debbie made his waning days in school tolerable. Although he had been accepted at Greysport (immediately dropping the long-awaited letter on the coffee table and tearing out to find Debbie for a celebratory fuck), he still kept up his efforts in school, afraid that something might go wrong.

It never occurred to Dan that his connection with Debbie might not be serious. He thought of getting her to move out on her husband and go with him to Greysport, which he told her about at length as they lay on damp sheets between sessions.

"I've never heard you talk so much at once," she said after listening to him.

"It's great," Dan said. "You'll love it."

He realized months later, while in bed with Candy, that Debbie had given him a look when he'd said that, and that he had missed the meaning of it completely. His anger about the realization made him take it out in a rough tussle with Candy, who seemed, forthrightly, to enjoy the energy he brought to it.

Debbie had hinted around that he should slow down, that he shouldn't take things so seriously, but Dan simply talked over her. As his eighteenth birthday approached, he built up his anticipation about what the two of them would do together. He had money, and thought about taking her over to Greysport, getting a hotel and showing her around. How could she fail to love the place, after living here on the river for so long, trapped in a marriage which was merely convenient, at best.

It was difficult for him to concentrate in school, or while working at the bar. If Debbie came into the bar when he was there, he respected her wishes that he act as if there were nothing between them. It was part of the fun of it, she'd said. It was like being a spy. Dan found it easy to keep on a stony face in public, but when they were alone, he became another person entirely.

It was just days before his birthday when he finally attempted to have an earnest conversation about leaving with him when he was done with school, she made plain her point of view.

"I can't leave here," she said, apparently mystified by his seriousness. "No. Oh, no. I'm married. I have a job."

"You have a shitty husband," Dan pointed out. "You have a shitty job."

"Yeah, well, they're *mine*," she said, with a little flare of anger. "You're just a kid."

Dan grunted and shook his head. "So I'm good enough to fuck you, but that's all?"

"Jesus, Dan," she said. "You're great. You can do way better than me. I'm ten years older than you and married. You have so much in front of you, don't you know that?"

Dan wanted to hit her, to smash her television, to throw her coffee table through the window. He did nothing, only sat there, breathing heavily, staring at her. After awhile, he got up and walked out, ignoring her when she called his name.

He remained strong for three days. With his mind in a welter of images of sex and revenge, he went through the alleys in the dark to her back door. She let him in and they argued; she had to tell him three times to keep his voice down, once sticking her head out the back door to see if neighbors were listening. He finally begged for pity sex, which she gave him. When he came, he felt like crying, and the fact that she had not come made him feel even worse.

He had made it through his birthday dinner at Emilio and Solveig's, then taken the truck down by the swollen river to drink, brooding in the cab while it rained. When he had gotten very drunk, he drove back into town, the street blurry through the rain and the booze. He parked the truck a few blocks away from Debbie's house, staggering the rest of the way to stand in front of it in the rain.

Debbie's husband's truck was parked in the driveway, lights on in the house. Dan stood in the rain, his hair plastered to his head, looking at the light from the windows, waiting to see some movement, a glimpse of Debbie. Twice he heard her laughter, and wondered if she were laughing at him.

In the end, he had walked over, pulled out his knife, and flattened all the tires on the husband's truck. He had gone home much later after sitting for a long time in the cab of the pickup, and had sobered up just enough to remember forever what he said to his grandfather in the kitchen.

He wished he'd been *more* drunk; he didn't want to remember. In Greysport, when he found himself thinking about it while up on the roof or down at the beach, he grabbed a beer or did a shot, worked out or went to Vnuk's, found Charlie (who always had diversions in mind), or took Candy into his room. And that was the good thing about Candy: she could only please him, never hurt him.

With Charlie, in their rhythm as roommates, Sunday afternoons and evenings became the time they were most likely to be anything approaching contemplative. After breakfast out somewhere in the mid-afternoon, they often returned and lazed for awhile, until Dan began to sketch or paint, and Charlie picked up a book.

Everything from informal sketches of ideas to finished drawings and large paintings accumulated on the walls. Some sketches were Charlie's; in his polymathic way, he was a pretty fair artist, but had neither Dan's fascination nor his hypnotic obsession with it. He was usually reading between three and ten books at once, from physics to Mayan archeology, Aristotle to Jefferson to Marx to Philip K. Dick. There was a certain intellectual cross-pollination between the two young men, but Dan found safety and refuge in art. Try as he may, he knew he could never keep up with the superball bouncing of Charlie's mind.

But paint he did, at least until Charlie got hungry for action and tore him away from it. Doing acid and drinking, listening to the Talking Heads (great acid music) and Elvis Costello, he tore through canvasses and paints, linseed oil and turpentine. The subjects were usually morbid or bizarre, executed in a way that even Dan himself would admit was fairly well done. His work almost always got Charlie's approval. Soon paintings began to take up the wall space of the large apartment above the book line. When they had parties, people began to comment that the apartment was becoming an art gallery. Charlie was more protective of the art than Dan was, and became enraged when a careless cokehead punk from Vnuk's, at one of the pre-dawn parties, had bounced off a wall, putting one of his elbows through a canvas.

Charlie's response had not one instant of hesitation. "You dick!" he shouted at the hapless mohawked young drunk.

"Well, what do you have shit on the walls for, man?" the punk was unwise enough to reply. "We're fuckin' *partyin'* here!"

"It's our *home*, you ignorant fuck!" Charlie grabbed him by the shirt, slapped and backhanded him, twisted his arm up behind his back and kneed his coccyx before tossing him out onto the fire escape.

"Don't come back," he said as the punk limped away. "I mean it."

People were more respectful after that. Dan simply took the torn canvas, applied duct tape to the back, brushed gesso on the front, and executed another painting which texturally incorporated the patched hole. When he was done, he showed Charlie.

"Excellent!" Charlie said.

Jim only showed up once that summer. It seemed that he was caught up in his own social life in White Birch Pointe, and he intended to go with his father to visit Gigi in Provence. It was also obvious to Dan that there was some tension between the brothers, although Charlie hadn't said anything about it. When Jim mentioned going to France, Charlie seemed disgusted.

"What are you brown-nosing the old man for?" Charlie asked him.

"I'm not brown-nosing him, douchebag. I want to see Gigi, and I want to go to Provence. Why would you not want to go to Provence? What the *hell*."

"He's also taking an honors biology class for high school this summer," Charlie said to Dan, indicating Jim with a jerked thumb, shaking his head and smirking.

"It's *interesting*, man!" Jim said. "I've got an interesting teacher and I'll get college credit for it."

"Brown-nose."

"Charlie..." Jim's look said that he'd lost his patience with his brother's badgering.

"Okay, okay," Dan said. "Let's just have some fun here, have a couple of beers and a joint. I'll get the beers." As Dan walked from the room, he caught the communication, fraternal and non-verbal, which took place as he went to the refrigerator: Jim's look said don't be such an asshole while Charlie's said, pooooor little brown-nose.

It took some doing on Dan's part to distract the two brothers from their seeming animosity. They had always worked so well together that Dan had referred to them as co-units, so to see them quarreling was uncomfortable. He had no idea what to do about it, having no siblings himself, so he simply tried to keep distracting them. Once they'd had a few beers and smoked some weed, Dan responded (atypically) to Jim's questions about his growing work.

"I'm not sure that art isn't pointless, but it *is* distracting," he said, not wanting to completely disregard Jim's appreciation.

"You've got a gift," Jim said. "You've got to use it."

"I suppose," Dan said

"Just like Charlie," Jim said, raising his voice to make sure Charlie heard in the next room, "Charlie could be a doctor, physicist, a writer…"

Charlie made a fricative noise of disgust from where he sat.

"What, Charlie," Jim said. "You could."

"Sure I could. If there were any point to it."

"What, are you a nihilist now?"

"I'm suffering from anomie," Charlie said. "Or enjoying it."

"What's that?" Dan and Jim asked simultaneously.

"Look it up." Charlie drank from his beer and read a book as they talked.

Dan and Jim shared a look: that's Charlie. They let it go at that.

They went for Mexican food again at Charlie's favorite place (which had quickly become Dan's), the little hole in the wall called Perrito's, after the nickname of the owner, a Mexican with a long pony tail, a red beret, and a habitually worn Che Guevara t-shirt. The place had eight or ten tables and a long bar, where Charlie and Dan preferred to sit. Perrito sat in his habitual spot at the end of the bar, a perpetual margarita in front of him, either staring expressionlessly off into space, or deigning to talk to the customers he thought important. Charlie said that, as long as he had been coming here, he had never seen Perrito do a second's work, leaving it all to the people behind the bar and working the tables. Perrito lifted his chin at Charlie and Dan when they came in.

"You speak Spanish, right, Dan?" Jim said.

"Some."

"What's 'perrito' mean?"

"'Little dog'."

"I hope that's not what they're serving here," Jim said.

"If they are, you won't care," Charlie said. "It's that good."

The woman who took care of them that evening was the one who usually did, and they had a warm relationship with her. Kaye was apparently of partial Latin extraction, but had beautiful, sad, sky blue eyes. She was about Dan's mother's age, he guessed, although of an entirely different demeanor; kind, attentive, nurturing. Where Dan's mother had been thin, Kaye was plump. She knew what he wanted for lunch, knew when he wanted a beer, and perhaps tequila, if it seemed like that kind of night. Dan looked forward to talking to her, and had spent afternoon hours in the hot summer slowly drinking beers and chatting. She had told him that, when she was young, she was engaged to a lovely boy who was killed in the Korean War, a boy from her home town. She had been shattered by his death, and had left the town for Greysport, the memories being, as she said, "too punishing." After some time in the city, she married a man she thought would do, perhaps because it was time and it was expected of her, but she finally realized that she was still in love with the dead boy, and that she always would be. When her husband showed tendencies toward being abusive, she kicked him out with a savage finality that must have made his head swim.

This was a weekend night, though, and Kaye had no time to chat, simply setting the three up with Greysport Lagers, not bothering to ask Jim for ID.

"Okay, this place is great," Jim said.

"*Told* ya," Charlie said.

When they seemed on the verge of a small sibling quarrel, Dan was inspired to divert their attention by changing the subject to their older siblings; they seemed to find gleeful unity in disparaging them.

"Hugh's studying voice and working in a gay bar," Jim said. "Occasionally, he and the other Raging Queens go and kick some hetero ass."

"Anyone who tries to roll homos down by the port is flirting with disaster," Charlie said.

Dan almost didn't want to ask about Gigi, who had only been superceded in his mind only by the stratification of sex experiences he'd had between his time with Gigi and the present. He asked why she was living in France.

"Probably to see if she could break her addiction to being a slut," Charlie said.

"Yeah," Jim laughed. "After fucking every guy in Greysport, including the winos, she was forced to seek greener pastures."

"Gigi went on a series of assorted sordid sorties..." Charlie started.

"With an army of smarmily harmful charming barmen..." Jim added.

"Interested in giving her a reamin' with their screamin' steamin' semen demons!"

Dan's diversion had worked so well the brothers were joined in their derision, laughing together, but he found that it was his turn to get angry. "Hey, that's your sister, man!"

This stopped the brothers' laughter.

"You're right," Jim said

"Yeah," Charlie said. "Gigi's cool."

"We can always rip on the old man," Jim suggested.

Charlie affected a posh English accent and said, "Let's, shall we?"

Seeing as the old blowhard was Dan's least favorite member of the Gates family, Dan was soon laughing along with the other two.

They got drunk. They tripped. They went to one of their favorite places, the Underground, a network of bars built beneath an ornate old theater, the bars linked by hallways leading to a bowling alley, a poolroom, a dart room, and a lounge, all with long bars and plenty of young patrons. When this became claustrophobic (as places will when one is tripping), they trotted out and piled into the car.

They trolled through Portview looking for Mike. They ended up in Cary at one of the steelworkers bars, where the collapse of the industry was making people even surlier than usual. Although there were some cautionary looks among the patrons when the trio walked in, all skepticism dissipated when Charlie bought the bar a round of drinks.

"I thought all you punk fellas was fags," one suddenly amiable unemployee said.

A flicker crossed Charlie's face, and Dan knew it was about Hugh.

"Not all of us," Charlie said, earning a look of appreciation from Jim. "Dan here's a fag, though."

There was a pause.

"You a fag, son?" the unemployee asked.

Dan regarded him and said, "Ask your dad if he knows me when you get done sucking his dick."

The bar erupted in cheers and laughter, and even the unemployee had to chuckle. Jim calculated afterwards that they were bought twice the amount of Charlie's original outlay.

"Exactly my plan," Charlie said.

Just before dawn, they ended up on the roof of the Kicking Pig having the traditional tail-end beers. Any tensions between the brothers seemed to be alleviated and they talked humorously as the sky got pink in the east. To the north, west, and south, the city rolled out in grey and misty blocks, quiet before the dawn, street lights glowing, a coal boat moving out of the harbor in the distance. Dan was distracted for a moment watching this, but Charlie and Jim's conversation regained his attention when Charlie summed up a thought by saying, "...with the slick-lipped avidity of a midnight pud-pumping windowlurker."

The phrase came out of Charlie's mouth so effortlessly that it was the delivery as much as the phrasing that had Jim and Dan leaning on each other, laughing.

"What?" Charlie said, deadpan.

Dan laughed. "You should be a writer."

"See?" Jim said.

Charlie snorted. "Writers are assholes," he said. "Like I want to be pacing pensively on the beach, lost in my self-important thoughts."

"Why would you have contempt for writers?" Dan asked "You read constantly."

"You think art is useless and paint constantly," Charlie said.

Dan frowned and shrugged. "Point taken," he said.

Charlie was on a line of thought, though, and not to be deterred. "No, really," he said. "I don't want to *write* stories, I want to *live* stories, okay? That's why I always liked your family, Dan. They lived their stories. We have the misfortune to exist in a time where there isn't a war, and because of it we're forced to live these timid, castrated existences, and to make matters worse, we'll probably all get smoked in a global thermonuclear war. I want an *actual* war. I want some action. I want to get right up to the *edge*, man. I want my goddam stories."

"I'm thinking that Dan's grampa wouldn't see it that way," Jim said.

Mention of Willy (and the way Charlie and Jim seemed to turn to him for a ruling) made Dan disengage from the conversation and walk away across the roof, but not before he overheard Charlie say to Jim, "I think you touched on a delicate subject."

Charlie sought his stories, though, and didn't seem too particular about how he attained them. Their perpetual nightlife became little more than a systematic trolling for experience, often ending with nothing but a substantial buzz, but sometimes yielding material for a new tale. Dan was certainly susceptible to this sense of quest, especially after the deadening time he had spent on the river. Often, they worked out with weights and hit the heavy bag before leaving for the evening, and when they ran down the fire escape at sunset, taking the steps two or three at a time, running through the alleys to where the 'Cuda was parked on the cathedral square, they felt as if they were being released to run wild in the summer night.

"Cry havoc!" Charlie would shout, "and let slip the dogs of war!"

They struck gold one night in a little bar in a desolate neighborhood of factories and run-down houses, the bar overcoming the local malaise by having such a huge selection (it was the first time Dan had Chinese beer) at such cheap prices that the place was always packed. The Red Lantern had become one of their favorite haunts.

Dan and Charlie got to know the owner, a short, bald man named Pete Kleinmetz, who enlightened the two on his approach to business, "Location, location, location?" he said, "Feh! Volume, volume, volume! A changing array of good products at low, low prices!"

It was usually a good place for frontloading, although there was occasionally some drama. They had come through the door that night to see a young man standing on his head next to the jukebox and trying to drink a beer upside down, and were watching this in amusement when two beefy biker women got into a brawl. This was no slapping and hair-pulling affair, but two solid women in leather vests punching each other in the face with their fists. The sound of the blows made even Charlie wince. Skirting the brawl, the boys made their way through the bar full of cheering patrons to where Pete was already filling up a pitcher for them.

"You could use a bouncer or two, Pete," Charlie said over the clamor.

"Don't I know it," Pete said. "And there's no point in calling the cops, because they'll never be here fast enough to stop the disturbance, only fast enough to make a report that could lose me my license."

"That sucks," Dan said.

"That's business."

The fight was soon over, though, the two bloody and red-knuckled women dragged apart by friends.

And that was just the warm-up, the opening bout for the evening. The trouble for Dan and Charlie started when some associates of the local chapter of the Guardians of Nocturne came in, the other customers giving them a wide berth. There were six of them, not including the women, and none of them wore the patch of the motorcycle club, but had biker paraphernalia in abundance.

"Great," Pete said. "Just what I need."

"I hate bikers," Charlie said. "Fucking joiners. And these douchebags are clearly exceeded by their reputation."

Dan watched them fixedly, taking note of the deference of the people around them. He shook his head and drank his beer.

Charlie went to peruse the jukebox and Dan went to men's room. When he came back, one of the bikers was sitting in Charlie's seat, and the biker's girlfriend sitting in Dan's. He thought about saying something to the woman, but decided to be chivalrous, excusing himself to reach over and get his beer. He had left, after all, when Charlie had gone to the jukebox, leaving no one to save their places.

He smiled at the woman and she smiled at him, rather suggestively at that.

"You got a problem?" the biker said. He had a grizzled beard and ponytail, bad tattoos on his arms.

"Nope. I was sitting here, but the lady can have my place."

"Damn straight she can," the biker said. "She can sit anywhere she wants."

Dan smiled. He knew how it was going to go when he got that wonderful feeling, all hot and light. "She could sit here. You couldn't."

The biker's eyes widened at such effrontery. "What do you think you'd do about it?"

106

Dan couldn't help but smile more, and kept his voice pleasant. "I'd kick your fat ass, scooter boy."

There was nothing the biker could do but come at Dan. He shoved Dan, and Dan shoved back.

"Hey!" Pete bellowed over the bar. "Knock it off!"

For an instant, Dan thought the little man sounded like his grandfather. Dan looked over at him and the biker punched Dan in the cheekbone.

Dan was off balance, and the blow staggered him back a few steps. When he turned his focus back to the biker, ready to pounce, there was a blur and there was Charlie, pounding the biker in the face with all his strength, left-right-left-right. People scattered, and the biker's descent to the floor was slowed only by the seven abruptly emptied barstools he knocked over as he fell. When he did hit the floor, he stayed there.

Charlie turned around, laughing triumphantly. This lasted an instant before the other bikers converged on them.

Later, Dan and Charlie tried to piece together what happened. They didn't contradict each other, but the sequence of events was fuzzy. They ended up fighting back to back, taking a hit here and there, and when one of the bikers lay on the floor from a kick to the groin and another had sat down cursing after a thumb to the eye, the remaining three formed a wary triangle around Dan and Charlie.

Pete called it. "Okay, everybody! It's all over!"

Dan glanced at him, and Pete said, "Boys, do me a favor, will you? There's more of them than there are of you, so maybe it'd be easier if you both just left."

"Jesus, Pete!" Charlie said. "That's not fair!"

"Help me out here, guys," Pete said.

Dan said over his shoulder, "How 'bout it?"

Charlie sighed. "Okay," he said.

As they walked out, the crowd parted before them. Dan jerked a fraction of an inch towards one of the remaining bikers, who flinched.

They walked two blocks to where the 'Cuda was parked, got in. Charlie started the engine, and when the Clash tape in the cassette deck started playing, he turned it off. They sat listening to the rumble of the engine, looking out at the street.

"Well," Charlie said. "That just won't do, will it?"

"Nope," Dan said.

"We've got the stuff in the trunk."

"Yes!" Dan said, cheered up. "Yes, we do!"

They roared up in front of the Red Lantern, screeching to a stop across the street. Charlie popped the trunk, and they got out and went to the back of the car, Dan pulling out a baseball bat, Charlie a three-foot length of heavy chain. They stood in the street in front of the open door of the bar. Music from the jukebox came out, but Charlie bellowed loud enough to be heard.

"Come on out, you fucking pussies!" He swung the chain in a circle, round and round.

"This'll even things up, you cocksuckers!" Dan roared.

They carried on in this manner until a couple of bikers came over to the door of the bar, one holding a hand over his eye. Patrons were looking out every one of the windows facing the street.

"Come on! What the fuck!" Dan shouted. "Let's go!"

"You fucking invertebrates!" Charlie yelled. "You're pretty fucking tough when you outnumber someone aren't you? Real badass motherfuckers!"

"Come on!"

"We're right here!"

They continued their taunts until the bikers turned around and walked away from the door, leaving it empty. When Dan and Charlie, laughing maniacally, got in the car and roared off, people were still watching them out the windows, their heads turning to follow their taillights.

The bikers, humiliated, never came back to the Red Lantern. Pete said they left as soon as they could do so without completely losing face, perhaps sending someone out to make sure that the two punks weren't lurking in the shadows. When Dan and Charlie went to the bar on a weekday afternoon a few days later to apologize, it was Pete who apologized to *them*. They never paid for a drink there again, which was notable, because Pete was a notorious skinflint. He also asked them to work occasionally as bouncers, taking Charlie's suggestion. Dan could use the money and the free drinks, but Charlie did it for the fun and the notoriety, not to mention the hope of future incidents.

The brawl at the Red Lantern immediately became one of Charlie's favorite stories. It did nothing to abate his search for more, but had apparently left a bad taste in his mouth about bikers, or joiners of almost any kind, for that matter. Dan went along with this to a certain extent, but knew that his old friends Stumpy and Nubby Schommer were members of the same motorcycle club out on the river, so they couldn't be all bad.

Charlie fulminated about joiners for some time, praying for there to be a demonstration by the local American Nazi Party.

"Those miscreants," Charlie said. "I'd love a shot at some of them."

If either of them had known the specifics of Willy's run-in with Pfister and Pfelcher at the Oakwood Medium Security Facility, and had further known that relatives of Pfister and Pfelcher belonged to this group, their response might have been more assertive.

There were also black gangs on the northwest side of Greysport, and Latino gangs south of Portview. Charlie drew the line at interfering with these groups.

"First," he said, "they might be dealing with a level of bullshit that we know nothing about. They might be doing it out of self-preservation, out of a feeling of social abandonment. So that's the philosophical aspect. From a pragmatic point of view, those guys are starting to get really well armed, so they probably have more guns than we do. And people. We've got the rifle you got from your grampa. So far."

Dan thought about Jorge and Darnell, his old friends from Portview, and wondered if they might be caught up in the gang life. "We're outgunned and outnumbered," he said, "and they haven't done anything to us."

"Right. Good point. We'll keep those guys off the list until they transgress against us. When they do, Los Reyes Latinos the Brothers of the Rising and all those jagoffs better watch their ass."

"Yeah," Dan said. "They'd probably be deeply afraid of a couple of quarrelsome punk rockers."

"Better be," Charlie said, and they laughed. In an hour they were out in search of a fresh adventure.

The next good story they acquired didn't involve joiners at all, but a loner. They had both admitted that they were having too much fun to go to the University that semester, and had decided to get drunk at a bar downtown which catered to the more mainstream students. The bar had an Irish name that both of them assumed was phony, a name so forgettably contrived that they simply referred to the place as O'Irish's, or The Bar of Paddy McX.

"I've got a little Irish in me," Charlie said.

"Drop trou, and I'll put a little Scottish in ya," was Dan's obligatory reply.

As Charlie saw it, there was a positive factor in that the place, in season, was packed with defilable sorority girls. The negative factor was that, of course, where there would be sorority girls, there would be fraternity boys.

"Now *those* are some joiners," Charlie said. "The sorority boys. Fucking rich kids."

"Pardon me for mentioning this," Dan said, "but *you're* a rich kid."

Charlie gave his best menacing look. It was pretty good, but Dan laughed.

Charlie relented. "You're the only one who would laugh at me when I focus my death ray on them," he said.

"Whatever," Dan said.

Dan wouldn't have minded beating the shit out of a mouthy rich kid, but that wasn't the way the evening went. Even more disappointing was the fact that they had gone to the army surplus store where Dan had gotten his current wardrobe, there to do some shopping. Dan had gotten a sap, a few Bundeswehr t-shirts, and a watchcap for the winter. Charlie had gotten a large, lock-blade folding knife (always having liked Dan's) and some brass knuckles. Dan wondered which would come into use first, each being on Charlie's current to-do list. Dan wasn't even sure which of them Charlie had brought to O'Irish's that night, if not both, or which would be used, if not both.

It ended up being the knife, and it wasn't used on one of the fratboys, nor was it used by Charlie. Dan wouldn't have used a knife on a fratboy in any event; they were witless and spoiled, but certainly not deserving, in most cases, of more than a stern, epiphany-inducing beating in an alley. A rapist of drunk girls, Dan and Charlie agreed, would be another matter entirely. That was not how the evening was to go.

The bar was lively, with a long, deep layout ending in a balconied upper level with pool tables. Dan had once seen a pint glass dropped from the balcony onto the head of a fratboy who was emerging from one of the restrooms at the back; the fratboy had laughed at the blood trickling from under his baseball cap and ordered another round. Dan and Charlie had had to give him points for obliviousness.

Charlie had dressed down for the night, hoping to score with a sorority girl, combing his hair back, wearing a simple black t-shirt and khaki fatigue pants. Dan dressed as he normally would, never being as flamboyant as Charlie when in full regalia. He was still dating Candy, which eased his motivation to find other women.

The sorority types in attendance that evening were not, apparently, to Charlie's liking, and it had become one of those occasions where the two might get nothing more than a good buzz. They were in the process of finishing their second pitcher and getting ready to leave when Dan noticed someone in the bar far more out of place than they were themselves.

Shuffling along among the crowded tables was man who resembled a large version of Charles Manson. Perhaps thirty-five, with grey in his beard and clothing slightly better than those of a vagrant, his look of insanity might have been a pose, an attention-getting device, but then again it might not. Dan nudged Charlie, indicating the man with his chin.

The man approached a table of young strangers, leaned towards them and said something that could not be heard over the jukebox and general racket, but was greeted by looks of scorn and disgust.

"Eeeeew!" some of the sorority girls squealed audibly over the din, and the man grinned and continued on. He looked like he could be dangerous, and that got Dan's attention. There was an institutional vibe about him, like someone out on parole who wanted female attention whether the female wanted it or not. The look Charlie gave him said he felt the same way.

When the man approached another table closer to where Dan and Charlie sat, they were now able to hear some of what the man said. It sounded like, "…with a real man, not with these puppies."

"Get *out* of here!" one of the sorority girls said. Another girl was looking around, perhaps for a bouncer or the attention of a bartender. The bartender was swamped, and there was no bouncer.

Dan stood up from his barstool to go over to the table, but Charlie put his hand up.

"Allow me," he said, but Dan, suddenly suffused with the feeling of lightness and heat, beat him to it and slipped through the crowd over to the table and the institutional man. Charlie didn't follow; ganging up was something joiners did.

Dan came up to the institutional man and said, "Time to leave."

The man turned on Dan, glaring. His breath was rancid, and there were puckered white scars on his face. "What are you, the bouncer?" the man asked.

"Sure," Dan said, shrugging.

"You're a fucking puppy," the institutional man said, leaning forward stepping up the intimidation of his glare as if he were trying to make his irises vibrate. "I eat puppies like you for breakfast."

The young women at the table watched, riveted.

"For breakfast," Dan said. "Original."

The institutional man barked at Dan and went to shove him, putting his weight behind it. Dan easily stepped out of the way and snared the man's arm in his favorite wristlock, hustling him toward the door. The institutional man howled and swore enough to get the attention of everyone in the bar. Charlie followed Dan out the door.

Out on the sidewalk, Dan shoved the man and told him to be on his way.

"Fuck you!" the man said. "You don't know who I am! I've killed people! I don't have to take shit from a puppy like you."

"Get going," Dan said, "or I'm going to have to fuck you up."

The man lunged at Dan, who grabbed him by the collar, slapped him in the face, and shoved him into a parked car. As Dan stood back shaking his head, the man came at him again. There was a flurry of blows, but one shot from the institutional man actually grazed Dan's jaw.

"Goddammit!" Dan cried. "All right, that's enough! Beat it!" Dan snapped the heel of his hand into the man's chest, sending him backwards into the street, where he sat down hard and cracked the back of his head into the bumper of a parked car.

Surprisingly, the man got up and came at Dan again. Dan shook his head, reached into his pocket, and clicked out his lockblade knife. When the man dove at Dan again, his hands outstretched, Dan moved the blade of the knife with a flick of the wrist, slicing the palm of the man's hand.

The man recoiled, holding the wounded hand in a fist against his chest. "Fuck! You asshole! Cut me! You fucking cut me!"

"I told you to beat it," Dan said reasonably.

The man cursed and trotted down the sidewalk, away from Dan, his wounded hand dripping blood.

Charlie approached from where he stood by the door, the entry behind him crowded with witnesses, as were the windows. "Chivalry is not dead," Charlie said.

"I don't know about that," Dan said, "but at least I got to cut a scumbag with a knife."

"Beat me to it," Charlie said. "Asshole."

Most of the bar had seen what had happened, and Dan was now a hero. Charlie appeared to be chagrined for a moment, but dropped it when it was apparent that they were seen as a duo. They were invited to sit at the table with the most recently offended sorority girls, and the bartender set Dan and Charlie up with pitchers and shots. Perhaps the young women were accumulating their stories, too, the ones they would someday be able to tell about their wild years at the University of Greysport.

Dan went back to the bathroom at one point, leaving Charlie to talk to the young women. They were not really Dan's type, a little too wholesome, a little lacking in edge. Charlie's approach was more omnivorous, and he filled the gap Dan left, putting his arms around two of the girls.

"Your friend's a hero," Dan heard one of them say.

"Yeah," Charlie said, "that's Dan. I, on the other hand, am fated to be a god."

The girls laughed at this.

Dan went back to the men's room, ignoring those who made comments or tried to high-five him. Finding the place empty, he went into one of the stalls, closing the door behind him. Standing on the toilet seat, he took the knife from his pocket and pushed up one of the panels of the suspended ceiling, placing the knife on top of the adjacent panel before settling the first one back into place. He hopped down off the toilet seat and took a leak before returning to where Charlie sat with the girls, holding all their attention with his considerable charm.

Dan wasn't in much of a mood to talk, and was soon nearly forgotten. They were still at the table, Charlie getting cozy with two of the girls, when two cops came in.

They walked right up to Dan, and one of them, a large black guy, said, "Could we have a word with you outside for a moment?"

"Sure," Dan said.

Charlie followed them out to the street. The girls from the table, the bartender, and a few dozen others packed the windows to watch.

The institutional man sat in the back of one of the squadcars double-parked by the curb. With a freshly bandaged hand, he pointed at Dan through the open window and said, "That's him! That's the motherfucker!"

"I'm going to have to pat you down," the cop said. "Would you mind putting your hands up on the wall here?"

"Okay."

Dan relaxed and let them search him. This procedure produced only his wallet, keys, and the pen and small notepad he kept in his cargo pocket to jot down ideas for paintings. The cop began to copy the information from Dan's driver's license into a notebook of his own.

"No knife?" the cop said.

"I don't have a knife," Dan said.

"The man in our squad here says that you cut him with a knife."

"Well, that's bullshit," Dan said.

Charlie walked up said, "The dude was hassling a bunch of young women who were just minding their own business, so Dan took him out of here and tossed him in the street. Maybe he cut his hand on some broken glass or something. Maybe he isn't cut at all."

"Oh, he's got quite a gash," the cop said. Some of the people from the bar stood watching in the doorway, and the cop raised his voice and said, "Anyone see a knife?"

A chorus of voices defended Dan; not only was there no knife, he had been the hero of the hour.

"That motherfucker cut me!" the institutional man cried from the back seat of the squad car.

"Yeah, all right," the cop said to the institutional man. To Dan, he said, "Look, I know what you're trying to do here, okay? Next time, just call us."

"Sure," Dan said.

When the cops drove off, the institutional man was cursing and gesticulating at Dan through the back window of the squad car. Charlie smiled amiably at him and gave him the finger.

"Where's the knife?" Charlie muttered.

Dan told him. Charlie laughed quietly through his nose.

"Let's get some more free drinks," he said. "And some sorority girls."

In spite of the consumption of alcohol, the girls were still not Dan's type. Charlie, on the other hand, was deeply engrossed with two of them, his arms around them, taking turns kissing them both. When it was apparent that he was oblivious to anything else, and Dan slipped out the back and walked the long distance to Vnuk's, taking alleys most of the way. There he found Candy, who gave him a look which said he'd been naughty, but that she was glad to see him.

In spite of constant infusions from Charlie's supply of cash, the side money from the occasional bouncing gig at the Red Lantern (none of the nights there turning out to be as eventful as the had hoped), Dan's money got low enough by the end of the summer that he had to start looking for a job. Borrowing Charlie's car to drive around to interviews, he found employment in a matter of days as a security guard at the coal-burning power plant in the industrial area just south of downtown. The Ashipinakwa River came down from the north, the Meskwackee River from the southwest, both emptying into the harbor, and the huge power plant, brutal in the functionality of its architecture, a pair of two-hundred-foot smoke stacks rising from the bulk of the building like horns, sat at the walled and paved confluence of the two rivers. Dan was given a uniform and a hardhat, and told to report for duty for second shift, on the Tuesday after labor day weekend. No problem, Dan thought. I could walk there from the Kicking Pig, take the bus in bad weather.

Charlie was a bit dismayed that Dan had gotten a job, but decided to make the most of it.

"I guess it's not the end of the world," he said. "But we definitely have to have a blowout before you start work."

The blowout started Friday afternoon and barely ceased, except for periods of sleep from mid-morning until midafternoon, until the Tuesday morning after Labor Day. Dan connected with Candy once or twice, finding her in his bed Sunday afternoon and staring at her for a moment before remembering what they had done together when they'd gotten home that morning. It made him think about the conversation he'd had with his grandfather on the subject of sex, the one where Willy had advised him to have threeways before he was married. He wondered if his grampa had ever done anything as nasty as he and Candy had just a few hours before.

On Sunday, knowing that Dan had a full-time work schedule looming ahead, they partied until Vnuk's closed, then at the beach with some of the regular gang. After that, they descended on their favorite bar near the port when it opened at six in the morning, doing a few lines of coke in the alley before going in. The bar was not closed for Labor Day, and was in fact open in anticipation of regulars having the day off, although it was obvious from the bartender's face when he opened the door precisely at six and the bar was flooded with punks that this was not what he had bargained for.

They were at it until almost noon. The more faint of heart began to fade, leaving the bar in ones and twos, and soon Dan had had enough.

"I've got to go, man," Dan said. "Got to get some sleep."

"Come on," Charlie said. "Don't be such a pussy."

"No, seriously. I've got to start a job tomorrow."

"Yeah, but that's not until tomorrow," Charlie said. "Tomorrow afternoon, in fact. It's still morning, and the day before."

"What are you, the undead? I'm going home."

Although he had gotten a second wind sometime mid-morning, walking out of the dark bar and into the sunlight was like being slugged between the eyes. Dan groaned as if he *had* been, squinting, reeling with the recognition of how drunk he was. He took alleys all the way home, trying to avoid the merciless sunlight.

Amazingly, Charlie woke him up late that afternoon. "Come on, man. Let's go out for a hair of the dog."

"Are you fucking kidding me?" Dan shouted, trying to hide under his protective orange sleeping bag. "I'm sleeping! Get out!"

"Pussy," Charlie said. Dan went back to sleep for what felt like five minutes before Charlie came back.

"Come on," he said. "Get up. Getupgetupgetupgetupgetup."

"Go away."

"You know I'll keep doing this. Getupgetupgetupgetupgetup."

"All *right!*" Dan shouted, barely able to open his eyes. "At least have the goddam common human decency to bring me a beer and a couple of hits of speed."

"Yessir! Can do!"

Soon they were roaring out into the high sun of the late afternoon in the 'Cuda.

On Tuesday afternoon, Dan showed up for his first day at the power plant with a hangover which he hoped would kill him. He had planned to take the bus in the future, but Charlie felt a bit remorseful for helping Dan get into such a state, and dropped him off in front of the place. Both of them had forgotten the power plant's position in the river valley, that it was built between a cattle yard and slaughter house on one side, and a tallow-rendering plant on the other. The day was hot and the stench was unbelievable.

"You look a trifle ashen," Charlie said, gagging once as Dan got his pack out of the backseat.

"Thanks," Dan said. "Always want to make a good impression."

"You're cute in your little uniform, though."

"Fuck yourself," Dan said, willing down the urge to vomit. He got out of the car and waved weakly as Charlie drove off.

Dan stood up straight, unconsciously following Willy's instructions, marched himself into the front door of the power plant.

He was trained by the young man he would be replacing, a third year law student at Greysport University. Russ Torrance, a navy man, sized up Dan's situation quickly, but seemed amused by it. "This is a bad place for a hangover," he said with sympathy.

The giant plant building was surrounded by a high chain link fence. Behind the plant itself was a large area for the storage of coal, offloaded from coalboats that came up the river from the lake and tied up behind the plant. The immense pile of coal was tended by bulldozers, stacking the mineral in a manner which resembled a black Mayan pyramid.

The plant had two guards on duty at all times, one of whom sat at a guard shack during the day shift, another in the lobby of the building. For second-shifters like Dan, one of the team sat at the guard shack until six in the evening, at which time he met the other guard in the lobby, both of them taking hourly turns to check the perimeter of the property.

"Other than that," Russ told him, "there's nothing to do. It's the best study job in the world."

When Dan did his first perimeter check, he tried to keep himself erect and neat-looking, a surprisingly difficult task. He put on his hardhat and ventured out with a nod to Russ, who smiled and shook his head pityingly.

Out behind the coal pile under a hazy orange sky, the roar of a nearby highway overpass constant, the reek of the slaughter house and tallow plant got to Dan and he hung on the cyclone fence, retching.

"Oh, man," he moaned. "Hoo, baby."

When he got back to the lobby, he guzzled cold water from the fountain and sat down at one of the two desks at the guard station. Russ was studying, and when Dan got a book from his pack, Russ looked at him and smiled.

"This is the job," he said.

The first shift was horrible, but he was feeling better when he got off at midnight. Before long, he was used to the place, even with the miasma from the meat industry. He got to know all the people who worked around the plant, and to have a certain affection for the filthy place itself, with its enormous turbines resembling something from a 1930s science fiction movie, and the immense smokestacks reaching up into the night, especially impressive if seen in fog or, as the seasons changed, falling snow.

The job paid enough, gave him time to read and sketch, and his partner, a tall dark Punjabi named Ramu, an engineering student, was amusing enough to be around. On their first night together, they had made formal introductions and sat at their respective desks, Dan reading a novel while Ramu read a book with indecipherable text and colorful panels. Ramu, a practicing Sikh, wore a long black beard and maroon turban along with his security uniform. Dan didn't know which clashed more, Ramu's look or his own. At one moment during the evening, both of the young men between their turns at rounds, they looked up from their respective books, their eyes meeting.

Dan had friends of many backgrounds who had been accused of being, in those heated days, terrorists. The least logical of these was a Welsh bartender at the Underground who had pale skin and grew pitch-black facial hair like a slow explosion, seeming to ripple almost visibly up from under his shirt to envelope his face. He'd been accosted on Lake Drive by Southside racists after missing his noon shave, the latter apparently convinced by his swarthy growth that he was ready to blow something up.

"I'm just hairy, man," the Welshman had said.

"Well, come on," Dan replied. "It's like a werewolf movie."

The Welshman had shrugged. "They'll soon find others to hate," he said.

Ramu had apparently been one of them. The fact that he had a beard *and* a turban (of any variety) was enough to classify him as a member of a terrorist organization, and it was only Ramu's fighting ability that had gotten him out of some tight spots. Dan didn't know this when he tried to make a humorous inroad with his new partner. Their eyes met over their books. Dan waggled his eyebrows and said, "Nice hat."

Dan was astounded by Ramu's response, and would always remember from that first exchange Ramu's juicy accent, which sounded as if he were trying to speak with unusual intelligence and fluidity while holding a large, heavy sourball under his tongue.

"What de fuck, my friend!" Ramu said, bolting up from his chair and leaning forward on his desk on his large, brown fists. "I have taken enough of dis shit from you assholes! *Madarchod!*"

"Easy, man!" Dan cried, laughing and holding up his hands. "I was just kidding!"

"It's not a fucking *hat!*" Ramu strongly pronounced the "g" in "fucking".

Dan snorted.

"What is so fucking funny!"

"Man, I was making a joke! Easy, motherfucker!"

"It is *you* who are the motherfucker, sir! *Madarchod!*"

Dan spread his hands. "Sorry, man. I figured you got hassled for bullshit like that. Bad joke. You don't have to be a jagoff about it."

"I'm not being a jagoff," Ramu said, settling down. "I was merely responding in a way that seemed to call for some manner of jagoffery in kind."

While contemplating that last sentence, Dan asked, "What does *madarchod* mean?"

Ramu gazed at him a moment, his face expressionless. Dan was beginning to think the bearded young man was trying to stare him down when Ramu said, "It means 'motherfucker', motherfucker." He kept his face serious until Dan laughed.

"Useful," Dan said.

"Yes it is."

"You like beer?" Dan asked.

"Of course I do," Ramu said. "If it is good Indian beer. Strong stuff. I am not a jagoff, you know."

"Or a *madarchod*, for that matter," Dan said. They were friends after that.

Charlie was cut off by his father for his shiftless ways, not the first time it had happened, apparently. Henry Gates had begun to compare Jim favorably to Charlie; seemingly the younger brother had "straightened himself out" and was ready to start college immediately after high school.

"I guess I've got to show I can live a straight life," Charlie said, "if I want to get have any access to the Gates bucks."

"Here's your chance to become working class," Dan told him, "just like you always wanted."

Dan talked to a supervisor, and Charlie soon had a job at another power plant in South Greysport. Charlie loved it. Aside from doing his simple rounds, he devoured books at a rate that soon had them piling up even deeper in their apartment. He weeded out the books he thought to be inferior and took them to the gigantic used bookstore downtown. On the occasions which he didn't buy more books with the money, he bought a case of beer, which the two drank on the roof of the Kicking Pig.

After a few months of Charlie being consistently employed, Dr. Gates seemed impressed, and had the two up to White Birch Pointe for dinner, which the young men, all too used to eating canned goods and carry-out, were eager to do.

"The Gates of Gates," Charlie said ritualistically as they pulled up the driveway to the mansion. Dan was so used to their run-down apartment, their shady neighborhood, the black and purple environs of Vnuk's (always with the faint whiff of urine and vomit, no matter how the staff cleaned it), the subterranean confines of the Underground and the less-than-pleasing ambience of the power plant, that parking in front of the mansion and walking in was a bit surreal. Dr. Gates greeted them in the living room by the grand piano, the whole place perfect and ablaze with light.

"Charlemagne!" Dr. Gates cried. Charlie gave him a dead-eyed look. "And young Huck! Back with us at last. Fix yourselves a drink!" Charlie went immediately to the sideboard, got out two crystal glasses, filled them to brimming with scotch, handing one to Dan.

"Working at a power plant!" Gates said as they talked before dinner. "How rugged! This will teach you so much about how the world really works."

"I already know a lot about how the world works, Dad."

"Well, this will give you great insight."

"You never actually *worked*, though, right? You flew through college and right to grad school because everything was paid for by *your* dad? Or do I have that wrong?" Charlie drank down half of his whisky.

"Oh, now! Hah! How are things with you, Dan?"

"Just fine, sir." In reality, Dan wanted nothing more than to be in the kitchen with Elpidia.

Jim came down for dinner, greeting the two warmly, although when he said something about how much he had to do for his upcoming exams, Charlie scoffed a bit, and Jim gave him a look. The tension still existed. Dan thought about asking after Elpidia, but got a feeling that one didn't do such things. Dan asked later, and found out that Elpidia had been let go

At the end of the evening, Hugh showed up, and Charlie was able to talk him into going down to Vnuk's. Hugh seemed hesitant, but apparently did it on Dan's behalf.

Wearing a black leather jacket, the lanky Hugh escaped anything more than the occasional suspicious scowl. The bill for the evening was two girl bands, the first being Vaginoraptor, who was opening for the Armageddon Sluts.

"This is typical fare?" Hugh shouted at Dan over the din.

"Don't you love it?" Dan shouted back.

"It has a certain charm," Hugh laughed.

When Dan woke up in the morning, it took him a few moments to remember having gone to dinner at the Gates's, or doing cocaine with Hugh at two in the morning. It was a Saturday, though, and he could be lazy. He rolled over and went back to sleep.

Dan and Candy drifted apart, although they might get together for an occasional night. In a few months, he wouldn't even be sure who had broken up with whom. Charlie began dating the drummer from the Armageddon Sluts, a young woman who called herself Pummela on stage, but whose real name was Pamela Scott. She chainsmoked and drank heavily, keeping herself from collapsing with lots of coke and speed.

"The sex is unbelievably twisted," Charlie informed Dan, who preferred, at this point, to keep his life uncomplicated through a series of one-night stands.

And so their time was frittered away. They did what many young men and women will do, putting their plans on hold for another week, another month, which then becomes a year and then perhaps a decade. Dan and Charlie vowed to get into school, though, Charlie himself especially having big ideas, although what those big ideas were changed constantly.

Dan consistently painted, although more than once he literally put his application materials for Greysport University on the shelf when Charlie turned on the television and fired up the bong.

Nearly every day before going to work, Dan took the bus to the bridge that crossed the rivers in the industrial area to Perrito's, to whose food he was now addicted. Kaye was almost always there, and almost always complained about her lazy boss, who sat, almost always, staring enigmatically off into space with a margarita in front of him.

"The margarita wasn't even invented by a Mexican," Kaye told Dan. "What a fucking phony." She knew what Dan wanted to eat, though, and on slow days leaned on the bar and chatted, which Dan found comforting.

Dan saved enough money to buy a used van from the fleet of vehicles for the power plant. Charlie, amazingly, still had his job, which he claimed was a good place to get some peace for eight hours a day, and gave him cover in case anyone inquired about his finances. Most of his money still came from dealing, though, so he was flush. When Dan bought the van in April, not long before his birthday, Charlie made a trade with someone he knew from Vnuk's to paint it.

"It's an early birthday present," he said. Dan accepted, but only after Charlie convinced him it was fitting, seeing as he benefitted from Dan's help and knowledge a great deal when they worked on the 'Cuda on weekends.

Dan had the van painted plain black, which cut down on the expense of the trade. The guy who did the job often airbrushed barbarians and buxom, swordwielding warrior women on similar vehicles.

"That's all you want?" the guy asked.

"Yeah." Dan said.

Charlie said, "You don't want it black with, like, a yellow and orange nuke exploding on the side?"

"Too obvious," Dan said, "and too memorable in case of the commission of a crime.

And although Dan had only been half-joking, Charlie had snapped his fingers and pointed at Dan, saying, "Right!"

They customized the inside of the van in a functional manner, and when Dan took it down to the north side of the entrance of the port, just across from the abandoned warehouses, it was his portable home, his cozy cabin on wheels.

Partying again resumed at the Kicking Pig when the weather warmed up. The after-bar parties had a shifting cast, although some members remained consistent. Pummela from the Armageddon Sluts was often there, although Dan preferred it when Charlie slept at her apartment; the stench she often left in the bathroom in the morning was more than enough to make him hope for her absence.

"Damn!" she would call down the hall after such an event. "What a log! Should stick a flag on the top of this fucker and salute it as it goes down!"

Dan would cover his head with a pillow and wait until the two left for breakfast.

"She's quite a lady," Dan once said to Charlie, who laughed hard.

"I should take her home for Thanksgiving," he said, "although it's traditional to serve poultry, not pork."

"I'm sure Henry would be impressed," Dan said

Often in attendance at the Pig parties was a trio of short-haired, muscular thugs who dressed like Dan in sleeveless t-shirts and fatigue pants, looking more like mercenaries than anything else, often responsible for fights at Vnuk's, but whom Dan found amusing; he would have liked to pack them in the van and take them out to MacDougal, there to loose them on the innocent populace. Jerry, Chris, and Jimmie referred to themselves as The Three Horsedicks of the Apocalypse, and so they became known.

Chris seemed particularly volatile. In the middle of one loud party, Dan had been showing him (unadvisedly, he immediately realized) his rifle.

"Is it loaded?" Chris asked.

"Yeah," Dan said. His desire to have a loaded weapon around was connected, rationally or not, to the need to have a pipe or a brick handy back at 718 Pier.

"May I?" Chris said, holding out his hand politely.

"Sure," Dan said, and handed over the rifle.

"Just a moment," Chris said. He excused himself, walked over to an open window facing the alley, pointed the rifle up at the black sky, and fired off a quick succession of rounds. The booms echoed down the alley and off surrounding buildings, and the party was suddenly silent except for The Clash on the stereo. The song ended at that moment, leaving a few seconds of complete silence.

"Hey, it *is* loaded!" Chris shouted, and cackled with laughter. Jerry and Jimmie looked at each other and laughed the same way. The next tune began and everyone at the party began talking at once.

"Jesus, give me that!" Dan said, yanking the gun out of Chris's hands and hiding it in his bedroom.

"It's okay, I aimed out over the lake."

"If some guy on a tanker gets a round in the skull, I'm not taking the bite for it," Dan said.

Dan was surprised that the police didn't show up.

"That's the beauty of living in this neighborhood," Charlie commented. "the cops don't give a shit what goes on."

Chris tried to redeem himself later that same evening with his half-assed attempt to a solution to the Irv Klubertanz problem. Irv was an intelligent young man, often morose when drunk (and usually drunk), who worked as a tombstone engraver in the summer, between semesters as a student at GU. Whether through affectation or some kind of stylistic disability, the only clothes he wore, ever, were janitor's uniforms. He varied the color between olive, khaki, navy, and grey, but the clothing was always the same. He'd had Dr. Gates as a professor, and implied that Gates, although informative, had a tendency to be long-winded and self-impressed. The fact that Charlie was Gates's son seemed to fascinate Irv.

"Charlie's cool and kind of scary," Irv slurred at Dan one night. "I can't believe they're related."

119

"They are," Dan said. He kept his mouth shut about Charlie's origins, knowing that subjects like his family background and mansion of origin weren't things he necessarily liked to have brought up.

Dan and Charlie had begun to like Irv when he told them a story at a party before he was too drunk to be comprehensible. Irv struggled with the meaning of his existence, a subject which was amusing at first, but began to age with constant repetition. It was fresh, the first time, though.

"So, I talked to all kinds of people," Irv had explained. "Priests, rabbis, philosophers. No one could tell me anything that made sense, that seemed to have any real application to my life. It was all just bullshit, the perpetuation of comforting illusions. Finally, I was at a family reunion down in Cary. Most of my family worked in the steel mills or in auto plants. They're not fancy people, but they've been through a lot. Survived everything, wars, death, deprivation, you name it.

"I was bummed out, sitting off to the side of this backyard cookout by myself, when I saw my grandfather doing the same. He's, like, the patriarch, you know? A World War One veteran, union steward, been in labor riots, you know, all kinds of shit.

"He was a messenger in the war, relaying packets by motorcycle to the front and back. One time he came upon a little depression in the landscape he had to pass through, to drop off his packet, right? Only thing was, the depression was filled with mustard gas. He has to get these dispatches back to headquarters, and there's no other way to go, okay? And he only has goggles, no gas mask. So he calculates the distance, hyperventilates for a bit, revs up the bike and hauls ass through the gas. He almost makes it to the other side before he lets out his breath in a burst, and inhales a bit of mustard gas. It fucked up his lungs, but he still got the packet of dispatches back to headquarters. Got some kind of medal for it. Family legend.

"So there he is, sitting off to the side of the party like an aged version of myself. I'm feeling too bummed out to be embarrassed by asking him questions, and go throw myself at his feet to explain my plight.

" 'Grampa,' I said, 'you're a wise man. You've lived through everything, lived a life as hard as it has been rewarding. You've seen everything, birth and death and success and failure. I'm searching, searching for some kind of meaning, and I just feel lost.'

"I think I was kind of emotional, and I had to pull it together, because that kind of shit doesn't fly with the old dudes, you know? So I *got* my shit together, put on a soldier's face and said, 'Just tell me, Grampa. What's it all mean? What's life all about?'

"He sat there for some time, kind of pondering the question and sucking his teeth. Finally he says, 'Irv?'

"And I go, like, 'Yes, Grampa? What is it? What does it all mean?'

"And he says, "Irv...it don't mean shit.'"

Dan and Charlie had howled with laughter. Dan could see that Irv had meant the story to be meaningful, to be deep, but when they began laughing, he soon smiled and was laughing along with them. The lasting effect of the story on Dan, however, was to taint him with a feeling of guilt for not calling his own grandfather. He made himself feel better with the thought that he would call Willy when he was firmly situated in school.

Repeated exposures to Irv's alcohol-fed depressions soon stripped them of their charm, however.

"Try carving tombstones for a living," Irv would mutter. "See what that does to your *soul*."

It got to the point that, when he shifted away from their often enjoyable conversations to his ruminations on the pointlessness of existence (his, not anyone else's) Dan simply walked away.

Irv was being fairly annoying the night of the rifle incident, though, going from talking about the horrors of tombstone engraving to yet another monologue about the pointlessness of his life. Irv was drunk enough to be reeling as he sat, and Dan, Charlie, and Chris watched in amusement.

"I really just don't see the meaning of it," Irv said, drinking a beer and smoking a filterless French cigarette, which he had to guide to his mouth with care. The front of the evening's grey janitor's uniform was spotted and speckled with drizzled beer and bits of ash. "Why bother to continue? It's pointless."

"That's the point," Charlie said, laughing.

"What?"

"That's the point, that it's pointless."

"What?" Irv was mystified.

"Since it's pointless, you're free. Any social codes or structures are meaningless, which means that adherence to them is meaningless. The opinion of those who adhere to such structures is also meaningless, because they're abstractions. They don't exist. The only real laws are those of survival and adaptation."

"I like the way you think, man," Chris said, and clapped Charlie on the back.

Charlie ignored Chris and continued. "So you're always talking about being a tombstone engraver, right? Right?"

"Yeah," Irv said. "Yes, I am." He seemed to derive some dignity from this, meaningless or not.

"And the tombstones you've carved for people, how long do you think they're going to last?"

"Hundreds of years!" Irv said, making a sweeping gesture with his beer and splashing some on a nearby girl in fishnet stockings, who yelped.

"And do you think that any of the people planted under those stones are going to be remembered in hundreds of years?"

Irv thought about this, and a melancholy look pulled down his face. Dan thought of Ingrid's tragedy mask.

"I don't want to live, man," Irv said, on the verge of tears.

"You idiot," Charlie said. "You're completely missing the point. You're free! Drink, for tomorrow we die!"

Now Irv was visibly struggling with tears. "Dan, you've got that gun. Just kill me."

"No," Dan said.

"Please, man. Just kill me."

"I don't like you well enough," Dan said.

"*I'll* do it," Chris said obligingly. This was his first attempt at rectifying his previous *faux pas*.

Irv hung his head and began to blubber. Dan, Charlie, and Chris looked at each other in amused contempt.

"Just fucking kill me, man. One in the ol' brainpan!" Irv dropped his cigarette butt on the floor and put an index finger to his temple. "Right in the head! *Poozh!*"

"Oh, for fuck sake," Charlie said. He grabbed Irv by the collar of his janitor's shirt and jerked him to his feet. "Come on!"

"Where are we going!" Irv cried.

"Shut up and get moving!" Charlie said. He grabbed one of Irv's elbows as well and walked him to the door to the fire escape.

Chris gave Dan a delighted look and called the other two Horsedicks. Dan went out the door after Charlie.

Protesting all the way, Irv was taken up the fire escape to the roof. Charlie seemed to nearly lift him off his feet. Dan was right behind him, and a crowd soon followed, rattling up the stairs. Charlie took Irv right up to the edge of the building in front, pushing his upper body over the waist-high brick wall. Buses and cars moved by on the street several stories below, a snatch of music drifted up from a passing car. A semicircle of partiers watched.

"You want to fucking die, you dick?" Charlie said. Irv didn't answer, so Charlie shook him by the neck. "I'm asking you a question. Do you want to die or not? If you do, just fucking jump! Do it! Jump! Quit fucking whining and jump!"

"I don't want to," Irv said quietly.

"What?" Charlie said.

"I don't want to."

"Push him off!" Jerry said.

"*I'll* do it," Chris said.

"Are you going to jump or not?" Charlie demanded. "There's the solution to all your problems, that pavement down there, a few convenient seconds away. I'm sure one of your buddies would be glad to carve you a stone, but they might as well do it in chalk, because you're going to be forgotten in far less time than usual. Are you going to do it?"

"No," Irv said.

"*Are* you?"

"No!"

"All right," Charlie said, letting him go. "Then shut up about it."

"Okay."

"If you're not going to kill yourself, what do you want to do?"

Irv thought about it. "Have a beer, I guess."

"Great idea! I'll take a beer over suicide any day! Anybody got a beer?" One was handed over from the small crowd. Charlie opened it and gave it to Irv.

"Okay, Jumpin' Irv," Charlie said. "And no more of this shit. I mean it. Enjoy your life, change it, or end it. And give the first two a try before pussying out."

"Okay," Jumpin' Irv said, smiling a little, his face still wet from tears. Charlie clapped him on the back of the neck. People filed down off the roof, back to the apartment.

"Well, *that* was disappointing," Jimmie said, and Dan and the other two Horsedicks laughed.

"Man," Chris said, shaking his head. "*I* would have done it."

"What, jumped?"

"No, tossed him off." Chris snorted. "Dumbass."

The name Jumpin' Irv immediately stuck, something that the unfortunate Irv Klubertanz would have a hard time living down.

Above all, Dan had a feeling of liberation in his life. Even a year after leaving Willy and the river, he didn't take it for granted. He had a job, his own money and vehicle. No one could tell him what to do, he told himself; he was free.

The very idea of Willy filled him with oppression, though, and he procrastinated on calling. Willy was a tough old man, but witnessing his slow decline had left Dan with an unspoken weight of obligation that only beers and bongs could abate. After several of each, especially on a weekend night, a little acid or speed or the occasional line of coke got him revved up enough to run down the fire escape and into the night. Once there, he didn't think about Willy at all.

Dan had a revolving door of girlfriends, and with his feeling of freedom came a sense that he didn't necessarily have to treat anyone all that decently. He went along with Charlie on this on a logical level, although when he dumped a girl in an unkind manner, it often left a bad taste in his mouth which he tried to banish. Sometimes they dumped *him*, but he had learned his lesson and was careful to avoid going out with women he seriously liked. Sexual attraction was one thing, admiration another.

As summer approached, Charlie got dumped for the first time that Dan could remember, and by the skanky Pummela of the Armageddon Sluts. Charlie admitted he had seen it coming. One of the band's catchy little tunes, *Hose Me, Daddy, I'm Dirty* had taken off, and now the band was getting a great deal of exposure and was looking at a record deal. Pummela was seen in short order with the bass player from a national band of some note.

"She was just too classy for me," Charlie said, laughing, about the break-up.

"Yeah," Dan said. "She made Audrey Hepburn look like a hillbilly."

"Like Icarus, I flew too close to the sun," Charlie laughed. "And I plummet, oh, and I plummet."

He plummeted right down to the Bar of Paddy McX to troll for sorority girls in search of adventure. They still got free drinks for their night of heroism, so Dan went as well.

It was after a long night of partying that they came to a bar they had often driven by while returning to the Kicking Pig from South Greysport. Standing in a brown field among factories and steel mills on the downswing, it wasn't quite seedy and dilapidated enough for them to have found it attractive. On that particular night, however, it had the added bonus of seven Harleys parked outside, lined up neatly alongside the building in a gravel parking lot.

"Look," Charlie said in a chipper tone, "joiners!"

"Oh, man," Dan said. He felt a little tired after a protracted evening of boozing, and wasn't sure he was in the mood for drama. They'd worked the door at the Red Lantern the night before and had a couple of set-tos, and Dan was feeling as though his resources were depleted. A couple of lines of blow lifted his combative spirits.

Dan would later think that it was only Charlie's love of his brother Hugh which kept him from simply walking into the bar, holding up his fists, and declaring, "All bikers are faggots!" Charlie would say himself that he had nothing against faggots. If someone had said, "All faggots are bikers!" that would have been an entirely different story.

The group in this bar, with their "old ladies" in tow, wasn't an amoebal node of the Guardians of Nocturne, but one of their rivals in the area, the Outcasts. Charlie didn't set in to insulting the name immediately, but walked to the bar after smiling his way through the room. This might have been normal in the north woods, or out on the river, or somewhere in the farmland in the middle of the state, but in Greysport, anyone going around smiling for no good reason was immediately suspicious.

Dan beat Charlie to the bar and ordered two beers from the nondescript bartender, rather than the customary pitcher. Charlie gave him a questioning look, and Dan said quietly, "I'm betting we won't be here long enough."

Charlie frowned and nodded in agreement. They drank their beers and assessed the room: working people having a beer, a few barfly women in their forties or fifties, and Outcasts either playing pool or watching the game. Dan and Charlie shared a code of eye movements that said none of the women present were attractive enough to plausibly start a fight over.

One of the Outcasts reminded Dan of Mike, if Mike had had the decency to grow a beard and a ponytail. The resemblance warmed Dan to the task, knowing that, when Charlie was in the mood for adventure, he would not be deterred. Dan watched for his opening. When the jukebox had gone silent after a Stones tune, and the Outcast in question was chalking his cue, Dan went over and put in a couple of selections, chosen for their ability to annoy bikers. He started with *Killer Queen* by Queen. He didn't think that, if the situation were properly handled, they would get around to listening to his second selection *I've Got a Brand New Pair of Roller Skates*.

Dan was almost surprised by the effectiveness of his choice. He glanced at Charlie, who was trying not to grin.

"What the *fuck*?" one of the bikers said when the music came on.

"Jesus," Ponytail said, continuing to chalk his cue. "Who listens to this shit?"

"We do," Dan said. "What have you got against Queen?"

"They're a bunch of fags," Ponytail said, "and they play faggy music."

"Oh, come on now," Charlie said. "What have you got against fags?"

The bikers seemed taken aback by such a question, some looking at each other in puzzlement, others chuckling in disbelief.

"What have I got against *fags*?" Ponytail said, looking around at his cohorts. Any of them who had been sitting got up and drew closer to the pool table.

"Yeah," Charlie said. "What have you got against fags?"

"Well, they like dick," Ponytail said slowly, as if perplexed at having to explain. His brothers in leather muttered in agreement.

"Shit, even your mom likes dick," Dan said, surprised at the low combustion level of the situation and sharing a look with Charlie. "Even if she's a dyke, she liked dick well enough for *you* to be here."

"Excellent point," Charlie said, and they clinked beer glasses.

There was a moment of baffled silence. One of the barflies snickered.

"Are you fuckers crazy?" a fat biker said.

"No," Charlie said, "we just like Queen. And I bet you do, too. You just don't want to admit it to your buddies. Come on, you've done a little time, right? Sucked some dick in the joint? Fucked a guy or two, maybe taken it in the ass to return the favor? It's not like you're *gay* gay, just *prison* gay, right? Man's got to survive, after all."

This was actually enough to overcome the bikers' disbelief that they were being insulted. The fat one came around the pool table at Charlie from the right, another two coming at Dan from the left. Dan grabbed a ball from the pool table and drew his arm back to pitch it. Charlie picked up a pool cue. The barflies and other patrons drew back and tried to get out of the way.

Ponytail bellowed, "Okay, *what the FUCK!*"

It was loud enough for everyone to freeze; it would later remind Dan of Willy's ability to do the same thing, only better. Ponytail reached back under his leather, pulling a .45 automatic out of his waistband and chambering a round. His cohorts backed away as he walked slowly around the bar, pointing the gun at Charlie, then Dan.

Dan was too surprised to find a gun trained on him to be afraid. He simply realized that he might be about to get shot. He glanced at Charlie, whose face was expressionless.

"I think you're right, Nasty," Ponytail said over his shoulder to the fat biker. "I think you two are fucking crazy. Are you fucking crazy?" He stood six feet away, holding the .45 on them, first one, then the other.

"Now, this is my brother-in-law's bar, right Gary?"

The nondescript bartender cleared his throat. "Yep," he said.

"And we come here to play a few quiet games of pool without having to put up with any bullshit. And we don't want to fuck up my brother-in-law's bar. So, we want you just to back the fuck up out of here and go away."

Neither Dan nor Charlie moved.

Ponytail came closer. He stood before them, putting the barrel of the .45 first to Charlie's forehead, then to Dan's, pushing off with it and jerking Dan's head backwards with the force of the motion before taking the gun away.

Ponytail leaned closer and muttered, "If there weren't any witnesses here, and if it weren't my brother-in-law's bar, I'd just put a slug in both of your heads and drop you in the river."

"What would you do," Charlie said as quietly, "strap our corpses to the back of your hog?"

Ponytail laughed. "Shit, kid. You *are* fucking crazy. You got a death wish. That or you got your balls from a fucking quarry."

The wordless thought flicked through Dan's mind that the biker was right, on all counts. He didn't think about his own lack of emotional response. Charlie's face was still impassive, with the slightest trace of a smirk.

Ponytail spoke loudly enough to be heard by everyone in the dingy bar. "Tell you what, guys. You just apologize and we'll let you go."

Dan looked at Charlie and saw that he, in all reality, was unwilling to make the apology.

Ponytail saw this and said in a low voice. "Okay. You're tough guys. Couple of big fuckers, I'll give you that, along with being crazy. You ever want to look at becoming Outcasts" -Charlie snorted, Ponytail paused but ignored it- "you come look me up. But right now, I got the gun. So get the fuck out."

The two backed out of the door. Out in the dark parking lot, with the sound Melanie chirping on the jukebox, they crunched across the gravel to the 'Cuda. They stood for a moment, looking at each other over the top of the car. Charlie unlocked his door.

"Fuck," he said. "This is like the time at the Red Lantern."

"Except we didn't kick anyone's ass."

"Exactly."

Dan shrugged.

They drove off. Charlie turned onto the deserted street and headed north. He drove half a block and pulled over for a second, saying, "That just ain't gonna do it."

"What?" Dan asked.

Charlie didn't answer. He made a U-turn, the tires of the car spitting gravel. Pulling into the parking lot of the bar, he drove counterclockwise around the back of the building and back towards the street. Cars were parked on the gravel, motorcycles were parked side by side, neatly diagonal, backed into their spaces close to the building.

"What are you doing?" Dan said.

"Watch this."

Charlie punched the gas and aimed at the bikes. Dan braced himself. He would later remember the sensation of his eyes being open as wide as they would go.

Charlie didn't hit the bikes straight on, however, and swerved the last moment, crashing into only the last foot or so of them. From where Dan sat, he could see handlebars and mirrors flying, turning over. The thump of the 'Cuda smashing into the Harleys was a sickening delight. A headlight went out on the 'Cuda. Charlie roared away.

They left the bikes as wreckage. Charlie pulled out of the parking lot and headed north again on the empty street. Dan looked back out the rear window, "Ohhhh fuck." The door of the bar opened, bulky backlit figures piling out, and Charlie took off. They drove a hundred yards before they realized the car had a flat on the front left tire.

"Shit!" Charlie said and laughed, shaking his head.

"Not funny!" Dan shouted, laughing in spite of himself. "They could be piling into cars from the parking lot and coming after us! Take a right here, we've got to hide the'Cuda!"

Charlie did, struggling to steer as the flat tire twisted and warped, shuddering around and around in the wheelwell. Soon it was obvious that they were driving on the rim. He pulled into an area of warehouses and drab little homes, going down the street with the rim grinding on the pavement. They were fortunate enough to find what appeared to be an empty warehouse, and drove over dead weeds around to the back, where Charlie parked by a garbage-strewn loading dock.

"Okay, let's change the tire and blow out of here," Charlie said, getting out of the car and going around to the trunk.

"If they didn't see that we got a flat, they won't be looking for us," Dan said. "It'll take them awhile to sort out their bikes."

Charlie laughed. "They're not going to be driving any of those bikes."

"Then it'd be smartest to assume that they're looking for us in cars."

"I suppose," Charlie said. He reached into the trunk to get the spare. "Huh. It's flat."

"Oh, shit!" Dan looked at Charlie, who spread his hands and grinned.

"Guess I forgot to check it," Charlie said.

They both began to laugh, a little at first, then harder and harder.

It took them hours to walk home. They stayed off the streets, using alleys and brownfields wherever possible. They knew the neighborhoods that might be less than friendly to a couple of white boys and skirted them, using the tallest buildings of downtown Greysport to give them direction. At one point, they had to cross a long, well-lit viaduct over the river and the industrial valley, the smokestacks of Dan's powerplant looming in the distance against the lightening sky. There was little traffic, but any car that passed was suspect, and they were glad to get back into the shadows.

It was almost light out when they trudged up the fire escape of the Kicking Pig. Silently, they rifled through the refrigerator, sharing out Chinese, Mexican, and Indian food, drinking prodigious amounts of cold water. Finally, they shuffled off to their bedrooms and collapsed.

They woke up groggily around midafternoon and got ready to rescue the 'Cuda. Charlie had a spare tire in their storage unit in the basement, and Dan parked his van in the alley while Charlie brought it out.

It was a Sunday, and the industrial area where they'd had their latest run-in was deserted. Dan found the bar, driving south past it, doing a u-turn coming back. The gravel parking lot of the bar was empty, but there was a pile of Harleys beside the bar, obviously dragged out of the way until they could be tended to. Dan and Charlie laughed, punching each other on the arm.

The 'Cuda, their old friend, had sustained some damage, but was not beyond fixing.

"It was worth it," Charlie said. "That's one of our better stories."

They fixed the flat and drove to Perrito's, where Kaye brought them food and beer, and Perrito himself sat enigmatically, a margarita in front of him. Neither were interested in further partying, though, as often happened on Sundays, and they went home, where they listened to Beethoven while Dan painted and Charlie read.

The incident with the Outcasts (which Charlie called The Night of the .45) led to a rather disastrous party, which in turn led the two young men to finally enroll in college, Dan, at least, for the first time.

After The Night of the .45, Charlie had been so impressed by the weapon that he had to have one for himself.

"That was a cool gun," he said. "Things would have gone differently if I'd been packin'."

This comment made Dan uneasy, but their largely unspoken philosophy of extremity prevented him from saying anything about prudence or caution. Instead, when Charlie brought home the gleaming, well-oiled gun, Dan got out the old rifle Willy had given him, and they went to a beach north of the city for target practice. Charlie brought M-80s, along with a twelve-pack of Greysport Lager and a pint of tequila in his backpack. Dan brought rifle ammo and more beer. It would be unseemly not to do so.

It was cool and cloudy for a summer day, and the two, well-armed in every sense, walked from Dan's van through breezy fields and down a wooded glen with a stream that cut through the bluffs to a deserted stretch of sand, a place they went from time to time to experiment with explosives and had named Terror Beach.

The beach was empty, with the closest witnesses being what appeared to be a young couple walking by the day's small waves perhaps a mile to the south. A few prefatory M-80s tossed onto the sand and blowing craters seemed to give the couple reason to turn around and head back in the direction from which they had come.

Charlie had read up, he said, on the use of a .45. They rapidly had several beer cans for targets, which Charlie refilled with water from the waves for weight and "splatter". His aim improved every time he shot. Dan, of course, had been raised around guns and wasn't sure he'd seen the like. Dan was not as good with the handgun as he was with his grandfather's rifle, but redeemed himself by backing far off down the beach and nailing a can with one shot.

Charlie was in love with the .45. "This gun is so cool," he said, drinking one of the last beers. "One of these days someone's going to piss me off and I'll ventilate him. Now *that* would be a maximal experience."

Dan snorted. "Right," he said. "I'm sure the ventilatee would feel the same way."

On the way back to the glen, Dan picked up the torn beer cans and stuffed them in his pack.

Charlie watched him with mild disgust. "That's not going to matter, man."

"Humor me," Dan said.

They went home for a nap, flopping into their respective nest. Although they woke up bleary, with enough speed, they were able to go to the Underground and to Vnuk's, staying out until the late weekend bartime.

The next morning, they got the information that led to the disastrous party. Professor Gates called to remind Charlie that he was going to France to visit Gigi with Jim, and that the house would be empty. He had asked Charlie to go, but Charlie had claimed that he couldn't take the time off of work. This wasn't true; he'd been on the verge of quitting, tired of the rigors of showing up somewhere punctually at the same time every day. Dan overheard the conversation from where he sprawled groggily in bed. Charlie sounded touchy, not being used to dealing with anyone at this annoying hour. Dan wasn't sure what they were arguing about, only hearing Charlie's side of the conversation.

"That's not the point," Charlie was saying as Dan wandered out into the living room. Charlie looked at him and rolled his eyes. "I *know* you think that. It's *because* you think that that I wonder why you ever got to teach at GU in the first place… Maybe I *do* have to be insulting, *Henry*. What you fail to grasp is that this species is feces, and we're doomed as a result. If you just *got* that you'd have a clearer

128

understanding of why I live the way I do…No… No. The point is that you don't even *try*, that or it's beyond you… Yeah… No… Okay, whatever. Yes, I'll look after the house. Dan and I are going to work on my car in the garage. Okay… Right… *Ohhhhhhh*-kay. Yep. M'bye."

Charlie slammed the phone in its cradle. "What a useless asshole," he said, shaking his head. "Too bad he doesn't have good ol' Six to live up to his dreams. It's obvious Homo Hugh and I have been disappointing sons. At least Jim's shaping up."

Dan had nothing to say, only raising his eyebrows commiseratingly.

"Wanna party up in White Birch Pointe? Venture through the Gates of Gates?"

"Sure," Dan said.

They actually did make the repairs in the giant garage at the Gates "manor", as Dan thought of it. The garage was well appointed with infrequently used tools, and as they drank beer and talked occasionally, Dan and Charlie were able to make all the repairs but the paint job, which Charlie was going to have done by the same person who did Dan's van. They closed up the garage and ambled up to the house.

It was obvious that Charlie's conversation with his father was on his mind, as much as he evinced contempt for what Henry thought. They talked about it as they rustled food from the kitchen.

"I'm a bit surprised at Jim," Charlie said. "He's all on track to go to school and do something *meaningful*. It's because of his stupid girlfriend. Her dad's an oncologist, and I think Jim was pretty impressed by that. That and the fact that he's, like, a *real dad*, all attentive and dependable and shit. Likes Jim and gives him approval. So now he's all on track for graduate school and everything."

"Huh," Dan said.

The two talked with the obliviousness of many young people out of high school with large ambitions and glowing (and often unrealistic) dreams, some with none at all, unified only by directionlessness. Whatever their visions of the future, grand or non-existent, with unaccustomed freedom they find themselves temporarily diverted. The diversion becomes habit, becomes their lives, and soon their job is their job, their life their life, and dreams of going on to something else become a fading itch. For all their debauched worldliness, Dan and Charlie were still too young to see the larger picture, to ask great questions. How many millions of the young lack the support, both financial and psychological, to push through the barrier of habit (and often hopelessness, often despair) to find out what they can really do, to grow some nascent talent they have within? How many bright and talented young men and women, through lack of opportunity or through simple hesitation, find themselves grinding through a life they might never have imagined? Then children come along, and the barrier is higher and deeper.

Although they did not yet see this part of the picture, they clearly understood their own context, how the extended group of friends connected to Dan and Charlie represented every variation on the spectrum of possibility. Some were poor kids who had gotten factory jobs and were glad to have them, some attended Greysport University with a little help from parents and part time jobs, some were students as serious about partying as they were about school (these mostly seen on the weekends), some were shady and slightly criminal, although their criminality had nothing to do with their intellectual abilities. Charlie was the one with the most stable financial background and the greatest intellectual capability, but with what appeared to be the greatest desire to squander it. The only reason he went through pulses of the desire to go back to school at all was that it represented an unaccepted challenge, as if Fate had thrown down the gauntlet, and he was being too chickenshit to pick it up. Dan remembered the look that had crossed Charlie's face when he heard of Jim's ambitions: it hadn't been one of jealously, as those of an obvious bent might expect. Dan wasn't even sure if Charlie was *capable* of jealousy. It was a look of disappointment, Dan knew, of disappointment in himself, as if he were staring at that discarded gauntlet at his feet.

"You want to know what I think?" Dan asked.

"Yours is one of about three opinions I *do* care about," Charlie said, "and I'm not sure at the moment that I know who the other two are."

"All right, then," Dan said. "I think that you'd go for a PhD if there were a gruellingly long, one-day test you could take to prove that you're intellectually worthy. One that might involve bursts of physical pain."

"Hmmm. Go on."

"You, yourself, are intellectually worthy and capable of kicking ass on such a test, but there *is* no such test, and you don't want to do the work."

"Right!" Charlie said, obviously cheered to be so clearly understood. "I'd do that test if I'd be done with it in one day, no matter how brutal that one day was. Problem is, to get a PhD takes a lot of linear effort, and that linear effort takes a sound belief that it all *means* something. This is a belief which I do not entertain, nor can I trick myself into entertaining it. Jim seems to have succeeded in doing so."

"And yet you're toying with the idea of going back to school," Dan said.

"Currently. And most of that is motivated by the delicious irony of doing so."

"Good old irony," Dan smiled, drinking his beer.

"Here's how I see it playing out," Charlie said. "For whatever reason, I get my focus and am able to decide on *one* thing, and *only* one thing, to which I could dedicate myself. This with all of us being afloat in a sea of fascinating ideas, okay? Could be genetics, could be geology, could be literature, could be filmmaking. Who knows. Computer science is going to be big, just you watch.

"Anyway. So I find my focus and keep it up, managing to overcome gaping chasms of deadly boredom, not to mention all the countless and wonderful distractions which present themselves: pussy, fighting, booze, drugs, their intensity all competing with the duration, the grinding duration, of intellectual pursuit.

"I discipline myself. I party only on weekends, just to let the dog out for a walk. I get into grad school, do my Master's, do my PhD. I get through with flying colors. Maybe I even get married and am all happy and shit. That's when it happens."

"Global thermonuclear war?" Dan asked, laughing.

"Sure. That or something else. Plague, maybe. We're overdue. The collapse of the oil economy; you know *that's* coming. Greenhouse effect? Already underway, and who knows how that shit will turn out. Some way, at any rate, in which we finally stumble over the fact that we're a bunch of fuck-ups, the most destructive species in the four and a half billion years of the existence of the planet. We finally bring down the house of cards."

"All that work for nothing," Dan said.

"You got it, buddy. Do some acid?"

"Sure."

"And let's have a party. I'm going to call some people."

Dan didn't try to talk him out of it; he knew it would be pointless. If Charlie was ever feeling too hemmed in by obligation, he would not be diverted from diversions. Dan later wished he *had* tried, for Charlie's sake.

It was a bit slow to start, but when the evening was really rolling, Dan wondered if Vnuk's and the Underground were both virtually empty; all of the regulars seemed to be at the Gates mansion. Partiers were spread throughout the house: in the kitchen, of course (no matter the circumstances, people will always party in the kitchen), seated around the huge dining room table, in the cavernous living room, where the tall French doors were open wide to the terraces, gardens, and the pool, which were crowded and loud with voices. Although he was fully and energetically tripping, Dan tried to keep people from going upstairs; he caught two people he knew, surrounded by a profusion of bedrooms, fucking in the upstairs hallway like dogs.

He snorted laughter and asked them to return downstairs when they were done. They agreed without interrupting their rhythm, and Dan simply walked past them. A girl with a green mohawk and safety pin ear rings was puking forcefully in one of the bathrooms, her pert ass wiggling invitingly in the air, a contradictory image. Dan would have held her hair back if it had been necessary; as it was, he merely asked her to clean up any mess that she might leave.

"Okay," she said, her voice reverberating in the porcelain echo chamber. She gave a brave thumbs-up, before vomiting again with a sound as if a bucket of corn niblets were being poured into the toilet from the top of a ladder.

Dan checked on Gigi's room, where he was pleased to find everything seemingly in place. It became one of those moments, when tripping, that he seemed to go through a door (in this case literally) into another chapter of the evening, even another reality, this one slow and contemplative. Turning on the lamp atop Gigi's desk by the window, he went back to the switch by the door and flicked off the overhead light. Outside the window came the sussurant sound of the crowd, punctuated, in a way in which the house itself would have seen as unfamiliar, with rowdy shouts and high-pitched shrieks and the occasional sound of breaking glass.

Dan remembered his first slackjawed impression of the place, remembered his irrational hope that Henry Gates would demonstrate some kind of decency, some ability to get things done, and would see to it that Dan would come to live here, see to it that Dan would be saved. Who could live in this place and not get things done?

It had not worked that way, though, and his grandfather had shaken himself out of his fossilized life and come to get him out of some kind of obligation. This possible life within the Gates of Gates had been erased, as was the real and ugly life that he had lived in Portview with Ingrid and Mike. He would never talk to *them* again, naturally. What he half planned for Mike didn't call for dialogue. Nor would he talk to Adriana or Darnell or Jorge, in their case out of simple embarrassment. That life was dead, as was his life on the river. He pulled a can of beer from one of the cargo pockets on his black fatigue pants, turning out Gigi's desk lamp. He sat watching out the window, unseen over the heads of the partiers on the terraces far below. He drank the beer, and another, thinking for awhile about his life, before realizing he was getting depressed. He decided to break out of this suspended animation and rejoin the living.

The girl with the green mohawk was curled up at the base of the toilet, gently snoring, and the two people who had been fucking like dogs were gone. As Dan emerged from the hall onto the balcony which Jim had once used to place the Christmas star atop the massive tree, stopping before coming into view. As he did, the Three Horsedicks of the Apocalypse came in through the front vestibule, casing the place with a wary air. An odd addition to their number was Jumpin' Irv. Jerry, Chris, and Jimmie had their usual mercenary look, as if they would appear more comfortable strapped with guns and explosives rather than merely being equipped with cases of Greysport Lager and two bottles of whiskey. Jumpin' Irv, with his customary janitorial panache, looked right at home with a large plastic bottle of vodka, a filterless cigarette in his yellowed fingers, more packs of butts in his shirt pockets. The fact that Irv was with the volatile trio didn't seem quite right to Dan, as if the Horsedicks had something predacious in mind. They seemed to be getting along well enough, though, at least for the moment. The four did not look up to see Dan, mostly concealed, on the landing.

Irv was not yet hammered, and spoke lucidly when he said, "Okay, what the fuck. I can see Professor Gates living in a place like this, but the notion that Charlie the Badass Gates grew up here is just weird."

"It's a trifle incongruous," Chris said.

"Charlie seems like he'd come from Cary or Portview or something," Jerry said.

Dan smiled; Charlie would have taken that as a compliment.

"Whatever," Jimmie said, walking out of view with a case of beer under his arm. "Let's get fucked up."

"Okay," Dan heard Jerry say before his voice trailed off, "but we don't bust anything up, and we fuck up anyone who does."

The four followed the sound of music, voices, and laughter. Dan gave them a few minutes before he went down the stairs.

The driveway was packed with a jumble of cars, with everything from an old Rambler spray-painted black and emblazoned with the circled A for Anarchy in drippy crimson on its hood and doors, to a Mercedes in front of the garage. The Horsedick's van was there, beige with a black lightning bolt on the front doors. More vehicles were on the street outside the gates, most of them not of the sort that one would normally see in White Birch Pointe, certainly not the type that would belong to anyone coming to a party hosted by Henry Bosworth Gates V. Dan wondered how long it would be before the cops showed up.

He looked around for Charlie, who was nowhere in evidence, not in the living room or out on the terrace, not in the kitchen, not in Dr. Gates's office. Dan was about to look for him in the poolroom or in one of the basements when he got sidetracked in the kitchen by a girl from the Underground who insisted that he join her for a shot of tequila and a line of blow. Dan felt as if he'd been too responsible in all his prowling around, and accepted cheerfully.

The simmering buzz from the acid was competing with that from tequila, beer, and whiskey, which was in turn kept at bay by more lines of coke. Dan was getting cuddly with the girl, an adorable, petite young woman named Amy, with bleach-blonde hair streaked with cherry red, which matched the lacquered red of her lips, the red getting smudged with repeated applications of her shotglass. She was laughing and leaning her head into Dan's shoulder, and Dan was thinking that Gigi probably wouldn't mind at all if he used her bedroom.

That was when someone came down the hallway from the front door, calling "Cops! Cops at the front door!"

There, Dan thought, nodding his head. With Charlie missing and himself as de facto second-in-command, Dan had no choice but to go to the front door and talk to the bored policemen of White Birch Pointe. He excused himself, telling Amy earnestly that he'd be right back. His fear was that the unchallenged cops were so bored that they might want to do more than issue a warning, and Dan thought that there must be at least some underage people here, not to mention a long list of illegal substances and weapons.

As he approached the front door, where the gold knocker was being diligently belabored, Charlie trotted up from the direction of the living room, looking clear-eyed and somehow refreshed. He slapped Dan on the back and said, "I'll take care of it!"

When Charlie walked through the vestibule to the large front doors, Dan was alarmed to see Charlie's .45 stuck, quite obviously, in the waistband of his pants at the small of his back. Charlie calmly opened to doors. Dan came up to stand behind his right shoulder. Two uniformed officers stood outside the door.

"Officers!" Charlie cried. "Hello! I'm sure you're here to talk to us about the noise, and I'll bet you'd like to see some ID just to make sure I belong here and am not some raiding Visigoth!"

Charlie reached into his back pocket for his wallet, touching the gun as he did so. He turned slightly and smiled charmingly at Dan before focusing the look on the cops.

"There *have* been a few calls," one of the cops said.

"Well, I'm Charlemagne Gates, as it says right there," Charlie said, handing over his driver's license. It was the first time Dan had heard him own up to the name. "And this house belongs to my father, Dr. Henry Gates."

It was another first: Charlie referring to his father with his name and title. Dan was surprised that Charlie didn't include his middle name and put The Fifth at the end of it for good measure. It was better than Charlie's more customary reaction of belligerence, especially with the .45 just feet away from the cops.

"We know Dr. Gates," said the first cop who spoke.

"If this is all too much of an annoyance to the neighbors," Charlie said, "I'll start to shut things down. It's just a bunch of college students, you know. I admit that we can get a little rowdy."

The cops seemed mollified, perhaps even taken aback, by Charlie's helpfulness.

"Okay," The first cop said. "That's great. We just wanted to stop by before things got out of hand."

"Maybe we should come in and take a look around," the other cop said.

"Oh. Jeez. Well, that's awkward," Charlie said, grimacing amiably.

"How so?" the second cop asked.

133

"You might not be able to tell from my appearance," Charlie said, "but I'm majoring in pre-law at GU, and if I let a couple of police officers, however well-intended, into my father's premises without his permission, or, more importantly, a warrant, I'd just never hear the end of it."

Dan recognized the look the cops exchanged. They were two working guys dealing with rich fucks. They did everything but roll their eyes. Dan admired their composure.

"Well, okay," the first cop said. "Try to get it under control, tone it down a bit."

"Certainly officers," Charlie said. "G'night!"

It seemed as though he was going to slam the door for a second, but he closed it gently as the cops walked down the steps and out to their cruiser. Charlie watched them through the peephole.

"Pre-law, huh?" Dan said as they walked back in to the party. "Is carrying a .45 a prerequisite?"

"Shoulda shot the motherfuckers," Charlie said.

"Why'd you have the gun in the first place?"

"I was playing glow-in-the-dark frisbee with some people down on the beach, and I thought it would be fun to shoot the frisbee. You know, in the dark."

Dan knew objection was pointless. "Sounds reasonable," he said.

The party degenerated from there. Dan missed part of the slide, taking the eager Amy up to Gigi's bedroom. He had just gotten her off when he realized that he would not be able to do so himself, and heard a commotion down by the pool. Dan left the suddenly drowsy Amy in bed, threw on his pants and boots and ran down to the terrace, the trip seeming to take forever.

Charlie was no longer so fresh, due to the speedy consumption of hard alcohol. He rarely got sloppy, in the manner of Jumpin' Irv, but he got a dead look in his eyes that Dan recognized, one that promised a disagreeable mood.

At the moment he was being belligerent with four young men, not from their circle, who had crashed the party and been found in the wine cellar by the Horsedicks. The latter had found the former (who looked like a hair band, wearing tight jeans, silk shirts, and leather jackets, one even sporting a lavender sash around his waist, a style considered unacceptably passe by the Vnuk's and Underground crowd), amidst several broken bottles. When interrupted by the timely appearance of the Horsedicks, the rockers had become indignant, which had annoyed the Horsedicks, as was evidenced by bruises, bloody noses, and a torn silk shirt or two. Pinioned by Charlie and the Horsedicks, they explained that they had been flummoxed to find no bottle opener in the midst of such plenty, and were experimenting with simply breaking off the tops of the bottles and pouring them carefully into plastic beer mugs so as not to swallow broken glass.

Dan was disappointed to have missed the fracas, and got filled in by Jimmie, who had one of the hair band boys in a painful wristlock. This young man was witless enough to say to Charlie, "What do *you* care, man? It's just some rich fuck's house, right?"

"It's my *dad's house*. It's *my* house, you asshole!" Charlie shouted. "Get them on their knees, guys."

The Horsedicks complied, with Dan's help. Music played in the background, ignored, as all the nearby partiers formed a circle and watched. That was when the .45 made its inevitable appearance.

Charlie had obviously learned something from his humiliation on the Night of the .45. He pulled the gun from his waistband and brandished it. Dan rolled his eyes. Charlie was merely being melodramatic, but, amusingly, people in the crowd gasped.

"This is my dad's house. It was my grandfather's house, my great-grandfather's house. We didn't get this place by being scrupulous. We've carted bodies out of here before."

Dan held one of the hair banders by the neck, and had to duck his head not to snort with laughter.

"So, you fucks come in here uninvited, and you disrespect *me*, you disrespect my *family*, and you fuck up my *house*?"

Muttered variations on apology followed from the rockers: "We didn't mean it, man," and "We're sorry," and "No disrespect, seriously."

Charlie crossed his muscular arms, rubbing the barrel of the gun against his cheekbone as if in contemplation. "What do you think I should do, Dan?"

"Only one thing *to* do, you ask me. Cap 'em. We'll dump 'em in the river before it gets light out."

"What do you guys think?" Charlie asked of the Horsedicks.

"Pop 'em," Jerry said.

"Ventilation time," Jimmie said.

"*I'll* do it," Chris said.

The quartet went into paroxysms of pleading. Charlie seemed to be weighing his options, listening both to the keening of the hair band and the muttering of the crowd.

"All right, all right, *all right!*" Charlie shouted. "I have a solution! Nobody has to get popped."

People in the crowd groaned, but the rockers looked up at Charlie, dewy-eyed with relief. The one with the lavender sash was actually crying.

Charlie said, "My solution, notable for its benevolence, is that you fucks are going to kowtow to my ancestors, kiss the ground at my feet, and vow to never do such a thing again."

There was a general babble of agreement among the hairy quartet, although one nudged another and muttered, "What does kowtow mean?"

Charlie heard this and gave instructions. The four did as they were told, then sat in kneeling positions. Charlie put the gun to their foreheads one by one, just as the ponytailed Outcast had done to him, saying, "Now, *never*...do *anything*...like *this*...*again*. You read me?"

The hair band boys almost literally fell over themselves apologizing and promising compliance.

"Okay," Charlie said finally. "Get 'em out of here. And not *through* the house. Around the side."

As the Horsedicks kicked and slapped the rockers around the side of the building, the crowd cheered. Someone handed Charlie a bottle of vodka, and he upended it, guzzling, while holding the .45 straight up in the air.

135

He shook his head like a bee-stung dog, belched, and handed the bottle to Dan, who also drank.

"Now those pussies have a good story, too," Charlie said.

"Share the wealth," Dan said.

"I'm getting groggy," Charlie said, then shouted, "Who's got some blow!"

The party thinned out in time, and in the small hours of the morning, most of the people left were quite drunk, even while bolstered by a variety of drugs. The driveway was mostly empty, the typical litter of a party scattered on the lawn. The carnage in the house was worse, but Dan was drunk enough to ignore it. He went around locking doors and making sure the place was at least safe, reeling a bit as he did.

He found Charlie, the Horsedicks, Jumpin' Irv and a half dozen others sitting or reclining on chairs around the pool. They were arguing, as young men might, about what it takes to be a man. The young women around seemed justifiably bored by the conversation, if not actually asleep.

"It's responsibility," Jumpin' Irv said, his words slurred as a result of his diligent drinking of vodka.

"Like you know what that is," Jerry said.

"Well, sure," Irv said, "I'm no glowing example, but I'm just young."

"You're just full of shit," Jimmie said.

"You've got to kill somebody," Chris said. "Real men have killed someone. Not just anyone. You don't go out and just blow off the head of some random person. But someone who's got it coming."

"Someone who needs it," Jerry added. "A child molester or a rapist or something. Then you've stood up."

Charlie was thinking about it, and said, "That's right. Seriously. Look at Dan's family. His grandfather was in World War One, and killed some freak after the war. Even though he did time for it. He stood up. And his father was in Korea, and who knows what kind of shit happened there. He was on the front lines, but never told anybody what happened."

"All right, now," Dan said. He noticed with a mix of emotions that the Horsedicks, Jumpin' Irv, and even a few of the drowsy young women, paid attention to what Charlie said.

"No, seriously," Charlie persisted.

"My dad was killed in an avoidable accident and my grandfather's just some boring hick, a loser. He has no fucking stories. We live right now."

"Ah, you just don't get it," Charlie said. "You don't even get your own family."

Dan hated it when Charlie was supercilious. "Fuck off. You don't get *yours*. You come from this and you fucking blow it."

Nobody talked to Charlie that way, not even Dan, and the Charlie's face said as much, taking on that dead-eyed look.

"Shut the fuck up," Charlie said slowly.

"Make me," Dan said back and walked closer to Charlie.

Apparently others felt the crackle.

"Guys, guys!" Jerry cried. "Easy! We're all friends here!"

"Be cool!" Chris said. "It's just the booze talking."

Dan ignored them, and so did Charlie.

"*Fuck* you," Charlie said, shoving Dan's shoulder.

"Fuck me? Fuck *you!*" Dan said, shoving Charlie harder.

Their old competition, from the first time Charlie had made a crack about Dan's dad and Dan had decked him, flared up, and they readied to go at each other. Dan's head was swimming with alcohol, and his vision tunneled down to Charlie's smug face. He wanted to kick it repeatedly.

Suddenly, Jumpin' Irv was between them, just as Charlie seemed to be going for the .45 in his waistband. Irv was blubbering, tears streaking his face. He got between them and pushed them apart, then stood there with his arms spread, palms outward, so drunk he could barely stand.

"Stop it!" Irv yelped, a bit of drool roping from his lower lip. "Just fucking stop it! You guys can't kill each other! You're…fuggin'…like my heroes or some shit! Knock it off! All this talk about killin'…ya wanna kill someone, kill me!"

Irv provided the distraction Dan needed, and he began to laugh. "Here we go," Dan said.

Charlie didn't laugh. Instead, he turned his dead focus from Dan to Jumpin' Irv. "You gonna start that shit again?" he said quietly.

"Fuggin'…damn skippy, man," Irv sniveled. "If you guys are gonna fight, just do it. Kill *me*. Use that fuggin' gun a yours. *Poozh*, right in my tormented fucking skull."

"You think I won't?" Charlie said. "You think I give a shit?"

"No! An' I don't give a fuck if you do!"

Charlie grabbed Irv by the front of the shirt with his left hand, producing the gun with the right. He pushed Irv back, holding the gun up in the air. Too drunk to walk backwards (or in any direction), Irv stumbled and fell to the ground close to the feet of the statue of Bacchus.

"You think I won't?" Charlie shouted over a chorus of pleading from the others. Dan moved closer to grab Charlie from behind.

"Do you think I won't! Tell me!"

Irv sprawled on the ground, whimpering. Charlie pointed the pistol at Irv for a second, Dan moved forward, and Charlie aimed at the head of Bacchus and fired. The granite head exploded, pieces scattering. The boom of the gun echoed off walls and down the terrace, the sound reverberating even after the clinking of the shell casing on stone. Then there was silence.

"See?" Charlie said reasonably. "I don't give a fuck."

He turned on his heel and walked into the pool room, the gun dangling from his hand. Most of those left exchanged wide-eyed looks, their mouths little O's.

"We better take this inside, in case the cops come back," Dan said.

The next afternoon, Dan woke up alone in Gigi's bed with poisonous hangover. He was relieved to find that Amy had left at some point, but couldn't remember when she had. He straightened up the bed and slipped out of the room. He was fairly sure that Charlie didn't know what had happened between him and Gigi and preferred to keep it that way, especially with the groggy sense of misgiving about the envenoms of the previous night.

137

Dan was drinking a glass of orange juice in the kitchen when Charlie wandered in his customary muddled and disheveled morning state. He looked around and shook his head with a fatalistic laugh. The carnage was everywhere. There were smashed bottles in the kitchen and remnants of food on the floor. Those who were merely polite had left beer, wine, and booze bottles on almost every available surface. It was like the chaos at the Kicking Pig, expanded into a much larger and more vulnerable space.

"What the fuck happened," Charlie asked.

"I'm not so sure," Dan said.

"Did you and I almost duke it out?"

"Maybe," Dan said.

"There was something about the .45."

"Oh, yeah."

They wandered from room to room laughing ruefully and cursing, bits of the night coming back to them.

To his credit, Charlie was immediately remorseful. Not so much about the damage to the house, which was extensive, but his drunken protectiveness of the place, his admission that this was where he was from.

"Don't worry," Dan said. "The whole thing with the .45 and those rockers solidifies your credibility."

"True," Charlie said, seeming cheered up by the thought. "That's a great story. What else happened?"

There were worse things than the cigarette butts ground out in witless places, roaches from joints crushed out on bookshelves and furniture, red wine and other liquids spilled on the carpet. They found an unflushed turd in Professor Gates's office bathroom; they laughed and howled as Charlie flushed the toilet with his toe. Someone had vomited inside the grand piano.

"Now that's going to be tough to clean out," Dan observed with a wrinkled nose.

The French doors to the terraces were wide open.

"I'm surprised seagulls didn't fly in here to find stuff to snack on," Charlie said.

All down the terrace was carnage. They looked out over it, shaking their heads.

"Maybe having a party wasn't such a great idea," Dan said.

Then they saw the headless Bacchus.

"Ohhhhh, *shit*!" Charlie said. He walked slowly down the steps and over to the decapitated statue, sitting at its feet. He picked up a chunk of the shattered head, a part which had an eye and the bridge of the nose.

He sat looking at the chunk for some time.

"I've got to get my shit together, man," Charlie said finally, hanging his head.

Dan sighed through his nose. "First we've got to try to clean this place up."

"Henry's going to disown me anyway. Let's just split. Henry can clean it up. Asshole."

"Henry won't clean it up," Dan said. "It'll be, like, Elpidia and Ng, or somebody else who never did anything to you."

Charlie squinted up at him. "Man, why do you always think of shit like that?"

Dan shrugged.

"We'd better have some coffee and breakfast first," Charlie said.

The cleanup took all afternoon and into the evening. The sun was going down when they were finished, having filled numerous garbage bags with the wreckage. Although the place didn't look too bad, there were some things which could not be concealed, cigarette burns, rings left on furniture from beer bottles, stains on the floor of the wine cellar where the rockers had broken bottles. Cleaning the vomit out of the grand piano was difficult and nauseating, and Dan wasn't even sure if the stench would ever go away. Again to his credit, Charlie had done most of the cleaning in that case, although Dan had helped out of solidarity, having done everything from cleaning up vomit in a bar to handling corpses.

The headless Bacchus was, of course, the worst part. As the sun went down, they sat exhaustedly in deck chairs, drinking bottles of beer and looking at the statue.

"Fuck," Charlie said.

"Gotta tell you, man. Sometimes you go too far just to make sure you've gone far enough."

"Got that shit straight."

They sat for a bit, contemplating the headless statue.

"I'm just realizing how much I liked that thing," Charlie said.

Dan said nothing, just took a pull off his beer.

Half an hour later, Charlie said, "I'm getting back in school."

It could have been interpreted as providence, but it was merely good timing that Willy called Dan just after the disastrous party and the decapitation of Bacchus.

Having avoided talking to his grandfather in so long, Dan spoke to him in what he thought to be measured and mature terms.

"Haven't heard from you in awhile," Willy said. "How are you doing?"

When Dan heard how weak and raspy his grandfather's voice sounded, he shut the thought down. In fact, it increased his contempt.

"Fine!" he said, keeping his tone the unfriendly side of neutral. "Got a job at the power plant, great place to live, you know."

Dan was certain about what his grandfather *didn't* say, that there was a power plant right up the river from McGregor Island, that he could be working there and taking over the bar at the same time. His grandfather didn't say that kids Dan knew without his talent were working there and doing just fine.

"Hey, that's great," Willy said. "But, you know, with your talent you should be…"

"Look," Dan said, sharply interrupting, "I get it, okay?"

There was a pause, and Willy said, "Sure. Just ask if you need any help. At all. And come home soon."

Home, Dan thought.

"I have to go to work," he lied.

When he hung up, he imagined Willy that very morning, out in his jonboat on the river before dawn, sitting and thinking as the avian wildlife slowly awoke, gradually adding each of their voices one by one to a crescendo, the ritual cacophony of dawn. There the old man sat, his hands clasped as the sky turned from slate to pink and orange. There he sat, no line in the water, no gun in his hand, just thinking.

Dan tried not to think about it, but the image came back to him throughout the day.

Charlie was a returning student, and had no trouble signing up for classes. Dan had already been accepted, back during his last stint on the river, and with Charlie's help was able to expedite the enrollment process.

Aside from art classes, Dan took things that looked interesting for breadth requirements. The process of looking through all the available choices was itself exciting, and it was hard to narrow down his choices; everything looked so interesting. Charlie suggested an Introduction to Philosophy class, and another in the History of Science. Dan also took Spanish, which he thought would be simple, what with his prior knowledge of the subject.

He went to bed early the night before his first day of classes, a rarity. It was strange to lie there in his messy room, mostly sober, trying to concentrate on reading by the lamp which he almost never used. The room was somewhere he usually just flopped down to crash out after partying.

His full schedule was a matter of some concern, having classes during the day and work at the power plant at night. With money he had saved, he had been able to pay his tuition in cash, so that was not a worry, but he wondered if he had waited too long, if he had somehow become stagnant. An unspoken part of his mind had the conviction that he needed to thwart what he imagined as Willy's negative prediction, that he had to go after his goal with vigor. Sleep didn't catch up with him until two in the morning.

To avoid the expense of parking his van, Dan took the bus to campus. It was strange to be up so early without some variety of hangover or afterbuzz. The campus was located on a bluff over the lake, north of downtown, and there was a fresh onshore breeze blowing under a clear sky. Some trees along the street, stressed by the fumes of traffic, were prematurely sporting autumn colors. Dan was one of the last off the bus, which had gotten steadily more crowded as it headed north. He got off and went to his first class, the location of which he had cased out several days earlier.

Dan did not look like a tyro (in fact, he caught one or two people giving him suspicious looks, as if he were there to steal something, or beat someone up), and felt protected by the fact, but there was a part of him that wanted to gape like a hick at the place. There was a vibe to the campus, an energy that he found... refreshing. The sidewalks between the buildings were crowded with students, all moving in a more or less organized manner between the many buildings spread out over several square miles. The architecture varied greatly, from stately brick and granite with actual ivy growing brightly on it, to more recent construction, the kind of project that had gone to the lowest bidder. Any imperfections were beside the point. Dan felt as if he were beginning something. The jaded part of him wanted, by habit, to sneer at this, but something stronger and more optimistic shoved it aside, and he allowed himself to feel hopeful and excited. This didn't change the bored and mildly threatening look that he kept on his face.

His first class was Intro to Philosophy. He strolled in with plenty of time before the bell, picking a seat in the back in a corner. As students trickled in, Dan watched them. Some looked young enough to be in high school, and Dan felt this sharply. Again he got a faint look or two, from a couple of girls with big hair and pastel clothes. He regarded them as they whispered together and sat down at the front of the classroom.

Dan was fingering the scar in his eyebrow when a kid came into the room who stood out a bit from the rest. Thin and of average height, he had curly red hair-ringlets, really- and huge green eyes, large, Dan thought, but not so big as to be outright weird, like some nocturnal primate. The kid wore black "slacks" (Dan noticed contemptuously) and, of all things, a purple silk shirt. To Dan's annoyance, the kid came straight back and sat next to him.

"Hey," the kid said, grinning with Bugs Bunny teeth and sitting down. "Philosophy, man! We're gonna be deep thinkers!"

Fuck, Dan thought.

"What are *you* doing in here?" the kid asked. "You get this mixed up with your parole office?"

Dan stared at him. The look which got an effective response from tough guys and ne'er-do-wells of every stripe (an unrecognized genetic gift from Willy) was apparently invisible to the kid.

"Tom Schwartz!" he said, extending a long-fingered hand.

Dan cleared his throat. "McGregor. Dan McGregor."

"Fuckin' punk hoodlums in my philosophy class! I *love* this shit! College is *great!*"

Dan sighed through his nose. He was about to tell the kid to fuck off when the professor came in, a small woman in an actual tweed jacket with curly hair and thick glasses.

"Hello, everyone!" she said sharply, immediately beginning to quell the hubbub of speech. "I'm Professor Steinmetz!"

The Schwartz kid knuckled Dan on the arm, to which Dan responded with an irritated "what the fuck?" look.

Schwartz was oblivious. "Great," he whispered of their professor. "Another Jew."

When Dan sat in his place after class, refusing to line up like cattle to leave, the Schwartz kid sat next to him.

"I see what you're doing," the kid said. "You're too cool to shuffle out. I'll just sit here with you."

Dan stared at the front of the room. A minute later, the kid said, "All right! Great! I'm heading out. Make like a baby and head out, right? Hah! See you later?"

"Guess so," Dan said.

"Okay!"

Dan waited a bit longer, just to make sure the kid was gone.

The History of Science class was in a gigantic lecture hall holding perhaps two hundred people. It was difficult to tell. The initial talk made Dan think that it would be interesting, if impersonal.

Spanish class was boring, and, he was alarmed to note, the art classes seemed boring as well. When he heard what they'd be covering in the latter, he wondered if he should even buy supplies; it was all subject matter that Charlie and Jim's Aunt Julia had covered with him when he was a kid. He wanted to comply with the program, but wasn't sure that he had the patience to sit through this basic shit. Densely bored within fifteen minutes, he took out a spiral notebook and a pen and

141

drew a caricature of the art teacher, who was a thin, middle-aged woman with frizzled black hair and ostentatiously goofy black glasses.

A purple-haired, zitty girl next to Dan glanced at the drawing, sighed sadly and said, "Fuck."

"What?" Dan said, used to the reaction and hiding the fact that he was pleased.

"My mom was right," the girl said. "I should go into nursing."

"Ah, come on," Dan said, touching her with his elbow.

Dan got on the bus after that first day of classes, getting off by the cathedral square where he parked his van. He went home first, tempted to take a shower, but sprawled out on the ratty couch for a bit. After forty-five minutes, he jerked awake. He dressed in a hurry, just short of panicky disorganization, grabbed his hardhat, ran down the alley and the side-alley to the cathedral square, and drove recklessly to the power plant.

"College boy!" Ramu said when Dan walked in.

"*Madarchod*!" Dan said, smiling. They were friends. Dan cracked his philosophy text, Ramu a book on mechanical engineering, and they studied together, the sounds of the power plant and its generators grinding and humming around them.

To class and to work. That became Dan's life, at least during the week.

The weekends were excluded from this pattern, as one might expect of a young person in his twenties. Dan was certainly the only one in any of his classes to show up with a deep cut on his lip (resulting, eventually, in a pale scar), or cut-up knuckles, or bruises on his arms. On Mondays he looked around, with sharply decreasing frequency, to see if there might be any classmate who had used a baseball bat to crack someone or bash out their car windows as they drove away in terror. There was no one he would suspect of ever having seen a corpse, let alone handling many of them. A few, just people he saw on campus, looked as if they might occasionally have come off an acid and tequila buzz on the beach as the sun came up over the lake, but they looked like posers and Dan didn't talk to them.

Charlie was indeed disowned by Henry, and even castigated by Jim, who stopped by on Saturday before going to dinner at his girlfriend Jenny's house.

"Dad is *pissed*, man," Jim said.

"Yeah, well." Charlie opened two beers, handed one to Jim.

"What the hell. And what happened to the Bacchus statue by the pool?"

"I kind of blew its head off with my .45."

Jim said nothing for five seconds. "What the hell'd you do *that* for?"

"That Jumpin' Irv dude was pissing me off," Charlie said.

"You should've blown *his* head off, then. Didn't he want you to before?"

Charlie bobbed his head and spread his hands. "I don't think his acquiescence would have flown in court. In retrospect, though, it seems that that might have been the better way to proceed."

"No shit. Way to go. Now Henry doesn't even want to *see* your ass. Great thinking."

Charlie was done placating. "Hey, back the fuck off. Who are you, *Mom*? Great role model. And she sucked anyway."

"You could've come to France and seen Gigi and stayed in Henry's good graces," Jim pointed out. "Now what are you going to do?"

"I'm going to work and go to school, doofus. Dan does it. Never hear him complain once about it. And his grandfather offered to *pay* for shit, too."

Dan, eavesdropping from his bedroom, felt a quick flash of pleasure.

"I don't need Henry and neither do you," Charlie said. "You should tell him to fuck off."

"There should be *some* benefit to coming from this fucked up family," Jim said. "I'll take what I can get."

"How noble of you."

When it sounded like things were getting too heated, Dan feigned obliviousness and wandered out of his room and stood between the two brothers.

"Now, boys," Dan said. "Can't we all just find common ground in a few beers and shots of whiskey?"

The brothers took him up on it, and they stood out on the fire escape looking out over the city, spread under a smoky sunset. The subject had been changed, and they talked about things of common interest, but Dan could see in the brothers' eyes that the tension between them had not gone away.

When Jim left, Charlie made a little fun of him for going to engage in wholesome activities, but then seemed to desist. After a few hours of frontloading, Dan and Charlie left to do things that were not wholesome at all.

Each day in September seemed long, yet the month slid by quickly. Dan was soon so used to his schedule that he wondered what he did before it.

His initial opinion of his classes was correct. The History of Science lecture was interesting, although impersonal. The art classes were grinding drudgery, as if Dan were forced, as a requirement, to practice tying his shoes over and over again. It was too late to change to a more stimulating class, and he needed the basic requirements for his degree at any rate. Dan stuck it out and never turned in anything but beautiful work. The professor recognized his talent and understood his plight, but could do nothing to help.

"Too bad you can't test out of this and move on," she said. "In my opinion, you should be in grad school. That's the system, though."

The most interesting class was philosophy. At the end of most classes, Dan walked away lost in thought. He often stayed behind and argued with Professor Steinmetz, an expert at rational argument, who quite obviously enjoyed tying students' minds in knots. The annoying Schwartz kid was often up there with him, making incisive points and getting lit up by the discussion. Steinmetz would cut them off when their time had run out, and they would walk out into the hall of the old building, exchanging a few words before going their separate ways. Schwartz often wanted to get together, but Dan claimed he was too busy.

Charlie was taking a general science curriculum, possibly aimed at pre-med. In spite of his scattershot approach in previous semesters, he had nonetheless been deft enough to drop the classes he had stopped attending due to diminished interest, and as a result had maintained an excellent grade point average.

"I should become a surgeon," he once said to Dan. "I bet a lot of sociopaths become surgeons. They can cut people and get well paid for it."

Dan didn't know if this was a joke or not, but gave a short laugh anyway.

143

"I'd be *Doctor* Gates," Charlie continued. "A *real* doctor. *That'd* piss Henry off. Put my little brother in his place, too."

Charlie managed not to quit his job, and was grateful to Dan for it. He saw the huge advantage of being able to study at work, and the boredom that awaited otherwise made the studying look attractive. This left them time after work to change clothes and go to Vnuk's or the Underground, where Charlie's reputation had grown after the night of the disastrous party.

When Professor Steinmetz began covering Determinism in Philosophy, Dan toiled through a grinding piece on Hard Determinism and found it to be irrefutable, and therefore debilitatingly depressing. Dan had, he was convinced, no free will; any thoughts to the contrary were an illusion. Reading this at the power plant on the Thursday night, the last night of his work week, he wandered out to his van after assuring Ramu that he would be all right.

He discussed it with Charlie, who took the book, flew through the reading, and understood immediately.

"Yet another thing to be cheerful about," Charlie said. "Everything matters even less than I thought it did yesterday. Isn't that liberating?"

Having hoped for Charlie to suggest a way out of the maze of depression he had entered, Dan snatched the book back and went to his room. Charlie called him out in awhile to do bongs and shots.

"Why not?" Dan said.

Dan was sure that Steinmetz had scheduled the reading so that the students who actually did it promptly would be able to shuffle around in a despondent malaise for the entire weekend. He ground through his Friday art class, feeling that if he stood up and walked out of the class, dropped it, and lived a few brief years as a wino in the empty warehouses by Portview, that it would never have been his choice in the first place, seeing as he had no free will.

After art class, relearning how to tie his shoes, he wandered in a daze to the student union. Everything that had happened since the Big Bang had led to the fact, in this tiny eddy of reality, that he wanted to drink beer, after all, and who was he to argue. He had no free will. I drink therefore I am, he thought.

The Rathskellar at the Union was straight from some Teutonic fever dream, down in the basement of a solid old building. It had heavy arches and smoke-yellowed walls with depictions of German gnomes up to no good, crappy paintings which were done by zealous students when his grandfather was his age, but which it would have been sacrilege to paint over. Heavy wooden tables were scattered under the arches, all carved with initials and crude artwork over the decades. It was a Friday afternoon, and the din was incredible, even for someone who was used to getting his ears blasted at Vnuk's. The air was layered with blue smoke, and some people smoked joints openly. Dan got himself a pitcher of beer and a soft pretzel and looked for a place to sit.

Occupying a small table was the Schwartz kid from Philosophy class. He, too, had a pitcher of beer (down to a couple of inches), and the remains of a soft pretzel. In front of him was a copy of the same text that Dan had been hunched over the night before. The kid had a tight look on his face, two vertical lines between his eyebrows.

He looked up from the text, stared off into space for a moment, and chugged down the better part of a mug of beer.

The kid looked about as despondent as Dan felt. When Dan was about to turn away, the kid snapped out of his trance and met Dan's eye. Schwartz's face lit up, and he pointed back and forth between their two pitchers of beer, then to the empty seat across the table from him. There was nowhere else to sit and Dan was ready to drink. He sighed to himself and gave a tepid smile before winding his way through the shifting crowd to sit down.

As Dan sat and poured a beer, the kid said, "Determinism, right? Am I right?"

Dan knocked back most of the beer. "It's been on my mind," he said.

"I could tell, man. I could tell. I said to myself, now there's a guy whose mind has been infected by thoughts of determinism. Fuck, I'm good!"

"You looked kind of depressed when I first saw you."

"Yeah," Schwartz said. "I'm depressed a lot. I see a therapist, the whole thing. Don't ask. Just kidding; you can ask. That's why I like diversions, anyway." He grinned rather evilly with his Bugs Bunny teeth and polished off his beer. "Speaking of that: smoke some weed?"

They bought pitcher after pitcher and smoked joint after joint. Tom Schwartz was not a big guy, and after awhile it occurred to Dan to be amazed at how much beer the kid could put away.

"You should see me with scotch or vodka," the kid said. "Come party at my parents' house. They're in Africa for the year, and wouldn't mind anyway."

They talked about Hard Determinism, the horrifying inescapability of the subject. Dan was as impressed by the kid's intellect as he was his ability to drink. He realized that a Friday night was slipping away from him, that he could be at Vnuk's or the Underground or the Red Lantern, but was having such a surprisingly good time discussing such a bleak topic that he simply put it off for another pitcher. And another. And a joint.

"At the moment," Schwartz said, "I'm feeling like an automaton, just going through the motions. Fortunately, I am an automaton which has been programmed to *drink*."

Dan laughed.

Schwartz said, "I told my therapist about you."

"Me?" Dan said. He was half offended, tempted to leave the table, but the kid was rolling up another joint of his really good weed. Furthermore, there was something in Dan that made him want to hear something good about himself, a fact he would never admit.

"Yeah," Schwartz said. "I told her about this guy who looked like he'd spent a lot of time in a prison weightroom but who was actually an *artist*, of all things…"

Praise made Dan uncomfortable, but Schwartz had just bought yet another pitcher, and lit up the joint as he began to talk. Dan disciplined himself to settle down a bit. He listened as the kid talked about his life, about his indulged childhood which quickly came to an end when he got into college and his parents immediately volunteered for an altruistic venture in Africa, leaving him keys to everything and a generous bank account.

Where do these people *come* from? Dan thought. First Charlie and Jim, now this.

It appeared that, once the Schwartz kid had gotten Dan's attention, he didn't much care whether Dan had anything to say or not. As the kid talked so openly about his fears and his self-loathing, his family history, the idea came to Dan that perhaps *he* had a fucked up background, that he himself had something to talk about. The Schwartz kid seemed to get some release from a sense of communion, though, and Dan, finding that he liked him, listened and nodded a lot. When he contemplated making such admissions himself, he could feel his brow knot up.

The Schwartz kid apparently noticed this. He pointed at Dan's head and said, "Determinism, right?"

"Yeah," Dan said. "What can you do?"

This struck Schwartz as hilarious, and he almost fell off his chair laughing.

Dan woke up on Schwartz's couch. The house was modern, sprawling, and horizontal, a prairie school place, airy and bright in the October morning. It took Dan a moment to get his bearings, then he realized that he had come back here with Tom to sample some of the rare booze that was kept around the place. Tom had also tried to turn him on to some jazz, which Dan attempted to enjoy when he realized that he liked the kid.

Padding around the comfortably messy house, Dan finally found the Schwartz kid snoring in direct sunlight in a large bedroom with floor-to-ceiling windows. After saying his name a few times, each one louder than the last, Dan realized he wasn't going to wake up. Gathering his few things, he went out to the driveway to find his van, remembering the blurry ride to the suburb Glenwood, north of White Birch Pointe and not so august.

It felt good to park the van at the cathedral square in the late morning light. The day was cool with a fresh scent coming onshore from the lake, and a few familiar winos hung out in the park. Dan walked through the alleys and up the fire escape to the apartment. He sighed when he came through the kitchen door. Maybe it was always like this: no home, just a succession of places where you lived.

Charlie got them temporary weekend jobs as security for professional wrestling. They wore their own black fatigue pants and kickboots, and were issued black t-shirts with SECURITY bluntly emblazoned on the back, with a smaller version over the left breast.

"This will be good for the freak show factor," Charlie pointed out.

Dan found that he liked the job as a warm-up for the activities later in the night. It was, he had to agree with Charlie, hilarious, and indeed excellent for the freak show factor. At one point, Dan and Charlie were ringside, watching both the match in the ring and the rowdy crowd. It was evident that what went on in the ring was rehearsed, that most of the wrestlers were in fact friends (they partied backstage after the matches), and that watching the crowd itself was the real entertainment. Dan was fairly certain he'd never seen such a collection of lowlifes, rednecks, and simpletons, ravening at the wrestlers, sometimes nearly apoplectic in their fervor.

The security supervisors were all off-duty cops, Dan was initially uneasy to note, who turned out to be older men with attitudes not unlike those of Dan and Charlie: they liked a bit of a dust-up, and always seemed to be in search of new stories. Dan's distrust of the cops lessened when they had to form a flying wedge to get a "heel" (Mortuary Mike McDonald, a wrestler who was currently a bad guy), out of the ring and to the locker room. Amid the roar of the crowd, under a fusillade of wax paper beer cups and other garbage, the off-duty detective in charge put Dan at the point of the wedge and Charlie to his right behind him, other officers and young thugs filling out the formation.

"Go, go, go!" the detective shouted, and they shouldered away from the ring and up the aisle through the surging crowd. An empty milk crate hurtled from a balcony above, just missing Charlie, who ducked, scowling up into the darkness.

"Fuck!" Mortuary Mike shouted, looking around with surprise and fear. "Being the heel sucks!"

They made it to a broad side passage, where Dan thought they were safe. Just yards away from the entrance to the locker room, though, a huge, beer-bellied man who looked like a trucker lunged toward them, his ferocity focused on Mortuary Mike.

"Take him out, take him out!" the detective yelled, and Dan body-checked the man into the concrete wall, where he banged his head and slid to the ground. Charlie kicked him for good measure.

"Atta boy!" the detective shouted.

Dan and Charlie looked at each other and grinned. He thought about the time he'd cut the psycho at the Bar of Paddy McX , and the reaction of the cop there. Maybe these guys weren't so bad.

"You fellas should become cops," the detective said once they were safely back in the locker room.

"Should become *wrestlers*," Mortuary Mike McDonald said, shaking his head and opening a beer.

Winter came on, and the end of the semester. Dan studied for his exams at the power plant; he and Ramu bent over their books, going through the routine they never had to discuss. The generators hummed and the hours passed. Dan was surprised when the third shift arrived to relieve them, looking at his watch and feeling as if he'd been awakened from a trance.

The art classes ended with a review of the work. There were exams in History of Science and in Philosophy, something simple in Spanish. Dan flew through the History of Science exam, the class having been so interesting that doing the required reading had not seemed obligatory. When he took the Philosophy exam, requiring essays in a blue book, he found himself in a zone of clear thought, and the writing poured out of him, his hand cramping as he struggled to get down the words fast enough to keep up with his mind.

That exam was his last, stuck at the tail end of the week on Friday. He and Schwartz had used all of the allotted time, and were the last two to put the blue books on the desk of Professor Steinmetz.

"I'm expecting good work from both of you," she said.

"Great class," Dan said. "Thanks."

The two went immediately to the Rathskellar to drink beer and smoke dope. Dan realized that the Schwartz kid had become his friend. He wondered how the gentle and friendly little guy would fit it with his thuggish group, but realized that he didn't care. Charlie and Jim had been his only consistent friends, Bobby Dolan being little more than filler in a barren time, and Jorge and Darnell part of a past that he'd rather forget. Tom Schwartz was, in effect, the first friend he had made in a time and place of his own choosing.

Tom, in turn, seemed to be overjoyed to have a friend like Dan. He talked about himself and his family again, the conversation a bit one-sided, but he was so amusing and intelligent about it that Dan just drank beer and lit another joint, the din of the Rathskellar roaring around them, *My Sharona* playing for the third time.

"My great-uncle," Schwartz was saying, "my dad's uncle, was a safe-cracker. They called 'em 'yeggs' in those days. Squinty the Yegg, they called him, although his real name was Benjamin Schulsberg. Did time for it and everything. You ever do time?"

"Surprisingly, no," Dan said, smiling.

"It'd suck to be in jail and infected with the idea of hard determinism," Tom said. "Then you'd be stripped of any *illusion* of free will you might have."

"No shit."

"Anyway, my great uncle Benjamin made a final score with my other great uncle Moishe the Kid- seriously, and he was a bad-ass- and they made some investments and started a couple of businesses. I think Benjamin was scared of his wife and had to go straight or something. Anyway, that was how my dad could afford to go to college, vet school, all that. That's why we've got a fair amount of money."

Tom waited for Dan to speak. When he didn't, Tom said, "You've got to have some stories in your family."

Dan shrugged. "Not much of a family, really. I'm pretty much on my own."

"Me, too. Parents off in Africa. Had a little brother, but he was born with some major birth defects and died as an infant. I don't even remember him."

"It's less complicated this way," Dan said.

"Yes! Right! And we can find solace in mind-altering substances!"

They clinked their beers together and lit another joint. The night ended again up in Glenwood. Tom was a musician, and showed Dan his numerous guitars, giving a detailed and often pointlessly digressive background on each one. Tom insisted on demonstrating his expertise, which turned out to be considerable. He plugged in a Fender guitar, rippling his long fingers expertly up and down, grinning at Dan with his big teeth. Dan couldn't help but laugh. Tom then moved on to demonstrate his prowess on the bass, popping and thumping away.

"You play anything?" Tom asked, setting the bass aside.

"A little piano," Dan said. "My grandmother played. She taught me a little."

"You never mentioned her," Tom said. "Where is she now?"

"Dead," Dan said. "Everybody's dead, pretty much."

The look in Tom's eyes was so stricken, so genuinely compassionate, that Dan wished he'd kept his mouth shut.

"Play some music I don't know," Dan said, slapping his knees and standing up.

The last thing Dan would remember was listening to Parliament, one of Tom's favorite bands, as loud as he could rack the stereo in the well-appointed basement of the house.

The next morning, Dan again woke fuzzily at Tom's house. After a few moments of consciousness, it seemed as though a heavy sense of dread and obligation were being pumped into his bloodstream. He slipped out of the house once more, driving

148

back downtown. Now that the semester was over, he knew that he had to deal with it, knew that he had to call Willy about the coming holidays, however much he had avoided thinking about it. He didn't want to hear the old man's wispy voice again, to hear the sound of the wind in it. He knew Willy's habits and schedule precisely, and called the bar when he was sure that Bob Two Bears would be there, but not his grandfather.

"I called the house and he didn't answer," he lied to Bob.

"Huh," Bob said. "Snowed here last night. He's probably shoveling or something."

"Must be it," Dan said. Oddly enough, it was good to talk to Bob. Dan filled him in on some of the more seemly points of his life, concentrating mostly on the college experience.

"I'm proud of you, kid," Bob said. Dan was surprised to find this instantly put a lump in his throat.

"Yeah, thanks," he said. "Anyway, tell the old man I can't get out of work. In fact, I have a part time job, too, so I won't actually have a day off." It felt bad to lie to the big man he'd known as long as he could remember, but it seemed that there was nothing else he could do.

"You should get out here pretty soon," Bob said. "Willy isn't getting any younger, you know. You should come out this summer."

"Yeah, I'll try. Just tell him I called."

Dan hung up. He drew a deep breath and sighed, his eyes wide, fixed on the phone. On the one hand, he felt despicable. On the other hand, he was off the hook, at least for the time being.

That night, a party developed at the Kicking Pig. Charlie had gotten a few kegs of beer from a customer at the Greysport Brewery, which they loaded into Dan's van from a side door of the plant.

"There'll be more of this," Charlie's customer said, punching him amiably on the arm.

They set up the kegs on the fire escape to keep them cool, although the weather was unseasonably mild and wouldn't get so cold as to freeze the keg's contents, which would get consumed fairly quickly in any event.

The usual crowd showed up, and the usual buzz accumulated to the usual music. Charlie went into a variation of his usual rant.

"We're dancing in the graveyard of our civilization, and it's our good fortune that at least we know it," Charlie said. "And, by the way, it's not the grassed-over graves, it's the open ones, the yawning, expectant cavities."

The distractions available to Dan often got in the way of his overall creative endeavors, that the tantalizing convenience of some new adventure (probably violent and dangerous, always exciting, and right there down the fire escape) usually presented stumbling blocks to his long term goals.

Tonight was different: creativity overrode diversion. Dan, his head roaring with beer, whiskey, and acid, loved the kind of bleak thought that Charlie was laying out, and took sudden inspiration from it. He had been smiling and laughing at what Charlie was saying, and then, Ding! there it was. In the midst of the party, tingling with the acid, he began pushing things away from the largest wall in the living room,

149

enlisting the aid of the Horsedicks to move books and shelves. He took down and set aside some of his older paintings, took milk crates and a board to make a platform. He stood on the platform and began to sketch on the wall, an outline taking up almost the whole surface.

Charlie laughed. "What's it going to be?"

"A mural," Dan said. "You'll see."

"Here we go," Charlie said. "Okay, folks, let's give the artist some room." He began herding partiers away from Dan's work area.

Liberated from the drudgery of the classroom, Dan was soon in the trance of creation. It would not be a meticulous work, being more impressionistic in style, and he worked quickly, putting down large blocks of color on top of the sketch. Over the hours, the skyline of Greysport emerged, not as it existed now, but what it might be like when the city was abandoned for a hundred years. Skyscrapers were rusted and glassless, grown with greenery. The Greysport Bank Tower, a familiar landmark, was not its usual white, but the brown of rust, the grey of exposed steel, the green of vines and other plant life which had obstinately taken hold. Birds circled in the air, making the place look like an aviary. Deer stood by the silver water of the harbor, watched at a distance by wolves hiding in the tall grass of what had once been a park.

Dan worked, oblivious to the people who looked on. Charlie and others brought him beers and shots, which he barely noticed but drank anyway. He was unaware when people moved on to other activities, and only realized that the apartment was empty shortly before dawn, when he noticed that the place was silent. He worked for another hour after that.

He was finished at the same time that Charlie came in through the kitchen door from the fire escape. "Holy shit," Charlie said, seeing what Dan had done. He put his arm around Dan's shoulder and shook his head admiringly.

Slipping off the frayed ends of the trip, Dan was exhausted but satisfied. They drank a beer and a shot apiece on the roof, not that either wanted to, but that it was ritual; they had to prove they were hardcore. After that, the two went to their respective rooms and threw themselves down to sleep.

Over the winter break, Dan found himself dividing his time between Charlie and Tom. It wasn't as if he and Charlie had any set routine; often Charlie was off with some sexual interest of the moment, or off to the bars, to come home late and sleep until just before his afternoon classes. With the long semester break, all bets were off, and Dan could never tell when Charlie might come home at all.

On their first Friday without classes, Tom came over to the Kicking Pig. Dan had had some trepidation about Charlie meeting his new friend, and was a bit relieved to find that Charlie wasn't home.

Dan had mentioned, once (in answer to a rather rare direct question from Tom), that he was studying art, but Tom had chattered obliviously over this bit of information, going off on a tangent about the kind of funk band he would like to start, which could have a part in the pornographic rock opera he was in the process of writing. Dan had smiled and listened to his friend, amused by his enthusiastic fantasies. He didn't talk much about art after that.

When Tom came into the disordered apartment, though, he had a different reaction. He smirked at first about the bottles and cans everywhere, seeming inspired and a little envious by the arena for partying, so different from his parents' large, lonely house. His eyebrows raised when he saw the hundreds of books. When he saw the mural, though, he stopped in his tracks.

"Holy shit!" he said. "Who did *that*?"

"I did," Dan said.

Tom looked at the painting, at Dan, back at the painting, back at Dan.

"*You* did?"

"Yeah."

Tom shook his head and whistled. He walked closer to the wall to investigate the brushstrokes, then backed up ten feet to get the overall effect, beer cans clanking on the floor behind his retreating heels.

"Wow," Tom said.

When he finally tore his eyes away from the big piece, he noticed the other artwork, everywhere on the walls. It took some time, and Dan could tell that Tom had spent hours in art museums.

Tom, atypically, was speechless. Finally, he was flipping through several canvasses which Dan had stacked carelessly in a corner.

"Well, shit." Tom said at last.

"What?"

Tom thought for a moment, and said, "First, I wouldn't think a big hulking lug like you would have any artistic talent at all. Then I wouldn't think that said lug would be so good."

Dan was pleased, but kept from smiling.

"I mean," Tom continued, "doesn't jibe. One look at you says you have a capacity for destruction."

"So, I've got a knack for art and for other stuff. Doesn't mean they're mutually exclusive."

"Guess not," Tom said. "Maybe I'm thinking stereotypically. And this is more than a knack."

While Tom returned his attention to some of the artwork, Dan went to the refrigerator and got two beers. He came back and handed one to Tom.

"You need a better environment to work in," Tom said. "This place has got to be too chaotic, as fun as it looks."

"Yeah, it can be."

"Look, we'll set you up at my place! Yeah! We've got studio space and everything!"

"Your parents won't mind?"

"They're gone for a year, man," Tom said, obviously getting excited about the idea. "Then they'll be home for a bit and gone for another. And they're big supporters of the arts anyway."

"You sure?"

"Yeah! It'll be great! I can practice my instruments and write my rock opera and you can paint! It'll be our own little artists' colony! Then we can get fucked up and philosophize!"

"Okay," Dan said. "Sounds good."

"Really? Excellent! We have to stock up on booze, though. I'll buy. My parents set me up with a fat account. You bring the hallucinogens."

"Can do," Dan said, laughing.

"This'll be great!" Tom cried. "This is the start of something big!"

Tom's enthusiasm was irresistible. It was also refreshing. Most of his other friends were too jaded to be ebullient about anything but partying, sex, and brawls, and here this kid wanted to start an artists' colony, of all things. Dan threw some clothing and a few books in his backpack, gathered his art supplies and his easel. He left a note for Charlie with Tom's address, and they took off.

If Sundays with Charlie were occasionally productive, his time at Tom's made it seem insignificant. Charlie was usually ready, after a few hours of reading, to badger Dan into leaving his work and go off in search of stories. Tom was different; in spite of his callowness (and having apparently forgotten his notions of determinism), he had something that Dan thought of as rare: hope for the future. It often occurred to Dan to pop the balloon of his optimism, but he admitted to himself that this was merely a habitual reaction to cheerfulness on his part, and that Tom was fine just the way he was.

The Schwartz's modern house in Glenwood was, in fact, set up with a studio towards the back to the house, with north-facing windows which opened up to a garden, now covered in two feet of snow. Tom's father was a talented amateur photographer, the walls covered with his work. His mother did beautiful work in ceramics, her pieces placed around the room on shelves and tables. Both had made valiant attempts at painting in watercolors and oils, and these, too, were in evidence. The room was sunny and peaceful.

"How's this?" Tom said.

Dan looked around and sighed, smiling. "Perfect," he said.

Dan set up, getting out a pile of sketches he'd been working on at the power plant. He had in mind a series of paintings which he would call Deformatorium, which dealt with mutated human faces and bodies in dim rooms, or outside institutional walls under the stars, gathered around a fire or under street lamps. The images gave him the shivers when he pictured them in his mind. When he tried to explain it to Tom, words were not sufficient, and he finally said, "You'll just have to see for yourself."

Tom left him alone, going off to the music room to work on ideas for his pornographic rock opera. At first, the quiet of the room was strange; Dan's ears almost roared with it. He realized that he rarely spent any time in places that were quiet; he was either at the power plant or in loud bars. At home, there was usually music cranked, whether it was being listened to or not. Even the rooms where he had his art classes had people talking and making other background noise, all of this over the hiss of a cheap radio. The only time he was anywhere silent was when he was at the beach by himself, and those moments were too rare, and not even this silent. For a second he thought about the quiet out on the river or in the woods, the hours of peace he had felt there, but shook the thought off. He stood for some time in the middle of the room, his mind seeming to spin like an unmeshed gear. Then he set up his equipment, and tentatively started in to work.

Who could say how long it took him to withdraw from distractions and sink into his own mind; it was not unlike falling asleep. Soon, though, he was in his trance, loving the scents of the linseed oil and turpentine, of the oils themselves, the sight and feel of the crimped tubes of paint and the brushes in his hands. Then he lost conscious thought to the instruments themselves, no longer contemplating the procedure, merely being it, living it. Part of him noticed that he could actually hear his brushstrokes on the canvas, it was that quiet. His focus tunneled down, excluding all but the work. Another part of him, far down beneath the thought of actual words, told him that if he did this long enough, he would find out the truth.

So entranced was he, and so habitual in the trance, that it did not occur to him to ask, *What truth?*

Outside the windows, there in the garden, the shadows of the trees moved blue across the snow, marking the hours unseen. Dan painted, hypnotized, chuckling occasionally at the demented vision moving from his mind, through his hands, onto the canvas.

When it got too dark to paint, Dan snapped out of it, blinking and looking around him. He went through the ritual of stopping, of tidying up, then wandered off through the house in search of Tom. He found him in the music room, sounding out notes on the piano and making notations on a pad of sheet music.

"Hah *hah*!" Tom cried. "The artist! How's it going?"

"Pretty good, I guess."

"Let's see what you got done," Tom said, grinning.

"You go ahead. I'm gonna stretch out on the couch here. My back is killing me."

Tom left the room and Dan flopped on the couch, groaning with relief. The dense muscles of his back and shoulders were knotted; he hadn't realized it until he'd surfaced from his trance.

Tom came back into the room at half the speed with which he'd left, shuffling in distractedly. He had a large whiskey in one hand, sipping from it, and another for Dan, which he set on the coffee table next to the couch.

"You are a freak, man," Tom said. "Freaky *good*. Disturbed, actually."

"I guess I do all right for a thug," Dan said, trying to make his friend smile.

Tom did not smile, though. "Thugs are a dime a dozen," he said. "You've got to be known for something better than that."

Something about this comment struck Dan as familiar, but he couldn't quite put his finger on it. He didn't worry about it. He decided to get drunk instead.

Finding himself in the right place at the right time, in the greatest creative flow he'd ever experienced, Dan decided to use some of the accumulated time off he had coming from work. Tom had suggested it, and lit up when Dan agreed.

"This is the beginning of something," Tom said, antsy with excitement. "Just you watch. You're going to be big. *I'm* going to be big. We'll eventually have to figure out a way to market you."

Dan blinked. "*Market* me?"

"Yeah. You know. So you can sell your work. Make a living at it."

Dan stared at him.

"What," Tom said, "you never thought of this before?"

"Can't say that I have."

Tom squinched his eyes shut and nodded quickly, tapping his temple. "Don't worry. I've got ideas. Lots of 'em. You just be your badass artist self."

They immediately fell into a routine of working in the afternoon and evening, then partying at night, on a low-key level that Dan found restful. It was such a pleasant change that Dan didn't feel he was missing much at Vnuk's or the Underground. If anything serious were to happen, Charlie would know where to find him.

Late Monday morning, he drove to campus and worked out hard at the gym, lifting weights, hitting the heavy bag, going for a swim. Tom, an incorrigible night owl, had been asleep when Dan had left, and was only starting in on a bowl of cereal when Dan returned.

"Man, you are huge," Tom said when Dan took of his flight jacket. "You should teach me how to work out."

And so Dan did. He thought it was the least he could do for Tom, who, he knew, had been pushed around once or twice in his life. Dan knew how that felt, of course, and thought for a moment about Mike Krapczak, his mother's husband. Now *there* was an unsolved problem, he thought. Tom would probably see it as an opportunity.

Tom had never worked any difficult or strenuous jobs, and aside from some downhill skiing, hadn't worked out much, either. Dan showed him the basics in the weight room, just enough to get started.

"You want to go slowly," he instructed his friend. "You build up too much lactic acid before your body is used to working out, and you'll be useless for a week. A disincentive like that stops a lot of people for good."

Tom appeared pleased at how much he could bench press until he saw Dan do it. Then he seemed taken aback.

"Man, you *are* a freak. On all kinds of levels."

Dan ignored this, saying, "You can do this. Takes time. You make a plan, then work the plan. Keep your ego out of it."

Tom's general cheerfulness could not be quelled, however, and he was in good spirits when they went to the locker room. They'd come in their gym clothes, putting their street clothes in lockers. They stripped down and went to the showers.

Dan had spent a lot of time in gyms, and, subsequently, in locker rooms. Fully heterosexual, it never occurred to him to check out the equipment of other males, although he would gladly have showered in the women's locker room (and hung out there, in fact) if such a thing were permitted. As it was, he showered up, simply ignoring those around him. He was doing just this, with Tom soaping up vigorously at the next shower, when an odd, wobbling motion in his peripheral vision caught his eye. Dan instinctively tracked on this motion, which led his eye to Tom's cock.

It was more than a matter of proportion. Yes, Tom was slim, and not a large young man. His cock, though, would have looked huge on a basketball player. Thick and heavy, it sprouted from his groin and hung almost to his knees. It was the flopping of this gargantuan tool that had caught Dan's eye.

"Jesus fucking Christ!" Dan shouted, the sound reverberant in the tiled shower. He clapped his hands over his eyes, then pulled them away, goggling in disbelief.

"What?" Tom said innocently, continuing to soap, his surprise appendage wobbling back and forth.

154

"What do you mean, 'what'? That's the biggest dick I've ever seen!"

Tom glanced down at his unit as if it were the most natural thing in the world. "Oh. Yeah. I hear that a lot."

"I mean, fuck!" Dan said. "And you call *me* a freak! Doesn't that thing give you a bad back or something?"

"Guess I'm used to it."

"You won't have to worry about working on your quads, lugging that trouser sturgeon around. You should do porno, man," Dan said, now trying to keep his gaze in an upward direction.

"Actually," Tom said, "it can be kind of a problem. Kept me from getting laid in high school."

"Trust me," Dan said, "that's not going to be a problem any longer. You need to hang out with older, sluttier chicks. I mean, damn. Makes me want to wash my eyes out with soap."

Dan did seven paintings in five days, all part of the Deformatorium series. At night, he and Tom listened to music and talked, played pool and darts in the recreation room. As Dan became more comfortable (and more drunk), he began to tell Tom about his life. The later it got at night, the more he spilled his guts. Tom was capable of endless chatter, but at times like these, he listened.

Dan told him about his father, how he had been killed in an accident and died out in the snow. He talked about how he was forgetting the way his father looked, or how his voice sounded, or how he laughed.

"His name was Gordon, Gordon McGregor. He was an artist, too," Dan said, keeping his face stony.

"Then you have a legacy to fulfill," Tom said.

Dan thought about this. "I don't even know what that *means*."

Tom began to explain, and Dan held up his hand. "I understand you. I just don't know if that concept has any meaning."

He told Tom about the poisonousness of his mother, about how his faded memories of his father were tainted even with that. He told about how he had lived with his grandparents after the death of his father, how they had nurtured him and made him feel as if he belonged. As he talked (and he never would have discussed this kind of thing with Charlie), some parts of his life became clearer in his understanding, in spite of the booze they had drunk and the dope they had smoked.

He told Tom about being ripped out of his home on the river, taken back to Portview with Mike. About how his grandmother had died and his grandfather had left him there. At that point he slowed down and stopped talking.

"It was bad?" Tom asked, his compassion real.

"Not so great, I guess," Dan said. "Somebody's always got it a lot worse."

"That's one way to look at it. I thought I had it bad until I started listening to you."

Dan snorted. "What's wrong with the life you've got?"

"I get lonely. Then I get depressed. Kind of start thinking black thoughts." Tom shrugged.

Dan visualized this thoughtful, intelligent kid wandering around the big house like a ghost, moaning softly to himself.

"Are you lonely now?" he asked.

"No, man," Tom said, smiling. "No, I'm not."

"Are you depressed?" Dan said in a loud voice.

"Fuck no!"

"Wanna do some shots and *bongs*?" Dan yelled.

"Yes!" Tom jumped up from his seat, fists in the air.

"Well, all right, then!"

After nearly a week of creative satiation, Dan thought it was time to take Tom to Vnuk's. He was unsure how his partners in crime there would react, but he didn't want to skulk around as if his friendship with Tom were something to be ashamed of. Nor did he feel as if he needed to try to perform the kind of make-over on Tom that Charlie had done on Dan himself. Dan had wanted to assume a new persona, to shed his life on the river, whereas Tom seemed content with his own *eclat*. Tom had a quiet style and polish that Dan knew he himself could never carry off, and the fact that Tom wore loose fitting slacks made a great deal more sense now. Furthermore, he was interested in different music, in jazz and funk. That was simply his style, regardless of what others might think. The fact that he would fit in at Vnuk's much less than Hugh did was annoying to Dan, making him think that much of the non-conformist ethos of his group was just another form of conformity.

They frontloaded before driving downtown, drinking whiskey and beer, doing a little speed for the boost. Tom seemed excited, sitting in the passenger seat of the black van. He was either oblivious to the fact that this place could be dangerous to anyone who went there, let alone to obvious outsiders, or he felt safe under Dan's protection. Either way, Dan wasn't sure he liked it. Dan parked by a bank of rotting grey snow across from the old bridge and they got out.

"This is so great!" Tom cried. "I always wanted to go somewhere like this!"

Oblivious, Dan decided. He was tempted to tell his friend to try to act cool, but he was amused by him at the same time. Let Tom be Tom.

Vnuk's was roaring along at full tilt, and Dan was pleased to see the Buggery Thugs onstage, knowing that Tom would be delighted by them. Dan lifted his chin in greeting to the bald lead singer with black greasepaint around his eyes, and the singer pointed at Dan, grinned evilly, and howled into the microphone.

"I'm gonna be deaf tomorrow!" Tom shouted. "This is great!"

Dan shouldered a path through the crowd for them. He ordered beers and shots at the bar, leaning forward to talk across the bartender's ear, giving him a joint. The bartender (whom Dan had met when on his first night at the bar) brought the drinks back, refusing payment from Dan, clapping his hand on Dan's forearm before looking after someone else.

It was impossible to carry on a conversation, so they stood by the bar and drank. The lead singer of the Thugs did a stage dive at the end of the set, but must have found a weak link in the crowded mosh pit, because one person collapsed, falling into others, precipitating the singer face first into the floor. Tom looked at Dan with astonished delight. The singer was immediately back on his feet, though, bleeding from smashed lips, grinning hugely, his teeth red. He jumped back onstage, grabbing the microphone.

"Thank you and good night!" he howled, droplets of blood flying from his lips.

Dan and Tom looked at each other and laughed.

"Now there's a showman!" Tom cried.

Dan knew for a fact that some kind of trouble was going to happen, but decided he couldn't just hover protectively over Tom. He was right, of course; he could almost have timed it on his watch. In the break while the next band set up, they tried to talk over the background roar of the bar, downing more beers and shots. Dan was again amazed by Tom's inhuman capacity to drink. He couldn't hold back the results of the liquid consumption forever, though.

"Where's the john?" Tom said finally.

Dan pointed back across the sea of spiked and dyed heads to the black hallway.

"Be right back!" Tom said cheerfully.

Dan remembered his first time here, with Charlie as his guide. Dan hadn't needed a bodyguard, but he was certain Tom did; he remembered how Tom had walked into the first day of philosophy class and set in immediately to giving Dan shit. A little brush with reality might do him good, Dan thought. He couldn't help but glance at his watch.

Sure enough, less than four minutes had passed before there was the unusual motion of a scuffle in the black hall. Tom was borne backward by a tall skinhead who Dan knew not by name but by his reputation for surliness that stood out even in a place like this.

The skinhead had Tom by his black silk shirt, holding him against the wall and shouting down into his face. The look on Tom's face was one of puzzlement rather than fear, as if he couldn't imagine what he might have said to create such a fuss. Dan could imagine quite well.

As Dan crossed the space between them, he could see that Tom was trying to argue rationally with the skinhead; by now, he knew that particular look on his friend's face. It was Tom's odd mixture of sophistication and innocence, perhaps, that made Dan feel protective, made his blood grow light and hot.

Dan didn't talk to the skinhead, didn't try to reason with him. He simply reached up and grabbed him by the shoulder, spinning him back against the black wall. The skinhead had time to blink once before Dan took him by the lapels and head-butted his nose. Dan could feel the crunch of cartilage through the crown of his forehead and jerked back before he could get more than a few drops of blood on himself. He pounded four mulekick blows to the skin's abdomen, then delivered a knee to the balls for good measure. The skin slid to the floor.

Tom stood looking down at the man with his mouth open, perhaps the beginning of a look of delight. The crowd closed around where the skin lay; a body on the floor was not an unusual occurrence.

"We should probably go," Dan said.

They retrieved their coats from the bar, making for the door as quickly as possible.

"That was excellent!" Tom shouted as the next band started up. "That was *so excellent!*"

Dan tried to act cool, tried not to laugh, but it was hard.

"Man, I always wanted to do something like that," Tom said as they climbed into the cold van.

"You don't want to do that," Dan said. "You're a good person."

"What does that make you?"

"A *maldito*," Dan said.

"A what?"

Dan ignored him and pulled away from the curb, checking in the reaview mirror to see if they were followed. The streets were empty because of the cold, though, and no one came out the door.

They were too jolted with adrenaline (not to mention speed and alcohol) to consider going back to Glenwood, so Dan took Tom to the Underground. They got lucky and found a parking space right under the marquee of the old theater.

"What are you parking here for?" Tom asked. "Isn't it a bit late for a movie?"

"How long have you lived in Greysport?"

"All my life."

"Well, you'll like this."

Going through the gold metal doors of the theater, they passed the locked doors to the theater itself and descended a wide staircase carpeted in plush red freckled with stains. The carpet stopped where the last step reached the gloomy bottom level, replaced by flooring of black linoleum. A labyrinth of halls split off, dimly lit. From one direction came to sound of bowling, from another the break of pool balls. Jukeboxes competed from one direction or another.

"Shit," Tom said, "it's like an underground town down here!"

Dan smiled and walked off. On a hunch, he went down the hall to the dart room.

As he had suspected, Dan found Charlie and the Horsedicks at a large round table in a back booth under a red glass tiffany lamp, Charlie's white-blonde spikes visible from across the bar. The table was littered with bottles and pitchers either empty or on their way there. A pretty young woman with a large black hairdo, heavy black mascara, and a tight t-shirt with a swastika on it sat next to Charlie, leaning towards him with one hand apparently stroking the inside of his thigh underneath the table.

Dan and Charlie hadn't seen each other in a week. They lifted their chins in bland salutation. The Horsedicks muttered greetings, making little effort to cover their obvious suspicions about Tom's appearance.

"Who's your girlfriend?" Dan asked Charlie.

"Megan," Charlie said. "Who's yours?"

No one laughed harder at this than Tom, who snapped his fingers and pointed at Charlie before introducing himself and holding his hand out to shake.

"Pleased to meet you, Charlie," Tom said. "Heard a lot about you."

"Huh," Charlie said. "I've heard next to nothing about you."

"That's Dan. He can be a taciturn fucker."

"That he can," Charlie said, as Jimmie said, "Oooh. *Taciturn*."

Dan was displeased but unsurprised at the group's reaction. Tom didn't appear to notice at all, simply introducing himself all around with a smile, and actually kissing Megan's hand.

"*Enchante*," he said. Megan ducked her head and smiled prettily.

"Love the swastika," Tom said with a charming smile. "Nice touch."

Knowing that Tom was Jewish and that his comment was sarcastic, Dan kept his face straight but snorted once with laughter.

Tom immediately told the table about how Dan dealt with the skinhead, exaggerating a little, making the story longer and more colorful. He either didn't know or didn't care about what his passive role in the story made him look like to this gathering of thugs. Unfailingly generous, though, he went off to get pitchers of beer and shots of whiskey.

"Where'd you find that little fuck?" Jerry said, starting in immediately.

"In the Rathskellar, after Philosophy class," Dan said.

"He's obviously handy when the shit goes down," Jerry said.

"Not everybody's a fighter," Dan said.

"Better be if he hangs around with us," Jimmie said, to a general grumble of approval.

"All right, knock that shit off," Dan said. "Tom's cool. Plays all kinds of instruments, and he's smart as a motherfucker. Can probably drink *you* under the table, you dumbfuck."

With that, he reached out and took Jimmie's beer from in front of him, drinking half of it off before setting it down. Jimmie smirked and nodded ruefully.

Charlie said nothing, just sat with his arm around Megan, regarding Dan impassively. Dan remembered the first time he had seen Charlie, sitting on his Aunt Julia's front porch with his brother Jim, reading comic books, the picture of jaded boredom. Bobby Dolan had approached him, and Charlie had sent him off with his tail between his legs, in a way that had lessened Dan's respect for Bobby ever since. He knew that the reason he'd become friends with Charlie at first was because he'd knocked him on his ass. Dan met Charlie's gaze, raising his eyebrows: *what are you going to do?*

Charlie, ignoring Megan nuzzling his ear, spread his hands and smiled.

Tom came back with tray of drinks, putting it in the middle of the table and handing shots out evenly. He then took all the empties, piled them on the tray, and took it back to the bar.

"You ought to be a bartender," Jerry said drily when Tom returned.

"I think I'm going to *own* a bar one day," Tom said, as if agreeing with the best notion he'd ever heard. "A whiskey bar!"

"Not a bad idea," Chris said, hoisting his shot in salute. He couldn't let things go on a positive note, though, and said, "Love your shirt."

"Thanks!" Tom said. "Silk. Want to feel it?"

"Nah, I'm good." He downed the shot.

"I like *your* look, by the way," Tom said.

Chris was wearing a variation of what Dan, Charlie, and the other Horsedicks had on, their usual uniform of some subfusc color of fatigue pants, a sleeveless t-shirt, most often black, frequently with a chaotic design of some sort. They all had nylon flight jackets (with an insulated hooded sweatshirt if the weather was cold enough), and they all wore some kind of heavy, treaded boots. In the bar, though, the coats were cast nearby, lots of muscular arms around the table. Tom's comment seemed earnest, though, so earnest that Dan couldn't tell if he were being made fun of along with the rest. He decided he didn't care.

Tom poured from the pitchers, keeping everybody's glass full. He yammered on obliviously while the tough guys exchanged puzzled glances. Dan watched, and Charlie remained silent.

"That reminds me of a joke," Tom said, talking fast from speed and booze and his usual state of excitement. "Guy goes into a diner, hearing they have the best chili ever. Says to the guy behind the counter, 'I'd like a bowl of your renowned chili.' Counter guy says, 'Sorry, but our last bowl went to that guy right there,' and points to another guy down the counter, who has a full bowl right in front of him. Second guy says to the first guy, 'I'm not going to eat this,' and slides it down the counter to the first guy. First guy says, 'You sure?' Second guy says, 'Yeah.' First guys sits down, starts eating the chili. When he's half way through the bowl, he finds a rat's ass in the chili. Leans over and goes, *blawwwp*," Tom mimed vomiting, "into the bowl, filling it back up to the top. Second guy says, 'Yeah, that's as far as I got, too.'"

It was the perfect joke for its audience. The table erupted in laughter; Megan emitted a high pitched squeal, Chris apparently had a hard time keeping from shooting beer through his nose. Even Charlie smiled broadly.

Dan had heard the joke; Tom had told it to him before, in almost the exact same way. For him, it was the second flash of his life on the river since he'd entered the Underground. He hadn't thought about it in years, but suddenly he remembered the time when he and Charlie and Jim had interrupted the hoods at the old hotel with a barrage of M-80s. He had later encountered the hoods in his grandfather's bar and was terrified, but had gotten in their good graces by telling a joke.

Tom was doing the same thing.

Dan smiled and clapped him on the shoulder.

They continued to drink, Tom taking on the role of the evening's entertainment. The Horsedicks seemed to accept him, and Megan clearly adored him. Only Charlie seemed unamused. At one point he managed to get a word in edgewise.

"So, you guys met in Philosophy," Charlie said.

"Yep," Tom said, still smiling along with the others' laughter after a joke he'd told.

"Have you read any Hiedegger?"

"Sure," Tom said.

What followed nearly amounted to an interrogation. Tom was able to hold his own even with Charlie, who was smarter than anyone Dan had ever known. At the same time, Tom matched Charlie beer for beer, shot for shot, in spite of being half Charlie's size. During a pause, Charlie stared narrowly at Tom, as if thinking he might just be acceptable after all.

Tom took this as an opportunity to get more drinks. Megan was almost passed out, and the Horsedicks were obviously drunk, Jimmie zoned out by the philosophy conversation, Jerry's head weaving, Chris's eyelids seemingly stuck at different apertures.

Except for Megan, they all roused when Tom returned, cheering his most recent purchase.

Tom raised a shotglass to Charlie, his expression a smiling plea for friendship.

"Tom," Charlie said, "in spite of my initial assessment, you seem to be a good guy."

"Thanks," Tom said, grinning. They clinked glasses, slopping a bit, and downed the shots.

"I still fear, though, that you wouldn't be much help when push comes to shove," Charlie said.

The grin on Tom's face diminished. Dan was suddenly infuriated. There was a twinge, a little wince of guilt, about his past failures at protecting the hapless.

"Hey!" Dan spat. "What did I say? Not everybody has to be a fucking fighter."

Charlie said, "Well, then, aside from being a good drinker, a fun guy, pretty smart, and, yeah, buying drinks, what does Tom bring to the table?"

"He's got...special powers," Dan said, first at a loss, then suddenly inspired. "Yeah. *Super* powers, even."

"Really? And what might those be?"

Dan nudged Tom and said, "Show 'em your super powers."

"What?" Tom said.

"You know," Dan said with a snort of laughter, a nod and glance at Tom's crotch. "Bring your *super powers* to the *table*."

"Oh!" Tom cried. "Oh, yeah!"

Tom stood up and pushed away some beer mugs and shot glasses on the wet table. Unzipping the long fly on his slacks, he reached in and fished out the entirety of his crank, which he then thumped onto the table with a splatter of spilled beer.

Megan came to. She stared for a second, her eyes shot wide open, and she screamed.

"Jeezizmotherfucking*christ*!" Jerry cried.

"Holy shit! Holy *shit*!" Jimmie backed up in the booth, his hands up.

"No fucking way!" Chris said, his brow furrowed, mouth agape. "There's just no *way*."

Tom stood at the table, his dick crossing a good portion of it. He leered, nodding, his tongue between his teeth, giving a double thumbs up.

Dan and Charlie fell on each other laughing.

"Super powers!" Charlie choked. "Man, you weren't kidding!"

Things only partially recovered to normal when Tom went to the effort of packing his meat away. Megan stared at him, wide-eyed, before saying, "I have to go find my friend Audrey. Audrey has to know about this."

After a question and answer period (everyone wondered what it was like to tote such a monster around), things quieted down and those left at the table began to realize how drunk they were.

Tom muttered in Dan's ear, "Think I should invite these guys back to my place?"

"No," Dan whispered. "Probably not a good idea."

They were just about to leave when Megan reappeared with a large, buxom woman with a dyed-red beehive hairdo by her side.

"Tom," Megan said, "This is Audrey."

"Pleased to meet you, Audrey," Tom said, with reflexive politeness.

"I hear you're a man of amazing gifts," Audrey said.

"Well, I..." Tom began.

161

Dan elbowed him, and could almost see the lightbulb come on over Tom's head.

"I…have some atypical qualities, I suppose."

Dan thought of trying to pick up a girl as the bar closed, but Tom's urgency to get home with Audrey was apparent. Dan drove the van while the two of them grappled in the back. When they got back to Glenwood, Tom almost ran with Audrey down the hall to his room.

"Thanks, buddy!" Tom called over his shoulder.

Dan went off to sleep in one of the guest rooms, horny, a little lonely, but satisfied.

Dan used up the last of his leave from work to party, telling himself that he deserved a break after the semester of work and school he'd just completed. The fact that the semester was only sixteen weeks long and he had used up a year's worth of vacation was something he ignored.

He found it difficult to evade responsibility entirely, though, and woke up at Tom's on Christmas day feeling almost nauseous with the guilty knowledge that he should call his grandfather. He found Tom in the kitchen that afternoon, and had a hard time pretending he wasn't gloomily preoccupied. He sat down silently at the kitchen counter.

Tom was cheerful about how the conditions of his life had improved. After his first night with Audrey (who, Dan was sure, was trying not to wince as she walked gingerly with Tom out to his car the next day), Tom had apparently seen a new world of possibility. She'd been over often since then, but had to work most nights as a bartender, giving the two young men time alone to follow their pursuits. Tom had become relentlessly cheerful.

"Gettin' some *stank* on my *hang*down, dawg!" he'd once said to Dan, sticking out his tongue and holding up the index-and-pinky-fingers devil's horns of rock. Dan had laughed, glad to have had something to do with it.

Where Dan's other friends would have ignored or not noticed his mood (which, it must be admitted, wouldn't look that different from habitual punk surliness anyway), Tom was often perceptive.

"What's the matter, man?" Tom asked Christmas afternoon. His tone of was one of genuine concern, and he handed Dan a glass of grapefruit juice.

"Nothing," Dan said.

Tom grinned. "Bullshit," he said.

Dan drank some grapefruit juice and remained silent.

"Let's see," Tom said. "It's Christmas Day, the inaccurately dated anniversary of the birth of the Christ Child."

Dan stared at him.

"It's a biggie for you goyim. A time of family get-togethers. Often dysfunctional, but family get-togethers nonetheless."

"I guess," Dan said.

"Now, it's easy to deduce that you're not going down to Portview to spend time with your dear mother and her loving husband…"

"Not without a gun."

"That'd be quite a holiday surprise," Tom said. "So, your only living relative, with whom your relationship is apparently 'complicated'"- Tom made air-quotes- "is your grandfather."

Dan remained silent, staring at his glass of juice.

"He's getting old, and it scares you—"

"I'm not scared of anything!"

"—and you make up excuses to avoid calling him, or seeing him…"

"Knock it off."

A few ticks of silence followed.

"You should call him," Tom said kindly.

"Knock it off, man! Seriously."

Tom opened his mouth, closed it again, nodded his head. He went and got two bananas, putting one on the counter in front of Dan, who left it where it was.

Tom left the room, coming back after awhile with the newspaper.

"You want a refill?' he asked, indicating Dan's glass.

"Only if it's got some vodka in it."

Tom smiled broadly. "Now you're talking."

A few hours later, when they had gotten a substantial buzz on, Tom offered to introduce Dan to a fine Jewish tradition: going out for Chinese food on Christmas.

"All the goyim are at home or something, doing their thing," Tom said. "They're sure as shit not in Chinese restaurants. It's great."

Regular Chinese food, at least the type most familiar to Americans, wasn't good enough for Tom, who insisted that they go out for dim sum, his treat. Tom put on clothes sharp enough to make Dan feel a little underdressed, but this abated when he realized he was too drunk to care.

Dim sum was a new thing to Dan, and Tom, who was so familiar with the restaurant that he was greeted at the door by name, guided Dan through the menu, finally ordering a good portion of it. Dan had the sense that Tom might be testing him a little, ordering items that might be a little off-putting to many people. Dan had eaten any number of strange things with his grandfather, Bob Two Bears, and Mr. Benitez, though, and was not to be dissuaded. They packed the food in, and left the place groaning.

When they got back to Tom's though, one glance at the telephone sent Dan back into his funk. His anxiety filled him so strongly that he excused himself and went to a back bathroom, trying to be quiet as he vomited his dim sum into the sink. He pushed the chunks down the drain past the stopper, rinsing the basin clean. He came back to where Tom was watching the television, certain that his friend had guessed everything, especially when Tom glanced meaningfully at the telephone.

Dan's mouth worked. He clenched his fists.

"I think I'm going to call my grampa," he said finally.

Tom smiled faintly. "Good man," he said. He poured Dan a whiskey before showing him into his father's study.

Playing the usual games of procrastination, Dan fiddled with things on Tom's father's desk. There were three cut crystal prisms intended to scatter light, a small yellowed skull with large fangs, which Dan couldn't figure out if it was real or a replica of a fossil. He acted to himself as if he was fascinated by these things until he blearily admitted his task.

Steeling himself, he took a blast of the whiskey. He breathed in and out rapidly like a woman delivering a baby. Picking up the phone, he dialed the number to the Eyrie, visualizing the electrical impulse sparking blue down the telephone line out across the plains and the hills and the woods to the dark nighttime river.

The phone rang and rang. Once he had dialed it, Dan grew drunkenly stubborn and refused to hang up.

Finally there was a click when the phone was picked up. There was a roar of sound, bar sound, laughter and clinking, loud voices. There was music in the background, which Dan recognized at the Ad Hoc Band.

Finally, a voice said, "Eyrie!" The person sounded young.

"May I speak to Willy McGregor," Dan said.

"What!"

Dan repeated himself, shouting.

"Just a second!" the young person said, and the sound became muffled.

A moment later, Bob answered. Dan knew his voice immediately. Dan knew he was too drunk; the sound of Bob's voice tore him with homesickness.

"I'm looking for my Grampa!" Dan shouted.

"Are you drunk?" Bob asked him, and Dan could tell he was smiling.

"Yeah!" Dan shouted back.

"You sound shitfaced, kid!"

"I am!"

"Call him at home," Bob said, laughing, and hung up.

This put Dan back in the same position. He sat with the phone in one hand, his finger depressing the hang-up button. He went through the same procedure: a blast of whiskey, a bit of hyperventilation. Finally, he punched the numbers into the phone.

It rang and rang and rang. Dan decided he would rather leave it off the hook on his end than hang up. He imagined Willy groping through the dark from the living room to the wall phone in the kitchen.

Finally there was a clatter. The voice was raspy and faint, but it was still his grandfather.

"Hello?"

"It's Dan."

There were five seconds of silence.

"Dan?" the old man said.

Dan swallowed. "Yeah," he said. "I was just calling to say Merry Christmas."

Another few seconds passed. "I was asleep," Willy said. "I was dreaming."

"Oh, I'm sorry," Dan said.

"No, no," Willy said, the wind in his voice. "I was dreaming about your grandmother…"

Dan interrupted. "I'm sorry I woke you up, Grampa," Dan said. "I'll call you tomorrow."

"No, wait," Willy said, but Dan hung up.

When he got up in the morning, it took half an hour for Dan to remember calling his grandfather. He had a vague recollection of the old man's tone. He felt sick for

164

having called at all, sick that he didn't talk for hours, that he didn't get in his van and drive to the river right that minute. He didn't tell the whole story to Tom, told only a tiny fraction of it, but Tom helped him quench these feelings with spicy Bloody Marys.

Dan misspent the rest of the holiday break, doing no artwork or anything else to prepare for the upcoming semester. He went back to work, partying every night afterwards, either with Tom or with Charlie and the regular crew. Taking Tom once more to Vnuk's (and keeping an eye out for a bruised skinhead), he still noticed a bit of a chill from Charlie towards Tom, although Charlie had been big enough to anoint Tom with the nickname Kickstand after the night at the Underground. The name stuck, and Tom was delighted.

Having to work on New Year's Eve, Dan nonetheless got out to the bars after midnight, powering down shots to make up for lost time. He ended up back at the Kicking Pig on New Year's day in bed with a young woman whose name he could not remember. He slept or feigned sleep until she left.

Tom introduced Dan to some of his own hangouts, which were considerably less boisterous (and populous) than Dan was accustomed to. They went to a jazz club, and Dan was bored out of his mind. He realized at one point that he wanted to start a fight at the bar with a man he didn't know but whose hat he didn't like, all because he was bored. He restrained himself, though, out of loyalty to his friend. He had much less problem listening to records by Parliament back at Tom's house.

Soon he had run out of time. Dan was familiar with the feeling of having to face the music. He gathered such things as he had at Tom's and drove back to Greysport, leaving Tom snoring, and Audrey snoring louder, in the sunlit bedroom. As he parked the van on the cathedral square, the thought crossed his mind that he had, at least, faced the music on his own terms. He went in to his ugly bedroom (*his* bedroom, though) and fell asleep.

The semester started again, and a new routine. There was less freshness to it this time, and Dan saw the grind that he had ahead of him, years until he finished. He got up every morning, though, taking the bus up to campus, taking it down to work after class. He and Ramu studied in the humming lobby of the power plant, and everything was much the same.

Dan and Tom had a class in medieval art together, Monday, Wednesday, and Friday, scheduling it for Friday afternoon so they could continue what was now their tradition of getting together at the Rathskellar after class. They frontloaded, and took it from there.

Charlie continued to be studious, still not speaking to most of his family members. Dan contemplated talking to him about it, but knew that Charlie would simply wave him off. Charlie also seemed to be cool on the subject of Dan's friendship with Tom, as if it represented (Dan conjectured) some kind of disloyalty, this where Charlie appeared to consider his own family members disloyal. They did professional wrestling gigs together, and worked the door at the Red Lantern on special occasions, always glad to have the free drinks.

Tom had a great deal of entrepreneurial ideas, always something new occurring to him as a possibility. He wanted to start a whiskey bar, as he had mentioned at the Underground, played occasionally with a half-assed jazz band, and wanted to start up a recording studio. He made chili which he was sure could be marketed on a national level.

"It's good, right?" Tom asked, after cooking up a large sample.

"Fuck, yeah," Dan said, although it might have been the margaritas informing him.

Seeing Dan's growing body of art not only increased Tom's belief in Dan's talent, but seemed to get the gears moving in his head.

"I should open an art gallery," he once said to Dan. "I could make you a star."

When Dan said nothing, Tom said, "Remember? Marketing?"

"Oh," Dan said. "Yeah. Sure."

This kind of thinking puzzled Dan; of the things he thought about or acted on in his life, business wasn't one of them. When Tom said something like this, Dan simply agreed, without giving it much thought.

In March, Dan had a surprising call late one Sunday morning. He wandered to the phone, which he was sure had been ringing for over two minutes. If Charlie was in his room, he had shown no signs of life.

It took Dan a few moments to recognize the caller's voice. At first, in his semi-conscious state, he thought the Latino accent on the other end was Perrito, the ponytailed owner of Dan and Charlie's favorite restaurant, the oppressor of their favorite bartender and caretaker, Kaye. Maybe something had happened to her. Then he got it.

"Mr. Benitez?"

"Yes, yes," Emilio said. "Are you awake now?"

"Not really," Dan said.

"*Los McGregor*," Emilio said, "*siempre la misma cosa.*"

Dan understood, but, in his fuzzy-headed state, said, "What?"

Emilio did not mince words. "Look. Idiota. You chood come back here. Your grandfather is getting older, and perhaps he isn't all that well. He says nothing to me, but he never did. All you pendejos don't talk enough."

"What?" Dan said, trying to swim up out of his residual buzz to engage in the conversation. "All what pendejos?" he asked.

"You!" Emilio said, and after all his years on the river, it still sounded like "Joo".

"Me?"

"Yes! And your father and your uncle...okay, maybe not Chief so much, but your father, yes. You and Willy certainly."

Dan tried to think. He wasn't sure if the conversation would make sense if he were, for some reason, alert.

"So, Mr. Benitez," he said, trying to get a pause in order to think, "What are you saying?"

"You chood come back here. You chood come home."

"This is my home," Dan said.

There was silence on the other end of the line. Finally, Emilio said, "We make our home, here or there. One is where we come from, one is where we live. Sometimes they are the same place."

"I guess," Dan said.

"This is where you come from."

"Okay."

"Your grandfather is where you come from."

Dan sighed. "Okay."

"So come home."

Dan felt some power when he said, "I'll see. I'll look into it."

"See that you do," Emilio said, immediately putting Dan back into the middle of the boat, sitting on soggy life preservers, with Emilio and his grandfather in the senior positions.

Emilio hung up.

"Fuck," Dan said, and went back to bed.

When he steeled himself to call out to the river (it was slightly easier this time), Willy said there was nothing wrong with him.

"Emilio always worries too much," Willy told Dan. "There's nothing wrong with me, and we McGregors are known for our longevity. I'll live long enough to annoy your kids."

"Really?" Dan said. Feeling that he was off the hook, he felt little risk in saying, "I could come out there if you need me."

"Well, come out soon, but not now. You're in the middle of the semester, right?"

"Yeah."

"And you've got a job."

Dan was about to say that he'd used up all his paid leave, but the fact that he'd spent none of it with Willy would look bad. He kept his mouth shut.

"Yep. Full time job." At least that was the truth.

"So just keep doing what you're doing," Willy said. "I'm proud of you."

Dan realized how hard he was breathing.

"And Dan?" Willy said.

"Yes?"

"I'm sorry that I couldn't come and get you sooner back then. It's just that--"

"It's okay," Dan said hastily.

"I'm just sorry for any bad things that--"

"Really! Grampa! It's all right. Don't worry about it." He went to change the subject: "You done any fishing yet?"

Willy paused before saying, "Dropped in a few lines with Emilio and Bob the other day, now that you mention it."

They talked banalities for a few minutes, the distance between them like a plain filled with dust storm. When they hung up, they did so politely.

Dan didn't know what to think about the conversation, so he tried not to think about it at all.

That night he had a dream (or perhaps just an unimpeded memory) of him playing The Claw with Willy when he was very little, when his father was still alive. The dream came to him just before he was fully awake, and echoed in his skull for days. He did drawings of it at the power plant, using charcoal, appropriately enough. He used the charcoal heavily, the only light spots being the gnarled hand of the adult, a partial glimpse of his face, and, mostly, the face of the child, who might either be in a state of extreme hilarity or in a similar reach of pain.

167

"These are beautiful, *madarchod*," Ramu said of the sketches. "Beautiful. What the fuck is wrong with you, my friend?"

"Fuck yourself," Dan smiled, already at work on another.

Tom's parents came home in April.

The buildup to their arrival sent Tom into a state of anxious frenzy. His parents had been gone for so long, leaving him to his own devices, that he had no idea of where to start to set the house to rights. He came to the conclusion that a massive cleaning was the only thing that would suffice.

Dan offered to help, which, Tom would fully admit, saved his ass. Dan had worked enough jobs that he knew *how* to work, unlike Tom. Being sent down to the Eyrie to clean up after drunks most weekends had given Dan both the knowledge and the stomach to clean what they found at the Schwartz household. Dan had mentioned to Tom his work at Feeney's, which certainly had strengthened his stomach. It was often necessary in this case.

They blew a Saturday doing it. Dan spent an hour on the piled dirty dishes alone. They bundled newspapers and magazines, gathered cans and bottles and outright trash, pizza boxes months old with vestigial cheese annealed like dried glue to the cardboard. In the end, they had several full bags of garbage, which they decided would be too conspicuous out on the curb, and took instead to a dumpster behind a nearby restaurant in the black van.

When they returned, they could see the dramatic change they had made on the house. It was neat and shiny, smelling of cleanser and wood polish.

"Amazing," Tom said. He was still nervous, looking around, inspecting things.

"My folks aren't home until tomorrow night," he said. Let's have a few drinkies. And then a few more."

"What are you so worried about?" Dan asked him. "Your parents are cool."

"They've just been gone so long," Tom said. "I don't want to disappoint them.

This kind of thinking was strange to Dan; he made a fricative sound with his lips. "How would you disappoint them? You're doing well in school, you run everything here, including the finances. Place looks great, no fire damage or anything. You're fine."

Tom's eyes looked almost haunted, and he shook his head in nervous denial.

"You're not Jewish," he said.

"Whatever *that* means," Dan said, downing half of his drink.

When his parents returned, Tom nearly went into seclusion. Even on a Friday after medieval history class, he begged off.

"Nah, man," Tom said. "Gotta spend time with the folks."

Dan shrugged, keeping his face blasé.

And so his friendship with Tom faded for the time being.

When he walked in to Vnuk's later that night, finding Charlie, the Horsedicks of the Apocalypse, and even an unusually cheerful Jumpin' Irv, he was welcomed back with howls of approval. He saw Candy at the bar, sporting a hairdo that faded orange from the roots to snow-white at its farthest extremities (not to mention matching orange nail polish), all of which went with her black vinyl miniskirt, white t-shirt, combat boots, and white skin.

Dan gave her a nod of appreciation, and she looked him up and down, smiling. He walked back to the boys at the table, thinking about the time in the museum and smiling.

"Candy!" Charlie shouted over the din at Dan.

Dan smiled.

"When did I ever steer you wrong?" Charlie yelled.

"Usually!" Dan bellowed back, and they both laughed.

Having become used to the more low-key style of partying he'd been doing with Tom, it felt good to be unbridled, good to be with friends where nothing he did would be considered outrageous, and could not itself be outdone. He downed a hit of speed with a huge jolt of tequila, chased with pint of beer down in one long gulp. Before the end of the night, Dan had stood on top of the table howling, his pants around his knees, Candy and a friend of hers laughing at the bar. Although most nights at Vnuk's were loud and wild, this got boring after awhile, and Dan was fortunate enough to have returned on the night where a crowd of black gangbangers from the west side shouldered through the front door looking for trouble, an intentional turf infraction, more young men looking for their stories. Their ouster was spirited though, Charlie and Dan fighting side by side, the Horsedicks howling like Cerberus split into three separate entities, yet fighting as one, as if they'd been trained for it. Jumpin' Irv was capable of distributing a good thumping, when jarred out of drunken despondency. At one point, he was swinging at one of the gangbangers with a leg he had torn from a barstool, which made Dan and Charlie look at each other and laugh, in spite of the chaos.

The invaders were eventually repelled, and the whole bar was cheering.

"See?" Charlie said. "You come back, and immediately something great happens. This is going to be legendary."

"Good thing those guys didn't come strapped," Dan said.

"Soon everyone will have guns," Charlie said. "Whole gang thing is gonna change. It'll go from beat-downs to shootings."

"Think so?"

"Inevitable. Can't wait."

"Too bad you didn't bring your .45."

Charlie snapped his fingers and shook his head mournfully. "Really. It's sitting uselessly at home in an oily rag in a drawer. Coulda capped me some annoying gangbangers."

Dan laughed, but Charlie merely smiled.

They partied until dawn then wandered home. Up on the roof, all the snow had melted, and they watched the sunrise together. It was good to be home, such as it was. At least it was his.

Dan was the first to wake up in the afternoon, shuffling groggily out into the living room. The painting he'd done on the wall, he had to admit, looked even better in the daylight. Charlie came out not long after and stood next to Dan, again shaking his head.

"Beautiful," he said. "That's my happy place."

"Let's go get something to eat," Dan said. "Then I've got something to show you."

After breakfast at Perrito's, Dan took Charlie to reveal his surprise.

"We'll need beer," he said. Charlie sprang for a case, and Dan drove them down to the abandoned warehouses by the port, the same ones in which he had found refuge as a boy. They went through Portview, the scent of the brewery strongest today, with a hint from the chocolate factory. Dan wondered what he'd do if he saw Mike. Just to see what the effect on him would be, he drove past 718 Pier. He wasn't surprised to note that he didn't feel much of anything.

"Isn't this where you used to live?" Charlie asked.

Dan nodded.

Charlie pressed his knuckles into Dan's arm. "Fuck 'em," he said.

Dan nodded again.

He drove out to the warehouse through rusty gates. It was a cool, foggy day, although the sun was bright overhead, making the fog luminous. The inside of the warehouse seemed unchanged except for some recent graffiti; the sturdy brick walls and their large, glassless arched windows looking out over the water.

""Wow," Charlie said. "This is great."

Dan flicked his eyebrows up once. "Come on," he said, "check this out."

They walked out through one of the large arches and onto the concrete pier.

The waves were rolling in past the breakwater, gulls crying over head. Across the water, the city was obscured by mist. No lights were visible, or any motion, only the dim shapes of buildings hulking in the gloom

"It's like we're the last survivors of a gigantic plague," Charlie said, making his voice theatrically ominous.

"I knew you'd get it," Dan said.

They sat with their backs against the damp brick wall of the warehouse, the case of beer between them, imagining their city in ruins, listening to the waves, wind, and gulls. It was a happy place for both of them.

"Why didn't you ever show me this before?" Charlie asked.

Dan shrugged. He realized he'd been avoiding memories. It all seemed fine now.

Nearing eighty, Willy still got up almost every morning and went to work. He certainly didn't need the money and had let Bob Two Bears in on a well-deserved partnership, so his own presence was more habitual than it was necessary. The pains in his abdomen were back, shanking through him at irregular intervals, but he ignored them as much as he could. Willy went through his routine and out the door, never giving serious thought to seeing his doctor at the Veteran's Administration. He carried on out of habit, like most people.

On alternate mornings, he hit the heavybag or lifted weights, both of them pathetic endeavors. He imagined convincing himself that getting old was all right, that is was the normal course of things. He was disgusted with his inability to fully protect those within his reach. Another of his waitresses had had yet another conflict with a boyfriend (how long had this gone back?), and he had intervened forcefully for what, he hoped, was the last time. The only thing he had left was his will, a stern gaze, and (to his mind) a specious reputation, although he hoped that no one else guessed that.

At night, home after the ritual and distraction of the bar, he had increasingly frequent dreams of Mae being in the room. He struggled to wake up, but was sure that she was there in the shadows, decorating a darkened Christmas tree, or playing the reverberant piano in the unlit room, her silhouette against the sheers over the front windows. When he was sure he was awake, the living room seemed little different from the dream.

Not all his dreams of Mae were dark; those were the ones he had when between sleep and wakefulness. When he was fully in the other world, it was often sunny, and he had a great sense of the weather. It might be winter, brittle, blazing and bright, or a summer day so hot that he could feel moisture on his skin even in the dream. Mae was not old, nor was Willy himself, and the boys were there, down by the river or off in the nearby woods, their shouts and laughter audible, their images broken by fluttering leaves or dazzling sunlight on the water. There they played, young and brown, and they soon would be coming home for dinner.

Willy gradually withdrew from his responsibilities at the bar, he went to sleep earlier and earlier, looking forward to what his dreams might reveal, what might take place in the nighttime netherworld. In one dream, he found himself with young Mae on a hill in a stand of autumn maples, overlooking a broad white beach at the edge of what might have been the ocean, or one of the Great Lakes. The blue waves sighed and boomed, gulls wheeled and cried overhead. Mae's eyes were the picture of delight.

"Come look," she whispered. She took him by the hand, leading him through the trees. Not far from the beach was a cabin with a tricycle and small bike in the front yard, a stand of pines on the other side of the cabin. A screen door of hunter green swung open with the squeak of a spring, and from the cabin emerged a man in jeans and a workshirt. At first Willy thought it was Gordon, but then realized it was Dan; he had both of his earlobes, but a white scar in one eyebrow. He was grown, broad-shouldered and filled out, his face stubbly with whiskers, some of them grey. He drank from a cup of coffee and stretched contentedly.

Mae watched, her pale hand on the leaves of a bush in front of her. She turned to Willy and said, smiling, "There. Isn't that nice?"

Willy woke up on the couch and sighed. The dream was the best part of his day.

On a Sunday morning in early spring, Willy faced the real day grimly. He'd already slept so much that he could sleep no more, and sighed as he got up off the couch to get dressed. He had coffee and read the newspaper, then shuffled aimlessly out onto the front lawn. The lilacs were in bloom, and he walked over to his favorite bush, the one with the deep purple blossoms. Taking a branch in his gnarled hand, he pulled it gently toward his face, slowly breathing in the magical scent, exhaling, then slowly breathing in again. It made him think about how Mae had played the piano on spring evenings when he had sat listening on the front porch, the scent of the blossoms from this very bush drifting to him on the faint breeze. The scent of lilacs, and of apple blossoms, so strongly reminded him of Mae that it was almost as if he were smelling her hair.

This gave him an inspiration. He made a sandwich, put it in a baggie and a paper bag, poured himself a thermos of coffee. Getting in his pickup, he drove through the town and over the bridge, going north along the river road. He took the turnoff to Mt. Pleasant and wound his way up into the hills through the grotto of growing springtime leaves.

Out on top of the hills, he drove along the ridgeline to the orchard where he had taken Mae on a picnic, back when the boys were still alive. They had made love under the blossoms after the picnic. If there were a heaven, Willy would have spent the mornings with the boys on the river (and with Dan there, a toddler), and with Mae in the afternoon in the orchard. If there were a heaven.

It was Spring in that country. The wind picked up and the temperature dropped sharply. Billowing pewter storm clouds, limned with pale gold, came down from the northwest, growing in the sky as Willy drove. When he came to the orchard where he had stopped with Mae so many years ago, he pulled off the road, parked and got out. As he walked through the grass and among the trees, the grey wind loosed pale blossoms to sweep and fall around him.

Finding what he thought was the tree where they had had their picnic, where they had made love that day, he sat down and put his back against the trunk. It got colder, and he unscrewed the cap of the thermos and poured himself a cup of coffee. He sat and watched out over the orchard, over the hills, their apple trees in bloom for miles. The sky became dark with storm clouds, and still he sat.

After some time, it began to snow. Large flakes drifted down from the leaden sky and mixed with the windborne white blossoms, just as the melting flakes on his face mixed with the trails of his tears.

They were patient tears, those. Yes, and they were patient.

Willy wondered how to extricate himself without drawing undue attention. After his welcome home party following his release from prison, he didn't want a commotion to be made about his leaving. Mae told him in a dream how he should proceed, leaning over his ear in the grey predawn light. She described what he should do, and when he woke up fully, he went in to the kitchen and wrote it down before he forgot, then sat drinking coffee and reading the paper, content with the plan. It mystified him that his subconscious would send him solutions to the

172

problems in his life using an image of Mae as the messenger, but the plans were so clear and practical- typical Mae- that he didn't question the source, but merely complied.

The full dreams of her were poignant, though, so colorful and real, that he didn't want to wake up when he found himself in that world. In one, it was springtime, and he was walking up to the little hotel near Omicron Falls where he and Mae had first made love. He was walking to the door of their room, and could clearly see the number 11 on the door. The door opened, and Mae was there, smiling.

He awoke, excited, and decided that it was time for a trip even before the first long needle of pain shot through his guts. Willy took care of all the details the way Mae would have wanted, the way she had told him to, although he would never admit it to anyone. He tried to call Dan, but the number had been disconnected. This troubled him for awhile; he would have liked to see him. In the end, though, he felt peace that Dan was on his path, and that Willy and Mae had done all they could to ensure that he would some day be happy. He thought about the clarity of the dream with Dan near the beach, and found that this gave him a surprising amount of peace.

He told Bob he was leaving, to be gone indefinitely. He hoped that his gradual fade from the bar would make the event less noticeable.

Bob Two Bears was still huge and solid, almost unchanged except for his white hair, back, as ever, in a ponytail. Bob watched Willy somberly when he laid out his spare plan.

"Omicron Falls?" Bob said, deadpan. "Nice place."

"Mae and I went there a lot when we were young."

"I know," Bob said, staring at Willy until Willy dropped his gaze, certain that Bob had guessed his mind.

Willy cleared his throat. "Well, you hold down the fort."

To his surprise, Bob embraced him, strongly, then held him at arms' length.

"I'll be seeing you, Boss," Bob said, his words slow and quiet.

"Not if I see you first."

Willy was almost out the front door when Bob said, "Give everyone my love."

He almost gave in to the instant temptation to turn around, but walked out the door instead, closing it quietly behind him. Turning away from the place where he had first seen Mae, he walked slowly down the street.

"I'm pretty sick," he told Emilio, sitting on his porch overlooking the river. It was his last stop before leaving town, and he was a bit relieved to see that Solveig was gone.

"What, the flu?" Emilio asked, playing dumb.

Willy gazed at him long enough for his old friend to know his mind: there should be no bullshit between them.

"Oh," Emilio said at last. He looked off across the fresh grass and the flowers Solveig had planted. Nodding once, Emilio hung his head and started to cry.

"Knock that shit off," Willy said.

"No," Emilio said, sobbing.

Willy sat motionless. He had no sadness for himself, but felt it greatly for his friend, his brother. He wanted to tell him to be happy, but knew his words would have no effect.

When Emilio settled down, Willy said. "Everything's in order. You have all the stuff, the instructions. Don't act like it wasn't coming. I'm just going to leave town. On a *vacation*, okay?"

"You're just going to sneak out of town?"

"I don't want a big hoo-ha about this. So, in answer to your question, yes."

They sat for a long time in silence on the solid old porch. Willy remembered when he had first come up the river and found Emilio here, at this very place.

After some time, Willy said, "All those years ago I came here to find you. Right?" Emilio nodded.

Willy watched him for a moment before saying, "You come and find me." Emilio raised his head.

"Okay," he said.

"Then get Dan. That might take some creativity on your part."

"Okay."

They sat longer, then stood at the railing, side by side, as they had done over the decades together, in boats, in woods, in bars. Around tables of Thanksgiving, at gravesites, at the births of their children. Emilio's tears were gone, and the two old men were content together in their silence.

Before he left, Willy gave Emilio all his papers, keys and instructions.

"And Dan?" Emilio asked.

"He's a going to be good man," Willy said. "He just doesn't know it yet."

"Seems to run in your family," Emilio said.

Willy snorted and shook his head.

They embraced. Emilio had always been more comfortable with this than Willy, but now Willy hugged him back hard, kissing the white wooly hair on his friend's head. Emilio's breath hitched once, jerking his body with the suppressed sob, and he held on a bit tighter. When Willy let his friend go, let his brother go, Emilio's eyes were clear.

Willy waved once as he pulled away; Emilio raised his hand in return, and the fact that he smiled while doing so was peace to Willy's heart. He drove off down the driveway and through the trees.

He did not pass by the bungalow once more. He did not go to the graveyard where so many he had known now rested, their lives becoming forgotten. He did not go past the bar, and certainly not the sagging hulk of the old hotel. To get to the bridge from MacDougal Island, he *did* pass the park on the river where he had married Mae, but there was new playground equipment there, and what he still thought of as the new boathouse. The largest and oldest of the oaks in the park, once strung with festive lights for their wedding, was now dead and marked with orange spraypaint by the county parks department for removal.

He drove slowly across the bridge and away from the town, the place of his many years. When an impatient driver behind him rode his bumper, he pulled over onto the gravel shoulder by the slough and motioned the driver past, but the man still gave him the finger and laid on the horn. Willy laughed.

Driving north along the river, he first took a little detour away from the river road and up into the hills, for no other reason than to see the miles of apple blossoms. It was a cool morning and had just rained, but the clouds had moved off to the

174

southeast, towering black and grey, with peach, yellow and white on their sunward sides, and now the leaves and blossoms of the apple trees were pointed with millions of drops of water reflecting the sunlight, sometimes in prisms. Willy sighed, content. If he had stayed, the growing sense of a coming journey would have oppressed him, but here he was on the road, in a place which he and Mae had loved. It was almost as if she were beside him, and he found, again and again, his hand reaching out to place upon her thigh.

The little hotel near Omicron Falls had been some hours to the north, and he knew it would be disappointing if it weren't still there. A shot of pain went through him and he pulled over when he saw a cut-out from the highway with a sign reading Scenic Overlook. He turned off the ignition as another ripple of pain shook him. Deciding that his stoicism (and therefore his sobriety) was pointless, he went through his duffel bag and got out a bottle of whiskey and a small plastic container of morphine tablets. He put some of the tablets on his tongue, swallowing them down with a bolt of bourbon, and waited for the effect. Before long, the sharp beauty of the day was slightly dulled, replaced by a glow, warm and amber. Mae wouldn't mind, he thought.

Realizing that he had spent nearly an hour looking out over the river, he turned the ignition and got under way. It seemed like he was driving through an amber gel, like honey, a thought which amused him. Soon he was used to the feeling, driving without impairment, warmly buzzed with the pain at bay.

The hotel by Omicron Falls was still there, and even seemed well-kept and freshly painted, with vivid flowers blooming in large pots by the front door, carefully tended bits of gardening put everywhere possible. It looked better than he remembered it, actually; a pleasant surprise.

The young woman who owned it was a round and sunny-faced former hippie named Sue Rebello- hair dyed dark purple- who came around to the front door of the office when Willy entered and pressed a buzzer on the desk. She had gardening gloves on and a trowel in her hand, of which she rid herself before signing Willy in.

"Staying long?" she asked cheerfully.

"Not sure," Willy said.

"Here on business?"

"Not really." His reflex was to keep his business to himself, but there was something about her openness, her aura of kindness (perhaps it was the morphine), that made Willy feel candid. "I came here a long time ago with my wife, to go to Omicron Falls. We were young and stupid. Kind of a corny thing to do, I guess."

"Where's your wife now?"

It still took him a moment to say it. "She died."

Sue Rebello's look was genuinely compassionate. "I'm sorry. And it's not corny. It's sweet."

"Could I have room eleven? That's where we stayed, if memory serves."

"Of course. We've only got two other guests at the moment. We get more on the weekends. A lot of them come here for the same reason you and your wife did."

He checked into the room, putting his lightly packed bag on the dresser. He had anticipated it so long, had visualized it so frequently in his mind, that he was unsurprised at how normal it felt to be standing in the place where he had first made love to Mae. The room was sunny, and, when he sat on the bed's snowy trapunto quilt, he smelled clean sheets, and knew that the young woman with purple hair had recently let fresh air into the room. The furniture was new, and certainly the bed, but the room itself was the same. Pain sliced his guts as he unwrapped a drinking glass, filling it from the tap and swallowing the cold water.

After he took a nap, he went out and got into his truck, in search of a place to eat. He thought he'd have a few drinks, get some sleep, wake up early and see the falls.

A bar a quarter mile down the road- a place boasting cheese steak sandwiches and "the Best Burgers on the River"- looked good, unpretentious, and even a little rough; his kind of place. He went in and sat at the bar, ordering a beer and a large whiskey. No one knew him here. He was just and old man, the power of his peak years diminished by time and distance. Here he was no fading local legend, just comfortably invisible.

He talked a bit with the bartender (who seemed to consciously ignore the tremor in Willy's hand), then watched the television over the bar. As the night went on, the place grew more crowded. Young women came in, chirpy and cheerful, oblivious to the presence of an old man. Willy thought about them naked, about himself young. The still habitual warning image of Mae came into his mind and he loved it.

He ordered a hamburger, but only ate a few bites. After awhile, he pushed it away.

"Don't like it?" the bartender asked.

"Nah, it's great. Upset stomach." He ordered another beer and whiskey. "That I can handle," he said.

When he realized how drunk he had gotten, he went to pay up, pulling a folded stack of bills from his jacket pocket, all hundreds.

"Shit," he said to the bartender. "Sorry. Can you change this?"

The bartender grimaced, sucking air through his teeth. "Boy, let me check the register."

Willy stopped him. "Forget about it," he said. "Keep the change."

"Serious?"

"Yeah."

"Thanks a lot. I mean, a whole lot. My daughter…" he stopped himself and said, "Come back tomorrow and I'll take care of you."

"That'll work," Willy said, and walked out the door.

Drunk enough that he debated walking back to the hotel, he stood weaving beside the pickup truck. The booze and the painkillers had lessened his discomfort enough that he felt no pain at all; on the other hand, the image of his driving into the side of the lovingly tended hotel was an unpleasant one. He liked the young Rebello woman, and didn't want to disappoint her. In the end, he left the truck parked, and wove back to his room.

Feeling bleary in the morning, we woke up to a stab of pain. After taking a red and messy shit, he showered and dressed, went and got the pickup. He found a small grocery store a short distance from the hotel and picked up things that would be easy to eat and soothing to his stomach, apples, bananas, the makings for peanut butter and jelly sandwiches, a half gallon of milk. He also got a styrofoam cooler, and brought all of it back to room 11, getting ice for the cooler from the machine in front of the hotel's office. With the bar and the grocery store, he realized he had everything he needed.

He drove up to the falls and was surprised at the accuracy of his own memory. Two rivers banked with pines came together and flowed into a cauldron of red granite, their streams colored copper from iron and pine needles, roaring in a mist which settled as the combined waters then made their way to the river, the Big River, the River Itself. It was hypnotically beautiful, and Willy tried to remember what was on his young mind when he had taken Mae here. He could only recall her delighted reaction, kissing her here, *right here*, overlooking the booming water and the mist. Sitting on a fence rail, he looked down at this scene until he lost track of time.

Finally, though, some biological need breaking his trance, he left, the boom and rush of the water receding behind him as he walked through the woods.

A few days passed in this manner, and he was as happy as he could be. He was unconcerned when there was more blood in his stools in the morning. He sat by the river and read in the afternoon, wrote a poem or two. He went to the bar in the evening, chatting with the bartender, leaving most of his cash in an envelope in the room addressed to the purple-haired Sue Rebello, just in case something happened while he was out.

On a Thursday morning, he was driving idly along the river south of the hotel when he saw a young woman hitchhiking at the side of the road. A little chubby, with spiky hair, wearing jeans and a leather jacket, there was something about her that reminded him of Mollie Sletto.

He pulled over. "Where are you headed?" he called out the window. She hurried and jumped into the cab.

Introducing herself as Sherry, she thanked Willy warmly for the ride. She came from a town three hours to the south, she said, and was quick to divulge in a matter-of-fact way that her parents had kicked her out of the house and that she was on her way to the two cities a ways to the north, there to live with friends and start a new life. She said she had no money, and her clothing and a small backpack appeared to be her only possessions. This didn't seem to bother her in the least; in fact, she seemed excited and hopeful about her prospects in the cities.

"They've got a great punk scene there," she said, chomping then popping her gum. "There isn't jack shit in the shithole I come from."

Sherry did nothing to embellish the story; she wasn't looking for Willy's sympathy, just candidly explaining her situation. Willy liked the fact that she looked like trouble. She made him think of Dan.

As they approached the hotel, Willy made a snap decision. He pulled into the parking lot and parked the truck.

"Maybe I can help you out," Willy said. "I know you could use some money."

Sherry looked at the hotel for a moment, then at Willy. "I don't think I'm up for this," she said. "I might be broke, but I'm not *that* broke."

"What? Oh, it's not like that at all. I'll let you have some money, and you can just have the pick-up."

She blinked. Once, twice. She popped her gum.

"What?" she said. "Are you kidding?"

"Nope. Take it."

"What's the catch?"

"No catch. Just take it." He took some out of the thick sheaf in his shirt pocket.

The girl blinked. "You *are* serious."

"Yep. I'll even sign the title over to you."

She got over her disbelief slowly, as Willy rifled through the glove compartment, moving his wallet and some maps and receipts to get the title. She was still in a state of disbelief, asking Willy again and again if he were kidding. Willy assured her that he was not, and got her to fill out her information on the paperwork. She was effusive with thanks, which Willy waved off.

"How are you getting home?"

Willy sighed and looked out the window. "My wife's coming to get me, her and the boys," he said. "Either that, or I'll meet 'em down at the river. Don't worry, you just go ahead."

She had tears in her eyes. "You're a good man," she said, and kissed him on the cheek.

He wasn't sure he agreed with what she said, but he could feel that the little kiss had made him blush.

It wasn't until he was back in the hotel room that he realized she had driven off with his wallet in the glove compartment.

"Ah," he said to himself, "Doesn't matter."

When the pain got bad, Willy took morphine with whiskey. It was the worst in the morning, when the morphine had had time to wear off as he slept and the sharp pain woke him up. At those times, he took the painkiller and simply waited for it to kick in, often drinking whiskey to dull the wait. He had plenty of the drug, though, and like many people given a choice about putting an end to their pain, he decided again and again to wait another day. He thought about Doc and Harriet Ambrose and how peaceful they had looked. He thought about Mae on the floor of the living room, then in the bed, when his body had betrayed him by living. In his dreams, though, in his dreams, there was Mae, young again and smiling, and there she would always be, there with the boys, in sunlight or in shadow, in the wind or in a stand of trees, always waiting by the river. So he would decide, again, to see one more day. When he was ready, he would find a still place in the river, take all the pills with a bottle of whiskey, and lie down at last in the waters.

He realized he had waited too long when he woke up very early Tuesday morning feeling as if his intestines had been sliced by a razor. He staggered into the bathroom and pulled down his pants, sitting frantically on the toilet. Blood fountained from him, splashing into the toilet. When he thought it was finished, it started again. And again.

Finally it seemed to be over. Dizzy, cold, his head roaring, he struggled up in a panic. Disoriented, he pulled up and fastened his pants. The river, the river, he thought; there to be with them. He staggered across the room, the roaring overcoming him. He stumbled and fell to the floor, rolling over on his back. "Mae?" he whispered.

And he had a vision, of Mae and Gordon and Chief waiting for him, smiling, welcoming. Little Dan was there, but not a part of it, holding up his hands, wait, wait. Willy knew, *knew*, the boy would be fine. It all was so completely real that his last logical thought was one of surrender, of acquiescence. And just before Willy toppled out of the back of his head, out into everything, his final emotion was one of gratitude. There was nothing he could do about this, it was beyond him to hold on. He released his grip on all that he ever had, let go in relief, and fell away, away from space, away from time.

We touch people in the swirling current, our fingers brush each other and we are swept apart, sometimes we thrash in the water and hold on in spite of the strength of the current. Sometimes the current is gentle and it's easy to hold on.

We are surrounded by missed connections, and by important connections barely made. Willy might never have corresponded with Emilio after the War, and the barely-made connection would have withered and drifted away, as would the version of his life that took place out on the river.

Some lifelong connections are next to meaningless, other than the fact that, in the end, all we have is each other. As Willy once said, most of the friendships that occupy our lives come about by simple proximity; we work the same job, we live in the same neighborhood. This while the most important connection in our lives might have walked right by us in the opposite direction, but only a block away.

And sometimes we are fortunate enough to know the connection when we find it. Willy knew it when he first saw Mae, and he clung to her, held on tight. And their *lives* happened.

Dan would think about it later, but wasn't really sure if he recognized the importance of the moment he met Kate Driver. She was certainly different, but his relationships with women were muddled and confusing, going from one night stands and anonymous couplings to something more important, but not important enough for him to really care about. If a young woman he'd met at Vnuk's or the Underground got angry enough to tell him that he obviously didn't care enough and that she was leaving, he would tell her that he didn't care, and she left.

Dan met Kate when he'd accompanied Charlie to troll for sorority girls at The Bar of Paddy McX near the end of the Spring semester; Charlie wanted to score once or twice more before all the "defilable nubiles" left for the summer. Dan wasn't averse to this pursuit, and often joined in, both of them playing the shocking and dangerous young tough guys. Charlie worked at the role, getting tables of girls to squeal at his antics; with Dan there, comfortable in the guise of sidekick. He was still known for the night he'd cut a man in defense of some young women at the bar, and was content to be his withdrawn self as Charlie, all eyes on him, became more and more outrageous and entertaining.

She was an animated young woman with strawberry blonde hair, short and curvy with the posture of a gymnast or figure skater, standing near the jukebox with a couple who were obviously her friends. With his Dark and Moody persona as a great excuse to wander off in his own head, Dan ignored Charlie and the girls at their table, finding his eyes drawn to Kate as she talked to her companions, her face lightening up or scowling in mock fury, as she shoved the arm of the young man who cuddled up with his girlfriend. When she piped that there was money left on the jukebox if anyone wanted to put on some tunes, Dan perked up. She wasn't his type, exactly, looking a little too clean and wholesome in deck shoes, beige shorts and a light blue linen top and black sweater, but Dan was drawn to her. He walked over to the jukebox and stood next to her. Even in the smoky bar, she smelled clean.

"You sure?" Dan said to her.

"Sure," she said, "although I know exactly what you're going to put on, so I might as well just punch the numbers for you."

Dan nearly laughed. "What am I going to put on?"

"The Ramones, the Clash, something like that."

"How about a compromise? I won't put on any Clash, and you don't put on any Captain and Tenille."

The young woman laughed. "Captain and Tenille. Wow. Harsh. How about some Talking Heads?"

"I love the Heads," Dan said. "You don't look like you'd be a Heads fan. You look like you just got back from sailing."

"I *did* just get back from sailing. You look like you just got out of prison."

Dan laughed out loud. He'd heard this kind of comment before, of course, but out of her mouth he somehow found the comment flattering.

"What does a Talking Heads fan look like, anyway?" she asked. "Do you have to look a certain way to appreciate genius?"

"Guess not. Did you really just get back from sailing?"

"Yes. Did you really just get out of prison?"

"No." Dan laughed again.

"You look like it."

"You said that. What, are you rich or something?"

She snorted disgustedly. "Fuck no. I just like sailing. You look like you might have been on a boat once or twice."

Dan wondered how she might have deduced this. His best boat story, he thought, was the one about Sam Feeney's boat on the sandbar, and he contemplated telling her about it. "Once or twice," was all he said.

"I can tell these things. Watch out. I can see right through you. Kate Driver," she said, holding out a neat, pale little hand. Dan introduced himself and shook it.

They chose tunes together, having similar tastes, not identical, but overlapping. Charlie was sitting at the table of sorority girls, and when Dan glanced over, Charlie beckoned him with a wave of his hand. Dan held up his index finger and returned his attention to Kate. Dan thought she might be cooler than she looked. He pulled in her fresh scent as they stood close to each other and made their selections.

She bought him a beer. He bought her one back. They sat down at a small table together, and she began to tell him about her life with boats, how it went back down through her family's history to Ireland, and a few centuries before that. She told him that her family had come to the state when her grandfather had washed up on Denfer Island in the infamous Winter Storm of 1913, the commercial vessel on which he was employed going to the bottom of the frigid lake, her grandfather one of the few survivors.

"He made it to the lighthouse on Denfer Island before he could die of hypothermia," Kate said. "Tough dude."

"Was he little, like you?" Dan asked, smiling.

"Nope," she said, "big hulking SOB like you."

"You should meet *my* grandfather," Dan said, the words out before he knew he was going to say them.

She must have seen the frivolity drain out of him. She waited for him to say something.

When he didn't, she went ahead and asked.

"Where is he now?"

181

Dan almost asked to change the subject, but found that he wanted to talk to her.

"He lives on the other side of the state, out on the river," he said.

"Are you close?"

"We used to be," Dan said.

"Tell me about him."

And before he could think twice about it, he did, at least to the best of his knowledge, and only what he thought to be the good things. Within those confinements, he told her everything he could think of, even about Sam Feeney's boat, a story which she found hilarious, much to Dan's relief. It was as if both of them had passed a test. It also surprised him that he would do a lot to make her laugh.

He talked himself hoarse. She bought more beer, and he bought more back.

At one point, Charlie, sufficiently motivated by curiosity to leave the table of girls, who craned their necks to follow what he did, then leaned forward to talk excitedly. Charlie came over and introduced himself gallantly. Dan found himself a bit jealous of Charlie's style.

"You must be talking Dan's ear off," Charlie said to Kate.

"He's talking *mine* off," Kate said.

Charlie did a doubletake. "Dan? *This* Dan? Dan *McGregor*?"

"Yep."

"Holy shit. Dan, did you sustain a head injury or something?"

"No new ones," Dan said, and Kate laughed.

Charlie leaned on the table, chatting charmingly, saying only supportive things about Dan, who felt a bit nervous about Charlie's interest. To Dan's relief Charlie knew when to leave, but brought them shots of Irish whisky first.

"That's your friend?" Kate asked.

"My best friend."

Kate nodded. "Maybe you didn't *just* get out of prison, but in three to five you *will* have."

Dan was stunned, flatlined. He could feel the look on his face for an instant before Kate said, laughing, "Close your mouth, it's just reality. He's charming as all hell, but he's big trouble."

"Okay, how do you know that?"

"My mom says I have x-ray vision. I told you: watch it, I can see right through you."

When Kate said she had to leave, stating it with brusque finality after doing a last shot, Dan fell back on the good manners that his grandmother and grandfather had taught him.

"May I escort you to your car?" he said.

"Why, certainly!"

On the misty street outside the bar, it was suddenly quiet. They walked side by side; Dan liked the fact that she only came up to his shoulder. He resolved to walk her to her car without putting a move on her, and recognized that this was nearly unprecedented.

"What are you doing tomorrow that's so important?" he asked. "It's just past midnight."

"I'm going sailing," she said.

"You said you just *were* sailing," Dan said.

"Well, yeah, but I love it. I pine for it all winter."

"Huh."

"It's great. It's like a religion for some people."

"Yeah?"

"Seriously. You should try it."

"I guess I do have a lot of boating in my family," he said.

"Come with me tomorrow," she said.

Dan stopped walking.

"Really?"

"Sure. Guy like you could be handy on a boat."

"Well, uh, okay."

She took a notepad from her small purse and wrote down her number, slapping it on Dan's chest with the palm of her hand.

"Call me if there's some catastrophe that will prevent you from coming," she said. "You know where the community sailing center is at the marina?"

"Sure."

"Meet me there at nine o'clock."

She's a pushy little shit, Dan thought, trying not to smile.

"You can smile if you want to," she said, grinning herself.

Dan laughed and shook his head. "See you tomorrow, I guess," he said.

"You guess? You'd *better* be there, buster, or I'll come looking for your ass."

Dan held out his hand, and she took it, just as she had at the jukebox. Dan put his left hand out and clasped her tiny hand in both of his. She pulled him closer and kissed him on the cheek.

"I wouldn't invite you if I didn't have a good feeling about you," she said. "It's the x-ray vision thing. You know."

Dan nearly opened his mouth to inform her that he was a *maldito*, but decided to keep it shut instead. She got in to a little gold Opal wagon, flashed a smile as she turned the ignition, and drove off into the night.

Dan's greatest surprise to himself was that he told Charlie his plans and went home early, drinking a great deal of cold water and taking aspirin before going to bed.

It was strange to get up early in the morning, feeling pretty good. Dan left the apartment while Charlie was still asleep, the door to his dark room open enough that Dan could see not only Charlie's feet hanging off the end of his mattress, but the pale feet of a woman who used black toenail polish. From this Dan deduced that Charlie had not scored at the Bar of Paddy McX, but had been successful at either Vnuk's or the Underground. He laughed quietly and left, going out the kitchen door and down the fire escape, through the alley to his van. The marina was north of the harbor and the museums, surrounded by sports fields that ran up to the beach, not far from where Greysport University sprawled on its bluff overlooking the vast water.

The morning was crisp, with a good wind from the south. Dan stopped to pick up coffee and pastries on the way, getting to the marina ten minutes early. The sailing center itself was a small building with an office, a general purpose hall, a locker room and showers. Dan and Charlie had prowled around it a few times before in the middle of the night, looking for targets of opportunity. Next to the main building was a boat yard with vessels in dry dock, some obviously being repaired or having their hulls refinished. Dan backed his van into a spot facing the entrance to the facility, so he could be watching when Kate drove in.

He waited to drink his coffee, hoping Kate would show up before it got cold. He heard a sharp whistle from behind him, though, and craned his neck around to see Kate coming out of the boatyard wearing yellow foul weather gear, which went well with her light red hair and blue eyes. If he were prone to painting such cheerful things, it might have made a good picture.

"You're even early!" Kate called as she walked in quick little steps across the parking lot.

"Brought something, too," Dan said, holding up the cardboard container.

"You are a god," she said smiling, her skyblue eyes bright in the morning sun.

They sat at a picnic table on the lawn, and talked a little, but were mostly quiet, watching the gulls and enjoying the cheese danish and coffee. Kate tilted her head back, her face to the sun, a little smile on her face. Dan found that he wanted to take her hand, but held back.

Done with their breakfast, Kate led him down to a slip where their boat for the morning waited. She told him about the boat: "Fifteen and a half feet, sloop-rigged with a spinnaker, displacement two hundred and sixty pounds, draft three feet two inches..."

Dan didn't listen too diligently, though; he mostly just watched her as she talked, pushing a loose strand of red hair out of her eye, squinting against the sun. It made him smile to watch her, back under his stony face.

"Want a slicker?" she asked him. "It's a bit choppy. Gonna be some spray out there."

"I'm cool," Dan said. She looked him up and down. He'd worn fatigue pants, a t-shirt, and a nylon bomber jacket, and knew enough to wear sneakers instead of his boots.

"I suppose a tough guy like you isn't about to wear a life jacket," she said.

"If the sea takes me, she takes me," Dan said in a pirate voice. She laughed. He liked it.

Kate was about to show him how to untie the bowline, but Dan flipped it off with ease. He hadn't been on a boat in a few years, but his legs adapted to the roll out of lifelong habit. They pushed off from the slip, and Kate showed him how to raise the sail, which, filled by the wind, went taut with a snap. The boat heeled over, and they leaned to windward against it.

It was beyond exhilarating. Dan had a feeling in his chest, almost like the lightness he felt before a fight, but instead of fury, it was...what? Joy, perhaps. Maybe this is what joy feels like.

There was a small chop in the harbor, but when they slipped past the concrete end of the breakwater and were out on the rolling waves, the little boat seemed to hit its stride. Dan followed any instructions that Kate gave him, watching her as she sat confidently at the tiller, squinting up at the sail or out at the horizon. The whole experience, the sight of her, the sound of the boat as it thumped through the waves, the feel of its roll, of the cold spray, of the sun, the life-giving scent of the water, all of it made him grin so hard that he got cramps in his cheeks. They looked at each other and laughed.

"What do you think?" she piped.

"It's…" he started. He thought about it.

"It's what?" she called.

"It's majestic!"

"Yeah!" she said. "Majestic!"

They sailed for two hours. She showed him how to tack and jibe, talked to him about right-of-way. Again, he was only half-listening.

When they got back into the harbor and tied up at the marina, they were chilly and damp and happy. Kate changed clothes in the locker room, coming out in jeans, sneakers, and a black cotton sweater.

Dan took her to lunch at Perrito's, where the everpresent Kaye wrote an order for Dan's "usual" without having to ask: a Greysport Lager and a plate lunch, which consisted of refried beans and rice and a kind of beef stew with potatoes and green beans, all forked into hot, fresh tortillas and topped with copious hot sauce.

Kaye waited for Kate's order, and Dan said, "If I were to be sentenced to execution by firing squad and given the choice of a last meal, this would be it."

"How can I argue with that?" Kate said. "I'll have the same."

Kaye smiled and brought them two Greysports, giving Dan a look which said that she liked the young woman.

Kate loved the food and ate with gusto. When they were done eating, they sat at the bar, and this time Kate did most of the talking, which she did with humor and speed, pausing to take sips from her beer.

Her father, who was "a bastard" (Kate's words), had been a plant manager in a factory in Cary. Her parents had gotten married young, when Kate's mom had thought that her future husband was "the most exciting man" she had ever met. The Old Man was psychologically abusive to everyone, Kate's mother and three sisters, but appeared to draw the line at physical abuse to women. In traffic or out at a bar, however, he was perfectly willing to pick a fight if the other man was noticeably weaker or smaller.

The Old Man was bitter and angry at having ended up married with children, like many men of that generation. They were an impediment to his life, ungrateful, disrespectful brats. He had four lovely children and a fine wife, but was too poisoned in his own mind to see the happiness he had right at his fingertips.

"A small town hick at heart," again Kate's words, he'd acted like an asshole for years and expected everyone under his supervision at work to back down, but finally found out that the city guys meant what they said, that their threats were not idle. He'd eventually pissed someone off enough that he'd been savagely beaten in the parking lot of the plant and taken to the hospital in a coma. There had been no witnesses, and no one spoke up. After Kate's mother made the decision to take the Old Man off life support two weeks later, none of the members of her family were terribly sad. In fact, it was as if a pall had been lifted. When they'd gone to Kate's mother's family cabin on Denfer Island after his burial, they had said it had been for recuperation, but it had, in fact, been a celebration. The mother and all three sisters

185

soon changed their last name from Trompeter to the mother's maiden name of Driver.

"Do you think I'm terrible?" Kate asked Dan.

"You wouldn't ask me that if you ever met my mother and step-father," Dan said, and gave a brief explanation of that part of his story.

"I'm just not sure my step-father is worth going to prison for," Dan summed up.

"Just don't get caught, dummy," Kate said, smiling.

Dan laughed and shook his head in wonder. "You are a deceptively tough little shit, you know that?"

"Yep," she said.

She told Dan about her favorite place in the world, the family cabin on Denfer Island, which was a few hundred miles north of Greysport, off the tip of the peninsula that thrust out into the inland sea of the great lake like a thumb, accessible by ferry. Her story of it captured Dan's imagination immediately. The place was stratified with spooky legends. The oldest went back to a conflict between warring tribes of Indians (one of them the tribe from which Bob Two Bears and Faith-in-Full Goodforks sprang), a belligerent tribe crossing the treacherous straits to invade the island occupied by their more peaceful neighbors. The shaman of the peaceful tribe placed a curse upon the invaders, and, according to legend, a gale blew up as the attackers crossed the straits, sinking all of their canoes, drowning them all.

When the French occupied the area, more and more shipwrecks happened on the shifting shoals of sand around the island. The French named the strait Port d'Enfer, or Door to Hell. When the British, in turn, had occupied the island, this was anglicized to Port Denfer, which was then applied to small, safe harbor on the east side of the roughly horse-shoe shaped island.

Kate's grandfather came to the island with the famous Wreck of the Gullion Pinther during the proportionately legendary Storm of 1913. The Pinther was a commercial freighter which had foundered during the famous winter norther which had sunk ships all over the western Great Lakes, the frozen bodies of men washing up on shore for some time afterwards. Michael Driver had been an officer on the freighter, and had made it to the island on a dinghy after being pulled from the frigid waters by remaining members of the crew (others having been lost in the black depths), taken to the lighthouse and saved from hypothermia by being put into a large clawfoot bathtub.

In spite of the island's ominous history, he found it to be a beautiful place, perfect for planting apple and cherry trees in orchards among the hills clad with maple, oak, and pine. There he had made a home, having only one child, Kate's mother, before his wife had died. A simple, two story building with a friendly kitchen and a spacious porch, protected from with winds off the stormy lake by a stand of giant pine, it was the family retreat, the place of their holidays.

"You'd like it," Kate said. "I'm going to live there."

She was studying to be a teacher, and her plan was to finish school and pursue her profession on Denfer Island, making her home in the old cabin, where neither her mother nor her three older sisters were interested in living full time. She was getting her training in teaching grade school, with an additional emphasis in art education. Her interest in, and knowledge of, art itself was impressive, and Dan wondered if

186

he'd ever seen her in the halls of the art museum and not taken note. He was too embarrassed to mention in any detail that he was studying art, saying simply that he wasn't quite sure about his major. Indeed he felt that way, subjected as he was to the tedious spate of boring requirements necessary to the completion of the degree.

They went to the art museum together that afternoon, walking through the hushed marble halls, standing close to each other but not even going so far as to hold hands. It was unusual for Dan to be able to discuss the works in front of them in such a fulfilling manner; it seemed that she was as surprised by his knowledge as he was by hers. As she talked about a particular piece, his gaze drifted from the painting to her animated face. It made him smile to watch her talk.

They left the museum as the sun went down, and walked slowly in a maze of blooming lilacs on the grounds next to the museum. The lilac blossoms ranged from snow white to deep purple, and it was by one of these bushes under a lavender sky that he first kissed Kate. She had been walking slowly, a faint smile on her face, closing her eyes and taking in the scent of the blooms. Her eyes closed, she tipped her head back and inhaled.

"Beautiful," she said.

He delicately put his hand on her shoulder and she slowly opened her eyes. Leaning forward, he gently kissed her soft lips. The cynical side of him might have said that it was too sweet, too good, something contemptible and not to be trusted, but when she responded to him in the fragrant twilight in the maze of blameless lilacs, when she parted her shining lips and kissed him back, it was a flawless thing, impeccable, and he knew he was in love. And yes, he knew he was in love.

They went back to her small, neat apartment near campus, and there they first made love. It was slow and it was gentle, unlike anything he had ever done. The way she stroked him, the way she drew her small fingers lightly down his bare chest in the half-light of her bedroom was thrilling; he struggled not to squirm. Getting her to lie back on the bed, he knelt and licked her, her calves on his broad back. The desire to enter her was actually painful, but he licked her slowly until she was near climax, then stopped.

"Oh, no," she whispered. "Don't stop."

He moved her towards the center of the bed, kissing his way up her belly, slowly licking her nipples, kissing and sucking her neck, until he was on top of her. He hesitated. It would be the first time he entered her, the only first time. He contemplated it. It was delicious.

"Do it," she gasped, and he languidly slid into her heat. They both groaned as they merged. Starting slowly, they built intensity, looking in each other's eyes, feeling the slow sensation of every stroke.

Their orgasms overlapped. He stayed in her for some time, lightly kissing her lips, her eyes, her cheeks, her ears, her nose. He didn't want to withdraw, because it would end that first time. Finally, though, his arms grew tired from keeping his full weight off her small body, and he pulled out and collapsed on his back. They whispered to each other for an hour, smiling, laughing softly, touching.

Finally they pulled the covers up to their shoulders. Dan encircled her in his arms. When she fell asleep, with her small face against his chest, he watched her until he could no longer keep his eyes open, then moved his arm from beneath her head, softly resting her head on the pillow. He was afraid to wake her, but she muttered something unintelligible and turned over on her side.

They talked constantly. Yes, even Dan, *that* Dan McGregor. In bed, on a beach, in a park, they talked. They knew they were together (it was one thing they did *not* have to talk about), and it happened effortlessly. Kate said that she had had some trouble trusting men after the fine example provided by her father, and Dan, of course, had experienced a trouble or two of his own.

Perhaps it was because of his conversations with Tom, prefatory salvos of communication, and it certainly had to do with his unusual feeling of openness to Kate, however tentative. She was so open herself that he felt comfortable enough (although cautiously so) to respond in kind. When he began to tell her about his childhood, her gasps of astonishment and well-timed curses drew him out more.

"You poor thing," she said at one point, kissing his cheekbone.

He tilted his head, shrugged his shoulders, and gave a tough-guy frown- worse things have happened to people- but to be the object of such genuine feminine sympathy was…intoxicating. He wanted to lean toward her so that she would kiss his cheekbone again.

"It's not only so terrible to lose your father in such a way," she said, "but that Mike! What a scumbag. Reminds me of *my* father."

Dan laughed.

"You're a good man," she said.

"No," he said. "No, I'm not."

"Why do you say such things?" she said, slapping him lightly in the arm with the back of her hand.

Kate was not a pushover, though, and was the first to tell him he was wrong about his grandfather.

"Of *course* you're wrong," she said. "He didn't know where to find you. Your shitty mother was hiding you from him, don't you get that? He had no idea where you were. Think how he felt, especially after your grandmother died."

Dan *did* think about it. Intellectually, he felt a tickle in his mind that told him it was the truth, that he had been wrong. His guts, though, organs of habit, told him that he had been betrayed and abandoned. He shelved the notion, taking Kate out for Indian food instead. When they returned, she opened a bottle of liebfraumilch and they watched *I, Claudius* on public television.

Part of Dan was amazed that he could take delight in such domesticity. They made love, slept cozily, got up early, went sailing. Dan was so happy that he was positive something bad had to happen.

It was terrible to return to work. He walked numbly on his rounds or tried to concentrate on a book, ignoring Ramu's questions about his changed demeanor. Although the semester was over and his days were free, Kate's job at a daycare center on the south side kept her busy during the day. To make matters worse, she was committed to a vacation at the cabin on Denfer Island with her mother and sisters a few weeks after school was out. They made the most of their time together before she left for the island.

"We'll go up there for Thanksgiving," she told him on the street next to her car. She stood on tiptoe to kiss him before getting in her little Opal and driving off with a wave and a quick snap of smile.

Kate didn't see any of Dan's work until Tom pulled his surprise.

At a party at the Kicking Pig, one which was even wilder than usual, a few of Dan's paintings, which had been stacked against a wall, had nearly been crushed when a partier had slipped in spilled beer and crashed to the floor. Dan had ushered people away from the vicinity and up to the roof, but it was obvious that he had to come up with a different strategy for the storage of his work.

This had been before Tom's withdrawal, and Dan had mentioned it to him.

"Store it over here," Tom had said simply. "We have plenty of room."

On a Saturday afternoon, they had moved a vanload of his canvases to Tom's house. When Dan had expressed his gratitude, Tom said, "I should be your promoter."

Again, such a concept was foreign to Dan. He felt that he had an image to maintain, though, and said to his friend, "Whatever. Do what you want with this. I can make more."

"I might just take you up on that," Tom had said.

Tom had finally called when his parents had returned to Africa and Kate was on Denfer Island. Dan laughed to hear his friend's voice.

"Kickstand!" he yelled.

"You've got to come down to the student union," Tom said. "I've got a surprise for you."

Tom had rented, for a low student price, a small hall on the third floor of the union. The space was often used for the display of artworks of graduate students, but Tom had managed to attain it after the end of the semester. Inside, neatly hung on all the walls, were Dan's paintings. Tom even had a sign professionally made up to stand at the entrance:

The Dark Vision of Dan McGregor

Dan wasn't sure when he'd been more stunned. To see his own work, so professionally displayed (and with discreet price tags), washed him with such a tumult of emotion that he ended up showing none at all.

"Huh!" Dan said, walking into the space.

Tom was seated at a little table dressed all in black: slacks, silk shirt, light leather jacket. He grinned toothily.

"Huh?" Tom said, spreading his palms upward.

"Huh!" Dan grunted, wrinkling his nose and shaking his head.

"No, really," Tom said. "Come one, now. *Huh?*"

Dan shook his head. "Yeah, really. I don't know. It freaks me out."

Tom grinned again. "You said I could do whatever I wanted with them."

"Yeah, but…"

"Someone wants to buy the Deformatorium series for two hundred bucks."

Dan snapped his head back. "Two hundred bucks!"

"Yeah, man," Tom said, in the tone of someone gratified that another was finally catching up. "You're a professional artist."

Dan didn't know *what* to think. He ran his scar-knuckled hand through his spiky short hair.

"Da *fuck*!" he said.

"*Huh*?" Tom cried. "I *knew* you'd say that!"

When Kate returned from the island, Dan was beside himself. He considered not telling her about the little exhibit at all. If she hated the art, with all of her knowledge, what would she think of *him*? He finally came to the conclusion that he couldn't hide or defer it. He had to take her.

He was in front of her building when she showed up. She'd given a time when she'd be back, but it was only approximate, and Dan had waited with a book, feeling a bit nauseous, tempted to go across the street to a small bar and having a few beers.

Finally, she pulled up and parked. Seeing him, she smiled beautifully, and he strode over to the car as she opened the door. They embraced, and she took his head in her hands and pulled it down towards her, kissing his face all over as he wrinkled his nose and laughed.

It wasn't with enthusiasm, but with dread, that he said, "Look, don't go inside. I have something I have to show you."

"Huh?" she said.

"Just please trust me," he said.

At the Union, they took the elevator to the third floor.

"What is it?" she said.

"A surprise," he replied.

"What?"

"I can't tell you!"

When she saw his name on the sign and walked into the space, he saw her look disoriented for the first time.

"This is you?"

"Yeah," he admitted. He felt as if he were in mid flinch.

"Holy...*shit*!" she said, grinning. "This is *you*?"

She put all her weight into shoving his shoulders.

Dan relaxed and laughed.

Dan was surprised at who showed up at the little exhibition of his work. He spent a few hours every afternoon there with Tom before his friend locked the place up with the keys he had been temporarily issued.

The Three Horsedicks of the Apocalypse came one afternoon, all of them sidling in and spreading out as if they expected a sneak attack. They looked around and, to their credit, seemed to be taking it seriously.

"You know, man," Jerry said. "You're really good."

"It makes more of an impact when you see it in this kind of context," Chris said.

Jimmie just shook his head and whistled.

"And Kickstand put this all together?" Jimmie asked

190

"Yeah," Dan said.

The three exchanged glances.

"Little fucker's all right," Jerry said.

"Little how?" Chris said, and they all laughed.

Hugh and Jim came the next day, both looking prosperous. Dan grinned witlessly at the sight of them, but was at a loss for words at their compliments.

Hugh was taken aback.

"I had no idea!" he said.

"He's *always* been like this," Jim explained, apparently puzzled by Hugh's surprise. "Since we first *met* him. That's when Charlie and I knew he was something different, not just some river rat."

"Dark stuff," Hugh said to Dan. "Where does all of that darkness come from?"

Dan shrugged, avoiding their eyes. "Dunno," he said. "Too dark to see."

"Maybe you can get our brother to do something meaningful with *his* life," Jim said. Dan was a little put out with Jim's apparent disloyalty.

"He is," Dan said. "He'll surprise you one day."

Charlie was one of the last people to come to the little exhibit. He sauntered in and looked around, his leather jacket creaking as he moved forward and back, inspecting the paintings. He had seen most of the paintings, except for those executed at Tom's house. It was hard to read his expression: was there a little tightness around his eyes? Could he be envious?

"I always suspected it would come to this," he said. "Legitimacy!"

Dan smiled tentatively.

"Who knows where this could end up," Charlie said after inspecting the paintings.

"Who knows," Dan said.

"Good work, bro," Charlie said before leaving. His smile seemed genuine enough.

On the last day of the exhibition, Dan used the proceeds to take Kate and Tom out for drinks and food at a peaceful bar they all liked. Charlie begged off, claiming other obligations. Kate and Tom hit it off immediately, though, touching each other's forearms and laughing after only half an hour of drinks and conversation.

Tom proposed a toast.

"Here's to the start of something big," he said.

"Hear, hear," Kate agreed clinking glasses with Tom, and then with Dan when he slowly held his own glass up.

"We'll see," Dan said.

"Of course!" Tom said, drawing his head back, seeming baffled.

"It's like you don't think you deserve to be happy," Kate said.

Dan didn't say anything, simply downing his drink.

Dan and Kate spent most of their weekend nights at her neat little apartment. It only took Kate one exposure to the Kicking Pig to solidify this habit. Dan had nearly shuddered at the idea of bringing her there, but she had finally persuaded him.

"Just show me where you live," she said. "How bad can it be?"

"You asked for it," Dan said.

Fortunately, Charlie wasn't home. Dan was sure that the spectacle of the filth in which they lived would be bad enough without Charlie doing something boisterous.

They went up the fire escape and in through the kitchen door. Kate looked around and laughed.

Beer and liquor bottles, mostly empty, were everywhere. On top of the refrigerator, there were partially full beer bottles on top of the old refrigerator that had been there long enough to have a skin of mold on top of them. There was no wastebasket in the kitchen, only a stolen garbage can, nearly spilling over with garbage. The huge old sink was stacked with dishes, pots, glasses, and pans. Dan and Charlie's procedure, when they cooked at all, was to take plates and pots off the top layer in the sink, wash the items for use, and return them to their position afterwards, unwashed.

Kate laughed again.

"Holy shit," she said. "Bachelors."

Dan was relieved that she simply blamed the living conditions on his general demographic, rather than seeing it as an individual personality flaw. She walked through the place, laughing some more and shaking her head. Pizza boxes, some of them ancient, were scattered here and there, along with grease-stained Chinese food cartons. She liked Dan's art that remained on the walls, somehow unscathed, and loved the mural. She goggled at the size and amount of weights in the workout room, taking a jab at the heavy bag.

When she saw the cubby hole of Dan's room, she sighed.

"You poor thing," she said. "It's obvious that I'm going to have to take care of you."

"Okay," Dan said sheepishly.

Kate peeked once into Charlie's room. On his small desk sat not only his .45, the butt sticking out of an oily rag, but a large double-dong dildo.

She snorted laughter. "Nice!"

After looking around some more, smiling and shaking her head, Kate said "Didn't you help Tom clean up his place once?"

"Yep."

"So you do know how to do it?"

"It'd just get trashed again anyway."

"I see your point, but still…" she mimed vomiting, and Dan laughed.

"Forgive us," he said, "for we know not what the fuck we do."

And so it was that from the time Kate got off work on Friday until Dan returned to his own job on Sunday afternoon, they spent all their time together at her place. In her kitchen, lit by the setting sun, they drank wine while Kate cooked from *Mastering the Art of French Cooking* and *Larousse Gastronomique*. She was an astonishing chef; Dan had never experienced anything like it. She laughed with pleasure to see how the amazement on his face melted into zeal. When they did the dishes together, the feeling Dan experienced was so peaceful, so…wholesome, he guessed, that it made him almost as suspicious as it did happy.

They listened to music together. He introduced her to Smetana, not thinking about the fact that it was the same record that his grandfather had given him, the corners and faces of the cardboard jacket worn. Kate had him pay complete attention to Ralph Vaughan Williams's *Fantasia on a Theme by Thomas Tallis*.

"Sounds like sailing," Dan said of the piece.

"Yeah!" Kate said, obviously pleased that he understood.

Whenever they were driving they listened, again and again, to Elvis Costello's *Armed Forces*, taking it from her Opal to his van, singing along together to the tunes, especially What's So Funny 'Bout Peace, Love, and Understanding.

They went to the beach, going far up the coast, falling asleep on a blanket together under Dan's orange sleeping bag. Dan spent incautious amounts of money on dinners, in spite of Kate's protests.

It was the first time Dan told a woman that he loved her. He found that it was a difficult few words to choke out. He couldn't remember the last time he had said it to anyone; it was probably his grandmother, and the words hadn't meant the same thing, had never meant anything like this.

She said it first. They were on the beach together on a Saturday evening, watching the waves and the gulls. Dan had made a little driftwood fire, and they drank from a jug of wine.

She moved her gaze from the waves and looked at him directly.

"I love you," she said. It sounded like a simple statement of fact, something that made her happy.

She didn't seem like she needed him to say it back, only sat looking back out over the water. Dan wanted to say the same thing to her, parted his lips to do so. Instead, he put his arm around her shoulder, held her to him, kissed the top of her head. To tell her that he loved her would be to leave himself unprotected.

After a long time, Kate said, "I know you've had a hard time, Dan. You've felt so alone."

Dan said nothing. He drank wine and watched the sky.

"You can trust me with your heart," Kate said. "You can trust me."

After some time, he said, "Okay."

"All right then," she said.

The twilight deepened, the coals of the fire glowing more brightly. He had to say it before it got dark, so he could see her eyes. He lost his nerve.

"Maybe we should get going," he said, moving to stand up.

"Yeah," Kate said. "Let's go home."

It was that word that did it: home.

She stood up, and he looked into her eyes, the twilight reflected there, the orange light of the fire on her face.

"I love you," he said.

She smiled, shrugging slightly, closing her eyes for an instant.

"I know," she said.

And so they went home.

As much as Kate liked Tom, she soon developed an obvious dislike for Charlie. Dan wanted them to get along, but it was apparent that that was not to be. Dan wondered if the state of their apartment, the gun and the dildo had anything to do with it, but Charlie sealed the deal by getting into a fight at one of Kate's favorite nightspots on a muggy evening in early summer.

The Up and Over Pub was a place Kate liked to go after sailing, along with other members of the club. It was not the kind of deafeningly loud and rowdy place Dan usually frequented, but it was friendly enough. Dan sat at a large table next to Kate

193

with a group of her sailing buddies, listening to the conversation, still feeling like a bit of an outsider. He'd told Charlie where he was going to be, but hadn't expected him to show up.

Charlie walked in, tan and muscular in a sleeveless black t-shirt, white-blond hair spiky. The bar was getting crowded, and Charlie made his way toward the table, shouldering aside a couple of athletic-looking young men, but stopping and clearing a space for pretty woman trying to make it to a table with a pitcher of beer and a few glasses. The young men looked annoyed but reluctant to do anything about it, while the woman smiled sunnily and walked by.

Charlie didn't look like anyone in there, and, as much as his showing up gave Dan a twinge of trepidation, Dan also laughed to see him. Although he'd never been happier than during the time he'd been spending with Kate, he felt that he'd been a bit disloyal to his friend and missed the excitement he habitually provided. Charlie bought two pitchers of beer and brought them to the table, introducing himself before turning a chair around backwards to sit.

"So, what's the topic of conversation?" Charlie said. He topped off any glasses that were less than full before pouring himself one, which he immediately downed in one long pull, his adam's apple bobbing.

"We were talking about boats, actually," said Tim, a sunburned and handsome sailing instructor who Dan didn't think he liked. Since Dan had become a believer about sailing, though, he recognized that Tim had useful knowledge and wanted an amiable relationship with him.

Charlie smiled pleasantly enough to make Dan wary, but said nothing, simply pouring and downing another beer. The people at the table listened as Tim held forth for a bit. Dan held Kate's hand under the table and they exchanged an intimate glance. Dan looked at Charlie, who had a slight, amused smirk on his face. Charlie cut Tim off in mid-drone.

"Top off your beer for you, there, Tim?" he asked, smiling.

"Uh, sure. Charlie is it?"

"Yep."

"You sure can put it away, Charlie," Tim said a bit snidely.

Charlie ignored his tone and said, " 'Alcohol is the anesthetic that gets us through the operation of life'. George Bernard Shaw. That and it's hotter than a motherfucker out there."

"I love your colorful use of language," Tim said.

"I thought all sailors liked to drink beer and swear," Charlie said.

"Within reason, I suppose."

Charlie snorted. "This guy remind you of anyone, Dan?" he asked, jerking a thumb at Tim.

Dan noticed Kate's look, her lips parted, eyes a little too wide. She doesn't like where this is going, Dan thought, but said, "I guess he reminds me of one Henry Bosworth Gates the Fifth."

"My thoughts exactly," Charlie said.

"I had him for a philosophy class," one young woman at the table said.

"Do tell," Charlie said, leaning forward. "And what was your impression of the man?"

"A real blowhard, actually," the young woman laughed.

Charlie spread his hands and grinned at Tim, who glared back.

"Did he ever hit on you?" Charlie asked.

"No," the young woman said. "But he hit on one of my friends."

"Don't take it personally," Charlie said. "You probably weren't sitting close enough to the podium."

The young woman laughed again. "As a matter of fact, I wasn't. But eeeew, anyway."

"I hear you," Charlie said, reaching across the table and patting her hand. She smiled. Kate squeezed Dan's hand under the table. Kate had said that she had the same feeling about Tim that Dan did, but obviously wanted to keep the situation under control.

It was plain that Tim was put out by Charlie's commandeering of the conversation. He attempted to regain control, using a tone of voice that indicated he was accustomed to being in a position of authority. He turned the subject back to boats.

Charlie listened for a moment, downing another beer.

"Is this what you do," he finally said to Tim. "Just talk about boats?"

"Well, it's a point of common interest," Tim said huffily.

"Yeah, I suppose it is," Charlie said. "Hey, Dan, you ever tell these mopes about the time we stole a speedboat out on the river? Ran it up on a sandbar?"

Dan didn't know whether to laugh or be annoyed. Kate, who knew the story, said, "Maybe we should save that one for another time, Charlie."

"No, no!" Charlie said. "It's good. I believe we had given ourselves the mission of liberating a boat in the furtherance of blowing up a vehicle precious to some rednecks. We got shitfaced, however, and things went awry…"

"Really Charlie," Kate said. "Some other time."

"Okay, I'll keep it brief. Short version is, it looked like we were going to get caught. I was on probation for B and E…"

"What's B and E?" asked the young former student of Professor Gates.

"Breaking and entering," Charlie said, reaching across the table and taking her hand. "It's so sweet that you don't know that."

Dan laughed and Kate gave him a look. He gave her one back: that's Charlie.

"Anyway, my younger brother and I split at Dan's insistence. Dan got popped before he could get the boat off the sandbar and took the heat for us. Had to work in a funeral home handling corpses to pay off the damages. Now that's a friend."

He raised his glass, and Dan raised his back. They each arched an eyebrow and clinked glasses urbanely.

There was silence around the table as everyone looked at Dan.

"You have interesting friends, Kate," Tim said.

Kate smiled sweetly and said, "Thanks, I know." She leaned over to kiss Dan on the white scar on his eyebrow.

Charlie looked at Tim and Dan knew that look. He was about to get Charlie to leave the bar when a group of several burly rugby players, sweaty from the field, came into the bar loudly demanding pitchers of beer. One of them bumped soundly into Charlie's back in passing the table. Charlie sighed and smiled, and Dan knew what was going to happen.

Charlie patted the hand of the young woman. "Excuse me for a moment," he said, standing up and moving through the crowd. Dan watched, but the wall of backs closed, and from his seated position, he couldn't see where Charlie had gone.

Tim resumed talking but Dan wasn't paying attention. Nor were most of the other people at the table. It was only a couple of minutes after Charlie had left that the familiar sounds began. The scrape and clatter of a barstool falling to the floor, the sound of breaking glass, a woman's scream, followed, on this occasion, by a man's voice bellowing, "Fucker broke my thumb!"

Dan had no choice but to get up and take Charlie's side, but at that moment the crowd dispersed to let Charlie through, leaving two rugby players writhing on the floor behind him. Charlie was laughing.

He stopped at the table on the way out.

"No problem," he said dismissively to Dan. He then leaned over the table and said to the young student, "If the police ask you any questions, please be discreet." She smiled and ducked her head.

Before he left, Charlie pointed once at Tim and raised his eyebrows, a cautionary set of gestures. Tim tried not to look frightened, but his face paled.

"Later!" Charlie said, and walked out.

As the commotion resumed around the downed rugby players, the members of the group at the table turned their gazes towards Dan, their looks ranging from amusement to horror.

Dan shrugged and drank from his beer.

Later that night he assured Kate that she wouldn't need to spend much time with Charlie, a simple compromise. She didn't complain, didn't disparage Charlie, but Dan offered up the solution anyway. That was as far as he was willing to go.

"He's more than my friend, he's my brother," Dan said. "He's the whole reason I'm in Greysport in the first place. It's because of him that we met."

"Well, I owe him something for that," Kate said.

As much as Kate had her reservations about Charlie, it was apparent that she liked Tom *because* of the fact that he was odd, rather than in spite of it.

Tom had his periods of despondency, of course, but went into a real tailspin when his ulotrichous head of red hair began falling out in clumps. And he had only just turned nineteen.

"Same thing happened to my dad," Tom moaned to Dan and Kate over margaritas in the back yard of his house. "And I'm not even as cool as he is."

"Oh, you are *too* cool," Kate chided him, knuckling his arm.

"Just shave your head," Dan said. "You'll look like you're from the future."

Tom consoled himself with sex with Audrey, who had become as accustomed to Tom's size as she ever would. So impressed was she with Tom's accidental bequeathment that she had, on occasion, set it up so that she could share it with friends of hers who liked that kind of thing. "Size Queens", she called them. Tom was beside himself with joy about this. It made him forget, for a time, his depression about his hair, and he thanked Dan so profusely that it began to make Dan uncomfortable.

"So you've got a freaky big crank," Dan said. "Word was bound to get out eventually."

"You started the ball rolling, man," Tom said. "I am forever in your debt."

"Whatever."

Finding forgetfulness in sex wasn't enough for Tom, though, and he decided to throw a party for himself with the theme being The Death of My Childhood. It was to be a living wake, held late at night. He had engraved invitations made with black calligraphy on butter-colored paper, stating the date, time, and purpose, requesting that all attendees wear black in observance of the somber occasion. The only lighting was provided by dozens of beeswax candles, and the alcohol consumed was all dark in color: red wine, dark beer, rum and whiskey. The lighting and the neutral tones of the walls made the place look medieval. Dan and Kate smiled at each other about Tom's attention to detail.

Tom's hair had, indeed, been falling out in literal handfuls, so, after a short speech about his departed childhood, he asked Dan to cut off his remaining hair with electric clippers before shaving his head.

"I need an artist's eye for this," Tom said.

A group of Tom's friends formed a solemn circle. Some of them were members of his half-assed jazz band, many were friends from high school who had been engaged in a candle-lit game of Dungeons and Dragons in the kitchen or arguing about Star Wars and Star Trek before the little ceremony.

Dan had never done anything remotely similar to this before and was at first momentarily daunted by the prospect. After a few drinks (and lines of coke done in private with Tom), he realized that there was no real way for him to botch the job, and simply went at it. A circle of blackclad witnesses looked on gravely as Dan sheared off Tom's remaining red locks, which fell onto a black towel he wore around his shoulders. Tom sat erect, holding his chin up with great dignity. Dan then lathered up Tom's head with shaving soap and a brush (nothing from a pressurized can for Tom), and, now in the spirit of things, deftly shaved off the remaining stubble. Dan looked up in the midst of the process at the surrounding witnesses, and found Kate grinning from among them. Dan had to concentrate on not laughing. He finished the job and toweled off Tom's pinkly gleaming dome. Tom emerged from the experience with the look he would have for the rest of his life. He gazed into a mirror to see Dan's handiwork.

"And so it is done!" Tom declaimed. "Let us par-tay!"

Compared to the hard-knuckled, two-fisted partiers that Dan usually hung out with, the attendees of Tom's party were lightweights, drinking moderately and talking too much about the effects. Three of the guests (including a baby-faced kid of three hundred pounds who looked like a hobbit, and a skinny, pale boy with a bowl cut and a calculator on his belt) smoked dope from Tom's bong in the living room and talked about how stoned they were, who was more stoned than whom, and why. None of them drank much. Dan and Tom went at it with enthusiasm, though, and Kate occupied herself by getting involved in the game of Dungeons and Dragons. After several hours, she tore herself away from the game, and, taking one look at Dan, told him that she would be the one to drive home. She was amused by Dan's grogginess, and put him to bed.

In the morning, he woke up later than she did and was being stoic about his hangover. Willy had always said, "Never bitch about a hangover. You did it to yourself, so don't be a pussy about it."

Dan was sticking to this philosophy when she brought him breakfast in bed. Again, Dan thought this was all too good to be true, that, as a *maldito*, he didn't deserve such treatment and that something had to go wrong to end it. He wondered why she wasn't with someone better than him, but said nothing about it, wanting it to last as long as possible.

Kate had made him scrambled eggs with ham, onions, and tomatoes chopped, sautéed, and mixed in. There was toast and jam, orange juice and a bottle of hot sauce. Dan tried not to eye her suspiciously.

"How's my hung-over sweetie?" she asked as he sat up in bed so she could put the little breakfast tray over his knees.

"I'm okay," he said.

She watched as he ate, smiling. It wasn't a smile of adulation or worship, but one that was amused, as if by a naughty boy.

Kate wasn't a pushover, though, and her patience only went so far. When Dan had gone out with Charlie and some of the other regulars to Vnuk's after work on a late Wednesday night which had proven to be boring and ended up being drunk, he'd shown up at her apartment at four in the morning.

She wouldn't let him in. "I don't care if you do this," she said. "You have some wildness to live out of you. Just don't mix me up in it. I have to be to work in four hours, for fuck sake, and now I won't be able to get back to sleep. If you got this way with that Charlie, let him make breakfast for you."

Dan had dolefully shuffled away and slept in his van down by the port.

He didn't talk to her until Friday evening, feeling contrite but not wanting to seem desperate by calling her. When he finally did, she told him coolly that he could come over if he wanted to.

Dan apologized, which was difficult, as he wasn't in the habit of apologizing to anyone, for anything. She accepted it, although it was apparent that Dan couldn't behave any way he wanted to, as he had when involved with women he didn't care about.

He wanted to please her, and realized that she was the only person on such a list. For the rest of the summer, if he had adventures with Charlie and the Horsedicks, he kept her out of it. If he did acid and drank until eight in the morning with Tom, he didn't mention it unless she asked. He showed up once with a bruised eye and scabbed knuckles, and she just sighed through her nose and shook her head.

"Are you going to say that I remind you of your father?" Dan said. If something was coming, he wanted to get it over with.

Kate looked shocked. "Why do you say such things?" she asked. "You're nothing alike. You're kind and sweet and gentle…"

"Gentle!" Dan said, a bit indignant. Next she'd be calling him sensitive. "I get in brawls all the time!" He held up his fists as evidence.

"That's a boy thing, and a chivalry thing, whether you know it or not. You're kind and gentle to *me*."

Dan rolled his eyes.

"And you're talented," she said, but added: "Although I loved you before I knew you were talented."

"So I don't remind you of your dad?"

She blew air out of her lips contemptuously. "My dad was an asshole," she said. "You're the opposite of that."

Dan didn't contradict her. He figured he'd quit while he was ahead.

Charlie didn't seem to be that taken with Kate either, although, since he was too cool to talk about it, Dan wasn't sure why. It might have been that she didn't like anyone calling him on his behavior. Perhaps it was that he found her attractive himself. Charlie didn't say. He was merely distant after Dan disappeared for the weekend, or when he briefly mentioned Kate in conversation.

"There was a great brawl at the Underground on Saturday," Charlie informed him one Monday morning from where he was reading on the couch. "Cops came and everything."

"No shit?" Dan said.

"Yeah. You missed it."

Dan shrugged with his eyebrows. "Kate and I went sailing all afternoon. Then we went to a cookout."

"Mister Wholesome," Charlie said, not looking up from his book. "Mister *Domesticity*."

"Fuck off," Dan said amiably.

Things got back to normal with Charlie for three weeks in July just after the Fourth. Dan and Kate had spent an evening together that she had described as "romantic"; Dan himself had not yet become comfortable with the term. They had gone down to the park by the lakefront and watched the spectacular fireworks after a picnic dinner that Kate had put together, including wine and brie, baguettes and ham. After the fireworks were over and people dissipated from the park, leaving them alone, they had lain folded up in the blanket, her head on his chest. This created a warm stillness in Dan, a deep peace in his heart. He dreaded having to move. Eventually, though, the sun would come up, it would get hot out, and the grass of the park would become repopulated. The fact that Kate would soon be leaving for a seminar made it worse. He held her close and kissed the top of her head when he thought of this. He didn't want to move and didn't want her to leave; if this made him romantic in the eyes of his friends, he thought he'd learn to deal with it.

She kissed him at the airport for a long time.

"Oh, don't be so stony-faced," she said. "I'll be back before you know it."

"Okay," he said.

"And go do something destructive and reckless with your mutant friends while I'm gone."

He couldn't help but smile. "Well, that takes all the fun out of it."

"Okay, not *too* destructive and reckless, although they *are* mutants."

She turned around and waved before going through the gate to the plane; curvy and adorable, eyes like the sky and a sunny smile; she actually blew him a kiss. Then she turned and was gone.

Dan waited until the plane had taxied away, watched until it took off. At that point, there was nothing more he could do, and he shuffled away, feeling bleak. He would have been disgusted to see himself: in spite of his physicality, with his black spiky hair, black t-shirt and shorts, black boots (even his watchband), and blackest of expressions, he was yet another variation of the Doomed Romantic. As a true tough guy, though, he strove for imperviousness, and this picture of himself might have made him puke. At least he would have liked to think so.

He tried to erase all these feelings by finding his cohorts that night. Unable to locate them at the chaotic venue of Vnuk's (where an interesting band, The Cadaver Dogs, was playing) he found them immediately after that at the Underground.

Dan's greeting was the same as always, with welcoming cheers and a barrage of ballbusting. Charlie was in fine form and bellowed upon seeing him, slapped down his pool cue and howled like a werewolf, clenching his fists, arms corded, roaring at the ceiling. Everyone nearby knew Charlie, and either laughed along or smiled nervously.

After several shots, beers, joints, and lines, Dan began to feel liberated. What was he doing getting pussywhipped by that chick? It might have been Charlie who had initially made such an implication, but when Dan had consumed enough of everything, the thought became his own. It was wonderful to drive again through the deserted streets after bartime, stoplights blinking red or yellow, his van filled with comrades, as were the other vehicles in their caravan. They went to the beach with cases of beer and partied until sunrise, then, as of old, assailed one of the port bars when it opened. Dan rediscovered how he loved to hear Charlie rant, about nuclear holocaust, about plague, about the collapse of the oil economy. When the bartender tried to argue, Charlie, rather than being the bully he could be, took the man's arguments apart calmly, piece by piece. This necessitated the occasional trip to the bathroom for a bump of coke, but, as Charlie pointed out while they did a line together, the bartender was sober, and on his home turf. Whatever the bartender's protestations, he eventually began to agree with Charlie's points. He bought the two beers and shots in acknowledgement of this.

They drank until noon.

It was hot and brilliant when they left the bar. Dan staggered to his van, squinting and shading his eyes, putting on his darkest sunglasses from the glove compartment for the drive to the cathedral square. He parked, staggering exhausted through the alleys and up the fire escape to the familiar scent and squalor of his nestlike room. Allowing his joints to go loose, he let gravity take care of the rest, and fell like a crash-test dummy onto his unfresh mattress.

When he awoke in the late afternoon, his first conscious thought, even before the need to piss, was that of missing Kate.

Had he felt like that before? There had been homesickness and grief, betrayal and loss, all of which he did not consciously examine and did his best to hide.

The greatest thing, when about to explode into a painful and useful epiphany, many people find, is to avoid it altogether. Most people are cowards about such things; some are not. For a few weeks, Dan doubled down on his cowardice.

He did no drugs which might offer illumination, sticking instead to those which would obscure and obliterate his worries. He snorted heroin for the first time with Charlie, feeling an immediate bliss.

"We don't want to do this too much," Charlie advised, seconds before doing another line.

Wavy, wavy wonderful, calm and dreamy wonderful. It opened things up: I am in love. I should call my grandfather, he's a good guy. A hero. My hero. He should know I'm in love. It'll all be okay anyway. Right now is fine. I can do everything tomorrow. Everything.

The mixture of drugs left him, unsurprisingly, with such a sick and crunching hangover that whatever epiphanies he might have attained were wiped off with poisonous, virus-packed shit. He vowed never to snort smack again. The power plant that night was a drone of misery, even worse than his first day. Ramu regarded Dan and shook his head, tisking, and returned his attention to yet another book.

Due to youthful resilience, though, Dan went along with Charlie on a drug exchange only a few days later.

Charlie made a handsome amount of money dealing weed. He had developed a taste for drugs of a more compelling nature, and considered selling them as well, but the comparative legal risk seemed to ignite his smart side.

"Lot of money in coke, lot of money in smack," he explained to Dan. "Getting busted for such things might, just might, interfere with me going to med school. Rather sell high-end weed to mellower folks."

With Dan back in the fold (if only temporarily), Charlie asked him to come along for backup on a deal of several pounds of primo weed to members of the northwest side gang famously named the Brothers of the Rising, or BOR, as they were known in the press and on the corners.

The meet took place in an apartment not unlike the Kicking Pig in a neighborhood once new and progressive, with shops and restaurants lit up with inviting neon and the hope of a promising future. It was of course now squalid: Charlie said that the morale shot down and despair shot up in inverse proportion.

Dan was thinking about this when he went up the stairs to the apartment behind Charlie. He had a .38 (from the Horsedicks) in the back of his waistband, just as Charlie had his dependable .45, the Bacchus killer, in the back of his. They wore loose-fitting shirts to cover the guns, but nobody was fooled. Even the cops in the violent neighborhood would not have been fooled, and only would've jacked someone (especially white boys) upon provocation.

It was a tentative business arrangement, and both sides were a bit jumpy. Charlie's counterpart, a young man of equal age named Trey, shook hands ornately with Charlie when they came through the door. The apartment was spare and neat, with a few posters like Bob Marley and Marcus Garvey on the walls. Of the brothers in attendance, there was a disparity of styles, the main distinction being the guys in jheri-curl and protective shower caps, and the ones, fewer in number but obviously in charge of the transaction, wearing dreadlocks. It was the complete lack of posturing on the part of the latter group, their emotionless, quiet, and businesslike manner, that made them the ones to watch. Dan didn't know that two of the jheri-curl contingent were first cousins of his friend from the dismal Portview days, Darnell.

There were a few moments of tension, a typical scene. When the small backpack of money and the duffel bags of product exchanged hands, each side inspected what they had received. Dan wondered why the rastas would be suspicious- who would come into someone else's home territory to cheat them so obviously- but he realized that they were not worried. Business was business.

Things went well enough, actually, that Trey, the Dreadlock in Charge, offered them a couple of forty-ounce bottles of malt liquor, which Charlie accepted just as Dan was about to open his mouth to beg off. Being Charlie, though, he pounded the forty pretty quickly, leaving Dan to catch up.

They left with handshakes all around, Charlie and Dan going down the worn wooden stairs and out onto the hot streets to the van.

"I thought it might've been better to get out of there after the transaction," Dan said.

"Ah, they're okay guys," Charlie said. "It's the cops I'm worried about. Besides, it would've been rude to decline."

Three weeks turned out to be a long time. Dan missed Kate more than he had ever missed anyone, it seemed, and he was grateful for distractions. Art was a great one, and Dan had to admit that he had gotten next to nothing done whenever he spent lengths of time with Kate. The short term happiness of her presence was much more attractive (and easy), than it was to create something on a canvas.

"When do you actually do your work?" she had asked him once before leaving on her trip.

"Late at night," he said. "When I'm not with you."

"If I hadn't seen what you had done, I wouldn't think you were an artist at all."

"I guess I am, though," he said. "Don't worry about it."

The fact was that he seemed to have lost his momentum, and was beginning to feel badly about it. A little inspiration and time alone was all he needed, he told himself.

Late at night though, with Kate out of town, he was tripping pretty heavily and drinking a lot to keep the edge at bay. He began to obsess on the idea that he had lost his talent, lost it completely. The notion gained momentum, and soon was freaking him out so much that he left Vnuk's and stalked out, jaws clenching with the force of the acid.

Stopping at the Kicking Pig, he stuffed his backpack with cans of beer and a bottle of whiskey, in with his usual pad of drawing paper, zippered pockets of pencils and erasers. As he walked to the beach, his mind was fizzing with acid; people who walked by looked as if their shapes and colors shifted, their speech and barks of laughter seemed sharp and animal. He walked with an open beer, guzzling it and throwing it in a trashcan, taking his pack off his shoulder to open another, his ability to drink on acid always prodigious.

He crossed Lake Drive- the same street Hugh had driven up after rescuing him at the bar on that grim Christmas so long ago- and found himself in the comforting dark. His senses roared; shapes in the darkness seemed to be made of enlarged pixels of purple, magenta, and green, the susurrant sounds seemed at times to be those of laughter, then of breaking waves. He found himself taken by such a sound at one point (a rushing, a sighing), and looked up to see the most beautiful maple tree he had ever seen, its leaves rippling in the darkness. Fascination with this trapped him for some time- he had no idea how long- then the sound of the darkly flickering leaves reminded him of his initial mission, and he continued down to the beach.

Once there, he sat on a large rock at the edge of the sand, the waves coming in softy, yards away, on the mild pre-dawn breeze. To abate any possible heart-hammering paranoia, he drank from the bottle of whiskey. He opened a lukewarm beer and sipped it.

The sky showed traces of light over the lake, striking first the high, thin clouds, and gradually dim color seeped over the horizon. Soon it faded through gold to orange, with slow slashes of purple and ruby. While it was undeniably beautiful- he thought of Willy talking about the grandeur of the Cathedral of Nature- it was, nonetheless, nothing he would have enjoyed painting, nothing that would have fascinated him.

Just before the sun broke the horizon, an older couple of about thirty, dressed in a rather posh manner, walked past him and out onto the beach. While the man seemed to make pains to ignore him, the woman gave Dan a quick look of disdain, exactly the type of look he would expect a yuppie to give a spiky young punk in a ratty sleeveless t-shirt and black fatigue pants who happened to be holding a whiskey bottle.

Dan held up the whiskey bottle and said, "Happy sunrise."

The woman gave him a nasty look, but the man took her elbow and muttered something to her, marching her out onto the beach.

Dan realized he was coming down from the acid, getting that gritty, greasy, exhausted feeling which followed a good trip. He thought he'd have one more warm beer before walking home and crashing out until late afternoon. The first crescent of sun vibrated orange over the horizon.

Then the woman screamed. They were fifty feet away, standing just at the edge of the high point of the waves. The woman screamed again, running back the way she had come, right past Dan, her eyes wide and animal.

Shouldering his pack, bottle of whiskey in hand, Dan walked over to where the yuppie stood by the surf, watching something dark roll back and forth in the waves. As Dan approached, he could see that it was a dead man, dressed in a dark suit and maroon tie. One shoe was missing. The man's back was to the shore, but every time a new wave came in, it flung his shoulder towards the shore before allowing him to slump back to his curled position with the recession of the waves. Dan walked out into the waves for a better look. The dead man's skin was pale yellow, his hair black and lank, flowing in the water like seaweed. Eyes black and wide, mouth a dark hole which filled and drained of water with each wave. Dan thought about Mickey Potts's DB and sighed through his nose.

The yuppie was staring at the corpse, panting.

"Hey, man," Dan said. "It's a dead guy. It happens. You'll be just as dead as this motherfucker someday. Hope somebody cares."

The yuppie looked at Dan once and fled across the sand.

"Call the cops!" Dan called after him. "And don't be such a fucking pussy!"

Dan stood in the waves, watching the corpse and the quality of light on it in the changing glow of the rising sun. He waded out deeper into the water to see it from that angle, splashing away in order to keep his shadow off the form.

When the police showed up, he gave a statement. The yuppies were still there, looking shamefaced and stricken (the woman looked as if she had vomited, and was about to again), but Dan realized at one point that they had spoken well of him. Once the police had his information, they let him go. None of the cops said anything about his drinking whiskey, or casually opening a warm beer in front of them, or, for that matter, looking like a punk hooligan. Dan loved Greysport.

"We'll take care of it, kid," one cop told him. "Go on home. Take some vitamin C, helps ya get over the acid hangover."

"What about this hangover?" Dan said, holding up the whiskey bottle.

"You're on your own, buddy." He looked at the cop next to him and they both laughed.

"You should become a cop," the second one said.

"I do drugs and drink a lot," Dan said.

"Perfect," the first cop said.

"You're tough, that's what counts," the second cop said.

"Thanks," Dan said, smiling. "I'll keep it in mind."

With the acid dissipated and the sun up, Dan shuffled home. When he walked up the fire escape, the loudest sound was from his own apartment, a pumping punk anthem of some sort. Lights were on, beer cans, whiskey and tequila bottles everywhere. Full morning sunlight analyzed the room.

Dan took the needle off the record and turned off the machine. He went through the apartment, checking for damage and turning off lights. Going to the piled sink, he took a beer stein and filled it with cold water, drinking it down and repeating it.

In bed, he tormented himself for awhile, thinking of calling his grandfather and shying away in dread, before going to sleep.

When he awoke in the afternoon, he knew what he had to paint. After doing a few clarifying sketches, he started in on it. When, after eight hours, he realized he was getting tired, he did some acid. He went on a cycle for forty-eight hours, doing all paintings of drowned people.

Charlie came in at one point, seeing what he was doing and saying, "Man, what the fuck."

At the end of the summer, Kate took Dan to Denfer Island for the first time. It had been miserably hot for two weeks, the only respite being to dive into the freezing water of the lake, or to hide out in a nice cool bar. Work was miserable; even after the sun went down, the enormous black ziggurat of coal radiated heat, and the dense and humid air trapped the stench of the slaughterhouse and tallow plant. Dan ignored all of it and went through his rounds.

When Kate made the suggestion of the trip, her desire to show him her favorite place in the world had Dan scurrying to get his shifts covered at the power plant for a week, giving him almost ten days of vacation.

Denfer Island was over a four hour drive to the north, all of it along the coast. They set out early on Friday morning while it was still cool. They headed north on the expressway, the density of the Friday morning traffic decreasing as they went. It occurred to Dan that, a year ago at this time, he would probably be sleeping for another six hours, only to wake up with a hangover that would make him question the point of his existence. As it was, though, they sang along to a Talking Heads tape, Dan driving as Kate cut up an orange with his knife and handed him slices.

Once out of the city, Kate directed Dan off the highway, taking county roads over to the route which most closely hugged the shore.

"It takes longer," she said, "but it's worth it."

Dan didn't care. He looked over at her sitting on the passenger seat of the van in her green cargo shorts and orange t-shirt, tiny hiking boots and white socks. He would have driven around the rusting steel mills down in Cary all day if she'd asked him to. He would have hung out at the slaughterhouse.

There were little commercial fishing villages along the way, and the small industrial town of Port Martineau, which, Kate told him, had shipyards which had built submarines during the second world war.

Dan loved all of it. He wondered again why his grandfather had wasted his life out on the river.

They stopped at an abandoned beach with the stumps of a rotted pier and went swimming, coming back ashore for a picnic lunch which Kate had prepared. They proceeded at a leisurely pace the rest of the way up the coast.

By the time they reached the tip of the peninsula and the dock for the ferry to Denfer Island, it was getting late in the afternoon. Giant storm clouds, rayed from behind by the westering sun, were shouldering in from the horizon. They had to wait for the ferry to return from the island, and other passengers in cars or on bicycles, a couple on motorcycles, eyed the towering clouds as they approached. At last the ferry docked and its gates lowered to the concrete like drawbridges. They drove onto the ferry and the gates were raised behind them. Out they went onto the choppy water as the sky darkened.

Dan and Kate got out of the van and went to the railing to watch as they approached the island. Dan realized he was grinning.

"There are shipwrecks all over around here," Kate mentioned.

"Excellent," Dan said.

"I knew you'd like it," she laughed. "Lots of drowned people for you to paint."

It began to pour when the ferry docked in the little crescent-shaped harbor of Port Denfer. The other passengers, many of them obviously tourists, seemed disconcerted by this, scurrying to their cars as the clouds loosed their torrent. Those on bicycles and motorcycles seemed particularly dejected.

Dan and Kate got back in the van, laughing.

"Don't worry!" Kate shouted as the rain pummeled the top of the van like dozens of fists, "The cabin's as snug as a ship!"

"This is great!" Dan shouted back.

He couldn't make much of the little port through the downpour, although he could see blurs of neon here and there that he knew were bar signs and the glowing logo for Greysport Lager. It immediately got darker as they left the little town for the wooded roads.

"If the wipers work any harder," Kate said, "they're going to fly off!"

"Then we're *really* fucked!" Dan said, and they laughed.

It was a few miles from the little port to where the cabin sat in the woods on the northeast edge of the island. Kate directed Dan, who squinted through the windshield at the blurry centerline and occasional reflective markers barely visible among the thrashing branches of trees and seemingly living underbrush.

It became truly challenging when Kate had him turn off the rudimentary road and onto a drive consisting of two sandy ruts through the woods. It seemed to go on and on. At last they came into what appeared to be a clearing, as Dan could tell by the marginally improved light. He suddenly saw the cabin itself in the headlights of the van.

It was more than he had expected. Two stories, clapboard siding, with a large porch with wicker chairs and large dark windows, a cedar-shake shingle roof. Large pines stood behind it, moving in the wind. Dan parked so that Kate's door was closest to the cabin. She crouched and went back into the van to get her things and a few bags of groceries. Dan was more concerned with the two cases of Greysport and the large bottle of bourbon he had brought.

"Ready to make a run for it?" Kate said, grinning.

"Sure."

Kate bolted inside, but Dan took his time. When he came through the front door, completely soaked, he set down the cases beside the front door. Kate had turned on some of the lights.

The place reminded him of Emilio and Solveig's cabin on the river, although the artwork was nautical, lots of oils of sailing scenes on the varnished wooden walls. There was a big stone fireplace with brass tools and neatly stacked firewood nearby. The large common area had overstuffed leather chairs and sofa, and a long dining table with many chairs under a brass chandelier. Polished wooden bookshelves neatly packed with hundreds of books were placed everywhere possible. Brass nautical instruments were on the walls, and a brass telescope on a tripod near the front windows, which had polished wooden shutters. Warmly colored oriental rugs were placed under the dining room table and in front of the leather couch, going down a hallway to the back of the first floor and at the base of the steep stairs to the second. The place smelled of pine and sand and woodsmoke, and of course the singular fresh smell of the lake; even though they had just opened the front door, the scent came in gusts. Outside, the rain drummed down.

Dan sighed and smiled. "Wow," he said.

206

"Let's make a fire!" Kate said. "You do it, you're the pyromaniac. I'll put stuff away in the kitchen and fix something to eat."

Dan made a fire and found Kate in a kitchen with generous windows and an old gas stove with six burners. Pots and pans hung from a rack suspended from the ceiling, seemingly adjusted to people of Kate's height. She had set in to heating up some venison stew she had retrieved from the well-stocked pantry.

"Why don't you have a shot of whiskey and a beer until this is ready?" Kate said.

"Don't say stuff like that if you ever want me to leave here," Dan said.

Kate laughed and stood on her toes to kiss his cheek. "I can always count on you to get it."

"Guess so."

No sooner had they finished eating than the power went out.

"Wow!" Kate shouted in the sudden darkness.

"Excellent!" Dan cried.

Lightning flickered, illuminating coursing rivulets of water running down the windows, and the hulking shadows of trees thrashing like enraged sentries. Thunder tore through the sky.

They went around and lit candles. Kate took a flashlight from a drawer and got three brass lanterns from a closet. Soon they were sprawled on the thick oriental rug in front of the fire, reclining on pillows, as the wind whooshed and whistled around the cabin, Kate with a glass of red wine, Dan with a beer and a glass of whiskey.

Dan found that he couldn't resist the urge to go outside. Rather than trying to talk him out of it, Kate got enthusiastic about the idea. She found foul weather gear and rubber boots, and they dressed up like space explorers about to go out onto the surface of a hostile planet.

"You'd better go out first," Kate said, "so you can hold onto the screen door and keep it from getting torn off its hinges. I'll close the inside door."

"Okay!" With this teamwork they closed the cabin up tightly. Immediately, there was a gratifyingly startling clap of thunder and flash of lightning. They both laughed.

"This way!" Kate called, taking his hand like an insistent little girl and leading him up a sandy slope away from the cabin and into a stand of whipping pine boughs. Dan turned around once to see the cabin behind them, the windows warm with the light of the candles and lanterns.

The cabin, it seemed, was in a little bowl surrounded by trees. Once over the rim of this bowl, they walked through dunes topped with swaying dune grass. Kate obviously knew the way, which was good, because the darkness was profound, little glimpses of their surroundings provided by the flashes of lightning.

Soon these flashes showed Dan the roiling water of the lake, the waves black and edged with white as they curled and boomed into the shore. It was one of the most exciting things he had ever seen. Kate walked him along the beach, taking him by the hand and walking where the sand was firm at the farthest extent of the breaking waves. She led him along, a determined set to her little body, as if she were protecting him.

They reached a stony point and stood above the riotous waves. When lightning seemed to crawl from cracks in the clouds like electric spiders along the roof of a cave, Kate squeezed his hand in one of hers and pointed with the other.

"Look!" she cried.

Dan laughed in delight.

"Do you think you could paint that?" she shouted.

"Boy, I don't know!"

A flash of lightning showed him the smile on her rain-wet face. He bent and kissed her.

After some time, she led him back up the dunes and down through the trees to the warm cabin. They closed the door tightly behind them and took off the foul weather gear. Only at that point did they realize how drenched was the clothing they had worn underneath, where the rain had coursed in spite of their hoods, soaking their fronts and backs.

"We have no choice but to take off these sodden garments!" Kate declaimed.

"Our very survival depends upon it!" Dan cried.

Once her pale, curvy body was naked in front of him, Dan said, eyeing her perfect pink nipples and the soft amber hair between her legs, "Now I must keep you alive with the warmth of my own body! We have no other choice!"

"I'll get some quilts! And perhaps some flavored lubricants!"

Dan threw more split logs on the fire as Kate laid out quilts. They made love for some time in front of the fire, then fell asleep, exhausted, not even making it upstairs to bed on their first night in the cabin.

The next morning was quiet and clear. Dan woke with his face less than a foot from Kate's. In the peaceful light, she looked about fifteen years old. Dan couldn't help but grin as he watched her.

He got up, letting her sleep, and slipped on a pair of shorts and a t-shirt. Going out the front door as quietly as he could, he walked out onto the porch.

The mystery of the place began to dissipate in the daylight. There was his van, there the pine trees, and behind them nothing but blue sky. There were cherry and apple trees off to one side, and a two-rut driveway winding back off through the woods. Dan walked barefoot up through the pine trees and out to the dunes.

The view was stunning, majestic, a kind of majesty that dwarfed that of the river. The sky was fathomless, deep blue with high cirrus clouds, the rain gone. The scent of the morning air was so clean, so fresh, that Dan could almost taste it on his tongue. Involuntarily, he tried to taste it, touching his lips with the tip of his tongue. He breathed it in as slowly, a scent so subtle, so fine, that he felt that it could heal something in his lungs, in his bones, in his brain. It was like letting sun and wind into a musty room.

And what were the colors of the water stretching to the horizon? Teal, certainly, aquamarine and cerulean, cobalt over there, chartreuse over those shallows. He wandered out into the biting cold water, swells coming in up to his knees. Gulls cried overhead.

Beautiful, he thought. How beautiful. He felt a great peace, a stillness of joy. Crystal waves surged around his knees, and he laughed to himself. He stood like that for a long time, losing track, thinking not about the past or the future (where lie both regret and worry), but only of that very moment.

208

At the sound of a shrill whistle, he turned around and saw Kate at the top of the dunes, the pines at her back. She was about to whistle again, two fingers between her lips, but cupped her hands around her mouth instead, shouting, "Breakfast!"

Dan waved back and trotted up across the dunes, through the scented and shadowy pines and to the cabin. As he walked through the door, he nearly stopped in his tracks at the scent of pancakes and bacon and strong coffee. He sat down grinning at the sturdy table.

They walked down the beach after breakfast, looking for anything interesting which might have washed up on the shore after the storm. There was, indeed, a noticeable wrack-line of sticks and seaweed, and a few giant logs with roots protruding bonily, stripped completely of bark as if they'd been floating for decades. Kate found a plastic jug and a faded orange life preserver. Dan filled his front pockets with sea glass.

"Look," he said at one point. "Red one. Rare." He held the glass up to the light. It looked like a rough ruby.

"Pretty," Kate said, hugging his arm and putting her head against his shoulder.

They walked far down the beach and back as the sun moved higher in the sky. If Kate found any garbage, she picked it up to throw away. Dan used his knife to cut away part of the plastic jug so she could use it as a receptacle.

When they got back to the cabin before noon, the sun was near its zenith, and the clearing in the trees was bright, the sand hot under their bare feet. The interior of the cabin was cool and dim, though, and it was wonderful to walk inside.

Dan put the sea glass into a pickling jar as Kate began to make lunch. He put the jar on the windowsill where it caught the light.

After lunch, they took a book apiece from the shelves and went up to sit in the shade of the pines overlooking the water as they read, sprawled on the quilt Kate had brought. The place was secluded, no one up or down the beach. Dan and Kate shared a look and a smile, and they shed their clothes to do it under the shifting shadows of the pine boughs. After they'd both come, they pulled the edges of the quilt over themselves and fell asleep under the pines.

It was Saturday evening, and they listened to Kate's favorite radio show as they cooked garlic and rosemary chicken with mashed potatoes (which Kate made with herbs and *bacon*), along with a salad, and local cherry pie for dessert. As they listened to the last hour of the radio show, Dan drew sketches of Kate. He wondered for an instant what Charlie and the Horsedicks would think of him playing Monopoly with Kate for hours at the dining room table, and was quite sure he didn't give a shit.

They slept in the biggest bed upstairs, which had a view of the water over a grove of cherry trees to the south of the pines. Dan woke up to the pure morning light through the open windows and knew that he never wanted to live any other way.

They went to the beach every day, naturally. Kate's fair skin forced her to wear long sleeves and light pants for part of the day, but Dan wore shorts alone and got very brown. Kate loved it, she said, loved the look of his brown hands as they brushed her fair thigh or cupped her breast. She loved how the scar in his eyebrow remained white, kissing him there frequently.

They went into town to check out the few small bars. Dan's favorite immediately became one where Kate had worked summers as a teenager. Hell's Gate, whose name belied the owner's nature and the kind of bar he ran. It was the only place Dan had ever been in which Bach was playing as he walked through the door, a sound incongruous with the pine paneling and trophy fish mounted on the walls. There was, however, framed artwork in some abundance, and several large, disorganized bookshelves along many of the walls. Even better was the fact that the bar, deceptively narrow from the front, had a four-lane bowling alley in the back, alongside which was a wall adorned with dart boards. Dan laughed with delight.

The owner, a rotund man with a fu manchu moustache and a ponytail, waddled tirelessly behind the bar in an apron, seeming to keep up with his food specials with no noticeable effort. He had an enormous jar on the old backbar which contained pitted cherries from the island soaked in locally made vodka, and, for a modest price, a customer could get a shotglass of three cherries. There was a bit of a bite (and eventually a buzz) from the cherries, and Dan found that he had to limit his consumption of them.

When more customers came in later in the evening, the owner, Russ, might change the music to bluegrass or big band. On the other hand, he might not. Although he didn't resemble Dan's grandfather in the slightest, Dan knew they would've liked each other. The old bastard.

The days were full and brilliant, an hour seeming to take forever, while a day itself took no time at all. They used old Schwinn bikes from the cabin's garage (after Dan tinkered them up with some oil and simple tools, using a hand pump to invigorate the flattened tires) to pedal around the island, passing cherry and apple orchards, small cottages and tiny, rustic hotels. They rented a little Sunfish to take sailing, sliding through the waves, until they capsized into the frigid water due to an error on Dan's part. Kate just laughed, and showed him how to right the boat after waving off an offer of assistance from a passing power boater. Back on shore, Dan gave her a dry sweatshirt from his van, the garment engulfing her, while he stripped off his t-shirt and replaced it with a long-sleeved one of cozy flannel. He did insist on some of the high octane cherries from Hell's Gate, though, as soon as they were comparatively dry.

Far too soon for either of them, their vacation was over. They spent the last morning cleaning up and getting everything neat for the next people to stay there, either Kate's mother or her older sisters and their children. Dan sighed rather desolately as Kate locked the green front door. As they drove off, the concerns of his life in Greysport began to settle on him. He thought once about his grandfather, but pushed the thought away.

"Oh, cheer up," Kate said. "We could live here someday if we wanted to."

Dan looked at her. "Both of us?"

"Of *course* both of us!" Kate cried, shoving his shoulder. "What fun would it be without *you*?"

Dan thought he might have blushed. He'd never imagined that anyone would want to do something permanent with him, let alone someone like Kate.

They were a bit spent on the ride home, a little doleful. They kissed sweetly before they parted ways for the week. Dan sighed as he pulled up in front of the power plant, the stench of the tallow plant and the slaughterhouse heavy in the motionless afternoon air.

210

Ramu grinned at him when he came through the door. "Hey, *madarchod*," Ramu said, and Dan knew he was back to reality.

A new semester began. Dan paid his tuition in cash, which seemed to confuse the woman behind the counter. It irked him to hand it over; his classes this semester consisted mostly of requirements which he found boring.

The surprise delight of the term was a class in American History. The professor, Ryan Lannon, was a young man in his thirties with wild curly hair, a beard, and oval, wire-framed glasses, over which he peered at the class to see if his point were getting across. While Dan thought the lecture was fascinating, he saw a fratboy in a pink Izod shirt reading a student newspaper in class and spoke to him about it when the period was over.

"Don't do that shit," he told the fratboy.

"Why not?" the fratboy said.

"Because it's disrespectful. The guy knows more than you're ever going to, and he's trying to teach your lame ass something. So don't do it. Show some respect."

The fratboy drew back a bit from Dan, but tried to save some face. "What do you care, man? It's just a requirement."

"There are more requirements involved."

"Like what?"

"Like I'm going to *require* that you show some respect or I'm going to *require* that you get your ass kicked. Got me?"

The fratboy didn't say anything, only turned and walked away.

"You'd take this more seriously if your daddy wasn't paying for everything," Dan said after the boy's back. "You little cunt."

Not only did the fratboy show no disrespect towards the professor again, he never returned to class. Dan hoped that it had been something he said. He hoped he'd see him at the Bar of Paddy McX.

Ryan Lannon was so interesting that Dan considered bringing guests to sit in on the lectures. Kate, Charlie, and Tom would all have loved the odd man's discourses, which seemed, at times, to wander off on irretrievable tangents before the man brought all the seemingly disparate threads of his ramblings together, tied up in a neat knot at the end of the period.

In October, they were covering World War One. Dan found it so interesting and enlightening that he took advantage of the professor's office hours to talk to him about it. It became apparent that the man's students rarely did this, and he was pleased to talk to Dan, inviting him in to his disorganized nook, its shelves packed with books and papers, the walls covered with maps, photographs, and posters. Dan sat in a threadbare, comfortable chair and began asking questions from a list he had prepared. Before long, Lannon had taken the conversation off in interesting directions, as Dan might have predicted.

"I guess I never understood anything about this before," Dan said. "The more you know, the more interesting it gets."

Lannon clapped his hands together and held them up. "Exactly!" he exclaimed.

"My grandfather fought in World War One," Dan said.

"Really! Where did he fight? What battles was he in?"

"I guess I don't know. Maybe he told me, but I don't remember." Dan felt suddenly guilty, then hoped he caught himself before it showed.

If Lannon noticed anything, he waved it off. "It's typical. Don't feel bad. We know *some* of our parents' stories, little *bits* of our grandparents', almost *nothing* of our great-grandparents', if anything at all. Cemeteries are filled with forgotten gravestones where relatives once stood, vowing to keep memory alive."

This made Dan jerk his head back and stare at Lannon. Willy had once said the same thing, when he and Dan had been walking in the Coeur de la Riviere cemetery.

"Is your grandfather still alive?" Lannon said.

"Yeah."

"Ask him lots of questions," Lannon said. "That's where you get some real insight into history. Ask your dad."

"He's dead. Since I was a kid."

Lannon stopped moving, then slowly looked at Dan.

"I'm so sorry," he said.

"It's okay. I'm getting so I can't remember him."

Lannon moved in a way that seemed like he wanted to put his hand on Dan's. He stopped, though, leaning back in the swivel chair in which he sat, lacing his fingers behind his head.

"Then ask your grampa about your dad," he said. "Try to remember."

Dan shuffled out of the office and down to his bus stop. He got on the bus robotically, and nearly missed where he needed to get off, right across the bridge from the power plant.

The rhythms of his life soon dulled the sense of anything else. He nearly forgot about Denfer Island. He was with Kate as much as he could be on weekends, although sometimes she begged off, seeming to keep him at arm's length. He didn't ask why this was so, retreating into some place of invulnerability. Perhaps she'd figured out that he was a *maldito*.

On such occasions, he partied hard with Charlie and the Horsedicks and Jumpin' Irv, or, in a completely different vein, with Tom Schwartz. With the former, things were predictably unpredictable. One night, when the things had gotten boring, they were walking down the street when Charlie had announced that needed to piss. He'd walked up the steps to the round door of a Chinese restaurant, all its lights off, and dangled his dong through the mail slot to let fly. He withdrew his unit, the flap snapped shut, and he began walking away grinning. He'd only gone a few feet when the door of the restaurant was flung open from within, and out sprang a squad of Chinese kitchen workers, almost all of them bearing slicing or chopping instruments of some kind. Dan, Charlie, and the other hoodlums had run away, howling with laughter.

They weren't the type who liked to run from anything, though, even when they'd been wrong in the first place. Retribution, in this case, took the form of returning in the early morning, using a plan of the Horsedicks' devise. First, a fortuitous garden hose was run from a nearby alley and into the mail slot. The lads sat by for awhile, passing around a bottle of whiskey as the lobby of the restaurant filled with in inch or so of water. After a certain point- Dan wasn't sure what that was- the Horsedicks worked in concert to withdraw the hose, wind it up neatly. They then took a pipe bomb, which Chris had carried in the inside pocket of his bomber jacket, lit the waterproof fuse and threw it into the mail slot, recently violated by Charlie's dong. There was a pause, and then a dense boom, an instant's illumination of the windows, and the whole crew ran away laughing, this time with no one in pursuit.

Upon reflection, Dan wasn't sure if he liked the whole thing. Charlie, after all, had pissed through the mail slot of the restaurant. The fact that they had been chased with knives seemed only fair. He would have done the same thing to anyone who had so assaulted his grandfather's bar. So, he was sure, would Charlie.

The Horsedicks kept things interesting by doing more than brawling, doing acid, and drinking as if it were a stunt. One night they got it into their heads to throw molotov cocktails out into intersections in the early hours when oncoming cars were only a block away. They, too, had a van, flat tan with black lightning bolts on the doors, which they pulled into a parking lot after promising a show to the local punks. The rags were lit, the bottles lofted, and plumes of flame curled up into the night as the sparse traffic screeched to a halt. Charlie was obviously a bit put out; he'd been the one to start things with molotovs, so many years ago. Although he was too cool to say anything about it, Dan could tell what he was thinking by the dull, narrow look in his eyes.

Partying at Tom's was almost a respite, a cool, philosophical place where one did acid, drank good booze, and listened to classical music. Dan painted while Tom practiced guitar or piano. It wasn't that they didn't drink and do drugs, obviously. They did; they just did so in a manner that was productive.

When his schedule permitted, Dan stopped by Kate's daycare on the south side. At first, he had been reluctant to do so, although he wasn't sure why. He grumbled about it, but Kate persisted, pointing out that it wasn't far from the power plant, and he could just poke his head in the door.

"Aren't you curious about it?" Kate asked him.

It was simply not possible to say no to that little smile, to those blue eyes.

"I guess so," Dan said, smiling a little himself and dropping his gaze.

"You guess so?" She knuckled his arm.

"I'm curious. I'm *really* curious. I'm *overwhelmed* by curiosity, nearly *paralyzed* with it."

"I know!" she cried. "How could you *not* be!"

The daycare was in the neighborhood of Riverside, which could be interpreted to form a right triangle with Portview and the power plant. Dan pulled up on a Wednesday afternoon an hour before going to work.

It was not what would be described as a good neighborhood, being similar to Portview in many respects. The residents had made the most of it, though, and many of the brick and cinderblock walls of the area's buildings were painted with murals from poor to pretty good. The streets were lined with large old trees, now coloring with the cool fall weather. People had gone to the trouble of putting flowers in window boxes, and there was not much litter in evidence.

The daycare center itself had a mural overlooking its playground, which was enclosed by a high chainlink fence. The mural had a stylized rainbow and a flat blue sky, a lazily painted (in Dan's opinion) green hill, and a gaggle of cheerful multi-ethnic children in the foreground. As Dan regarded this mural, imagining something by Monet on the wall, double doors opened and a flood of screaming children, living models for the cartoon kids in the mural itself, issued from the daycare. Kate walked out with a large black woman. When she saw Dan, she lit up and smiled.

Kate let him in a side gate, opening a padlock to do so. She introduced Dan to her co-worker, Lateisha, who smiled shyly as she shook Dan's hand. They sat at a picnic table and watched the children while they talked.

"Nice mural," Dan said.

"We did it together," Lateisha said. "Me and Kate."

"Dan's an artist," Kate said. Lateisha raised her eyebrows, impressed, but Dan held up a hand and shook his head.

Kate nodded at the mural and said, smiling, "Think you can do better?"

"For the intended purpose? No. Not unless a big, sprawling thing with open graves was what you had in mind."

"Ooooh," Lateisha said, "and zombies."

Dan chuckled. "Zombies'd be good."

They all laughed. That was when the children noticed Dan, gravitating in, surrounding the table and jabbering questions. The kids were so funny that Dan found himself laughing out loud. Kate and Lateisha, with some effort, redirected the children's energy to different activities. Dan didn't move from the table, though, simply sitting and watching the children with a smile on his face, fascinated by the idea of what might be going on in their cheerful, sunny (and as yet unstained) minds. They scattered around the playground, chattering and screaming, all of them in their own way lacking any self-consciousness, doing, it seemed, whatever their bodies told them to do: walking jerkily, improvising little dance steps, running so fast they kicked themselves in the butt with their heels, squatting to investigate a bug on the ground. Dan watched, mesmerized, until he realized that Lateisha had left the table, and Kate was sitting watching him with a soft smile on her face. Dan smiled back and took her hand.

He stopped at the daycare more often after that.

Near the end of October, Dan had a dream. He was out on the river with his grandfather. They were in the jonboat, fishing. They were having a conversation, most of which Dan would not remember when he awoke. As Willy talked, Dan noticed that his father was on the shore a hundred feet away, back to the river, broadbacked in a workshirt. His father was shouting into the woods, and Dan couldn't tell if it were about a threat or in welcome.

At that moment, his grandfather held up a fish he had caught, huge, impossibly huge.

"Well, then!" Willy said. The giant fish thrashed in the boat, hanging over the gunnels. Dan was both amazed and terrified.

When the flopping of the fish slowed, Willy said, "See how the scales overlap, one after another?"

Dan didn't hear his own voice in the dream, but knew that he meant 'yes'.

Willy understood and said, "The scales are like our lives, overlapping, one over the next. See?"

Dan voicelessly agreed.

"And our stories are big and long," Willy said. "Bigger than you can think about. Bigger than a fish longer than this river, the head upstream in the future, the tail downstream in the past. All of our stories overlapping one over the next, none of them understanding the…"

Kate's alarm woke him up. He thought about the dream all day, about the overlapping of their stories, about his father on the bank of the river.

Greysport lived up to its name with approaching winter. It got dark early and the first flurries came down, although nothing stuck. There was beauty in this grimness, and there were times when he relished working at the power plant. Sometimes after work, he drove down to the abandoned warehouses by the port, cruising through the desolation slowly, listening to a somber tape. More than once he drove at a funeral pace past 718 Pier, looking up to see if the lights were on in a given apartment.

For all the luscious squalor of the city, the true and unadulterated beauty of Denfer Island was refreshed for him in November when he and Kate drove there for Thanksgiving. Kate had suggested that they go out to the river to spend it with Willy, but Dan rationalized both to Kate and himself that they would do it next year.

They took Kate's car, which was easier to keep warm. This time it was not an escape from the city heat, but a drive north under deepening clouds. The landscape was beautifully melancholy, the trees leafless, the fields brown. As they drove by abandoned beaches, the waves came in strong and grey, the water glinting out to the gunmetal clouds on the horizon, pale gold beams of sunlight breaking here and there through the overcast. It was nice to have Kate drive; Dan looked out at the scenery composing landscapes, identifying colors. The fact that his imaginary landscapes included distant dismal crucifixions or burnings at the stake (these bright plumes, a tiny, agonized black figure in their midst, over there on the horizon) he kept to himself, wary of the infection of his thought.

They came to the end of the peninsula, to the ferry launch. Flurries got thicker around them, the sky so heavily clouded that it seemed well towards dusk rather than mid-afternoon. The ride across on the ferry was bumpier than it had been the previous summer, although to the ferry captain, it was a matter of course.

"We do it in the dead of winter," the captain told them when Kate asked for Dan's benefit.

Dan was a bit nervous about meeting Kate's family. He thought back to the Thanksgivings of his childhood, when his grandmother was still alive, when he was still capable of happy illusion, of a child's warm view of the world. Whatever cheer these strangers might muster, he wanted to create a convincing portrayal of a young man who enjoyed such things without doubt, without irony. He was afraid he'd be unable to carry out such a deception, that Kate's sisters and mother would see him for what he was. Kate didn't object when Dan wanted to stop at the Hell's Gate bar for some vodka cherries and a couple of beers.

The rest of the family was already there when they arrived, the lights of the cabin glowing as they pulled in and up near the pines. It was the Wednesday evening before the feast, and although Dan had tried to rationalize coming on the day itself (so doubtful was he of his ability of sustaining the illusion of Pleasant Young Man), Kate just ignored him.

"Don't worry, you'll be fine," she said, seeming once more to see right through him. "They'll like who you are. You're surly sometimes, but it's a good surly."

Dan didn't know exactly what that meant, but was beginning to trust what Kate said even when he didn't agree with it, or even understand it.

There was activity in the kitchen, they could see as they approached. The shouts of children came from inside.

"Remember," Kate said, "six nieces and nephews. It'll be like the kids at the daycare, but way better."

Dan grabbed the two bottles of applejack that he'd bought without knowing why, and said, "I'll never remember their names."

"Sure you will. Eventually. Just call them 'hey, you' until you do. They'll love it."

"And your sisters' names?"

"Sue's the oldest, Ann next. Husbands Rick and Terry, respectively. Rick's the truck driving guitarist, Terry the hippie carpenter philosopher."

"Hippie carpenter philosopher. Right."

They went through the door to cheers. Three boys, ranging in ages from five to ten, took one look at Dan, seemed to sense something about him, and rushed to grapple with his thighs in an attempt to bring him to the floor. Two women in their thirties, red-haired, blue-eyed, sunnysmiled older versions of Kate, shouted from the kitchen as Kate ran to embrace them. Two men, one with an Elvis haircut and a workshirt, another wearing flannel and a ponytail, looked up from where they were talking over beers at the long dining table. A woman in her fifties, an older, matronly version of Kate, waded expertly through the chaos and handed Dan a Greysport Lager.

"Glad you could come, Dan," she said. To his surprise, she leaned over the grunting boys wrapped around his legs and kissed him on the cheek. "I'm Mary ."

There were only snacks that night, most of the preparations in the kitchen aimed at the feast the next day. Dan walked into the kitchen to introduce himself, pretending to ignore the boys clinging to his thighs.

"He's the Hulk!" the middle one said.

"Well, I'm Spider-Man!" the youngest one claimed.

Dan sipped his beer and shook hands with Sue and Ann, who gave Kate looks of what might be described as salacious approval. Kate gave a look back that said she knew. Three young girls, the approximate ages of the boys, were standing on chairs in the kitchen, trying to help their mothers. They noticed the exchange between the sisters. The oldest one piped, "Do you smooch him, Aunt Kate?"

"I sure do!" Kate said, smooching him.

The girls looked at each other. "Wooooooo!" they cried delightedly.

Step by step with a wide-legged stance, Dan dragged the boys back into the living room to introduce himself to the husbands. They laughed as he approached. The one with the Elvis haircut introduced himself as Rick and clinked the neck of his beer bottle with Dan's. Pony-tailed Terry took a look at the three boys grunting with effort at Dan's legs and laughed.

"Welcome to the club, man."

"What club is that?" Dan asked, smiling.

"The Male Attendants of the Driver Matriarchy," Terry said. "Right, Rick?

"Fuckin' A," Rick said, grinning. "I don't mind bein' no man-toy."

Dan snorted at this comment.

After a few beers, Dan was given the task of keeping the kids occupied. The thought flashed through his mind that this might be some kind of a test, a form of hazing (had Kate gotten him down to the daycare center as a warm-up?), but the kids' cheering reaction to the idea had Dan scrambling about how to keep them occupied. They looked up at him in anticipation, mop heads of red and brown and yellow hair, blue and green eyes alight with anticipation.

"Well, uh…" Dan said, looking over at the kitchen, where a quartet of redheads watched him, smiling. Kate gave him a thumbs-up and a tongue-out grin.

"Let's see…" Dan continued, "anybody want to learn how to draw cartoons?"

The kids roared, jumping up and down.

"I don't suppose there are crayons and paper around here," Dan said.

"Got 'em!" Kate called from the kitchen, producing the articles so quickly that Dan knew she had anticipated him and had them waiting around the corner. She put them at one end of the long dining table, Terry and Mick watching at the other.

"I'm too old for crayons," said Kevin, the oldest boy.

"I know, man," Dan said, tapping the boy's shoulder with his knuckles. "You're way too old for that. You should be drawing with a pencil, or even a pen."

"I'm pretty good," Kevin said.

"I'll bet."

Soon Dan had them all going, busily scribbling away. He leaned over again and again, giving pointers and drawing examples. He liked how they were oblivious of their poses in their concentration: this one stuck his tongue out as he drew, that one sat with her foot in an impossibly flexible position underneath her, another made faces and sound effects as he ground his crayon into the paper. Dan watched the children's progress, heedless of the conversation from the kitchen, or even the other end of the table.

"That is one of the most hideous monsters I've ever seen," he told Trevor, the youngest boy.

"Do you like my princess?" asked Tess, the middle girl.

"It's like something from a fairy tale," Dan said. "Draw the kind of prince you'd like to see."

"I don't need anyone to *rescue* me," Tess objected. The trait runs in the family, Dan thought.

"Then draw one *you* could rescue," he said.

"Okay!"

It was obvious that Dan's attentions gave the parents relief. When he looked up at the fathers, Terry mouthed *keep going* and Rick nodded, his eyes wide. Fifteen minutes later, he glanced up at the door to the kitchen to see Mary and Ann watching him, smiling.

The fire was large in the hearth, warming the place, and Dan took off his sweater, down to his sleeveless t-shirt. It was an unconscious action; he was merely hot. After awhile, Kevin noticed.

"*Wwwwwoh!*" Kevin cried. "You must be stronger'n shit!"

"Kevin!" a shout came from the kitchen.

"Sorry!" Kevin called back, but continued. "How much can you bench press?"

It amused Dan that Kevin knew what bench-pressing was at the age of ten. "Four hundred pounds or so," Dan said.

"*Wwwwwwoh!*" the kids cried.

"Could you pick up a car?" asked Olivia, the smallest girl.

"Maybe a really small one," Dan said.

Soon he was allowing the children to hang from his arms, which he held out into a T. Next he was holding this position while on his knees, with all six kids wrapped around his arms as he tried to stand.

"Betcha can't do it," Kevin giggled.

"Betcha I *can*," Dan said, getting to one foot, then the other, shouting "Grrrraaaahhhhh!" as he stood up, the laughing and screaming kids hanging from his trembling arms. As he stood like this, ready to buckle, he saw Kate watching him smiling, her eyes glittering.

With the kids so wound up, and the hour being what it was, he knew that he had to wind them back down. This he did by drawing caricatures of them in a way he thought they would enjoy, having seen their dispositions in their own drawings. This boy would be a gargoyle with batwings, this girl a princess with a tiara and the powers of levitation. Dan worked quickly, wanting to keep them interested. They crowded around watching, rapt.

Kate watched him in adoration. Dan grinned back at her, for the moment not suspicious of his happiness, so involved in what he was doing that he was simply happy.

Even when the kids were settled down, it was hard to get them to bed. The mothers, their respite over, herded them up the stairs. When the kids quieted down, the adults sat around the dining table, drinking, talking, and laughing. The families were intertwined, knowing each other well, and yet they did not make Dan feel like a stranger. Rather they pulled him in, made him feel at home, asked him real questions about himself. He held Kate's hand on top of the table.

One by one, people drifted off to bed. Dan and Kate settled down in front of the fire in a nest of quilts and pillows, as they had on the first night on Denfer Island. Before he fell asleep, it occurred to Dan that he had felt a little nervous before coming through the door of the place. In the fireplace, a knot in a burning log popped, and Kate snuggled up to him. He realized how ridiculous he had been.

It snowed more than six inches during the night. Barely awake, Dan could tell by quality of morning light coming through the window. He got as close as possible to Kate under the covers, looking at his watch, wondering when the kids would wake up and notice what had happened.

Kate awoke just as the first shout came from upstairs. Soon all the children were yelling and squealing, "Snow! It snowed!" A chaos of thumping came from the floor overhead, along with pleas from the groggy adults to keep it down.

"I'll make coffee," Kate said, kissing him before she got up.

Soon the kids were thundering down the stairs, looking around for coats, hats, and mittens, the older ones helping the younger get dressed,

"Dan! Dan!" Kevin shouted. "Come on! Snow!"

"Okay," Dan said, slipping on fatigue pants over his boxers.

Soon Dan and the six children were outside in the brilliant day. He led them up through the shadowy pines and down to the dunes all dazzling before them, down to the calm bright blue water. The children screamed with delight, running through the fresh snow. Dan watched them for a moment, involuntarily composing a painting in his mind, the bright fresh snow, the sky almost cobalt blue at its zenith, shading to pale towards the horizon, the water blue beneath it but the small waves themselves a transparent jade as they curled and hushed into the shore. He had no idea how to depict the fact that the air seemed to have more oxygen in it, that it made him feel both revived and soothed, made him want to laugh for no good reason. The kids seemed to feel the same, running across the gleaming beach, goofy and hilarious, shouting and laughing and acting like little idiots. Dan grinned until his face cramped.

"Don't fall in the water!" he called. "No death by hypothermia!" It was his grandfather's voice, his *father's* voice, he realized, popping out before he could consciously form the words. He found this both amusing and gratifying.

There was a snowball fight, as one might imagine, the Kids versus Dan. Dan didn't have to pretend too much that he lost, in spite of the protracted nature of the battle. He ultimately admitted defeat, sprawled at the feet of his conquerors with snow in his hair, in his ears, everywhere, the children grinning like puppies, panting and red-cheeked. At Kevin's instigation, they all piled onto him, wrestling. Dan tickled the girls and was a little more rough with the boys, pretending to do a savage knee drop with Kevin, who gurgled gorily and went through dramatic death throes. When they were all panting, laughing and exhausted, Dan got them to their feet and began walking in a cluster back to the cabin, where Kate, dependably, was making an enormous breakfast.

It was the best Thanksgiving that Dan had ever experienced, the best he'd ever even heard of. Whatever went on in the Gates mansion that day could not have eclipsed it. Dan offered to help in the kitchen, or to play Monopoly with Terry and Rick, but the children had taken a liking to him and would let him do nothing without them.

So there were walks on the brilliant beach, Dan fielding questions and making jokes with a swarm of children around him, all jockeying for his attention, the smallest taking turns on his shoulders. When they were inside, they took over the dining table with drawings, and soon most of the kitchen was festooned with them, held up on the walls with tape. One night Dan got a break when Terry, a native of the island, told the ghost stories he had heard as a child. There were a lot of them. Dan watched the kids' eyes by the firelight as Terry, his gift for language set loose, terrified them, made them gasp. Dan thought that he might have loved those kids.

But yes, the feast itself was unparalleled. It was Dan's first exposure to the Driver women and their cooking, but it was beyond his realm of experience, beyond anything he'd known during the best days of his childhood. The day of the feast, while Dan and his surrounding cloud of children were in and out of the cabin, he caught glimpses of the quartet working in synchrony in the sunny kitchen, Mary making suggestions brief and kind, and only when necessary. Kate worked with a towel over her shoulder and a strand of red hair in her eye, looking over to grin at Dan when she knew he was standing in the doorway.

When the feast was over and the kids were sprawled on the floor, Rick played guitar for them, or Terry told them stories. Eventually they got groggy, then drifted off to sleep. Dan sat at the table with Kate on one side, Mary on the other, Sue and Ann as close as they could sit. The sisters all drank wine, but Dan and Mary had the applejack he had brought. Time passed, Dan listening to the cadences of the women's witty, intelligent speech, all of them like Kate, their delivery and timing polished by the years like sea glass on the beach, by dozens of such gatherings after the merciful death of the father.

Dan and Mary ended up finishing most of both bottles of applejack. Dan had consumed perhaps two-thirds of that amount, but Mary was a small woman; he had to give her credit.

He'd been silent for over an hour, but in a lull in the conversation, the sisters smiling at each other, he said to Mary , placing his hand on hers, "I want to thank you for having me here, Mary ."

"Mom," she said.

"What?"

"Mom," Mary repeated. "Call me Mom."

Maybe it was the applejack, but Dan had a lump his throat. Dan resisted the urge to lean his head on her shoulder. He wanted to ask her forgiveness, for what he did not know. He could do no more than leave his hand on hers, if only for a moment.

When they left early Sunday so that Dan could make it to work in time, he felt a regret so deep it seemed almost like dread. If Kate noticed, she didn't say anything. So they went back to Greysport, back to the obligations they realized, back to the ones they did not.

Their lives resumed. On a Saturday night, Dan and Kate ran into Jim Gates and his girlfriend Jenny at their favorite Indian restaurant, coming in the door just behind the other couple as they waited to be seated.

Dan and Jim were overjoyed to see each other, thudding together in an instant bearhug while Kate and Jenny, strangers, were left to laugh together over the antics of their men. Introductions were made, and they all sat down together.

Jim still resembled Charlie, naturally, but it was only a family resemblance, not the slavish imitation of an adoring younger brother. He was in simple jeans and a black sweater, his hair cut in a practical fashion and left its natural honey blond, not bleached nearly white like his older sibling's. Nor did he have any of Charlie's demeanor of unpredictability; he was calm and polite, considerate of the feelings of the others at the table, especially Jenny's. She was pretty in an understated way, subdued in her dress and manner. It was obvious that they loved each other. It was only Jim's raucous laughter at a particularly funny comment that made Dan think of M-80s and stolen boats, car chases on a summer night. Other than that Jim had changed in a way that made Dan feel as if childhood was far behind him.

It was wonderful to see how Kate and Jenny hit it off. An astronomy student, daughter of two professors (who lived, Dan inferred, in a much more modest and realistic way than did Henry Gates, and were kind, interested, and supportive to boot), she was funny and vivacious. It was also obvious that Jim's relationship with her and her family had given him direction. Jenny and Kate were laughing together within minutes, exchanging embarrassing stories about Dan and Jim, who smiled at each other.

After dinner, the four went out for drinks. The women hit it off so well that Dan and Jim were able to talk at length, the subject coming around to Charlie. Jim had gotten to the point where he was rather disapproving of the way Charlie lived, and didn't hesitate to say so.

"I mean, it's great to go out and party once in awhile, you know? And I don't mind a brawl if there's some point to it. But Charlie, man. His whole living dangerously thing. I'd rather see it as his wild years than as his whole life."

"Smart guy," Dan said. "Got a lot to offer."

"Guys like us maybe have some energy to burn off before we can settle into our lives. I've got it. You've got it twice as much."

Dan laughed. "And Charlie's got ten *times* as much."

"Got that right. Jesus. But if you can be a successful artist and I can go on to become an oncologist, who *knows* what *he* could do."

"We're neither of those things yet," Dan pointed out.

"There you go, being Mr. Negative. People like that come from somewhere. Why not us?" Jim laughed and put his hand on Dan's shoulder. "You've always been so dark. You gotta give yourself a break, man. You're a good guy. And talented."

Dan sighed, smiling a little, shaking his head. "That's what Kate always says."

"Well, listen to her, genius."

"I'll give it a shot."

"Good. What to do about Charlie, though. As dark as you are, he's got all his negativity organized, categorized, and meticulously delineated. A guy who could be anything. A geologist, a playwright, an ichthyologist, you name it. *He* needs someone to listen to."

Dan looked at him. "Since when has he ever listened to anyone?"

"Okay. Got a point there," Jim said. He took a drink and was silent for a moment. "He'll come around, though. I still think he's the best of us."

When it got late, Kate and Jenny exchanged phone numbers, promising to get together; Kate obviously held no grudge against Jim for being Charlie's brother, liking him on his own merits and Jenny on hers. Dan felt oddly hopeful after his talk with Jim; it was interesting to hear the kind of things Kate said about him, coming out of the mouth of someone else he trusted, the words in slightly different form. It gave him something to think about, at any rate.

Dan maintained a positive attitude well into December, feeling good about the end of the semester, perhaps even about some kind of future with Kate. He began, tentatively, to suspect that things with her might last, that things would be all right. He dared to imagine, in short bursts, a happy future. He wasn't quite sure *how* to imagine it, but fell back on what his grandfather had said, that he should pursue the life he wanted, not the life he would merely accept.

When things went wrong, though, they went wrong quickly.

On the Monday night after the Thanksgiving weekend, Dan went out with Charlie to have a few beers after work. Charlie seemed to be in a contemplative mood, as happened from time to time. The fact that he wanted to go to a quiet corner bar that they rarely frequented told Dan that he had something to he wanted to talk about.

Charlie said nothing at first. Dan took advantage of this atypical silence to tell Charlie about his holiday on Denfer Island. He anticipated that Charlie might give him a hard time about the "domesticity" of the whole thing, but Charlie just slowly sipped his beer and nodded. Dan stopped talking and waited for Charlie to say something more. Charlie was lost in thought, and realized that Dan was watching him.

Finally Charlie spread his hands. "Nice," he said. "Sounds nice."

Dan narrowed his eyes and watched Charlie for another thirty seconds. "Nice, huh?"

"Yeah."

"Okay," Dan said. "What the fuck is going on?"

Charlie laughed tiredly. "It seems that my family is broke," he said. When Dan's mouth dropped open, Charlie continued. "Yeah. I don't know why I ever thought the Gates family status was permanent, but I guess it wasn't."

Dan tried to think of something supportive to say. "Well, you always kind of resented that status anyway."

Charlie smiled a little and laughed again. "I know," he said. "That's what I'm trying to get my head around."

They drank slowly as Charlie told the story. Professor Henry Bosworth Gates was to be a professor no more; the identity in which he had wrapped himself was gone. He had been slapped with two sexual harassment suits by young undergraduate women, and, rather than face any kind of inquiry, had simply resigned. Henry had managed to get all the children home for Thanksgiving, even Gigi, to tell them this. He had emboldened himself with substantial drink before doing so, but had first been able to fake his way through an artificially jolly dinner. Then he had broken down.

"He sat there and just sobbed," Charlie said, staring at the table in front of him, playing with the rings of moisture left by his beer glass. "I mean, I have contempt for the guy, but you don't want to see *that*."

"Contempt?"

"Sure. He's a vain, weak, cowardly windbag. Fucking useless. Never did back up a single thing he said. Remember back when you were living with your mother and that Mike dude in Portview and he had the chance to help?"

"I seem to recall something about that," Dan said drily. "He said he couldn't do anything about it."

"Bullshit," Charlie said. "He could have pulled some strings. Could've done *something*. He just didn't want to get his hands dirty."

"Huh," Dan said.

"Yeah. Still kind of sucked to see him that way."

Once the dam had broken, more of Henry's truth had flooded out. His vanity had kept him from accepting any investment advice, and for years, apparently, he had slowly lost the money he had inherited on frivolity and bad investments. He had taken out a mortgage on the house and had squandered that as well.

"Now he's got to sell the place," Charlie said.

Dan's mouth dropped open again. "Wow!" he cried. "What about all the stuff? Suits of armor, art work. Books! That piano! The, the…"

"Wine collection?" Charlie shrugged. "Auction, I suppose."

"Guess he can't do anything with the headless Bacchus."

"I don't know," Charlie said. "I'm pretty sure there's an armless Venus out there that's worth something."

They looked at each other and started to laugh.

"You always wanted to be working class," Dan said. "Now's your chance."

"Guess so!" Charlie laughed. "Apparently there's and upside to everything!"

Dan wanted to cheer his friend up. "There is! Even death! Seriously. Dead people are really, really relaxed."

"And they don't have to worry about retirement," Charlie said.

"And if your boss wants you to show up for work when you're dead, you *know* the guy's a dick!"

"Makes me want to go out there and *relax* somebody!" Charlie cried.

They laughed hard enough to cause other people in the bar to look their way. Dan might have worried about his friend were it not for his resiliency, a trait he had apparently inherited from his long-gone mother. It certainly didn't come from Henry, who would remain, as Charlie described him, vain, cowardly, and weak.

This was just a little wave though, almost like a warning, compared to the things coming down from upstream.

Since Dan had left the river, several people had told him to get in touch with his grandfather. Kate, Tom, Professor Lannon, even Charlie, from the echoing distance of his "anomie". Kate's persistence got him pondering it the most, though, got him thinking that he had nothing, really, to be angry at his grandfather about, that perhaps his anger was just an excuse that Dan had come up with to avoid, to cover up, a sense of responsibility, like painting over a canvas on which was painted a scene too brutal to contemplate. Kate had said that, one night in early December as they'd eaten dinner in her kitchen. She'd put it tactfully (as if sliding under his defensive radar), but in a manner that got Dan contemplating what she had said.

"Do you think so?" Dan asked her after some moments of silence.

"It's possible," Kate said. "*You're* certainly not to blame. Your childhood was confusing, to put it mildly."

"Huh," Dan said. He could feel his forehead knot up, the beginning of a headache.

"Think of it another way," Kate offered. "Your grandfather's old. There's nothing keeping him out there on the river. He could come and live with us on Denfer Island. It'd be a lot like where he grew up, from everything you told me."

"He could? Live with us, I mean."

"Sure!" she said. "It's just a thought. Let's go out there for Christmas, anyway, and see how it goes."

"You'd give up that time with your family?"

She spread her hands and widened her eyes. "He's the only one you have left."

We're all we've got, Dan thought.

Dan thought about it for a day before he decided to call. He went through the usual prefatory anxiety, sitting on the bed and staring at the phone, but finally dialed the number of the bungalow out on the river. He was startled by the three discordant tones preceding the announcement that the number had been disconnected. He dialed the number again. And again. Finally he checked with an operator from the phone company.

"Yes," the woman said. "That number has been disconnected."

In spite of the fact that it was cool in Kate's apartment, Dan began to sweat. He swallowed repeatedly, his lips feeling dry. Finally, he dialed the number for the Eyrie, letting it ring and ring before hanging up.

He had to ask directory assistance to get the number for the Benitez household. The phone was answered on the second ring by Solvieg. She sounded old, with a quaver in her voice.

"Hi," he said. "It's Dan."

"I'm sorry, who is this?"

"Dan."

"I'm afraid I don't know any Dan."

Oh, shit, she's senile, Dan thought. "Dan McGregor. Willy's grandson. Gordon's son. How are you Mrs. Benitez? Long time no see."

There was a moment of silence before Solvieg said, "Oh, my. *Dan*."

"Yeah! Hi! How are you? I'm trying to find my grandfather. There must be something wrong. His number is disconnected."

"Oh, my," Solvieg muttered. "Oh dear oh dear oh dear. Ding dong dammit. Let me get my husband."

Dan shouted into the phone, but she had set it down. It was several minutes before Emilio answered. Dan could hear Solvieg muttering agitatedly to Emilio before he finally picked up the phone.

"Hello, Dan," Emilio said. "We been especting a call from you for a long time."

"Sorry," Dan said. "I'm looking for my grandfather."

Emilio sighed. "I know," he said. "I have something to tell you."

Dan sat and listened as Emilio told him that his grandfather was dead. Emilio told him a few of the details, but it was too much to handle at the moment, too much for him to take in.

Sue Rebello, the gardening hotel owner in Omicron Falls, had found him in room eleven, where Willy had stayed with Mae so long ago. Willy lay pale on the floor, his shirt open, the old white scars exposed. The back of his pants were soaked with blood. His eyes were open, opaque as agate, his lips, almost smiling, parted as if to speak.

"Oh, no," Rebello said. "Oh, you poor man." She went to the office to call the Sheriff's Department. When the deputies showed up, they were less compassionate.

"Some old drifter, I guess," one of them said.

"No wallet," said another.

"He came in a pickup truck," Rebello said. "At least I thought so."

"No pickup out there now," the first deputy said. They would never know that Willy had given the truck to a girl who had reminded him of Mollie Sletto.

"Lookit those old scars. He must've been a tough old bum."

"Seen some shit, I guess."

"Ten to one he ends up in a county grave."

This statement ended up being accurate, as Emilio would eventually find out. The county coroner was a bitter man who worked with a small staff and a smaller budget and was going through a hate-poisoned divorce. When a woman of obvious farm stock was found beaten to death with a hoe, all evidence pointed to the woman's husband, a farmer with whom the coroner sympathized when the facts of the case came out.

"Bitch fucking deserved it," the coroner was heard saying to one of the Sheriff's deputies. The deputy laughed in order to show how world-weary he was.

The day after Willy's death, a ten-year-old boy driving a tractor flipped it and was crushed, thereby completely filling the coroner's schedule to a level of unpleasantness to which the lazy man was unaccustomed. The old bum found dead in his own bloody shit in the Rebello Hotel fell off his list of important things to do, and he had the old man planted in a pauper's grave just to close the case.

When Willy had left town that final time, it wasn't long before Emilio grew certain of what had happened, and didn't take much investigation to find out where Willy was buried. Emilio drove up to Omicron Falls and talked to Sue Rebello, who seemed relieved.

"I knew that man wasn't alone in the world," she had said. "I knew someone cared about him."

And when Emilio had seen where his friend, his brother, was buried (and of the circumstances, the coroner eventually being fired, and nearly tried, for dereliction of duty), he knew that Dan would come back to bear the weight of it, that Dan would take responsibility. He knew that this day would come, that he would tell Dan these tales. He knew what Dan's response would eventually be, when Dan didn't even know himself.

"I see," Dan said, holding the phone numbly to his ear. "I see."

"There is more to it," Emilio said. "You come out here and talk to me when you want to know the rest."

"Yes. Sure." Dan couldn't think of what to say, which of a hundred questions to ask next. He settled on one: "Where's he...uh...is he buried? Where's he buried?"

"In the wrong place. When you are ready, come and see me."

"I'll come out, Mr. Benitez."

Emilio didn't tell him that it was too late for such things. He simply said, kindly, "Yes. Come and see us, Dan. You come out and see us."

Emilio hung up before Dan could say anything else, although he tried.

"Mr. Benitez? Mr. Benitez!" But he heard only moment of silence followed by a dial tone.

He went out and sat down at the kitchen table.

"Well?" Kate said.

Dan cleared his throat. "He's dead. My grandfather's dead."

"*What*?" she cried. "Oh, *no!*"

She came to him, put her arms around his neck and clung to him. It could only be out of compassion for Dan that she soon began sobbing. When he did nothing, didn't move or speak for several minutes, she finally let go, sitting down in the chair next to him, her face wet with tears.

Dan ran his hands through his short hair. He released a small, low whistle through his pursed lips and thumped his hands on the table. His mouth was dry, his lips sticky. Kate put a hand on his wrist, a keen look of pain and concern in her eyes.

Dan forced himself to breathe slowly and deeply. He related what Emilio had told him in simple terms, all he knew of Willy's death. Then he simply sat in silence. Kate said nothing, just kept her hand on his.

"I don't know what I'm doing," Dan said at last. "I don't know what I've done. What have I done?"

"It's all right," Kate said.

"No it's not," he said. "It's not all right at all."

"It's all right," she repeated. "We'll figure out what to do."

He shook his head, feeling blank.

"See?" he said finally. "I'm a *maldito*. I told you I was."

"Stop that! You are not."

"I am," he said. "You know what it means? *Maldito*? It means cursed. It means damned. If I wasn't before, I surely am now."

"You're not! Stop saying that!"

They sat at the kitchen table for a long time. Every once in a while, Dan whistled softly, a windy, descending tone, and shook his head.

"I have to go," he said finally.

"No, you don't."

"I have to...do something. I have to go."

"You can just stay here," she said. "With me."

"No, I can't," he said, without even being able to say why.

Dan went immediately and without conscious motivation to find the lads at Vnuk's.

He fled an inarticulate sense that if he stayed at Kate's he'd have to confront too much. In the thought-deadening abandonment of partying, he was able to defer facing the things that lurked in his mind that had been there so long, that he had forcefully ignored until they became overwhelming. One of the things he didn't want to face was the unvoiced, inchoate conviction that he didn't deserve Kate, and that this was the thing that would end it. Something would end it, he had always thought, being undeserving of her. This was it.

So he avoided Kate. She called, and he ducked it. When she called at the Kicking Pig one afternoon and Charlie answered, Dan silently waved, motioning that he wasn't there. Kate and Charlie didn't like each other and would spend no time on chit-chat, so Charlie just told Kate that Dan wasn't home and hung up.

Charlie himself was almost neutral about the belated news of Willy's death, in spite of the fact that he held the old man in high regard. "Everybody's gotta go sometime," he said. "Too bad, though. Now we have to prove that we're men enough to fill his shoes."

That was all Charlie said on the matter. It was apparent that he had enough of his own problems on his mind.

Tom was different. He seemed as hard hit as if it was a loss in his own small family.

"That's terrible!" he cried, when Dan brought the news up almost conversationally in Tom's front hallway. "Are you okay? Why didn't you tell me right away?"

Dan shrugged. "Too late to do anything about it," he said blandly.

"Look," Tom said, going into the kitchen and immediately setting about making margaritas, "you're basically in shock. This is going to take some time to sink in."

"Maybe."

"It will. And when it does, I want you to remember you're not alone. You got *me*. Okay? Say it. You've got Tom."

"I've got Tom," Dan said, smiling a little. Tom was actually flustered, *discombobulated*, as Willy might have said.

"You're not *alone*, man," Tom muttered, cutting limes. It seemed as if he were, at least in part, trying to reassure himself. "Wow, what a mindfuck. But you're not *alone*. Got it?"

"Not alone," Dan said, absently repeating the words.

Dan finally talked to Kate just before Christmas. He met her at a bar near her apartment, rather than going into that place, their little enclave. The place where he had once touched happiness. *Home*, she had once said, let's go *home*.

"Let's go up to Denfer Island," Kate said. Her tone was tentative; she obviously felt the distance between them.

"I don't think so," Dan said.

Kate was persistent. "Why?" she said. "It'll be fun! Great food, lots of partying. We can cross-country ski on the beach. The kids will love to see you; they've been talking about you non-stop. I told my mom about your grandfather, and she's worried about you."

Dan sat back in his chair, pulling his forearm out from under Kate's little hand.

"Nah," he said. "I'm just going to stay here."

"Please come," she said. "Please."

"I'm good," he lied. "I'm fine."

Kate had once related a favorite quote to Dan, one from Eleanor Roosevelt: "No one can take your dignity without your consent." She had asked Dan to leave with her. She had pleaded as much as she was going to. And so, when he refused to go, she went to Denfer Island without him. As soon as she left, Dan thought that he should have broken it off with her, so that she could forget about him and go on to have a happy life. Keeping things going between them would only bring her down with him.

Things continued to go wrong in a way which Charlie claimed was statistically unsustainable. He was scheduled to pick up twenty pounds of weed and deliver it on the day before Christmas day to the dreadlocked Trey and the Brothers of the Rising. It had to take place in the afternoon before Trey and his crew had to attend family functions that evening.

Twenty pounds was a lot of dope. Charlie didn't say it, but Dan knew there was a lot of money riding on the deal. Charlie gave a volume discount to Trey, the Dreadlock in Charge, but made a lot of money in return. It was simply that he had to buy the dope from his main supplier himself, putting up all the necessary cash.

Dan agreed with the notion that he didn't need to know the identity of the supplier; there was less information which he could, theoretically at least, be leveraged into divulging. Dan and Charlie read the same kind of spy books, so there was a thrilling element of skullduggery to the very real and serious business at hand.

They were each other's oldest and most trusted friend (in spite of the occasional competitive friction as old as the friendship itself), so Dan took it as an acceptable factor that Charlie would not divulge the name of the main dealer, a man whom, Dan was able to put together over time, flew large quantities of weed in from parts unknown. What Dan did know was that the weed was unusually potent, and much sought after on the street.

Charlie enlisted the use of Dan's van, offering a rather large amount of money (two years of tuition, Dan figured), due to the fact that the van was nondescript. Charlie appeared to appreciate Dan's wisdom on this.

"Didn't I want you to have an orange nuke airbrushed on the side of it?" he asked, when getting Dan to do the move with him.

"Yeah," Dan said.

"That was stupid," Charlie admitted.

"Yeah," Dan said, punching his old friend in the arm. He wanted excitement. Excitement was distracting, a fact of which Dan was consciously unaware.

They picked up the duffel bags of weed at a house in White Birch Pointe that Willy would have described as "swanky". It wasn't nearly as large as the soon-to-be ex-mansion of the Gates family, but was swanky nonetheless. French provincial, white and stately in the soggy snow. Dan pulled into the driveway without comment. He just did it; he wasn't even aware of how much he needed the distraction.

With the December snow deep on the ground, melting on this grey day, the temperature above freezing, Dan pulled his black van up to the neatly shoveled sidewalk to the house. Charlie got out and went up to the front door, rang the bell. The door opened, and a man with grey hair, and artificial tan, and a fluffy white bathrobe opened the stormdoor to talk to Charlie. They smiled and laughed, seeming on good terms. When Charlie indicated the van with a sideways nod, the grey-haired man looked over. Dan lifted his chin at the man, who appeared not to notice. The man went back into the house, closing the front door.

The house had a three car garage, and, as Charlie walked back down the wet walk, the door closest to the house itself began to open automatically. Charlie nodded toward the opening door, and Dan drove forward.

In the other two bays were an Audi and a Mercedes. Dan pulled in slowly, Charlie motioning him on so that he nearly brought the grille of the van in contact with a pristine tool bench. No one had ever worked on a thing on that bench. There were a few obligatory beer signs on the wall, an unlit neon one for Greysport Lager, and two girls' bikes with pink, frilly tassels on the handlebars. Dan turned off the engine and waited as the garage door closed behind him.

After awhile, Charlie came out of a side door with some black duffel bags. He went to the back of the van and opened up the doors, throwing the bags inside. He slammed the doors.

"All right!" he called, and the garage door opened again. Charlie got into the passenger seat with a grin.

"Let's go!" he said. He waited, smiling, while Dan backed out.

"What the fuck was with that guy?" Dan asked, pulling out onto the wet black street.

"Can't say," Charlie said. "Although I'll admit he's weird. You know where we're going, right? BOR dudes from last summer?"

"Yep."

Dan drove south and caught the nearest artery to the freeway. On the freeway, he imagined being rear-ended by a truck, the back of the van smashed open and pound-bags of weed scattering on the pavement just before the police responded to a report of an accident. Traffic was fairly heavy, and he kept looking in the sideview mirrors for anything unusual. He got off the freeway and drove into the Hood with its run-down buildings and weedy lots, a place where he immediately felt more comfortable.

"Let's stop for some barbecue," Charlie said.

Dan might have been feeling like his hinges were a little loose, but this was going too far. "What, with all the dope in the van?" he said. He gave Charlie a little purse-lipped smile to show that he wasn't a pussy.

"Sure," Charlie said. "It'll be fine. Make it more exciting. I've got the .45, anyway."

"Fuck," Dan muttered. He had his knife, but had left the .38 behind.

They pulled into the lot of the Speed King barbecue, a place they frequented on that side of town. The drive-through had four inch plate-glass windows, and the lobby itself had a weaker glass installation of only an inch in thickness. They ate there a tiny percentage of the time that they did at Perrito's (the latter being home), but, at the right moment, it was the right place. They were always the only white people in there, which made it better.

Dan pulled into the lot, parked and locked the van. Charlie's smiling attitude annoyed him, but Dan, finding that he didn't much care what happened, was in the mood for some good barbecue. They got their food, heaping mounds of meat in a square styrofoam container with some red beans and a tiny token piece of white bread. They moaned and smacked over it while they ate. A few people came in from the neighborhood, giving the non-indigenous whiteboys a look before going to the counter.

They finished their food, tossing their containers in the garbage, still getting eyed up from some neighborhood folks. Dan went into the men's room to wash his hands. A large man came in, bumping into Dan seemingly on purpose. Dan gave the man a look both weary and humorous. The man snorted a laugh and lifted his chin at Dan, who went out the door.

Charlie was no longer in the restaurant. Dan looked out the window and saw him with the back doors of the van open, apparently checking the contents of the bags. Feeling a bit of alarm, Dan left the restaurant. Charlie gave him a snort and a tip, just like the man in the restroom. Dan got behind the wheel and started looking for a Talking Heads tape. It might have been somewhere on the floor; he couldn't believe the van had gotten so disorganized. He rifled around through the mess between the front seats.

When he sat back up, there was a gun to his neck. He might have thought that it was simply cold metal if he hadn't turned around slightly, seen the big white plainclothes cop, and seen, peripherally, the gun in the cop's hand.

"Hi!" the cop said cheerfully. "Want to step out of the van?"

Dan sighed. His immediate clear thought was that his grandfather would bail him out, but then he remembered that Willy was dead. The detective yanked him out by the collar of his jacket, had him put his hands against the side of the van and spread his legs. It was only then that he saw the unmarked squad parked at an angle behind the van, as if they'd rolled up silently while Charlie was checking the bags. Charlie was in a similar position at the back of the van, getting searched by another detective, this one short, fat, and black. People came out from the restaurant and from the sidewalks to watch the proceedings, staring frankly, some of them eating barbecue, enjoying the free show.

Dan and Charlie were friends long enough that when they looked at each other while being patted down, a slight widening of Dan's eyes asked Charlie about the gun. Charlie smiled a little and shook his head almost imperceptibly, the look enough to make Dan struggle to keep a stony face. The cops didn't search the whole van, missing Charlie's gun, although the white one found Dan's knife and put it in his own pocket.

"Naughty, naughty," he said to Dan, before handcuffing him and kneeing him in the back of the leg to get him kneeling on the ground, his face against the grimy side of his van. Charlie was in a similar position. He smiled almost imperceptibly, giving a little rise of his eyebrows.

At that moment, the black detective said, "My, my, my oh my! What have we here?"

The white cop said, doing a Monty Python's voice, said, "What's all this then?"

Both of the cops laughed.

Dan's eyes and Charlie's were locked. So this is how I go to prison, Dan thought. They've already got me for carrying a concealed weapon and possession with intent to deliver. Unless Charlie says something when they find the gun, I'll get it for that, too. Charlie wouldn't leave him holding the bag; perhaps they could be cellmates. Whatever the case, they were in the process of getting busted.

He was a bit surprised to find, quite consciously, that he didn't care. He'd miss Kate, but thought that their time was over anyway, that his sense of doom about it had always been correct. This would ensure that she had her freedom, and would go on to have a happy life.

They knelt like that for some time, their faces against the grime and winter roadsalt on the van. They could hear the two cops muttering for a few moments, then heard some shuffling, indefinable sounds. Dan looked over to see the white cop closing the trunk of the unmarked vehicle.

Both of the cops came and got them back on their feet. Each of them, as if it were common procedure, took them by the back of their jacket and banged their heads into the van.

"You motherfuckers are in a lot of trouble," the white one said.

"Yes, you most certainly are," the black one said in turn.

The look that Dan and Charlie shared said that they would not talk.

"Fortunately for you," the black one said, "we're conducting a survey of the quality of contraband in the area, and we're taking this...what...whole *shitload* back here into custody."

Dan was thinking about this when Charlie said, "Wo, wait. Can we work something out?"

The detectives looked at each other and laughed.

The white one said, "We're gonna work you into Greysport county jail, dumbfuck. Want that?"

"No, actually," Charlie said. "That would be inconvenient to my schedule at this time."

The detectives looked at each other again, and laughed even harder.

"So we'll just be taking our sample," the black one said. "And we'll get back to you motherfuckers later."

The white one took off their handcuffs.

"You're free to go," he said. "Try not to be so conspicuous in the future."

"Merry fucking Christmas," the black one added.

And they drove off, with twenty pounds of weed in the trunk of their car.

"Well," Charlie said. "Fuck."

They drove disconsolately to Vnuk's to get drunk. A band was playing that Dan had wanted to see, Afterbirth of a Nation, but he found that he wasn't that interested. They drank at the bar until it closed, snorting lines of coke from the table in plain view. They were the last to leave after the bright lights had been turned on, and had tried even the patience of their friends who ran the place. Finally, they sat in the van before dawn, drinking beer and glumly looking out over the lights of the harbor.

"I'm going to kill those guys," Charlie said.

There was that dead look in his eyes, and Dan believed him.

He woke up in his dark nest of a room on a gloomy Christmas afternoon. His grandfather was dead, his love with her family on a snowy, idyllic island, surrounded by children, by family. Gone; that was gone. He went to the bathroom to take a piss. Before returning he thought about the rifle in his closet, the one his grandfather had given him. He understood why suicides increased around the holidays, understood it on a deep level. If Charlie was right and nothing meant anything, what was the point of enduring misery? Why just play out the string to its shredded end? What made a person do such a thing, some sort of witless stoicism?

231

As dark as he felt, though, he stored such thoughts away. It would have to get worse for him to actually put his grandfather's gun in his mouth, reach down and pull the trigger. He always had that option, though, right there in the closet. After all, who would care?

As it was, he just went back to sleep.

The last time Dan tried to get Kate and Charlie to be friends was also the last time he would live at the Kicking Pig.

Dan was, day after day, in a dazed state, living in such a continual dark fog that it was difficult to make decisions. The fact that he and Charlie had been a whisker away from doing some serious time barely grazed his consciousness; it was like something he had watched disinterestedly on television. He did realize he was lucky that the two detectives were crooked, but didn't have much of an emotional reaction to his fate either way.

Charlie was not so phlegmatic. At the party at the Pig, he talked about murder, as he had been doing since the events of that day. Occasionally he invoked the memory of Willy, of his doing something extralegal in the interests of justice. When he caught Dan giving him the eye once, he hesitated for a moment then simply kept talking.

"Now there was a man who realized what had to be done and went ahead and did it," Charlie said, regarding Dan steadily as he did so.

At the night of the final party, he was on such a rant, with the Horsedicks nodding along with him.

"That's the fullest, the most extreme and intense, of life's experience," he said, "to take the life of another human."

"I'd do it," Chris said, to the laughter of others.

Dan had been standing silently next to Kate. She seemed, for the moment, to have given up on getting him to talk, not only about Willy's death, but about anything at all. Although Dan was only dimly aware that he was merely going through the motions of creating a bond between Kate and Charlie, he still realized that even that plan (which could hardly be said to be "conceived") was going awry. He shook his head wearily, wondering whether or not he should pull Charlie aside and ask him to tone it down, just as a favor. Normally, Charlie wasn't averse to a reality check from Dan, and he was certainly at his most pompous and most in need of it. Things had been different with him lately, though, so Dan hesitated.

Kate didn't. After listening for a bit, she shook her head, giving a little sneer of contempt, and shouldered through the people in front of her (all of them taller), finally through the wall of the Horsedicks.

"Been listening to what you've been saying, Charlie," she said, looking up at him, smiling pleasantly enough. Charlie was a foot taller, broad-shouldered and massive in front of her.

"Yeah?" Charlie said. His look was just the hostile side of neutral.

"Yeah. As usual, you're so full of cheerfulness and optimism."

"I *am* a radiant point of kindness and humanity," he said, smiling a little.

"It always shows," Kate said with a smile which was not quite hostile in return. "Charlie Gates: cheerful and optimistic."

Dan watched all this, more interested than he had been in anything for some time, which wasn't much.

Charlie cocked his head to one side, seeming to consider Kate's comments. Finally, he said, "Cheerfulness and optimism I see as nothing more than useful defense mechanisms of self-delusion. They assist in insulating the individual from the reality of the world."

"Wow. Profound," Kate said. "And what do you see as the reality of the world?"

All conversation stopped. People leaned toward the two to listen, like iron filings orienting towards a magnet. Someone turned down the stereo.

If Charlie noted this, he gave no indication. He simply answered: "The reality of the world? I see that we are the most virulently destructive species in the history of the planet. That not only are our lives pointless, but they are doomed in ways that previous generations would not have imagined. That in our greedy and rapacious short-sightedness, we are doomed to fall, the downside to that being that we will claw countless innocent species with us when we do. We, as a species, are filth. This species is feces."

The Horsedicks and others laughed at that, some repeating it.

"Here's the way I see it," Kate continued, undaunted. "Sure we're a problem, and you'd have to be crazy to deny that we're the most destructive species in the history of the planet. I'm with you on that. But to just throw up your hands and declare defeat is chickenshit. We've been the problem, but we can be the solution. *Only* we can be the solution. We're the only species with the power to fuck things up this bad, but we're also the only species that can fix it."

"We'll never fix it," Charlie said. "Don't you get that?"

"*You* don't get it. You claim we have the power to fuck things up irrevocably. What you're missing is the most important part of that sentence. Power. We have power. Unprecedented power. The power to create as well as destroy. We have the power to pull it all together. With sufficient effort and unity of vision, we could make a garden of this planet."

At that moment, Dan emerged from some of his darkness and remembered why he was in love with her.

"It'll never happen," Charlie said.

Kate put on a grandmotherly tone and said, "Not with that attitude it won't, mister."

Charlie snorted. "That's just head-up-the-ass idealistic bullshit."

"Maybe you don't recognize it because it's courageous," Kate said. "Truly courageous."

Charlie drew his head back, narrowing his eyes and smiling. "You calling me a *coward*?"

"Yes," she said, her blue eyes keen. "You could change, but yes."

Charlie's mouth actually dropped open in disbelief.

Kate wasn't done. "You're cynical about pretty much everything, Charlie. Did you ever wonder what would happen if you got cynical about cynicism?"

"No. Enlighten me."

"When you're cynical about cynicism, the only thing left is hope. How's that for enlightenment?"

Charlie snorted and shook his head, but looked away.

"You're such a tedious poser," she said to Charlie, and he slapped her.

Dan was over the people in the way and through the Horsedicks before he was aware of it. Charlie had an instant of wide-eyed recognition before Dan set in. Dan pounded Charlie in the face as he had done to others, left-right, left-right, hitting him even as he went down. Charlie thudded to the floor, scattering bottles and breaking glass. He lay on the floor, eyes fluttering, forehead furrowing for a moment, before his face relaxed.

"Wo, man," Jerry of the Horsedicks said.

"What the fuck," Jimmie said.

Dan stood over Charlie's form, saw that he was breathing.

Kate put her hands on his shoulders from behind, and he started.

"Let's go," she said.

He shook himself and came to. Turning around to Chris, he said, "We've been friends, right?"

"Yeah, man. Sure."

"If you're going to be here most of the night, watch my shit, okay? I don't want Charlie tossing it in the alley or burning it or anything."

"Sure, man. To do otherwise would be unethical."

Dan almost laughed, and left with Kate.

They went back early the next morning with Kate and Tom. Charlie's bedroom door was closed; they couldn't tell if he was there or not. Dan was worried about what Charlie might do if he woke up, not for himself but for Kate and Tom. Neither of them would be dissuaded from going up to the apartment with him.

"What's he going to do?" Tom said.

Dan didn't reply, merely raised his eyebrows and shook his head.

Dan didn't have much there; most of his paintings were at Tom's. The mural on the wall, of course, was permanent until another tenant painted it over. Some boxes of books, some bedding and toiletries, a few bags of clothes.

They made it down to the van in the alley without incident. When Kate saw the small pile of possessions in the back of the van, she shook her head and clucked her tongue.

"That's kinda sad," she said to Tom, who sighed and nodded. Dan was near the front of the van but overheard. He decided not to tell them to fuck off.

Kate hinted that Dan should move in with her, something they had discussed during happier times. Dan was brusque about it.

"I'm going to stay at Tom's for a bit," he said.

He ignored it when she tried to hide her stricken look.

They broke up shortly after that. Dan drank too much, ignoring her, leaving to her all the work of the relationship. He turned away from her sadness.

They were at Tom's house when it came. Finally she said, "You have some things to work out, and I just feel like I'm in the way."

Having seen it coming, having allowed it to happen, *caused* it to happen, Dan didn't even bother to shrug with indifference.

They were sitting in Tom's kitchen, a place they'd been happy before. Tom was puttering around in the nearby laundry room, trying to act like he wasn't eavesdropping. Dan didn't care about that either.

Kate was proud, though. She watched Dan for a few moments and said, "We have something here, you know."

Dan said nothing, didn't move his eyes from his glass of whiskey.

"Do you want to save it?"

Dan said nothing.

"Why do you want to *do* this?" she asked. It was as close to a plea as he had ever heard from her.

He could feel her watching him, but didn't meet her gaze.

"You will sort things out," she said, "and you'll try to come back to me. I might be there, and I might not. I'm not waiting."

She turned and walked out.

After a tactful interval of time, Tom came quietly into the kitchen.

"You sure about this?" Tom said.

That was when Dan shrugged.

Things got worse, statistically unsustainable or not. Just before the new semester was about to begin, Tom got sick.

At first, they thought it was a hangover. Dan had been shuffling around, sleeping and drinking too much. He got back to Tom's after work, and they routinely partied. The only effort Dan expended was working out, although that was only half-heartedly, and as a result of mental images of Mike coming after him in his room at 718 Pier. If it wasn't a workday, he ate some protein after his regimen, then waited a bit before doing a bong and having his first drink.

The night that led to the assumed hangover involved a party at Tom's attended by many of the people who had shown up for his mock funeral. Again, only Dan and Tom drank heavily. When he realized that he was bored by the party, Dan found himself having to strongly resist the urge to call Kate. His mind vacillated about her. Perhaps a life with her was the only way he would ever be happy, his only slim chance. He loved her though, and truly; because of this he thought the noblest thing to do would be to let her go, to not infect her, to not ruin her life with his. He walked away from the phone in the kitchen when Tom shouted at him to do a shot. In the middle of the night, when most of the partiers still in attendance were playing Dungeons and Dragons, he slipped out of the house and drove by her apartment, parking in front of a fire hydrant as snow began to fall. The lights were out. Again he wrestled with himself before driving away. The thought that she'd be angry with him if he showed up in the early hours, especially given the present circumstances, was what convinced him to pull away from the curb. He drove away thinking that she might not be angry at all, but relieved, finally deciding that procrastination wouldn't hurt in this case. Perhaps she'd miss him so much that she would come and convince him that he was wrong, that he should be with her. If he yielded to this, he would be back in the position of being responsible for the contamination of her life.

He took a long time driving back to Tom's house, tormenting himself with possibilities. The snow fell more heavily, and he found himself sitting at a green light, watching his windshield wipers and the snow. When he got back to Tom's, everyone had gone home. Tom was asleep on the couch with the television on.

Dan woke up in the late morning. He padded through the house in gym shorts and a t-shirt. Tom was not asleep on the couch, nor was he in his bed in the full sunlight. Dan found him in the bathroom, curled on the floor near the toilet with a damp washcloth over his eyes. The lid of the toilet was up, and although it had been flushed, there were streaks of vomit down its porcelain contours.

"Wow!" Dan exclaimed. "Are you okay?"

Tom didn't move, just limply pushed the washcloth into his eyes. "No. No I'm not."

If it hadn't looked so bad, Dan might have laughed. As it was, his sense of protectiveness took hold. "Do you want some ice water?"

"No," Tom said. "Wait, yeah."

"Okay, hang on," Dan went through the house to the kitchen, put ice in a glass and filled it with water, adding a slice of lemon. When he came back, Tom was retching over the toilet, although nothing but a strand of mucus came out.

"Shit," Dan said, wrinkling his nose. "You still want this?"

"Please," Tom said, extending a pale and shaky hand.

While he guzzled the water, Dan said, "I left for a bit last night. Did you drink or eat something weird while I was gone?"

"Nothing," Tom gasped, setting down the glass.

"Seems pretty bad for a hangover."

"This isn't a hangover. It's a demonic possession."

Dan laughed in spite of himself.

Tom drank some more water. "Mmmm, lemon. Nice touch." He drank the rest of it, the ice clinking back into the glass. Then he held up the glass rather urgently, and Dan took it, just before Tom vomited up the water into the toilet.

"It's not that it wasn't refreshing," he said to Dan, giving a wan smile.

Dan had to help him into the living room to the couch. Tom was painfully sensitive to light, and Dan drew the curtains. He was barely able to get his head off the pillow, due not only to the pain in his head, but the stiffness of his neck. Usually a fan of loud electronics, he could only tolerate the television being on low volume.

Dan brought him some broth, but Tom found it too painful to sit up to eat it.

"Maybe it's the flu," Dan said.

"Did you ever have the flu when it felt like wild animals were gnawing at your spine?" Tom muttered.

"No."

"Me neither."

Not long after it got dark, it was obvious that Tom had to go not to the doctor, but to the emergency room. At this realization, Dan's mind flatlined for a few moments; he had no idea what to do, and certainly didn't want the responsibility to do it. He could only imagine how his father would proceed in such a situation, but was certain how Willy would. That made things clear.

"Come on," he said.

"What?" Tom groaned.

"We're going to the emergency room."

236

Tom seemed to think about this for a moment and said, "I don't think I can move."

"I'll be right back," Dan said. He got on his jacket, went out and started his van. Opening its back doors, he arranged the little mattress and his sleeping bag in the back, leaving the doors open. Back inside, he helped Tom sit up, wrapping him in a blanket. It hurt Tom so much that he began to cry.

"I've gotcha," Dan said, lifting him gently in his arms. Placing him in the back of the van, Dan closed the doors and went back to lock up the house. He sped through the streets to Greysport Memorial, screeching to a stop in front of the doors to the Emergency Room.

At the front desk, he got members of the staff to bring a gurney out to the van. He helped move Tom onto it, ignoring the protests of the staff. Tom didn't want him to leave.

"I'm just parking my van," Dan said. "I'll be right back in."

He parked the van and sprinted back into the emergency room. Tom was already in an alcove, vomiting into a kidney-shaped plastic bowl held by a nurse. A doctor was trying to ask Tom questions, but he could barely respond. Dan filled in the gaps as best he could.

It came down to Tom getting a spinal tap to either confirm or rule out spinal meningitis. They got Tom to sit up and lean forward on a bedside table on wheels, his forearms on a pillow. Dan took his hands and held on tight.

"Just look in my eyes," he said to his friend.

When Tom's spine was pierced, his eyes went wide, then squeezed shut.

"Jesusmotherfuckingchrist," he whispered.

"Is that anything for a nice Jewish boy to say?" Dan asked, but he felt sick with pity for his friend.

They waited in the alcove for the test results. Tom was given painkillers through an IV. He seemed to panic a bit at first, then relax to it.

"Wow," he said finally. "This is great."

Since Tom was out of immediate misery, if not danger, Dan didn't mind that it seemed to take hours for the results to come back. In the meantime, they rolled Tom out of the alcove and up to a room. Dan tried to stop worrying (there was nothing more he could do), and was watching Tom sleep when the floor doctor called him out into the hall.

"Have any family members been notified?" the doctor, a young Asian guy by the name of Fung, asked Dan.

"Parents are in Africa," Dan said. "Can't really be reached."

"Well, this situation is serious. We need a family member."

"I'm his brother," Dan said.

"You're *his* brother?"

"Yep," Dan said. "Half-brother. Same mom, different dads."

If the doctor didn't believe him, he didn't seem to care. "Not much of a resemblance, you have to admit," the man said drily.

"Guess not. That's genetics for you."

"Yeah. Well, your *brother* has spinal meningitis, the bacterial variety. You know what that is?"

"Vaguely."

The doctor explained it to him, a thumbnail sketch. "Any questions so far?"

"What are his chances?"

"Well, this is dangerous. In his age group, one in seven survive, maybe less. Among the survivors, many experience an array of symptoms. This can lead to deafness, epilepsy, cognitive deficits. The body can throw off clots, which can lead to gangrene and amputation."

"*What?*"

"Yeah. Dangerous. His organs can shut down. Multi organ failure. Septic shock. The bacteria can double in number every twenty minutes."

"Holy shit!" Dan rubbed the stubble on his cheeks.

"Holy shit, indeed," the young doctor said.

"I should have gotten him in here earlier."

The doctor looked at him, sizing him up. "Ever seen anyone with meningitis before?"

"No."

"Are you a trained medical professional?"

"No."

"Then don't beat yourself up about it. You did a good job with little information. If he'd been alone, he probably would have died." Fung patted him on the shoulder.

This didn't make Dan feel much better. "What can we do?" he asked.

"We're already doing what we can for him. We need to do something for you."

"Me?"

"Yeah. This is communicable. You can pick it up just from being in close quarters. That's why it happens in college dorms. Any chance you drank from the same bottle or anything? Shared a joint?"

"I don't remember exactly, but there's more of a probability than a chance."

"Okay. We're getting you on some antibiotics. Immediately."

"Fine. Can I be in the room with him? I don't want to leave him alone."

The doctor regarded him for a moment, then said, "Seeing as you're his *brother* and everything, sure. We'll get you some isolation gear, gloves and a mask. Antibiotics first. And don't beat yourself up, as I said. You look like a guy who might have a capacity for self-torment."

Where did *that* come from? Dan wondered.

So Dan spent the first night in the hospital room with Tom. Early in the morning, when he thought things were stabilized, he went back to Tom's house and took a shower, falling asleep in the spare bedroom. He took a pack full of drawing materials and books back to keep himself occupied while he waited.

When he returned and went up to Tom's room, he stopped at the nurse's station to ask for an update. They told him that, while he was gone, Tom had gone into septic shock and was in a coma.

It was not a new thing in the world to wait by the bedside of a loved one in peril, to sit through the agony of the unknown. Willy had done it, of course, but had fallen short of his desire to beam such knowledge into the minds of his descendants, now numbering one.

238

Millions had gone through it before, billions, down through the corridors of time. Still, it was new to Dan, something that only experience could teach him. He sat next to Tom's right side in a mask and gloves and disposable gown, reminiscent of his time at Sam Feeney's. Watching his friend breathe on a respirator, he had plenty of time to burn himself with recriminations. He had failed Willy, he had failed Tom, he had failed Kate. The need to weep sizzled right behind his eyes. He sat stonefaced, though, staring redly at Tom, holding his friend's hand gently, avoiding the taped IV lines.

When he was told that he'd used up all his vacation time at the power plant and was expected to show up, he quit. He'd left nothing there, and gave a brief thought to saying goodbye to Ramu. He'd catch up to him someday; now he had to look after one of the few people left to him.

When he was told kindly to go home and get some sleep, he drove by Kate's first, sitting in front of her building. He wanted to know she was safe, to tell her what had happened, to be held by her, to lie on the couch with his head in her lap. Knowing he didn't deserve such merciful treatment, he drove back to Tom's after an hour. He drank and listened to the campus radio station as the sun was coming up. Costello's *Peace, Love, and Understanding* came on, and at first it made him think of Kate, of them driving together.

The one person he could think of who was strong, who was trusted, was buried like a dog in a grave out by the river.

Downing his bourbon, he leaned on his knees and pressed the heels of his hands into his eyes, wishing he could cry. It was full daylight out before he was drunk enough to sleep.

Dan tried every avenue available to get in contact with Tom's parents, playing the detective and following leads, leaving messages at various places in Africa, a vexatious task. He spent at least sixteen hours a day at the hospital, sometimes sleeping in a chair beside his friend. Reading aloud to Tom until he could read no more, drawing until his hand cramped, watching television, he passed the hours in the room, observing Tom's changeless state. The new semester started, and he hardly gave a thought to attending. He'd withdraw and get a refund when things resolved themselves. Back at Tom's house, in an hour before short sleep, he worked on drawings, cruel and eviscerating things: Willy's grave, Tom in a casket. His father, for some reason, back to the viewer, headless in a snowy clearing in the trees, lit by the dawn. He was disgusted with himself for doing it, but couldn't stop, soothed by the ritual of it, the flicker of his hand over the paper, and was terrified by his own ghastly images.

Perhaps he would not have felt so terribly alone if he had known that he was yet another McGregor to boil himself in the acid juices of his own regret. Perhaps not.

In spite of all his time at the hospital, Dan missed it when Tom woke up. Leaving his van in the parking ramp, he trudged into the entrance of the hospital and took the elevator to Tom's floor. He walked by the nurses' station, lifting his chin at the familiar people there. They smiled upon seeing him, he noted with some puzzlement.

Going into Tom's room, the first thing he saw was the back of Dr. Fung. He went around the foot of the bed towards his familiar chair, the chair he had sat in until his ass was sore, day after day, night after night.

239

"Hey, Dr. Fung," he said.

"Notice anything unusual?" Fung said.

Dan turned around and found Tom looking at him.

"Fuck!" Dan shouted.

Tom winced, then smiled.

"Volume," Tom said quietly.

Dan knelt beside the bed and took his friend's hand in both of his, carefully avoiding the IV tubes, but bending Tom's fingers and pressing the knuckles to his forehead. Right at that moment, he almost wept.

"Brothers, huh?" Fung said, grinning. "You sure you're not boyfriends?"

This made Dan laugh hard, washed with relief. "*Fuck* no!" he exclaimed. "You see the size of the *cock* on this guy?"

Even Tom laughed a little bit at that.

Tom could not be released until he was well enough, and deemed not to be at risk of infecting others. Dan spent almost as much time at the hospital as he had before, Tom being as alone as he was himself. Dan read to him from *The Lord of the Rings*, a mutual favorite, until his throat was raw or Tom fell asleep.

When Tom was feeling better, he talked to Dan about school.

"Man, because of me, you're going to miss a whole semester!" Tom said.

"Don't sweat it. I felt like I was spinning my wheels anyway. You gave me an excuse to take some time and think about shit."

"Okay, but what about your job?"

"I've got some money saved up," Dan said. "Don't worry about that either. Just buy booze. And acid."

"That I can do," Tom laughed weakly.

Tom was finally released from the hospital, rolled out to the entrance by an attractive nurse while Dan got the van. Dr. Fung had gone over instructions with Tom before his release, making sure that Dan paid close attention.

"You're lucky to have a brother like this," Fung said to Tom at one point.

"I know," Tom said.

Dan shook his head and snorted.

Tom's house was equipped with a Betamax, the first one Dan had seen. Tom was weak for some time, frequently seeming moody, but was able to watch movies endlessly on videotape. If his parents had also purchased an answering machine, Tom and Dan wouldn't have been surprised when they called from the airport.

Tom answered the phone, and Dan listened to his side of the conversation.

"What?" Tom said. "No, I'm okay. I'm *okay*. Got home less than forty-eight hours ago. Yeah... No... My buddy Dan, he's been with me the whole time... He *is* a good guy...Okay, thanks for the heads up."

It was a good thing that they had done the comprehensive cleaning months before, and had managed to keep on top of it. As it was, they had to do some sanitizing, getting rid of bongs, bags of weed and the like. Perhaps Tom's parents had guessed at this; it took them an hour to get home. Tom gave it fifteen minutes of stoic effort before Dan made him lie on the couch.

"What the fuck," Dan said, putting a blanket over his friend. "You almost *died*, man. I'll straighten up."

When Tom's parents came through the front door, tossing their bags on the floor and rushing in, Dan and Tom were trying to act casual, watching *Chinatown* on the Betamax. Mr. and Mrs. Schwartz were tan and fit, wearing not quite safari clothing, but something close to it, garments that said they had been elsewhere for a long time. They both wore bead necklaces. Tom's father was tall and lanky, his mother short and compact, both attractive. Dan realized the understandable nature of their priorities when they were brief with him (however pleasant), and went to kneel by the couch where their only son lay under the blanket which Dan had placed upon him.

Dan immediately felt unnecessary. The Schwartzes took over the care of their son, doting on him ceaselessly, seeming to make up for the time they had been away.

"They're feeling guilty," Tom informed Dan when they had the rare chance to be alone. If they were guilty, Dan thought, they hid it well behind their cheerful and competent activity. With all the time they had spent in trying circumstances in Africa, they seemed ill-disposed to useless wallowing in guilt.

Although Tom had given an almost deceptively spare synopsis of Dan's situation to his parents (who had responded by expressing their gratitude and going out of their way to make him feel welcome), Dan tried to make himself scarce. He regretted having quit his job at the power plant; the ritual of it would have been reassuring, as would the money it brought in. That bridge was burned, though, and he could have done nothing else at the time. The shadow that made him close his eyes and wince, at times, that made him hang his head in private moments, seemed to debilitate his motivation to change. That he lived on dwindling savings and the grace of this kind and oblivious family would have furthered his humiliation, and therefore his darkness, where he appeared to have reached a watershed.

He pretended that he had to work, though, spending the time away from Tom's (the Schwartzes', he would correct himself) at one of the libraries on the campus of Greysport University. He got back late enough that the parents were in bed, and he could stay up late with Tom and watch TV.

"It's good to see them," Tom said, "but I have to admit, they're starting to get annoying."

"Man, what the hell!" Dan said. "They came back from saving a *village* in *Africa* to dote on your ass! Don't take it for granted!"

"I guess I didn't think of it that way." Tom looked hurt.

Dan saw he had wounded his friend's feelings, and adopted the voice of a scolding black grandmother to say, "I guess you *di'in't!*"

Tom laughed and Dan felt better.

Dan was there when Tom first tried to convince his parents to go back to their village in Africa, where, they had let it slip, there was a crisis in their efforts to provide the village with dependable fresh water. It was apparent that the kind and energetic couple were torn.

"Seriously, I'm fine," Tom said.

His parents exchanged a skeptical glance.

"You have nothing to worry about," he said to them. "I'm tough!"

"Oh, you are not!" his dad said, laughing heartily, clutching his son's forearm.

Tom looked at Dan, a significant glance. The parents' eyes followed.

"Yeah," Dan said slowly, smiling and nodding. "Yeah, he is."

The parents looked at each other, the meaning of the glance impenetrable to outsiders.

"If you say so, then he must be," Mrs. Schwartz said at last.

They threatened to stay until Passover, but the crisis worsened in their village and Tom turned up the persuasiveness on his arguments. Finally they were convinced. After a farewell dinner and painfully protracted goodbyes, Dan took them to the airport.

Mr. Schwartz embraced him.

"You're a good friend," he told Dan.

"Tom's the good friend," Dan said. "I'm just trying to keep up."

Mrs. Schwartz hugged him and kissed his cheek, to Dan's embarrassed surprise.

"You *are* a good friend, and a fine young man," she said, reaching up to put her hands on his shoulders.

Dan sighed through his nose and shook his head. Fine young men don't leave their grandfathers to die alone, he thought in a flash so quick that words of it didn't even form in his mind. He found that he wanted to ask her for forgiveness, just as he had felt with Kate's mother. Now, though, he had something specific for which he needed to be forgiven.

He watched them walk into the terminal, waving back before they went in the doors and were lost from view.

Dan picked up the habit of walking on the beach at Glenwood's eastern edge when Tom's parents had been in town. It became a ritual, whatever the weather. In spite of his misery, the crisp wind and the sound of waves always made him feel somewhat better. As he crunched through the rimed and hardened snow along the small hills of jagged ice accumulated by the freezing of pounding waves, part of his focus was always turned back into his head, there to gaze upon a welter of recurring images.

Willy was there, and Mae. His father smiled in dim images, mostly impressionistic; sometimes there was an ominous flash of a clearing, of naked trees and snow red in the dawn. Charlie popped up, and Dan found that he wanted to talk to his friend somewhat more than he wanted to punch him in the face. Kate was there so much that she burned behind his eyes; her laughter, her mannerisms, the way she curled up with a book on her couch under the amber tiffany lamp, the way she chewed something delicious, bobbing her head from side to side in little movements of delight. The way she sounded when she came. How it felt when her hot, sweet breath whispered in his ear, right in his ear, making him wriggle with delight, that she loved him. She loved him.

He had thoughts of Mike Krapczak from time to time, and thought about what Charlie said about killing someone. It wasn't the maximal experience of it that Dan would enjoy, though, but the feeling of having justice. Mike had to have contributed largely to his mother coming to get him in the first place; she was greedy, but she was lazy, and Dan was certain that Mike had had a great deal to do with taking him away. Dan felt little about his mother, no love, no pity, no grief, no hate, only a slight but customary nausea at the idea that every other thread of him was one of hers, as if something dirty were woven into his being. She was weak and she was rotten, and she was in his veins. Without Mike in the picture, though, she wouldn't have come to take him away, and Dan would have been there in his grandmother's final days (she had kissed his head, kissed his cheeks until he squirmed, held him on her lap when he was little, made him soup when he was cold and tucked him in and read to him at night. Perhaps it was his Dan's absence that had killed Mae, which in turn had left Willy alone. It gnawed at Dan to think of Mike walking around Portview with a smile on his face.

All of these thoughts had no traction, though, made no progress, just rolled around and recombined, the same elements again and again, like dark beads and broken glass in a kaleidoscope. Although he revealed only a tiny fraction of what went on in his mind to Tom, his friend had suggested that he keep a journal so he could make progress in his thinking, not having to come to the same conclusion again and again. Dan agreed it was a good idea, but procrastinated on it. He painted and drew his visions, his nightmares; he thought in images. Writing his thoughts would have been a difficult habit to develop.

When he had been on the beach long enough, he often went down to Perrito's for some cheap food and a couple of beers. He went around noon to avoid Charlie, although part of him wanted to have an encounter to find out whether Charlie was his friend or his enemy, and to take it from there. These thoughts tangled with the fact that not only had Charlie slapped Kate, but that Dan had knocked Charlie out, an event which had caused great turmoil in their circle. Kate was not hurt, but Charlie had lost face terribly. Dan's feelings on those events were so muddled that he conveniently decided not to think about it. At Perrito's, though, he always watched out the windows when he sat at the bar.

He could spend hours talking to Kaye when business was slow, feeling a kinship to the round woman. Kaye, in turn, told Dan that he had always seemed familiar, although she couldn't put her finger on why. Again, he didn't reveal too much, but there was something in the leisurely cadences of her speech, in the knowledge that she, too, had suffered sadness, which made him feel comforted. They didn't discuss much detail; usually they didn't talk at all, perhaps only doing a crossword puzzle together, or exchanging sections of the newspaper. If a customer came in and sat at the bar while Kaye was thus distracted, Perrito, planted in enigma behind his eternal margarita, would clear his throat to get Kaye's attention. Kaye would get to her feet, sharing a dark look with Dan before moving slowly down the bar to take the customer's order. When business was taken care of, she would slowly amble back.

"At least I trained the asshole to get his own margaritas," she muttered, nodding down the bar as Perrito did just that.

Dan often found himself antsy for action, contemplated going to the Underground or Vnuk's, but was uncertain how this might be received. As much as he enjoyed Tom's company, his wise and insightful commentary and his depraved imagination, Dan still, as Kate had said, had some wildness to live out of him.

Time slipped by quickly with little to anchor it. Tom was still recovering from meningitis, at turns weak and cranky, sometimes feeling energetic and seeming like his own self. In one of the latter periods, Dan convinced him about the necessity of working out, and Tom went out and bought a gym full of weights and equipment, following Dan's advice and setting up a dedicated room in the sprawling house's finished basement. Tom's dedication was spotty, though; he only went at it in spurts, and usually after Dan's lengthy exhortations.

"What is it with you?" Tom panted at the end of one workout.

"What do you mean?" Dan said, sweating himself, but inured to the routine.

"Whatever motivates you to pound it so hard?"

Dan set down the sixty-pound dumbbells with which he'd been doing curls. "I just never like being a victim, I guess."

"Why?" Tom gasped. "Right now I'm thinking that being a victim takes a lot less effort, and it's usually over with in seconds."

"Yeah," Dan said, "but it leaves a mark."

Tom thought about that for a moment before saying, "Okay, that's a good point. One that would best be followed by some nourishing bloody marys."

And that was the way the time elapsed. Dan worked out regularly, suspecting, as his grandfather once had, that his strength would eventually be needed. Tom was less regular, and would never be, as he said himself, a "big, hulking brute", but Dan suspected that there was something better balanced about Tom's psyche, something that allowed him to accept things the way they were.

They pursued their projects. Dan was able to entrance himself in a painting, just the way he had that first time at Tom's, when the sun had moved across the sky, shadows bending blue across the snow, without his conscious awareness of it. With every piece he did, he seemed to be getting closer to some kind of truth about himself, closer to some epiphany, but the epiphany always seemed ten or twenty more pieces away, an ever-receding goal. The process was hypnotic, though, and deeply satisfying, seeing his ability increase to transmute some figment of his mind into a window of imagination through which others might look, and in looking, understand. Tom understood, perhaps better than Dan did himself.

"You always make me see the world differently," he said. "More dark, more mysterious, more beautiful. More horrible and excellent, all at once. You see it from your point of view, as the creator. I don't think you get the effect of your work on others; you're so lost in your own mind."

Dan, never comfortable with praise, shrugged this comment off. When Audrey showed up, Dan greeted her and politely declined her offer of being set up with one of her friends. When the two went to Tom's bedroom, Dan put on headphones and continued painting. Listening to *Fantasia on a Theme by Thomas Tallis* and *The Moldau*, his vision sometimes blurred with tears which never quite fell, yet his face was immobile, locked down in stone. He would cry if he could. Sometimes the sadness seemed to vibrate in his nerves as he painted, and one morning he had awakened on the couch to find Audrey weeping in front of what he had painted the night before, a subfusc scene of a small boy apparently stranded on a foggy bank at twilight. He feigned sleep until she left.

Tom had his own style of productivity. He claimed to have a short attention span, but seemed to be capable of pursuing several objectives at once. "Multi-tasking", he called it, the first time Dan had ever heard the term. So, in a room which had developed into his office and music studio, Tom went between working on his pornographic rock opera (*O! Coprophagio!* Tom had told Dan, giggling), to designing the layout, theme, and alcohol collection of his whiskey bar, to trying to

244

put together a funk band and determine the line-up of their music, and to looking into what would be involved in starting up a commercial kitchen from which he could market his own brand of chili. For this last, he had already requested, and was studying up on, everything that was necessary in the city of Greysport to establish such an enterprise. He didn't seem deterred by the complicated requisites and codes set up by the Board of Health and other governmental entities.

"People a lot dumber than me have done all this stuff," he pointed out when Dan shook his head at all the explained complexities. "Why shouldn't I be able to do it?"

"No idea," Dan said. He tried not to smile; Tom's obtuse optimism amused him.

It was on one such productive night that Charlie showed up, sometime after midnight on a Saturday halfway through March, the snow melting slowly during a few days of fog and misty rain. Tom was thumping away experimentally on his bass guitar while Dan worked on sketches for a large painting, having just stretched and applied gesso to a very large canvas. The theme of the painting, he thought, was wonderfully somber: a funeral held on the banks of a black river in October, the water reflecting the color of the leaves: orange, red, copper, yellow, brown, dark gem tones and rust. Shadowy figures would stand indistinct in the misty graveyard, the large, tilted stones would convey a sense of mossiness and decay. Were the dark figures standing in wait?

It was delicious, and the scene was as vivid as memory in Dan's mind. The theme itself was more than a nod to Dan's hero, Caspar David Friedrich, but when the idea came to him, he knew that there was only one way to satisfy that itch. Scratch it 'til it bleeds, he thought.

When Dan described the idea to him, Tom asked, as he usually did, "Man, *where* do you *get* this stuff?"

Dan replied customarily by smiling, shrugging, and spreading his hands.

The comradely creative silence was interrupted when they realized that someone was ringing the doorbell and pounding on the door on the other side of the house. They looked at each other with narrowed eyes. Nobody showed up at Tom's unannounced. In fact, nobody showed up much at all.

They padded down the hall, Dan following Tom, who turned on the porch light and looked out through the peephole.

"Holy shit!" he said. "It's Charlie Gates!"

Dan stopped moving. The skin between his shoulders prickled, the sensation flowing up his neck and making his scalp tingle.

"Does he have a gun?" Dan said, just as Tom said, "He's all messed up!"

Tom opened the door before Dan could stop him.

Charlie's face was bruised and cut, he had a split lip, and one eye would be black in the morning. There was dried blood in his white-blonde hair, on his t-shirt and jacket; one knee of his pants was torn, the knee itself bloody.

He limped through the door, his shoulders held stiffly at an angle that suggested further injury. He gave the old Charlie grin nonetheless.

"Thanks, Kickstand," he said. "Hey, Dan, what's up?"

His offhand tone made Dan laugh; part of it was Charlie's seeming indestructibility; part of him wanted to knock Charlie out again for slapping Kate, part of him felt relief that they still appeared to be on speaking terms. Dan realized how much he had missed his anarchic friend, simultaneously the most and least trustworthy person he had ever known. The state of Charlie, all other considerations aside, flushed Dan with a surprising surge of protectiveness. Dan and Tom tried to help him into the kitchen, but he brushed off their assistance.

"It's cool, I'm good," he said. "Could use a blast of something strong, though."

While Tom got him a drink, Dan stood in front of his old friend, waiting for him to say something. They were too cool to mention any slapping or knocking out. Charlie lifted his chin in thanks to Tom and took a large gulp of whiskey.

"So?" Dan said finally.

"So, what?" Charlie said, deadpan.

"So what happened?"

"What do you mean, what happened?"

Dan held up his hands to indicate Charlie's state.

"Oh, this?" Charlie said. "Nothing much."

Tom snorted laughter.

"Had to be something," Dan said.

"Well, yeah. I totalled the 'Cuda."

"No *shit*?" Dan and Tom cried simultaneously.

"Yep. Down by the port. Cops are looking for me, definitely. I couldn't go home, and they'd never look for me up here in Glenwood. I had your address…"

"Stay as long as you like," Tom said automatically.

"How'd you get here?" Dan said.

"Took some evasive action after the accident, laid low for a bit, then took a cab."

"Okay, start from the beginning."

Charlie sighed. "All right. I finally got Jim out to have some fun…"

"*Jim* was with you?"

Charlie held up his hand. "I'll get to that. But yeah. Got his ass out to have a few beers. He's just been too damn serious lately. It's because of that girlfriend of his, that Jenny. Not that I have anything against her; she apparently helped Jim find some kind of intellectual linearity…"

"Would you get to the point?" Dan laughed.

"I would, if you'd stop interrupting. So, she's out of town, and I get him out to have a few beers. You could tell he was like a dog off its leash. He started lightening up, having some fun. We did some blow, although the pussy acted guilty about it at first."

"Where's Jim now?" Dan insisted.

"I told you. I'm getting to that."

Charlie told the story while Dan and Tom listened.

The brothers had been at the German bar with the iron chandelier, the crossbows and swords. They had started out a little tensely, Charlie implied, until Charlie had followed the first round of Hefe-Weisses with shots of Baronjaeger. Then the brothers had begun to disparage their incompetent father (lazy, vain, and useless, they both agreed), and soon were laughing together, hard, just like the old days. They went into the men's room to do a little blow.

Dan and Tom looked at each other: these things were normal.

As Jim loosened, Charlie took him to lower- and lower-rent places, just to ascertain his brother's current level of tolerance.

"I knew when he showed up in a black t-shirt and black leather jacket that he was ready to go," Charlie said. "He wasn't looking like his new, straight self."

"But where *is* he?" Dan insisted.

"I *told* you!" Charlie laughed. "I'm *getting* to that!"

They ended up down by the port, not far from where Dan had lived.

"718 Pier. There's another address I remembered," Charlie said. "Just like Tom's."

Having found no beefy, flat-topped terrorizers in the neighborhood, they had gone to a few more bars. At this point, at least according to Charlie's telling, Jim had begun to get a bit belligerent. Dan found it somewhat hard to believe, especially after how Jim had seemed at their last meeting. He let it pass.

"Yo, Kickstand," Charlie said, holding up his glass. Tom immediately filled it to brimming.

Charlie freely admitted that he had suggested a car chase.

"It was like that time out on the river, Dan. Remember that? With the rednecks?"

"What time?" Tom asked eagerly.

"Later," Dan said.

"In this country," Charlie said, "any story has to have a car chase."

And so they did. It was a simple as pulling up to a couple of Latinos in a hot car at a stoplight and revving the engine. The car of their opposite numbers, young men of about the same age, was an orange Road Runner, and they gunned their engine in return, smiling smugly back at Charlie and Jim. There was no threat to it, no territoriality; it was just a meeting of two sets of young gearheads, cocky and soaked with testosterone.

The light turned green and the two cars peeled out, tires screeching on the damp pavement. Onlookers on the sidewalks stopped and stared as the two cars roared by, neck and neck.

Charlie and the driver of the Road Runner exchanged quick glances, the other driver's eyes wide, as were his friend's. Jim, one hand braced on the dashboard, was laughing and grimacing, watching the street and wincing when cars nosed out from cross streets and stopped suddenly, when pedestrians jerked back between parked cars. The 'Cuda and the Road Runner were at times inches apart, the engines roaring.

Charlie howled, while Jim clenched his teeth in a rictus of terrified mirth, chanting "Shit-shit-shit-shit-shit-shit!"

Doubling down, Charlie pressed the gas pedal to the floor and pulled away. A stop light turned yellow then red in front of them.

"The light!" Jim shouted.

"I know!" Charlie shouted back.

The driver of the Road Runner stood on his brakes and the car screeched and shuddered to a stop, heaving forward on its springs, as Charlie blew through the red light, cross traffic howling to a stop at different pitches, car horns sounding.

"We win!" Charlie yelled. "Fuckin' pussies!"

It was then that they saw the squad car at the side of the street. They shot past it.

The squad's lights and siren came on. The cop waited for a break in traffic and powered after them.

Charlie glanced in the rearview mirror. "Ooops," he said.

"Oh, shit," Jim said. "And we're drunk."

"I guess we've got a car chase now," Charlie said. "At least we snorted all the blow."

"You gonna pull over?" Jim looking over his shoulder at the squad car, which was almost two blocks behind, and being held up by the jaded and uncooperative drivers who lagged in getting out of the way. Some of them might have even lagged on purpose.

"Nope," Charlie said, and accelerated. Jim's eyes were wide, and he pushed himself back in his seat.

Flashing on an opportunity, Charlie took a sudden sharp left turn through a gap in traffic in front of a bus, intending for the bus and other vehicles to block the squad, which was closing the distance behind them. This worked; Charlie screeched into an alley, the bus blocking it behind them as it moved forward. They could hear the squad's siren and the frustrated honking of the cop behind the wheel. It only took ignoring the Do Not Enter sign at the end of the one way street.

"It's one way!" Jim yelped.

"I'm only *going* one way!"

Charlie accelerated again and barreled down the empty side street that lead to the port. Visualizing the bridges over the rivers, the alleys and empty warehouses, he hatched a plan, knowing he could get away if only he could put the cop far enough behind them.

It worked, at least for the moment. When the cop got through traffic and turned onto the empty street, the Gates brothers in the roaring 'Cuda were blocks ahead. Charlie bellowed laughter and accelerated again.

"Hope they don't have the plates," Jim said through gritted teeth, glancing back and forth, with wide eyes, at the street in front and the cop behind.

They shot out of a cluster of warehouses into what amounted to a clearing, an open space with warehouses on the other side, brownfield dead grass and a weedy parking lot in between, bisected diagonally by train tracks. A freight train was grinding along the tracks from the right, an unknown length of cars linked behind the engine. Charlie looked at the train, into the rearview, back at the train, and did an easy calculation. He punched it.

"Fuck!" Jim said.

Charlie got the car over the tracks with thirty feet to spare, thumping over the rails.

"Just like in the movies!" Charlie shouted.

It wasn't all that close, and not all that much like the movies. Nonetheless, the brothers were laughing (the cop cut off behind them), speeding down the street, when Charlie drove through a stop sign and a tow truck approaching from the right smashed into the 'Cuda.

The impact turned the car into a flattened capital C, shattering all the glass in it and sending it skidding eighty feet into an empty gravel lot, spinning counter-clockwise. Charlie's door popped open and he was thrown out, rolling over cracked pavement and into a stand of dead weeds and a heap of rotting snow. The smashed 'Cuda came to a rest twenty feet away. It was over in about three seconds.

Charlie was knocked unconscious for a few moments, waking to the sound of the long freight train still rolling slowly by. He got up on one elbow and looked over at the 'Cuda. The hood was bent upwards, steam boiling up as radiator fluid drizzled green into the empty lot. All the windows were shattered, and no part of the car's body was not buckled or dented.

Charlie got to his feet and shuffled over to the car. Something was wrong with his knee; he nearly had to drag his leg behind him. Liquid was dripping in his eye, and when he brushed his forehead with his hand, it came away bright with blood. He got closer to the 'Cuda, which hissed and ticked.

The driver of the tow truck, the front end of his vehicle smashed, had pulled over to the side of the street not far from where Charlie had been thrown into the weeds. He was a fat man with a fu manchu moustache and a hat with a dixie flag on it.

"Jayziz Christ!" he cried. "Jayziz motherfucking Christ! Did you see *that*?"

"I was in it," Charlie said.

"Wow! Wow! Wow! Jayziz Christ!" the man jumped up and down, flapping his hands. Charlie continued to limp over the vehicle.

The fat man scampered next to him. "I didn't...were you *driving*? Didn't you have a stop sign?"

"It wasn't your fault," Charlie told him. The freight train continued to clatter slowly down the tracks a block away.

"Is there somebody in there?" the fat man said. "Is there somebody else *in* there?"

"Yeah," Charlie said.

"Wow! Wow! Christ! I'd better call an ambulance!"

Charlie looked into the twisted 'Cuda. Shattered glass was everywhere, flecked with blood that got more thick and dense as it got closer to Jim, who seemed to be at the center of a vortex of it. Charlie could see by the asymmetry of his brother's head, by the angle of it, by the bits of yellow-white that stuck out from under his matted hair, that his brother wouldn't need an ambulance.

When the trucker got back to the smashed 'Cuda after calling for an ambulance on the tow truck radio, the train was just passing, sounding its horn far down the track. The first police car showed up, but the trucker found himself alone in the weedy lot.

Having told his story, Charlie sat, watching their reactions.

"Ohhhhh, fuck!" Dan said. He slowly put his hands up to his head.

"No, no, no," Tom said, looking like he was about to cry. "Oh, no."

"It's okay," Charlie said. "Doesn't mean anything."

Dan stared at him.

"Of *course* it means something!" he said. "Your brother is dead. Jim's dead."

Charlie gave Dan a pitying look. "It doesn't mean anything because *nothing* means anything. When are you going to get that?"

"What?" Tom asked, shocked. "I mean, *what*?"

"You're a smart guy, Kickstand," Charlie said. "I thought you'd get it. It's like this: people imbue their stupid lives with some *big cosmic significance*" -he hunched

249

his shoulders and fluttered his hands, miming superstition- "because they can't handle the emptiness, can't handle how pointless it really is."

"There's a point, man," Dan said. "And Jim's dead."

Charlie stared at him. "You're just like everyone else, burdening yourself with senseless misery. You're free, and you don't even know it."

"You're just avoiding reality," Dan said. The clear image of Jim's crushed body lying in a morgue cooler somewhere pierced his mind and he gave a low and mournful whistle.

"No," Tom said, "No, no, no. This is so bad."

Charlie gave Tom a bland glance, finished the glass of whiskey, then raised his eyebrows, indicating the bottle.

"Of course," Tom said.

Charlie refused to answer further questions, so they sat in silence in the kitchen, each in their own thoughts. Dan was often lost in his own head, but when he looked at Charlie, the harshest description of the look on *his* face might have been "wistful".

"What are we going to do?" Dan said finally.

"Let's talk about it in the morning," Charlie said. "I'm wiped."

Tom showed him to a spare bedroom, where Charlie threw himself down, and appeared to be asleep almost immediately. Dan checked on his old friend, his old nemesis, once or twice during the night before going to sleep himself. He placed a clean t-shirt, socks and underwear, folded neatly, at the foot of the bed for Charlie's use.

In the morning, though, Charlie was gone.

Dan got a cheap black suit for the funeral of Jim Gates. Tom tried to get him to buy something more expensive, but Dan shook it off.

"You should go with some style," Tom said.

"I don't have that many people left to die on me," Dan said. "It's not like I'd use it much."

Although Tom barely knew Jim, he offered to go along to the service. Dan convinced his friend that it would be better if he went alone.

The cheap dress shoes he had bought chafed his ankles through the thin socks as he went up the sidewalk to the large funeral home in White Birch Pointe, an austere building of grey stone and black trim which actually reminded Dan of the Gates mansion itself. Or the former Gates mansion, he thought. As the dress shoes wore through his socks and the skin over his ankle tendons, he thought about what a witless and stupid expense they'd been. Why would anyone wear shoes like this? he wondered.

The sidewalks were wet with melting snow, and he realized that he was shuffling along, looking at the concrete squares and the feet of others. When he raised his head, he was surprised to note the number of people who were filing into the funeral home, drawn down the sidewalks from both directions, coming from the far side of the funeral home's packed parking lot. He even recognized Scotty, Ian, and Joel, the neighbor kids who had showed up at the mansion when Dan had run away from Portview. They were talking amongst themselves as they went slowly up the steps and into the building. Scotty looked smug and derisive, and Dan remembered wanting to pound the kid's face with his fists. He felt the same way now. When

Scotty looked over, Dan met his eye. Whether or not Scotty recognized him, he dropped his gaze and the look on his face changed.

The funeral home was a familiar place to Dan, although he had never been there before. There were faint odors he recognized, and he knew the kind of bier and casket that stood at the front of the room, knew what had gone on to set up the place and its somber ambience.

"Gotta make it kinda fuckin' dignified, kid," Fred Turner had told him at Sweeney's. "Gotta give the DB a good send off. That's what people pay for. Show biz."

The DB at the front of the room had been his friend. Jim had never been a nemesis; rather he had been Dan's cohort, mutually dwelling in Charlie's roaring aura. He had been kind and funny, had buffered some of Charlie's intensity right from the beginning. Although he could be wild, yes, he was bright and he was kind.

Dan hoped to blend in with the growing crowd. He picked out Elpidia, his friend from the Gates kitchen, and Ng the gardener, amiable accomplice and eraser of the boys' misdeeds. There were faces from Jim and Charlie's mutual friends, and those who looked like teachers and professors.

In the front row sat Gigi, beautiful in black, tragedy making her pale skin luminous. A sexual image popped in to Dan's head, and he crushed it in disgust. He imagined Gigi in a portrait by one of the Dutch masters, and then in one of his own composition.

Gigi sat next to Jim's girlfriend Jenny. They were holding hands and had been crying. As Dan watched, Jenny began to sob and leaned to rest her head on Gigi's shoulder. Gigi laid her cheek on top of the girl's head and put her arm around her, patting her shoulder as she wept.

On Gigi's other side, almost unrecognizable, sat Henry Gates. He seemed deflated and grey, and was oblivious to those who filed in front of him, bending towards him and talking softly. Dan had moved out of the flow of people and was standing watching this when he saw Hugh moving towards him through the crowd. Impeded by those who wanted to talk to him, Hugh slipped away with a few gracious words.

When Hugh stood in front of Dan, they embraced. The gaze they exchanged was so desolate that words would only violate it. They embraced again.

"No Charlie?" Dan said.

"Nope," Hugh said. "Charlamagne's a no-show. But there are cops." He nodded toward an opposite corner at the back of the room. Two men in overcoats and cheap short haircuts stood there with bored expressions. One covered a yawn with the back of his hand. Dan was a bit surprised they weren't the detectives who had stolen Charlie's stash.

Dan and Hugh stood side by side for a moment, watching people file in to the seats.

"I saw Charlie the night of the accident," Dan told Hugh softly. He told him about what Charlie had said.

There was nothing for Hugh to say. He exhaled through his nose, softly shaking his head.

"We'll talk later," Hugh said finally. "I have to take care of some things."

Dan stopped him. "I'm sorry, man," he said. "I could have done something."

"No, you couldn't," Hugh said. He kneaded Dan's shoulder and went off through the crowd.

Perhaps Hugh was right. Perhaps there was nothing Dan could do to change what had happened. The notion of his powerlessness to protect his friend made his eyes burn. Then another thought: suppose Charlie's right? Suppose all my sadness and guilt are meaningless, something from which I could free myself if I only had the will?

As people settled, it became apparent that the time was nearing when speeches would begin over Jim's coffin, something which would doubtless have made Jim laugh. When he imagined Henry Gates overcoming his grief to give a speech that was more about himself than his dead son, Dan had a clear mental image of Jim howling with laughter about Donna's reaction to the M-80s out on the river. Jim's face was tanned, teeth white, hair golden, an improbably perfect boy. With the sound of Jim's laughter so strong in his mind, Dan almost laughed himself. Then his mind wandered; moments later it had reset to helplessness and grief.

Before Henry Gates could get up to speak, Dan slipped out the back.

He went back to Tom's and changed clothes hurriedly, putting on his sturdy boots, his fatigue pants, sweatshirt and jacket. He had the kind of watchcap and gloves that Willy had always worn, and pulled them on as well.

Soon he was down at the beach. The temperature had dropped, and it began to snow. The waves sighed to the shore, their white rims glowing under the luminous sky. The winter icepack, seeded with sand, was beginning to break up in the spring warmth. As he sat on a freshly exposed rock, a slab of ice the size of his van broke off the greater mass of ice and slid into the waves with a boom and a spray of water. Dan watched this, thought of a painting, then slid back to thinking about all that had gone wrong and everything he had done, and not done, to cause it.

It wasn't productive, perhaps, but had the benefit of being habitual. At least some things were dependable.

The way in which Charlie had been intermittently supportive of Dan's artistic efforts had been, over the years, salted with his comments about its pointlessness, as one might imagine. Nothing Charlie said impeded Dan in this regard; if he had an inspiration, or was feeling that itch, that "cacoethes", as Charlie called it, nothing his friend said could deter him, and Dan went ahead and got in the spell, whether it was pointless or not. Dan might eventually be prematurely broken out of his trance when Charlie needed to kill his boredom, but he was usually able to resume later, although this called for varying degrees of effort.

Strangely, Tom's entirely positive reaction, his visions of a glowing future, sometimes made Dan pull away and seek distractions. Tom currently had the idea of an "art bar", as he called it, a place where local artists could put up their work, have it seen, and (hopefully) sold.

"I see it as a sprawling place," Tom said, lost in the mania of his vision. "There will be a few bars on different levels, artwork everywhere. Black walls, dark carpeting, subtle spotlights on the art, the bars little glowing islands of inebriation and interesting talk. You with me?"

"Yeah."

"Good, because you figure prominently. This is where your art is going to take off. Pretty soon you'll have rich guys in bidding wars over your stuff. Then you get commissions. Then you're off."

"What's in it for you?"

"Ten percent."

"Sounds fair."

Although Tom's enthusiasm was a little disconcerting, Dan didn't worry about his vision actually coming true. Tom might achieve much of what he set out to, but things like that didn't happen to people like Dan. This was a feeling rather than an articulated thought. If Dan had been pressed to clarify this feeling, he almost certainly would have used the term *maldito* yet again. As nearly involuntary as it was for him to create his visions, a mirror-image part of him, just as strong, wanted to pull him in another direction entirely.

A great pull in The Other Direction came that summer in the form of the Greysport Riots. The Riots, and their legendary severity, were made possible by a confluence of events, all streaming downhill towards each other like separate flows of spilled gasoline combining in a flood and trickling inexorably toward a match lit by two cops and a gangster.

The first flow of gasoline arose from a labor dispute in the steel industry, a dispute which was more or less traditional. Samuel Dixon had started the first steel mill in Greysport in 1903. His competitor, Edwin Butz, had started another a few years later. By the time Willy had gone to Europe in the Great War, the two captains of industry had realized the advantages of pooling their resources and had joined their companies. Both of them had short tempers when it came to treating their workers fairly, and were adamant in their stance against unions. Strife broke out again and again over the years, with the magnates using their power to have police sent in to knock the heads of strikers, who fought back in the early years. In 1980, the company policy remained in effect, although the union had won victories over the years, victories which diminished the rate at which the Owners accumulated great wealth, victories that The Owners were driven to disassemble. The steelworkers had currently been on strike at the Dixon-Butz foundry for over a month, the union holding out for a raise in pay, safer conditions, and better benefits while the head of Dixon-Butz itself, making three hundred times the annual wages of the lowest paid union member, was trying to break the union. When scabs tried to cross the picket lines, skirmishes had broken out and the police had been called. So far, nothing too serious had happened, although tensions continued to build. The Union workers had t-shirts printed up and distributed, bold white print on black cotton, saying: FUCKED AGAIN BY DIXON-BUTZ. Even the cops laughed at that one. The t-shirts soon became de rigueur among the denizens of Vnuk's and the underground. Dan and Charlie both had them, although, being temporarily estranged, they hadn't consulted on the matter.

At the same time, conflict had been on the rise between rival motorcycle gangs, the Outcasts and the Guardians of Nocturne. Skirmishes had happened here as well, but nothing more serious than a few bare-knuckle dust-ups, or maybe the use of a baseball bat or a chain, nothing that Dan and Charlie wouldn't have participated in if they had been so inclined. If Dan had kept in contact with Stumpy and Nubby

Schommer, they might have told him that things were going to get more serious, that the Guardians were gearing up with everything from handguns to AK-47s, the River Chapter itself on call, and a bloodbath in the offing.

Other traditional rivalries among the underclass seemed to be heating up with the weather. Black gangs were going after black gangs, Latino against Latino, Latino against black, and so forth, with Vietnamese gangs, Chinese, Koreans all in the mix of territorial rivalries, many going against each other across racial lines (skinhead acquaintances of the Three Horsedicks of the Apocalypse were in on this), all fizzing at the edges as if the walls of cells under a microscope had all become electrified and acidic. Perhaps the greatest rivalry was between the Brothers of the Rising and the 47th Street Badass Niggaz, although the friction between Los Reyes Latinos and Los Salvajes Locos came in a close second. All the participants were apparently blind to the fact that they had far more in common than that which divided them, and the fact that they fought amongst themselves worked perfectly for the top two percent of society, the Owners, who really ran things. To be fair, it should be noted that any of the Owners could easily be bumped off their pillar by a single bullet from the lowest of gangbangers, something about which they maintained a small but constant level of terror. The Owners had played things well, though, and would, as usual, sit the riots out.

Some mounting tensions were understandable. Gaybashing and fagrolling had been on the increase down by the port, and the Raging Queens were gearing up for retribution, knowing the location of a redneck bar where such forays often originated. Hugh Gates now sang with the Civic Opera, but was able to strip away his cultivated veneer when necessary. He was a hard and trained fighter underneath.

"I'm like a gay Batman," he'd told Dan at a get-together not long before the riots.

What really set it off was what often does, an injustice (perhaps only a perceived one) too large to be ignored. It revolved around a police brutality case in which a young asshole was not-so-inadvertently killed by a couple of somewhat older assholes of a different race and profession. The incident itself had happened the previous winter, the real fallout happening after several days of brutal summer heat. Dan had blankly watched the news coverage of the initial incident right around the time he had broken up with Kate.

LeShawn P. Singleton was a cocky young dickhead who thought of himself as a gangster. A big guy, he'd been a linebacker in high school and done some boxing, considering himself tough even when he didn't have a gun. Joe Pulaski and Doug Dougan were cocky young dickheads who thought of themselves as cops. LeShawn slung drugs and did some small-time crimes, sponged off his mother and had three children by three different girls, acknowledging his parentage of none of them. He never stinted on getting himself the most expensive fashions, though, never mind the fact that the fashion would have passed in no longer than three months.

Joe Pulaski and Doug Dougan were thicker than thieves, sometimes actually *being* thieves. They stole from crime scenes, from homes and businesses that had been burglarized, then simply added what they had stolen to the list of missing items on their police report. They stole from suspects routinely, and never, ever, paid for drugs. Falsification of police reports was, for Doug and Joe, routine, as was drug use, drunkeness on the job, and fucking around on their wives. They were friends with the cops who had ripped Charlie off. One of their favorite activities was to give a good beating to perpetrators (even witnesses), and none of *them* dared to speak up. Joe and Doug knew how to cover themselves in their reports and testimony, were considered expert witnesses in court, and would make a point of coming at anyone who testified against them. It might be noted that their favorite joke was the Juicy Interview. This involved going to the home of someone they needed to talk to for information regarding a case they were working. If the conditions were right, one of them would keep the interviewee in the living room or other part of the house, while the other would wander into the kitchen with an air of studious professionalism, all with the intent of opening the refrigerator and pissing in whatever juice container they might find, then coming back out to the interview to nod with concern as the talk was concluded.

LeShawn P. Singleton had just sold some drugs when he was pulled over by Officers Pulaski and Dougan. An anomaly, he had no weapon in his Cadillac, no drug paraphernalia, nothing to incriminate him but a large (although legal) amount of cash. Nothing would have happened if he had confined his anger and kept his mouth shut.

Joe and Doug pulled him over on the pretext that he had taken a right through a red light without the benefit of a turn signal or coming to a complete stop. This was merely convenient; they would have pulled him over if he had done nothing, then fabricated an excuse. Their real aim was to bust LeShawn for anything they could; they were profiling him, based on accurate and time-tested perceptions.

Joe approached on the driver's side while Doug came up from the right, both leaving their holsters snapped as they walked up. LeShawn radiated hostility out the rolled-down window of the Caddy. Joe Pulaski, out of endless practice, radiated the hostility right back, focusing a narrow beam of icy professionalism.

"What the fuck you pull me over for, man?" LeShawn barked, starting off on the wrong foot. "I di'int do nothin'!"

"You ran a red without coming to a complete stop, and without using a turn signal, sir," Pulaski said. "License and registration, please."

LeShawn fumed about this, but pulled his heavy winter jacket aside to get his wallet out of his back pocket. Joe stood behind the driver's side window, sharing a grin with Doug over the roof of the vehicle.

When LeShawn handed over his papers with a surly glare, the curl of his lip revealing a gold tooth, Joe laughed as he walked back to the squadcar to run LeShawn's name for warrants. That was only their first approach; if no warrants came up, they'd try to trick LeShawn into letting them search his car.

"Mother*fuck*er!" LeShawn said out the window as Officer Pulaski walked away. Pulaski heard this, turning slightly, but stopped himself from looking back or responding. This was going to be good.

As he ran the information, Doug Dougan came around the side of the squad. "Let's jack him," he said.

"I thought I'd try to do it legitimately before we made something up," Joe said.

"Wise. Very wise. Any warrants?"

"Nope. Plenty of priors, no warrants."

LeShawn sat in his car and fumed some more. He was cautious and intelligent, but hotheaded, and the fact that he knew that his car was clean, as was he (except for a nose full of blow) gave him the leeway to let his hotheadedness come to the surface. He looked at the two cops in his rearview, catching them grinning.

"Those mother*fuckers*!" he said. "They *laughin'* at my ass!"

He made the mistake of getting out of his car and walking back to the squad. He wasn't cursing under his breath, and was, in fact, muttering loud enough that a few of the half-dozen people at the bus-stop a few yards away took notice.

Doug Dougan noticed as well. "Ah, fuck," he said to his partner. "Check this shit out."

LeShawn was a large young man, bigger than either Joe or Doug, and walked back to the squad rolling his shoulders, pointing at the two as he said, "I done tol' you, I di'int do nothing! I'm a busy motherfucker, so gimme back my license so's I kin be on my way!"

This really got the interest of the bystanders. The cops looked at each other, shaking their heads. They got out of the squad.

"Return to your vehicle, sir!" Doug intoned. "Now!"

"I ain't got *time* for this shit, dog! Gimme my damn license! I know my damn rights!"

The three of them came together. Joe said quietly, "Know your damn rights, huh? You got the right to get your fuckin' head busted, you don't get back in that pimp-ass Caddy."

The onlookers came closer, sensing drama. LeShawn noticed this and suddenly felt heroic.

"I know my rights, motherfuckers!" he shouted. "I will not stand for this oppression!"

"Put your hands behind your back, sir," Doug declaimed for the onlookers. "You have the right to remain silent..."

Rather put his hands behind his back or remain silent, LeShawn took a swing at Joe, who bobbed back, avoiding most of the blow but taking enough of it on the cheekbone that it knocked off his cap. The onlookers cheered.

Doug took out his baton and chopped LeShawn in the kidney. People in the crowd shouted.

"Leave that man alone!" one yelled.

"Police brutality! Police brutality!"

"That motherfucker hit a black man!"

LeShawn grunted at the hit, but got Doug in the jaw with a left.

"Fuck!" Doug shouted.

The two cops regrouped, falling back on training and experience and going at LeShawn with their batons. One hit a knee, the other a collarbone. A crack to the back of his skull made LeShawn stagger, but the young man was nearly as tough as he thought he was and swung again.

"You're resisting arrest!" Joe shouted. "Lie on the ground with your hands behind your back!"

Doug saw the anger of the onlookers (who could become the basis of a mob) and took the seconds required to say into his radio mike, "Officers need assistance. And

256

an ambulance." He gave the location and went back to assist his partner, who was being slammed into the squadcar by LeShawn.

They chopped at his knees and his elbows, at his forearms when he covered up his head. Finally he went down as the sound of approaching sirens echoed down the snowy streets. LeShawn was coked up and pissed off, though, and refused to submit. Joe opted for a variation on the sleeper hold, and used the L of his baton to apply to LeShawn's carotid arteries. Doug helped hold him down as Joe cranked the hold hard, grimacing as he did so.

"Nighty-night, motherfucker," he gritted, giving a few extra jolts to LeShawn's neck. Sirens approached, both police and ambulance. A bus drove by and left, letting people off, although none got on. The original onlookers informed the newcomers, who became angry themselves.

Both cops were pumped with adrenaline, one of the reasons they had sought the job in the first place. Joe used this additional energy to make sure LeShawn was really out, while Doug got up, shouting at the crowd to back off. When LeShawn was finally compliant (not to mention completely limp), Joe put the young man's large hands behind his massive back with some effort and clicked on the cuffs. He stuck with the suspect while other cops took care of dispersing the crowd.

LeShawn was out cold, sure enough. When one of the paramedics checked him out, he said to Joe, "Dude ain't breathin'."

Joe exhanged a subtly tense look with his partner. "What?" he said. "Fuckin'...*what*?"

The paramedic shrugged. "Hate to be the bearer of bad tidings, man, but he ain't."

"Fuck!" he said, looked over at the onlookers, who were now behind a police cordon, spread out, but still obviously angry. "Well, get him on the ambulance and get him breathing again!"

"Yeah!" Doug said. "Don't do it in front of *these* motherfuckers."

The paramedic and his partner loaded LeShawn P. Singleton into the ambulance and closed the doors, driving away without the siren. They made a halfhearted effort to resuscitate him, but LeShawn was already dead.

The verdict didn't come in until the following summer, when Dan and Tom watched events unfold on the television in Tom's living room. Tom seemed appalled. Dan was entranced, enthralled, *pulled* toward it.

If the acquittal of officers Pulaski and Dougan had come back in another season, in the fall or the winter, for example, or during a mild stretch of the summer, things might have gone differently. Even if it had been at the beginning of the heat wave, the results might not have been the same. As it was, though, there was a city full of people already pissed off and short tempered. Domestic abuse, bar fights, assault and murder were all up, and that wasn't even including the tensions that existed between all the aforementioned parties.

"This could get interesting," Tom said. His tone was wary and weary.

It *could* get interesting, Dan thought.

Dan went to the kitchen to get a few more beers. He found himself staring out the front window, and realized that part of him was looking for Charlie. He shook his head. Of course he should stay here with Tom, who wouldn't get involved in any of the chaos that might follow. Dan thought he might go by the daycare center where Kate worked, just to see if she was okay, but it was a Friday, and she would probably leave before things got bad, if they got bad at all.

Of course they *did* get bad.

As the sun went down orange and smoky over the industrial sprawl west of the city, the rioting started in the black neighborhoods a few miles from downtown. It wasn't all in reaction to the verdict of the court, but to decades of hopelessness, of soul-gutting poverty and humiliation, of anger which had simmered long without relief. All of it was combustible, all of it went up.

People began smashing the windows of stores in their own neighborhoods. Once the first window was broken, it was easy to throw a cinderblock through the next. Some people looked around and saw their neighbors doing things so out of character that they weren't sure they were seeing the same people. There was the sound of liberated howling, though, of wild laughter, of smashing glass and sirens, of relief and release and revenge, and suddenly the sense of oppression was gone, usurped by a roaring freedom. Friends and neighbors and enemies alike climbed empty handed through the broken windows of stores only to come out grinning with armloads of things useful and not useful: TVs and booze, snack cakes and roller skates, malt liquor and meat, stereos and cough syrup, diapers and showercaps. The people were smiling and laughing, ignoring the approaching sirens and shouting to each other about their acquisitions. Fearless they were, with far too many of them for the police to arrest.

Delegations opened fire hydrants against the heat and children danced in the showering water in the streets as looting went on a block away. Water pressure diminished, and when the fire department roared out to extinguish buildings set alight, there was not enough force in the water to do the job. Teams in squadcars were sent out to shut hydrants, but these teams were chased off with fusillades of bricks and bottles and the occasional gunshot.

Arrests were made here and there where it was safe. This happened enough over the course of the first night that the jail got overcrowded, but those arrested were still just a tiny fraction of the population who thronged the streets, dancing and drunk and free in the remaining streetlights, and the firelight from burning buildings, and cars in intersections, and bonfires built in the middle of the street.

When the riots started in the neighborhoods, the tension at the picket line outside of Dixon-Butz also ignited. Scabs tried to cross the line, and union members stopped them. Fights broke out, and it all turned into a melee. Police coverage of the event was minimal, as forces had been pulled off to deal with chaos elsewhere. Violence gained momentum. A scab was pulled from his truck and beaten, but this stopped when an executive was spotted trying to leave from a side exit of the plant in his gold Mercedes. He was pursued by strikers on foot and crashed his car into a lightpole in his panic. The windows of his car were smashed out, the body beaten and dented. He was dragged from the vehicle and pounded himself, until one of the strikers took pity and got his companions to compromise. Rather than letting him go, the strikers acceded to the savior's idea of simply stripping the man naked and duct-taping him to a telephone pole.

Jumpin' Irv was the first casualty during the riots from among Dan and Charlie's network of friends. He was arrested when things first started going, although it was in a northwest suburb, far away from the action, and not directly related to the riots themselves.

As much as he could be low man on the totem pole among the Vnuk's and Underground crowd, he was capable of being belligerent and bullying when back in his own safer neighborhood of Finster's Corners, among friends from high school. They were less attracted to the wild lifestyle that Irv often pursued, satisfied to stick to their own suburb. When Irv went out there, he got to act like a bigshot.

He drank a lot in front of his old friends to prove how tough he was. To demonstrate his intelligence and sophistication, he tried a trick on one of them that Charlie had tried on him.

"There are two kinds of people," he stated in a tone of authority, "those who believe that there are two kinds of people, and another, which doesn't exist, who believes there is only one."

Charlie had said this to Jumpin' Irv when he was in a befuddled condition, and the statement had made him more befuddled still.

When Irv tried the line himself, one old friend squinted at him for a few moments, before tilting his head to one side and saying (just as Irv had), "*What* now?"

"Exactly!" Irv said, pleased to see someone look as stupid as he had felt when Charlie had said the same thing to him.

Irv held forth, amusing friends with the stories of his wild buddies in the city. He even told the tale of the time when Charlie had blown the head off the statue of Bacchus, changing things around so that he, himself, was more heroic and the story more frightening. His old friends shook their heads in wonder, buying him more drinks. Irv accepted with kingly magnanimity. The TV over the bar showed muted images of the riots going on in other areas of Greysport, but almost everyone ignored it.

When Irv left the bar, he was quite drunk, yet sober enough to walk a straight line, to speak fairly coherently, and to think he should drive. The heat outside made it worse; cold air might have straightened him up.

The trouble was that, once out on the sidewalk, he couldn't find his car. Unable to remember where he had parked it, he wandered up and down the streets, sweating through his janitor's uniform in the muggy air, getting more and more angry. It finally dawned on him that the car had been stolen. This made him livid.

He hated to go back into the bar to use the payphone, having made what he considered to be an impressive exit, but he had to report the car stolen and get a ride from one of his old friends. He didn't explain what had happened when he came through the door, but kept his dignity about himself and went to the phone booth, holding up an index finger, a plea for pause, to his old friends on the way.

Calling the number for the suburb's police, he got right through; the suburb of Finster's Corners was a boring one, which was why Irv preferred Greysport. He gave the operator at the police station a description of the car and its license plate number, his name and home phone.

When he got out of the phone booth, he stood in front of the table full of comrades and announced that he needed a ride back to the city. His friends insisted that he have another drink, which led to three. Then one or two more; no one would give him a ride unless he capitulated.

Finally, one of his old buddies agreed to give him a lift. They left the air-conditioning of the bar, and the heat outside made it seem like they were on a planet with higher gravity and a denser atmosphere.

"Jesus!" Irv moaned.

"What kind of car do you have?" his friend asked, jingling his own car keys.

"Blue Valiant," Irv said.

"It's right there," the friend said, pointing across the street to where the car was parked in a shadowy space equidistant from two street lights.

"Shit!" Irv cried. "How did I do that?"

"You're hammered," his friend said amiably.

"No, I'm not," Irv said. "I've just got a lot on my mind."

"Okay, if you say so."

Irv thanked his friend for offering to help, got behind the wheel of his Valiant, cranked the ignition, and took off. Four blocks later, he got pulled over by a bored suburban cop who was almost gnashing his teeth with excitement about the possibility of arresting a car thief. The cop called for backup from his best friend, who showed up almost immediately and boxed Irv in. An hour earlier, the two had been discussing their chagrin at not being part of the riots downtown. At least they had this.

Irv produced his driver's license and registration, telling the cops affably that it had all been a misunderstanding. They agreed that these kinds of things did, indeed, happen, but they also couldn't help but notice that Irv was wasted. With the additional drinks that he had had after re-entering the bar, he was now unable to even walk a straight line. It was bad enough that he almost fell over during the mandatory sobriety test. The cops put Irv in handcuffs and took him down to their diminutive police station. After booking him, taking his fingerprints and mugshot, they put him in a tiny holding cage little bigger than a closet. Here Irv had time to get morose. He was even crying when the cops came an hour and a half later to take him down to

Greysport County Jail, seeing as their little station was too small to have cells of its own.

Irv was searched again before his admission to the jail. A deputy with a small flashlight clenched between his teeth had him drop his janitor's pants, bend over, spread his cheeks, and cough. The deputy squatted behind him and watched Irv's flexing anus as he did.

As depressed as he was, Irv found this amusing. At least he didn't do *that* for a living. "Like your job?" he asked the deputy with a smirk.

"Fucking *love* it," the deputy said. "Can't *wait* to come in to work."

Irv was put into a large holding cell which was already beginning to fill up with arrestees involved with the riots. As the night passed and the cell got more crowded, the noise level rose. None of his new cellmates resembled janitors, in fact none of them resembled Irv much at all. If they paid attention to him, their gazes were less than friendly.

Irv moved into a corner, sitting down and avoiding eye contact, and began to wait for sobriety, and for his arraignment the next morning.

Three Horsedicks of the Apocalypse were not ones to watch the opportunity of the riots pass. They didn't do what Charlie wanted to do, which was to use the cover of the riots to go out and seek revenge. The Horsedicks were more practical; they had looting in mind.

Their first target was one which Jerry had identified; a warehouse at the port which he knew contained thousands of brand-new television sets from Japan. The trio was aware that police all over the city had been rerouted to the riots themselves. When things had started up, they had been playing pool and drinking cold beer in the sanctuary of their local bar. A Breaking News segment interrupted a baseball game, and the patrons of the bar went silent to watch. As if sensing something on the wind, like wolves, the Horsedicks had looked up from the pool table, back and forth between each other, and begun to smile.

So as conflict burst out the boys geared up. They cruised slowly with their beige van down to the port. Larcenous pragmatists at heart, they thought that they would profit first and get anarchic later. With Jimmie at the wheel, they pulled up to the twelve-foot chain link fence to their targeted warehouse, there under the bridge which spanned the harbor. Jerry stood lookout while Chris took boltcutters to the simple chain which locked the nondescript fence in front of the place. They shorted the electrical system and the alarms, and were soon inside the warehouse itself. Jerry and Chris opened the loading dock doors, and Jimmie backed the van up to the dock.

They were quick and skilled; it was one of the things they did well. They packed the van efficiently with TVs, leaving only inches of clearance before they shut the rear doors. They never fought any more about who would sit in the back seat; as a matter of habit and practicality, they judiciously took turns. This time Chris sat in back, surrounded by the brown cardboard and black print of boxed televisions behind him, beside him, and right up to the roof.

Chris did insist, however, that they pull over when he spotted a city vehicle parked on the side of the street as they went through an underpass. Profit was one thing, a target of opportunity another. It was only a car belonging to the Department of Public Works, but the Horsedicks were, in a way that they never dared to reveal to

Charlie, only vague and misdirected anarchists, as spectacular as the demonstrations of their nebulous philosophy might sometimes be.

"A moment, please, lads," Chris said, sliding open the side door of the van. He got out, and, taking a bandanna (always useful) from one of the cargo pockets of his fatigues, he flipped open the cover over the city vehicle's gas cap, unscrewed the cap and threw it aside. Into the empty fill tube, he stuffed the bandanna. He then took a lighter from another sidepocket and lit the bandanna, which seemed to sputter a bit, but then lit quite well.

He got back in the van and said blandly, "Okay."

They wanted to drive off like heroes in an action movie, paying no attention to what happened on the street behind them. They were not that cool, though; when the flame from the bandanna ignited the gas fumes in the Public Works vehicle, which ignited the gas itself, first with just a *whuffff* and then a genuine explosion, they had to pull over, instead of driving away with the looks of stony professionalism that all three of them wanted to affect. Chris couldn't see anything out the rear windows, the van being packed with TVs, and Jimmie and Jerry could only see in the rearview mirrors on the sides of the van.

Jimmie didn't pull over soon enough. They all piled out, though, immediately after the muted explosion (again, not like in the movies), but still were doubled over laughing at the results. The car burnt merrily, its flames contributing to the toxic heat.

"Next time," Jerry said, "let's just watch the whole thing." They all concurred. Jimmie took backstreets and alleys to their secret storage place. It might have been overly cautious, seeing as riots raged throughout the city, shots fired, people killed, cars (even buildings) ablaze in more conspicuous places. They all agreed, though, that occasional caution increased their overall odds, for there would certainly be times when they would not be cautious at all.

On the morning of that day, Jumpin' Irv Klubertanz was released from Greysport County Jail. He wasn't arraigned; he was simply released.

"Lucky day, Klubertanz," a deputy (not the same one who had inspected his spasming bunghole) said. Irv, haggard from a stupefyingly long night of jail-rape apprehension (and vastly hung over to boot), was too baffled to ask any questions; he was merely relieved. The deputy answered for him, nonetheless.

"You're kicked out," he said cheerfully. "We got too many assholes in here to deal with a simple drunk driver."

"What about my charges," Irv asked. "What about the cops in Finster's Corners?"

"We'll take care of it."

Jumpin Irv was dumbfounded, not quite believing his luck.

"Fuckin'....thanks, man," he said to the deputy.

"*I* didn't do it," the man said. "I'd rather have a dozen of *you* in here than a thousand of *these* assholes, let me tell you."

Irv summoned the capacity to keep his mouth shut. He retrieved his personal articles (after another head-pounding wait; everything involving the cops apparently took forever) and found himself on the street. Painfully tired, he wanted nothing more than to go home and go to sleep. The shame of his own irresponsibility, however, his loserliness, made him think that the most adult thing he could do would be to take a cab, go back to Finster's Corners, and retrieve his Valiant.

It appeared that cabs waited, vulturelike, outside the jail, hovering for the recently released, who might be immoderate with their grateful tips. He was picked up immediately, and on his way back to Finster's Corners, the scene, he thought, of his most recent transgression. In spite of the heat, the wind blasting in from the freeway through his open window was as reviving as pure oxygen itself. The breeze was from the south, bearing the stink, from that particular direction of the compass, of the tallow plant and slaughter house near which Dan had worked. He rested his head back on the questionable seat of the cab, exhausted, relieved by the wind, already hot in the morning, booming in the window and lifting his greasy hair. He barely noticed when ambulances and police cars screamed past in the other direction.

Back in Finster's Corners, he had the driver stop in front of the bar. Irv, did, indeed, tip the man immoderately; the driver thanked him and drove off, leaving him alone on the quiet, steamy street. He was dazed with fatigue, monumentally depressed. He found though, that he was entertaining none of his usual bleak tendencies, no thoughts of suicide, even of nihilism. He found that, as bleak as he felt, he recognized that the worst was over, that he was out and free, alive and unsodomized.

In spite of this revelatory feeling, if the bar had been open, Jumpin' Irv might have been tempted to go in and have a drink, drawn by that wordless voice that had gotten him into such a predicament in the first place. In the hellishly long night in the holding tank, though, he'd been contemplating the aimlessness of his life, thinking that perhaps the people he associated with didn't contribute to his overall well-being, and that he didn't contribute to it much himself. The fact that the bar was closed made it easy to turn around and go down the street to his Valiant.

The car was already so hot inside that he didn't dare sit on the vinyl seats, let alone touch the steering wheel. He opened the front doors to let the humid air in, leaning on the trunk and smoking a filterless cigarette.

When his grandfather had told him the story about his time in World War I, Irv thought, perhaps he had only been trying to be humorous when he had told Irv that life "don't mean shit". Maybe his grandfather had only wanted to see the look on his face. Maybe not.

Irv felt strangely buoyed, though. There were all kinds of possibilities; look what had just happened to him. If ever a situation had seemed hopeless, that was it. Yet here he was on the beautiful summer morning, on a quiet street next to his car. He could get in and drive in any direction. Who knew what might happen next.

When he smoked the cigarette down to where it nearly burned his yellowed fingers, he flicked it in the gutter and got in the car. He drove slowly back to the freeway, finding something cheerful on the radio. *Walking on Sunshine* by Katrina and the Waves came on. Irv did not, as he usually would have, flick it off, feigning disgust. He had always liked the song, but would have hidden it from his friends. *Fuck* my friends, he decided.

Bobbing his head to the music, he got onto the onramp and headed south on the freeway. Greysport lay to the south, and west of downtown, south of downtown, inverted cones of smoke roiled slowly into the summer sky, indicating the areas of the riots.

Irv lit another cigarette with the Valiant's lighter. He tapped the steering wheel with his free hand. Although he was exhausted and hung over, he still felt happy, unusually optimistic. If I can be optimistic in this state, he thought, what would it be like to wake up with a simple good night's sleep?

He approached an overpass where two kids stood just over his lane. He often saw kids in the same position, standing there to wave at traffic, but flipped them off in return. As he approached, he decided he would wave to them, do something positive.

There was a truck in the lane in front of him, which is what the kids might have been aiming for when, acting as a team, they lofted a bowling ball over the bridge's fencing up into the air and down onto the cab of the truck.

Irv's instantaneous reaction was one of amazed mirth. The bowling ball crunched the roof of the cab with a sound audible even over the freeway traffic, bounced up, seeming to freeze for a fraction of a second, then appeared to accelerate towards Irv's windshield at head height.

Irv had time to flinch and scream before the ball punched through the glass.

Dan woke up late that same muggy morning feeling that he was missing out on something. Watching the television with Tom the night before, seeing the growing chaos on the local channels, he had continued to feel that itch, that pull toward chaos, toward the things that he had never seen. When he looked over at Tom, though, he saw that his friend did not share the pull; Tom was clearly saddened by what he saw. That was because, Dan thought, Tom was not a *maldito*.

He continued work on his latest (and biggest) piece. After what, in recent months, had become a deadening lassitude, a desire to do nothing but drink, do drugs, read and watch TV, he pushed himself through a barrier. The barrier itself consisted of mental images of Willy, dead and alone, of Kate weeping in the kitchen of her apartment in the late afternoon sun. Images even of his mother, of Mike Krapczak, of Jorge and Darnell.

Once through the barrier, he lost himself in the current project. A room-filling triptych, it consisted of three huge canvasses, each four feet in height, eight feet in width. The construction of the frames and stretching of the canvasses themselves had been problematic.

The scene depicted was one of an autumn marsh fire at night, the long, dead grass billowing amber flames, some reflected by black water, cattails often in silhouette, but bright and clear on the opposite side of the flame. On the central canvas (the other two being its arms, the life of the paintings diminishing to the left and right extremes, or growing towards the center, depending on the point of view), stood dark figures amidst the marsh grass, sometimes amidst the flames themselves, sometimes ablaze. Were there pyres among the flames? Was it some kind of ritual? Dan left that up to the viewer, or the "witness", as he called them to himself, privately. Over all of this flaming landscape, though, was a gibbous moon, gelid and detached, afloat in a sheet of pale blue and silver cirrus clouds, untouched by the insignificant drama beneath it.

Dan had no idea what someone else might think of it. He had little idea of what he thought of it himself, only knowing that he had successfully summoned, from somewhere deep, a kind of mystery, a kind of dread, a kind of beauty. He knew that Kate would understand, where he, himself, did not.

He painted until he was nearly finished (needing, really, only his signature, although he could have tinkered forever), but he was too exhausted to go on. When his eyes felt like smoldering charcoal briquettes (closing them, he could nearly feel his eyelids sizzle), he acknowledged his point of diminishing returns and blearily cleaned up his tools. Standing back, almost asleep on his feet, he felt a profound satisfaction, one that nearly kept other emotions at bay.

Tom was already asleep, so Dan had watched the television for a bit with a big whiskey and a hefe-weiss before stretching out on the couch and falling asleep himself. When he awoke the late next morning, about the time that Jumpin' Irv was getting out of the county jail, he turned on the news. In spite of his satisfaction with his work, the pull exerted itself again. Helicopter footage of cars burning in intersections, of buildings ablaze with no firefighters in sight, reports of looting and beatings and murder, all made his eyes widen, his nostrils flare, and his breath deepen.

Later that morning, they were watching the news, Tom clucking his tongue and shaking his head, while Dan was feeling the need to get in his van and simply drive toward it.

Tom, always perceptive, apparently sensed this, shifting his gaze from the television to where Dan sat, enraptured, on the couch.

"Man, it's gonna get bad down there," Tom said. "Stay here. Paint. One of these days you're going to do this for a living, but not if you fade at every temptation."

Dan wrestled with it. His rational mind told him that Tom was right, but a more primitive side of him, something atavistic and dark, exerted that familiar pull in the other direction. There was no harm in sitting here thinking about it, he told himself.

He wondered where Charlie was. Charlie had disappeared after the night of the accident, and only rumors of him had surfaced since. Even knowing him as well as Dan did, he didn't have any idea of where to find his friend, although Charlie apparently always knew where to find *him*. Dan went to the Underground and to Vnuk's, even reuniting temporarily with Candy for some nicely raunchy sex, made pleasant only by the fact that Dan's mind was usually too altered by booze and drugs to have images of Kate interfering with what he was doing. When he woke up after such a night, though, he often had an image of being in bed with Kate in the sunlit bedroom of the cabin on Denfer Island, of them walking in the morning on the beach. Such thoughts made his face feel numb and his guts feel greasy. He would pull himself out of bed and get on with going through the motions of the day, the day he deserved.

When Dan looked out Tom's kitchen window and saw an unmarked black Chevy Impala police cruiser pull up at the curb in front of the house, he had a moment's consternation. He could see nothing through the tinted windows, but the vehicle's subtly ominous appearance was one that would have made him check his speed if it had pulled up behind him on the freeway.

When the driver's side door opened and Charlie got out, Dan snorted with laughter.

Charlie had changed appearance, toned it down enough, seemingly, to avoid attracting the focus of the eyes of a police officer. Although he wore customary khaki fatigue pants and a black t-shirt, the clothing was simple and unadorned, washed and clean. His hair was cut short, and he wore dark aviator glasses. He might have been a young man fresh out of the military, going into the police academy. Dan was sure that this was the intent.

Dan should have expected Charlie to show up. His appearance now established it as a pattern. Charlie had said that he always knew where Dan was (keeping the source of his information mysterious), and this seemed to prove it. Here was his old friend again, just in time. Dan's life had been too productive, too fulfilling, even without Kate.

Sometimes he thought of things that Willy had said, that Kate had said. He pondered the possibility that perhaps he might be able to sneak into a happy life. He even thought of calling Kate, instead of driving past her apartment or the daycare. Each time he drove away from where she lived and worked, it felt like he was increasing the distance between him and a possible happy future. There was something perversely fascinating about it, like the desire to stick his tongue to frozen metal. When he drove away from Kate's haunts, he was moving away from something good, putting himself back in a twilight area where he could be pulled over the event horizon and into the darkness altogether.

When Charlie knocked on the front door, the pull was so strong that it felt to Dan like relief.

Dan opened the door and Charlie strode in.

"Been watching the news lately?" he said, as if they had spoken to each other yesterday.

Dan remained deadpan. "No. Why? Did I miss something?"

They were both laughing when Tom came down the hall in his bare feet. Tom knew at a glance what Charlie's presence meant. He kept the dislike off his face, but lifted his chin in greeting.

"You gonna finish the triptych today?" Tom said.

"It's finished," Dan said.

Tom looked at Charlie and back at Dan. "You don't need to do this," he said.

Dan squinted and tilted his head to one side.

"Sure he does," Charlie said. "This is our time."

Dan went into his room to get ready and Tom followed.

"Come on, man," Tom said. "This is trouble."

Dan put on his black fatigues and a black t-shirt. Tom wasn't cut out for this kind of thing, he told himself. He still felt guilty leaving. Tom's big eyes regarded him mournfully. Dan grunted in exasperation. He put on a grey baseball cap, making a production out of it so he could stall to think. Then he had an idea.

"Look, man," he said. "Come here."

He thumped down the hall in his boots, Tom following him silently. Dan came to the triptych, which looked even better in the daylight than it had the night before. *Maldito* or not, he had to admit that he could paint. He took the linseed oil-impregnated rag off his palette of paints. Loading a brush with orange paint, he went to the lower right corner of the central panel of the triptych, an area in black shadow from the depicted flames, and signed his name, orange on black.

"That's all I had to do," he said. "It's done. It's yours. If anything happens to me, keep it, sell it, whatever. Same with all of my stuff. I don't care. It's yours."

"Come on, man," Tom pleaded. "Something bad is going to happen."

Dan stopped in front of Tom and looked him in the eye. "I have to see what's out there," Dan said. "This is something I have to do."

He was hoping that Tom would be distracted, wouldn't follow him back to his room, but Tom *did* follow him. He had no choice but to get the .38 from his sock drawer. Charlie was waiting.

"*Oh*, no," Tom said. "Come on, man. This is bad. Don't do this."

"I'll be okay," Dan said, not sure if he were lying or not.

Charlie had gone out to his car. Dan walked down the sidewalk in the muggy heat, got in slammed the door. He didn't look back to where Tom stood for a moment on his front porch before turning into the house and closing the door behind him.

Charlie grinned at Dan and pulled away from the curb slowly, slowly, as if to increase the tension.

Charlie's plan was simple, if vague: he was going to find the detectives that had stolen his cargo of weed and kill them. The thought of it made Dan feel light-headed. When he remembered his face being planted in the salty grime on the side of his van while the two detectives searched it, he felt the heat of humiliation. It was the same feeling he had whenever he thought about Mike Krapczak.

Although Charlie's plan was amorphous (atypically so), Dan didn't think he had anything to contribute. Charlie knew the precinct the detectives worked out of, knew the general hours of their shifts. Under the circumstances of a riot, they could be deployed, in uniform, anywhere in their district, assigned any number of tasks.

"I figure our best chance of finding them is just to head towards the flame," Charlie said.

"What do we do when we find them?"

"Watch and wait."

They had some time before it got dark out, and it was Charlie's plan to get a little lubricated first. He headed downtown, towards the cathedral square, parking in the alley behind the Kicking Pig. Dan knew what he had in mind, and when Charlie popped the trunk, Dan reached in to get the twelve pack there, while Charlie retrieved the bottle of whiskey. They took the fire escape stairs two at a time to the rooftop of their former home.

They sat together on the low wall at the front of the building, at exactly the spot where Charlie had once shown Jumpin' Irv his limitations. Charlie reached in a cargo pocket and pulled out a prescription bottle, taking off the cap and shaking out a couple of hits of speed apiece. Without commenting on this, the two downed the speed with a gulp of whiskey followed by a chaser of beer.

The sun burned down the sky through a brown and orange haze, its edges wavering in the heat as it became oblate at the horizon. The grey buildings faded into the steamy smog to the west, and here and there a wash of smoke floated slowly skyward on the hot wind from the south. Police and fire sirens could be heard from different directions, and once or twice the sound of gunfire, as if the sound carried better in the thickness of the air.

Charlie looked at Dan and grinned. "It's not Ragnarok," he said, "but it'll do for the time being."

They barely spoke. Dan didn't ask his friend where he had been, or how he felt about Jim, or his family. He didn't ask about being on the run. Nor did Charlie ask him about anything, about Kate, about his grandfather, about the future. They just sat and watched, beginning to tingle on the speed, drinking from the whiskey bottle, draining can after can of beer, which they tossed aside on the roof.

When it was dark, they left the roof of the Kicking Pig for the last time.

Almost twitchy with speed, they slowly cruised the streets for hours. Some neighborhoods seemed unscathed, with people out on the porches and stoops, talking and passing brownbagged bottles. Children played, running back and forth on the sidewalks, from the light under streetlamps and back into the shadows.

Only blocks away from one such peaceful setting, they found a police barricade at an intersection. A corner store had been looted and burned. The store was surrounded with yellow crime scene tape, while cops and firefighters stood around the blackened, sodden wreckage, perhaps relieved that this was their most dangerous duty for the moment.

Charlie was as alert as a raptor, his focus burning through the windshield as he appeared to assess and discard each cop present. He parked the Impala and got a short-sleeved brown shirt from the trunk. Putting it on and leaving it unbuttoned, he reached under the driver's seat and took out the .45, which he slipped into the waistband of his pants, pulling the brown shirt over it in back. He did this while standing twenty feet away from the distracted cops. Dan took the small .38 out of the glovebox and put it in the front pocket of his loose fatigues. He followed Charlie's lead and walked up to the barricade.

"Hey!" Charlie called to a cop standing a few feet away, writing on a clipboard.

The cop turned. Dan saw that the reaction on the man's face wasn't the one he might have given had Charlie been sporting his customary look. There was no suspicion there; his immediate reaction to Charlie's appearance was one of neutrality.

"Yeah?" The cop said.

"Any idea where Detective Vandenburg is tonight?"

"Vandenburg," the cops said, thinking about it. "Narcotics? Works with Jackson?"

"Yeah. He's my uncle."

"Who knows. You may have noticed that the situation is a little chaotic at the moment. Everything's up for grabs."

"Knowing that fat-ass Jackson," another cop said, "they're probably off eating a burrito somewhere."

"That's Jackson for you," Charlie said, laughing.

"If I see him, who shall I say is looking for him?"

"Don't bother," Charlie said. "I'll find him at home."

As they walked back to the car, Dan said, "What are you going to do if you find him?"

"I'll improvise."

Charlie reasoned that the detectives would not be at home, not under the present conditions. They both lived in the suburbs, away from the current action, which they would not miss. He wanted to get them both at once, at any rate.

And as they roamed the city, passing burned-out cars, shops with shattered windows, fights in the streets, it did not feel as if hunting two cops was wrong. If it felt like anything at all, it felt like fate.

In the end, though, Charlie's impatience, aided by amphetamines, won out.

Just after midnight, he said, "Look, we're going to have to postpone this. These circumstances won't last forever, and we've got to use this cover to get some payback. Any ideas?"

"Sure," Dan said. "Let's go to Portview."

Charlie barked a laugh and slapped Dan on the arm with his knuckles.

"I was waiting for you to say that!" he shouted.

"You were, huh?"

"Yep!" Charlie said. "It was just a conclusion you had to reach on your own."

"What about Vandenburg and Jackson?"

"Some other time. The good thing about revenge is that the longer it takes, the less connection you have to it."

Dan had always known where to find Mike Krapczak; he simply hadn't been committed enough to do anything with the knowledge. Now, after a night of frustrated hunting, of adrenaline and other useful chemicals, they were both practically vibrating with the need for action. They headed south for Portview.

On the way, they drove through Riverside. Dan had Charlie drive by Kate's daycare. Charlie didn't know where she worked, and Dan didn't tell him. They rolled by the building, the street quiet, the mural and the playground in shadow.

"What do you want to come by here for?" Charlie asked.

"No reason," Dan said.

They also drove by the Tienda Lopez. Two young men sat on stools in front, one Latino, one black. Both had baseball bats between their knees, and forty ounce bottles in brown bags on the ground in front of them. Dan recognized his old friends Jorge and Darnell, out guarding the tienda. He put his hand up to the side of his face as they slowly drove by.

"Hood rats," Charlie said.

Dan remained silent.

Dan gave Charlie directions, a left here, a right there. Soon they rolled past 718 Pier. Dan craned his neck to look up at the darkened windows of the old apartment.

"Does your mother still live there?" Charlie said.

"I think of her as Ingrid," Dan said.

Charlie laughed. "Okay. *Does* she?"

"I don't even know."

"Do you care?"

"Nope."

"That's the spirit," Charlie said.

"Take the next left, then find a place to park."

Dan had always known Mike's favorite bar; he just hadn't been ready (as Charlie had understood) to act on the information. It was a typical southside neighborhood dive, its small windows glowing with the neon of Greysport lager and other local favorites. The little brick-faced nook didn't even have a sign on the front which gave it a name, although the locals knew it as Lupenko's. Dan had often spied on Mike as he entered and left the bar.

"That's it," he told Charlie.

"I'll pull around the corner."

As anticlimactic as their hunt for the two detectives had been, on this venture they had immediate results. Leaving the car, they walked around the corner and down the sidewalk to Lupenko's. A denizen of the neighborhood approached from the opposite direction, and Dan lowered his head so the brim of his baseball cap covered his face. Charlie kept his chin up as they walked past.

Looking in through one small window, the neon glowing on their faces, Dan immediately spotted Mike Krapczak. As big and meaty as ever, quite a bit thicker around the middle and with a little grey apparent in his cropped hair, he sat at mid-bar, right next to the taps. Dan couldn't hear what he was saying over the country music on the jukebox, but he knew he was holding forth about something. Dan could not remember seeing Mike so jovial. He turned and faced the window (apparently not seeing them), and Dan could tell that he was drunk from the boarish pinkness of his eyes, a look that appeared amiable at the moment, but, Dan knew, could change in a second.

Seeing Mike after so long made his hair stand on end. He felt a rush of terror as if it were programmed into him. This rush made him ashamed, which made him angry.

"That's the guy?" Charlie said. "Looks like a two-legged pig with a crew-cut?"

"That's the guy," Dan said.

"Fuck," Charlie said. "No wonder you ran away."

Dan stared at Mike through the window.

"Time for some extra-legal justice," Charlie said.

"How are you…" Dan began, but Charlie held up a hand and went into the bar, the noise increasing for a moment as the door opened and closed.

Dan watched as Charlie went into the din of the bar and walked up to Mike. Charlie managed to look official, and pulled from a cargo pocket a small notebook, which he flipped open while talking to Mike, who leaned forward listening and nodding. Charlie indicated the front door of the bar with a nod of his head, then turned and headed toward it. Mike said something to the bartender, set down his beer, and followed Charlie out.

"…just had a few questions," Charlie was saying, "and thought you could help."

"Sure thing," Mike said, the sound of his voice jolting Dan's system with adrenaline. Before Mike could speak again, Dan said, "Hey."

Mike turned and faced Dan. "Yeah?"

Dan drove his fist so hard into Mike's stomach that the big man bent over and vomited. Charlie laughed, but stood back, leaving things to Dan. While Mike was coughing and retching, Dan got him in a wristlock, leading him around the corner to a garbage-strewn empty lot, dark under a few big trees. When Mike seemed to be catching his breath, ready to speak, Dan grabbed him by his greasy neck, forced his head down, and kneed him in the face. This laid Mike out, his face immediately covered in blood.

"What did I do?" Mike croaked. "What did I do?"

Dan kicked him as hard as he could in the ribs, perhaps breaking one or two. Mike grunted, then groaned.

"Get up," Dan said quietly. "Get up and face me, you piece of shit."

"You're not cops," Mike wheezed, rolling over to support himself on an elbow, looking up at them through the blood dripping from the fresh laceration on his forehead.

Charlie howled. "Not cops! Not cops! Excellent! We are clearly dealing with a genius!"

Mike didn't recognize Dan. "Come on, son," he begged. "You've got the wrong guy."

"Don't call me *son!*" Dan barked. He pulled out the .38 and cracked Mike on top of the head with the butt of the gun. Blood flowed immediately from the shorn scalp.

"All right, all right! What do you want me to call you?" Mike cried.

Dan thought about it. "Sir," he said.

"Okay! Okay!"

"Say it."

"Okay! Sir!"

Dan held him by the collar and gently ground the muzzle of the .38 into the temple of his tormentor.

"So, I'm thinking I should kill you," he said.

"For *what*?" Mike whimpered.

"Sir."

"For what, *sir*."

"You don't know?"

"Fuck, no," Mike yelped. "How the fuck should I know?"

Dan cracked him in the head once more with the butt of the gun. Mike howled.

Dan bent over and whispered, "I will shoot you in the head just to shut you up. So shut up."

Mike did so, averting his eyes, whimpering.

"What do you want me to do?" Mike quavered after a long silence.

It was the quaver in the man's voice that reminded Dan of Mike's reaction when Ingrid had had a miscarriage, when Mike had bent over the kitchen table and sobbed. And there in the dark lot, his tormentor at his mercy, no witnesses in sight, Charlie watching wide-eyed with anticipation, Dan felt a flicker of pity. More than a flicker; he felt compassion. Mike was stretched at his feet, his face bloody, his pig eyes avoiding looking at Dan's face or at the gun. It was at that moment that Dan knew he wasn't going to shoot him. In fact, he felt a flash of disgust with himself for ever thinking that he might. Another idea occurred to him.

"Piss yourself," Dan said.

"What?"

"You heard me. Piss yourself." Dan cracked him on the head again, this time with the short barrel of the gun.

"Jeez! Fuck! Well, okay!"

"Do it!" Dan said.

"I'm tryin'!" Mike said. "Ain't never had to piss my pants with a gun to my head before!"

"If you don't get going pretty quick, you'll never have to worry about it again."

Mike whimpered and grunted, and soon a dark stain was spreading in his crotch.

"Jesus," Charlie laughed.

"Keep going," Dan said.

"I ain't got much left," Mike grated.

"I got some," Dan said. He cracked Mike at the base of his skull with the butt of the gun. Mike gasped, and fell back on the ground. Dan put the gun in a pocket and stepped on Mike's neck. As Mike moaned, Dan unbuttoned his fatigues, pulled out his penis, and pissed on Mike's face. Dan got some on his boot, but it was worth it.

When Dan was done, he said, "Give my regards to Ingrid!" He kicked Mike in the head; he couldn't resist. Then he turned and walked from the lot.

Charlie ran up beside him. "What, you're not going to pop him?"

"No," Dan said.

"Why not?"

"Because that's enough," Dan said.

"What! After all he did to you?'

"We're even."

"Shit, *I'll* do it. You want me to do it?"

"He's not yours. He's mine. Leave him alone."

Charlie squinted at Dan, his mouth open. "Man, this is your chance! This is *it*! You're blowing it!"

"We're even. I'm good. Let's go."

They got back to the car, slamming the doors. Charlie started the engine and squealed out of the parking space. Dan got beers from the back seat and handed one to Charlie.

"Whiskey, too," Charlie said. He drank from the bottle and handed it to Dan. He drove fast, the humid air coursing in through the open windows.

After awhile, Charlie said, "I'd have to categorize that whole thing as anticlimactic."

Dan didn't say anything, just looked out the window and drank his beer.

Charlie kept at it. "That was your chance, man," he said. "That was it."

"I took it as far as it needed to go," Dan said.

"Well, I gotta say. You're the last person I thought would pussy out."

Dan looked at him. "I didn't pussy out."

"First Jim, then you. Jesus. I can't count on anybody."

"What, are you going to kill me too?" He regretted the words as soon as they were out.

"*Watch* it!" Charlie said, his tone suddenly dead. "Fucking...*watch* that."

They drove in silence. Dan could practically see the gears turning, fast, in Charlie's head. He scowled and clenched the wheel.

Although Charlie's master plan had gone awry, and the backup plan had not gone to his satisfaction, there were always targets of opportunity. As they crossed the bridge over the Ashipinakwa River, the tires of the Impala rumbling over the steel grate, a stoplight turned green ahead of them on the nearly deserted street. The only other vehicle in sight was a taxi, coming from the left and going through the light after it had turned red.

"Now, see?" Charlie said, jamming on his brakes to avoid the taxi. "What the fuck. Everybody's got to be an asshole."

He laid on his horn. A meaty, tattooed arm came out the open window of the cab, along with a big fist and upraised middle finger.

"Goddammit!" Charlie said, he accelerated, pulling up on the right side of the cab.

"Hey! Asshole!" Charlie shouted. "What are you flipping *me* off for! You just ran a red and cut me off!"

The cab driver, a large, fat man with long hair and a beard, gave Charlie a bored glance and called, "Fuck off."

Charlie slammed the steering wheel with his hands. "Fuck off? *You're* telling *me* to fuck off? Pull over, you fat piece of shit! Fucking pull over!"

"Didn't I just tell you to fuck off?" the driver called back, laughing.

"*Pull the fuck over!*" Charlie didn't shout, he shrieked. Dan pulled away in his seat, his eyes wide.

"You asked for it, asshole!" the driver called back.

The man turned into an alley not far from the bar they used to go to after watching sunrise at the beach. He drove up and parked by a dumpster, Charlie pulling up behind him.

The guy got out of his cab. He wore a short-sleeved workshirt and jeans, and had a black aluminum baseball bat in his hand. He was perhaps ten years older than Dan and Charlie, and looked like someone who dealt with confrontations with tired pragmatism. Waggling the bat in a rhythm which might mimic his pulse rate, he stalked back toward the Impala.

"Da *fuck*, man!" the cab driver shouted, spreading his arms and holding up the bat. "I'm right here! Let's go!"

Charlie got out of the car and pulled the .45, standing behind the open door.

"Come on," Charlie said.

Dan got out on his side and said, "No!"

The guy lowered the baseball bat to his side, dropping his arms. Charlie shot him in the chest.

"No!" Dan shouted.

The guy grunted, looking down at his chest. There was a small hole in the workshirt. He looked at the hole and back at Charlie.

"Da *fuck*, man?" he said, looking down at his chest again. His mouth worked as if he were having trouble catching his breath. Blood began to spill into his shirt as if someone were pouring out a bottle of wine behind it. It came in pulses. The guy shuffled over to sit down on the greasy back stairs of a restaurant, using the utilitarian railing to help him sit.

Dan watched, motionless, breathing hard. Then he moved forward to help the guy.

Charlie swiveled and pointed the .45 at Dan.

"Stay," Charlie said.

He turned back to the guy, who sat panting on the greasy steps, the front of his shirt filled to dripping with blood.

The guy coughed once. When he grimaced, his teeth were red. He looked up at Charlie and said, "What'd I ever."

Charlie shot him twice more in the chest. Dan watched, jumping at the decibels of the shots. The shell casings tinked on the hood of Charlie's car. The guy wheezed and toppled over, rolling as if boneless down the steps, his neck catching at the base of the railing, stopping the descent.

Charlie swiveled, turning the .45 on Dan

"Toss your .38 over by that dumpster," he said.

Dan did as he was told. The gun clacked and slid on the pavement, coming to rest against one of the dumpster's rubber wheels.

Charlie walked over, took Dan by the collar of his shirt and bore him back against the brick wall of the alley.

"You were going to help that guy?" Charlie said.

Dan didn't reply. He just watched Charlie's eyes

Charlie held the gun up to Dan's jaw. "I could kill you for any number of things," he said. "I could kill you for fucking Gigi and lying about it. You think I didn't know about that?"

"I didn't lie…"

"Shut the fuck up. I could kill you for decking me when we were kids. I could kill you for being too stupid to realize what you had with Kate. I could kill you for decking me *because* of Kate, you stupid fuck. The fact that, just now, you were going to help that useless piece of shit over there tells me you're a tergiversator. You know, an apostate. No? Too complex? That you're *disloyal*, dumbfuck. Having come to that sad conclusion, I have to inform you that I *will* kill you if you say anything about *this*." He jerked his head towards the body. Charlie held the gun to Dan's neck, gripping the collar of Dan's shirt in his hand and bouncing him off the brick wall for emphasis. He let Dan go and went over to the dead man, taking the wallet from his back pocket, all the time watching Dan, keeping his gun trained on him. Going to the taxi, he retrieved what appeared to be a cigar box filled with bills. Charlie put the wallet in the cigar box and came back to Dan.

"This guy appears to be the victim of a robbery," Charlie said. "That's going to be the story."

Charlie put the gun back to Dan's neck.

"If you ever see me again," he said, "you'd better avert your fucking eyes, or I'll put a bullet in both of them. Then I'll kill Kate just for the fuck of it, because she's a cunt."

Charlie shoved Dan against the wall and walked down the alley. Dan watched him get in the Impala and back out of the alley. He chirped the wheels and drove off, gone from sight.

Dan stood in the roaring silence of the alley. The only sound came from the taxi's dispatch radio, a scratchy voice calling out intersections, cab numbers, and addresses. Dan stood staring at the dead man for some time. He finally snapped out of it, realizing that he should fear discovery. He went over to the dumpster and picked up his gun, pocketing it. He was careful to step over the man's pool of blood, which had gained enough volume to send a tendril down toward a storm drain. He didn't need to take a last look before he fled down the alley. He was sure the image of the man would be with him forever.

By Monday afternoon, the riots had been quelled. The National Guard had been called in to support the overwhelmed police department, and soon peace was restored. The Outcasts and the Guardians of Nocturne had gone at it, as had Los Reyes Latinos and Los Salvajes Locos.

Charlie's customer from the Brothers of the Rising, the dreadlocked Trey, was organizing an armed looting tour of White Birch Pointe and other rich suburbs, when a carload of the 47th Street Badass Niggaz performed what amounted to the first driveby shooting in Greysport, at least since the days of Prohibition. Some of the Brothers were killed, some wounded, but also killed was one of Trey's young nieces. This called for retaliation, and plans to steal from the rich were forgotten. Torn away from his other plans, Trey shot three 47th Streeters himself.

By the time the riots were over, thirty-eight had been killed, more than twelve hundred injured, and nearly thirty-five hundred arrested.

When the bowling ball punched through Jumpin' Irv's windshield, he had flinched just enough to avoid having his head splattered by the ball, which ended up in the back seat of the Valiant. As a result of his reaction, though, Irv had piled the car into the concrete wall of the freeway, just under the bridge from which the two kids had tossed the ball in the first place. Although the car was totaled, Irv considered himself fortunate.

The Three Horsedicks of the Apocalypse narrowly averted disaster themselves. After doing some productive looting, they made the mistake of making one more foray. This last one was to Little Viet Nam, a neighborhood given that name for obvious reasons, where the looting of liquor stores got a flash in the news. The lads had gone over to steal some party supplies, not knowing that the local Vietnamese, unaccustomed to taking much shit, had organized, and were mounting defenses of their properties. The three lads were trying to make off with some cases of Tsing Tao beer when the cinderblock storefront of the place they were looting was suddenly pocked with buckshot and rounds from a rifle, the local defense force firing on them with fortunate inaccuracy from the roof across the street. The three dropped their loot and ran pell-mell down the littered street and into an alley making it back to the van with a squad of angry young Asians on their heels. They shouted and laughed all the way back to their warehouse hideaway, where they decided to plug in one of the stolen TVs and get drunk while watching the news coverage, rather than becoming news themselves.

The strike at Dixon-Butz continued, although a tone of civility now prevailed. Officers Pulaski and Dougan went back to work as if nothing had happened. Among all the chaos, no mention was made in the local media of the robbery and murder of a veteran cab driver.

The day after Charlie killed the cab driver, Tom could obviously tell that something bad had happened. Dan wouldn't talk about it, although Tom persisted.

"Was it bad?" he hectored.

"Yeah," Dan said. "Yeah, it was bad."

"Did you do something bad?"

"Could've been worse."

"Did Charlie?"

Dan looked at him. "You don't want to know," he said. "For your own safety, you don't want to know."

Dan didn't doubt what Charlie had said. At first, he was nervously vigilant, waiting for Charlie to show up at Tom's. Now he understood what Bud Sletto's threat had meant to Willy, what Willy had been ready to sacrifice in protection of his family. Dan often sat at night outside Kate's apartment, drinking coffee, waiting for Charlie to show up.

For weeks afterward, Dan trolled the streets and alleys in the van looking for him, Willy's rifle between the seats covered with a strategic assemblage of fast food wrappers and newspaper. He kept the .38 in his pocket.

From time to time, he drove by the police station, thinking of saying something. Once, he actually parked and went in. The lobby was thronged with people, the cops behind the counter looking overworked and jaded. When Dan realized he had no idea what to say, that he would possibly be incriminating himself, he turned around and walked out.

So Charlie had disappeared, and no amount of searching turned him up. Dan didn't know what he would have done if he'd found him, but he was careful to be armed. He longed to talk to Kate, but believed that he had poisoned her life enough, even endangered her enough, already. While he thought about things, he painted a few portraits of her from memory.

There were only a few activities he took part in. He worked out, wanting to stay prepared. He drank with Tom, although he refused to talk about what had happened, refused to talk about much of anything. At night, he drank and watched television with Tom, often half-listening while Tom chattered. It occurred to him that Tom's yammering was meant to be soothing, perhaps even meant as a way to draw Dan out. Tom would never forget what Dan did when he was sick, would never forget Dan for simply including him. Dan would watch him talk about his plans and about their future, all of it so positive, so unrealistic. It was as if Dan had turned down the volume on Tom's speech and watched his lips move, watched his animated face. He would smile a little at his friend's groundless optimism.

He walked on the beach, which soothed him somewhat, although when left alone with his own mind, he cycled through images again and again. Charlie with the .45 up to his neck. The dead cab driver. Willy out there in the dark. Kate: endless images of Kate. He painted; if he wasn't painting or watching television or in some other way occupying himself, he sat staring at nothing.

Dan thought about Tom's optimism, about Kate's. He went back and forth in his thinking; was he right or were they? Was Charlie? Was his gloom an infection? If it was, then it appeared that people like Kate and Tom were impervious to it. His grandfather had lived through everything (this belated realization weighing upon him), and yet he never seemed beaten. Was Dan himself beaten? How could that happen? Was he not the grandson of Willy and Mae McGregor, the son of Gordon McGregor? Yes, Ingrid was his mother, but if he just gave up, would he not be like her, more truly her son than he was his father's, than the grandson of Willy? His mother's consistent demonization of Willy seemed to have percolated into his consciousness until it was a form of habit, as had Mike's contempt. He now saw that they were wrong, that they might have intentionally lied. Even if they were merely uninformed, the result was the same.

A child still existed in him, wounded and astonished. Why would someone do that?

The man that grew in him, though, said that it happened all the time, that misery was constant and a matter of degree. Even Kate, with her sunny outlook, did not come to it unscathed. With a father who was such an asshole that he was beaten to death in a parking lot (which Dan found darkly amusing), she was positive about her lot, so much so that he could almost assign colors to her presence and its work on his heart: orange and gold, he thought. They were orange and gold. It made him visualize a biology film from high school showing busy, healthy cells, pink and active under the microscope.

And Tom. An only child, as Dan had been, yet with such a difference. Even though he was a victim in high school, he remained (Dan searched for the word) unvanquished.

These people, these people he loved. How were they similar?

I am lost, he thought. I am lost. He thought about going down to the beach, or back to the river, putting the .38 to his head and pulling the trigger.

That would be his mother, though; that would be Ingrid. After a point, certainly after her beauty had faded, her life, by default, would be about waiting to die. She was too cowardly even to kill herself in the bathtub, to overdose on valium and vodka. He could not be like that.

So Dan decided that he would not die. At least not voluntarily.

What, then, was there to do?

There were the things he could not change, and there were the things he could. What was left that he could change? What of his misdeeds, committed either through his actions or his inactions, could he set to right?

He awoke one morning realizing that he must move on. He'd had another sad nightmare, one which began to blur as soon as he awoke, but left him panting in bed. Out in the back yard, though, the morning was cool, scented with the onshore breeze from the lake.

Dan was first drawn to Kate. It was irrational, he knew. Just to see her face, though, see her smiling in the sunshine, just once, and tell her that he was beginning to understand. There was only something he had to do first.

When he pulled up two blocks away from the daycare center, Dan vomited from anxiety.

"Great," he gasped, wiping his mouth with a left-over fast food napkin, rinsing it with a can of pop.

Kate was not there. He spoke to Lateisha, who, he noticed, still appeared to like him.

"She's up at that cabin," Lateisha said. "Where have you been? She's been sad about you."

This statement made Dan feel like vomiting again. Lateisha saw this and said, "You okay?"

"No, I don't think so," Dan said. He realized that he felt relieved by the candor of his comment.

"You don't think so?"

"No, I do not."

"Well, *do* something about it," she said, a little disgust showing.

"Okay," he said. He got up and left.

"Wait!" Lateisha called, "I didn't mean to…"

"You're right!" Dan shouted over his shoulder.

At Perrito's, Kaye got him his Usual, brought it to where he sat at the bar. The place was empty but for two of Los Reyes Latinos sitting off in a corner, talking quietly but with apparent gravity. Dependably, Perrito himself sat in his usual placid state, with a margarita in front of him, possibly contemplating eternity.

In spite of the taciturn nature of their relationship, Kaye seemed to perceive Dan's state of mind.

Although he said nothing, when he was sitting with a clean plate and an empty beer in front of him, Kaye came and rested her hand on his.

"It'll be okay," she said.

He came back to himself and said, "What?"

"It'll be okay," she repeated.

"Really?"

"Yes. But you have to make it so."

It was as if she'd read his mind. It was something Kate would have done.

When he left, he felt as if it might be his last time in the place.

Back at Tom's, he got ready to go. Tom watched forlornly.

"You can do whatever you want with these," he said, waving a hand at the paintings. "You always liked them, so I didn't feel like I could just take them to the beach and set them on fire."

"Jesus, don't talk like that."

"I don't know if I'm going to do art anymore."

Tom's mouth dropped open. "Why the hell not?"

"I'm not sure I'm good enough."

Tom laughed. "Can't you just look at your own work and see that you're gifted?"

"It's not that kind of good."

This seemed to puzzle Tom, who just shook his head and let it go.

"So do what you want with them," Dan said.

"Thanks," Tom said.

He took only one painting, a small one of Kate that he had done from memory.

The young men embraced. Tom asked him if he needed any money, and Dan lowered his head and said, "Yeah, okay."

"Don't feel bad," Tom said, going into his father's study, opening a bottom desk drawer. "I didn't do anything to earn it. This is an advance. We're going to make a shitload from your art." He grinned his Bugs Bunny grin.

Although Dan's face felt numb, he snorted laughter. "If you say so," he said. He pocketed the roll of bills.

Tom walked him out to the van, which was now empty but for a few possessions: some clothing, books, a sleeping bag and camp stove. His art supplies. His rifle and the .38. He put the portrait of Kate in with the rest.

"Do what you have to do and come on back," Tom said.

"Thanks," Dan said. "Keep track of Kate when she gets back in town. Make sure she's okay."

Tom agreed, and Dan got in the van and drove off.

Although on some unacknowledged level he knew what he had to do, where, ultimately, he had to go, he headed north toward Denfer Island. The heatwave had dissipated, and it was pleasant with the windows down as he drove out of the city. Soon he was driving down the highway, fields and woods alternating on the landscape, a Talking Heads cassette playing, the lake always blue and vast on his right.

The first night away from Greysport, he scouted around back roads off the highway and found a gravel lane that dead-ended next to the lake. After some fishermen left at sunset, he had the place to himself, building a driftwood bonfire, roasting cheddarwurst and drinking beer as the stars came out. He stared at the fire and listened to the waves, but none of it distracted him from the images in his mind's eye, there as indelibly as though they'd been burned into his retinas. The body in the alley. His grandfather, Willy, back there behind his eyes no matter where he looked. The fact that Willy was almost always smiling and happy in his mind somehow made it worse, as if his actions (and inaction) would erase that happiness.

In the morning, he got up and walked down to the grey dawn beach where small waves rolled in. Except for gulls, annoyed and sent flying by his presence, he was alone on the sand. Although it was slightly chilly, something in him wanted a cleansing, a catharsis, and he went back to the van to retrieve his bottle of spearmint soap and returned to the water. Stripping off his shorts, he waded out naked, still somehow shocked by the cold of the water, then dove and swam out chest deep, lathering himself up, panting in the cold waves until his body grew accustomed to it. He returned to the shore, invigorated, put on his shorts and a t-shirt, eating an orange and guzzling water from a plastic gallon jug.

He had read that indecision was sometimes a symptom of depression; if this was true, he was probably depressed. He felt little different from how he had during his years in Portview or during his last stretch on the river, and only suspected that something might be amiss due to the contrast with his happy times with Kate. He imagined that some people might feel that happy most of the time, and again found himself wondering who was wrong, the happy people or himself.

Due to this indecision, he took his time going up the coast, staying the next two nights at state parks, the first with his van parked at a campsite under some giant pines, reading by lantern at the site's picnic table. He walked away from the lantern at one point as the wind began to gust in the boughs, and as his eyes adjusted to the darkness, he saw that towering thunderclouds were coming in from the west. He spent the night cozily in the van, reading as rain drummed on the steel roof overhead.

The next day was sunny and cool, the blacktop roads of the state park steaming as they warmed in the light of the rising sun. He left and got on the road again, driving up the shore to the next campsite, spending that night among dunes near the beach.

Everything about it reminded him of running away from Portview; he was in a place of solace, but the knowledge that the solace was temporary, that he still had so much to face, seemed to coat his guts with a thin film of nausea. He wanted to sleep just to stop his thinking. He curled up in his sleeping bag and moaned, images bobbing up again and again, like pale corpses to the surface of black water. The wind hissed in the dune grass around him, and he contemplated getting up and guzzling from his bottle of whiskey just to knock himself out. He tried to force his mind to pleasant images, the thought of Kate laughing on the beach by the cabin, of her holding up a soup spoon for him to sample what she was cooking at the stove. The sound of the wind and the waves, usually a reliable anodyne, had little effect. Somehow, he finally fell asleep.

Dan awoke too early to the cry of gulls and the weight settled on him again as soon as he remembered where he was. He clenched his teeth and put the heels of his hands to his eyes. Within an hour, he had showered and brushed his teeth at a campground facility and was on the road again. When the local radio station played *Carry That Weight* by the Beatles, he forced himself to listen to it, staring dazedly out the window as he drove north down the highway.

Dan parked the van in the lot for the ferry to Denfer Island. From his limited stash of money, he splurged on a submarine sandwich from a stand set up to prey on those waiting for the ferry's return. The sandwich was delicious, but as soon as he had eaten it, he realized that he'd done so too quickly to enjoy it, and regretted it.

He sat in the open side door of the van, watching the ferry come and go over the hours. He sat there still as the sun set, brilliant and orange with cirrus clouds of puce, salmon, and lavender; he thought that Kate might be watching the sunset from the island, imagining that she might be thinking of him at the same moment as he thought of her.

When it was dark, he drove far enough away from the ferry that he was able to find a store with cheap jugs of red wine. He bought a crate of four, thinking they might get him through the next few days. Never did he have a clear idea of where those days might take him.

Driving back to the ferry landing, he sat in the parking lot and cursed himself for his cowardice and indecision, filling his plastic coffee mug again and again with wine. The island was out there, just visible even in the starry darkness beyond the dark waves, and he'd been too much of a jagoff to get there.

Morning came, and with the screech of gulls and the sun in his face, he realized that he had parked next to the public beach adjacent to the ferry landing. He groaned with the hangover he had acquired, squinted against the midmorning sun, and realized that a kid was staring at him through the open side-door of the van.

"What the fuck?" Dan said.

"Are you a punk rocker?" the kid asked.

"Get the fuck out of here!" Dan shouted, and the kid fled.

Doing a hundred sit-ups and two hundred pushups on the sandy asphalt of the parking lot nearly made him vomit, but he did them anyway. He thought about the legend of his shadowed father, thought about his grandfather (no, put that away), and did his exercises as a cleansing, punishing thing. Sweating heavily, he watched the ferry arrive, load its cars, bikes and passengers, and return to the island. He ran across the beach in his black shorts, through the multicolored umbrellas and towels and beachballs, ran through them and dove into the cold waves.

Still close to vomiting, he ate an orange and left the ferry landing, wearing only his shorts, his hair in spiky disarray. Before he could give it any thought, he drove back down the peninsula and up the other side of the bay, stopping only for gas. When he found a state park, he pulled in and took a shower at the camping facilities, ignoring the scowls and suspicious looks of those in earth tones and hiking boots. He slept on the beach, all beaches now home.

At a thrift store, he bought three flannel shirts, six t-shirts, and a pair of olive drab fatigue pants. He also bought a pair of scissors and a mirror; in a state park bathroom, he cut his hair down past the dye-mark, which was very short indeed. Cutting the hair on the back of his head was surprisingly difficult, and he snipped the index finger of his left hand with the scissors. In the end, though, the effect was good.

One of the t-shirts was faded green with cracked yellow print depicting a jumping bass on a hook with the cheerful statement *"Fishin'!"* over it. It made so little sense that Dan found it funny, and had to hide his laugher when wearing it into a little store to find food and beer.

"Catchin' any?" the old woman in cat's eye glasses behind the counter asked him.

"Nah," Dan said. "Not really."

The t-shirt became his favorite. He blended right in.

However stingily he minded his roll of cash, it began to get small, and he started to look for a job. The scent of an industrial port, small as it was, brought him to Port Martineau, a town he'd driven by before with Kate. There was that sharp tang of pitch he recognized, and perhaps the sour odor of fermented grain. He knew the town before he came over the rise to see it.

Port Martineau was a squalid little place, and had been famous for the construction of submarines during the Second World War. Dan was unmindful of that history, wanting only a job. The foreman in charge of hiring at a commercial dock checked out Dan's size (and certainly the *Fishin'!* t-shirt) and appeared to come to a conclusion.

"Ever drive forklift before?"

"Sure," Dan lied.

"Start tomorrow."

Sleeping in his van, it wasn't hard for Dan to wake up early and get jittery with coffee before the new job. He knew he'd screw up if he weren't fully awake, though, and resentfully spent a bit of money for some coffee at a stand outside the chain link fence surrounding the dock.

This would be one of his most lucid memories of the job. Other factors would fade; his cursory training, the accidents before he gained expertise, the occasional conflict with the other workers; all these memories would dissipate in time. In fact, the job seemed so temporary that he was conscious of this, and spent most of his days driving a forklift around the loading dock, his body going through the motions of the job while his mind was elsewhere entirely.

Getting a room at a dingy boarding house not far from his job, he holed up after work reading anything distracting on the narrow, squeaky bed. He became a regular

281

at a small used bookstore, getting familiar enough to the people who worked there that they knew his name and exchanged small pleasantries. At a dimestore, he picked up cheap art supplies almost compulsively (although he nearly put them back), and spent evenings and weekend afternoons doing sketches and watercolors of the industrial scenes in weedy lots around the little port.

A few nights a week he went to one of the many little bars in the town with other people from work. He had more than one opportunity to become entangled with young women from the town, but none of them interested him. The image of Kate dogged his memory, and when he drew or painted something strictly from his memory, not his imagination or surroundings, more than half the time it was Kate. Sometimes he found himself staring at nothing, wondering how things could ever have gone so wrong. Catching himself, he would heave a deep breath and find something, again, to distract him.

When he dreamt about Willy, he had no idea that he was carrying on a family tradition of such things. In the dreams, Willy was usually across a street or an empty lot, perhaps a body of water or a slough on the river, up a hill or standing among sunlit trees. Willy was forever trying to tell him something, but his words were indistinct, or covered by a competing sound. "What?" Dan would cry. "Grampa! What? Say it again!"

His grandfather would then be gone, though, and Dan would swim up to consciousness, bursting through the surface of his sleep to a smoky feeling of desolation.

At the end of the fall, the port's business slowed down, and, being the last person hired, he was the first to be laid off. Leaving behind dozens of books and stacks of drawings and watercolors, he gathered his few remaining belongings and left without saying a word to any of the people he had come to know, driving away from the water and into the woods of the north.

Perhaps to provoke a psychological reaction in himself (Dan was unsure of his own motives), he drove to the town where his father had died, where his grandfather had come to rescue him the first time. He still had relatives there; for all he knew, his mother might have left Greysport and returned. He hadn't the slightest inclination to find any of these people, though, and after spending some time parked in the van, watching the comings and goings at the lumber mill, he drove off, feeling nothing at all. Even the thought of going back to the clearing where his father had had his accident left him feeling blank, and in the end he convinced himself that seeing the place in the woods would be pointless.

With the money he had saved working in Port Martineau, he got a room in a boarding house for a few weeks, giving himself time to think. He walked in the woods during the day, taking long and exhausting hikes, and came back to the little room hoping to sleep without dreams.

Out of boredom, Dan went out to a local bar one night and got drunk, the evening becoming more and more blurry as it went on. He woke up in a slovenly bedroom next to a woman with bleached blonde hair (with inch-long black roots) who outweighed him by twenty pounds. She snored away, prone on the couch, her large, dimpled ass uncovered, her legs spread, revealing a surprisingly hairy black snatch. He gingerly gathered his clothes to sneak out, and almost blew it by laughing when the woman farted wetly. It was only when he was getting dressed in the living room that he realized he was actually in a trailer park. He nearly kissed his van in relief when he found that it was parked outside, and didn't stop driving until he had put a hundred miles behind him.

Dan was astonished to find a casino in the middle of the North Woods. Driving down the state highway, the dense trees suddenly opened up, revealing a cluster of large brown buildings in the midst of a giant parking lot, all of it identified by a giant sign: Ashipinakwa Casino. It was such a strange sight in the middle of the endless forest that Dan was immediately drawn in. He parked in the lot and made his way across the blacktop, threading through tour busses and avoiding occasional carloads of seniors looking for parking for their Buicks and Cadillacs.

The inside of the casino was surreal, with loud carpeting in what might have passed for Native American patterns, giant chandeliers hanging from the tall ceilings. Banks of hundreds of slot machines stretched across the floor, more than half occupied by an odd assortment of people, often smoking with one hand while operating their machine with the other, utterly fixed on the rolling symbols in front of their eyes. The din of ringing bells was incredible. Other areas had blackjack and roulette tables, all attended by employees in black slacks, vests, bowties, and impeccable white dress shirts. Dan immediately felt as if he had done a small dose of acid. The place was huge, with bars and restaurants, lounges and seating areas, meeting rooms and convention halls. And more was under construction. He wondered where all the people came from. It was so strange that it was fascinating.

It was there at the Ashipinakwa Casino that he got his next job. They were taking on security guards, and he was hired on the spot. The fact that he had worked security at professional wrestling tournaments in Greysport got the attention of Leo Whitehorse, the man who would become his direct supervisor. An overweight Native American, Leo was a fan of professional wrestling.

"You met Steelmill Stanley?" Leo asked, discarding Dan's application on his buried desk.

"Yeah," Dan said.

"How about Mortuary Mike McDonald?"

"Sure," Dan said, unable to keep from smiling.

"Did you have to keep them apart?"

"I hate to tell you, but most of those guys are friends backstage."

"No!"

"Yep, 'fraid so."

"Well, damn," Leo said, shaking his head.

Dan was given a uniform at no charge from the Nation, as Leo's tribe was called among themselves. During his training, he was filled in on the history of the place.

"Started as a bingo parlor," Leo told him. "Just took off as laws changed about casinos on reservation land."

The job paid surprisingly well, and had good benefits if one put in the time. As profits increased, so did the benefits to members of the nation, although non-native employees were also treated well. Dan even got a neat little room in quarters for temporary workers until such time as he could find another place.

"Things used to be bad around here," Leo told him. "Now that we've got this going, we have better schools, great health care, you name it. Anyone who wants can go to college. Gambling people come from all over to make their Donation to the Nation, as we say. And it's all because of Mr. Goodforks."

Faith-in-Full Goodforks (now *there's* an odd name, Dan thought) was the superintendent and driving force behind the entire operation. A lean and energetic man with a broken nose, very white teeth, and a long grey pony tail, he was kind and patient with everyone who worked there, never too busy to hear about someone's problems, never too lofty to clean up abandoned drink glasses or to empty an ashtray. Leo explained that Goodforks had been in trouble as a young man, even done a little time, but had straightened himself out and become the pride of the Nation. One of the first things he had done when he had started to make money was to buy back ancestral lands at the Goodforks River near its confluence with the Ashipinakwa and put them in trust as a preserve.

"I'll show you the place sometime," Leo said. "It's beautiful, and saved by Mr. Goodforks. Don't let him hear you call him that, by the way. He'll tell you that he's no better than anyone else. He is, though."

Dan saw the perpetually busy Mr. Goodforks from time to time. On the first occasion, Dan was standing at a post by one of the entrances to the casino. Goodforks came in through the double doors, walking so fast that the beer-bellied heating and air-conditioning man following him could barely keep up. Goodforks saw Dan, did a double-take, and stopped in his tracks, cutting off the beer-bellied man with a politely raised hand. Goodforks stared at Dan.

"Evening, Mr. Goodforks," Dan said.

"Please call me Faith," Goodforks said automatically. He squinted and tilted his head. "Do I know you?" he asked.

"Don't think so. I just started here. Name's Dan." He held out his hand and Goodforks shook it.

"Huh," Goodforks said, shaking his head. "You look familiar."

"I'm not from around here," Dan said.

"Well. Weird. Nice meeting you anyway, Dan." Then his attention was turned back to the man with the beer belly and he was gone. The strange thing was that Goodforks seemed familiar to Dan as well. He put it down to having heard the unusual name somewhere before, or perhaps having read it in the newspaper, and let it go at that.

Dan worked a double shift on Thanksgiving, for the generous overtime, certainly, but mostly to keep himself busy. It was a big day of work for members of the nation, as well; a surprising amount of people came in from all over the state to gamble on that day, a new tradition which appeared to be gaining momentum. Late on the afternoon of Thanksgiving, Dan was standing off to one side of a bank of double doors as three busloads of gamblers bustled in to make their Donation. He was shaking his head in wonder when he realized that Mr. Goodforks had appeared at the other side of the doors, neatly dressed in a grey suit, greeting people as they came in. Dan's eyes met with those of Mr. Goodforks, and the man grinned and flicked his eyebrows up mirthfully, a shared joke. Goodforks turned back to greeting gamblers, then was gone again on his constant round of activity.

The double shift was tiring, and Dan kept going with constant infusions of coffee. He traded positions with other guards and took a dinner break with Leo Whitehorse, but most of the time while he was watching the gamblers get the money sucked out of their pockets, he retreated into his mind.

He envisioned Kate and her mother and sisters at the cabin on Denfer Island, the warm kitchen glowing, the Driver women busy over steaming pots at the stove, the children running in and out. He was disgusted at his own longing to be a part of such a vision, it was so corny, so unoriginal (he told himself), although it kept popping up in his head. Putting these thoughts out of his mind, he pondered the chainsmoking gamblers getting justifiably fleeced by the Nation in a way that amounted to racial revenge, and as he walked down the aisles between banks of loudly clanging slot machines, he was amused by the notion that all of these people deserved to lose their money, and that most of them would.

Five minutes later he had a luminous vision (as if for a painting he would like to render in tones of gold and brown, orange and red), of himself carving turkey at the cabin the way Willy had shown him, Dan himself carrying on the tradition, as Kate watched him, smiling, and her nieces and nephews clamored at the kids' table. He snorted and shook his head at his own witless sentimentality. The work of Norman Rockwell would only have been acceptable if his subject matter had involved more hangings and autopsies, perhaps a drowned person here and there. He snorted again. Sometimes he disgusted himself. The visions seeped back in as soon as he let his guard down. One of walking on the stormy grey beach with Kate after the big dinner, kids running on the sand and shouting over the sound of the waves, was particularly distracting. He forced himself to snap out of it.

Working a double on this day itself wasn't so bad, and could be considerably worse. Jim, for example, was dead, so that could have turned out better. Hugh and Gigi might be having a dolorous get-together, the first time they would do it alone, because Charlie certainly wouldn't be there. Tom and his family together was too pleasant an image to contemplate, so he moved his mind on. If Ingrid and Mike were still together, it was no stretch of the imagination that they were sloppily drunk in a dive in Portview. The thought of Ingrid sobbing over her lost son, other patrons rolling their eyes in tired disgust, was an amusing one indeed. Bitch.

And Willy. Thanksgiving was almost a holy day for his grandfather; not that he was religious, but that family was everything, the reason for his existence, Dan now saw. And Willy was…where he was, and his father and grandmother and uncle….

Towards the end of his second shift, his legs were tired, his eyes stung from smoke, and all the coffee he had consumed had made his stomach uneasy and gotten him grinding his teeth on a tired piece of gum until his jaws ached. He punched out and went back to his room to change into street clothes, then came back to a bar on the second floor of the complex which was reserved for watching sports. No sports were on at that hour, so the bar was quiet. After a few beers and a shot or two, he began to feel better. Leo Whitehorse found him, dressed in his own street clothes, pulled out one of the padded barstools and sat down.

They talked about the job, as workers anywhere will do. Although Dan had the sense that he and Leo held little in common, they had enough: their work, and experience in hunting and fishing. Leo's approach to things was uncomplicated and kind-hearted, something to which Dan realized he had grown unaccustomed. Leo reminded him of people out on the river, but was too friendly to be made fun of about it.

When the bartender, a cousin of Leo's, told them that he had to close down, Leo invited Dan to the Nation's celebration of Thanksgiving the next day.

"We always do it the next day," Leo said. "After Easter, Christmas, whatever."

"Man, I have some stuff I have to take care of," Dan lied. "Thanks, though."

Dan had the next day off, and by late morning found himself by the parked van, down a long sandy road in a clearing among a great tract of pines. He sat there feeling blank, poking at a smoky fire of pine logs with a stick. Next to the fire, he had placed a pot of chili from a can, and drank a beer as he waited for the chili to heat. The sky was dark grey and boiling with swift clouds, the air hissing cold through the pines, and he zipped his jacket up to his chin. The temperature was just warm enough for sleety rain, which began as he was finishing his chili. Bits of whitish sleet fizzled into the fire, and when it got heavy enough, he went into the van and closed the door. While lying to Leo, he'd said that he had to be gone for most of the afternoon, and now had to stay gone. He thought about what Leo and members of his family might be doing, and wondered why he couldn't have simply accepted the invitation. What was wrong with him?

Dan climbed into the van and slid the door shut, then got into his orange sleeping bag (sniffing it for the residual scent of Kate) and zipped it up to his chest, huddling there reading to pass the time, listening to the ticking of sleet on the roof of the van. He waited until twilight, when it became too dark to read. By the time he drove back to the casino complex, it was snowing. He parked the van not far from the loading dock and slipped up to his quarters through service corridors, hoping all the time that no one would notice.

The job was pleasant enough, although the boredom took a Zenlike patience to overcome. Occasionally someone got drunk and had to be escorted from the complex, or became upset after a losing streak at blackjack, roulette, or anything else at which one could make their Donation to the Nation; these people received the same treatment. Compared to the chaos Dan had seen already in his young life (although it didn't feel young to him), the altercations at the casino were tedious and routine.

Only one incident gave him pause. In a trancelike state of boredom at an unimportant post, a coded page came over the PA system and the radio on his belt almost simultaneously, signifying trouble at a group of blackjack tables. Jolted awake into the hope of action, any action, Dan raced down the garishly carpeted aisles through the ringing slot machines, the heads of gamblers turning as he ran.

When he burst into an empty space between the slots and the blackjack tables, he saw Leo and another guard standing on either side of a large man with spiky blonde hair and a black leather jacket, his back to Dan, who was abusing the cowering young woman who had been dealing cards at the table. It was Charlie.

A jolt of terror rang down his nerves to his fingers and toes, and Dan sprinted across the carpet. "Hey!" he shouted. "I'm right here!"

The instant before Dan's fist made contact, he saw that his target wasn't Charlie at all, but a man with a reddish beard and surprised expression, turning to face Dan's voice. Dan's blow was in mid-trajectory, though, and crunched into the man's left cheekbone, sending him to the floor and Dan over him with the momentum.

Dan scrabbled back to his feet and over to where the man lay on his back, raising his hands to his face. In the time it took to reach the man, the desire to kill Charlie turned into anger at being tricked, and Dan straddled the man, ready to beat dents into his temples.

"Wo, Dan!" Leo shouted. "Be cool, be cool!"

The red-bearded man cringed looking up at Dan, his left eye already contused. "The *fuck*, man!"

Thwarted, Dan tried to settle the bloodlust in his chest, but not before flipping the man over, putting him in a painful wristlock, and thumbing the pressure point under his ear.

"Don't fuck with our people, asshole," he said.

Dan was a hero after that.

What ruined it all was when Mr. Goodforks discovered Dan's talent as an artist. The good part lasted through the holidays and well into spring, with Dan becoming well-liked, not for his personality, but because he would pick up a shift anytime someone else from the security department needed time off. Then came the incident with the man he thought was Charlie, said man being arrested for assault and drunk and disorderly. Mr. Goodforks thanked him for his fervor, as had nearly everyone else, but the attention and Dan's embarrassment at it faded over the ensuing weeks. He punched in early and punched out late, often feeling anxious and at loose ends when he had a day or two off.

And it was those days off that got him into trouble. When he began to relax in the environment of the casino, he started to doodle when stationed at particularly boring posts, simply out of lifelong habit. With Dan, though, no doodles were simple, and the more bored he got the more elaborate and amazing the doodles became. Many were sharply accurate and unflattering caricatures of customers, informed by the ingestion of hallucinogens. He put them in drawers and hid them in his locker when he didn't simply throw them out, but some were eventually found, even retrieved from the garbage and passed around. It annoyed Dan to see some of his work posted on the bulletin board next to the time clock, or in the security meeting room.

"And here I thought you were just some thug," Leo said one day.

"I *am* just some thug," Dan said, not wanting to feel as angry as he did. He took the drawing Leo was admiring and tore it up.

"You don't have to be so hostile," Leo said, either ignoring Dan's state of mind or unaware of it. "You should go to art school or something."

Dan left the room before he could say something he regretted.

He felt so bad about his behavior to kindly Leo that he relented to his pestering and showed his friend a stack of his work, including watercolors that he'd done in the deliciously gloomy woods around the casino, back on the long sandy roads which had become his retreat. The mystery of the woods made his fingers itch, made them seem to want to pick up pencils and brushes on their own, like something from an episode from *The Twilight Zone*. On his rare days off, he couldn't help but get to work. And the work piled up. One watercolor he did late at night in his quarters, inspired by the notion of his hands having lives of their own, was of the severed appendages modelling for each other and painting in their own blood, while Dan stood in the dark background, staring round-eyed at the stumps at the ends of his arms. He chuckled as he painted it. And the work piled up.

It was in April when all of this came to a head. His friend Leo stood in his quarters, not acting at all victorious while going through sheaves of Dan's accumulated work. Dan forced himself to stare out the window, trying not to pay attention to Leo's grunts and muttering, his whistles and soft oaths.

"This is nuts," Leo said finally. "I mean, what are you doing here?"

"Fucking...*working*, man!"

"Well, you're a...I'm not sure *what* you are, but you shouldn't be working here."

"*You're* working here."

"I can't do *this*," Leo said, holding up some of the sheaf.

As it often did, the attention made Dan feel as if he were being applauded by a crowd for masturbating in public. "I like working here," he said.

"Yeah, and we like having you but, really, man." He held up on stack of work and shook his head, smiling.

"Whatever," Dan said. "Let's go get some beers."

Two days later, Dan was paged from his post to the security office. Leo sat behind his permanently cluttered desk, his feet up on a stack of papers, fingers laced behind his head.

"Showed Mr. Goodforks some of your stuff," Leo said, smiling. He flicked his eyebrows up in a way he might have learned from Goodforks himself.

"What stuff?"

"Your artwork."

"You *what*?" Dan barked.

"What are you pissed off about? This is a genuine opportunity! The new construction they're finishing is going to be an atrium, right? They want sort of North Woods scenes painted on the big walls under the windows. Mr. Goodforks was going to hire some bigshot from Greysport to do it, but thinks you'd be better, wants to give you a chance. And that's on the strength of your talent alone, okay? He says he was sure he knew you from somewhere, and now he knows where, so there's only one thing to do. You're family. You've got the job."

"What did you do a thing like that for!"

"Are you shitting me? You'd make a lot more money than working security. Get your head out of your ass." There was no anger when Leo said it; he was nonplussed and a little amused.

"Thanks a lot, Leo," Dan said. "Goddammit, I thought you were my friend."

"I am, dumbass! Why do you think I did this?"

"Fuck," Dan said, and left the office.

Packing had become easier with repetition. It helped to keep things simple; if you don't have much, you don't have much to pack. As quickly as he could, Dan jammed things in his duffel bag. He tidied up his quarters and put his uniform on hangers in his closet, and was out the service corridors and into his van before Leo Whitehorse and Faith-in-Full Goodforks could find him.

And so Dan came at last back to the river. He was far north of MacDougal Island, where the river was almost narrow, and worked his way down slowly, perhaps in trepidation, but drawn back nonetheless. He shied away from examining his motives, but where he could have made the entire trip in less than a day, he stretched it out, stopping in places that attracted him. The pull to return to MacDougal Island was only slightly stronger than his dread of doing so.

Omicron Falls was beautiful. He seemed to remember a family story about it, but the details escaped him. There was a pleasant little hotel with an early garden being tended by a short, round woman with purple hair, but Dan drove by it, intending to camp instead. He found a nice spot on a slough under fresh-leafed trees, and made beans and kielbasa sausage for his dinner. As he got closer to the island, places which provoked memories became more persistent, and he noted with some puzzlement that most of the memories were happy.

Soon, he had run out of miles on the banks of the river, and unless he were to turn around or drive away completely, it was time to go into the town itself. He couldn't simply keep halving the distance between himself and his destination.

His mouth watered with nausea as he crossed the bridge. He had been gone long enough that his memories had become imprecise, brushed into blurriness and slightly altered, but driving across the bridge brought them back into focus. Although he wanted to avoid the inconvenience of being recognized, he knew that he had been through a few changes of appearance in the years since he had left; he dressed differently, had gotten bigger. He hadn't shaved since he left the casino, and, with the addition of a baseball cap and dark glasses, he hoped that he wouldn't turn heads. The thought of being recognized by Bobby Dolan, or almost anyone else, for that matter, filled his mouth with saliva, a sure sign that he was close to vomiting from anxiety.

There were only three people whom he wanted to see: Bob Two Bears, and Emilio and Solveig. No one else was of any interest, he told himself, but he felt, underneath, a wordless shame.

He'd had an unformed plan to go into the alley behind the bar and sneak in the back entrance in search of Bob, but was shocked to see that the bar had apparently been sold. Not only had the front of the place been renovated, forever ruining its warm and comfortable look, but the name of the place was different: *Whitey's*, a new, cheerfully painted sign said on the front of the building, which had been painted an appalling but thematically consistent white. The front windows had been made larger, as had the door, in an apparent attempt to create an airy atmosphere. It was obvious that the bar had different owners by these developments alone. Bob would never have tolerated such a thing. Dan hadn't realized how much he had loved the place.

He drove slowly enough, in that slow little town, that a driver behind him politely tapped his horn. For this to happen, the man had to have been following Dan for some time. Dan pulled over and waved him past, then sat staring out the windows of the van at his surroundings.

Bluff Street had not changed, although perhaps some trees were bigger, street signs rustier, houses smaller. He tried to sneer at what he saw, but when he pulled up in front of the old bungalow, he was pulsed with a feeling of homesickness so strong that it startled him. He remembered when Willy had rescued him the second time, in Greysport, remembered coming back and falling on the bed in his old room, his father's room, and sleeping with a sense of peace that he hadn't had since those days. In some way, he had resented Willy saving him. As he had done so many times before, almost unconsciously, he closed his eyes and whispered, "Forgive me."

Dan thought that his slow cruising might strike some as suspicious, and sped up a bit, driving past the bungalow, past Julia's old house. He snorted with laughter at the memory of Mickey Potts getting bonked on the head by the loose gutter, then was immediately saddened by the thought of Jim's death.

He turned around the corner and back into the alley where Charlie had once hidden the damaged 'Cuda (and where Bud Sletto had fled Willy's approach that forgotten Christmas night). He parked the van behind the old garage and got out, walking slowly down the broken concrete of the alley.

Where his sandbox had once been now stood a vegetable garden, newly planted for the spring, labels for the vegetables sticking out of the soil. A birdbath and a bird feeder had been set up on the lawn beneath the kitchen window, a trellis laced with morning glories off to the side.

In a trance of fascination, of memory, he walked around the garage and onto the driveway, heavy with the feeling that if he walked up the back steps and into the kitchen, his grandfather and grandmother would be sitting at the kitchen table, talking and holding hands, listening to the radio with the newspaper and half-finished cups of coffee between them.

Leaning on the fence, lost to the world, he almost jumped when a woman's voice said in a stern tone, "Can I help you?"

On the back steps of the bungalow stood a middle-aged woman in a floral dress, beauty-parlor hairdo and suspicious expression. A dishrag was in one hand, the other held open the storm door.

"Can I *help* you?" she repeated. A vertical line of displeasure drew her plucked brows together over birdlike eyes.

"No," Dan said. "I just...I used to...." It occurred to him to tell her who he was, but, acknowledging the dim view some of the people of the town had taken of his family, he wasn't sure if it wouldn't do more harm than good.

"Used to what?" the woman said.

"Nothing. Sorry. I'm leaving."

"You'd *better* leave. I don't like the looks of you. We don't need anybody like you around here...."

"Okay."

"...and if I see you back here, I'm calling the Sheriff's Department."

"Okay! *Okay*, I said," Dan said, walking away. "Jesus."

"Don't you take the Lord's name in vain!" the woman cried. "Get out of here!"

Dan had an image of Charlie stalking through gate of the fence and punching the woman in the face, dropping her. As it was, though, he walked around the garage, got in the van, and drove away.

He knew that he had to go to the home of Emilio and Solveig Benitez, but after this humiliating encounter with the woman at his old home, he just didn't have the stomach for it. He drove down the road toward their little enclave on the south side of the island and parked by the gravel turnoff to their drive, across from their mailbox. On a subverbal level was the notion that, if he sat there and they saw him, he wouldn't have to make a decision; they would take him in. He sat there for awhile, feeling as miserable and cowardly as he had at the ferry to Denfer Island. After some time, he finally drove away.

He parked on a gravel siding on the bridge, right near where Bobby Dolan had been fishing the time they had hitchhiked to Black Marsh. When a Sheriff's Department cruiser approached, Dan remained calm, loosening his muscles and looking bland. He hadn't done anything illegal (although it would be better if the van weren't searched), and he could probably drop his name and show his ID to get out of immediate trouble. When the deputy in the cruiser only looked at him once and drove on into town, and Dan knew that the woman's threat had either been idle or she hadn't seen the van. After nearly an hour, the deputy drove back across the bridge and took a left, driving up the river road. Dan knew that the deputy probably wouldn't be back that night. He decided to get drunk. Just to be on the safe side, he drove over the bridge and took a right, finally parking at a spot where he had once fished with his grandfather.

It got dark, and he listened to the radio in the van on battery power, starting the engine from time to time to keep the battery charged. The stations were terrible, with the one glowing exception of public radio. He drank beer and whiskey and listened to classical music, hoping they'd play Smetana's *Moldau*, or Ralph Vaughan Williams's *Fantasia on a Theme by Thomas Tallis*.

After awhile, he lit a joint from his dwindling stash, able to enjoy the weed now that he was getting drunk, and glad that he'd had the sense not to smoke any before the weird experience of being in the old town.

When it was quite late, an hour from bartime, he was drunk enough to think it was a good idea to go to the old bar. The fact that it had been changed from the Eyrie to a fern bar called Whitey's made him more and more angry. At the same time, he thought he could sneak up into the old bedroom above the bar and sleep somewhere familiar. He wanted a fight, he wanted to sleep. The two thoughts did not conflict with each other, but traded off with the drunken changes of his attention span.

At this point in his life, Dan was good enough at driving drunk to keep it between the lines, under the limit, and rubber side down. He thought he'd learned that expression from Willy, and it made him laugh. He rolled through the town, concentrating on his driving and drinking a beer. Taking a back street and two alleys, he approached the bar from behind. The classical music on public radio had changed to jazz, which annoyed him, and he bent forward to dial the radio, steering with his left hand holding a beer, the wrist controlling the steering wheel.

He found "Black Betty" playing on an otherwise shitty station and whooped in delight.

"Fuckin' A!" he shouted out the window, and punched the gas. He roared up the alley, the old brick walls swishing by him out the open windows, went to turn to park by the back door of the old bar. Misjudging his speed and the braking ability of the van in his inebriation, he skidded and slammed into the back wall of the bar, right where Willy had once slapped around a con man decades before.

There was a smash and a tinkle of glass (a headlight), and Dan sat at the steering wheel for a moment, stunned. He checked, feeling his forehead and looking down at his chest, and found that he was unhurt. Thumping music came from the bar, but that

291

was all. Realizing how drunk he was, he nonetheless took a good pull from the bottle of whiskey, which would be the last thing he would remember the next day, that and an image of the old hotel on the bluff in the headlights of his van, the building having collapsed.

Before dawn, he woke up cold to the prefatory sounds of waking birds. A robin, a cardinal, other birds were echoing calls in the distance. His teeth were covered in film and his mouth tasted foul. Moaning a bit, almost silently, he thought only about his misery until he realized that he was not in his van. In fact, he had no idea where he was.

Sitting up with a start, he looked around in panic. He was on a cushioned wicker couch on a porch, and he knew in the next instant that it was the porch of the old bungalow. Willy and Mae's bungalow. Forcing himself to be calm and get his bearings, he rubbed his eyes to clear them, trying to breathe slowly. He looked through the screen, and saw that the van was not on the street in front of the bungalow. At that moment, a light turned on through the sheers over the front windows, back in the once-welcoming kitchen. Early risers.

"Holy shit," he whispered.

As silently as possible, he gathered up his sleeping bag. There was an empty beer next to the wicker couch, and he picked that up as well. Walking on the edges of his feet, he crept over the creaking boards of the porch. The old spring on the screen door creaked and hummed as he eased the door open, creaked and hummed in reverse as he eased it shut.

He hoped the van was in the alley. If he went down the driveway, he could be seen from the kitchen windows, so he slipped across the dewy lawn toward Julia's old house. As he rounded the hedge between the two yards, the front door of the bungalow opened and a fat man leaned out, looking up and down the street. Dan watched from behind the lilac bushes, and saw a paper boy approaching from a few doors down. Waiting until the fat man went back in the bungalow, he darted across the lawn, down Julia's old driveway, and into the alley. To his sickened relief, he found the van parked there, right behind the old garage. He turned the key in the ignition and the van started a bit too loudly. Loosing a sigh of relief, he drove slowly down the alley, trying to think inconspicuous thoughts. Through the streets of the deserted town, the sky pink and orange in the east, he rolled over the river and back to the old fishing spot where he had gotten drunk the night before.

When he woke up that afternoon and started driving with no destination other than North, the radiator on the van began to steam. He pulled over onto a side road near some small fishing cottages and waited for the radiator to cool, he inspected the van. He found that the broken headlight, cracked grille and dented bumper weren't the only damage; the collision with the wall of the old bar had run the radiator into the fan, or vice-versa. He swore luridly, cursing himself, and topped off the radiator with water from one of the jugs in his van.

A mechanic in the next town wanted to charge a sum greater than half of his remaining money for the repair, and Dan couldn't do it. The option of going back to the Benitez household to ask for help flickered through his mind, followed by a twist of nausea which he could only quell with a promise of procrastination. A sudden inspiration came to him.

"Hey" he said to the mechanic. "Do you know of a blacksmith forge around here? Maybe in Mt. Pleasant?"

"Sure," the man said. "The Heffasis Forge, something like that. Bikers, but okay. Some of that huge Schommer clan, Stumpy and Nubby. Thought blacksmiths would die out, but they're making a pretty good go of it. Good fellas. Veterans."

"Can you give me directions?" Dan asked. He topped off the radiator before he left.

A few miles north along the river, then up the serpentine coulee road, through the bluffs and the trees, up and up, the trees in summer forming a green tunnel overhead, past occasional roadside quarries, high cliffs and steep drop-offs, up and up through more trees and then out at last into the sunlight on top of the bluffs, the view suddenly huge under the sky, long grass shifting in the wind in rippling patterns, apple orchards stretching away. Here on these windy bluffs over the river lay the hamlet of Mt. Pleasant, long home to many members of the prolific Schommer clan.

The town was almost extinguished in the influenza epidemic in 1918, the contagion racing through it and wiping out two-thirds of its hardy and self-sufficient people. In the following years, buildings were abandoned, houses and barns fell to ruin. Some were occupied off and on enough that they still existed. By the '60s the town had been home to a hippie commune, and would eventually become a small but successful artists' colony, large enough to justify a tiny post office and the sinecure of the blue-clad, long-haired bongster who lurked in back. Mt. Pleasant had apple blossom festivals in the spring, art fairs in the summer, and apple harvest festivals in the fall, always with food and music, home made wine, hard cider, and applejack. It goes without saying that there were bales of weed, both foreign and domestic, the latter being unusual for the length of its pedigree, breeding, and generations of care. Other adult diversions were available, mostly of the organic variety, along with some fine acid.

It was in Mt. Pleasant that Dan came at last to Dwight and Don, aka Stumpy and Nubby Schommer, the grandsons of Willy's longtime employee Runty Schommer. Back from Viet Nam, each of them maimed, they had inherited the property from a great-uncle who was proud of their service (and ignorant of their shame and anger about it), gladly taking it as a place of refuge and recuperation.

The property was sprawling, with a farmhouse and outbuildings, along with acres of woods and fields running along the tops of the bluffs. Built on a slope near one of the bluffs, the farmhouse was an old Victorian heap with a dank stone basement set in the hillside, three floors, complete with cupolas, reaching up in peeling-paint splendor. There were gaspingly beautiful views from its upper floors, especially from the roof's highest point, a ten foot square reached by ladder and surrounded by a wrought iron railing, good for watching meteor showers, lunar eclipses and river traffic, for doing bongs and drinking hard cider.

Two barns and a large shed stood down the hill from the farmhouse, all perched on the bluff which dropped down to a heavy stand of old oak woods. One barn was mostly empty when Dwight and Don took it over, housing only a few arcane farm implements from another era, the uses of which would be indecipherable to most people. The brothers would later use it as a grow room for the pot seedlings they would plant on the sunny hillsides atop the bluffs, one of the many ways in which

293

they would augment their income, as well as providing their own stash. The distilling operation was another project, although this took place in the basement of the same barn, reached by a ladder down through heavy plank floors.

The next building was the shed, where they kept most of the tools for outdoor use: chainsaws and circular saws, lawnmowers and hydraulic jacks, red five gallon gascans and many containers of paint and stain; fertilizer and ladders, picks and shovels, wrenches, screwdrivers, and socket sets. It had the pleasant chemical smell of an old hardware store.

And down the hills from the house were vegetable gardens, flower gardens and vineyards, large and prolific, Nubby's pride and obsession.

The real masterpiece, though, the place Dan would love, was the blacksmith shop. The last building, farthest down the slope from the house on the hill, the shop was in the basement of the barn. Built into the slope, so that one side had small windows looking out through the heavy stone walls and over the oaks growing at the base of the bluff, while the stone on the opposite side held back the earth beneath the gravel drive to the barn above, where sat their aging and much cobbled and modified yellow tractor. The shop had two large doors, one going out the side of the shop and up the slope to the barn itself, while the other opened out the back of the shop to a broad concrete platform, testing ground for any number of experiments in metal sculpture and wrought-iron forging, also home to heaps of metal in various states of rusting decay. To one side stood an old concrete mixer used for knocking the slag off forged metal objects, a deafening enterprise when it was running. The platform was also a fine place to watch the sunset after a day's work, a spot where one could have a few beers among the sculpture and ironwork, where one could stand at the edge and piss, unobserved, over the trees below.

All of it was accessible by a long gravel road named Enchanted Valley, the signs for which had been altered to read Disenchanted Valley by the Schommer brothers. The turn-off to the gravel driveway had a large sign, functionally painted, reading:

Haphaestus Forge

7700 Disenchanted Valley Rd.
Mt. Unpleasant

Schommer Family Prop.

Customers Welcome. Trespassers Will Be Violated.

This was the place to which Dan pulled up, the radiator of his van steaming. He parked the van on the drive between the outbuildings, turned off the ignition and got out and stood there long enough for the steam to begin to dissipate. The rhythmic clanking of metal on metal and the fizzing sound of welding from inside the blacksmith shop ceased. There was motion in a little window in the heavy stone wall of the building, and Dan knew he was being watched.

Two tall figures emerged from the large door of the metal shop, each wearing leather aprons, earrings, and dark ponytails. One wore a bristling black beard, welding glasses on the bridge of his nose, and cutoff jeans exposing a prosthetic leg. The other had bib overalls, a dense fu manchu, and a heavy cross-peen hammer in his right hand. His left arm, from just below the elbow down, was prosthetic, with a leather-covered stump from which emerged curious blackened tongs holding a cooling piece of tool steel.

The latter man grinned, his teeth white under the hanging black bristles. In spite of the grin, his tone was not friendly.

"Who are ya? What the hell ya want?"

The other man walked out a few more steps, his gait made asymmetric by his prosthesis.

"You idiot," he said he said to his brother. "That's Dan McGregor."

With Dan's radiator was repaired, he was asked to stay for awhile. And so it was that Dan came to live for some time in Mt. Unpleasant, living and working at the Hephaestus Forge.

Dwight, missing a leg, could not shed the nickname Stumpy, nor could Don get rid of the handle Nubby, especially since the loss of his arm. Branded all those years ago by Barnacle Brad, the names had even cropped up in the service, and stuck all through Viet Nam. Some of their brothers in arms were now living on the river, members, with Stumpy and Nubby, of the local chapter of the Guardians of Nocturne. They had given up on shedding the appellations, but drew the line at putting them on the sign for their business.

"That old bastard must have been prophetic," Stumpy said of Barnacle Brad.

"That will puzzle me for the rest of my life," Nubby said. "How could he know?"

"I don't think he knew he was going to end up legless himself," Stumpy said. "So he couldn't have been all *that* prophetic."

Dan didn't mention his run-ins with members of the same motorcycle club's Greysport chapter, at least not until much later. The fact that they were honored members gave him pause at first, but he soon saw that, in spite of their physical modifications and the weight of their additional years, the Schommers were still the same.

Both of them were completely forthright about their debt to Willy, who had tried to warn them away from foolish adventure.

"He told us," Stumpy said. "Got to admit."

"Wise man," Nubby said.

"Too bad nobody listens to wise men until it's too late," Stumpy said.

"That's humans for ya."

Stumpy had gone to Viet Nam first, and soon found himself in firefights in the bush. He had all the adventure he had sought and more, yet was unable to call it quits when he had had enough.

"Be careful what you wish for, as they say," he said as they drank home made apple wine together that first night.

Out of loyalty alone, Stumpy had nearly "re-upped", taking another tour of duty simply to look after his brothers in arms, all while deriding his younger brother for volunteering at all.

"Just like your dad and uncle," Stumpy said to Dan. "You'd think people would learn."

His tour of duty had ended when he was walking point and stepped on a mine. The explosion had flipped him up into the air, the jungle whirling around him, and landed him in the undergrowth while an ambush had opened up around him. Stumpy had managed to tie a tourniquet around his abbreviated limb before passing out. All of his comrades had been killed and he himself left for dead, only to be found nearly so by an American patrol the next day.

"My reasons for re-upping were erased at the same time as was my ability to do so," Stumpy said. "It's better to be redundant than redundant."

Where Stumpy's intelligence had remained intact (he read constantly: poetry, astronomy, philosophy), Nubby had come back a little…altered. He was dreamy and sometimes drifted off to another place, and at no time was he happier than when he tended his different varieties of plants.

"Maybe I'm a little goofy," Nubby said. "but I don't worry about stuff as much as Mr. Personality here." He indicated Stumpy with his prosthesis and drank from his glass.

Not to be outdone by his brother, Nubby had been in the bush as well, talking his way out of a behind-the-lines assignment. He was three months from the end of his tour of duty when, in a cataclysmic firefight, he had fired on a Viet Cong soldier, killing him. An instant later, one of the soldier's comrades, standing just beside him, had returned fire at Nubby, at such a shallow angle that the round from his AK47 had hit Nubby's left hand where it gripped his rifle, shredding the hand and glancing off the M16, then grazing Nubby's head before exiting his helmet from the inside.

"The noise of an AK is almost enough to kill you by itself," Nubby said. "Should go after deer with AKs; they'd drop right over without being hit. As it was, I was knocked out by the round and covered with so much blood, especially from the head wound, that my buddies thought I was a dead. I coughed, that's what saved me. They choppered me out. Don't remember any of it. Brain injury. They just told me about it later, when I woke up a hand short. Eventually they fitted me with one of with *these*." He held up the prosthesis on his left hand, now holding a joint which he passed to Dan.

They had recuperated in the VA hospital in Black Marsh, the same one Willy had gone to for his cancer treatment. Stumpy had gotten out first, looked up some old friends and joined the western chapter of the Guardians of Nocturne, some of whom had approached him even before his tour of duty. His intelligence and ferocity made him enough of an asset as it was, but the prosthetic leg gave him so much credibility that he was accepted immediately after a short (and nearly token) apprenticeship.

The price was that he had to give up any hope of being called Dwight, resigning himself to the probability that "Stumpy" would be carved on his tombstone.

When Nubby came home, he received the same treatment, welcomed into the open arms, previously even in number, of the Guardians of Nocturne. Eventually more of the extended Schommer clan would join the club, which amounted to an alternate system of law and justice, providing a kind of feudal protection to the happy colony of hippies and artists in Mt. Unpleasant. The kind of rednecks that Dan, Charlie, and Jim had encountered in Black Marsh wouldn't have dared to interfere with the residents of the little fiefdom.

Stumpy and Nubby, though, were fairly safe, unless one had done some harm to the weak or innocent, which was likely to go unnoticed by the putative authorities. In such instances, even Nubby's kind goofiness was known to coalesce like quick-frozen water vapor into something sharp and hard. When Stumpy and Nubby began to trust Dan enough to talk about these kinds of things, when they heard some of his own stories, they knew he was like them and welcomed him. Considering their shared history, this took no longer than the first half of the first night.

At one point, Dan felt comfortable enough to begin to ask hesitant questions about his grandfather. Some thought he had simply left town, but the rumors varied as to where, some saying the East Coast, some the West, others the Great Lakes (there being no rumors, apparently, which did not involve water). Those closer to the truth, like Stumpy and Nubby, had it on good authority that Willy, very ill, had gone on a final quest and died in an unknown location, only to be buried elsewhere. It seemed that anyone with the inclination to do something about Willy's final estrangement from his home figured that it was someone else's responsibility. Emilio was the last logical choice next to Dan, but he was too old. Dan felt the invisible pointing of fingers.

Perhaps Stumpy and Nubby saw the effect that this news had on Dan, who found himself staring at his wine glass. In his peripheral vision, he thought he picked up nonverbal communication between the two, but ignored it. As Stumpy filled Dan's glass, Nubby cleared his throat to get Dan's attention.

"So, you want to be a blacksmith?" Nubby said.

"What?" Dan said, a bit bewildered after his reverie, along with a few hours of drinking on an empty stomach.

"Yeah!" Stumpy said. "Good *idea*. You've got some art skills, right?"

Stumpy's memory was foggy, or he was trying not to embarrass Dan, who hesitated before saying, "Some."

"And you're obviously the third known generation of Mighty McGregors in these parts," Stumpy said. "The rigor of the task would be nothing to you."

"If you say so," Dan said. He thought about the proposition for a moment. "I could see doing something practical."

"Practical," Nubby said. "Your grandfather slew a troll with a hammer. Like Thor. You guys are practical, all right."

"You can stay here," Stumpy said, giving a wink to Nubby which Dan caught.

"Okay," Dan said, dropping his gaze.

That was the last time the conversation was either pragmatic or dolorous for the evening. With Dan's immediate worries taken care of, his mood improved, and things relaxed and got humorous. Later in the evening, Dan had one thought: that he was not worried about Kate or Charlie or his grandfather or anything else before he did another shot of Schommer's Home Vodka and several hits of Schommer's Riverview Weed.

Dan awoke on their couch to the sound of clanking pots in the kitchen. He covered his head with the knit quilt and tried to go back to sleep. Soon he heard the clump-*clump*, clump-*clump* of Stumpy coming down from one of the upstairs bedrooms and into the kitchen. Some muttering went on in the kitchen, which Dan tried to ignore. Soon Stumpy came into the living room and over to the couch, clump-*clump*, clump-*clump*, the sound changing from hardwood to carpet. There was a thump on the coffee table in front of the couch, and Stumpy said, "Welcome to your first day as a blacksmith. Here's some coffee. It's how we function."

When they had eaten a hearty breakfast, they ambled down the hill to the shop. It was apparent that this was the way they did it most of the time, a silent ritual, anything that might be said about it having been talked out long since.

"We'll start you out simple," Nubby said, setting Dan up with a hammer and tongs in front of a gas forge ten feet from the door of the dark and, to Dan's eye, messy shop. Stumpy went off in a far corner and resumed the welding he had been doing the previous evening, sparks and blue lightning producing flickering shadows on the heavy beams and hanging tools around him.

Nubby showed him how to shape concrete nails into hooks, heating them in the forge until the steel was orange, holding the hot metal with tongs while pounding the head of the nail flat, then tapering the tip down as well, before holding it over the edge of the anvil and bending the tip around until it formed a curl. The nail was then reheated and withdrawn from the forge, the curled tip dipped with a small explosion of steam in the "quench bucket", a small bucket of water, cooling it. The rest of the nail was still hot, easily bent into the shape of a J in a special jig cranked into a vise. The flattened top of the J was later drilled and cold-rivetted onto a piece of forged flat stock, varying in length, but about the width and thickness of a yardstick, heated and ornamentally curled on the ends.

Dan picked it up quickly.

"Hey, you're pretty good," Nubby said. "He's good!" he shouted across the shop at Stumpy, who pulled down his goggles to look at them and give a thumbs-up.

"Make a hundred of those," Nubby said. "Start five at a time, work up to ten."

Dan shrugged, and went at it with a will.

They had named the forge after the Greek God Hephaestus, deity of blacksmiths, sculptors, artisans, technology. Stumpy told him that Hephaestus was lame, hated by his mother for being so, and considered grotesque by the perfect gods of Mt. Olympus.

"That's why I like him," Stumpy said.

As a *maldito*, Dan had to like the ostracized god as well, and liked Stumpy for liking him.

When they had taken over the forge, their first idea had been to use it as a money laundering operation for their marijuana sales, but both of the brothers had taken to it more and more seriously. They sold their work at art fairs, and, given increasingly complicated commissions and unable to resist a challenge, their skills had increased with repetition and necessity. Both of them pored over books on the subject, at times travelling to learn from any master who would teach them, until they had become masters themselves. In that German bar in Greysport, Dan had often downed volumes of hefe-weiss under a giant, medieval-looking chandelier suspended from the ceiling by heavy chains, never knowing that the masterful work had been created by friends.

After he had forged a thousand hooks, Nubby told him that his work was too perfect.

"People want to buy this stuff because it's a little rough," Nubby told him, his manner kind. "Your work is starting to look like a machine did it. Lighten up."

The labor was tiring and filthy, but kept him so busy that he had time to think of little else. A stereo with a cassette deck sat on a heavy beam above the chaos of the shop, and throughout the day, the three of them listened to classical music on the public radio station, or any of the mishmash of uncategorized tapes that was kept in a grimy box on the beam next to the stereo.

At lunch, they washed up with soap and icy water from a hose by one of the outbuildings (an old milkhouse) and straggled up to the house to eat in the sunny kitchen. Black beans with venison on tortillas was a favorite, and Dan would find that the brothers ate them with handfuls of chopped garlic in the winter, their belief being that this would strengthen their immune systems for the trial of working in the freezing shop on snowy mornings before the heat of the forges could penetrate the cold. That winter, Dan would be able to smell either of them coming if he stood downwind.

The three of them got along well, and Dan began to feel at home. He was given a room which had been intended to be an office, but instead was stacked with boxes of unread papers, stored for reasons which neither of the Schommers could remember. Dan emptied the room out, leaving a desk and a chair, throwing an old mattress on the floor with his orange sleeping bag on top of it. The room had windows which looked out over the vineyard, rows of grape vines rolling away down the hill to the woods and Disenchanted Valley Road.

There was that familiar humming bass note of unfaced music down deep in his mind, but if he worked hard and long he could keep himself distracted. From the plentiful scrap metal to be found on the premises, he fashioned dumbbells and a chinning bar, and eventually got a used heavy bag, which he hung from the rafters of one of the outbuildings. He got into the habit of working out in the early morning on the concrete platform outside the shop, and as the sun rose and burned the dew from the grass, a cacophony of birds singing in the woods down the bluff. Without Kate, he was as happy as he supposed he could be.

When he thought of Kate, though, or when he thought of Charlie, when he thought of his grandfather (each sparking a completely different emotion from the other two, a triumvirate of balanced miseries), he pounded something redhot in the shop. The feel of the hammer and the tongs, the ring of metal on metal, heaping up the pounded steel, all of it became as soothing as a mantra. The day done at last, he shuffled up to the house with Stumpy and Nubby, where they took turns taking showers, scrubbing up thoroughly before sitting down in refreshing clean clothes to a dinner of things from the woods and the garden, drinking wine under a framed print of Rubens's *Vulcano* on one wall.

"In the day we pay homage to Hephaestus," Stumpy said from time to time. "At night to Dionysus."

"Not that Greek shit again," Nubby would say, and they all laughed.

In the summer, they got their lunch fresh from the garden, taking it up to the cool of the house, simply rinsing the dirt off the vegetables in the sink. On blazing hot days, Dan pounded in front of the roaring forge, keeping an old milk jug filled with icy water from the milk house hose, guzzling it empty repeatedly. He ran with sweat, taking his headband off again and again to wring it out to mere dampness. At the end of the day, he went up to the milkhouse, near which an abandoned clawfoot bathtub sat in tall grass. Stoppering the drain, he filled up the tub and stretched out in the cold water, soaping himself with liquid mint biodegradable soap under a sulphurous summer sunset. Even in his peacelessness, he found momentary quiet in such a ritual.

Biker duties seemed to be light for Stumpy and Nubby, although they were gone most weekends on runs with other Guardians of Nocturne when they didn't have an art show to attend. Occasionally, a grizzled and tattooed Guardian or two would roll up the gravel drive in a thunder of loud pipes, looking for one or both of the Schommers. There were also frequent weekend parties, populated with bikers and biker chicks, along with hippies and members of local communes, all of whom got along in a manner which Dan found surprising. Dan suspected it was because all of them were living in a way which was more or less at right angles to straight society, something with which Dan, of course, identified.

Stumpy and Nubby had liaisons with any number of biker girls, there seeming to be free-flowing relations in the club not unlike the mosh-pit sexuality of the scene at Vnuk's. Although some of these healthy and willing young women seemed interested in Dan (as did some of the hippies from the little hamlet), Dan only responded occasionally, after some lengthy partying, and then avoided further contact. Waking up under his sleeping bag or out in a field with a young woman whose name he barely remembered, he felt bad about himself and bad for her, responding by ignoring the woman until she went away. This mystified and annoyed some of the young women, and Dan felt a little guilty, but less so than he would if he had strung one or more of them along. The thought of Kate made his throat tighten, and the memory of driving away from the ferry at Denfer Island made him want to smash his head into a wall to jog the memory loose.

Dan did find moments of great peace in this place close to the sky, finding some sense of community, of inclusion. Stumpy showed him the science of distilling and of the cultivation and breeding of marijuana plants. Nubby was more than proficient at the latter as well, but seemed to cede that to his brother.

"Gives him an excuse to be alone up in the hills," Nubby explained. Nubby's true gift was for the growing of all other living things. Starting a garden for purposes of self-sufficiency, he discovered he had a gift for it, expanding the garden each year after he had gotten home from the war. Soon he had expanded from the strictly practical growth of plants in the vegetable garden and had a wildly profuse flower garden every summer, beauty for the sake of beauty.

300

"If I could paint this," Nubby told Dan as they walked in the untamed garden one summer evening, "I would. I'd make it last. These come and are gone."

"Maybe that's what makes it beautiful." Dan said.

Nubby thought about this. "I guess so," he said. Knuckling Dan on the arm with his remaining hand, he said, "Phi*los*opher."

Nubby had also started his endeavor of the vineyard some years before, and although it was a project that had turned out well and continued to grow, it was obviously frustrating for Nubby from time to time.

"Never grow white wine grapes in this northern environment, Dan," Nubby said one evening in the vineyard before sunset. "*Never*. It'll break your heart."

Dan hadn't the slightest inclination to do so, but said, "Okay."

Nubby went on to talk about French hybrids, red hybrids, and why whites wouldn't grow. He talked about leon millot and foch, the Phylloxera epidemic in France. Dan only half listened, following his friend as he walked along the rows of the vineyard, trimming here, picking there, the sunlight as gold and orange as Kate's aura, illuminating floating pollen and the grapes on the vine. There was the sound of the breeze and of crickets, the fresh scent of grass. Up on the front porch of the house, Stumpy sat in a chair with his good leg stretched out long on a stool, reading a huge book in the setting sun, a glass of wine on the table next to him, the refracting sunlight setting it ruby.

This is almost it, Dan thought; almost. Then he wondered what Kate was doing at that exact moment, if she might be walking on the beach, perhaps with some other guy. That thought popped Dan's bubble, and he got Nubby to leave off his task and go up to the house and drink some wine. They sat down on the porch with Stumpy, who was off in his own world.

"Did you know," Stumpy said, "that Iceland has the oldest parliament in the world? Yeah. The Althing. Dates back to the 10th Century. Isn't that interesting?"

"*Very* interesting," Nubby said disinterestedly.

Dan laughed. For all his bristly and piratical appearance, Stumpy was bookish, and always had been, far before the cultivation of this appearance. His look had nothing to do with this bookishness, any more than Nubby's had anything to do with his skill with growing things.

"How come you never went to college?" Dan asked Stumpy.

"I could've gone to school on the GI Bill. Been a lawyer or something."

"Why didn't you?"

"I figured I would've worked five hundred percent harder to be maybe five percent happier," he said. "And I'm not even sure about that five percent. Would that make any sense?"

Dan gave it honest thought. "I guess not."

"And how much more do we need than *this*?" He spread his hands. They looked down the hill at the vineyards and the garden glowing in the nearly horizontal rays of the sun. "If the shit hits the fan and society collapses, we'll be able to hold on. Would I be able to do that if I were a lawyer?"

"I see your point," Dan said.

"Thought you would."

The sat on the porch drinking wine in companionable silence, listening to the crickets, watching as bats began to fly out from under the eaves of the barn.

The blazing summer ground to a close with Dan having successfully procrastinated on going to see Emilio Benitez. If he kept busy and distracted enough, he found that he didn't necessarily feel like a miserable, disloyal coward.

In late September, preparations began for the traditional fall fete at the forge, the Feast of the Harvest Moon. General plans were laid out weeks before, but the serious preparations began the *night* before, with Stumpy and Nubby readying to use posthole diggers to excavate cylindrical holes from the hillside next to the farmhouse for luau pits. Whereas they were both adapted to the work in the shop (or to riding motorcycles, for that matter, the bikes modified to operations by the limb-losing brothers), the use of shovels was difficult for them, especially Nubby. They weren't the type to ask for help, though, so Dan simply walked up to them and took the tools away, asking how they wanted the holes dug.

The idea was to dig the holes while starting a bonfire nearby. When the fire was roaring, large stones were put in it, and left there to heat overnight. The pleasure of it, Stumpy explained, was that the process gave them an excuse to stay up late, tending the fire and drinking hard cider as the sky got dark. Dan woke up in his sleeping bag, covered with a poncho against the dew of the chilly autumn morning, the mound of glowing coals nearby, the sky purple and orange in the east. What *kind* of orange was that, he thought, what *kind* of purple, the involuntary questions of a painter, however much he tried to resist the pull. He lay with his fingers laced behind his head, contemplating the changing color of the sky. Indigo, amethyst, he thought. Pumpkin, orange peel. When the sky brightened to a pale autumnal gold, he piled more wood on the fire and wandered up to the house for his first cup of coffee.

About mid-morning the preparations began in earnest and members of the Schommer clan began to ascend the bluff. Sisters Darla and Diane, the middle children, picked apples and made pies from scratch. Older brothers Dave and Dwayne, suspicious of the luau idea, prepared to fire up grills made from fifty-five gallon drums, split in two, hinged, and fitted with grates. Dave and Dwayne were comrades in their overall conservatism, and skeptical about the food that Stumpy and Nubby intended to prepare, having brought dozens of bratwurst, hot dogs, and sausages so that people would have, as Dave put it, "something normal to eat."

Stumpy and Nubby were aware of the older brothers' skepticism (or timorousness, as they saw it), and refused to let such a challenge go unanswered. Along with the usual game that they customarily served at such events, meat that any huntsman was honor-bound to eat, they had planned a few surprises. Nubby had shot a pesky groundhog with a .22, cleaned it and saved it in the large freezer in the basement. The night before the feast, as Dan and Stumpy had tended the bonfire, he had cubed the meat and simmered it in pear wine with sautéed garlic and onions until it was quite tender, and now made it into a large meat pie with red potatoes, carrots, and peas, sharing the joke with the sisters as they baked in the kitchen. Both women were revolted but amused.

Not to be outdone, Stumpy had prepared rattlesnake. While up in the hills tending some of his beloved pot plants, he had stepped on the unfortunate creature while walking along a sunny path. He might have felt the snake underneath him if he'd trodden upon it with his good foot, but had only sensed some instability under his prosthesis. He'd had no warning; it is a misconception that rattle snakes, shy and reclusive animals, always use their rattle before striking, or that they always inject venom when striking. It was with a primate horror that he looked down and saw a snake as thick as one of Dan's upper arms, and he was too startled to move before the snake struck. Luckily for Stumpy, the snake bit his prosthetic leg, where it fangs stuck long enough for Stumpy to bend down, grab it behind the head, and dispatch it with the machete he carried to trim brush. Stumpy had thrown the carcass over his shoulder and limped back to the house, where he skinned and dressed it, putting it in the freezer next to the groundhog. Before the feast, he took it out to thaw, then marinated it in lemon juice, garlic, and hot paprika for a day before putting it on shishkabob skewers. This was too much for Darla and Diane, who squealed in revulsion with Stumpy revealed the origin of the meat. Dan had to admit he was interested.

For the luau pits, all three blacksmiths and numerous guests had prepared meat and game of a more traditional variety. Venison, duck, goose, pheasant, all dressed with the stipulation that this event was to be special, that meat was not to be simply thrown on a fire and gnawed on by a pack of growling cavemen. Bikers, hippies, farmers, rail- and bargemen had all spent days at the unaccustomed task of researching recipes, and the results were interesting. Two separate recipes for duck l'orange, one for cider-braised pheasant, medallions of venison tenderloin marinated in red wine, garlic, and black pepper, the list went on and on. When asked to contribute, Dan made a Canada goose, stuffed with fresh apples, garlic, and rosemary from the garden, along with a few oranges from the co-op in Mt Pleasant, the only ingredient not raised in the garden or nearby orchards. More mundane contributions included a marinated roast suckling pig and a barbecued side of beef.

All the meat that wasn't going onto the grills went into the luau pits. First put in oven roasting bags then wrapped in foil, the large lozenges were put by the cylindrical holes. For the goose, Dan had gotten around the possibility of dry meat by pouring in a cup and a half of the pear wine before sealing the bag. The stones, which had been heated all night and into the next morning in the fire, were scooped up and dropped in the holes, then covered with Swiss chard. The meat was carefully placed in the holes, then covered with canvas, with dirt then shovelled on top.

Many of the more conservative revelers were skeptical about this procedure. Older brother Dave, an electrician, was so unbelieving that he went so far as to drop a heat sensor down in one of the pits, with a wire leading up to a readout which he could consult. He shook his head and grumbled, saying that at least he had bratwurst to eat.

Trestled tables were set up in long rows between the vegetable and flower gardens, covered with white table cloths and fresh cut flowers in mismatched vases. Chairs and wineglasses were scrounged from anywhere, many of the attendees bringing their own. Kegs were tapped and cases of wine brought out as fresh vegetables were harvested from the garden and taken to the kitchen, where Darla and Diane maintained order and gave directions. Their most attentive assistants were two bikers named Ratzass and Dirty Dick, each of whom had had food preparation experience from working in the cafeteria at Oakwood Medium Security Facility and restaurant employment after their release. They were eager to help, listening dutifully to the bossy sisters, nodding with inclined heads to the women's instructions. In an attempt to make a favorable impression, they began a conversation about the correct preparation for mirepoix. The discussion became so heated (Dirty Dick advocating the use of ham or bacon, Ratzass saying that no meat should be used at all), that the two Guardians began a shoving match. The sisters intervened to break it up, small and determined between the two, experienced with brothers but outmatched. At that moment, Dan walked into the house, saw this unlikely tableau, and broke it up, shoving the bikers apart.

"Cool it!" Dan said. "Don't we all have stuff to do?"

His manner was apparently sharp enough that he made his point, and both Ratzass and Dirty Dick agreed, a little shamefacedly. Dan began making his way to the door before he could laugh out loud.

"You should become a Guardian, Dan," Dirty Dick called after him.

"Thanks," Dan said over his shoulder, "but I'm not much of a joiner."

Grills smoked and the bonfire was again laden with wood as the sun slid down the western sky. A nonsensical variety of music played from speakers set in the open doors of the barn above the shop, ranging from bluegrass to Beethoven. Dave checked his thermometer, and found that the temperature of the pits had gone up consistently and was now well over the range where the meat was safe. He raised his eyebrows and frowned, nodding. Stumpy and Nubby elbowed each other and clinked their glasses of wine.

The preparations complete, Stumpy and Nubby came out of the house dressed in feast regalia, both wearing black leather pants and frilly cotton shirts, with skull and crossbone bandanas covering their heads. Through their connection with a maker of prosthetics in Black Marsh, they had different artificial limbs for different purposes, consulting with the technician and doing the metal work themselves. Nubby had different hands, one for blacksmithing (blackened toolsteel tongs with a leather cover for the wrist of the device), one for the motorcycle, and one for formal occasions, the latter of which he sported this afternoon. It was made of stainless steel, with what appeared to be emeralds at the joints, this matching his favorite green glass wine goblet. For his part, Stumpy had fashioned a leg attachment which resembled the claw of an eagle grasping a ruby-red glass sphere the size of a cueball, protected on the bottom (Stumpy had told Dan) by a black rubber pad. Dan was one of the first to see them as they emerged from the house onto its front porch. He laughed and shook his head while others saw them and began to applaud. The two bowed like courtiers. Dan noticed the older brothers exchanging weary looks.

"May I have your attention!" Stumpy cried. When all eyes were on them, Nubby intoned, "It is now time for the sacred anvil blast!"

Dan had known about the anvil blast for months. A tradition among blacksmiths dating back centuries, it involved upending a large anvil on top of a cross-section of tree stump, then filling the conical hole in the base of the anvil with black powder. A fuse is put into the black powder, and a smaller anvil placed right-side-up on top.

The two blacksmiths, showmen to the bone, had done this enough that they knew to build anticipation of the event, and to wait until later in the afternoon when the guests had had enough to drink and suspense was given time to grow. The crowd murmured as Dan, at a nod from Stumpy, joined them in walking down to where the anvils were set up fifty feet from the door of the forge. People rearranged themselves in a rough circle a safe distance from the action, and Dan was given the honor of handling the matches.

"And now..." Stumpy called out, "...the lighting of the fuse!"

Nubby nodded, and Dan struck a match, touching it to the end of the fuse. It lit for a moment, then sputtered and went out.

The three blacksmiths looked at each other, and Nubby cried, "And now, the re-lighting of the fuse!"

This time the fuse caught, the sparkling flame sputtering up along its length. The three got out of the way, Stumpy doing a hop, skip, and jump repeatedly until he was clear.

The fuse fizzled its way up to the two anvils, ten inches left, then five, three, two, one...and nothing.

"Shit," Dan said.

Stumpy held up a forefinger and tilted his head. "It's not-"

The black powder ignited with a boom that Dan felt as an expanding hemisphere, a bubble of sound, rippling across the contours of the landscape, blowing grass and leaves and the hair of people back in a wave. The roll of it had to be audible, finally, up in Black Marsh and down on MacDougal Island. The smaller anvil, a seventy-pound lump of steel with no aerodynamic properties whatsoever, hurtled improbably skyward, spinning dreamily as it went. The faces of the crowd turned upward in unison, gape-mouthed in mirth and astonishment, as the anvil reached an apex of perhaps sixty feet before stopping its ascent and dropping back to earth with a whump, burying itself in the grass in a small, fresh crater. There was an instant of silence, then dogs began to bark, people started to laugh and shout and applaud all at once. Dan fell to the ground laughing. It would go down as one of the funniest things he had ever seen.

Stumpy and Nubby looked at each other, nodded, and cried simultaneously, "Let the feasting begin!"

Dirty Dick and Ratzass, with two other Guardians, had extracted the meat from the luau pits, and, after some arrangement, loaded it onto a table fitted with long poles, so that the meat was carried along like roasted royalty on a palanquin.

On cue, Stumpy and Nubby began to sing "America the Beautiful". They sang the first line slowly, in clear and confident baritone voices.

Oh beautiful for spacious skies...

By the time they started the second line, a few among the hippies, biker, and farmers, quick to catch on, stood up and joined in.

For amber waves of grain...

On the third line, all had stood, the riverrats, rail and bargemen, all stood, all sang the song, gathering in strength and conviction, harmonizing, putting their arms around one another, smiling.

For purple mountains majesty
Above the fruited plain
America, America
God shed his grace on thee
And crowned thy good
With brotherhood
From sea to shining sea

There seemed to be confusion about the verses that came after this, and there was in instant of pause.

"One more time!" someone cried, and they sang it again. Joyously. At the end, people embraced.

Dan was disgusted with himself to find that he was touched. There had been so much turmoil and conflict in the country; there would doubtless be more to come. Here, though, on this golden day, the many different people stood together on the bluff and sang this familiar song, and when they sat down to eat and drink together, they were, for a short time, family.

As people lined up to fill their plates from the tables of steaming food, a sedan drove up from Disenchanted Valley Road, up between the parked Harleys and pickups and hippie vans. A biker stood with his hand up, talked to the driver, and let the vehicle pass, pointing out one of the few spots left close to the farmhouse.

Dan was standing next to Stumpy, talking about what needed to be done next, as good hosts will. Stumpy said, "My dad brought my grandfather. Didn't think he'd show up."

Sure enough, Shorty Schommer got out of the driver's side of the car and went around to open the door for Runty, who, Dan was surprised to note, was even smaller than when he had last seen him. The fact that the old man, whom Dan had known from Willy's bar since he was a child, had shown up at all gave him a moment's pause, a little constriction in his throat. He was more than close enough for Emilio and Solveig to arrive, to force upon him the thing he had been avoiding. The circles of these people overlapped; it could happen. He scanned the driveway and the road, but no one else was approaching. Not wanting to reveal his thoughts, he said nothing.

"Hi, Dad," Stumpy said. "Grampa, glad you could make it."

"Had to wait 'til that damn noise was over," little old Runty said. "I haven't liked an anvil blast since I was a kid."

They shook hands, affectionate embraces being the sole province of the youngest generation of Schommers, and not all of them (Stumpy and Nubby didn't even try the biker bearhug with elder siblings Dave and Dwayne, who would've recoiled as if the perpetrator of the offense were covered in pigshit).

Dan stood ten feet away with a beer in his hand, the sight of three generations of a family together overwhelming him for a moment. He snapped out of it enough to begin slinking away when old Runty said, "Stop right there!"

Dan knew the old man was talking to him and turned in resignation.

"I'd know a McGregor anywhere," Runty said. "Jeez, you've gotten big."

"Yessir," Dan said, moving forward and extending his hand.

306

"I heard you were here," Runty said, taking Dan's hand. "It's one of the reasons I came."

Dan expected castigation; he wouldn't even have been surprised if the geezer had called him *maldito*. Instead, he was encouraged by the old man's warmth. Runty might have shaken hands for an instant and be done with it, but he held the grip warmly, reaching out with his left hand and touching, almost kneading, Dan's right arm.

"It's good you're back on the river," Runty said. "You don't need to be in a place like Greysport, what with the riots and all. Place like that is dangerous."

"Yessir," Dan said. "I have to go, though. Gotta help with some things."

"You do that. Talk to me later."

The feast proceeded under a goldening sky. Dan went up to the barn and stuck in the tape of Beethoven's Sixth, The Pastoral, after momentarily resisting doing anything so obvious. When the music was playing and he looked around, he saw that not only did no one notice, but that the selection of music appeared to illuminate the scene along with the sunset, and as he came back out of the barn, he stood for a moment, regarding the long tables of varied people in their hubbub of conversation, the rattle of silverware on plates made in the local kiln, with the clinking of glasses, no two alike, created by glass workers right in Mt. Unpleasant. Dan wondered what the fatalist, catastrophist Charlie would make of the scene. He filed it all away, thinking that he could paint it, putting in a hanging or crucifixion in the background just to make it his own.

Along with the drinking, joints were passed casually. If any of the many Schommer relatives present might have been offended, it was apparently treated as if they were visitors in another land, and that the customs of the natives were to be tolerated. As Dan drank and feasted, he noticed that Dave and Dwayne were sharing a joint with Runty and Shorty, perhaps one of the strangest things he had seen in a long time. When he looked at them again, they were all leaning upon each other in a fit of hilarity.

One of the hippies (actually a glassblower who had provided many of the wine glasses), covertly gave Dan a hit of blotter, which he downed with a glass of wine before going to the tables of food, where the crowd had dissipated.

The first thing he tried was the groundhog pie and rattlesnake shishkebab. The groundhog was excellent; Dan heard that comment from another brave epicure that they would have it twice a week if they could, that Swanson's should have groundhog pot pies.

"I'd like to see the advertising for that," Dan said, and people laughed.

The rattlesnake was tangy and surprisingly good, made better by the apparent disgust of some of the hippie girls who cringingly bore witness to Dan's feat of culinary courage. Dirty Dick took this as an inspiration, and plucked the eyeball out of a roast pig and ate it, feigning delight. At this, the girls simply left, turning their backs, their slender hands thrown up in disgust.

"That was great," Dirty Dick said.

"What, the eyeball or those girls' reaction?" Dan asked.

"The girls' reaction," Dirty Dick admitted. "The eyeball nearly made me puke."

Dan wandered away, a glass of dandelion wine in his hand.

The shifting murmur of conversation, disconnected bits here and there intelligible, sounded like water in river rapids, with the occasional spike of laughter or a shouted word. The landscape glowed in the amber light, and the riotous flowers in the garden, purple and burnt orange, sky blue and dark yellow, seeming to glow, to move nearly with sentience in the slight breeze. Dozens of beeswax candles were lit in wrought iron candelabra along the tables and Dan felt as if he were dollied backwards from the scene, observing from a remove the sense of joy, of community; he was not apart from it, but seeing it as if floating slightly above, like a benevolent ghost observing the happiness of his descendants.

The flowers and the landscape glowed under the sky, wineglasses catching the sunlight like pellucid gems, this one topaz, that one ruby. There was poetry in the light shining through a biker's hoisted glass beer mug; what would Rembrandt have done with the scene?

Dan thought that this might be his favorite day without Kate, this a nearly perfect moment, delicate, ephemeral. He tried to pull it into his mind, widening his eyes and slowly looking around. Keep this, he thought. Keep this. This is nearly it.

The perfect moment did, indeed, flee quickly, as they always will, leaving only the search for the next one. The light changed, the sky grew dark, and soon the only illumination was that of the many candles on the table and of the bonfire, piled high with dead wood and ringed with partiers, their silhouettes black, fronts washed with orange.

Tired of avoiding him (and emboldened by his earlier kindness), Dan sat with old Runty Schommer, listening to the old man, saying little about himself.

"So howdja like living in Greysport?" the old man had begun when Dan pulled up a folding chair next to where Runty was comfortably seated, well attended by grandchildren and great grandchildren.

"It was all right," Dan said.

"Went there once or twice," Runty said. "Dwight and Don's dad lived there for awhile, worked in a steel mill. I always thought the place was too big. Like it here. Guess you came to the same conclusion."

Dan shrugged.

"Might've thought you had something left to do out here, huh?"

"Maybe."

It was apparent that Runty was comfortably inebriated. Dan's taciturnity didn't seem to bother the old man at all; in fact, he apparently took it as a vacuum into which he could expand. As Runty talked about his ailments and his dislike of "that asshole Reagan", Dan realized how much he was getting off on the acid, and thought that he would sit politely for a bit and soon excuse himself. He was readying an excuse, looking for a gap in the flow of words, when Runty, in a conversational right turn, began to talk about Dan's family.

"When I first saw your grandfather, I knew he was something different," Runty said.

Dan's plans for a polite departure dissipated and he eased back a little in the folding chair "How so?" he asked.

"He looked different, at least for around here. Looked like someone who'd come after you in a port town when you were behind on your payments to a loan shark.

308

But smart? I'll tell *you*. And he was the only man on this river who had any kind of chance with your grandmother. She was a beauty, and took shit from, well, guess who?"

"Nobody?"

"Nobody!" Runty cackled. "You got that right. Only the two of them could've produced someone like your dad and your uncle, rest their souls."

Although the party continued at full strength, Stumpy and Nubby came up with their father and pulled up chairs. Soon Dan was being basted in the folklore of his family, hearing things that any of its members might have been too modest to relate, or that they thought were somehow not worthy of note. He found that his grandfather and grandmother had set up scholarship funds, put former employees through college, set up other employees with downpayments on new homes when they got married, shown others how to manage their money.

"Didn't you know any of this?" Nubby asked Dan.

"Not really," Dan said.

"It's all true," Stumpy said. "All of it. Real widows and orphans shit."

"You probably heard a lot of bad stuff, especially after that whole Bud Sletto thing," Runty said. "A lot of people were going to have it in for your grandfather anyway, seeing as he was a rumrunner and all."

"It's not wrong to defy a bad law," Stumpy said. "Might be illegal, but not wrong."

"Sometimes it's wrong *not* to defy a bad law," Runty said, and the murmur of agreement made Dan smile.

The talk went on, and people came and went, everyone having something to add. As the acid came on more strongly, Dan drank straight from a bottle of dandelion wine to keep from being overwhelmed by the chemical, torn between his fascination with these newly revealed stories and the desire to be invisible, unknown, his old self.

Finally Shorty mentioned to Runty that it was time to go. Runty creaked to his feet and said, directly to Dan, "People need heroes. People need those who will do extraordinary things."

"I suppose so," Dan said.

"*You* could do extraordinary things."

Dan sat in his chair and hung his head. Runty's words and the acid made his hair stand on end. "I don't think so," Dan said. "I'm not like that."

"Sure you are," Runty said. And, as if he'd read the back of Dan's mind, added, "You go talk to Emilio Benitez, see if he doesn't bear me out."

Dan was relieved when the old man left; nowhere in the conversation was there any mention of Willy's death, or of his final resting place. It was as if the subject were taboo, at least within earshot of Dan. He knew what small towns were like, however, and knew that it had been talked about. Perhaps people were simply waiting to see what he would do. The only real source of information would be Emilio Benitez.

Maybe it was a coincidence that the party (as it had become after the feast) got rowdier when Runty left, waiting out of respect for the old man's frailty, but rowdier it got. Dan accepted another hit of acid, and only realized after forty-five minutes that he was roaring with it. He slipped away from the party and went up to the house, through rooms and upstairs, finally to the ladder and up to the ten-foot square that was the highest part of the roof.

The sprawling view was stupendous. From this altitude, there was still a smudge of purple and dark red on the horizon, this being reflected on the water of the river, which was not visible from the grounds around the forge itself. Dan again had the feeling of being a spirit, this time at a greater remove, hovering over the party below, the community of linked people, sisters and brothers of Stumpy and Nubby, their cousins and nieces and nephews, greatgrandchildren of Runty, all mingling in with the other people in attendance, all connected, all a community.

Dan knew himself to be outside of it, walled off forever, like the ghosts he had heard about, roaming and restless, unable to find their way from one world into the next. The loneliness of it pierced him momentarily, then he thought that he was exactly where he deserved to be.

He had brought a bottle of the homemade vodka, and took a warming pull from it. A rush of goosebumps rippled over his skin from the vodka and the acid, and he lay on his back, looking up at the limitless casting of stars. They did not appear merely as the roof of the world, as ancient mythologies would have told it, but deep into time, into space, the greatest distances of all, billions of motes in a lucid lens of infinity. And that was not all; he sensed other dimensions of reality behind it, as if he could peel away the edge of the sky and reveal a kaleidoscope reality, a gemlike clockworking of cathedral glass, the luminous jewelry of reality shifting and sliding in incomprehensibly giant and unknowably tiny interconnected gears, gleaming and glinting gold and ruby, sapphire and emerald. The reality that shunned him below was only the reflection off a facet on one small gem; he did not need to be part of it. He could belong to the greater reality, could peel back the sky and reveal it, to topple up into it, to fall away from this tenuous gravity and away into the glowing stained glass sky.

He could peel away the face of this sad reality and enter the true realm. If only he had the right hands.

Dan tripped into the early morning, falling asleep only briefly before the birds, thousands of them, began to sing with the coming of dawn. He stumbled across the roof in the grey light, seeing the forms of those asleep down on the grass below, in sleeping bags and covered with blankets among the litter of bottles and plates on the trestled tables, the burnt-out candles, and the deep ashes of the bonfire.

Creeping down the ladder, he walked quietly through the old house, down the stairs. People were crashed everywhere; in the living room, he heard muffled, tender conversation and hushed laughter. Surprisingly, no one was in his bed. Dan flopped down and went to sleep.

Waking in the afternoon, he got up to help with the post-party cleaning. It appeared that many who had spent the night were willing to pitch in; the spirit of camaraderie from the night was apparently, for the time at least, no illusion. Dan thought with a bit of longing about the old days at Vnuk's where, even after a night's chaos at that place, he could simply stagger home. Even so, he sighed, drank some Hephaestus Forge coffee, and got to it.

310

The exhausting work done (made worse by an acid hangover), recuperative partying began. There was plenty of leftover food, and Dan soon had lost his hangover in a pleasant afternoon buzz. As evening approached, though, people started to acknowledge that it was a Sunday, and began to wander home.

It was only the next day, as Dan woke up to another Monday morning feeling stunned and unfocused, that he realized it was time to talk to Emilio Benitez.

He put it off until the weekend. The weekdays were rainy and cool, good weather for forging. Much of the time, the three were silent in the shop, each doing their allotted duties, happily distracted and hard at work. They ate dinner together at night, once going down to the little river town of Fountainville for hamburgers. Young women came and went out at the forge, and the usual array of bikers and members of the Schommer family.

On Friday night, Dan sat with Stumpy on the front porch and told him what he was going to do.

"I was wondering when you were going to get around to that," Stumpy said.

"You were?"

"Sure. You're a man with a mission, whether you know it or not."

Dan squinted at him, but decided not to ask what that meant.

On Saturday morning, Dirty Dick, Ratzass, and another couple of the Guardians roared up the drive to get Stumpy and Nubby for a run to a meeting in Greysport, something that would keep them gone until Monday afternoon. Dan came down from the house to see them off, a cup of coffee in his hand.

"Sure you don't want to become a Guardian?" Dick called to Dan over the roar of his engine.

"Pretty sure," Dan said loudly, although Dick's leer made him laugh.

" 'Kay!" Dick said, revving his engine. "Just say the word, and you'll be wearing a patch and be riding a sweet machine like this before you know it!"

"I like my van." Dan called. "Gives me someplace to put my beer. And guns. And bodies."

"That *is* useful," Dirty Dick shouted.

Soon they were gone in a racket that made Dan wince. They tore onto Disenchanted Valley Road and away, off through the gold-dusted autumn leaves, leaving Dan alone in the ringing silence, thinking about what he had to do.

Dan drove down to MacDougal Island that Saturday morning. He didn't call first; to simply show up seemed like a cleaner way to do it. He crossed the bridge to the town feeling nauseous with anxiety, so busy thinking about what he would say to his grandfather's best friend that he barely noticed the town when he drove by it.

The trees along the drive to the Benitez home seemed more dense than when he had last seen them, hiding the house and other buildings completely. He drove slowly along the gravel track through the trees and into the clearing in front of the house. Everything looked as it always had, in fact it seemed better, an idealized version of itself, everything freshly painted, neatly varnished, squared away.

Dan sat in the van, breathing slowly and deeply for a few moments before getting out and walking up to the front porch. He took a deep breath and knocked, his hand trembling, then stuffed his fists in his pockets.

311

Emilio came to the carved front door. His skin was dark brown from the sun in his garden, his curly hair completely white. He wore silver-rimmed glasses, a snow-white linen shirt and khaki pants, and walked with a polished and beautifully carved cane. Emilio had managed a great elegance in his old age.

"Well." The old man said. "Why don't you come in."

The inside of the sturdy old house was so much the same, so comforting and perpetual, that Dan was stunned by it, although he had a strong tug of longing for the cabin on Denfer Island, and, of course, for Kate.

He thought Emilio might be angry with him, but when Emilio went to embrace him, Dan found himself hugging the old man so hard that Emilio grunted. Dan relaxed his arms and apologized. Solveig came in from the kitchen, clapped her hands in delight, letting out a little cry. She looked neat and healthy, wearing a beige wool skirt and sweater, the perfect partner to Emilio. Grown side by side over the decades, they seemed to lean on each other like two old trees. Dan restrained himself from hugging her as hard as he had Emilio, instead holding her gently in his arms.

Solveig stood back, saying, "Look at how big you are. What a handsome man!"

Dan's throat tightened. He felt a sob deep within himself, and kept it there. Solveig scolded him lightly for his absence, and Emilio, perhaps sensing Dan's unease, gave her a look to quiet her.

"I came to, to talk to you about my grandfather," Dan said.

"I know," Emilio said. "Come in and sit down."

It was difficult to begin. Dan searched for words for a moment while the old couple sat patiently. He thought of what Willy would say when Dan was faced with an unpleasant task or duty: "Just march yourself up there and do it."

To open himself, to make an admission of all that he had done wrong, and the wrong he had done through his inaction. It was this that made him nearly choke: the admission, the acknowledgement of his weakness. In the eyes of the old couple patiently watching him, though, there was no recrimination, only kindness, only love.

"I should have been here." He spat it out. "I should, I should have looked after Grampa. He always looked after me."

"You were just confused," Solveig said.

"And young," Emilio added, his small shrug indicating the inescapability of this condition.

Once Dan had started, it came out in a torrent. "I said some things that I couldn't take back, and now I can't fix it at all. I was wrong. I was so ashamed of myself, I just ran away, and I made it worse, I made it worse."

Emilio watched him until he was silent.

"Willy understood," Emilio said quietly. "Your grandfather understood."

This idea stunned Dan. He stared at Emilio, at the floor, back at Emilio. "You think so?"

"Of course. He told me about the argument you had, and some of the things you both said. He knew that you would feel badly about it."

"He did?"

"We're old. We seen everything. You think you're the first young person to do something he regrets?"

Solveig said, "Everyone has regrets."

"Not like mine," Dan said.

"Some even worse," Emilio said. "You think your grandfather didn't have regrets?"

"I told him he'd never lived through anything."

"I know," Emilio said with a kind smile. "We laughed about that. Your grandfather lived through *everything*."

For the next hour, Emilio and Solveig told Dan about the lives of his grandparents, leaving out very little. They verified what Runty and others had said about them, things Dan would never have known. They talked about his father and uncle, from the time of their birth, through their childhood and youth. They talked about the weight of their deaths, about how this weight had nearly crushed Dan's grandparents.

As the old couple talked, Dan could visualize the faces of Willy and Mae McGregor. He had seen them only as his grandparents, not as people who had lived through such storied years, people who had once been as young and frightened as he. Dan looked around at the many framed pictures on the luminous walls, the Benitez family at various ages, black and white and in color. Many of the McGregors. A framed drawing done by Dan as a boy, of Solveig. A few photos of a daughter who was a young dead-ringer for his friend and commiserator from Perrito's, Kaye. There was his dad. There were his grandparents. There were the grandchildren of these kind people before him. Dan felt on the verge of grasping something.

To spare Dan's feelings, Emilio didn't tell him everything, filling in a bit more than what he had said when Dan had called him from Kate's apartment. In fact, Emilio had told no one about the actual circumstances of Willy's death and burial, not even Solveig. Knowing the McGregor gift for self-torment (but also their gift for resilience), he told the facts in a terse and unembellished manner.

When he had talked himself out, they sat quietly in the sunlight of the living room. A faint fall breeze with a hint of woodsmoke and the scent of burning leaves came in through the open door, and mallards could be heard from where they bobbed by Emilio's dock. Dan sat with his forearms on his knees, hands laced; he stared at the floor.

"I have kept something for you," Emilio said.

Dan raised his eyes. "For me?"

"Yes. From your grandfather."

"What is it?"

"You have to help me get it," Emilio said. "I'm too old, and it's heavy. Only a strong young man like you could carry it."

Dan followed Emilio down into the stone basement of the cabin. Do all old men have the same kind of workshops? he wondered. It smelled like his grandfather's shop, even had the same kind of tools, cans and jars of screws and nails. There were a great deal of wood carving tools, but no weights, no heavy bag.

Emilio used his cane to tap at something in the shadows under the workbench.

"There are two trunks down there," he said. "A heavy one and a light one. They belong to you. Perhaps you would like to take them up to the front porch and examine the contents."

313

Dan knelt down and looked under the bench. There he found two wooden trunks of medium size, old, handles tarnished, covered in dust. They seemed familiar, especially in the context of the workshop. Then Dan realized that they were, in fact, from under the workbench in the old bungalow, something he had seen in the background when lifting weights or hitting the heavy bag, seen so often that he failed to see them at all.

"What the hell," he said, pulling them out. One was quite light, but the other had some heft to it, and would seem especially heavy to an old man.

"They've been waiting for you," Emilio said. "Go through the lighter one first."

Dan stacked the light trunk atop the heavy one, taking them up the stairs. Emilio followed slowly, saying, "See? I knew you were strong enough."

Dan set the trunks in front of one of the chairs on the porch, the light one on top of the heavy. He sat staring at the thick dust for a moment, thinking before opening the first one. Emilio came out with a damp rag and began to wipe off the dust, but Dan took it away from him gently and finished the job.

"I will leave you alone," Emilio said. "Come and find me when you are done."

Dan opened the first trunk.

Inside were stacks of papers, different shapes, different colors, different ages. They were not legal documents or ledgers, but large sheaves of different sheets, from pages of legal pads to those the size of letters to slips from pocket notebooks. There were even numerous cocktail napkins of various shapes and sizes. All of them had only one unifying factor: his grandfather's handwriting.

"Huh," Dan said. They were poems. Stacks and stacks of poems. "Wow."

There were everything from short notes and fragments to something that looked like an epic poem, written in a single spiral notebook; Dan set this aside. Wait; there were more of these.

There were love poems, poems about death. These seemed too heavy in content for the moment, so Dan set them down for a moment.

He read a love poem to his grandmother:

For Mae
Where is it that we love
Here in this physical world
Is it shape or shadow
Real or illusion
It is your face I love
Your eyes bits of sky
Apple blossom cheeks
Rose petal lips
Scented autumn hair
The curves of you
The taste of you
Right here in my arms
But what is it that lies beneath
Our reality unseen
Is it Heart, is it Soul
Is it a deeper place of Energy

And there are we bound together?
My Heart feels your Heart
My Soul longs for your Soul
My Energy is bound forever with yours
I have no fear in this physical world
For in the reality unseen
We are one
Our energies bound
Come find forever
With me
And another:
This I loved about you
Above all
Your languid hand
In the water's current
Lips kissed by the sun
Eyes illuminated
Stained glass to the sky
You would be my love
You would fill my empty soul
You would hold me up
And into the sunlight again
All possibility
And all hope seen
Through your cathedral eyes
And another:
Here I floated aimlessly
The life behind me left
Past dead was I, abandoned,
Unburied, and bereft
Yet here I found you waiting
On this unenvisioned shore
You held me to your glowing breast
And I wandered never more
A valkyrie, you picked me up
From the meadows of the dead
Your kiss sparked light and breath again
Alive, I raised my head
This gentle land our kingdom
Our boys beside us stand
And through the wheeling of the seasons
We behold our golden span

Way to go, Grampa, Dan thought. It made him think of the hallucination he'd had on the roof of the Schommer brothers' house. It made him think of Kate's eyes. Our minds must be similar, Dan thought. Another apparently was written after Mae had died:

I only truly saw
What the light of her held back
Her blazing light
Orange, gold and yellow
Held back the black
I had known before
Yet when she left
Was blacker still
Yet when she left
Collapsed with gravity
With weight
So dense that it clutched
To my skin and down
And through
To my bones
And into them
To my skull
And into it
To my brain
My mind
Her light had kept it
All at bay

Dan furrowed his eyebrows; he had thought his grandfather was so tough.
One was entitled *For Mollie*:

There she was
An unloved girl
Pale in cruel light
Slack in death
The spasms past
Alabaster, blue,
and black
A daughter there
May she sleep
May she sleep

The name Mollie seemed vaguely familiar to Dan. He seemed to remember Willy saying something about her, perhaps up in the Coeur de la Riviere cemetery, another forgotten grave.

There were countless poems describing the local landscape. Reading one, he could see it clearly enough that he could have painted it from the vision it induced in his mind:

Lavender and orange snowy sunset
The blackbone trees sharp silhouettes
The river runs orange and the far hills
Are dark, here and there a light
Shades from orange to umber in the darkening twilight
The eagle, huge black serrated wingspan
White head and tail, gold beak
Described arabesques over the still water
Plunging for prey, serene, methodical, elegant

He liked another one:

There are the silent, still-dark mornings
When the woods lie in slumber
Darker than dreams
The river slides by, silent and wide
Down to the sea
And the land holds its breath
Before sighing and stirring once more
The rhythm, the ritual
Of endless days
The forest then breathes with the croak of a crow
His brothers then stir and they speak
In a rasping chorus
Of laughter or of condemnation
And the geese murmur and converse
First one, then dozens, encouraging their flock to flight
With the pinkening of the morning sky
Shimmering on the surface of the ancient river

As if Willy had planned it, Dan found a packet of humorous jottings, among them a few limericks.

There was an old homo named Jack
Whose overused anus was slack
With his legs spread apart
He'd no pressure to fart
And the turds toppled out by the sack

Dan had no idea who Jack was, but the limerick made him snort. He liked the next one:

There was a Norwegian named Hansen
Who eschewed any female romancin'
His desires, instead,
Went to lutefisk in bed
Which he handily then stuck his lance in

He wondered if it pertained to an old guy who had hung around the Eyrie when Dan was a boy, a man whose shiftless brother had been crushed by a boulder, as he remembered it.

The last one in the batch, although not a limerick:

These are my favorite things to wear:
My pallid ass and pubic hair
For dressed like this I needn't wait
To grab my dick and masturbate

Dan laughed out loud at that one, although the thought of that wizened old tough guy beating off provided Dan with an indelibly disturbing image, something which made him wince and snicker at the same time. He tried to cleanse that thought with an image of his grandfather as a young man beating off, which was somehow worse. He remembered, though, that Willy had actually encouraged him whack off, where other senior figures would never have even acknowledged the existence of such an activity.

Then he got to more somber things. There were a series of what were labeled as song lyrics for the Ad Hoc Band. One read:

Please don't weep beside my grave
Don't you weep beside my grave
For I have done bad things
Yes, I have done wrong things
Please don't weep beside my grave
Don't you grieve me when I'm gone
Don't you grieve me when I'm gone
There in the water's embrace
Will my conscience erase
Don't you grieve me when I'm gone

It went on, verse after verse. He realized that he had heard the informal band play it when he worked at the bar. Did they play it the night he found his grandfather weeping in the basement? There were more poems about remorse. One was entitled *On Killing*:

To kill a man
Is a fine thing
Trust me
I know
The death of rage
The death of fear
The death of want
Wrought by your hands
Your bloody hands
The death of love
The death of friendship
The death of possibility
Wrought by your hands
Your bloody hands
Held up to the sky
Held up to the rain
To the thunder
To the lightning
Washed clean
Never clean
Never clean again

One was entitled *For Thanksgiving*:

For the things I have not done
Please please forgive me
For the wars I have not won
Please please forgive me
For the things I have not said
Please please forgive me
For the dreams laid down to dread
Please please forgive me
With things undone when I stood still
A fraction of my crime
Transgressions I committed
Are the burden of my time
For the things I said in fear
Please please forgive me
For the anger I held near
Please please forgive me
For succumbing to my rage
Please please forgive me
For my comfort in my cage
Please please forgive me

319

Dan put this one with the other similar pieces, his heart thudding.

"I forgive you, Grampa," he whispered.

Some were more hopeful:

We all are born with an empty cup
Fill it with what you will
Fill it with love
Fill it with hope
Fill it with bilious swill...

This one continued for two pages, but was ultimately about having the will to be happy, in spite of evidence that worked against such a pursuit. He thought of Kate, and what she thought about cynicism and hope. She'll never meet him, Dan thought.

The work went on and on. There was the beauty of the land. The birth of sons, the death of sons, leaving Dan breathless with sorrow. Poems from after Mae's death that made Dan wonder how the old man could have survived such grief, made him wonder why he would want to.

Oh, Dan thought at last. For me. He did it for me.

There was a poem about the first time Willy had held Dan in his arms. Dan thought about how is grandfather, a stoic man, not given to weepy effusion, had shown Dan love. In his "confused" years, as Solvieg might have called them, Dan had often thought that his grandfather hadn't loved him at all. Of course he had, Dan realized. Of course he had. And he had shown it every day. When they had been out on the boat or up in the woods, what had been going on in that man's mind, what was churning there in the skull behind that craggy and impassive face. A great deal, apparently. When Willy had looked at Dan, had he looked at him with love? Dan's mind knew the answer, yet his chest seemed to remain empty, facts without knowledge.

There was one poem that gave him the most pause, the one, over the years, he would love the most. It appeared to have been well-handled, the paper yellowed and creased. It was entitled *The Young Oaks*.

Cover that cold sacrificial stone
With dust and dirt and grass
And grass again and soil, my friend
And then be oaks at last
And when the oaks fall down
And then the young oaks grow at last
Let soil be deep upon the stone
And peace be there at last
And peace be there at last, my friend
And peace be there at last
Lay down with stone the weary bones
And peace be there at last

Dan read that one again and again. He looked out at the river, thinking, and read it once more. His back stiff, he leaned back in the carved wooden chair and watched as the westering sun changed the color of the trees across the river. Time passed, and he watched and thought, watched and thought.

He was so lost in contemplation out on the Benitez's front porch that he scarcely noticed that it had gotten dark. Emilio gently nudged him from his reverie; Dan jumped when he came back to himself. Dan went to take the trunks back into the house, grunting once when hefting the weight of the second one.

"Did you look in the heavy one?" Emilio asked him.

"No," Dan said, "I got...distracted."

"Your grandfather always did that," Emilio smiled. "You want to look now?"

"I already have a lot to think about."

"Oh, go on," Emilio said. "Go ahead."

Out of politeness, Dan complied. The heavy oak box had been hidden in plain sight for years. When Dan opened it, he had the same response Emilio had had half a century before. He whistled. The old trunk was full of stacks of gold coins: quarter eagles, half eagles, eagles and double eagles. Dan only recognized that they were gold.

"Wow," Dan said, the visual non sequitor of it flatlining his mind. "What the hell."

"It's yours," Emilio said. "Your grandfather left if for you."

"What...is it real?"

"Yes. Those are actual gold coins. From when Willy was not much older than you, running booze up the river."

Dan looked at the stacks of coins, at Emilio, at the coins, back at Emilio.

"And he held onto it all this time?"

"Yes. Your family always lived simply."

Dan stood staring. Finally, he said. "Well, *I* can't take it."

"Why not?"

"I just can't, that's all."

"But he left it for you," Emilio persisted. "So why can't you take it?"

Dan spread his hands. "I just...I...I don't *deserve* it."

"*Es tipico*," Emilio muttered to himself, smiling and shaking his head.

"Pardon?"

"It's typical," Emilio said loudly. "Most people, or a lot anyway, would ask how much it was worth. That doesn't even occur to you. You just think you don't deserve it."

"Well, I don't."

Emilio looked at him levelly. "Ask yourself," he said, almost in a whisper, "*why?*"

Dan opened his mouth a couple of times before saying, "I just have things to do that...need doing."

"Such as?"

Dan blinked a few times. "Well, I'm not sure. I just know I can't take that. At least not right now. Right now I definitely can't. *You* keep it. He was *your* friend."

"It's yours," Emilio said implacably. "He was your grandfather."

321

Dan sputtered about it, without any logical argument. They stood in silence together for some moments. Finally, Dan said, "I...I don't know."

"Don't know what?"

"I don't know what I should do," Dan said. He looked at Emilio, searching his eyes. "What should I *do*?"

Emilio put his hand on Dan's shoulder. "What you *need* to do. You will know. You McGregors have always been a people of...unusual gifts."

Dan left with the location of Willy's grave. It was a strange sensation to have opened himself up as he had, to tell some of the things that were most shameful about himself, and to be accepted nonetheless. That Kate had seemed to love him in spite of himself was one thing; these people he had known his whole life; they seemed like the representatives of Willy and Mae. Feeling partially unburdened, and with a clear destination, he felt unusually focused, understanding, in glimpses, how lost and adrift he had been.

He went back to the old house at the Hephaestus Forge for some things, his sleeping bag, a change of clothes. He stopped only in Fountainville for gas and a few provisions, then drove north, crossing the river at Black Marsh with not much of a drive to Omicron Falls.

It was not hard to find Bluff Haven Cemetery. He pulled in to a gas station for directions, and the attendant produced a detailed map, complete with topographic lines, and showed him where it was.

"I don't think anyone gets buried there anymore," the attendant said.

"This would be a county burial," Dan said, and was surprised by the look on the attendant's face.

"That makes it...uh, less good," the man said, went on to tell Dan about the rumors and the press regarding the coroner and his burials. The information only served to make Dan feel worse.

"Thanks," he said.

The road to the cemetery could not be missed, marked as it was in the no-nonsense manner of rural people: Cemetery Road. Placed at the base of this sign (as if put there, Dan thought, to remove any room for vacillation on his part) was an old rectangular metal sign, rusted, but with gold letters on a black background that read Bluff View Cemetery. The road led into the trees and up the bluff.

He had faced Emilio, summoned the courage to do it after denying for so long that it had to be done, or that it had weighed on him. There remained this to be confronted. He hesitated at the side of the road, both hands on the steering wheel as he stared at the sign to the cemetery. A car drove by. Dan turned the van onto the road leading up the bluff.

The hedges in front of the cemetery were so overgrown that Dan at first drove by the gates. He turned around onto what looked like a fire road, came back and parked. The wild hedges obscured a heavy stone wall, and large gates, the sturdy work of long-dead blacksmiths, with a carefully crafted wrought-iron arch overhead spelling in large, rusted letters the cemetery's name. The gates were ajar, unable to move due to rust and years of deepening grass. Dan walked through the gap of the leaning gates, and headed through the grass among the huge oaks and neglected tombstones. There were a few mossy crypts just inside the fence on the high part of the grounds, put there long ago when people of importance were buried here, their names inscribed and now forgotten. Dan walked down the slope to the far end of the acreage, past tilted obelisks and broken tombstones, the details of their engravings softened by the rains of years, down the slope to where the graves were more recent and less proud, near where the vinegrown fence was close to the edge of the bluffs. Down to the paupers' graves.

There weren't many such graves; there was no big city nearby, and people mostly took care of their own, a thought that gave him a pang, made him wish it hadn't occurred to him. The cemetery showed no signs of being tended, and the long grass nearly obscured the cheap, flat concrete markers. Then he found the newest, perhaps last such marker in the cemetery.

WILLIAM J. MCGREGOR

This was all it said.

Dan stood over the little rectangle. He didn't know whether he should weep or beg forgiveness, shout or scream or fall to his knees. Perhaps there would be a thunderclap, perhaps the shade of his grandfather would tap him on the shoulder. Nothing happened. Dan simply stood there, his cheeks and forehead feeling pinched. He stood there watching the shadows of the grass, moved by the breeze, on this grandfather's name on the concrete marker, there in a forgotten cemetery on a lovely October day.

In the end, he spent the night. He parked the van out of sight on a nearby fireroad farther up the bluff, not wanting to risk the small chance that he might be interrupted. In the van, he ate a cold can of beef stew, then brought his sleeping bag, a twelve pack of Greysport Lager in a cooler, and a bottle of home made vodka from the forge. He wanted to weep, to hear his grandfather's voice, but nothing came to him. He sat there drinking with eyes so dry they stung.

The wind picked up as it grew dark, and he sat cross-legged in front of the gravestone with his sleeping bag around his shoulders, a beer to one side and the bottle of vodka held with one hand between his legs, the other hand palm down on his thigh.

After a few hours he was very drunk. He talked to his grandfather out loud, imagining his responses, and somehow this was soothing. Even as drunk as he was, though, sitting alone above the bones of his grandfather, his hero, even with no witnesses so that he could shout as loud as he wanted, he still could not utter, could not even whisper, the words that he wanted most to say: "Forgive me."

Dan slept on Willy's grave, the wind snatching leaves from the large trees overhead, whisking them away. Some piled against the side of Dan's sleeping bag, on which he had tightened the drawstring to keep out the cold, leaving a hole through which he could breathe. Dan was drunk enough to pass out at first, but woke up before dawn having to piss, waiting until the need was nearly unbearable before getting out of the cozy bag to walk away on the frosty grass to relieve himself. Too groggy to walk back to the van, huffing with the chill, he got back in the bag and zipped it up as quickly as he could, trying to get back to sleep. Part of him thought that he might have a dream about Willy, some kind of message, a sign. The only thing that came to him was something between vision and dream, perhaps the creativity of the hypnopompic state, an image of shadowed shapes standing in the darkness of the autumn trees, of the patiently waiting dead. Perhaps it was his imagination, something he might have painted himself.

When it was fully light, he lay in the sleeping bag staring up at the trees, getting warmed by the rising sun. Although it was comfortable and peaceful, the notion of the strangeness of where he was soon began to leech into his mind, his grandfather's bones resting just beneath him. The thought of it roused him, and he got out of his sleeping bag and stood up into the dizziness of a severe hangover, wondering what was wrong with him to have slept in such a place, to find such a thing comforting.

Dan spoke to his grandfather without the benefit of alcohol, the notion of it more comfortable now. "I will be back, Grampa," he said. "I'll return." He knelt and touched the little concrete slab. As to what he might do upon his return, he had no idea.

He walked away through the long grass of the cemetery, out through the rusted gates. Soon he was down on the river road heading south.

Winter came and the three men forged stock to create an inventory for art shows, working on a few special commissions together, a long railing, a series of wall sconces, and a gigantic chandelier for a house on the lakefront in Greysport, not far from where the Gates family had lived, as Dan recognized from the address.

A blizzard hit before Christmas, moaning down from the north, and Dan was the first to trudge down through the deep powder to the shop in the morning, firing up the gas forge for the immediate warmth. The huge oak cask which held water for quench buckets (into which the tip of a piece of ironwork might be dipped, so that another part, still red-hot, could be bent or twisted) had frozen to the depth of a few inches, and Dan had to smash through it with his hammer in order to get water for the day's work.

Soon Stumpy and Nubby came down, dressed, as Dan was, in heavy woolen trousers, insulated boots, and jackets. As the shop warmed and the serious forging began, the men were down to t-shirts alone under their leather aprons, although still wearing the woolen trousers, only their upper bodies being really warm. When Dan walked away from the forge to cut metal, the sweat froze on his arms. Soon AC/DC was playing loudly over the speakers in the shop, although, after lunch, Dan changed things up by playing Beethoven's Ninth. The men pounded away in synchrony with the chorus, in synchrony with each other, metal ringing on metal, hammer on steel on anvil, a poetry of movement, the men realizing the magic of the moment, Stumpy and Nubby grinning whitely through their black bristles. They laughed out loud at the beauty of it.

There was a moment when the tape ended coincidental to a small stretch of silence in the shop; Dan walked outside through the heavy door of the shop and stood bare-armed in the deep snow in his heavy boots, tongs in his left hand and a hammer in his right. It had begun to snow again, gently, with flakes as big as quarters settling slowly from the grey sky. Dan looked across the silent white landscape, the naked trees standing black, fields and gardens and vineyard snowy and asleep. Again he had the feeling almost of peace, almost of having reached a destination.

What would Kate think of such a place?

He held up the tools in his fists and saw that his arms were steaming. Now *there's* a painting, he thought. I could do a triptych, he thought, of five forearms and one prosthesis. Inside the shop, Nubby put on a tape he liked, Jethro Tull, the one with the lyrics about heavy horses, brewing heavy weather. Dan shuddered and went back in to the forge.

Dan lay low for the holidays, in spite of Stumpy and Nubby's request that he come along for family events. He also turned down invitations to hippie galas in the town, wanting to read instead, and to work on secret sketches of ideas for paintings. These he kept hidden, not wanting to repeat the events of the casino.

While he had had no guiding vision in the cemetery where lay his grandfather's bones, now Dan often had the dream about his grandfather, thematically the same, although the settings were different, where Willy stood on the other side of some gulf, talking or shouting in a way that Dan was unable to hear. In one such dream in February, Willy was down the hill from the shop, standing in the snow, saying something across a distance of perhaps fifty yards, gesturing for emphasis.

"What?" Dan called. "*What?*"

Willy seemed to repeat himself, slowly and deliberately, but Dan couldn't make out the words, and soon the wind howled and the falling snow became so dense that Willy was lost behind it. Dan awoke to realize that the dream had been affected by the wind outside, laden with snow and strong enough to make the windows thump and rattle. It took him some time to get back to sleep.

The three men were snowed in the next day, but were caught up enough in their work to declare a day off. After a large breakfast, Dan stoked the woodburning stove in the kitchen, and they sat around the table with large mugs of coffee, Nubby reading a dog-eared science fiction novel which Dan had suggested to him, whereas Dan, in return, rather grudgingly read a western which Nubby had gotten for him from the house's bulging and disorganized bookshelves. Stumpy was reading a book about literature.

"Did you know that Dostoyevsky wrote *Crime and Punishment* because he was so in debt from gambling that he desperately needed an advance?"

"I did *not* know that," Nubby said.

"It's true."

"Very interesting."

They spent the day in that manner. In the late afternoon when it was getting dark, they made a pot of venison stew with thawed meat from the freezer and canned vegetables from the garden. Dan brought up plum wine from the basement, and after dinner they drank and played Monopoly, smoking the occasional joint.

Dan drank a bit too much, and although Stumpy and Nubby were not the type to criticize such behavior, they each had to snap Dan out of small trances as he stared off into space.

"Earth to Dan," Nubby said once when it was Dan's turn to roll the dice.

"Sorry," Dan said, and returned his attention to the game.

When Nubby won, the three sat around the table in the warmth of the stove, reading their books. Dan found that he was in a trance of thought again when Stumpy startled him by saying, "You okay? You got the thousand yard stare, man."

"Yeah, I'm all right," Dan said. He had been thinking about how deep the snow might be on Willy's grave.

The next day, they went back to work in the shop, Stumpy claiming to be bored in the house. Nubby bundled up to follow his brother, saying, "Come on down, if you get restless."

Dan stayed in the house, drinking coffee and thinking. He finally got dressed and left the house, squinting in the brilliant sun and trudging down to the shop through the deep and silent snow.

As he walked up to the open door of the shop, he could hear the roar of the gas forge, and the voices of Stumpy and Nubby. He hesitated, though, looking up at the eaves of the old barn where a huge crystal stalactite of ice refracted the sunlight. He overheard what the brothers were saying.

"We have to look after him," Stumpy said.

"Yeah, I love that kid. And we owe it to the old man."

"Tell you one thing," Stumpy said. "He's a hurtin' unit. He's taking a 'round the world guilt trip on a hijacked plane of reality."

"Poor fucker."

Dan backed away from the door a dozen steps and made a production of coughing before walking up to the door of the shop. Stumpy and Nubby had stopped talking when he came in. Dan walked over to the forge and held up his hands to warm them.

"We gonna pound some hot metal today?" Dan said, trying to sound hearty.

"Oh, yeah."

"You bet."

Dan didn't mention what he had overheard, simply locking it away with a mound of other things.

Spring came in fits and starts, the usual way of the North. First there would be a day in the seventies, then one of cold and blustery temperament. There was a late snow which melted almost immediately in the next day's warmth, followed by two days of rumbling thunder and gravid clouds. Dan went down to the shop in a poncho, delighting in the sound of thunder, the smell of things coming alive again. It was so dark outside at noon that they kept lights on in the shop, and it reminded Dan of afternoons in Mr. Kinder's classroom in Greysport.

At night, though, he often could not sleep, and would lie in his little bed. As the world came alive again, as the landscape transformed in the slow green watercolor wash over the black and white of winter, Dan thought of the dead yellow grass over his grandfather's unwanted grave, and the new sprouts coming up long again to obscure the marker. There would be no peace there, he thought. There would be no peace.

Dirty Dick, friend of Stumpy and Nubby, long a member of the Guardians of Nocturne Motorcycle Club, was killed on Memorial Day weekend of that year.

It was Sunday night, and Dick had the next day off at the auto shop where he was a mechanic. He had had a few beers in Black Marsh, not even enough to catch a buzz, and was roaring south down the river road to go to a kegger party at the Hephaestus Forge, where he could drink as much as he wanted and spend the night, crashing out in the vineyard in his sleeping bag.

The driver of a pickup truck headed in the opposite direction had not decided to be so moderate. A recent high school graduate, Scott Schnagl was a trainee butcher, and had spent the day at a park on the river, helping to man the grills while preparing bratwurst that was made at his own shop. He wasn't a bad kid, and had a peaceful life in front of him. He stayed too long at the park, however, and had consumed enough beer that he was weaving on the way home. His parents were an oppressive duo, hardliners in the local church who took a dim view of Scott pursuing his love of beer. He had gotten an apartment with a friend from high school in Black Marsh and was feeling liberated. He thought, since no one could tell him what to do, that it might be okay to tip a few more on the way home.

Scott's pickup was old and pulled to the left, causing him to constantly fight it to keep it straight. This wouldn't have been a problem to a more experience driver, but that wasn't Scott. He was drinking a beer from the six-pack on the bench seat beside him, tilting the can up to get the dregs, when the road curved to the right, his truck pulled to the left, and Dirty Dick roared over a rise.

Scott Schnagl's pickup went five feet over the centerline just as Dirty Dick approached. Dick swerved at the last second, but not fast enough, and the pickup clipped him, shearing his arm off at the shoulder and sending him skidding down the road and into a ditch. It happened so quickly Schnagl wasn't even sure what had happened, but got control of the truck and pulled off to the side of the road. His windshield was shattered by the disembodied arm, blood splattered down the door and side. In a panic, Scott almost fled, but then backed up along the shoulder to point his headlights at any wreckage or victims that might be there. Aside from the presence of a few motorcycle parts, shattered mirror and a bit of the handlebars, Scott found nothing until he came upon the arm off on the gravel on his side of the road. This was enough to make him vomit, with great force, all the beer and brats he had consumed that day.

To his credit, Scott Schnagl did not flee. He followed the long skidmarks down the highway to where they had shorn off some grass, but was unable to find either the motorcycle or Dirty Dick. He was not accustomed to dire circumstance, and it was fifteen minutes before he remembered that he had a CB radio in his truck. When memory seized him, he ran back and called for help. Then he took all the evidence from his car and tossed it into the tall grass and retrieved a jug of Koolaid left over from the picnic from where it sat in the back of the truck. He guzzled the Koolaid, vomited again, guzzled more and waited for help.

Dirty Dick was conscious for a few minutes after being sideswiped, lying in the tall grass and looking up at the trees illuminated from underneath by Scott Schnagl's headlights, listening to the boy run up and down the side of the road. He was in shock, and felt no real pain, but had a sense of commiseration for Stumpy and Nubby at having lost a limb. When enough blood had left his body, he lost consciousness and died, never to prepare mirepoix again.

When the Sheriff's deputies finally arrived, illuminating the scene redly with their rotating toplights, they found Scott Schnagl sitting pale and sober on the tailgate of his pickup. He had covered the arm with a tarp, but had drawn the line at finding Dirty Dick's body. The deputies saw the state of the young man, a clean-cut boy, and, seeing that the DB was a biker, would've let Scott off completely if he hadn't insisted on his own wrongdoing.

Scott Schnagl was given a ticket for inattentive driving. Fearing reprisals from the Guardians of Nocturne, he left the state for good.

A biker funeral is not unlike a Viking funeral, a fact to which many bikers would attest. Dirty Dick was beloved among his clan, and in preparation for his funeral, Guardians of Nocturne roared in to Black Marsh for days before the event. From all around the area and from neighboring states, representatives or whole chapters came to the local chapter headquarters in a warehouse in Black Marsh. As a demonstration solidarity, members of other biker clans attended as well, providing a mix of patches in the jam-packed and overflowing funeral home. Dan didn't know that this put some of the bikers on edge, and he stood among them, a rare civilian of biker age, without concern.

The funeral hall selected was the largest one available in Black Marsh, making Sam Feeney's look tiny in comparison. The streets were lined with neatly parked hogs, and the hall itself had kegs tapped long before the funeral began. The outnumbered local police, along with two of the sparse Deputies, parked in a strip mall across the street from the funeral home, looked on uneasily.

Dan had been to too many funerals for such a young man, but this was the loudest and rowdiest he had experienced. He had liked Dirty Dick a great deal, but was so numbed by other events, other concerns, that he could do little but shake his head and sigh upon hearing the news of Dick's death on Memorial Day. The bikers around him, in black leather and worn denim, wild hair and tattoos, were boisterous even before the kegs were set up, at which point they roared. When a local brother provided barrels of funeral ale (a tradition borrowed from the Vikings) the brothers howled. Whiskey was brought out, and Dan drank in somber salute with Ratzass, who had been crying on and off all morning. An overly enthusiastic member fired a .38 into the ceiling of the hall, and Nubby and a few others had surrounded him, making sure he understood that such activity was frowned upon.

When Dan went up in the line to look at Dick in the casket, shuffling along in a queue of bikers, he felt nothing but a desire to get back in line to the keg.

Speeches were made at a podium on a platform, most of them loud and orotund, having to do with fights and bikes, drinking and women, Dirty Dick's aplomb in all categories. There was no respectful silence after the speeches, not even applause, only howls. Dan imagined similar clamor, accompanied by the beating of sword on shield, at such an event among actual Vikings. He smiled, he laughed, he drank. He howled along with the rest, as loud as he could, until his throat hurt. Here he could be anonymously loud, here he could salute death. It occurred to him to join.

Outsiders were not trusted among these men, and no hearse was to be used. Although Dan was not a member and wore no patch, Stumpy had asked him if his van could be put to use to transport the casket. Dan had to admit disappointment that Dirty Dick was not to be put on a pyre.

Stumpy was strangely formal in his request. "I know you're not officially a brother," he had said, "but Dick liked you, and you're with us. If it's not too much of an imposition, that is."

"Not at all," Dan had replied. "I'd be honored."

When the speeches were done, brothers closed the lid of the casket. Funeral home workers moved to do their job, but were blocked by stone-faced bikers buzzed on funeral ale. None of the funeral home people were willing to take their job so seriously as to contradict such a phalanx, and were pleased to accept when offered free beer.

Many more brothers lined up to carry the casket than were needed, but Stumpy and Nubby were two of them, and in the front. An instant of confusion ensued when Nubby had to explain that he needed to be on the left side of the casket. "I have to use my right arm," he said. "See? The left one is detachable." He apparently didn't feel the need to point out that he had worn his formal arm.

The casket, made light by many bearers, was taken out to the loading dock and slid into Dan's van. Ratzass, whose bike was being repaired by Dirty Dick in his shop at the time of his death, rode shotgun, giving Dan directions to the cemetery north of Black Marsh. Ratzass cried along the way, quaffing occasionally from a giant mug of the funeral ale, calming down before looking back at the coffin and beginning to cry again.

Aside from a procession of the honor guard on motorcycles in front of them, two abreast and six long, a line of bikes stretched out behind them, hundreds of them, also two abreast, tatterdemalion warriors rumbling on their way to bury a brother. When they passed through residential areas, people came out to watch. Little children covered their ears, although some ran alongside on lawns in an attempt to keep up.

They reached a shady, well-tended cemetery (nothing like the abandoned Bluff Haven), and Dan followed the honor guard to where a bier was set up with chairs and a black awning. Here the final ceremony was performed, and brothers passed by the re-opened casket one last time, saying a word, putting in a bottle of whiskey or a can of beer or a porno magazine. Stumpy paused over the box and dropped in a dozen neatly rolled joints of his best weed. Dirty Dick's colors were given a final arrangement, and the casket was closed for good. Guardians lowered the casket into the grave themselves, and Guardians took the shovels to drop the earth down into the rectangular hole, lining up to take turns at the privilege.

Of course more partying took place back at the warehouse, and as loud as it got, the police didn't dare interfere. Dan commented on this to Nubby.

"Are you kidding?" Nubby said. "They'd have to call for backup from the National Guard, and even then *they'd* have a problem."

Later in the evening, Dan found himself sitting off in a corner alone, a beer and a whiskey forgotten in front of him as the wake raged on. Although he had liked Dirty Dick, the man was not his grandfather, and the differences in the manner of their departures could not have been more stark.

And who was there to change it? Only him.

Soon his second summer working at the forge had passed, and although he was not content, Dan felt powerless to move. He worked out of habit, as he imagined most people did, *lulled* by habit, his circumstances acceptable enough for one more day, and one more day, and one more day after that.

He felt disquiet, though, wondering what was going on with the people he'd left behind in Greysport.

His insomnia increased, and sometimes he had nightmares so ghastly that he was afraid to go to sleep at all. He often got up and slipped outside, walking barefoot in the dewy grass in the vineyard, or out to the moonlit concrete platform outside the shop, standing among the metal shapes and looking up at the sky.

His grandfather's poems stayed with him, especially the one entitled *The Young Oaks*. If only he could talk to his grandfather about what it had meant, about what had made him write it. Had his grandfather, after everything he had lived through, attained some state of peace? Could Dan himself? What must he do? Dan closed his eyes and tried to sleep, breathing deeply and slowly, methodically, trying to relax his muscles and fade off, perhaps to find answers there. Perhaps to be visited by Willy. Just tell me, Dan thought. Tell me what I should do.

When at last he started to float into sleep, he was suddenly aware of it. This is it, he thought; I'm going to sleep. And the clarity of the thought woke him up again.

"Goddammit!" he would say, starting up and looking at the glowing numbers of his clock. He finally slept for a few hours before dawn, waking up when he heard the sounds of Stumpy making coffee in the kitchen, the soft thumping of his asymmetric gait. Groaning, he got up to start another day.

Dan was often exhausted at work, but with enough of the strong coffee that was brewed in the kitchen, he bulled through it. There was a tradition in the forge that, if a blacksmith happened to sizzle himself on red-hot metal, he was honor-bound to run immediately over to any other smith present and hold the burned flesh and hair under the nose of his companion for his appreciation. Dan was making a series of twisted pieces of square stock for a set of candelabra, putting the metal in the roaring gas forge until it was orange, withdrawing it with tongs, and dipping the ends swiftly in the quench bucket before putting one cooled end of the piece in a vise and twisting the other end so that the hot metal in the middle was made into the form of a helix. Nubby was next to the door of the shop, talking to one of the hippie women about the upcoming apple blossom festival. The woman, named Annie, with a sweet face and blonde hair, was a weaver, knitter, and fabric artist, kind-hearted and soft-spoken, and it was fairly clear that Nubby was smitten with her.

Dan was fatigued, though, and had been dazedly cranking out the little helices, something he had done so many times that he hardly had to think about it. He had the process down to an efficient series of machine-like movements: steel from the forge, quench one tip, quench the other, put in vise, twist the metal, remove from vise, straighten piece, set aside, repeat. He was about to remove the current glowing hot piece from the vise when the tongs in his left hand slipped off the metal. He nearly dropped the tongs, and in a reflexive move, he turned to catch them in his right hand, and in so doing, drove his left forearm into the hot metal with a hiss.

"Yah!" Dan cried, recoiling. It didn't hurt as much as he expected (the nerves being cauterized), leaving the sizzled skin with a feeling of hot tightness, as if molten

331

candle wax had been dripped across it. There was in instant smell of grilled steak and burned hair. Remembering tradition and honor, Dan trotted across the floor of the shop to hold the burned limb under Nubby's nose.

"Ah!" Nubby said, sniffing deeply. "Good one! Now you know why I've got this leather cap on my prosth…"

It was only then that the two men noticed that Annie's kind face had gone wide-eyed and pallid, her throat working visibly.

"Hey!" Nubby said. "Let's go take a look at the garden!" He took Annie gently by the arm and walked her outside, saying quietly over his shoulder to Dan, "You might want to put some aloe on that."

It got so that Dan only had some hours of sleep if he drank enough in the evenings to pass out. Then, just as had happened during his night in Bluff Haven cemetery, he awoke having to piss. After that, he usually spent the hours until dawn in a stew of self-recrimination. When one of the Schommers began stirring in the kitchen, he would sigh and get up.

He avoided the annual Feast of the Harvest Moon, feeling vaguely ashamed of himself for his inaction (what action was there?) and unwilling to have another conversation with old Runty. Instead he went camping, although he came up with an excuse for leaving, overcoming the earnest protests of his friends. He had the feeling that Stumpy understood his need to leave, and might have said something to Nubby, who soon stopped pestering him.

Before he left, Stumpy said to him, " 'Solitude affects some people like wine; they must not take too much of it, for it flies to the head.' Mary Coleridge."

"Uh, thanks," Dan said, clapping his friend's shoulder before getting into the van.

Stumpy came up to the door of the van, grinning through his bristles, and said, " 'Alone, alone, all, all alone, alone on a wide, wide sea! And never a saint took pity on my soul in agony.' Samuel Taylor Coleridge. Did you know he was, like, the great uncle of Mary Coleridge?"

"Nope." Dan was terse; he wanted to get on the road, and Stumpy was beginning to annoy him.

"You're not alone, though. You *got* that, right?"

"Right. I should shove off."

Stumpy put his broad and gnarled hand, its nails, calluses, and creases permanently blackened from the forge, on the burn scar on Dan's forearm where it rested in the open window of the van.

"You're not alone, so that last quote doesn't apply to you. You know one that does?"

Dan told himself that Stumpy was merely trying to be helpful. "No. What does?"

" 'Such strength as a man has he should use.' Seneca. Think about it."

"Okay," Dan said. He put the van in reverse, and as he backed away, Stumpy's fingers slipped off his arm. The strange man waved as Dan backed, did a Y turn, and drove off onto Disenchanted Valley Road.

Bluff Haven Cemetery seemed somehow more abandoned than when he had first seen it, although this time he walked directly to his grandfather's concrete marker. The little stone itself was covered with leaves, and he brushed them away angrily, this stone somehow not yet ready to be obscured.

Sleeping on the grave that night as he had before, he again woke up long before dawn, gathered his things and drove off, having coffee and eggs at a little café whose lights were coming on just as he drove past.

For the next two nights, he camped in a state forest in a little site with a firepit. He had stopped at a used bookstore and picked up a thick page-turner of a novel, something that would provide him with a world other than his own. He read and drank and read and drank. When it got dark, he read by the light of a fire, and of a lantern he placed on the campsite's picnic table. He was engrossed in the story, unable to stop reading, however much things ground away in the back of his mind.

October came as a relief after the summer. It got cool out, and they stopped blacksmithing for awhile and harvested from the garden, the hills, and the vineyard, making wine and canning fruits and vegetables, hanging pot plants upside down to dry. Annie was around a great deal, her cheerful presence welcome in such a masculine setting.

Dan liked to talk to her in the kitchen as she baked bread. Something about it reminded him of sitting in the Gates's kitchen in Greysport when he had run away, being in the comforting presence of Elpidia. Dan watched Annie make the bread from scratch, and soon the kitchen was filled with that warm and wholesome scent. The overall feel of the kitchen in her presence lowered his guard so much that he didn't even mind when she began asking questions about girls.

"Why don't you date anyone around here," Annie asked, and although the question was direct, her manner made it disarming.

"I don't know," he said, embarrassed, but not shutting her down.

"There are plenty who are interested, you know. And the more aloof you are, the more interested they become."

"I suppose."

"You love someone back in Greysport, don't you? Someone you can't be with."

"Who told you?"

"You did," Annie smiled, "just now."

Dan snorted and hung his head.

Stumpy and Nubby, arguing about something pointless, came in the front door, and Annie gave Dan a sympathetic look before their conversation was broken off. They made spaghetti for dinner, with spicy venison sausage and lots of wine. The fresh bread was delicious. Kate would have loved it.

In the end, it was Stumpy who gave him his inspiration. After a day of work, Dan sat on the porch with a glass of wine, looking down at the vineyard where Nubby paced, inspecting his vines. Stumpy was drinking wine as well, a large book open across his knees. Nubby came up onto the porch and poured a glass for himself from the bottle on the little table between the chairs. He sat down, easing his shoulders.

"Did you know," Stumpy said, "That William Butler Yeats was buried in France in a small private ceremony in 1939, then exhumed almost ten years later and moved back to County Sligo?"

"No, I did *not* know that," Nubby said. "Very interesting."

Dan laughed. "For some reason, I thought that was Shelley."

"Nope," Stumpy said. "Shelley drowned in the Mediterranean and was cremated on a beach on a big pyre, actually not all that far from where Yeats was first interred."

"Huh," Dan said, but Nubby was setting up a chess board and he wasn't really paying attention.

When an owl hooted in a tree outside his little bedroom in the early hours, Dan started awake, knowing exactly what to do.

The next day, he tried to tell Stumpy and Nubby his plan. It had been more difficult to talk to old Sam Feeney on the phone, asking questions as indirectly as he could make them about the technicalities involved. Feeney, always kind, had guessed what Dan was up to and told him what he wanted.

"You're a good grandson," Feeney had said.

"No, I'm not."

"This is a fine thing you're doing," Feeney said.

"We'll see."

Dan hung up after promising to keep in touch.

With Stumpy and Nubby, though, he had hemmed and hawed until Annie came in, and somehow her calm presence again made him open up. When he said, in the simplest terms possible, what he intended to do, there was a long pause around the table. Even though these were people with a relaxed relationship with the law, he thought he might have gone too far in speaking.

"You *have* to do it," Stumpy said finally, rapping the table with his knuckles like a judge rendering a verdict. "I wouldn't want to leave things like that, if I were you."

"Fuck the law," Nubby said. "Do what's *right*."

Dan looked at Annie, who simply put her warm hand on his, her smile compassionate.

"You want any help?" Stumpy asked.

"No," Dan said. "I'll do it myself."

Dan remembered something his grandfather had said about when his grandmother had died. He cleared his throat.

"No, wait," he said, "Annie..." He dropped his eyes.

"How can I help?" she asked.

Dan looked up at her keenly and said, "I need a quilt."

He left in the afternoon of a mid-October day, driving first down to MacDougal, to make preparations on his grandfather's bluff, Maiden Bluff. This was a good month for such things, as his Willy had taught him. The bluff seemed forgotten, the path to the top narrow and on the verge of becoming overgrown. The view from the top was as beautiful as ever, and Dan paused there, gaining strength from it, and certainty.

Dan drove north along the river in the van, a shovel and pick and other equipment rattling in the back every time he hit a bump in the road. He listened to the public radio station and its evening selection of classical music, he opened a beer and did a hit of acid; it would be a long night, and he could see no other way to do it.

The sun set over the river to his left, and a cool front came in, lifting and moving the foliage at the base of the bluffs to his right. He knew he was retracing the track of his grandfather's last trip, and wondered what was on the man's mind as his drove this very road. What conviction he had had, what strength. If only Dan had known.

He came at last to the cemetery, the wind strong as it got chilly. Although the road up onto that bluff seemed rarely travelled, he parked the van on the fire road, far enough up that it was concealed. Taking what he needed from the back of the van, he slipped on his full pack and gathered things up, then walked heavily laden down the fire road and across to the gates of the cemetery, through the tall grass bending in the wind, past the autumn trees and tilted gravestones to the little concrete marker that bore his grandfather's name.

Dan put down his pack and all the other things he had brought, and stood staring at the marker. Reaching into his pack, he retrieved a beer, opened it, and drank half of it down. He walked a few feet and set the beer can on top of a stout fence post and looked out past the edge of the bluff, to the space of sky and river in the darkness beyond. Then he turned back and picked up the shovel next to the grave.

Methodically, he outlined a rectangular shape in the sod with the shovel and removed the chunks of sod from the grave, setting them out of the way. When a large neat patch of earth was exposed, he set down the shovel and took up the pick, and without hesitation swung it behind his shoulder, over his head, and deep into the center of the plot of black earth.

As he dug, he thought about how he had looked at the lines of the old man's creased and sunburned face, looked into his pale, sad eyes, and had failed to see what was there, what that lovely face had meant.

Dan dug deep into the black earth, loosening it with the pick and tossing it out with the shovel, onto the growing pile. The work went faster than he had thought it would; he was soon up to his hips in the hole, down to a t-shirt in spite of the chill. He stopped, and leaned with both hands on the haft of the pick, catching his breath. The trees roared nearby and across the open spaces of the place, clouds slid overhead so heavily that their motion seemed almost audible, a low sound like the dragging of granite. He didn't want to stop, but as it got darker, he climbed out of the hole and lit his lantern. He jumped back in and dug some more, the deep scent of the earth real and good. For a brief moment, he felt content. He had embraced everything at last, and he felt content.

His imagination gave him visions of what he might find. At one point, he scrambled out of the grave and ran to the fence, clutching the top of it and vomiting over its side, leaning on the top of the fence with a rope of drool running from his mouth. He forced himself to breathe deeply. It had been so long; there would be nothing but dust and bones. He drank a beer to rinse his mouth and to keep the acid in its place.

When he was chest deep in the hole, shovelling out the loose earth, the tip of his shovel struck something of a different texture, soft and giving, but not soil. He knelt down, moving aside the loose earth with his hands, brushing away the residue. The thing felt like...rubber. His dread confirmed, he cleared away the earth, searching for the object's edge, and found something like a seam. He pulled it with both hands and it came up out of the loose soil. It was a bodybag.

"Those motherfuckers," he said.

They had done it, the coroner and his minions, just as Sam Feeney had confirmed. They had taken his grandfather out to a forgotten graveyard and dropped him in a hole like a lost dead dog.

"Those motherfuckers," he said again, hurrying to free the body bag, almost beginning to sob. He stopped his immediately, shaking his head in sharp jerks.

Dan carefully removed the lumpy bodybag from the bottom of the grave, picking it up gently. It looped in his arms into an M, and objects inside slid and thudded into the downward ends. He set it in the grass beside the grave, opposite the mound of piled earth, and climbed out next to it, then took both corners of one end of the bag and pulled it over the soft, dark grass and left it several paces away.

He picked up the shovel and circled the grave to the mound of earth, and began shovelling it back into the hole, working steadily but stopping once or twice to drink from his beer.

"Sure wish you could have one of these beers with me, Grampa," he said.

Before too long, he had filled the hole in, but the dirt was loose and convex, so he walked back and forth on the grave, tromping down the dirt with his heavy boots. When it looked better, he got the sod he had set aside and put it neatly back in place. With rain and a little time, this lonely place would look the way it had.

Dan went over and lay down in the grass beside the bodybag, resting for a moment. "I'm tired, Grampa. I mean really tired. You know what it's like. Almost done now, though, huh?" He looked up at the moving leaves and the running clouds, listening to the sound of the wind hissing in the grass. He was soon asleep.

He awoke with a gasp, panicking, his hands clutching the long grass beside him, his heart thudding. He cursed himself, and held up his watch, thumbing the button that lit its face. Only fifteen minutes had passed. There were still several hours until dawn. He was shaking. "Jesus, sorry, Grampa," he said to the bones beside him. "I almost blew everything." He felt better for the sleep.

He stood up, and, kneeling carefully, picked up the bodybag, carrying it slowly up the hill through the graveyard, his back very straight, his legs swishing in the grass. He walked under the living trees and by the mossy crypts, out through the leaning gates of the cemetery. He crossed the gravel road and went up into the trees on the fireroad, coming up along the right side of the van. He rested the bodybag on the ground for a moment, then opened the side door of the van. Gently, he set the bag in the back, onto the quilt that Annie had given him, stretching it out on one half of the sewn fabric, folding the quilt over it. He placed his hand on the large, round lump in the bag and said, "I'll be back in a minute," and went back down into the cemetery to get the tools. The concrete headstone he slipped into the pack. Bringing everything back, he put the pack on the passenger's seat, and set the tools next to where Willy's bones lay wrapped in the quilt. His grandfather had liked tools, Dan thought, and wouldn't have minded.

Dan slid into the driver's seat and put the key in the ignition, starting the van. "Almost done, now," he said, and put the van into reverse and backed it out onto the road, then headed down the road the way he had come.

He parked the van at the base of the bluff at the head of MacDougal Island. Sliding open the door, he gently removed the quilt and the bones. There was enough of a moon that he could see along the trail to the top, but he brought the lantern, looping it over one forearm as he carried his burden, now surprisingly light. The pack on his back was heavier.

He came to the place where he had made a pyre of hickory and cedar, old fence posts of white oak dried by years in the sun. The high stack of wood was neatly laid, so that pieces across the top created a bier, and here it was that he laid the bones of his grandfather. He lit the lamp and set it aside, although it would soon be unnecessary.

Dan straightened out the quilt and the bag inside it as much as he could, trying to make it dignified. From the brush near the bluff he took a can of kerosene, carefully circling the bier and soaking the wood, soaking the quilt which Annie had made. He stood for a moment, regarding what he had done. Then he went over to the pack and took out the headstone, which he placed back among the oaks that Willy had long ago planted, soon to be covered with leaves, to be covered with grass.

From the pack he also withdrew a bottle of Willy's favorite whiskey and two cut crystal glasses. Pouring both glasses two fingers full, he set one atop the quilt, and took one for himself, drinking slowly from it.

Then he said the words that he had learned from his grandfather, for they were fitting, for the McGregors were water people:

Waves will run under endless sun
Long after deed of man is done
Take my grandfather, set him free
Softly, softly to the sea

With that, he took out a box of matches from his pants, lit one and held it to the wood. The flame guttered for a moment, then caught, spreading quickly. Dan stepped back and watched, drinking from his glass of whiskey.

The flames grew higher. They touched the corners of the quilt, which began to smoke. Soon the quilt was entirely ablaze, and Dan was forced to stand back farther from the heat. The cleansing flames caressed the bones of Willy McGregor, enfolding them, taking them in, freeing them. Ashes rose in a spinning column on the strong autumn wind, glowing and sparking at first, but then cooling, falling like grey snow over the broad waters of the epic river, falling on the waters and blending with them, at last to be carried away, at last to be returned home, softly, softly to the sea.

And finally did Dan McGregor weep. Slowly at first, a single sob. Tears lensed his eyes, and now he let them fall as if to clear his vision. And something within him broke, perhaps the fear of his grief. He sobbed three times, five times. He fell to his

337

knees before the flames, curling on himself, his sobs turning into a howl. He screamed with it, he drooled. Something set free, something set loose.

He howled and wept and tore at the grass, watching the flames of the pyre through his tears. And his sadness was right and he was just in his grief, for he knew at last that some things were lost and lost, were irretrievable beyond the ability to describe it, gone from life, gone from time, soon gone from memory, a golden span swept away forever and gone. And those who remained were tilted on a slippery edge, barely knowing their moment in the sun. And Dan wept for that as well. It was all precious.

Dan came down from the bluff that morning slightly altered. Although he recognized the permanence of his grief, and the weight of past misdeeds which could not be undone, there also was a feeling (and he had to admit it might be the acid), that he had broken free from a spell, or from the leaden weight of a darker future. He felt that he had changed his course, had lifted a curse, even only if that curse had been self-imposed.

He felt less ashamed.

It took time to get used to the idea of having done something so large, to have changed fate of his own volition. Going back to the Hephaestus Forge, he had announced to the Schommer brothers and to Annie that his mission had been accomplished.

All three seemed somber and unsurprised.

"We knew you'd do it," Stumpy said. "Not most people. Just you."

"You're a McGregor," Nubby said.

Dan kept silent about their misplaced adulation. Although, he thought, maybe I'm simply not as bad as I imagined I was. Maybe I'm not such a *maldito*.

Annie merely smiled and hugged him. Dan allowed himself to relax in this embrace. He allowed himself to hug her back.

He knew his time on the river was finished, that he had crossed over into something new, but still felt tentative in his altered self. There had been times after strong trips on hallucinogens that he had felt different, maybe permanently so, but this was something else, something more profound. He forged steel in the shop, the rhythms of it hypnotic, yet all the while the possibilities were whirling in his mind. He thought about Kate, about Denfer Island, about Tom and Greysport. When he thought of himself, as a matter of habit, as a *maldito*, he told himself to shut the hell up.

Maybe I am a good person, he thought. Maybe I am. People try to tell me so. Maybe I can live up to that, can come to deserve it. Perhaps I can deserve, as Willy said, to go after the life I want, not merely the one I accept.

So he forged, lost in thought, as the weather got cold and the first flurries came. He didn't know that the Schommer brothers watched him in the shop, exchanging glances.

In the beginning of November, Dan was sitting at the kitchen table when Stumpy tossed a magazine down in front of him. The logo was familiar: that of Greysport Magazine. That wasn't a jarring sight; it was the picture on the cover of Tom Schwartz with his gleaming bald head and Bugs Bunny teeth, dressed in sleek black leather and silk, now sporting a neatly trimmed goatee.

The caption read "Entrepreneur Tom Schwartz and his Salon de Refuses."

"What the fuck!" Dan shouted. "This guy's my friend!"

"I know," Stumpy said. "Says so in the article."

"What!"

Dan paged frantically through the magazine to the article itself.

It seemed that Tom had gone ahead with his plans to start a whiskey bar and recording studio. He'd tried marketing his own brand of chili, hummus, and jerk sauce. This hadn't panned out, but had educated him enough to pull off the other ventures, which were successful. There was no mention of a pornographic rock opera.

When asked what had spurred such a young man to these multifarious efforts, Tom had a short answer.

"I had a brush with death," Tom was quoted as saying. "Spinal meningitis. It changed my priorities."

The main subject of the article, though, was Tom's art bar, which had become a nexus of art activity in Greysport. The work of a young local artist, one Dan McGregor, had gotten the place its initial recognition, his dark and visionary work provoking a bidding war among the city's financial elite, including scions of both the Dixon and Butz clans. All bidders were convinced that young McGregor's art was beyond value, especially since the artist himself was "missing and presumed dead, possibly killed in the riots, his body never recovered".

Dan had been washed with dread at reading his name in the article, but seeing that he was dead, the pressure was off. He read the passage aloud to Stumpy, and to Nubby and Annie, who had just walked in. Grinning, Dan held his finger up to keep from being interrupted. There was a brief description of Dan's work, and some small, terrible photos to boot. He thought that the last triptych was done a particular injustice. He grimaced at this.

"Man, that sucks," he said. "you can't reduce three four-by-eight panels into some little snippets at the bottom of a page in a magazine."

"People might get the general impression," Nubby said helpfully.

"Doesn't matter anyway," Dan said.

"Why not?" Annie asked, concerned.

"Because I'm fucking *dead*! Says so right here!"

The all laughed hard at that, Dan so hard that he started to cough and had to be given a glass of wine.

It was only when things had settled down that Dan noticed the date on the magazine.

"Hey," he said, "this is from May."

The other three exchanged glances.

"It was my idea not to tell you," Stumpy said.

Dan spread his hands.

"We always knew about you," Stumpy said. "When you showed up here, it wasn't just your radiator that needed repair."

Dan snorted and drank some wine. "Oh, yeah?" he said. "Okay."

Nubby sat down next to Dan and put his good hand on the white and puckered burn scar on Dan's forearm.

"There were some conclusions you could only reach on your own," Nubby said.

It occurred to Dan to be angry, to feel betrayed. He thought about it for a moment, though, and said, "Thanks. Thanks, you guys."

They sat around in silence for awhile, all of them smiling.

"So, you're a big artist now," Annie said.

"Not that it'll do me any good," Dan said. "I'm dead after all."

They all laughed again, none as hard as Dan.

340

Perhaps our minds, from a deep and unknown level, sometimes send us the messages we need to hear; there is a clockworking of golden gears and an unseen kaleidoscope of gems, another facet of the hidden reality Dan had glimpsed on the roof of the Schommer brothers' house, tripping and beset with visions there on that summer night. Certainly there are other aspects of reality that remain hidden, not in the mind but in the fabric of the Universe, not supernatural, merely unseen and uncomprehended, but real nonetheless, like the existence of protons and neutrons to a Neanderthal roaming the ancient Doggerland.

Wherever it came from in his reality, just before Thanksgiving that year, Dan finally had another dream, a dream in which he spoke to Willy. And to Mae. And to his father.

As often happened in such dreams for Dan, water was nearby. There was a blue horizon through a scrim of perfect trees, the glint of motion and the sound of waves. Willy was by his side, a version of him the way he might have been when Dan was a boy. There was no sense that they could not talk, or that they would be interrupted.

"Good to see you, son," Willy said, putting his hand on Dan's neck.

"We can talk?" Dan asked.

"Of course we can," Willy said. "I have to show you something first."

They approached a picnic table in the shade of a lush oak. Upon it, Willy opened a hardbound atlas, which only then (in the evasive logic of dreams) had Dan noticed that he carried.

"Look," Willy said. "We were here." He pointed with his brown and gnarly finger to Mac Dougal Island, there in the curve of the river, topographical markings showing elevation of the surrounding bluffs.

"Yes," Dan said. "The river."

"Yes," Willy said. "Now we're here." Dan followed his finger as it moved northeast across the map, up to Denfer Island.

"That's where we are?" Dan asked. He looked up into his grandfather's eyes.

"I love you, Dan," Willy said. "Always remember I love you."

"I'm sorry, but..." Dan almost laughed, "could I have that in writing?"

Willy *did* laugh. "I understand," he said. In the wide blue of the atlas which depicted the vastness of the great lake around Denfer Island, Willy wrote in his strong hand, *I love you very much. Grampa.*

Dan was about to weep when he heard his grandmother's voice.

"Would you two come and eat?" she called.

Mae stood across the grass at another picnic table, this one spread with a checkered cloth, laden with bowls and platters of food and jugs of cider. There, too, sat Dan's father, Gordon McGregor, young and whole, and with his brother, Chief.

"Dad?" Dan said, and now began to cry.

Gordon stood up, came around the table, and held Dan in his arms.

"Oh, how I've missed you," Gordon said, holding Dan's chest to his neck. "I was afraid you were lost. But now you can go home."

And he was surrounded by them, taken in. His grandmother kissed his cheek.

"Home," they said. "Go on home."

Dan awoke in the grey before dawn, his face wet with tears. He felt clean, though, washed out. He knew that he was free, free to pursue the life he wanted, not merely

341

the one he would accept. It was what all those who had gone before him would have wanted him to do.

There persisted this unusual and tentative feeling; Dan supposed it might be called Optimism. Hope, perhaps. If he kept a kind of perfect, delicate balance, he thought he could get the feeling to continue. As he hurriedly packed a few things, he wondered when he might last have felt this way. Certainly it had been before his father died; not since then. He tripped over the gloom of this thought, but only for a moment. He had to change the habits of his thinking. I am *not* doomed, he told himself again and again. I am *not* cursed.

Stumpy, Nubby, and Annie were not surprised by his departure, only, it seemed, by the speed of it. They watched him from where they sat around the kitchen table, the place of so many days and nights, of the prefatory healing of his heart. And although leaving this place made him wistful, he knew at last that it was not Home.

"No breakfast?" Nubby asked.

"No *time*," Dan said. "Just coffee, please."

As Nubby poured him a cup, Annie smiled and said, "We are witnessing a man in love."

Dan smiled and ducked his head, then drank some of the strong coffee.

"Okay," he said. "Gotta go." He embraced Annie, and Nubby, kissing Annie's cheek but pretending to gag at Nubby's greasy bristliness. They laughed.

He turned and faced Stumpy, who put his hands on Dan's shoulders. "You go *get* this," Stumpy said, taking Dan in his arms, embracing him strongly. "You go *get* this, bro."

Dan began to cry, but laughed at the same time. He looked at Nubby and Annie and saw that they were doing the same.

"Thanks, you guys," Dan said, snuffling. "Just...thanks."

"Fuck off, man," Nubby said, blowing his nose. "You made me get snot in my moustache."

Dan laughed and tears ran down his cheeks. He turned and went for the door, picking up his things.

Outside, it was a grey morning, with flurries in the air. Dan fairly skipped down the steps to his van, throwing his bags and his grandfather's rifle in the sliding side door. He turned around once more to wave at the trio standing on the porch, then got in the van and drove off down Disenchanted Valley road, laughing once more about its name.

Realizing he had nearly forgotten something, he stopped at a phone booth at a gas station beside the river. He called the Benitez home (with immediacy, not hesitation), Solveig answered. He told her what he was doing, and rather than chastising him for leaving just before Thanksgiving, she said, "Oh, well, *fi*nally! You had me worried!"

Emilio got on and said, "Good boy. I'll watch after your things for you. Give us a call when you get settle."

"Yes sir," Dan said, smiling about the old man's use of the language. And he was off, first along the river, then up into the hills, over the grey and brown landscape, through denuded apple orchards.

He retraced the route he had taken before. It seemed he had always been bruised, in one way or another, during this trip. It was strange to drive through the gloomy landscape, feeling whole and hopeful. Never had he felt so intensely these unusual emotions.

Quite some distance from the river, he got on the first real highway. This led to the interstate, and the first green and white signs were for Greysport, with lesser destinations underneath, those always changing, Greysport remaining the same.

Soon he was in the careless and disorganized outlands of Greysport, where grim tract housing was interspersed with bleakly functional industry in a massive, mutant checkerboard, with jets seeming to float down like zeppelins to the airport.

The traffic condensed at this point, and Dan groaned. After so long out on the river again, sometimes not leaving the forge for weeks, he had to acclimate himself once more to urban driving. Forcing himself to slow down and be calm, he breathed slowly in through his nose, out through his mouth. He put Greysport's classical music station on the radio, breathed some more.

He forgot about all of this when someone cut him off with no turn signal, causing him to slam on the breaks, driving for both of them. He bellowed out the window, and then thought about the last time he was with Charlie. I'll get there when I'll get there, he thought.

When he did get there, it was too late.

The daycare center was getting ready to close, a bit early for the holiday. The flurries had come in across the state, swirling around the van as Dan coasted to the curb to park, rather than screeching in and bumping up over the curb and running in the door, as he visualized doing. He put the van in park and walked calmly into the building.

It was his fortune that Lateisha was at front desk. She dropped her eyes, shook her head, and laughed. She looked up at him with affection.

"You always seem to come here when it's too damn late," she said.

"What does *that* mean?" He felt sick to his stomach and sat down across from her.

"She got married," Lateisha said.

The only reason Dan didn't vomit was that he'd only had coffee out on the river, on what seemed a long ago morning.

"*She what?*" he whispered.

Lateisha was grinning, but this faded immediately, and she dropped her eyes. "I'm sorry," she said. "I was trying to be funny. That and you made her sad. She didn't get married."

There was an instant where Dan felt angry, but this was quickly supplanted by relief, then mirth.

He stifled a curse and said, "Don't *do* that!"

When Lateisha saw that he was laughing, she laughed, too.

"I'm sorry," she said. "She's my friend. I had to mess with you a bit. She *did* just break up with somebody, though."

"Yeah?"

"Yeah. I think you're the only one she'd take up to the island."

Dan grabbed her chubby hands and kissed them each, twice.

"So where is she?" Dan said.

"Headed to the damn cabin, genius," she said, drawing her head back and giving him a quizzical look. "She only left, like, an hour ago."

"Okay," Dan said. "Okay. No offense, but, uh, 'bye."

"You be good to that girl!" Lateisha shouted before the door closed.

"Can do!" Dan called back.

Maybe I can catch her, Dan thought. Of course I'll catch her, where's she going to go?

Even with these rational thoughts, he couldn't seem to slow down. It wasn't as if he'd pull up next to her on the freeway, but he couldn't quell his impulse to at least try to drive fast.

This was made difficult by the holiday traffic, masses of people scurrying to leave the city. On this stretch of freeway, they were going Up North. As the snow came in from the west, it now turned to sleet over the city, and the driving was getting treacherous. Then it got icy. The wind direction turned inland off the lake and it began to snow heavily.

"Fuck," Dan muttered, inching along in the traffic.

Ten miles north of the city, the traffic started moving again, lightening as people dispersed to the suburbs along the way. As if to make up for lost time, some people started to race, which even Dan, in his urgency, refused to do. He could see his grandfather shaking his head and saying, "You spend more time in a ditch than you do taking it easy."

Some people, it seemed, would not have listened to such advice from their forebears even if it had been given. On the other hand, there were those who drove too timorously and were prone to slide off the road, or sideways in traffic, prompted by nothing more than their own fear. Both of these types came to a confluence a mile ahead of Dan, when one of the timorous panicked, standing on the brakes unnecessarily and skidding from the right lane into the left, where some hothead had just passed on the left shoulder, angry at the incompetence of his fellow drivers, and pounded into the left front quarter panel of the former car. The ensuing carnage brought traffic to a complete standstill, although no one was hurt.

Dan wasn't hurt, either, but wondered what a stroke felt like. Holding the heels of his hands to his temples, he sat in traffic, staring through the exasperatingly rhythmic squeak of the windshield wipers (the ticking of his lack of progress), shifting from open-mouthed disbelief to short bursts of screaming profanity. It made no sense; he should be patient, but he had a vision of pulling up beside Kate's little gold Opal wagon and waving goofily to her, just to see her laugh.

Finally, the obstruction was cleared, and the things began moving and dispersed. Soon the traffic was actually light, although the heavy clouds dimmed the light, the snow obscured his view, and the slippery highway kept him from driving as fast as he wanted.

The weather changed as he went north. Two hours away from Denfer Island, the highway was actually clear, although the wedge of huge clouds which blocked his rearview mirror was now muscling in over his left shoulder.

"Shit," he said, and punched the gas.

It was this lack of patience that got him pulled over, just, he realized, as Willy would have told him.

When the toplights of the cruiser lit up (just as he passed the exit sign for Port Martineau), Dan's strange feeling of hope was cracked. Here it is, he thought, right here. What was I thinking with all this *optimism* bullshit. This is what I am, what I am destined to be, a fucking jailbird. There was weed in the car, not to mention acid, his grandfather's loaded rifle, and (he had noticed before getting on the Interstate to Greysport), a case of hard cider from the Hephaestus Forge, put in back by the brothers when he wasn't looking. Thanks a lot, motherfuckers, he thought irrationally.

Dan watched in the rearview as the trooper, in a mountie hat and sunglasses (It's snowing out, douchebag, Dan thought), walked up beside the vehicle. Dan already had out his driver's license and rolled down the window, holding it out to the cop, keeping his vision out the windshield.

The cop took it, studied it for a moment, and said, "So, what's the big rush?"

What Charlie would have done in such a situation, Dan thought too quickly for verbalization, would be to charm the guy, just like the cops at the door the night of the explosive beheading of Bacchus. Dan knew he didn't have that level of artifice. That old feeling of doom settled right in. So he told the truth.

"A girl I love is up on Denfer Island. She is, potentially, the best thing that ever happened to me. I haven't been happy too much, and she makes me happy, so I'm going for it."

He thought about the gun and everything else. The trooper held Dan's license for a second and said, "*Vive l'amour*, man."

"What?" Dan said.

"It's French," the trooper said.

"Yeah, I know," Dan said. "I was just taken aback."

The trooper handed back his license.

"Consider this a warning," he said.

"Okay," he said.

"Just be cool," the trooper said.

"*Vive l'amour*," Dan said.

"Hold that thought," the trooper said over his shoulder, walking back to his cruiser. Smiling, Dan pulled out and drove away. Okay, he said to himself, I'm not a jailbird today. Maybe I'm not even a *maldito*, although *that* thought might take some getting used to.

As Dan approached the tip of the peninsula and the dock for the ferry, the front of snow crunched in. This far north, and with the lake effect, there had obviously been much more snowfall than in the southern part of the state. Dan waited at the dock, thinking of the time he had slept in this very van that summer so many months ago, immobilized by his fear, his indecision, his guilt. It's amazing I didn't just kill myself, he thought.

Now, though, he waited with a few other people, sitting in their cars for warmth, as the sturdy white body of the ferry emerged from the gloom, Denfer Island barely visible in the distance. Dan tried to calm himself with slow breathing as the ferry lowered its drawbridges and allowed the vehicles to come on board. Dan sat in the van, not hearing the radio, drumming on the steering wheel with his fingers. This is all or nothing, he thought. How I live my life will be decided in the next hour.

The ferry ride to Denfer Island always seemed long, and that had been when Dan was in a state of happy anticipation. It was the anticipation mingled with a sense of dread that made the trip seem to take even longer. Where Dan might once have procrastinated on approaching this bifurcation to possible futures, he now wanted it over, for better or worse.

Finally, the ferry came into the little port. Dan almost laid on the horn when the car in front of him did not move the instant the drawbridges touched concrete and the safety lights turned from red to green.

Most of the boats were dry-docked for the winter, put in rows outside or in boat shacks, dimly visible in the growing darkness. The flurries got heavier as Dan drove by the Hell's Gate Bar, where the neon signs were on and warm light glowed from within. The part of Dan that always made him procrastinate tugged at him to go in for a couple of relaxing beers and high-octane cherries, but he resisted and drove off into the dark.

The drive reminded him of the first time he had been on the island, during the summer storm. He knew his way now, though, and forged through the darkness, his wipers going, whipping snow lit by his headlights the most brightly visible thing outside the windshield.

Coming to the cabin's rutted driveway, he again felt an impulse to drive away. What am I doing, he thought; I'm a guy who'll fight almost anyone, go anywhere in Greysport without fear, but I have trouble summoning the nerve to go up to the door of that cabin. Kate is there; *Kate*. Drive, chickenshit.

Dan went down the lane through the woods in to the clearing in the pines, and there was the cabin. Among the other vehicles parked haphazardly under the pines on snow and sand and pine needles, was Kate's little gold Opal wagon. Dan instantly knew what people meant when they said their heart skipped a beat. His mouth went dry and he was filled with dread.

I dug up my grandfather's bones and set him free, he told himself. I am Dan McGregor. He got out of the van and walked up to the door of the cabin. Inside, he could hear laughter and children, the sound of music on the radio. He didn't hear Kate's voice, but heard Mary, Kate's mother.

One deep breath. Another. The bad voice seemed to want to spin him around by the shoulder and walk him back to the van. He bunched a fist and knocked on the door. In his nervousness, though, he pounded rather than knocked.

"Shit," he muttered.

"What the hell was that?" came a male voice from inside.

Dan squinted, not recognizing the voice.

The door opened, and it was Kate's brother-in-law Rick (the guitar-playing trucker) standing there.

"Well, look what washed up on the beach," Rick said.

Dan stood frozen in the doorway. Then the kids saw him, and the moment of silence was broken with their cheers and laughter. This petered out when Kate came in from the kitchen, drying her hands with a dish towel, a puzzled (perhaps annoyed) look on her face. The kids and Rick looked back and forth between the two. Kate smiled, and they cheered.

When she crossed the room and Dan came in from the door in a flurry of snow and they embraced, the kids went wild. Sue and Ann came in from the kitchen, and Mary stood up from where she was making a fire.

Dan took Kate's head gently in his hands, fingers up through her red hair. He kissed her cheeks and her eyes, her nose and her ears, her forehead and her chin as she tried to kiss him back, gasping with laughter, her face wet with tears. He held his head up to breathe, his arms around Kate's shoulders, hers around his middle, holding him so tightly that it was as if she were trying to crush him.

"I'm back," Dan said.

She moved her head back to look at him, then clung to him again, tighter than before. "I know," she said.

Soon they were all around him, patting his back or kissing his cheek or, in the case of the boys, trying to wrestle him to the ground by his legs. Rick and Terry broke the boys up so Mary could get over to him, although the little girls held his hands and looked up at him, wanting his attention.

Dan thought Mary might be angry with him for having abandoned her daughter, but when Mary crossed the space between them, she was smiling.

Dan began to stammer, "I'm sorry that I…I'm…I'm sorry, Mary…."

"You're forgiven," she said. "And call me Mom."

Mary stood on her toes to kiss him on the cheek.

As the kids clamored and the adults talked over them, someone handed Dan a beer.

Kate released her tight little grip on him, her sky blue eyes looking up at him, and said, "Welcome home."

They walked on the beach in the snow to have the privacy to talk. The kids wanted to come so badly that they had to be physically restrained by the adults.

It continued to snow and the wind whickered across the icy beach, into the dune grass and the pines, the naked cherry and apple trees, all of them moving in the cold wind.

Kate had not waited for him. She had (as Lateisha had said) just broken off the third relationship she'd been in since Dan had left. She implied that she was only seeing someone out of boredom and loneliness, out of the desire to get her life moving again. Although he didn't like the idea of anyone else sleeping with Kate (the notion gave him the Hot and Light feeling, in fact) he himself had not been celibate, and had no fair reason to complain. He'd simply left, after all.

"I just got rid of the last guy," Kate said. "He was boring. But I guess, next to you, most guys are boring."

The compliment made him duck his head and blush. He imagined that he'd have to get used to it.

"I wasn't sure that you'd be back." Kate explained. "I wanted you to be, I had *faith* that you would be, but no rational reason to *believe* it."

"I understand," Dan said.

"Don't you ever leave me again," she said.

"Never," he said, and held her close.

Thanksgiving dinner the next day was nearly surreal in its excellence, even exceeding the last one held at this very spot. At one point, during the meal's preparation, Dan had to pull Kate out on the porch and get her to talk him down.

"This is too good," he said to her. "Stuff like this doesn't happen to guys like me. Something bad has to happen."

Kate slapped his arm with her knuckles. "Why does something *bad* have to happen?"

"I don't know. The other shoe's going to drop."

"No it *isn't*. You deserve to be happy as much as anybody else. More than a lot of people, even."

"You think?"

"Of course. It's random, at any rate. Good people die young and bad people die old, or vice-versa, any combination you can come up with. All we can do is be kind, ethical, and prudent, and the rest is out of our control."

"I guess."

"You guess. You're being superstitious, and superstition is a jinx."

Dan laughed at this, and Kate laughed at his laughter.

So Dan relaxed and let it flow over him. If he felt gloomy, he found something productive to do. He helped with Kate and Mary and the sisters in the kitchen, and soon was thinking of nothing but the project at hand. He made a cranberry sauce by simmering fresh berries in dark rum and brown sugar, letting it bubble until the berries broke down and the sauce reduced. Watching the sauce, he found himself thinking about when Willy had shown him how to make it. He stirred the sauce, and realized it was the first time in years that he had thought about Willy without being anxious or angry or guilty, only wistful. Only his memories of Willy remained, their time together irretrievably gone. Willy would want him to be right here, though, right here, and to love the time he was in, not to spoil it with poison about the unchangeable past. Be right here, he could almost hear Willy whisper.

So he did what Willy told him to do.

"Oh, Mary!" he said, remembering something. Mary's look corrected him.

"*Mom*, I meant," he said. "*Mom*. I brought us something from out on the river."

He went out to the van and brought in the case of hard cider in the back of his van, courtesy of the Schommer brothers.

Mary pulled her head back and spread her hands. "Well," she said, "what're we waiting for?"

It was opulent. Food was brought from the steamy kitchen out to the sturdy dining table: venison, duck, goose, ham, turkey of course. Side dishes put on trivets. The reactions of the children reminded Dan of the happy days with Willy and Mae; new memories were being forged. He helped to serve the children, and even talked little Olivia into eating green beans.

It was happy and boisterous, funny and loud.

And when he looked at Kate, there was patient love in her eyes.

After Thanksgiving, Dan moved in with Kate immediately. Before they could relocate to Denfer Island, Kate had to finish her Master's degree, Dan his bachelor's. It seemed pointless to go back to the Art Department, seeing he was already successful as a painter. Instead, he went back to Ryan Lannon and asked the delighted man to be his advisor as Dan worked on a degree in History.

Kate had been a bit tight financially, and seemed reluctant to tell Dan about it. When she did, he snorted.

"We don't have to worry about that," he said. He told her about the treasure of Willy's coins, and she gasped.

"Like, an actual treasure chest of coins?"

"Pretty much."

Then he told her about how much money Tom had made from the sale of his paintings. Kate knew about this success, of course, getting together with Tom regularly during the period of Dan's absence, but Tom had been too discrete to disclose any numbers. Dan was embarrassed to even mention it.

"What is it with you just falling into money?" Kate laughed

"I have *no* idea. It's not like it ever happened before."

"There are worse things that could happen."

Dan hesitated before saying, "I just don't think that I deserve it. *You* do, but me…" he squinted and waggled a hand.

"I'll help you get over that kind of thinking," Kate said. "And as for the money, we don't need that much. Maybe we could do something good with a portion of it. Help somebody out."

That struck Dan as a good idea. He put it on the shelf; they had time to think about it.

Once back in school, Dan found that he was older than almost all the other students. This didn't bother him at all. His grandfather and his father never finished their degrees, and he found himself in a time and a place where he could enjoy his studies. He and Kate spent quiet evenings in the kitchen and the living room, each with their own texts, making notes, sometimes holding hands.

He had become, as Charlie had once said, Mister Domesticity. His life with Kate was quiet and productive, and he liked it that way. Even if he had wanted to return to it, the old life had dissolved. Vnuk's had burned to the ground, and an arson investigation had revealed that the cause was accidental, old wiring being the culprit. The Horsedicks of the Apocalypse had hit the road after the riots, selling their stock of stolen goods and moving on to new adventures. Irv Klubertanz had become an accountant, of all things, and was living back in the suburb of Finster's Corners, and engaged to be married. Dan had little contact with the old gang. Even Candy was rumored to be married.

Dan and Tom Schwartz simply resumed their friendship, although it had taken on new dimensions. Apparently inspired by his brush with death, Tom had become startlingly focused. While he finished his bachelor's degree, his whiskey bar had taken off, as had his recording studio. Although he had "postponed" his idea of a pornographic rock opera, he had started a funk band. In having tryouts for the band, he had met his true love, Carolynn, a zaftig girl from the East Coast with beautiful eyes and a magnificent voice.

The two couples had gone out for dinner and Kate and Carolynn laughed together across the table.

"Thanks for getting me out of my rut back there," Tom added.

"Likewise," Dan said, placing his hand on his friend's.

Tom's greatest success was the art bar, which had gotten so much attention in the press. Tom had no problem with this, and became adept at giving interviews, something Dan abhorred. When Dan returned to Greysport, he had wondered about how he would change his status from "missing and assumed dead" after the riots. Tom had handled it with the media, making Dan's disappearance seem mysterious and perhaps having something to do with the artist's life being in danger. More details than that, Tom would not divulge.

"My client prefers to keep such matters private," Tom said.

Dan would grudgingly go to art openings and try to get away as quickly as possible. Sometimes his destructive voice tugged him in the direction of getting drunk and starting a fight at such an affair, but he steered clear of such behavior after talking to Kate about it.

"Don't listen to that voice," Kate said. "It lies when it tells you that you don't deserve to be happy."

At such affairs, Dan had a glass or two of wine and answered a few questions before making his escape. When asked about where he had gone after the riots and why he had gone there, he said little, but stuck to giving the general impression that his life might have been in danger, as were those of loved ones. More than that he wouldn't say.

Charlie was still missing, though, out there in the world. He had not contacted the remaining members of his family, he was simply gone. The fact that Charlie might read any interview Dan gave helped to keep his interviews short.

When it came to doing something good with the treasure Willy had left him, Dan and Kate came up with various ideas. They decided to put some money into the renovation of Kate's daycare center in Riverside, with Lateisha in charge of the project. They also looked into setting up a scholarship program for kids in that neighborhood and in Portview. They did what they could to keep their efforts anonymous.

One good deed came to Dan in a dream. In it, he had been out at Emilio and Solvieg's cabin on the river, the time that he had read Willy's poems. He had been too overwhelmed at the time to make the connection while looking at the photographs on the walls of the place. The realization came to him in his sleep.

When he awoke, he blinked a couple of times and said, "Holy shit."

Kate was just waking up and said groggily, "Holy shit what?"

It was a Saturday, a day they often went out for breakfast or lunch, sailing afterwards when the weather permitted.

"Don't have any breakfast," he told her. "I'll buy you lunch at Perrito's."

"When do you want to go?"

"As soon as they open."

"What's going on?"

"It's a surprise."

They were standing in front of the door to the place when it was unlocked by a kitchen worker. Perrito himself had not yet sat down at his place behind the bar with his perpetual margarita. One of the other workers was behind the bar putting the cash drawer in the register. Dan groaned with frustration.

"What is it?" Kate asked.

"A surprise, I told you."

The worker told them that Kaye would be in momentarily. Dan sat at the bar, fidgeting, and ordered the both cans of pop.

When Kaye came around the corner and walked behind the bar, she smiled when she saw Dan and Kate. She began to greet them when Dan snapped his fingers, pointed at Kaye and said, "Where did you grow up?"

"Not in Greysport."

"Where, then?"

"Out on the river."

"Are your mom and dad Solvieg and Emilio Benitez?"

Kaye's eyes narrowed and her mouth dropped open.

"How did you know that?"

"And your name's not Kaye is it?"

"No, it's Katita. I sign my timecard with a K, and it became my nickname."

Kate was mystified, and said, "What the hell's going on?"

Dan laughed, shaking his head, and said, "You were almost my aunt."

"Huh?" both women said.

Dan held up his hands and shook his head. "My last name's McGregor. Gordon was my dad, Willy my grandfather. You almost married my uncle Dan, who everybody called Chief."

"What?" Katita gasped.

Dan grinned and nodded.

"He's telling the truth," Kate said.

"You would have been my nephew," Katita whispered, tears coming to her eyes.

"Yeah," Dan said.

Katita came around the bar and held Dan in her arms.

At that moment, old Perrito himself came into the bar, going behind it to get himself a margarita. He sipped from it and sat down, regarding this tableau. "Why the hell are you on that side of the bar," he said, "and hugging a customer? Get back to work."

"Shut up, old man," Katita said.

As often happens, Katita and her parents had developed a habit of estrangement. This had begun with their fight about Chief's death, and was solidified when Katita, finding no men like Chief, had come to the realization that she preferred the company of women, a fact that she thought her parents would find intolerable. Dan assured her that this was not the case, and Katita soon arranged a visit to the elderly couple, the first time in many years.

When she got back, Dan and Kate started plans to help Katita open up her own restaurant, with a business plan drawn up by Tom Schwartz.

Dan and Kate were married on Denfer Island, but not in the way they had planned. Their notion was to perform the ceremony just through the pines by the cabin that would become their home, down on the broad beach. It wouldn't turn out that way.

Although it was a day in mid-May, and they had every reason to believe that the weather would be clement, it was still the North, where Spring was fickle. The house was packed with the Driver family, Sue and her husband, Ann and hers, and the whole gang of increasingly unruly kids. Not a single one of this last group took the event for granted; they had been in love with Dan since that first Thanksgiving, been depressed when Kate had almost evasively answered their questions about the break-up.

For two days before the wedding, guests arrived with each successive ferry. Dan was there to greet each wave, often finding people who knew him, but not each other, standing side by side or parked next to each other as the ferry docked and its gates went down.

Tom and Carolynn stayed at a little hotel, and Dan knew that the Schommer brothers had arrived by the roar of their bikes, Annie on the back of Nubby's, and some young rocker chick on the back of Stumpy's.

Bob Two Bears showed up later that afternoon, finding Dan in the Hell's Gate, where he was having a few beers with Tom and the Schommers. When Bob came through the door, backlit by the sunny day, his silhouette was unchanged; Dan knew him instantly. It was only in the following bearhug that Dan could see the changed, the leathered face and the snow-white pony tail. The held each other at arms' length and embraced again.

When the Emilio and Solveig Benitez arrived, driving slowly off the ferry in their pick-up truck, Emilio with a flower in the lapel of his ancient suit, Solveig with a boutonniere and a well-preserved floral hat, Dan was waiting for them. He hugged them gently, as they were frail, and escorted them to the best little inn on the island, happy that they were used to little. Katita joined them that day with her girlfriend, staying in the same inn.

The day of the wedding itself, Dan woke up with a hangover after partying at the Hell's Gate Bar. Kate was nudging him, and he could smell coffee.

"Wake up, my husband-to-be!" Kate sang, her voice suspiciously cheerful.

"What's up?" Dan said, squinting at his watch.

"We can't have the wedding at the beach," Kate said cheerfully. "The wind changed. It's gale force from the north and really cold!"

"What!"

"Yep! Old people and children will die of hypothermia! Wouldn't that be great?"

"No," Dan said. "I love the Benitezes. I'm even rather partial to your nieces and nephews. I don't want any of them to die. May I have that coffee, please?"

Dan went out to inspect the situation at the beach. Indeed, the wind was whistling in across the open water, hard enough to make him squint, to perturb and almost instantly chill the coffee in his mug.

"Well," he said, coming back into the cabin. "*That* ain't gonna work."

"I already have a plan," Kate said. Dan smiled at her; she was charmingly smug.

So they had the wedding at the Hell's Gate Bar. Dan paid for the services of the place in real gold, a few of the double eagles that Willy had left him. He did it with Emilio standing by his side, so that the old man could witness the significance of his actions.

"Well done," Emilio said. "Your grandparents would be proud."

"Really?"

"Yes," Emilio said, closing his eyes and nodding. "Very proud."

Dan raced around the island to tell everyone of the change of plans while Kate, her mother and sisters, along with Lateisha, Carolynn, Katita, Annie, and even Solvieg saw to the decorations of the bar. Stumpy and Nubby vanished with Dan's van and came back with it stuffed with fresh flowers, which the women adeptly distributed around the bar. The immediate crisis was averted.

They'd gotten a Unitarian minister to perform the ceremony, not that either of them were religious in any way. The woman was an islander, a post-hippie of the dumpy variety, with hair that was washed, at most, twice a week. She was inexpensive, though, and Kate and Dan liked the pan-cultural nature of her approach to things.

The fact that the minister had been back on the peninsula and had missed the morning ferry had complicated things, however. They received the news just as clouds piled in from the north and a lashing, icy rain came down.

Dan and Tom were in the bar, setting things up, when Kate told them.

"Goddammit," Dan said.

Tom shrugged. "At the end of the day," he said, "You'll still be married."

"Yeah," Dan said. "Yeah! You're right!"

Dan asked Russ, the owner, for a couple of beers. As people showed up for the wedding, having adjusted to the change of plans, they all responded to the invitation to get drinks at the bar. Things soon got jovial, small groups began bowling, playing pool and darts. Dan had the surreal pleasure of seeing people he loved but existed in different contexts in his mind all combining and recombining in different conversations. Seeing Bob Two Bears, Nubby Schommer, and Tom all standing and laughing around the pool table made him gape in astonishment until he stopped himself. Then he turned around to see Emilio, Solvieg and Katita talking to Kate's nieces and nephews. It was dreamlike.

People were almost put out when the unhygienic minister arrived. Some of them actually booed.

Dan went in a back room and put on his suit, with Tom's assistance.

"You look like a hitman," Tom told him.

"Perfect," Dan said.

When Kate came in from a little room off the bowling lanes, her mother and sisters in attendance, Dan experienced the same feeling that his grandfather had so long before, that so many other men have had. His breath hitched, and he fell in love again.

Kate walked slowly along in a pearly silk dress she'd bought at a resale shop. Nubby (it could only be his voice) whooped from somewhere in the bar. Everyone laughed, and Kate smiled, her cheeks pink.

The ceremony took too long, the minister droning on and on, doing more than she had said she was going to. Kate gave Dan a look which said she felt the same, a bit of a glaze to her eyes, although her smile was patient.

Then they were married. Then they kissed.

The bar echoed with cheers. Russ put on the stereo, loudly, the Chorus from Beethoven's Ninth. Kate and Dan waved like royalty with only a bit of irony, then went and mingled with their guests. Russ changed the music to something danceable. Dan took turns with Kate's mother, then her sisters, then her nieces.

Finally, he danced with Solveig, slowly and cautiously. He was touched when she put her head to his chest. When the song was over, they stood a bit apart.

353

"I always knew you'd find your way home," Solveig said, and Dan found himself close to tears.

It was a good life, and Dan knew it when he looked out on his golden span. Due to Tom's work, he made enough money from his art that they were more comfortable than he ever thought they would be. Kate taught at the little school, getting Dan to give occasional demonstrations in art, or lectures in history. Dan was pleased to be told that he made history interesting.

In late 1985, Kate told Dan that she was pregnant. Had it happened before, had a young man receiving such news been so washed with a flood of conflicting emotions, ones of joy, of possibility, of incredulity, of raw fear, that they canceled each other out, leaving the young man blank? Of course it had, millions of times. It was new for Dan, though.

"Oh," Dan said upon hearing the news. "Good."

"Well?" Kate said, the smile fading from her face.

"Well, what?"

"Is that all you have to say?"

"Okay: *wow*."

He got up and walked out of the house without a coat, through the pines and onto the beach. He watched the water for awhile, listening to the waves and the cries of the gulls. Then he ran back into the house.

Kate stood smiling in the kitchen.

"Wow!" Dan said.

"I knew you were going to do this," Kate laughed.

"WOW!" Dan shouted.

"*There* you go!"

"*WOW*!" Dan bellowed. He picked her up and danced around the kitchen with her in her arms, her head back, both of them laughing.

With Kate's mother and sisters living in the Greysport area, all of them wanting to get in on the action, it seemed practical to go down to city for the baby's birth. There was no hospital on the island, and, although Kate was confident in the local doctor's ability, Dan was too worried about all the possible negative outcomes. They stayed at Tom and Carolynn's house, it being the most spacious, when the baby was nearly due. The Driver matriarchy, now a unified clan with the Schwartzes, came and went in well-timed shifts.

The baby was born at Greysport Memorial Hospital on July 23rd, 1986, weighing in at eight pounds, seven ounces. They named him William, Will for short. He was a strong boy with all the right parts. He bellowed when he cried, with two vertical lines on his forehead, his tiny lower lip protruding like that of a belligerent boxer.

Any nihilistic thoughts or notions of pointlessness, any lack of purpose or sense of disconnection that Dan might once have had (wisps of it still whispering somewhere in his system) were blasted away like mold spores before a hot bright wind the first time he held that squalling baby in his arms. He was grounded, screwed to the Earth as if he had put down the deep and powerful roots of a giant oak, one capable of shrugging off any roaring storm.

They resumed their lives on the island, Kate teaching and Dan painting, both of them adapting to the needs of Wee Will (as they called him), who appeared completely unconcerned about the sleeplessness of his parents. Even when they were exhausted, though, they looked at each other and laughed. And when they awoke in the morning, it was in the bedroom on Denfer Island, the sun rising over the lake outside their unfettered bedroom window. In sunshine or in storm, they awoke warm together in the giant bed.

The next child was Ben, born August 24th, 1989. He did not have his brother's combative temperament, seeming, instead, philosophical and contemplative. Even as a newborn, he seemed to regard the world with assessing eyes.

Their last child was Emily, born December 19th, 1992. She was a bit colicky at first, but according to Kate, was also independent and resourceful.

"How can you tell she's those things?" Dan said to Kate, who held the baby in her arms.

"X-ray vision," Kate said. "Haven't you been paying attention?"

When the children were older, the family divided their time between Denfer Island and Greysport, not wanting to deprive the children of opportunities. Kate set up a program where she could swap positions with another teacher from the city, usually one just out of school, for a semester. They had enough money to keep an apartment on the East Side of Greysport. Will, Ben, and Emily showed varying degrees of adaptability, with Ben, in his removed and analytical way, being the most reluctant. When he got used to the idea, though, he thrived on it. Emily was still a toddler, and apparently capable of adapting to almost anything.

Dan never got used to going to his openings at Tom's gallery. Tom himself was a natural promoter, and it was to that that Dan owed his success. If it were anyone but his friend who asked him to go through such motions, he would have declined. Tom was Tom, though, and Dan could never resist his Bugs Bunny grin, especially when it came with a glass of scotch. By the time Emily was in kindergarten, Tom and Carolynn had their own child on the way.

Will was the leader of the children, although Dan thought that Ben, with his calm rationality, might have made a better one. Emily could scarcely be led, at any rate. With her white-blonde hair (in defiance of the Driver matriarchy's genes) and her mother's sky-blue eyes, her perfect little angel face, she fooled strangers into thinking she was something that she certainly was not. Kate had discovered her one day at a year and a half old after she had gotten into Kate's makeup, having taken red lipstick to the walls of the bathroom, to her arms and legs, and to most of her face. Kate had interrupted the process sternly but dissolved into laughter, having to go get a camera to take a picture of Emily, whose face reflected the fact that she resented the interruption.

It was as Solveig, had said at the wedding: he had, at last, found his way home.

There were the illnesses and accidents, the moments that tried them and gratified them. With many young couples and new parents, the distribution of labor regarding child rearing was a bone of contention. Not so with Dan and Kate; all of it was their duty, all the time. They would raise confident and conscientious people, those who had a sense of purpose. There would be no sense of "anomie" (a word that Charlie had taught Dan); Will, Ben, and Emily would all feel that they belonged, that they were necessary, that they were treasured, that they were loved. Any negative lessons or examples from their own childhoods, Dan and Kate agreed, would be turned on their heads.

There were some things, naturally, which Dan could not do. Nursing the kids when they were young, for example. There were some things it was merely difficult for him to do: changing diapers was the worst. He initially found this task to be so disgusting that he could barely bring himself to do it at all. He remembered what Mary had said about Kate's father, saying that he would simply shrug and turn away, not having a thing to do with it, calling it "women's work". That, of course, would never do.

He saw Kate eye him the first time he was expected to change Will. He hesitated, feeling like vomiting, then summoned some part of himself that he had discovered while working at Sam Feeney's. If he could handle corpses, he could handle *this*, he reasoned.

Kate was an old hand at changing babies and had shown him how to do it. The first time he had to do it by himself, she stood by him like stern supervisor who has keeping a bland face over a well of disapproval. Dan mustered his courage, though ("March yourself up there and do it," he would hear Willy say) and cleaned little Will's bottom while the boy squiggled and wiggled, put on the baby powder and was ready to follow with a diaper, when Will kicked both of his little legs at once, held them in the air, and farted liquidly with a force that not only undid all Dan's work but spattered his pants as well. The stench was awful.

"Holy shit!" Dan cried, jumping back a foot, holding the back of his hand over his mouth and gagging. Kate doubled over with laughter, staggering around the room. As soon as she could get her breath back, she said, "Finish the job."

While the baby giggled, Dan repressed a grimace and went back to it.

He got used to it quickly, though. By the time he had to change Emily, he could have done it in his sleep and with one hand. He wondered what his grandfather and father would have thought about this, supposing that they would have nodded in weary solidarity, and laughed at the more disgusting mishaps. The brothers-in-law, his great friends, got it.

"It's the price of being a man-toy of the matriarchy," Rick said, and they all snorted and shook their heads.

When the children got older, there were more ways that he could contribute. He read to them constantly, made them breakfast, made them lunch when they came in from the beach in the winter, or when he could manage to get them home in the summer. He let the kids "help" him working out in the little gym he had made in the outbuilding which held his painting studio. He taught them all how to draw, talked to them constantly about science and history. Little by little, he taught them how to fight.

"It's just a necessary skill," he'd say. "We are people who protect the weak, who do what's right. Family tradition. But your life has to be about more than just fighting. You've got to do more than that, do something positive."

Dan thought less and less about Charlie Gates over the years. When he was in Greysport, Dan had at first kept an eye out for him, but had become desensitized to this watchfulness over time. The mishap of mistaken identity at the casino years ago was an example of what might happen if he were overly vigilant. And these days, as

Kate had pointed out, he could be sued if he went around beating people up. At any rate, he imagined that Charlie had taken another identity, that he had moved away, perhaps even to another country.

Still, things happened which raised his hackles. Charlie had once said that he'd wanted to sever the head of some opponent (Dan couldn't remember who) and toss the head in the dryer at a laundromat at three in the morning when the place was empty, plugging the machine with five dollars worth of quarters.

Charlie had imagined how it would sound: "Buh-dump-da-dump. Buh-dump-da-*dank*-dump. Buh-dump-duh-dump-duh-dump."

Charlie had grinned and Dan had laughed a little. Dan didn't laugh when, years later, he read in the paper that a head had been discovered in exactly the same circumstances in a laundromat down in Cary.

Where had Charlie gone? What was he up to? Dan was old enough to know that sometimes there was no justice, there was no closure, that some things could never be fixed. John and Robert Kennedy had been assassinated, while Josef Mengele had drowned swimming, and Augusto Pinochet was walking around free. Charlie was not a monster; he had once been Dan's closest friend.

There was only so much one could do. Dan had already gone to unusual extremes to make things right in his life; he had to be at peace with that.

Still, the question of Charlie's end perplexed him intermittently. He spoke to Hugh and Gigi from time to time, and neither of them had any idea of Charlie's whereabouts. They had both moved on with their lives, seemed reasonably happy and content. Dan never wanted to upset them by telling them about the murder during the riots; the fact that they had lost two brothers, that they shared the care of their aging, discredited and disoriented father, was surely enough.

In mid-December of 1997, Dan was on Denfer Island working on a commission project. The work was for a movie in production, the plot involving characters struggling for survival in a post-plague world, vastly depopulated, where farm lands had become prairie or were returning to forest, and cities were being subsumed by nature. It was a perfect project for Dan; he could use ideas he had invented for the mural on the wall of the Kicking Pig when he was fizzing on acid at a party a decade and a half before, the vision itself having come from his time at the abandoned warehouses by Portview.

Kate was with the children in Greysport, planning to come back for Emily's birthday (on a Friday that year, the last day of school) and the Christmas holiday, when the Driver clan would descend upon the island for their customary celebration of the holidays. As difficult as it was to leave, Dan had come up early to work without interruption on the project.

Barring those distractions of family, it was not hard for Dan to concentrate on his work these days. To come into his silent studio, regardless of the time of day, he would often push through a membrane of hesitation, the old counterproductive desire to get drunk or shoot guns, to do anything that did not move his work forward, before he got down to the task. Once through that membrane, however, he saw connections and ideas, and was soon lost in his creative trance, living in the beauty of that moment, worry and regret at bay.

It could even be said that he had succumbed to a kind of lassitude. He had noticed, from time to time, evidence that there had been trespassers on the property, something that irked him. The beach was for everyone, but he had noticed, most recently, footprints in the snow up under the pines, stopping there as if someone might have been watching the cabin. He could not deduce the time of day that the tracks were made, and there was no other evidence of the person's habits, no cigarette butts or candy wrappers. The prints came up from the beach; it seemed as if the person who left them had leaned on one of the pine trees; the edge of a boot in the snow, the other foot solidly planted, gave Dan the image of someone with his shoulder against the bark of the tree, leaning there with one foot crossed over the other. When he tracked the prints back to the beach, they crossed from the snow to the sand, where waves had eradicated them.

Dan was, at that moment, in a mode which he thought of as "productive procrastination"; he didn't have to get drunk or shoot guns to avoid necessary work. The cleanliness of the house and the apartment in Greysport were evidence of that, something which would never raise a complaint from Kate. The children were given chores simply for the discipline that was in it, for the sense of contribution; it would be easier for Dan to take out the garbage himself than to grate on Will to do it (three requests before he raised his voice), easier to wash the dishes than to get Ben and Emily to work on it together, which often ended in something messy.

He thought about this as he walked down the beach with its first layer of snow, still thin before the ice pack had built up. The tracks he followed were those of a large man, feet bigger than Dan's and with a practical tread, perhaps combat boots. Where the prints were dissolved, Dan walked down the beach in the direction they seemed to be headed, to the southeast.

After a mile, Dan came to a spot where a stream wandered down the beach. The stream led up to a culvert, next to which was a parking lot for summer beach-goers. Dan thought that the person on his property might have parked there, but could find no evidence of their presence, no prints, nothing. He gave up actively thinking about it, and walked back to the cabin along the beach, thinking about having pea soup and a ham sandwich for lunch, listening to the waves and watching his condensed breath on the breeze. Dark clouds began to tower in from the north, changing the colors of the water and the waves: black and grey, pewter, lead, and silver, pale blue and turqouise. At one point, he realized he had stopped with his feet just above the waves, transfixed by the shifting interplay of cold colors.

The studio had gas heat which he kept at fifty degrees in the winter to keep things from freezing; he kept his paints close enough to the heater that they would remain soft. It also had a wood-burning stove, which heated the space beautifully, and reminded him not only of his time at the Haphaestus Forge but of his escape to the abandoned guardhouse of his youth, there in the industrial wasteland. Everyone in the family but Will thought that he kept the studio too cold in the winter. He started a fire in the wood-burner and put some Radiohead on his cheap sound system, cobbled from pieces of garage sale junk he had resurrected.

Dan didn't regret leaving the mural behind at the Kicking Pig those many years ago, when he had left Charlie knocked out on the floor. It wasn't as if he could take it with him, after all. The way it existed in his mind was perhaps better than the original version, which, he imagined, had long since been painted over, again and again, by any number of tenants, each coat further blurring the already deeply coated fixtures of the place. If Dan mentioned it to Tom, his friend would probably consider it a horrible loss, but Dan knew that there was better work stored right behind his eyes. It might not have mattered to him if he had known that the mural had never been painted over, that successive tenants had preserved it as a cherished asset of the old building. The most recent tenant had lived there for nearly eight years, and the presence of Dan McGregor's work was one thing that kept him from moving.

He and Kate had enough money, and he wouldn't have worked on the current project if it hadn't fascinated him. It did, though; he spent the afternoon sketching out concepts straight from the abandoned buildings around the port. It would have to be from memory; many of the old structures were being renovated turned into condos, restaurants, and galleries. Tom and his wife had one. The thought of this made Dan a little wistful, being a big fan of bleak urban decay.

It was dark outside when he left the studio, after straightening up his equipment (a satisfying ritual), checking on the wood-burner, turning down the gas heat. It was snowing again when he went out the door. He called Kate in Greysport, and talked to all of the children. Will came on first; at eleven, he was pushy, literally, shoving the other kids out of the way to get on the phone. Dan tried not to laugh out loud, and gradually got him to hand to phone over to little Ben. He could hear Emily in the background as well, piping her desire to talk to Daddy. It nearly broke his heart. He talked to her about her day, told her he loved her, and, with difficulty, hung up.

After a modest dinner, a glass of whiskey and two beers, he watched the television.

An hour went by. The wind picked up, whistling around the cabin, much as it had the first night he had come here with Kate in the midst of a storm. The thought of the tracks in the snow up under the pines began to aggravate him; the new snow would erase any evidence, just as the waves had on the beach. Suppose someone was up under the pines, watching him right now?

He finished off the rest of his whiskey, setting the glass down. Realizing he was a bit drunk, he laughed about what he was thinking and went to the hall closet off the kitchen. It was here that he kept his grandfather's rifle: the Springfield M1903 Caliber 30.06, oiled and preserved, his precious artifact. He only used it when hunting deer with the other "boytoys" of the Driver matriarchy, Rick and Terry, but now, perhaps because of the booze, he took it down from its place above the lintels of the closet door off the kitchen, where were housed crates of empty canning jars, boxes of winter hats and children's snowpants, where were kept old jackets for freezing strangers who might wash ashore as from wrecks like that of the Gullion Pinther. There above the lintel on the inside of the closet, on a blacksmithed rack, sat the Springfield in its case.

Dan realized he was being melodramatic, but Kate and the kids were gone, and he had a bursting flash of liberty; it was nice not to be someone's good example from time to time. He took the gun down out of the closet, over to the long dining table, and unzipped its case. Pulling it out, he held it aloft, gleaming, venerable, his heritage as much as his art was. He slipped on his boots and walked out the door into the dark.

"Who's out here!" he called.

The wind, bearing large snowflakes, whispered around him. He left the rough circle of light from the cabin, wearing nothing warmer than his black sweater. He scuffed through the deepening snow up towards the pines. Was someone up there?

"Who's out here!" he called again, adding, "I'll *shoot* your ass and, like, drop you in the drink! Or something." He laughed out loud to himself. It was one of the luxuries of being alone.

The pines were dark and the night was cold. He should have put on a jacket. Thinking about walking up into the pines and finding nothing, he began to lose interest. Suppose there were tracks up there, though, under the pines in the snow? Tracks which faced the house, then turned away? One thing years on the island had taught him was this: things didn't happen here. At least not much; a neighbor had gotten drunk at the Hell's Gate last summer and driven his Volvo into the little harbor. A summer tourist had beaten his wife and been arrested. There had been a murder ten years ago. It was tame. No one found heads being slow-roasted and tenderized in a laundromat dryer. Any stories that had happened on the island, back before the French to the island's original inhabitants, all become fodder for his brother-in-law Terry's ghost stories, but, in reality, the island was pretty tame.

He watched out into the dark for awhile, until he went from shivering to shuddering. Finally realizing his ridiculousness, he turned around and went back to the cabin.

There was a bit of a hangover the next morning, certainly. He was alone, though, and had no obligations to cook breakfast. He woke up a bit blearily, thumping the back of his hand on the space in the bed usually occupied by Kate. The space was cold and neat, and he had a flash of thought about his grandfather. Rest, old man, he thought. I'll be along. Just not for quite some time.

The kids' rooms were empty as well. Clouds moved from under the sun, and Emily's room was suddenly brilliant; it was messy, toys and books everywhere, lots of pink and lavender. The boys rooms were messy as well, but with color schemes dominated by black and camouflage. Will's room had art and writing supplies. On his desk was a story he was writing which was a fairly obvious theft from *Lord of the Rings*, to which Dan had introduced him. He insisted on writing the story longhand. Ben, only eight, thought this was anachronistic; why Will didn't write on a computer was beyond him. Ben's room reflected his techie tendencies. His computer was surrounded by little electronics experiments, and he had a TV set up to play video games. It was pointless to punish him by sending him to his room, which was where he liked spending a great deal of his time anyway. Dan shook his head, smiling, and went downstairs.

Some sharp coffee, some ham and eggs; these brought him back from his fuzziness. He thought of the drama of the night before and wondered what he might have been thinking. He suited up against the cold (after the snow, the temperature had dropped overnight), and went up the slope to the pines.

If there had been any boot prints under those pines, they were gone now, obscured by the fresh snow and the wind. Feeling happy in a way that might once have seemed impossible, Dan strode out of the pines and into the sunlight, dazzled by the freshness of the air, which seemed, as always, to cleanse what some might identify as a soul. He went down onto the abandoned beach, closed his eyes, felt his feet on the snow and the sand beneath it. He felt the cold on his face, took in the scent of the huge water. The only thing missing was Kate and the kids.

When he was at peace, he went back to the studio to work.

It was at lunch when his surprise visitor showed up.

Dan was heating up some beef stew in the kitchen when the knock came at the door. Nobody ever knocked here. All arrivals were anticipated.

Dan had just gotten off the phone with Kate. She had taken the kids to the mall in Greysport, mostly to shop for Christmas presents.

"I had to get Will to take Emily off for half an hour, so I could get her some stuff."

Dan, who hated shopping and malls, who depended on Kate for this among many other things, said simply, "Good."

"So you're okay?" she asked.

The sound of her voice softened him. "Well, yeah," he said. "I miss you like hell, but I'm getting things done."

"Okay," Kate said. "We'll be home soon."

They made little noises to each other, co-evolved utterances which would have embarrassed the kids. Dan didn't care. When he hung up the phone, he missed them all so much that it hurt.

The beef stew was beginning to steam and bubble. Dan turned off the heat and poured a pint glass of water. The knock at the door startled him, made him think, for a moment, that someone had washed up onshore, or that it was a daytime ghost from the Gullion Pinther, up from the depths and here to seek refuge.

At the door, in silhouette by the sun, stood a large, bulky man in an army surplus jacket of olive drab, a knit cap pulled down to his brow. Longish brown hair, perhaps dirty blond, sprouted out from under the hat, dangling by the man's reddish beard. Dan was reminded for a second of Kurt Cobain, if he had put on huge size and weight.

Dan's impulse was to help. If he had lived in Greysport for the last fifteen years, it might have been otherwise.

He opened the door to the stranger.

"May I help you?" Dan said.

The man raised his eyes to meet Dan's. It took a few seconds to realize that he was looking at Charlie Gates.

Dan stared at him. "Charlie?" he said after several moments.

"Your astute powers of perception remain unabated," Charlie said.

Dan felt the blood rush to his head and the hair stand up on his neck.

"You look, literally, as if you'd just seen a ghost," Charlie laughed softly.

It occurred to Dan to ask Charlie if he *was* one. Instead, he just stood there, mute.

"It's cold out," Charlie said. "Aren't you going to invite me in?"

With no other idea of what to do, Dan did. "Where are my manners?" he said, trying to think. Dan was too stunned, too civilized by the kind behavior of Denfer Island, to refuse. In the more vicious days of his youth, he might have kneed the man at the door in the balls, kicked his legs out from under him, and gotten him in a chokehold before asking any questions, just to be on the safe side. This instinct had

361

faded; he fell back on good manners, and the hardwired instinct to be cool. "Come on in."

Charlie took off his jacket and hung it on a chair at the head of the large dining room table. Under the jacket, he wore a green down vest and a plaid shirt, under which, yet again, appeared to be long underwear. He had on khaki pants and hiking boots. Dan knew that the soles of the boots would match the prints in the snow going down the beach, the prints up under the pines.

It was only by the eyes that Dan recognized Charlie Gates. Those eyes were the same, with their look of both distance and intensity, in spite of the redness there. The folds of his eyelids, nonetheless, were puffy. His cheeks were fat, his nose had gotten rather bulbous and was laced with a few purple, broken veins. When he loosed the snaps on his down vest, it seemed to be with relief; a round belly protruded under the taut plaid shirt, the buttons under some strain, the gaps between revealing his long underwear.

The fact that Charlemagne Gates sat at that sacred table was such a conceptual *non sequitur* that Dan continued his default to good manners.

"So," he said, "beer?"

Charlie spread his big hands, "Of course."

Dan went into the kitchen and opened two beers. Out of habit, he also poured two whiskeys, a couple of fingers each in crystal glasses.

He brought all this out to the table, even while thinking that the table was being contaminated.

Charlie looked at the beer and the glass of whiskey in front of him and said, "Whiskey? At *this* time of day? Well, I'd hate to be rude." With that, he downed half of the dram.

They regarded each other over the table. Charlie's eyes were unreadable; some of it appeared to be appraisal, some of it the old dead look he had when on the verge of violence. None of it was about love and friendship.

Dan retreated into a McGregor face of stone, his baffled mind clicking through possibilities, thinking about Kate and the kids and the conceivable reality of Charlie's threat.

He sipped from his whiskey and drank from his beer, just as Charlie did.

"You appear to have done well for yourself," Charlie said eventually. "Young Huck from the river, the poor kid from Portview."

Dan stared at him. "What. The fuck."

Charlie laughed, sitting at the head of the table as if he had made it and the chair himself.

"How did you find me?" Dan asked.

"I always know where you are," Charlie said. "I knew you'd be here alone, and I'll bet Kate's back in Greysport with the kids. Probably going to do some Christmas shopping."

Dan hoped the look on his face conveyed minor resentment rather than actual fear. Charlie must have seen something there.

"Don't worry," Charlie said. "I just wanted to catch up with you."

Dan knew Charlie well enough to realize that, at this point, he barely knew him at all. Charlie was calculating, Dan thought, perhaps playing chess while Dan was on the board in Candyland. What was he here for? Dan was obviously not a threat to him, not after all these years. Was Charlie actually as downtrodden as he appeared, or was it part of a stratagem? After everything, Dan still wanted to help his old friend, but the massive, protective love of his family superseded all that.

Was it *that* which Charlie hated and desired? Did he hate Dan at all? Looking across the table at his friend, his enemy, trying to divine the truth from his lidded eyes, Dan could draw no conclusions.

They talked about banalities. Perhaps it was something that had been customary in the Gates household; from Dan's experience, he would say that it seemed to be. Charlie had been untrustworthy even as a friend, what was he now? Did he have the .45 in the waistband of his pants? To sit in this place, in his *home*, and talk to Charlie Gates was so strange that his mind needed time to grasp it. All he could do was keep up with the banalities.

They finished their whiskeys and a few more beers. However strange it was to be sitting in his home with the ghost of his old friend, Dan found that his curiosity vied with his apprehension. Dan asked Charlie questions, but Charlie was usually evasive and indirect. Dan couldn't get out of him where he'd been for all the intervening years, what he'd been doing, where he'd gotten the new scars in his eyebrow and on his upper lip. Dan was forthcoming in his answers to Charlie's questions; he loved his life and was not reluctant to talk about it.

They never talked about the murder. They never mentioned Jim. Charlie was becoming relaxed, or at least allowing himself to appear to be. The deepest thing they talked about was the meaning of their lives.

"I guess I'm still with Jumpin' Irv's grandfather on that," Charlie said. "I believe his exact quote was, 'Don't mean shit, son.'"

In spite of his misgiving, not to mention the strangeness of the entire situation, Dan laughed at this.

"I take it you don't agree?" Charlie asked, watching him through narrowed eyes.

"No," Dan said. "It means something. I agree with *my* grandfather on that one."

"A wise man. What did he say on the subject?"

"He was pretty succinct in one of his poems."

"Do you remember it?"

Dan recited it:

"We all are born with an empty cup
Fill it with what you will
Fill it with love
Fill it with hope
Fill it with bilious swill."

Charlie raised his eyebrows, frowned and nodded. "It's no Keats, but it gets to the point."

"My life means something," Dan said. "To me. To Kate and the kids. It means something."

"Subjectively speaking, of course. *Ob*jectively speaking, we're all just bacteria on a mote which orbits a nondescript star."

"You've always said stuff like that."

"Yep. I've taken the *bilious swill* option and I stand by my decision," Charlie laughed. "If your life doesn't mean anything, then neither do your transgressions."

"My life means something," Dan said.

Charlie smiled slowly. "And your transgressions?"

"They mean something, too.

Charlie leaned forward, seeming genuinely interested.

"Then what do you do about them?" he asked.

"Atone," Dan said. "Set things straight, or try your best to do so."

"What if you've done too much for that?"

"You can try, Charlie. You just have to try."

"Fill it with love, fill it with hope, huh? And that worked for you?"

"I guess so, yeah. So much that I want to live as long as I can."

"That must be a strange sensation," Charlie said. "For years I've been willing to die, but the Universe has refused to cooperate. The time of your death is out of your hands, anyway."

Dan wondered if there were a double meaning to that, saying only, "I suppose so. I just want to try to help my odds."

Dan shared the beef stew with Charlie, putting bread on the table, more whiskey and beer. In spite of his rough appearance, Charlie couldn't cover up the neat table manners he had acquired in the Gates mansion, site of many stately, empty dinners.

After they had eaten, Dan said, "So what is it that you want, Charlie?"

"I told you," Charlie said. "I just wanted to catch up with you."

"Based on what happened the last time we were together, I feel the need to point out that that sentence could be taken in different ways."

"Sometimes a sentence can only be taken one way," Charlie said.

Yet another ambiguity. The slight smile on Charlie's face, though, told Dan that he was being toyed with.

"Maybe I should stick around," Charlie said. "Meet your wife and kids."

"I don't think that'd be such a great idea."

"No?" Charlie said. "I guess I can see your point. Kate never liked me all that much anyway."

Dan didn't say anything.

"How about this, then. We go over to the beach for some target practice?"

"What?"

"Yeah. You know, like we used to do."

"I don't know," Dan said. "I have a lot to get done."

"Come on, now. Don't disappoint me. If you do that, I'll feel *obligated* to wait around to visit your little family."

Dan's heart thudded in his chest, and he began to feel hot and light.

"What do you want, Charlie?" he said.

"Target practice. What did I just say?"

"What, did you bring your .45?"

"Old Trusty," Charlie said. "Of course I did."

"That's all?"

"No. I got a twelve gauge pump I've been dying to break in."

"Where is it?"

"I left it leaning next to the front door outside. Didn't want to freak you out."

Dan sat watching him, listening to his own heartbeat. He tried to remain impassive, tried to slow his breathing.

"You still have the rifle you got from your grampa, right?" Charlie said.

"Yeah."

"Anything else?"

"Not really."

"Big artist. Maybe you could bring some paint brushes."

Dan didn't say anything. He thought about his grandfather and Bud Sletto. You never know where it'll come from, Willy had said.

"Well, come on," Charlie said. He slapped his knees and stood up, buttoning his vest. "Get your rifle and meet me on the beach. You don't want to disappoint me, do you?"

Charlie put on his jacket and went out into the cold, closing the door behind him. A cloud moved away from under the sun, and suddenly the day was brilliant. Sure enough, Charlie bent to the side and stood back up with a twelve gauge shotgun.

"See you on the beach!" he called through the door.

If there had been room to sprint in the house, Dan would have done so. Rushing back to the closet, he put on his jacket, no time for gloves and hat. Reaching up over the door, he got down the old rifle and took it out of its case. He made sure it was loaded and went for the door.

Outside, he saw that Charlie was already standing among the pines, tracks leading up through the snow.

Charlie racked a round into the chamber of his shotgun and shouted, "Come on, laggard!" He turned and trotted off through the trees, lost from view almost immediately. Dan ran up the slope and into the green pine shadow, the scent thicker than ever before.

Was Charlie hiding behind a tree? Dan looked around, forcing himself to move deliberately, cautiously. Although the snow was not as deep among the pines, had even been blown thin by the wind coming up over the ridge, Dan could still track Charlie's boots. He lost the tracks once or twice on stretches of pine needles, but found them again. Fifty yards beyond the pines, there was a large clearing among the rolling dunes where a brush fire had been accidentally set on the beach by a camper the summer before, burning all the dune grass and killing a few saplings. The tracks seemed to be leading in that direction. It would be a tactical mistake on Charlie's part; he would have less cover among the denuded dunes, and knew that Dan was a superior shot.

Charlie was out there; Kate and the kids were coming home. Dan couldn't live with the threat. Whatever the consequences, he had to take care of it now.

He headed toward the edge of the pines, on toward the clearing. After a moment of hesitation, he left the cover of the trees.

Charlie's shotgun fired, and Dan fell back in the snow.

At that moment, Kate was having difficulty keeping track of the kids in the mall. She had stopped to have Ben blow his nose in a tissue; a cold had him producing a seemingly endless dual stream of mucus, which Will had pointed out.

"Gross," he said, miming vomiting, which made Ben laugh until Kate covered this up with tissue.

"Blow!" she said. Ben complied immediately, with glutinous sound effects.

"Oh, man!" Will said, wrinkling his nose in disgust.

It was only when Kate had thrown away the gloppy tissue that she noticed Emily was missing.

Will was the oldest, and was used to herding the other kids around. Ben, however, was the more conscientious. When they realized that Emily had wandered off, Will sighed and rolled his eyes, whereas Ben, Kate knew, was genuinely concerned.

People walked around the crowded mall, distracted by their tasks. Kate flicked between looking at the knee-level of adults for Emily, and checking out the faces of adults themselves, trying to see, in an instant, who might be the one to do harm to her child.

It's my fault, Kate thought.

She sent Will off looking. He instantly seemed to be doing it almost as a formality, sauntering along and occasionally tilting his head back to call, "*Ehhhhh-mily*," their habitual cry for the frequently missing girl.

Little Ben stood by, obviously anxious. Kate squatted down and looked him in the eye.

"Ben," she said, "where do you think she is?"

Ben had only been waiting for that focus.

"I know!" he said, and went off, dodging his skinny little body through the crowds, Kate followed urgently, terrified of losing another one.

Of all the many stores Ben could choose on that level of the mall, he went straight for a department store. Kate followed him through the crowd, shouldering people and apologizing. She caught a glimpse of Ben dodging through knees to the men's department, and followed him. There she lost him in the circular racks of men's clothes.

"Ben!" she called, ignoring the looks of holiday shoppers around her.

She didn't have to look too long before Ben came back, pulling the reluctant Emily by the wrist.

"Where did you find her?" Kate asked.

"In a rack of men's belts," Ben said. "She likes belts"

"It's like a jungoo," Emily said.

Kate smiled and laughed, closing her eyes for an instant, the hit of relief like a familiar drug. "Like a jungle?"

"Yeah, like a jungoo."

Kate laughed and picked the child up. Holding Emily in one arm, she held Ben's hand and walked back to the concourse of the mall, where they waited half an hour for the independent Will to return.

Dan checked himself and found that he was not shot. He rolled over to the base of one of the pines, keeping his rifle next to his chest. He moved his head, slowly and slightly, exposing one eye around the bark, trying to get a glimpse of the clearing, then ducked back before Charlie could get off another round. He waited, listening, smelling the pine resin and the lake. Waves crashed into the shore, driven by a cold wind from the north. There was no other sound.

Dan counted to thirty, to sixty, to one hundred and eighty.

"Charlie?" he called.

There was a time in his life when he would simply have charged the clearing, a time before Kate and the kids. A time when he had been pointless.

After waiting another two minutes, he called Charlie's name again. There was still no reply. Dan looked around the tree and could still see nothing. Keeping his back to the bark, he gradually got to his feet, the rifle at port arms, his finger on the trigger.

Slowly, he came out from around the tree. Moving through the pines, he went to the edge of their area and looked out over the brilliant, snow-covered dunes. The light dazzled him for a moment. He could see no human form out there, no olive drab jacket, no knit cap just over the ridge of sand and snow, a shotgun barrel, black hole portentous, pointed at him, blue eyes behind it.

Charlie's prints led up and over the first dune, although the contour of the snow and sand, of the similar patterns repeated behind it, were not interrupted by any part of a human shape. Pointing his rifle in the manner he had been taught while hunting as a boy, Dan went parallel to the tracks, on edge for a trap to be sprung.

Finally coming around that first dune, he found Charlie. His friend had gone over the crest of the dune and sat down in the snow. There, he had put the barrel of the shotgun in his mouth and pulled the trigger.

Charlie's head was missing from the eye sockets up. One ear was still attached, the other had to be among the blood and tissue scattered across the snow and the dune behind him. Brains had landed here and there, looking, in the brilliant sunlight, like partially-cooked skinless chicken. Charlie's shredded and sodden knit cap lay a dozen feet away.

Charlie had fallen sideways into the snow. It wasn't until the tips of Dan's boots touched the blood that he realized how long it had taken his father to bleed to death there in that clearing behind the lumberyard one frigid dawn, how much blood a living heart could pump out, something he had never realized until this moment.

The police department on Denfer Island consisted of two men, Officer in Charge Craig Tyler and his second and last in command, Barry Mills. That was as it should be; Officer Tyler was a sharp and inquisitive man of about Dan's age, Mills was some years younger, not nearly as intelligent, but a perfect subordinate in the tiny police department. Mills may have had a bit of hero worship for his friend and superior, Dan thought. One or both of them stopped by from time to time for a cup of coffee, or a beer after work.

Their duties were usually light. Tyler took care of his minor official duties, while Mills was more frequently on patrol, logging two or three times as many miles as his boss, going round and round the island, checking out the little port with its boats in the summer, the visitors' center, the empty cabins in the winter. Dan thought that the job had to be mind-numbing, that if one were to be a cop, Greysport would be the place to do it. Mills was amiable, though, if not too bright, and seemed content with his lot.

When Dan called in the DB in the dunes, the entire police force of Denfer Island (both of them) came roaring out to the northeast corner of the island, lights flashing and sirens howling. When they pulled up in front of the cabin, Dan was waiting. He was so overwhelmed by what had happened that he didn't have to pretend to be calm.

"You didn't have to hurry," Dan said to Craig Tyler. "The guy's already dead."

Tyler smiled. "Nothing ever happens around here. We've got to make the most of it."

"Where's the dead guy?" Mills said, almost jumping with excitement. He was a small ex-Marine with a neat moustache which he touched with the tip of his tongue when he was agitated. His tongue darted in and out now as if he were trying to catch flies.

"Come on, I'll show you," Dan said. He led them up through the pines and over the dunes to where Charlie's nearly headless body lay in the cold.

"Ho-lee shit," Mills said walking over to the body.

"Don't step in anything," Tyler said.

"Right," Mills said, squatting down for a better look and emitting a low whistle.

"Did you know the guy?" Tyler asked Dan.

Dan had made his decision, and created a cover story, before making the call. "No," he said. "He must have come to my door when I was back in the shop. Heard the shot, followed the tracks."

Typical of the mercurial weather on the lake, clouds obscured the sun again and it began to snow in big, heavy flakes.

"Hey, Barry," Tyler said.

"Yep?"

"Better go back and get the camera out of the squad. Looks like some of our evidence is going to be snowed over.

"Right."

Mills trotted back over dunes and into the pines.

"You don't seem too freaked out by this," Tyler observed.

Dan opened his mouth, but Tyler pointed at him and said, "Oh, yeah. Funeral home job when you were a kid."

Dan shrugged. "That and your odd drowned guy, body in an alley, that sort of thing," Dan said.

"You've seen way more than our buddy Mills, there," Tyler said, squatting behind Charlie's body. "He was a Marine, but worked as an orderly."

Tyler flipped up the flap on Charlie's back pocket and took out his wallet. Opening it, he looked at the driver's license.

"David Grimsby," he said. "Greysport."

Dan took in a deep breath and let it out slowly.

The snow came down more heavily, nearly obscuring the waves, which had turned from deep blue to the color of metal. Dan walked back to the house when the two men began gathering evidence. By the time the county coroner's van arrived from the ferry, Dan was back in the house watching from one of the front windows, a cup of coffee in his hand. The snow had covered all of his tracks, and certainly the blood on the beach as well.

Kate was the only person Dan told about the body's true identity.

"Oh, no," Kate whispered. "Oh, that poor, lost man."

That was Kate, Dan thought, loving her still more. She would shed tears for someone like Charlie, where others might celebrate his death. Dan knew that it was only her healing warmth, her light, that had made him whole. He might easily have ended up like Charlie.

They decided not to tell anyone the truth of what had happened. Surely Hugh and Gigi would be happier thinking that Charlie was cheerfully alive in Buenos Aires or in Prague (whatever their imaginations and conjecture would present to them), rather than knowing the loneliness of his real fate.

David Grimsby had no living relatives, something which, Dan was sure, Charlie had taken into account. He was buried in a well-maintained grave back on the peninsula, in a proper, simple coffin, which was then lowered into a concrete vault, as dictated by law. Dan knew where the grave was, and visited it once a year. It was not far from the beach, adjacent to a state park where the glittering water could be seen through the trees.

"Look at this day," he would say to the stone which sat in the trimmed grass. "Do you see what you missed? Look at this day." He would tip back his head and spread his arms, and breathe in deep.

In the spring after Charlie's death, Dan bought young oak saplings at a nursery on the peninsula and brought them back on the ferry, enough young trees to fill the bed of the pickup. On a sunny afternoon, he and Kate took the kids up to where the fire the summer before had burned some saplings. It was only yards away from where Charlie had fallen, up where the soil was better, and the young oaks could take root. They planted many more than had been lost to the flames. The trees took root, and over the years, they grew.

And so their golden span spread out before them, to last however long it would. Dan began teaching Will how to drive a stickshift in the summer when he turned fourteen. Will took to it immediately, with only a few stalls and false starts. They drove for practice on the island's inner roads; away from the beaches, it was away from the tourists, went Dan's reasoning. They passed Barry Mills at one point, and Dan had a momentary flashback to the intense feeling of seeing a cop when he was doing something illegal. Will, after all, was too young even for a learner's permit. Barry just waved as he passed, and Dan snorted laughter through his nose.

"What's funny?" Will asked.

"Nothing," Dan said. "Keep your eyes on the road."

A week later, during another practice drive, a tourist coming from the opposite direction was obviously distracted by the kids fighting in the back seat his car. He appeared to turn around to swat or separate them, and came across the centerline.

"Watch it!" Dan shouted.

Will adroitly drove up on the gravel shoulder while sounding his horn. The tourist jerked his steering wheel and righted the direction of the car.

"Be sure to take your half out of the middle!" Will bellowed out the window at the passing car. Dan laughed out loud. It was something his grandfather used to say. Perhaps, Dan thought, he said it himself. Where else would Will get it?

He and Kate talked about everything, any chance they got. They cuddled and laughed together at night and in the morning. They walked and went skiing on the beach, went swimming and sailing. The last thing took a bigger and bigger part of their life. They kept a thirty-foot sailboat in the little harbor, and all the kids were adroit at the sport, especially little Emily.

If they had an argument, it was minor, and they never went to bed without finding a solution. Once or twice the arguments were bad, something Kate would later blame on hormones. Dan, afraid of his own temper, never gave voice to it, never gave it a chance to escape from its dark oubliette, way down there inside him.

"Let's not say anything we can't take back," he would say quietly, before pointing out that Kate's anger was justifiable.

"Always be sure to have the last word," he advised Tom over the phone. " 'Yes, dear'."

Even the worst argument was a short one. One night in bed during a storm, when Will was working on a story, and Ben was playing video games with Emily, Kate and Dan talked about how they loved the kids.

"I hate it when people say to their kids, 'I love you all equally'." Kate said.

"I know."

"I couldn't love them any more than I do, but I love them all for different reasons. So it's not the same."

"Okay," Dan said.

"I love Will because he's reckless..." Kate said.

"Although it worries the hell out of you."

"Yeah. And he's imaginative and heroic, just like his dad."

Dan sighed through his nose and shook his head.

"I love Ben, because he's so smart and sweet and thoughtful," she said.

"Don't forget funny. He gets funnier all the time."

"So does Emily."

"Yeah," Dan said, leaning over to kiss her for no reason but habit. "Emily's just this little...*dynamo*."

"And Will? He takes himself a little too seriously. Again like his dad."

"What?" Dan acted shocked, then thought about it for a moment. "At least he's not a *maldito*."

370

Kate slapped his arm with the back of her hand. She stared him down.

"I told you never to say that again," she said.

His eyes wide, Dan held up his hands. "Sorry!"

"If you're not a *maldito*, what are you then?"

He didn't answer.

"Come on. Spit it out. What are you?"

"I'm a..."

"Say it!"

He took a deep breath and released it, saying, "I'm a good man."

"That wasn't so hard, was it?"

"Yes," Dan said. "As a matter of fact, it was."

Before Kate, before the kids, Dan hadn't known there was so much love out there. He hadn't had it from his mother. His time with his father had been too short. He supposed Willy and Mae had felt towards him the way he did to the kids, but he had been too young and confused to perceive it.

And the island was a place of ghosts, who seemed to take their turns leaning over Dan's sleeping form to whisper their stories in his ear. If ghosts they were, they were strangers, but from these dreams came paintings. And although Headless Grimsby became one of brother-in-law Terry's ghost stories, Charlie never visited Dan in his dreams. Dan's dream of his reunion with Willy and Mae, with his father Gordon and Uncle Chief, was one of the last he would have of them over the years, as if their ghosts had seen him happy, and departed.

And yet there was peace on the island, now. There was peace.

On September 11th, 2001, Ben's twelfth birthday had just passed. Dan was in the house having his morning coffee, listening to public radio before going out to the shop. He was dressed as usual when on the island, in jeans and a flannel shirt. His new beard was coming in with more grey than the last time he'd grown one. He grimaced when he saw this in the mirror, but Kate insisted she liked it, so he let it keep growing.

Kate and the kids were at school, the way his mornings normally went. He walked out on the front porch for a moment with his cup of coffee, scratching a bit at the new beard. He could hear the sound of waves through the pines, could hear the cry of gulls, his sound of freedom. Listening to this, he stretched with contentment. A passing thought came to him about Willy and Mae, about how they would have liked it here. Willy had been dead for twenty years, Mae even longer; he still missed them, but felt peace about it. Especially on days like this.

He went back through the hunter green door, past the long dining table and into the kitchen. The familiar voice of the announcer on the radio was saying that, in New York, a plane had crashed into one of the towers of the World Trade Center. It struck him as such an odd thing for the announcer to say that Dan wasn't sure if he'd heard correctly. He went into the living room and turned on the television, the first time he would see the images.

Dan sat down, mesmerized. He was watching when the other plane hit.

It was like something Charlie would predict, something Dan had anticipated himself. Watching it, though, it looked strangely benign, peaceful, a beautiful day on the East Coast, except for the pillar of smoke pouring skyward from the incongruously burning buildings.

Charlie would've predicted a nuclear device, if just a small one. The only thing that was surprising was the unexpected form catastrophe took. The catastrophe itself, Dan found, was not surprising at all.

It was only when he saw footage of people jumping from the building that his catastrophist objectivity was shattered.

"Oh, no," he said. "Oh, no."

Kate and the kids came home from school in the mid-afternoon. Dan had barely moved, only getting up for more coffee and to take a piss. Kate and the kids had heard what had happened, of course, but clustered around where Dan sat in front of the television, instantly as fixed on the televised images as Dan had been for hours.

He cooked dinner for everyone, although none of his family seemed very hungry. Emily sat on the couch on one side of Kate, Ben on the other. When Kate quietly wept, Emily asked her, again and again, what was wrong.

"A bunch of people died, dumbass," Ben muttered.

When Ben said this for the first time, he was ignored.

The second time, Dan broke out of his daze.

"Hey!" he barked. "Knock it off."

Will, fifteen and getting muscular, pulled up a chair and sat next to Dan. When Dan put his hand on his son's solid back, Will didn't rest his head on Dan's shoulder as he might have done until recently. Instead, he clapped his hand on Dan's back in comradely gesture. When they exchanged a gaze, Dan saw in his son's eyes a look which might once have been seen on his own: a look of anger, of determination, perhaps even of hate.

"The facts are not in on this, Will," Dan said, "although at this moment, I'm as pissed as you are."

"Somebody's got to do something about this," Will said, his eyes wide, his breath seemingly deep and thorough. It occurred to Dan that the boy might feel light and hot.

And when it was obvious that the country was going to war with Iraq, Dan and Kate despaired, looking at each other with blank dread.

"I'm going," Will said. "I'm going to enlist."

Dan and Kate looked at each other, then at Will.

"No you are *not*," Kate said.

"I am," Will said. "It's not your choice. This is my time."

And the oaks grew just above the beach, as did those planted on the bluff over the river. They were young and they grew strong. They would be, with their generations, witness to the ages until the glaciers came again. And their leaves and their acorns, when they fell on the water, would be borne upon the current, softly, softly, to the sea.

THE END